THE PHENOMENON OF
A WOMAN OF SUBSTANCE

Leaving a career in journalism, Barbara Taylor Bradford gained international fame with the publication of her first novel, *A Woman of Substance*. Immediately, it was a publishing landmark. A hardcover bestseller (three months on *The New York Times* bestseller list), it has sold to-date more than three million copies in paperback, logging a record-breaking 45 weeks on *The New York Times* mass market bestseller list. Also a bestseller in England, France, Italy, Holland, Spain, Germany and Portugal, as well as 22 other countries, *A Woman of Substance* has been translated into 11 languages and was produced as a major television mini-series. When the acclaimed sequel, *Hold the Dream*, was published, it too became a worldwide bestseller and mini-series. Mrs. Bradford's heroine, Emma Harte, is one of popular literature's most enduring and captivating characters.

"A LONG, SATISFYING NOVEL OF MONEY AND POWER, PASSION AND REVENGE . . . IT TELLS THE DRAMATIC AND OFTEN MOVING STORY OF EMMA HARTE, WHO RISES FROM SERVANT GIRL TO BECOME AN INTERNATIONAL CORPORATE POWER AND ONE OF THE RICHEST WOMEN IN THE WORLD. INTERWOVEN ARE THEMES OF HIGH FINANCE, ROMANCE, AND REVENGE, SET AGAINST THE SWEEP OF 20TH-CENTURY HISTORY."

—*Los Angeles Times Syndicate*

Bantam Books by Barbara Taylor Bradford
Ask your bookseller for the books you have missed

ACT OF WILL
HOLD THE DREAM
VOICE OF THE HEART

A WOMAN OF SUBSTANCE

Barbara Taylor Bradford

BANTAM BOOKS

TORONTO · NEW YORK · LONDON · SYDNEY · AUCKLAND

*This low-priced Bantam Book
has been completely reset in a type face
designed for easy reading, and was printed
from new plates. It contains the complete
text of the original hard-cover edition.*
NOT ONE WORD HAS BEEN OMITTED.

A WOMAN OF SUBSTANCE

*A Bantam Book / published by arrangement with
Doubleday & Company, Inc.*

PRINTING HISTORY
Doubleday edition published April 1979

A selection of Doubleday Book Club and Literary Guild, May 1979

*From "The Poems of Yurii Zhivago," Hamlet, from Doctor Zhivago, by Boris
Pasternak, translated by Max Hayward and Manya Harari. Copyright © 1958.
Reprinted by permission of Pantheon Books, a Division of Random House, Inc.*

*From "The Poems of Yurii Zhivago," Hamlet, from Doctor Zhivago, by Boris
Pasternak, translated by Max Hayward and Manya Harari. Copyright © 1958.
Reprinted in Canada by permission of William Collins Sons and Company
Limited.*

Bantam edition / June 1987

ISBN 0-553-26534-2

Published simultaneously in the United States and Canada

*Bantam Books are published by Bantam Books, Inc. Its trademark, con-
sisting of the words "Bantam Books" and the portrayal of a rooster, is Registered in U.S. Patent and Trademark Office and in other countries. Marca
Registrada. Bantam Books, Inc., 666 Fifth Avenue, New York, New York 10103.*

PRINTED IN THE UNITED STATES OF AMERICA

KR   0 9 8 7 6 5 4 3 2 1

For Bob and my parents—
who knew the reasons why

ACKNOWLEDGMENTS

Many people gave assistance to me during the writing of this book, but it is to Miss Carolyn Blakemore, senior editor of Doubleday & Company, New York, that I am most deeply indebted and whom I must thank first. For three years she gave unstintingly of her valuable advice and time, and her encouragement and belief sustained me at all times. But apart from her moral support, I am grateful to her for her technical skills as an editor, her good taste and sense of style.

I would also like to gratefully acknowledge invaluable help from the staff of the Reading Room of the British Museum, as well as the staffs of the following: Leeds Public Library; Bradford Public Library; Armley Public Library; the Newspaper Microfilm Division of Leeds Public Library; Bankfield Museum, Halifax; Kirkstall Abbey House Museum, Leeds; Fountains Hall, Studley Royal, Yorkshire; Temple Newsam House, Leeds; the Imperial War Museum, London; the New York Public Library. In particular I must thank Mr. Ernest Hall of Leigh Mills, Stanningley Bottom, Leeds, for devoting hours to showing me around old portions of the mills and supplying pertinent information regarding conditions in the Yorkshire woolen mills at the turn of the century; my thanks also to Mr. Ronald Jacobson, Export Liaison Manager of Marks and Spencers, Ltd., London, for providing old photographs of the original Marks and Spencers' Penny Bazaars in Leeds, and for information regarding the founding and development of that company.

I owe special thanks to Mrs. Susan Watt, formerly London editor of Doubleday & Company, whose research was always meticulous and efficiently and promptly supplied, often on very short notice. I would also like to thank all of those friends who helped in a variety of ways: Mr. Ronald M. Sumrie, chairman of Sumrie Clothes of Leeds, for introductions to woolen mills in Yorkshire; Mrs. Frances Lyons Barish of New York, for giving me access to her father's World War I diaries, for generously typing and duplicating relevant parts; Miss Pauline V. Delli Carpini of New York, for general assistance with the preparation of the final manuscript which saved me untold hours; Mr. Eugene H. Winick of Ernst, Cane, Berner & Gitlin, New York, for legal advice regarding wills, trusts, and estates; Mr. Morton J. Mitosky of New York, for advice about the same; Mr. and Mrs. Eric Clarke of Ripon, who drove me across Yorkshire on numerous occasions and reacquainted me with old childhood haunts; Mr. and Mrs. Eric Fielding, my gracious hosts on my various research trips to London; Mr. Peter W. McGill, chairman of AP Publishing, Sydney, who supplied me with detailed maps and vital research material about Australia; Mrs. Joan Feeley of New York, for typing a long manuscript most meticulously; Mrs. Charlotte Wendel, who helped to keep me physically fit; Mrs. Janet Shiff of Chicago, who diligently proofread major portions of the finished manuscript. I would like to express my gratitude to Mrs. Joy Klein of New York, not only for her friendship but also for her extraordinary understanding of my obsession with this book, which was expressed in countless ways. Also, my most sincere thanks to Mr. Paul Gitlin of Ernst, Cane, Berner & Gitlin, New York, and to Mr. George Greenfield of John Farquharson Ltd., London, my literary representatives for many years and both dear friends whose confidence and support I deeply appreciate.

Finally, I owe a special debt to my parents, Mr. and Mrs. Winston Taylor of Leeds, for their encouragement and dedication to my project. They also spent many months seeking out old books and newspapers and their vivid recollections of Yorkshire in the early 1900s provides much of the background for this novel. And my gratitude to my husband for his understanding and belief.

New York, 1978

CONTENTS

CONTENTS

The value of life lies not in the length of days, but in the use we make of them: a man may live long, yet get little from life. Whether you find satisfaction in life depends not on your tale of years, but on your will.

—MONTAIGNE, *Essays*

I have the heart of a man, not of a woman, and I am not afraid of anything . . .

—ELIZABETH I Queen of England

PART ONE

The Valley
1968

He paweth in the valley and rejoiceth in his strength:
he goeth on to meet the armed men.

—JOB

ONE

Emma Harte leaned forward and looked out of the window. The private Lear jet, property of the Sitex Oil Corporation of America, had been climbing steadily up through a vaporous haze of cumulus clouds and was now streaking through a sky so penetratingly blue its shimmering clarity hurt the eyes. Momentarily dazzled by this early-morning brightness, Emma turned away from the window, rested her head against the seat, and closed her eyes. For a brief instant the vivid blueness was trapped beneath her lids and, in that instant, such a strong and unexpected feeling of bittersweet nostalgia was evoked within her, she caught her breath in surprise. It's the sky from the Turner painting above the upstairs parlor fireplace at Pennistone Royal, she thought, a Yorkshire sky on a spring day when the wind has driven the fog from the moors.

A faint smile played around her implacable mouth, curving the resolute line of the lips with unfamiliar softness, as she thought with some pleasure of Pennistone Royal. That great house that grew up out of the stark and harsh landscape of the moors and which always appeared to her to be a force of nature engineered by some Almighty architect rather than a mere edifice erected by mortal man. The one place on this violent planet where she had found peace, limitless peace that soothed and refreshed her. Her home. She had been away far too long this time, almost six weeks, which was a prolonged absence indeed for her. But within the coming week she would be returning to London, and by the end of the month she would travel north to Pennistone. To peace, tranquillity, her gardens, and her grandchildren.

This thought cheered her immeasurably and she relaxed in her seat, the tension that had built up over the last few days diminishing until it had evaporated. A sigh escaped her lips, one of mingled weariness and relief. She was bone tired from the raging battles that had punctuated these last few days of board meetings at the Sitex corporate headquarters in Odessa; she was supremely relieved to be leaving Texas and returning to the relative calmness of her own corporate offices in New York. It was not that she did not like Texas; in point of fact, she had always had a penchant for that great state, seeing in its rough sprawling power something akin to her native Yorkshire. But this last trip had exhausted her. I'm getting too old for galavanting around on planes, she thought ruefully, and then dismissed that thought as unworthy. It was dishonest and she was never dishonest with herself. It saved so much time in the long run. And, in all truthfulness, she did not feel old. Only a trifle tired on occasion and especially when she became exasperated with fools, and Harry Marriott, president of Sitex, was a fool and inherently dangerous, like all fools.

Emma opened her eyes and sat up impatiently, her mind turning again to business, for she was tireless, sleepless, obsessive, and expedient when it came to her vast business enterprises, which rarely left her thoughts. She straightened her back and crossed her legs, adopting her usual posture, a posture that was contained and regal. There was also an imperiousness in the way she held her head and in her general demeanor, and her green eyes, as cold as steel, were full of enormous power. She lifted one of her small, strong hands and automatically smoothed her stylishly cut silver hair, which did not need it, since it was as impeccable as always. As indeed she was herself, in her simple yet elegant dark gray worsted dress, its severeness softened by the milky whiteness of the matchless pearls around her neck and the fine emerald pin on her shoulder.

She glanced at her granddaughter sitting opposite, diligently making notes for the coming week's business in New York. She looks drawn this morning, Emma thought, I push her too hard. She felt an unaccustomed twinge of guilt but impatiently shrugged it off. She's young, she can take it, and it's the best training she could ever have, Emma reassured herself and said, "Would you ask that nice young steward— John, isn't it?—to make some coffee please, Paula? I'm badly in need of it this morning."

The girl looked up. Although she was not beautiful in the accepted sense of that word, she was so vital and arresting she gave the impression of beauty. Her vividness of coloring contributed to this effect. Her glossy hair was an ink-black coif around her head, coming to a striking widow's peak above a face so clear and luminous it might have been carved from pale polished marble. The rather elongated face, with its prominent cheekbones and wide brow, was alert and expressive and there was a hint of Emma's resoluteness in her chin, but her eyes were her most spectacular feature, being large and intelligent and of a cornflower blue so deep they were almost violet.

She smiled at her grandmother with eager brightness and said, "Of course, Grandy. I'd like some myself." She left her seat, her tall slender body moving with a facile grace. She's so thin, Emma commented to herself, too thin for my liking. But she always has been. I suppose it's the way she's made. A leggy colt as a child, a racehorse now. A mixture of love and pride illuminated Emma's stern face and her eyes were full of sudden warmth as she gazed after the girl, who was her favorite, the daughter of Emma's favorite daughter, Daisy.

Many of Emma's dreams and hopes were centered in Paula. Even when she had been only a little girl she had gravitated to her grandmother and had also been curiously attracted to the family business. Her biggest thrill had been to go with Emma to the office and sit with her as she worked. While she was still in her teens she had shown such an uncanny understanding of complex machinations that Emma had been truly amazed, for none of her own children had ever displayed quite the same aptitude for her business affairs. Emma had secretly been delighted, but she had watched and waited with a degree of trepidation, fearful that the youthful enthusiasm would dissipate. But it had not waned; rather, it had grown. At sixteen Paula scorned the suggestion of a finishing school in Switzerland and had gone immediately to work for her grandmother. Over the years Emma drove Paula relentlessly, being more harsh and exacting with her than with any of her other employees, as she assiduously educated her in all aspects of Harte Enterprises. Paula was now twenty-three years old and she was so clever, so capable, and so much more mature than most girls of her age that Emma had recently moved her into a position of significance in the Harte organization. She had made Paula her personal assistant, much to the stupefaction and irritation of Emma's oldest son, Kit, who worked for the Harte organization. As Emma's right hand, Paula was privy to most of her corporate and private business and, when Emma deemed fit, she was her confidante in matters pertaining to the family, a situation Kit found intolerable.

The girl returned from the galley kitchen laughing. As she slid into her seat she said, "He was already making tea for you, Grandy. I suppose, like everyone else, he thinks that's all the English drink. But I said we preferred coffee. You do, don't you?"

Emma nodded absently, preoccupied with her affairs. "I certainly do, darling." She turned to her briefcase on the seat next to her and took out her glasses and a sheaf of folders. She handed one to Paula and said, "Please look at these figures for the New York store. I would be interested in what you think. I believe we are about to take a major step forward. Into the black."

Paula looked at her alertly. "That's sooner than you thought, isn't it? But then your reorganization has been very drastic. It should be paying off by now." Paula opened the folder with interest, her concentration focused on the figures. She had Emma's talent for reading a balance sheet with rapidity and detecting, almost at a glance, its strengths and its weaknesses and, like her grandmother, her business acumen was formidable.

Emma slipped on her horn-rimmed glasses and took up the large blue folder that pertained to Sitex Oil. As she quickly ran through the papers a grim smile settled on her face and there was a gleam of satisfaction in her eyes. She had won. At last, after three years of the most despicable and manipulative fighting she had ever witnessed, Harry Marriott had been removed as president of Sitex and kicked upstairs to become chairman of the board.

Emma had recognized Marriott's shortcomings years ago. She knew that if he was not entirely venal he was undoubtedly exigent and specious, and dissimulation had become second nature to him. Over the years, success and the accumulation of great wealth had only served to reinforce these traits, so that now it was impossible to deal with him on any level of reason. As far as Emma was concerned, his judgment was crippled, he had lost the little foresight he had once had, and he certainly had no comprehension of the rapidly shifting inner worlds of international business.

As she made notations on the documents for future reference, she hoped there would be no more vicious confrontations at Sitex. Yesterday she had been mesmerized by the foolhardiness of Harry's actions, had watched in horrified fascination as he had so skillfully maneuvered himself into a corner from which Emma knew there was no conceivable retreat. He had appealed to her friendship of some forty-odd years only once, floundering, helpless, lost; a babbling idiot in the face of his adversaries, of whom she was the most formidable. Emma had answered his pleas with total silence, the basilisk, an inexorable look in her pitiless eyes. *And she had won.* With the full support of the board. Harry was out. The new man, her man, was in and Sitex Oil was safe. But there was no joy in her victory, for to Emma there was nothing joyful in a man's downfall, nor was she vindictive.

Satisfied that the papers were in order, Emma put the folder and her glasses in her briefcase, settled back in her seat, and sipped the cup of coffee. After a few seconds she addressed Paula. "Now that you have been to several Sitex meetings, do you think you can cope alone soon?"

Paula glanced up from the balance sheets, a look of astonishment crossing her face. "You wouldn't send me in there alone!" she exclaimed. "It would be like sending a lamb to the slaughter. You wouldn't do that to me yet." As she regarded her grandmother she recognized that familiar inscrutable expression for what it truly was, a mask to hide Emma's ruthless determination. My God, she does mean it, Paula thought with a sinking feeling, but nevertheless she asked somewhat tremulously, "You're not really serious, are you, Grandmother?"

"Of course I'm serious!" A flicker of annoyance crossed Emma's face. She was surprised at the girl's unexpected but unequivocal nervousness, for Paula was accustomed to high-powered negotiations and had always displayed nerve and shrewdness. "Do I ever say anything I don't mean? You know better than that, Paula," she said sternly.

Paula was silent and, in that split second of silence, Emma became conscious of her tenseness, the startled expression that lingered on her face. Is she afraid? Emma wondered. Surely not. She had never displayed fear before. Paula was not weak. She was not going to turn out like the others. Or was she? This chilling possibility penetrated Emma's cold and brilliant mind like a steel blade and it was so unacceptable she refused to contemplate it. She decided then that Paula had simply been disturbed by the meeting, perhaps more so than she had shown. It had not disturbed Emma; rather it had irritated her, since she had found the bloodletting unnecessary and a waste of precious time and therefore all the more reprehensible. But *she* had seen it all before, had witnessed the rapacious pursuit of power all of her life, and she could take it in her stride. With her strength she was equipped to deal with it dispassionately. As Paula will have to learn to do, she told herself.

The severity of her expression did not change, but her voice softened as she said, "However, I won't send you alone to Sitex until you know, as I already know, that you can handle it successfully."

Paula was still holding the folder in her hands, delicate hands with tapering fingers that were also competent hands. She put the folder down with swift graceful movements and sat back in her seat. She was regaining her composure and, gazing steadily at her grandmother, she said quietly, "What makes you think they would listen to me the way they listen to you? I know what the board thinks of me. They regard me as the spoiled, pampered granddaughter of a rich and powerful woman. They dismiss me as empty-headed and silly, a brainless pretty face. They wouldn't treat me with the same deference they treat you, and why should they? I'm not you."

Emma pursed her lips to hide a small amused smile, sensing injured pride rather than fear. "Yes, I know what they think of you," she said in a much milder tone, "and we both know how wrong they are. And I do realize their attitude riles you, darling. I also know how easy it would be for you to disabuse them of their opinions of you. But I wonder, Paula, would you want to do that?"

She looked at her granddaughter quizzically, a shrewd glint in her eyes, and when the girl did not answer, she continued: "Being underestimated by men is one of the biggest crosses I've had to bear all of my life, and it was particularly irritating to me when I was your age. However, it was also an advantage and one I learned to make great use of, I can assure you of that. You know, Paula, when men believe they are dealing with a foolish or stupid woman they lower their guard, become negligent and sometimes even downright reckless. Unwittingly they often hand you the advantage on a plate."

"Yes, but . . ."

"No buts, Paula, please. And don't you underestimate me. Do you honestly think I would expose you to a tenuous or dangerous situation?" She shook her head and smiled. "I know what your capabilities are, my dear. I have always been sure of you. More sure of you than any of my own children, apart from your mother, of course, and you've never let me down."

"I appreciate your confidence, Grandmother," Paula replied steadily, "but I do find it hard to deal effectively with people who don't take me seriously and the Sitex board does not." A stubborn look dulled the light in her eyes and her mouth became a thin tight line, an unconscious replica of her grandmother's determined expression.

"You know, you really surprise me. You have enormous self-assurance and have dealt with all manner of people, on all levels, since you were quite a young girl. It has never seemed to disturb you before." Emma sighed heavily. "And haven't I told you countless times that what people think about you in business is unimportant. The important thing is for you to know who you are and what you are. And frankly I always thought you did."

"I do!" Paula cried, "but I am not sure that I have your capacity for hard work, or your experience."

Emma's face darkened. "Yes, you do. Furthermore, you have all the advantages of education I never had, so don't let me hear you speak so negatively of yourself again! I'll concede experience to you, but only to a degree. And you are gaining more of that every day. I'll tell you in all honesty, Paula, I would have no compunction in sending you back to Sitex tomorrow—and without me. Because I know you would handle yourself brilliantly. After all, I raised you, I trained you. Don't you think I *know* what I created?"

A carbon copy of yourself and a copy is never quite as good as the original, Paula thought dryly, but said, "Please don't be angry, Grandmother." Her voice was gentle. "You did a wonderful job. *But I am not you*. And the board is very aware of that. It's bound to affect their attitude!"

"Now listen to me!" Emma leaned forward and her narrowed eyes were like green glass slits underneath the old wrinkled lids. She spoke more slowly than was her custom, to give weight to her words.

"You seem to have forgotten one thing! When you walk

into Sitex in my place, you walk in there with something they have to take seriously. Power! Whatever they think of your ability, that power is the one thing they cannot ignore. The day you take over from me, after my death, you will be representing your mother, who will have become the single largest stockholder of Sitex. With her power of attorney you will be controlling twenty-five percent of the preferred stock and fifteen percent of the common stock of a multi-million-dollar corporation." She paused and stared intently at Paula, and then continued: "That's not ordinary power, Paula. That's immense power, and especially so in one person's hands. And don't you ever forget that. Believe me, they won't when it comes to the crunch. They didn't yesterday. But in spite of their unparalleled behavior—and I am beginning to realize just how much it did upset you—they were unable to ignore me and what I represent!" Emma sat back in her seat, but she kept her eyes shrewdly focused on Paula, and her face was implacable.

The girl had been listening attentively to her grandmother, as she always did, and her nervousness was ebbing away. For she did have courage and spirit, and not a little of Emma's resoluteness. But the virulence of the fighting at Sitex had indeed appalled her, as Emma suspected. As she gazed at her grandmother, reflecting on her words, she marveled at her again, as she had yesterday. Emma was seventy-eight years old. An old woman. Yet she had none of the infirmities of the aged, nor their loss of grace. She was vital and totally in command of her faculties. Paula had watched her grandmother's performance at Sitex with awe, had been amazed at her invincible strength, but most of all she had admired her integrity in the face of incredible pressure and opposition. Now Paula wondered, with a cold and calculating objectivity, whether she would ever have that sense of purpose, that icy tenacity to manipulate those men as astutely as her grandmother had. She was not sure. But then some of the nagging doubts were dispelled as she recognized the truth of her grandmother's words. Finally it was her own driving ambition that ultimately overcame the remnants of nervousness.

She spoke with renewed confidence. "You're right, of course. Power is the most potent of weapons, probably more so than money. And I'm sure it is the only thing the Sitex board does understand." She paused and looked at her grandmother directly. "I'm not afraid of them! Don't think that, Grandy. Although I must admit they did disgust me. I suppose if I was afraid, I was afraid of failing you." The smile she gave Emma was full of sureness and the troubled look had left her face. "I guess that's what my sudden nervousness was all about, but it's all gone now, Grandy."

Emma leaned forward and patted her hand reassuringly. "Don't ever be afraid of failing, Paula. It's stopped more people achieving their goals than I care to think about. When I was your age I didn't have time to worry about failing. I *had* to succeed to survive. And always remember what you just said to me about power. It *is* the ultimate weapon. Power, not money, talks. Money is only important when you're truly poor, when you need it for a roof over your head, for food and clothes. Once you have those essentials taken care of and go beyond them, money is simply a unit, a tool to work with. And don't ever let anyone persuade you that power corrupts. It doesn't always, only when those with power will do anything to hold on to that power. Sometimes it can even be ennobling." She smiled briefly and added with great positiveness, "And you won't fail me, my dear."

"I hope not, Grandy," Paula said, and when she saw the challenging look that swept over Emma's face, she added quickly, "I know I won't! But what about Harry Marriott? He's the chairman and he appears to hate me."

"I don't think he hates you, Paula. Fears you, perhaps." Emma's voice was suddenly flat and devoid of expression, but there was a dark gleam in her eyes. She had many memories of Harry Marriott, none of them very pleasant, for she had crossed swords with him innumerable times in the past.

"Fears me! Why?" Surprise made the girl's voice rise noticeably, and she leaned forward towards her grandmother, giving Emma her full attention.

A flick of contempt touched Emma's face as she thought of Marriott. "Because you remind him too much of your grandfather and that unnerves him. Harry was afraid of your grandfather from the very beginning, when they formed the original Sydney-Texas Oil Company and started drilling. Your grandfather always knew what Harry was and Harry instinctively knew that he knew. Hence his fear. When your grandfather left the Sitex stock to me it was with the understanding that I would never sell it as long as I lived. I was to hold it in trust for your mother and any children she might have. You see, your grandfather had great vision, Paula. He recognized years ago that Sitex would become the major company it is today and he wanted us to benefit from it. And he wanted Harry controlled. He wanted my rein on him always."

"I don't think he can do any more damage at Sitex. He's been rendered virtually powerless, thanks to you. Grandfather would be proud of you, darling," Paula said, and then asked with some curiosity, "Do I really resemble him—Grandfather, I mean?"

Emma looked at Paula quickly, a searching expression on her face. They were flying into the sun and a passage of light, very intense and golden, came in through the window. It centered on Paula as she was speaking. To Emma, her hair seemed shinier and blacker in this golden light, hanging in languorous folds like swatches of velvet around the pale still face, and her eyes were bluer and more vividly alive than ever. His eyes. His hair. She smiled gently, her eyes lighting up. "Sometimes you do, like right now. But mostly I think it's something in your manner that flusters Harry Marriott. And you have no cause to worry about him, Paula. He won't be there for long." She turned to the briefcase on the seat and began sorting her papers. After a few minutes she looked up and said, "If you've finished with the balance sheets of the New York store I'll have them back. By the way, do you agree with me?"

"Yes, I do, Grandy. They've made a marvelous turnaround."

"Let's hope we can keep *them* on the straight and narrow," Emma said as she took the folder from Paula. She put on her glasses and began studying the figures from the Paris store, already calculating the changes that would have to be made there. Emma knew the store was running into trouble and her mouth tightened in aggravation as she concentrated on the damning figures, and considered the moves she would make on their return to England.

Paula poured herself another cup of coffee and, as she sipped it, regarded her grandmother carefully. This is the face I've seen all my life and loved all my life, she reflected, a wave of tenderness sweeping through her. And she doesn't look her age at all, in spite of what she thinks. She could easily pass for a woman in her early sixties. Paula knew that her grandmother's life had been hard and frequently painful, yet, surprisingly, her face was incredibly well preserved. Paula realized, as she looked at Emma, that this was due in no small measure to the excellence of her bone structure. She noted the webs of wrinkles etching lacy patterns around her grandmother's eyes and mouth, as well as the two deep lines scoring down from her nostrils to her chin. But she also saw that the cheeks above these lines were still firm, and the green eyes that turned flinty in anger were not the rheumy wavering eyes of an old woman. They were alert and knowing. And yet some of her troubled life *is* reflected in her face, she thought, observing the indomitable set of Emma's mouth and the pugnacious tilt of her chin. As she continued to gaze at her, Paula acknowledged to herself that her grandmother *was* austere and somewhat stern of eye, to many the basilisk. Yet she was also aware that this autocratic bearing was often softened by a beguiling charm, a sense of humor, and an easy naturalness. And, now that her guard was down, it was a vulnerable face, open and fine and full of wisdom.

Paula knew that even those who were afraid of her grandmother found it hard to deny that she was a woman of great charisma, and few could resist the force of her compelling personality. Paula had never been afraid of her grandmother, but she recognized that most of the family were, her Uncle Kit in particular. Paula remembered now how delighted she had been when her Uncle Kit had once likened her to Emma. "You're as bad as your grandmother," he had said when she was about six or seven years old. She had not fully understood what he had meant, or why he had said it, but she had guessed that it was a reprimand from the look on his face. She had been thrilled to be called "as bad as your grandmother," because surely this meant that she, too, must be special like Grandy and everyone would be afraid of *her*, as they were afraid of her grandmother.

Emma looked up from the papers and broke into Paula's thoughts. "Talking of energy, Paula, how would you like to go to the Paris store when we leave New York? I really think I have to make some changes in the administration, from what I see in these balance sheets."

"I'll go to Paris if you want, but to tell you the truth, I had thought of spending some time in Yorkshire, Grandy. I was going to suggest to you that I do a tour of the northern stores," Paula remarked, keeping her voice casual and light.

Emma was thunderstruck and she did not attempt to disguise this. She took off her glasses slowly and regarded her granddaughter with a quickening interest. The girl flushed under this fixed scrutiny and her pale ivory face turned pink. She looked away, dropped her eyes, and murmured, "Well, you know I'll go where you think I'm most needed. Obviously it's Paris." She sat very still, sensing her grandmother's surprised reaction.

"Why this sudden interest in Yorkshire?" Emma demanded. "It strikes me there is some fatal fascination up there! Jim Fairley, I presume," she added, refusing to be deceived by Paula's ready acquiescence to her suggestion.

Paula shifted in her seat, avoiding her grandmother's unflickering stare. She smiled falteringly and the flush deepened as she said defensively, "Don't be ridiculous! I just thought I ought to take inventory at the northern stores."

"Inventory, my eye and Peggy Martin!" Emma exclaimed, reverting to the vernacular of the North. And she thought to herself: I can read Paula like a book. Of course it's Fairley. Aloud she said, "I do know that you are seeing him, Paula."

"Not anymore!" Paula cried, her eyes flashing, her lips shaking. "I stopped seeing him months ago!" As she spoke she instantly recognized her mistake. Her grandmother had so easily trapped her into admitting the one thing she had vowed she would never admit to her.

Emma laughed softly, but her gaze was steely. "Don't be so upset. I'm not angry. Actually I never was. I only wondered why you never told me. You usually tell me everything."

"At first I didn't tell you because I know how you feel about the Fairleys. That vendetta of yours! And I didn't want to upset you. God knows, you've had enough trouble in your life, without me causing you any more. When I stopped seeing him there seemed to be no point in bringing up something that was finished. I didn't want to disturb you unnecessarily, that's all."

"The Fairleys don't upset me," Emma snapped. "And in case you've forgotten, I employ Jim Fairley, my dear. I would hardly have him running the Yorkshire Consolidated Newspaper Company if I didn't trust him." Emma gave Paula a searching glance and asked quickly, curiously, "Why did you stop seeing him?"

"Because I . . . we . . . he . . . because," Paula began, and hesitated, wondering whether she dare go on. She did not want to hurt her grandmother. But in her crafty way she's known about our relationship all the time, Paula thought. The girl drew in her breath and, knowing herself to be trapped, she said, "I stopped seeing Jim because I found myself getting involved. I knew if I continued to see him it would only mean eventual heartache for me, and for him, and pain for you, too." She paused and looked away and then continued with the utmost quiet: "You know you wouldn't accept a Fairley in the family, Grandmother."

"I'm not so sure about that," Emma said in a voice that was hardly audible. So it went that far, she thought. Unexpectedly she felt unutterably weary. Her cheekbones ached and her eyes were scratchy from fatigue. She longed to close her eyes, to be done with this silly and useless discussion. Emma tried to smile at Paula, but her mouth was parched and her lips would not move. Her heart constricted and she was filled with an aching sadness, a sadness she thought had been expunged years ago. The memory of him was there then, so clearly evoked that it bit like acid into her brain, and her whole face underwent such a sudden change her bones seemed to stretch under her skin. And Emma saw Edwin Fairley as vividly as if he was standing before her. And in his shadow there was Jim Fairley, his spitting image. Edwin Fairley, usually so elusive in her memory, was caught and held and all the pain he had caused her was there, a living thing. A feeling of such oppression overcame her she could not speak.

Paula was watching her grandmother intently and she was afraid for her when she saw the sad expression on that severe face. There was an empty look in Emma's eyes and, as she stared into space, her mouth tightened into a harsh and bitter line. Damn the Fairleys, all of them, Paula cursed. She leaned forward and took hold of her grandmother's hand anxiously. "It's over, Grandy. It wasn't important. Honestly. I'm not upset about it. And I *will* go to Paris, Grandy! Oh, Grandy darling, don't look like that, please. I can't bear it." Paula smiled shakily, concerned, afraid, conciliatory. These mingled emotions ran together and underlying them all was a sickening fury with herself for permitting her grandmother to goad her into this ridiculous conversation, one she had been avoiding for months.

After a short time the haunted expression faded from Emma's face. She swallowed hard and took control of herself, exercising that formidable iron will that was the root of her power and her strength. "Jim Fairley's a good man. Different from the others . . ." she began. She stopped and sucked in her breath. She wanted to proceed, to tell Paula she could resume the friendship with Jim Fairley. But she could not. *Yesterday was now. The past was immutable.*

"Don't let's talk about the Fairleys. I said I would go to Paris," Paula cried, clinging to her grandmother's hand. "You know best and perhaps I should look the store over anyway."

"I think you *must* go over there, Paula, to see what's going on."

"I'll go as soon as we get back to London," Paula said swiftly.

"Yes, that's a good idea," Emma agreed rather brusquely, as glad as Paula to change the subject, but also instinctively pressed for time, as she had been all of her life. Time was a precious commodity to Emma. Time had always been evaluated as money and she did not want to waste it now, dwelling on the past, resurrecting painful events that had taken place some sixty years ago.

Emma was in a constant hurry to move forward and now she said, "I think I must go directly to the office when we arrive in New York. Charles can take the luggage to the apartment, after he's dropped us off. I'm worried about Gaye, you see. Have you noticed anything peculiar when you've spoken to her on the phone?"

Paula was sitting back in her seat, relaxed and calm again, relieved that the subject of Jim Fairley had been dropped so promptly. "No, I haven't. What do you mean?"

"I can't pin it down to anything specific," Emma continued thoughtfully, "but instinctively I know something is dreadfully wrong. She has sounded edgy during all of our conversations. I noticed it the day she arrived from London and called me at Sitex. Haven't you detected anything in her voice?"

"No. But then she has been speaking mostly to you, Grandmother. You don't think there is some trouble with the business in London, do you?" Paula asked, alarmed.

"I sincerely hope not," Emma said, unable to keep the concern out of her voice, "that's all I need after the Sitex situation." She drummed her fingers on the table for a few moments and then looked out of the window, her mind awash with thoughts of her business and her secretary, Gaye Sloane. In her sharp and calculating way she enumerated all of the things that could have gone wrong in London and then gave up. Anything might have happened and it was futile to speculate and hazard wild guesses. That, too, was a waste of time.

She turned to Paula and gave her a wry little smile. "We'll know soon enough, my dear. We should be landing shortly."

TWO

The American corporate offices of Harte Enterprises took up six floors in a modern office block on Park Avenue in the fifties. If the English department-store chain Emma Harte had founded years ago was the visible symbol of her success, then Harte Enterprises was the living heart and sinew. An enormous octopus of an organization, with tentacles that stretched half around the world, it controlled clothing factories, woolen mills, real estate, a retail merchandise company, and newspapers in England, plus large blocks of shares in other major English companies.

As the original founder of this privately held corporation, Emma still owned 100 percent of the shares of Harte Enterprises, and it operated solely under her aegis, as did the chain of department stores that bore her name, with branches in the North of England, London, Paris, and New York. Harte Stores was a public company, trading on the London Stock Exchange, although Emma was the majority shareholder and chairman of the board. The diversified holdings of Harte Enterprises in America included real estate, a Seventh Avenue dress-manufacturing company, and other stock investments in American industries.

Whilst Harte Stores and Harte Enterprises were worth millions of pounds, they represented only a portion of her fortune. Apart from owning 40 percent of the stock in the Sitex Oil Corporation of America, she had vast holdings in Australia, including real estate, mining, coal fields, and one of the largest fully operating sheep stations in New South Wales. In London, a small but rich company called E. H.

Incorporated controlled her personal investments and real estate.

It had been Emma's custom to travel to New York several times a year. She was actively involved in all areas of her business empire and although she was not particularly distrustful of those to whom she had given extraordinary executive powers, confident of her own shrewd judgment in these choices, there was a canny Yorkshire wariness about her. She was impelled to leave nothing to chance and she also believed that it was vital for her presence to be felt in New York from time to time.

Now, as the Cadillac that had brought them from Kennedy Airport pulled up in front of the skyscraper that housed her corporate offices, Emma's thoughts reverted to Gaye Sloane. Emma had instantly detected Gaye's nervousness during their first telephone conversation when she had arrived from London. Originally Emma had thought this was due to tiredness after the long transatlantic flight, but the nervousness had accelerated rather than diminished over the last few days. Emma had noted the tremulous quality in Gaye's voice, her clipped manner, her obvious desire to terminate their talks as quickly as possible. This not only baffled Emma but disturbed her, for Gaye was behaving totally out of character. Emma contemplated the possibility that personal problems might be upsetting Gaye, but her inclination was to dismiss this idea, knowing Gaye as well as she did. Intuitively Emma knew that Gaye was troubled by a business problem, one which was of some import and one which ultimately affected her. She resolved to make her talk with Gaye the priority of the day's business.

Emma shivered as they alighted from the car. It was a raw January day, and although the sun was bright in a clear sky, the wind was sharp with frost and Atlantic rain. She could barely remember a time when she had not felt icy cold all over and sometimes it seemed to her that her bones were frozen into solid blocks of ice, as if frostbite had crept into her entire being and petrified her very blood. That numbing excruciating coldness that had first invaded her body in childhood had rarely left her since, not under the heat of tropical sun nor in front of blazing fires nor in the central heating of New York, which she usually found suffocating. She coughed as she and Paula hurried towards the building. She had caught a cold before they had left for Texas and it had settled on her chest, leaving her with this hacking cough that flared up constantly. As they swung through the doors into the building, Emma was for once thankful for that furnace-like heating in her offices.

They took the elevator up to the thirtieth floor, where their own offices were located. "I think I had better see Gaye at once, and alone," Emma said as they stepped out of the elevator. "Why don't you go over the balance sheets of the New York store with Johnston and I'll see you later," she suggested.

Paula nodded. "Fine. Call me if you need me, Grandmother. And I do hope everything is all right." Paula veered to the left as Emma continued on to her own office, moving through the reception area quickly and with agility. Emma smiled at the receptionist, and exchanged cordial greetings with her, as she swept through the double doors that led to her private domain. She closed the doors firmly behind her, for she did not subscribe to this American custom of open doors in executive offices. She thought it peculiar and distracting, as addicted as she was to total privacy. She threw her tweed coat and her handbag carelessly onto one of the sofas and, still holding the briefcase, she crossed the room to the desk. This was a gargantuan slab of heavy glass on a simple base of polished steel and it was a dramatic focal point in the highly dramatic office. It was angled across a corner, looking out into the vast and lovely room, facing towards a plate-glass window. This covered the whole of one wall and rose to the ceiling in a glittering sweep that presented a panoramic view of the city skyline, which Emma always thought of as a living painting of enormous power and wealth and the heartbeat of American industry.

She enjoyed her New York office, as different as it was from her executive suite in the London store, which was filled with the mellow Georgian antiques she preferred. Here the ambiance was modern and sleek, for Emma had a great sense of style and she had decided that as much as she loved period furniture, it would be unfitting when juxtaposed against the slick architecture of this great steel-and-glass structure that pushed its way up into the sky. And so she had assembled the best in modern furniture design. Mies van der Rohe chairs were mingled with long, slender Italian sofas, all of

them upholstered in dark leather as soft and as supple as silk.
There were tall steel-and-glass étagères filled with books,
cabinets of rich polished rosewood, and small tables made of
slabs of Italian marble balanced on polished chrome bases.
Yet for all of its modern overtones there was nothing austere
or cold about the office, which had a classical elegance and
was the epitome of superior taste. It had, in fact, a tranquil
beauty, a softness, filled as it was with a misty mélange of
intermingled blues and grays, these subdued tones washing
over the walls and the floor, enlivened here and there by
rafts of more vivid colors in the cushions on the sofas and in
the priceless French Impressionist paintings which graced
the walls. Emma's love of art was also evidenced in the
Henry Moore and Brancusi sculptures and the temple heads
from Angkor Wat, which were displayed on black marble
pedestals around the room. The great soaring window was
sheathed in sheer bluish-gray curtains which fell like a heavy
mist from the ceiling, and when they were open, as they were
now, the room seemed to be part of the sky, as if it was
suspended in space above the towering concrete monoliths of
Manhattan.

Emma smiled as she sat down at the desk, for Gaye's
handiwork was apparent. The long sweep of glass was neat
and uncluttered, just the way she liked it, bare except for the
telephones, the silver mug of pens, the yellow legal pad she
favored for notes, and the practical metal extension lamp that
flooded the desk with light. Her correspondence, interoffice
memos, and a large number of telexes were arranged in
respective files, while a number of telephone messages were
clipped together next to the telephones. She took out her
glasses and read the telephone messages and the telexes,
making various notations on these, and then she buzzed for
Gaye. The minute she entered the room Emma knew that
her fears had not been unfounded. Gaye was haggard and she
had dark smudges under her eyes and seemed to vibrate with
tension. Gaye Sloane was a woman of about thirty-eight and
she had been Emma's executive secretary for six years, although she had been in her actual employ for twelve years.
She was a model of diligence and efficiency and she was
devoted to Emma, whom she not only admired but held in
considerable affection. A tall well-built woman with an at-

tractive appearance, she was always self-contained and placid, usually in command of herself.

But as she walked across the room Emma detected raw nerves being barely controlled. They exchanged pleasantries and Gaye sat down in the chair opposite Emma's desk, her pad in her hand.

Emma sat back in her chair, consciously adopting a relaxed attitude in an effort to make Gaye feel as much at ease as possible. She glanced at her secretary kindly and asked quietly, "What's wrong, Gaye?"

Gaye hesitated momentarily and then said rather hurriedly, feigning surprise, "Why, nothing, Mrs. Harte. Truly, I'm just tired. Jet lag, I think."

"Let's forget about jet lag, Gaye. I believe you are extremely upset and have been since you arrived in New York. Now come along, my dear, tell me what's bothering you. Is it something here or is there a problem with business in London?"

"No. Of course not!" Gaye exclaimed, but she paled slightly and looked away, avoiding Emma's steady gaze.

This did not go unnoticed by Emma, who tensed in her chair and leaned forward, her arms on the desk, her eyes glittering behind her glasses. She became increasingly conscious of the woman's suppressed emotions and sensed that Gaye was troubled by something of the most extreme seriousness. As she continued to study her she thought Gaye seemed close to total collapse.

"Are you ill, Gaye?"

"No, Mrs. Harte. I'm perfectly well, thank you."

"Is something in your personal life disturbing you?" Emma now asked as patiently as she could, determined to get to the root of the problem.

"No, Mrs. Harte." Her voice was a whisper.

Emma took off her glasses and gave Gaye a long, piercing look and said briskly, "Come, come, my dear! I know you too well. There is something weighing on your mind and I can't understand why you won't tell me about it. Have you made some sort of mistake and are afraid to explain? Surely not after all these years. Nobody is infallible and I'm not the ogre I'm supposed to be. You, of all people, should know that by now."

"Oh, I do, Mrs. Harte . . ." The girl broke off. Her voice was shaking and she was close to tears. Her heart was pounding with such increasing speed she thought it would explode against her rib cage.

The woman sitting opposite Gaye was composed and in absolute control of herself. And she was no weakling, Gaye knew that only too well. She was tough and resilient, an indomitable woman who had achieved her phenomenal success because of her formidable character and her strength of will, plus her resourcefulness and brilliance in business. To Gaye, Emma Harte was as indestructible as the coldest steel that could not be twisted or broken. But I am about to break her now, she thought, panic taking hold of her again.

Emma had watched Gaye carefully, noting with her usual acuity the passing emotions that flooded her secretary's face. She had seen, with gathering disquiet, the twitching muscles and the fear in her eyes. Emma stood up decisively and crossed the room to the rosewood bar, shaking her head in perplexity. She opened the bar, poured a measure of cognac into a small glass, and brought it back to Gaye.

"Drink this, my dear. It will make you feel better," she said, patting the woman's arm affectionately.

Tears sprang into Gaye's eyes and her throat ached. The brandy was harsh and it stung her throat but she was suddenly glad of its rough taste. She sipped it slowly and remembered Emma's kindnesses to her over the years and at that precise moment she wished, with great fervency, that she was not the one who had to impart this news. Gaye realized that there were those, who had dealt with Emma as a formidable adversary, who considered her to be cynical, rapacious, cunning, and ruthless. On the other hand, Gaye knew that she was generous of her time and money and understanding of heart. As she was being understanding now. Perhaps Emma *was* willful and imperious and even power-ridden. But surely life had made her so. Gaye had always said to Emma's critics, and with the utmost veracity, that above all the other tycoons of her caliber and stature, Emma Harte had compassion, and was just and charitable and infinitely kind.

Gaye eventually became aware of this prolonged silence between them, of Emma's fixed stare. She put the glass down on the edge of the desk and smiled weakly at Emma. "Thank you, Mrs. Harte. I do feel better."

"Good. Now, Gaye, why don't you confide in me? It can't be all that terrible."

Gaye was paralyzed, unable to speak.

Emma shifted in her seat and leaned forward urgently. "Look here, is this something to do with me, Gaye?" Her voice was calm and strong.

It seemed to give Gaye a degree of confidence. She nodded her head and was about to speak, but when she saw the look of concern enter Emma's eyes, her courage deserted her again. She put her hands up to her face and cried involuntarily, "Oh God! How can I tell you!"

"Let's get it out in the open, Gaye," Emma said brusquely. "If you don't know where to begin, then begin in the middle. Just blurt it out. It's often the best way to talk about something unpleasant, which I presume this is."

Gaye nodded and began hesitatingly, choking back her tears, her sentences disjointed, her hands twitching nervously, her eyes staring and wide. She spoke rapidly in bursts, wanting to tell it all now, and get it over as quickly as possible. It would be a relief, for it had preyed on her mind for days.

"It was the door. . . . I remembered . . . I went back. . . . I heard them talking. . . . No, shouting. . . . They were angry . . . arguing. . . . They were saying . . ."

"Just a minute, Gaye." Emma held up her hand to stop the incoherent flow of words. "I don't want to interrupt you, but can you try to be a little more explicit. I know you're upset, but slow down and take it calmly. What door?"

"Sorry." Gaye drew a deep breath. "The door of the filing room that opens onto the boardroom in London. I'd forgotten to lock it last Friday night. I was leaving the office and I remembered I had forgotten to turn off the tape machine, and *that* reminded me of the door. I went back to my office, because I was leaving on Saturday night for New York. I unlocked the door at my side and walked through the filing room to lock the door at the other end."

As Gaye had been speaking Emma had a mental image of the filing room in the executive suite of offices in the London store. It was a long narrow room with filing cabinets banked on either side and rising to the ceiling. A year ago, Emma had broken through the back wall of the filing room into the adjoining boardroom and added a door. This measure had been to facilitate easy access to documents that might be needed at board meetings, but it had also turned out to be a useful little artery that linked the boardroom and the executive offices and so saved a great deal of time.

Apprehension tightened Emma's throat. Gaye had obviously heard a conversation of vital importance or she would not be reacting in this frightened way. Innumerable questions ran through Emma's mind, but she reserved them for later. She nodded for her secretary to continue.

"I know how particular you are about that door being locked, Mrs. Harte. As I walked through the filing room from my office I noticed that the door was not simply unlocked but actually open . . . ajar. That's when I heard them . . . through the crack in the door. I didn't know what to do. I was afraid they would hear me closing and locking the door. I didn't want anyone to think I was eavesdropping. So I stopped for a moment, and then I turned off the light, so they wouldn't know I was in the filing room. Mrs. Harte, I . . ." Gaye paused and swallowed, momentarily unable to continue.

"Go on, Gaye, it's all right."

"I wasn't eavesdropping, I really wasn't, Mrs. Harte. You know I'm not like that. It was purely accidental . . . that I heard them, I mean. I heard them say . . . say . . ."

Gaye stopped again, shaking all over, and her mouth felt suddenly tight and dry. She looked at Emma, who was sitting perfectly rigid in her chair, her face an unreadable mask.

"I heard them say, no, *one* of them said that you were getting too old to run the business. That it would be hard to prove that you were senile or incompetent, but that you would agree to step down to avoid a scandal, to prevent a catastrophe with the Harte shares on the Stock Exchange. They argued about this. And then he, that is, the one who had been doing most of the talking, said that the stores had to be sold to a conglomerate and that this would be easy as several companies would be interested in a take-over. He then said that Harte Enterprises could be sold off in pieces . . ." Gaye hesitated, and looked closely at Emma in an attempt to discern her reactions. But Emma's face was still inscrutable.

The sun came out from behind a bank of gray clouds and streamed into the room, a great cataract of brilliant light that was harsh and unrelenting. This unremitting light was a shimmering presence in the room, bouncing off the steel and glass and marble furniture with enormous intensity, flooding that vast space with a white brilliance that made the room look alien, unreal, and frightful to Emma. The searing light seemed to pierce into her brain and she blinked and shielded her eyes against it.

"Could you close the curtains please, Gaye?" she murmured, her voice a hoarse whisper.

Gaye flew across the room and pushed the automatic button that operated the draperies. They swept across the soaring window with a faint swishing sound and the penetrating radiance in the room was softly diffused. She returned to her chair in front of the desk and, gazing at Emma, she asked with some concern, "Are you all right, Mrs. Harte?"

Emma had been staring at the papers on her desk. She lifted her head slowly and looked across at Gaye with blank eyes. "Yes. Please go on. I want to know all of it. And I am perfectly sure there *is* more."

"Yes, there is. The other one said it was futile to battle with you now, either personally or legally, that you couldn't live much longer, that you were getting old, very old, almost eighty. And the other one said you were so tough they would have to shoot you in the end." Gaye covered her mouth with her hand to stifle a sob and tears pricked her eyes. "Oh, Mrs. Harte, I'm so sorry."

Emma was so still she might have turned to stone. Her eyes were suddenly cold and calculating. "Are you going to tell me who these two gentlemen were, Gaye? Mind you, I use that term loosely," she said with biting sarcasm that was icy. Before Gaye had a chance to reply Emma knew deep within herself, deep down in the very marrow of her bones, exactly whom Gaye would condemn when she opened her mouth. And yet part of her was still disbelieving, still hopeful, and she must hear it from Gaye's own mouth to truly believe it. To accept her own damning suspicions as fact.

"Oh God, Mrs. Harte! I wish I didn't have to tell you this!" She took a deep breath. "It was Mr. Ainsley and Mr. Lowther. They started to quarrel again, and Mr. Lowther said that they needed the girls with them. Mr. Ainsley said the girls *were* with them, that he already talked to them. But that he had not talked to Mrs. Amory, since she would never agree. He said she must not be told anything, under any circumstances, because she would immediately run and tell you. Mr. Lowther then said again that there was nothing they could do about

taking over the business whilst you were still alive. He told
Mr. Ainsley that they would never get away with it, because
they did not have the power, or enough shares between
them, to gain control. He said they would just have to wait
until you were dead. He was adamant about this. He also told
Mr. Ainsley that he himself was entitled to the controlling
shares of the Harte chain and that he was certain you would
leave him these shares. He then informed Mr. Ainsley that
he intended to run the Harte chain and that he would never
agree to sell the stores to a conglomerate. Mr. Ainsley was
furious, almost hysterical, and started to scream the most
terrible things at Mr. Lowther. But Mr. Lowther eventually
calmed him down, and he said he *would* agree to the sale of
Harte Enterprises, and that would bring Mr. Ainsley all the
millions he wanted. Mr. Ainsley then asked if Mr. Lowther
knew what was in your will. Mr. Lowther told him he didn't
know, but that he thought you would be fair with them all.
He did express some concern about Miss Paula, because she
was so close to you. He said he didn't know what she had
been able to wheedle out of you. This upset Mr. Ainsley, and
he grew very excited again and said that they must formulate
a plan of action now, one which they could put into operation
after your death, in the event that your will did not favor
them."

Gaye paused breathlessly, poised on the edge of her chair.
She felt sick, although now that she was telling her story the
awful shaking had mysteriously ceased, and her limbs were
perfectly still. But she felt drained and empty as she regarded
Emma expectantly.

Emma could not speak or move or think, so stunned and
shaken was she now. The room, which had been washed with
filtered sunlight a few moments ago, had darkened around
her as Gaye was speaking, and the warm air, that suffocating
air, had become as cold as the Arctic. As she reflected on
Gaye's words the blood rushed to her head and a faintness
settled over her. She was lost, adrift, and every bone in her
body felt weighted down by the most dreadful fatigue, a
fatigue that was leaden and stupefying.

Her heart, her weary heart, moved and shifted within her,
and it seemed to Emma that in that instant it withered and
turned into a cold, hard little pebble. An immense pain
flooded her entire being. It was the pain of despair. The pain

of betrayal. Her two sons were plotting against her. Robin
and Kit. Half brothers who had never been close were now
hand in glove, partners in treachery. She was incredulous
and aghast as she thought: God Almighty! It's not possible. It
can't be possible. Not Kit. Not Robin. They could never be
so venal and exigent. Never. Not my boys! Yet somewhere in
the recesses of her mind, in her innermost soul, she knew
that it was true. And that anguish of heart and soul and body
was displaced by an anger of such icy ferocity it cleared her
brain and propelled her to her feet. Dimly, distantly, she
heard Gaye's voice coming to her as if from a cavernous
depth.

"Mrs. Harte! Mrs. Harte! Are you ill?"

Emma leaned forward across the desk, which she gripped
tightly to steady herself, and her face was drawn and pinched.
Her voice was low, almost a hiss as she said, "Are you sure of
all this, Gaye? I don't doubt you, but are you certain you
heard everything correctly? You realize the seriousness of
what you have recounted, I'm sure, so think very carefully."

"Mrs. Harte, I am absolutely sure of everything I've said,"
Gaye answered quietly. "Furthermore, I have not added or
subtracted anything, and I haven't exaggerated either."

"Is that all?"

"No, there's more." Gaye bent down and picked up her
handbag. She opened it and took out a tape, which she
placed on the desk in front of Emma.

Emma regarded the tape, her eyes narrowing shrewdly.
"What is this?"

"It's a tape of everything that was said, Mrs. Harte. Except
for whatever occurred before I went into the filing room. And
the first few sentences I heard. They are missing."

Emma looked at her uncomprehendingly, her eyebrows
lifting, questions on the tip of her tongue. But before she
could ask them, Gaye proceeded to explain more fully.

"Mrs. Harte, the tape machine was on. That's why I went
back to the office in the first place. When I went into the
filing room, and heard them shouting, I was distracted for a
minute. I turned off the filing-room light so they wouldn't
come in and see me. It was then that I saw the red light on the
machine flickering and I went to turn this off, too. But it
suddenly occurred to me to record their conversation, since I
was getting the general drift of it, and realized its impor-

tance. So I pressed the record button. Everything they said after that moment is on here, even the things which were said after I closed the door and couldn't hear clearly."

Emma had the irresistible desire to laugh out loud, a bitter, hollow laugh. She resisted the impulse, lest Gaye think her raving mad and out of her senses, or hysterical at the most. The fools, the utter fools! she thought. And the irony of it! They had chosen her own boardroom in which to plot against her. That was their first and most crucial mistake. An irrevocable mistake. Kit and Robin were directors of Harte Enterprises, but they were not on the board of the department-store chain. They did not come to board meetings at the store, and so they did not know that she had recently installed sophisticated equipment to record the minutes, another time-saving device. It liberated Gaye for other duties and she simply typed up the minutes from the tapes when it was convenient. The microphones were hooked up under the boardroom table, hidden for aesthetics rather than for any reasons of secrecy in the elegant Georgian room with its fine antiques and paintings of great worth. Emma looked down at the tape on the glass desk and to her it was an evil thing, lying there like a coiled and venomous snake. She shivered as she sat down behind the desk, her eyes not leaving the insidious little spool which was the instrument of their undoing, of their ruin.

"I assume you have listened to this, Gaye?"

"Yes, Mrs. Harte. I waited until they left and then I played it back. I took it home with me on Friday and it hasn't been out of my sight since then."

"Is there much more on it? More than you have already told me?"

"About another ten minutes or so. They were discussing . . ."

Emma held up her hand, utterly exhausted, unable to hear any more of this ghastly dialogue. "Never mind, Gaye. I'll play it later. I know quite enough already!"

She stood up and walked across the room to the window, erect and composed, though her steps were slow and dragged wearily across the thick carpet. She moved the curtains slightly. It had started to snow. The crystal flakes fell in glittering white flurries, swirling and eddying in the wind, brushing up against the window and coating it with a light film as delicate and as fine as white lace. But the flakes were rapidly melting under the bright sun, running in rivulets down the glass and turning into drizzle before they reached the ground. Emma looked down. Far below her the traffic moved in slow unending lines up and down Park Avenue and the scene was strangely remote. And everything was hushed in the room, as if the entire world had stopped and was silent, stilled forever.

She pressed her aching head against the window and closed her eyes and thought of her two sons, of all her children, but mostly of her adored Robin, her favorite son. Robin, who had become her antagonist after they had clashed a few years before about a take-over bid for the chain of stores. A bid which came from out of the blue and which she did not want to even discuss, never mind consider. When she had refused to talk to the conglomerate involved, he had been vociferous in his condemnation of her, exclaiming angrily that she did not want to sell because she did not want to relinquish her power. She had met resentment from him in such virulent proportions that she was at first incredulous and then truly infuriated. What nerve, what gall, she had thought at the time, that he would dare to dictate to her about her business. One in which he did not have the slightest interest, except for the money it brought him. Robin, the handsome, the dashing, the brilliant Member of Parliament. Robin with his long-suffering wife, his mistresses, his rather questionable male friends, and his taste for high living. Yes, Robin was the instigator of this deadly little plot, of that she was quite sure.

Kit, her eldest son, did not have the imagination or the nerve to promulgate so nefarious a scheme. But what he lacked in imagination he made up for in plodding diligence and stubbornness and he was uncommonly patient. Kit could wait years for anything he truly wanted, and she had always known he wanted the stores. But he had never had any aptitude for retailing, and long ago, when he was still young, she had maneuvered him into Harte Enterprises, steered him towards the woolen mills in Yorkshire, which he ran with a degree of efficiency. Yes, Kit could always be maneuvered, and no doubt Robin is doing just that, she thought contemptuously.

She contemplated her three daughters and her mouth twisted into a grim smile as she considered Edwina, the eldest, the first born of all her children. She had worked like a drudge and fought like a tigress for Edwina when she was still only a girl herself, for she had loved Edwina with all her heart. And yet she had always known that Edwina had never truly felt the same way about her, oddly distant as a little girl, remote in her youth, and that remoteness had turned into real coldness in later years. Edwina had allied herself with Robin at the time of the takeover bid, backing him to the hilt. Undoubtedly she was now his chief ally in this perfidious scheme. She found it hard to believe that Elizabeth, Robin's twin, would go along with them, and yet perhaps she would. Beautiful, wild, untamable Elizabeth, with her exquisite features and beguiling charm and her penchant for expensive husbands, expensive clothes, and expensive travel. No amount of money was ever enough to satisfy her and she needed it as constantly and as desperately as Robin.

Daisy was the only one of whom she was sure, because she knew that of all her children Daisy truly loved her. Daisy was not involved in this scheme of things, because she would never be a party to a conspiracy engineered by her brothers and sisters to slice up the Harte holdings. Apart from her love and her loyalty, Daisy had the utmost respect for her and faith in her judgment. Daisy never questioned her motives or decisions, because she recognized that they were generated by a sense of fair play, and were based entirely on judicious planning.

Daisy was her youngest child, and as different in looks and character from Emma as the others were, but she was closely bound to her mother and they cared for each other with a deep and powerful love that bordered on adoration. Daisy was all sweetness and gentleness, fine and honorable and good. At times, in the past, Emma had mused on Daisy's intrinsic purity and honesty and worried about it, believing her to be too open and soft for her own safety. Emma had reasoned that her goodness could only make her dangerously vulnerable. But, eventually, she had begun to comprehend that there was a deep and strong inner core in Daisy that was tenacious and unyielding to any form of pressure. In her own way she could be as implacable as Emma, and she was unshakable in her beliefs, brave and courageous in her actions, and steadfast in her loyalties. Emma had finally recognized that it was Daisy's very goodness that protected her. It enfolded her like a shining and impenetrable sheath of chain mail and so made her incorruptible and inviolate against all.

And the others know that, Emma thought, as she continued to gaze out at the skyline of Manhattan, her mind in a turmoil, her heart flooded with despair. She was still shaken; however, the stunned feeling that she had been bludgeoned about her head and her body was slowly dissipating. She discovered, too, that although she had been thunderstruck initially, this reaction was also a passing thing. She actually felt no sense of surprise now at Gaye's story. It was not that she had ever anticipated these actions of her children, for in all truth she had not. But few things came as a surprise to Emma anymore and in her wisdom, understanding, and experience of life, family treachery was not surprising to her at all.

Emma had come to believe long ago that ties of blood did not assure fidelity or love. It's not true that blood is thicker than water, she thought, except in Daisy's case. She really is part of me. She remembered a conversation she had once had with her banker, Henry Rossiter. It was years ago now, but it came back to her quite strongly, each nuance and tone so clear it might have taken place only yesterday. He had said grimly that Daisy was like a dove that had been flung into a nest of vipers. Emma had shuddered with revulsion at his ghastly and savage analogy. To dispel the hideous image he had conjured up before her eyes, she had told him that he was being melodramatic and overimaginative, and she had laughed, so that he would not observe her true reactions. Now on this January day, in her seventy-ninth year, she recalled Henry's words, which had been so ominous, as she contemplated the first four children she had borne and raised, and who had turned on her. A nest of vipers indeed, she thought. She turned away from the window abruptly and went back to her desk. She sat down and her unflickering eyes rested on that vile tape for a moment, and then she lifted her briefcase onto the desk, opened it, and dropped the tape into it without further comment.

Gaye had been watching with some consternation, her face grave. She was disturbed by Emma's appearance. Her countenance was now glazed over by a kind of hard grimness, and she looked haggard and drawn. The fine bones of her face, always very prominent, were so gaunt and close to the surface of her skin they appeared almost fleshless. Her naturally pale face was ashen. The spots of rouge stood out like raw smudges on her cheeks, and her lips had turned livid under the gloss of the red lipstick. Emma's wide-set green eyes, usually so clear and so brilliant and so comprehending, were now clouded with dark pain and disillusionment and the agony of fully acknowledged betrayal. To Gaye her face had taken on the overtones of a death mask, and she knew that this abrupt and drastic change in Emma's appearance was wrought by the painful thoughts of her children and the heinous treachery they planned.

Gaye thought there was something fragile and vulnerable about Emma at this moment and she looked so very old, and Gaye had the desire to run and put her arms around her. But she refrained, afraid Emma would think of it as an intrusion, for she knew that there was an unremitting self-reliance and intense pride in Emma's nature, which was forbidding, and she had an innate sense of privateness about her personal affairs.

Instead Gaye groped for consoling words to express the depth of her understanding and her devotion, but she could not find the right ones to articulate the full extent of her sympathy and her concern, so unnerved was she by Emma's appearance. And so instead she asked quietly and with some tenderness, "Do you feel ill, Mrs. Harte? Can I get you anything?"

"I'll be all right in a few minutes, Gaye." Emma attempted a smile. She bent her head and she felt the prick of tears behind her eyes. Eventually she looked up and said, "I think I would like to be alone for a little while, Gaye. To think. Would you make me a cup of tea and bring it in shortly, in about ten minutes, please?"

"Of course, Mrs. Harte. As long as you are sure you will be all right alone." She stood up and moved towards the door, hesitating briefly.

Emma smiled. "Yes, I will, Gaye. Don't worry." Gaye left the room and Emma leaned back in her chair and closed her eyes, relaxing her rigid muscles. First Sitex and now this, she thought wearily, and then there is Paula and her lingering interest in Jim Fairley. Always the past coming back to haunt me, she reflected sadly, although she knew deep within herself that no one ever escaped the past. It was the burden of the present and of the future and you carried it with you always. Was this all her fault? Was she to blame? And what would she do? She searched her mind for answers as she contemplated her children again.

Years ago, when Emma had been a young woman and had seen traits developing in her children which alarmed her, she had thought: It's *my* fault. I have made them what they are. Some I've neglected, others I've loved too well and too hard, all of them I've indulged and spoiled for the most part. But as she had grown older and wiser, her guilt was diluted as she came to believe that each man was responsible for his own character. Eventually she had been able to acknowledge to herself that if character did determine a man's destiny then every man and woman created their own heaven or hell. It was then that she had truly understood what Paul McGill had meant when he had once said to her, "We are each the authors of our own lives, Emma. We live in what we have created. There is no way to shift the blame and no one else to accept the accolades." From that moment on she had been able to come to grips with her mixed and frequently turbulent emotions about her children. She had refrained from agonizing over them and she had stopped blaming herself for their weaknesses and their faults. They alone were responsible for what they had made of their lives, and she was enabled to shake off the feeling that she was culpable.

All this came back to her now as she remembered Paul's words and she thought: *No, I'm not guilty. They are motivated by their own greed, their own vaunting and misplaced ambitions.* She rose again and crossed to the window, a degree of firmness returning to her step, the resolute expression settling on her face. She looked out absently. It had stopped snowing and the sun was shining in a clear sky. After a few moments of contemplation she returned to her desk. She knew what her course of action must be. She buzzed for Gaye, who responded immediately and came into the room carrying the tea tray. She set it down on the desk in front of Emma, who thanked her, and then went and sat in the chair opposite the desk. She *is* dauntless, Gaye said to herself as she gazed at Emma, noting the calm expression in her eyes, the steady hand that poured the tea.

After a moment Emma smiled at her. "I'm feeling better,

Gaye. I think you had better make three reservations on any plane leaving for London tonight. I know several airlines have early evening flights. I don't care which one it is, just get us on a flight."

"Yes, Mrs. Harte. I'll start calling right away." She stood up to take her leave.

"By the way, Gaye dear, I am quite certain Paula will wonder why we are returning to London sooner than expected. I shall tell her I have urgent business that needs my attention. I would prefer her not to know anything about this . . ." She paused, searching for the appropriate word, and laughed bitterly. "This plot, I suppose we should call it."

"I wouldn't dream of mentioning it to Miss Paula or anyone!" Gaye exclaimed vehemently.

"And, Gaye . . ."

"Yes, Mrs. Harte?"

"Thank you. You did the right thing. I am very grateful to you."

"Oh, Mrs. Harte, please . . . what else could I do? I was simply afraid to tell you because I knew how much it would distress you."

Emma smiled. "I know, dear. Now see if you can get us on a plane."

Gaye nodded and left the room. Emma sipped the tea, her mind crowded with thoughts. Thoughts of her business, her children and her grandchildren. The family she had raised, the dynasty she had created. She knew what must be done to preserve it all. But could she do it? Her heart fluttered. She quailed as she envisioned the days ahead. But this was a fleeting emotion, and she knew she would find the strength somehow. It struck her then how ironical life was. Her sons had made an irrevocable mistake by plotting in her own boardroom. Admittedly they had chosen what they thought was a propitious time, early evening on a Friday, when everyone had left. Even so, she was aghast at their utter stupidity. There was another flaw in their plot and it was a flaw that was fatal. *They had underestimated her*. And, finally, by a twist of fate, she had been forewarned of their treachery. Now that she was prepared, she could handle the situation most effectively, anticipate their next moves and forestall them. She smiled grimly to herself. She had always been something of a gambler in her business, in life in general, and once again she was holding the equivalent of a straight flush. Her luck was holding. She prayed that it would hold long enough.

THREE

Henry Rossiter pressed the telephone closer to his ear, as if better to hear the woman's voice, concentrating on her words, straining and attentive, for although Emma Harte's voice was well modulated as always, she spoke more softly than usual.

"And so, Henry, I would appreciate it if you would come over to the store at about eleven-thirty this morning. I thought we could chat for about an hour and then have lunch here in the boardroom. If you are free, of course."

He hesitated and it was almost imperceptible, but he knew Emma had caught it and he said quickly, "That's fine, my dear, I shall be glad to come over."

"Do you have another appointment, Henry? I would hate to inconvenience you."

He did, and it was an important luncheon date that had been arranged for some time, but he was hardly going to offend his most important client, who also happened to be one of the richest women in England, possibly in the world, since it was hard to truly estimate her real worth. He knew that she was astute enough to realize he would have a previous appointment, so he refrained from the tiny white lie and, clearing his throat, he said, "Yes, I do, but it is easy for me to cancel it, if you wish, my dear."

"Good. I appreciate it, Henry. I will see you at eleven-thirty then. Goodbye, Henry."

"Goodbye, Emma," he murmured, but she had already hung up.

Henry had known Emma Harte for almost forty years, long enough to fully understand that there was always an imperious demand beneath her soft-spoken requests, that they were really commands uttered in the most dulcet of tones and the most charming manner. That inbred charm had carried her a long way, as Henry was the first to acknowledge.

He stared at the onyx inkwell on his desk, pondering her words. She had said nothing unusual and he had been unable to detect any undertones of disquiet or anger in her voice, and yet a peculiar sense of foreboding had descended upon him as they talked. Henry was not without shrewdness and perception, and, being the ultimate banker, he was always carefully attuned to his clients, fully conscious of their basic characteristics, the quirks and foibles of their personalities. He had to be, since he was handling their money and usually much of their business, and he had come to realize years ago that the very rich could also be very difficult, especially about their money.

It struck him suddenly that it was Emma's unexpected invitation to lunch which puzzled him. It was unprecedented and therefore, to him, somewhat alarming. Emma, as he knew only too well, was a creature of habit. She rarely had luncheon dates and when she did they were carefully planned days before. This digression from her normal routine was decidedly odd and the more he pondered on this, the more Henry was convinced something was amiss. And yet he had spoken to her three times since her return from New York a week ago and she had been her usual self, brisk and business-like and, on the surface, seemingly untroubled.

He took off his glasses, leaned back in his chair, and wondered if she was dissatisfied about the way the bank was handling her business. Henry had always been predisposed to worry, especially about the bank, and lately this had developed into a chronic condition. "There's probably a simple explanation for the invitation. I'm just imagining something is wrong," he muttered aloud with a degree of irritation; nonetheless, he pressed the intercom and told his secretary to ask Osborne to come in and see him immediately.

Tony Osborne, and two other officers of the private bank, supervised Emma Harte's business affairs in England, both corporate and personal. All of them were answerable to him and he reviewed Emma's affairs twice and sometimes three times a week. Osborne often chided him for using so much physical manpower and was continually insisting they should use computers to deal with the Harte holdings. But Henry did not trust computers, being conservative, even old-fashioned, in his ways. Furthermore, he thought that the supervision of something in the region of three hundred million pounds, give or take a few million, was worth any amount of manpower it might cost the bank. Emma was demanding and she was shrewd, probably shrewder, in fact, than any banker he knew, including himself. Henry needed to be absolutely sure they could answer any questions at any time, which is why the accounts were under daily surveillance. Henry wanted all that salient information right at his fingertips, night as well as day, if necessary.

Osborne interrupted his thoughts as he knocked on the door and glided into the room. Conceited young pup, he's too egotistical and ambitious by far, and too smooth, Henry thought, regarding the immaculately tailored young man before him. But what can you expect from scholarship Eton?

"Good morning, Henry."

"Morning, Osborne."

"Quite a beautiful day, isn't it? I think spring is going to be early this year, Henry. Don't you agree?"

"I'm not a weather vane," Henry murmured.

Osborne missed the snub or chose to ignore it. However, his manner became a little more businesslike and his voice was a shade cooler. "I want to talk to you about the Rowe account—" Tony began.

Henry held up his hand and shook his head. "Not now, Osborne. I called you in because I have just spoken to Mrs. Harte. She asked me to go over to the store later this morning. Is everything in order? No problems?"

"Absolutely not!" Osborne was emphatic in his surprise. "Everything is under control."

"I assume you have been keeping an eye on her foreign holdings. Did you go over them yesterday?" Henry played with the pen on his desk, still somewhat beset by worry.

"We always do on Monday. We checked her American and Australian interests, and all are steady. Sitex is doing well. There's actually been a rise in the price since the new president went in there. Look here, Henry, is something wrong? What's up?" he asked, disquiet apparent in his voice.

Henry shook his head. "Nothing that I am aware of, Osborne. But I do like to be completely current and informed before I see her. I think I'll take a look at her accounts with you. Let's go to your office."

After an hour and a half of concentrating on the most pertinent of the Harte accounts, Henry was totally satisfied that Osborne and his assistants had been both precise and diligent in their work. All of the English figures were current and the figures for the foreign Harte holdings were as up-to-date as they could be with the changing world markets, the different time zones, and the rise and fall of stock prices. At exactly eleven sharp, for he was punctilious about time, Henry put on his black overcoat, picked up his bowler hat and umbrella, and left the office. He stood on the steps of the bank, sniffing the air for a moment. It was cold but crisp and sunny. Osborne was right, it was a beautiful day for January, spring-like in its clear freshness. He walked swiftly down the street, swinging his umbrella jauntily, a tall, handsome man in his early sixties, whose serious and dignified demeanor belied a sharp sense of humor and a flirtatious nature.

Henry Rossiter had a cool and refined mind, which was also quite brilliant. A cultured man, he was an art connoisseur, a collector of rare first editions, a devotee of drama and music. He could also ride and shoot like the gentleman he was, and he was Master of the Hunt of the county where his ancestral home was located. The product of a rich and old Establishment family, landed gentry, in fact, he was today a curious amalgam of upper-class English conservative principles and international sophistication. He had been married twice and was currently divorced, which made him one of London's most eligible bachelors, much in demand by chic hostesses, for he was entertaining, charming, and adept in all the social graces, and something of a bon vivant. In short, he was attractive and lethal, a success both in business and in society.

Henry hailed a cab at the corner and got in. Leaning forward, he said to the cabby, "Harte's, please," and sat back, relaxed and confident that Emma could have no complaints about the bank. Absolutely none whatsoever. He still could not fathom the reason for her sudden invitation, but he had shed his incipient worry. *Wimin*, he thought with fond exasperation, unpredictable creatures at the best of times! He truly believed all women were quite impossible, having been baffled, confused, and bewitched by them all of his life. But now he felt compelled to readjust his thinking in this direction, as far as Emma was concerned. He simply could not, in all honesty, label her unpredictable or even impossible. Head-strong, yes, and sometimes even stubborn to the point of rigidity. But mostly he knew Emma to be prudent and level-headed, and circumspection was undoubtedly her most basic characteristic. No, "unpredictable" was not a word he would ever associate with Emma.

As the cab pushed its way through the congested traffic towards Knightsbridge, Henry's thoughts stayed with Emma Harte. They had been friends and business associates for many years and had enjoyed a compatible and mutually re-warding relationship. He had always found Emma easy to work with, for her mind was logical and direct. She did not think in that convoluted female way, nor was her mind clut-tered up with the usual womanish nonsense. He smiled to himself. Once he had told her that she did not have a mind like a woman at all, that it was more like a man's. "Oh, is there a difference?" she had retorted with some asperity, but there had been an amused smile on her face. At the time he had been a trifle hurt, for he had meant it as a great com-pliment, in view of his disparaging opinions of women, or rather, their intellectual capacities.

He had been entranced by Emma from the first day they had met. Then he had thought her to be the most fascinating woman he had ever encountered and he still did. Once, long ago, he had even believed himself to be in love with her, although she had never been aware of his feelings. He had been twenty-four and she had been thirty-nine and that most desirable of all creatures, the experienced older woman. She had been extraordinarily striking in her appearance, with her luxuriant hair coming dramatically to a widow's peak above a broad forehead and enormous vividly green eyes that were bright and alive. She was filled with a tremendous energy, a robust vitality that was infectious, and he was always buoyed up by her vivacity and her incredible optimism. She was a refreshing change from the insipid and constrained women he had been surrounded by all his life. Emma had a sardonic wit, a capacity for laughing both at herself and at her trou-bles, and an innate gaiety and zest for living that Henry found remarkable. From then, until this very day, he had been continually staggered by her lambent intelligence, her prescience, and her unconquerable determination. And he had always been susceptible to that natural charm of hers, a charm which Henry knew had been consciously distilled over the years, and which she had learned to use with consummate skill, carefully exploiting its effects to the fullest for the most propitious results.

For almost thirty years he had been her financial adviser. She always listened to him carefully and appreciated his suggestions and they had never quarreled in all of this time. In a peculiar sort of proprietary way he was inordinately proud of Emma and what she had become. A great lady. An unparalleled business success. It was a well-established fact that Emma Harte's London store surpassed any other in the world, not only in size but in the quality and variety of its merchandise. Not without reason she was known as one of the great merchant princes, although few knew, as Henry did, the enormous and crippling price she had paid for her success. He had always felt that the foundations of her immense retailing empire were compounded of her own self-sacrifice and dogged will power, her genius for selling, her instinctive understanding of the public's whims, an unerring eye for recognizing trends, and nerve enough to gamble when necessary. He had once told Tony Osborne that the bricks and mortar of the store were wrought from her great vision, her amazing facility for finance, and her uncanny ability to rise from the most impossible situations to triumph. And he had meant it. As far as Henry was concerned, she had done it all alone, and the London store, of all the stores she owned, was a towering testimony to her invincible strength.

" 'Ere we are, guv," the cabby said cheerily. Henry got out, paid the fare, and hurried down the side street to the staff entrance and the elevator that would take him to the top floor and Emma's executive offices.

Gaye Sloane was talking to one of the secretaries in the outer reception office when Henry walked in. She greeted him warmly. "Mrs. Harte is waiting for you," she said as she opened the door to Emma's office and ushered him inside.

Emma was sitting at her desk, which was covered with papers. He thought she looked oddly frail behind it. She glanced up as he came in, took off her glasses, and stood up. He realized that her frailty had only been an illusion created by the large heavy desk, for she moved towards him swiftly, lightly, full of vitality, her face wreathed in smiles. She was elegantly dressed in a dark bottle-green velvet suit, with something white and silky at the throat caught in an emerald pin, and emerald earrings glittered at her ears.

"Henry darling, how lovely to see you," she said as she took hold of his arm affectionately. He smiled and bent down to kiss her on the cheek and thought: She seems self-possessed and well enough. But he detected a drawn look around her eyes and she was paler than usual.

"Let me look at you, Emma dear," he said, holding her away from him so that he could regard her more fully. He laughed and shook his head in mock bewilderment. "You'll have to tell me your secret, darling. I don't know how you do it, but you look positively blooming."

Emma smiled, her eyes merry. "Hard work, a clean life, and a clear conscience. And you shouldn't complain, Henry. You look marvelous yourself. Come on, darling, let's have a sherry and chat." She led him over to the comfortable arrangement of chairs and a sofa in front of the fireplace, where a roaring fire blazed. They sat down opposite each other and, picking up the decanter, Emma poured sherry into two crystal glasses.

"Here's to that great man whose name is Emma," he said, lifting his glass to touch hers before taking a sip of the dry sherry.

Emma threw him a quick, surprised glance and laughed gaily. "Why, Henry!" She laughed again and then said with some amusement, "With all due respect, I am not Catherine the Great and you're not Voltaire. But thank you, anyway. I assume you meant that as a compliment."

Henry smiled broadly, a little taken aback at her quick response, but delighted with her. "Is there anything you don't know, my dear? And yes, of course I meant it as a compliment."

Emma was still laughing. "There's a lot I don't know, Henry. But one of my gallant grandsons got here before you. He said exactly the same thing to me yesterday. And when I complimented him on *his* compliment, he had the good grace to tell me the source. You're a day too late, darling!"

Henry chuckled with her. "Well, we obviously think alike. And which grandson was it?" he asked, always curious about Emma's large and unorthodox family.

"I do have a few, don't I?" Emma said with a fond smile. "It must get confusing. It was Alexander, Elizabeth's son. He

was here yesterday afternoon, down from Yorkshire and in a
real uproar about his Uncle Kit, who was being extremely
stubborn about putting new machinery into one of the mills.
It is a costly move, but eventually it will save us a lot of
money and step up production. Alexander was quite right
and I sorted it out in the end, without too much of a
bloodbath."

"He's a bright boy and devoted to you, Emma. Incidentally, talking of Christopher . . ." He paused and smiled.
"Excuse me, Emma, I never could call him Kit. Anyway, to
continue, I ran into Christopher a few weeks ago and I was
somewhat surprised to see him with Edwina and Robin. They
were dining at the Savoy."

Emma had been relaxed, regarding Henry with affection,
amused at his gallantry. Now she tensed, but she kept her
face open and bland. "Oh, really. I'm glad to see my children
are getting along together at last," she said lightly, while
carefully storing that piece of information at the back of her
mind.

Henry lit a cigarette and went on. "I was surprised because
I didn't realize Christopher was friendly with the other two.
And frankly I didn't know Robin was still thick with Edwina.
I thought that was a temporary situation created when there
was all that trouble about the take-over bid a few years back.
Actually, I never did understand that liaison, Emma. I always
thought those two detested each other until they became so
chummy. Obviously it's lasted."

Emma smiled thinly. "You say you don't understand their
friendship, Henry, yet I discovered long ago that dark and
desperate plots make for very peculiar bedmates. You're right.
Of course, they did dislike each other intensely, but they
haven't been out of each other's pockets since that trouble
with the conglomerate."

"Mmmm. It was a funny business, wasn't it? But thank God
it all blew over. Well, as I said, I thought it rather odd to see
the three of them together," he finished, and sipped his
sherry, totally oblivious of the disturbing thoughts he had
stirred up in Emma.

She regarded him carefully, a shrewd look in her eyes, and
said with great casualness, "Oh, I don't think it's so odd,
Henry. To tell you the truth, I've heard on the family grape-
vine that the three of them are planning a gathering of the

clan for my birthday," she lied blandly. "I suspect they were meeting to discuss the arrangements."

"I thought your birthday was at the end of April."

"It is, darling. But that's only a couple of months away."

"I hope I get an invitation," he said. "After all, you'll need an escort and I have been your most constant admirer for nigh on forty years."

"You will, darling," Emma replied, relieved that the awkward moment had been so easily bridged. "But I didn't ask you here to chat about my offspring. I wanted to talk to you about a couple of things . . ."

The telephone rang and Emma stood up abruptly. "Excuse me, Henry. It must be Paula calling from Paris. That is the only call I told Gaye she could put through."

"Of course, my dear," he said, standing up also. She crossed the room to her desk and he sat down, relaxing in front of the fire, enjoying his sherry and his cigarette, his mind at ease. Emma looked tired, yet he could not detect any outward signs which indicated that she was troubled. In fact, he thought she seemed rather gay. He glanced around the room as she continued her telephone conversation. He envied Emma this office, which was more like a library in a stately home than a place of business. With its paneled walls, soaring shelves of books, magnificent English paintings, and handsome Georgian antiques it was a gracious retreat, one which he would have liked to own and work in himself.

Emma finished her call and he stood up as she rejoined him by the fire. She had a folder of papers in her hand which Henry could not fail to notice. She placed the folder on the table next to her chair and sat down. Henry settled back in his chair and lit another cigarette.

"Paula sends her love, Henry. She's in Paris, taking care of a few things at the store for me."

"Delightful girl," Henry responded, a note of admiration in his voice. "She's so like Daisy, sweet and open and uncomplicated. When is she returning?"

Emma did not think Paula was uncomplicated at all, but she resisted any comment about her granddaughter. "On Thursday. Another sherry, Henry?" she asked as she started to pour it into his glass.

"Yes, thank you, darling. You said you wanted to talk to me about a few things, before you took Paula's call," Henry remarked lightly, wanting to get down to business. He eyed the folder curiously. "Anything serious?"

"No, not at all. I would like to liquidate some of my personal assets and I thought you could handle it for me," Emma replied, her voice casual, her face relaxed. She sipped her drink slowly and waited, regarding Henry intently, knowing only too well how he would react.

In spite of his anxiety earlier, he was taken by surprise. He had not expected this at all. He put down his glass and leaned forward, a serious expression clouding his eyes, a worried pucker creasing his brow. "Do you have problems, Emma?" he asked quietly, fixing her with a penetrating, questioning look.

Emma met his gaze directly. She looked him straight in the eye and said firmly, "No, Henry. I told you I want to liquidate some of my own assets. For personal reasons. There are no problems. You should know that, darling. After all, you handle most of my banking business."

Henry reflected for an instant, his mind rapidly reassembling all those figures he had seen that morning. Had he inadvertently missed something of vital importance? No. That was not possible. He breathed a little more easily, and cleared his throat. "Well, yes, that's true," he said thoughtfully. "In fact, I looked over all of your accounts before I came over. Everything is in good order. Very good order. As a matter of fact, things have never looked better," he finished in all truthfulness.

"I need a little cash, Henry. Ready cash. For personal reasons, as I said. So, rather than sell any shares, I thought I would get rid of some real estate, jewelry, and part of my art collection."

Henry was so flabbergasted he was momentarily rendered speechless. Before he recovered sufficiently to make a comment she handed him the folder. He took out his glasses, put them on, and looked at the lists inside, startled and apprehensive. As his eyes ran down the assets he remembered his foreboding earlier in the morning. Perhaps his instincts had been correct.

"Emma! All this doesn't represent a little cash, as you casually call it. These assets represent millions of pounds!"

"Oh, I know. I figured about seven or eight million pounds. What do you think, Henry dear?" she asked calmly.

"Good God! Emma! Why do you suddenly need seven or eight million pounds? And what do *I* think? you ask me. *I* think there is something wrong and that you are not telling me. You *must* have problems I can have no way of knowing about!" His gray transparent eyes blazed as he endeavored to control his anger. He was certain she was hiding something, and it annoyed him.

"Oh, come on, Henry," Emma clucked. "Don't get so excited. Nothing's wrong. Actually, I only need about six million for my . . . shall we call it my personal project? I prefer to sell these things, since I don't need them anyway. I never wear that jewelry. You know I'm not overly fond of diamonds. And even when it's sold I'll still have more than enough that is decent for a woman of my age. The real estate is cumbersome. I don't want that either, and I feel this is the perfect time to sell and make a profit. I'm being rather smart really," she finished on a self-congratulatory note, smiling pleasantly at Henry.

He gazed at her in astonishment. She had the knack of making all of her actions sound admirably pragmatic and it generally maddened him. "But the art collection, Emma! My dear, you put so much love and time and care into gathering these . . . these masterpieces. Are you sure you want to let them go?" His voice had taken on a saddened, wistful tone. He glanced at the list in his hand. "Look what you're listing here. Sisleys, Chagalls, Monets, Manets, Dalis, Renoirs, and Pissarros, and a Degas. *Two*, in fact. It's a fabulous collection."

"Which you so generously helped me to acquire over the years, through your contacts in the art world. I am grateful to you for that, Henry. More than you will ever know. But I want to liquidate. As you say, it's a fabulous collection and so it should bring a fabulous price," she said crisply, adroitly throwing the ball back to him.

"Oh, indeed it will!" Henry asserted, the banker in him suddenly taking over. "If you are absolutely certain you want me to sell the collection I can do so very easily." His voice became enthusiastic. "Actually, I have a client in New York who would love to get his hands on these paintings. And he'll pay the right price, too, my dear. But, Emma, really! I don't know what to say. It seems such a shame . . ." His voice trailed off weakly, for he suddenly recognized that she had manipulated him rather cleverly, and turned his attention away from her reasons for selling.

"Good," Emma said hurriedly, seizing the opportunity to further promote Henry's enthusiasm, his banker's instincts. "What about the real estate in Leeds and London? I think the block of flats in Hampstead and the East End factory property will go for a good price."

"Yes, they will. So will the office block in the West End. You're right, of course, it is a good time to sell." He concentrated on the various lists she had given him, making swift mental calculations. She had underestimated the overall worth, he decided. The paintings, the real estate, and the jewelry would bring about nine million pounds. He put the folder down, and lit a cigarette as his anxiety accelerated.

"Emma, dear. You must tell me if you have problems. Who else is there to help you but me?" He smiled at her and reached over and patted her arm fondly. He had never been able to remain angry with her for very long.

"Henry, my darling Henry. I don't have problems," Emma replied in her most conciliatory and reassuring manner. "You know I don't. You said yourself things have never looked better." She went over and sat next to him on the sofa and took his hand. "Look here, Henry, I need this money for a personal reason. It has nothing to do with a problem. I promise you. Please believe me, Henry, I *would* tell you. We've been friends for so many years, and I've always trusted you, haven't I?" She smiled up at him, using the full force of her charm, her eyes crinkling with affection.

He returned her smile and tightened his hand over hers. "Yes. We have always trusted each other, in fact. As your banker, I realize you have no business or money problems as such, Emma. But I simply cannot understand why you need six million pounds and why you won't tell me what it's for. Can't you, my dear?"

Her face immediately became enigmatic. She shook her head. "No. I can't tell you. Will you handle the liquidation of these assets for me?" she asked crisply and in her most businesslike manner.

Henry sighed. "Of course, Emma. There was never any question about that, was there?"

She smiled. "Thank you, Henry. How long will it take to liquidate?"

He shrugged. "I don't really know. Probably several weeks. I am sure I can sell the art collection within the next week. I also think I have a client who would buy the jewelry privately, so we avoid a public sale. The real estate should move fairly easily, too. Yes, I would say a month at the most."

"Excellent!" Emma exclaimed. She jumped up and moved over to the fireplace, standing with her back towards it, regarding Henry, an amused glint in her eyes. "Don't look so miserable, darling. The bank is going to make money, too, you know. And the government, with all the taxes I shall have to pay!"

He laughed. "Sometimes I think you're quite incorrigible, Emma Harte."

"I am! I'm the most incorrigible woman I know. Now, let's go into the boardroom and have lunch, and you can tell me about all your latest lady friends and the exciting parties you've been to whilst I have been in New York."

"Splendid idea," he said jovially, although he was still riddled by that strange apprehension as he followed her across the office.

The following day Emma began to feel unwell. The cough she had developed in New York still troubled her and there was a tightness in her chest. But it was a whole week before she succumbed, and for that entire week she assiduously refused to admit there was anything wrong with her normally robust health. Imperiously, she brushed aside the fussing of Gaye Sloane and her daughter Daisy. She refused to deviate from her usual work schedule and religiously went to the office at seven-thirty every morning, returning to her house in Belgrave Square at seven in the evening. Since she was accustomed to working in her executive suite at the store until eight-thirty and sometimes nine o'clock at night, she felt this relatively early departure was a great concession on her part. But it was her only one.

Sometimes, at the end of a day, as she poured over the mountainous pile of balance sheets, stock reports, dividend sheets, and legal documents, she was wracked by coughing that exhausted her and left her weak and listless for a while. To Emma, the rasping cough was ominous; nevertheless, she carried on, pressed by a feeling of tremendous urgency. It was not the routine business matters that troubled her, for these she dealt with quickly, precisely, and with her own brand of shrewdness. It was the pile of legal documents, prepared by her solicitors at her bidding, that were her gravest concern. With them spread out before her on the huge desk, illuminated by the shaded lamp, she would sometimes balk at the enormity of the work still to be accomplished. She would think: I won't finish! There's not enough time left. And her mind would be frozen by momentary panic. But this mental paralysis was a passing emotion and she would continue to work again, with speed, diligence, and astuteness, reading and making notations for her solicitors. As she worked one thought would run through her head: The documents must be irreversible, irrevocable! They must be watertight. I must be sure, absolutely sure that they can never be contested in a court of law.

Often the pains in her chest and rib cage became razor sharp and almost unbearable. It was then that she was forced to stop working for a while. She would get up and cross the luxuriously appointed offices, so wracked by pain that she was temporarily unaware of their gracious, timeless beauty, a beauty she had patiently created, and which normally gave her a great satisfaction. She would open the tiny bar and with trembling hands pour herself a brandy and then rest for a short time on the sofa in front of the fire. She did not especially like the taste of brandy, but since it warmed her and also seemed to deaden the pain briefly, she thought it the lesser of two evils. More importantly, it enabled her to go back to her desk and continue working on the legal papers. As she pushed herself beyond physical endurance, she would fume inwardly and curse the treachery of her body, which had so betrayed her at this most crucial time.

One night, towards the end of the week, she was working feverishly at her desk when she had a sudden and quite irresistible urge to go down into the store. At first she dismissed the idea as the silly whim of an old woman who was feeling vulnerable, but the thought so persisted, clamorous and compelling, she could not ignore it. She was literally overcome with an inexplicable desire, a need, to walk through those vast, great halls below, as if to reassure herself of their very existence. She rose slowly. Her bones were afflicted with an ague and the pain in her chest was ever present. After descending in the lift and speaking to the security guard on duty, she walked through the foyer that led to the ground-floor departments. She hesitated on the threshold of the haberdashery department, regarding the hushed and ghost-like scene that spread itself out before her. By day it glittered under the blaze of huge chandeliers, with their globes and blades of crystal that threw off rays of prismatic light. Now, in the shadows and stillness of the night, the area appeared to her as a petrified forest, suspended in time and space, inanimate, frozen and lifeless. The vaulted ceiling, cathedral-like in its dimensions, was filled with bluish lacy patterns, eerie and mysterious, while the paneled walls had taken on a dark purple glaze under the soft, diffused glow which emanated from the wall sconces. She moved noiselessly across the richly carpeted floor until she arrived at the food halls, a series of immense, rectangular rooms flowing into each other through high-flung arches faintly reminiscent of medieval monastic architecture.

To Emma, the food halls would always be the nucleus of the store, for in essence they had been the beginning of it all, the tiny seed from which the Harte chain had grown and flowered to become the mighty business empire it was today. In contrast to the other areas of the store, here at night, as by day, the full supplement of chandeliers shone in icy splendor, dropping down from the domed ceilings like giant stalactites that filled the adjoining halls with a pristine and glistening luminosity. Light bounced back from the blue and white tiled walls, the marble counter tops, the glass cases, the gleaming steel refrigerators, the white tiled floor. Emma thought they were as clean and as beautiful and as pure as vast and silent snowscapes sparkling under a hard, brilliant sun. She walked from hall to hall, surveying the innumerable and imaginative displays of foodstuffs, gourmet products, delicacies imported from all over the world, good wholesome English fare, and an astonishing array of wines and liquors, and she was inordinately proud of all she observed. Emma knew there were no other food halls, in any store anywhere in the world, which could challenge these, and she smiled to herself with a profound and complete satisfaction. Each one was an extension of her instinctive good taste, her inspired planning and diligent purchasing; in the whole hierarchy of Harte Enterprises, no one could lay claim to their creation but she herself. Indeed, she was so filled with a sense of gratification and well-being that the pains in her chest virtually disappeared.

When she came to the charcuterie department, a sudden mental image of her first shop in Leeds flitted before her, at once stark and realistic in every detail against her retinas. It was so compelling it brought her to a standstill. That little shop from which all this had issued forth; how unpretentious and insignificant it had been in comparison to this elegant establishment that exuded refinement and wealth! She stood quite still, alert, straining, listening, as if she could hear strong and vibrant sounds from long ago in the silence of this night. Forgotten memories, nostalgic and poignant, rushed back to her with force and clarity. Images, no longer nebulous and abandoned, took living form. As she ran her hands over the rich polished oak counter it seemed to her that her fingers touched the scrubbed deal surface of the counter in the old shop. She could smell the acrid odor of the carbolic soap she had used to scrub the shop every day; she could hear the tinny, rattling clink of the old-fashioned secondhand cash register as she joyfully rang up her meager sales.

Oh, how she had loved that poor, cramped little shop, filled to overflowing with her own homemade foods and jams, bottles of peppermints, and stone jars of pickles and spices.

"Who would have thought it would become *this*?" Emma said aloud, and her voice echoed back to her in the silence of the empty hall where she stood. "Where did I find the energy?" She was momentarily baffled. She had not thought of her achievements for so many years now, always too preoccupied with business to fritter away her time ruminating on her success. She had long ago relegated that task to her competitors and adversaries. Because of their own duplicity and ruthlessness they would never be able to comprehend that the Harte chain had been built on something as fundamental as honesty, spirited courage, patience, and sacrifice.

Sacrifice. That word was held in her brain like a fly caught in amber. For indeed she had made tremendous sacrifices to achieve her unparalleled success, her great wealth, and her undeniable power in the world of international business. *She had given up her youth, her family, her family life, much of her personal happiness, all of her free time, and countless other small, frivolous yet necessary pleasures enjoyed by most women*. With great comprehension she recognized the magnitude of her loss, as a woman, a wife, and a mother. Emma let the tears flow unchecked and in their flowing a measure of her agony was assuaged.

Slowly the tears and her rasping breathing subsided. As she gathered her scattered senses, in an attempt to calm herself, it did not occur to Emma that she had willingly renounced all the things for which she now grieved, through her driving ambition and overriding desire for security, a security that always seemed beyond her grasp, however rich she became. There was a dichotomy in her character which she had never been able to come to grips with. But such thoughts evaded her this night, as she struggled with an unaccustomed sense of loss, feelings of loneliness and despair mingled with remorse.

Within a short time she was totally in command of herself again, and she was mortified that she had given way to such negative feelings, such self-pity; she despised weakness in others and it was an emotion she was not familiar with in herself. She thought angrily: I am living what I alone created. I cannot change anything now. I simply have to go on to the end.

She pulled herself up, erect and straight-backed and proud. She thought: Too much of me has gone into this. I will not let it pass into the wrong hands, unworthy, careless hands that will willfully tear it down. I am right to plot and scheme and manipulate. Not only for the past and for what it has cost *me*, but for the future and for all those who work here and take pride in this store just as I do. Her momentary weakness was replaced by a glacial determination, and with her head held very high, Emma left the food halls. Her feet echoed hollowly as she crossed the tiled floors and returned to her palatial offices high above the great store.

The events of the past few weeks had proved to her that great dissension about the control of the business and the distribution of her wealth would arise within her family after her death, unless she circumvented the dissident members of her family before she died. Now she would finish the last of the legal documents which would prevent the dissolution of this store and her vast business empire; documents carefully drawn which would unalterably preserve all of this and her great personal wealth as well, ensuring its passing into the right hands, the hands of *her* choice.

The following Monday morning, the pains in her chest were so intense and her breathing so impaired Emma was unable to leave her bed. It was then that she allowed Paula to call Dr. Rogers, her London physician. The preceding weekend, most of the documents had been signed, witnessed, and sealed, and now Emma felt she could allow herself the indulgence of being ill. After Dr. Rogers had examined her, he and Paula had been huddled at one end of her bedroom, their voices muffled and barely audible. She overheard a few words, but she did not have to eavesdrop; she had suspected for the last few days that she had again contracted pneumonia, and what she overheard only served to confirm her own diagnosis. Later that morning, they took her by ambulance to the London Clinic, but not before she had elicited a promise from Paula to bring Henry Rossiter to see her that same day. Henry arrived in the late afternoon, aghast to find her in an oxygen tent, surrounded by all manner of equipment and fussed over by starchy, antiseptic nurses and concerned doctors. She smiled inwardly at the sight of Henry's white face and worried eyes that betrayed him so easily, since she was aware of Henry's dependency on her or, rather more accurately, her business. He clasped her hand and told her that she would soon be well again. She had tried to return the pressure of his clasp, but she felt so weak her hand hardly moved in his. With a stupendous effort she asked him in a whispery voice if everything would be all right. But he misunderstood, believing her to be referring to herself, when in fact she was asking him about the liquidation of her assets which he was handling. He kept up his soothing talk, reassuring her over and over again that she would soon be home, until she was indignant and fuming with impotent rage.

It was at this precise moment that Emma realized that she was utterly alone, just as she had always been alone when portentous matters arose. Through all the vicissitudes of her life, whenever she had faced the gravest problems imaginable, she had been totally abandoned and so forced to depend entirely on her own resources. And she knew that she could only rely on herself now to accomplish the few remaining tasks which would preserve her empire and her dynasty. To do that she had to live, and she determined then not to succumb to this ridiculous sickness invading her weak, old woman's body; she would live and breathe if it took all of her strength. Every ounce of her will power would be brought to bear. It would undoubtedly be the greatest effort of will she had ever exercised, but she would *force* herself to live.

She was tired though now, so very tired. Dimly in the distance she heard the nurses asking Henry Rossiter to leave. She was given some medication and the oxygen tent was placed around her again. She closed her eyes. She was falling asleep and as she drifted off she felt herself growing younger and younger. She was a young girl again, just sixteen, back in Yorkshire, running on her beloved moors high above Fairley Village, to the Top of the World. The heather and the bracken brushed against her feet, the wind caught at her long skirts so that they billowed out and her hair was a stream of silk ribbons flying behind her as she ran. The sky was as blue as speedwells and the larks wheeled and turned against the face of the sun. She could see Edwin Fairley now, standing by the huge rocks just under the shadow of the crags above Ramsden Ghyll. When he saw her he waved and went on climbing upwards towards the ledge where they always sat protected from the wind, surveying the world far below. He did not look back but went on climbing. "Edwin! Edwin! Wait for me!" she called, but her voice was blown away by the wind and he did not hear. When she reached Ramsden Crags she was out of breath and her pale face was flushed from the exertion. "I ran so hard, I thought I would die," she gasped as he helped her up onto the ledge. He smiled. "You will never die, Emma. We are both going to live forever and ever, here at the Top of the World." The dream fragmented into hundreds of infinitesimal pieces and slowly began to fade as she fell into a profound sleep.

FOUR

Emma lived. Everyone said it was a miracle that a woman of seventy-eight years of age could survive yet another attack of bronchial pneumonia and the varied complications that had accompanied it this time. They also expressed amazement at her incredible recuperative ability which had enabled her to leave the London Clinic at the end of three weeks. Emma, when these comments were repeated to her, said nothing. She simply smiled enigmatically and thought to herself: Ah, but they don't realize that the will to live is the strongest force in the world.

After two days of enforced rest at her house in Belgravia she impatiently left her bed and, disregarding the advice of her doctors, went to the store. This was not such a foolish act of defiance as it seemed on the surface, for although she could be empirical she was not reckless and she also knew her own body intimately, could gauge her strength with accuracy, and now she knew herself to be fully recovered. She was greeted warmly by her employees, who for the most part held her in affection. They took her sudden return for granted. It was Paula who hovered nervously around her, cosseting, worried and concerned.

"I do wish you would stop fussing, darling," Emma said crisply as Paula followed her into her office, murmuring something about endangering her health. Emma took off her fur-lined tweed coat and put it away in the closet. She stood for a few moments warming her hands by the fire and then she walked across the room in her usual energetic way, a buoyant springiness in her step, her carriage perfectly straight and autocratic as always. She was self-assured and completely at ease with herself.

The black waves of shock and despair which had engulfed her after Gaye's revelations of her children's plotting had subsided, admittedly slowly and painfully, but they had subsided. The sinister imputations that could be drawn from that damning conversation on the tape, and her acceptance of their treachery, had only served to anneal her mind. She saw things with a cold and clear objectivity, exactly as they were, unclouded by needless emotion. During her illness, as she had drawn upon her iron will, ruthlessly fighting to live, she had come to terms with herself. And a great peace came flowing into her one day like a flood of warm bright light and it gave her solace and renewed inner strength. It was as if her brush with death had reinforced her spirit and her dauntless courage. Her vitality had returned, accompanied now by a quiet calm that surrounded her like a protective shell.

She took up her position behind the great carved Georgian desk, back in command of her domain. She smiled lovingly at Paula. "I'm quite recovered, you know," she said brightly and reassuringly. And indeed she looked it, although this was partially due to the illusion she had patently and rather cleverly contrived that morning. Noting her pallor and the tired lines around her eyes and mouth as she dressed, she had shunned the dark somber colors she generally favored and had selected a bright coral dress from her wardrobe. This was made of fine wool, softly cut with a draped cowl collar that fell in feminine folds around the neck. She was fully aware that the warm color and the softness of the neckline against her face was flattering, and with a few carefully applied cosmetics she had completed the effect. There was a robust healthy glow about her which Paula did not fail to notice.

Paula realized this was created by artifice to some degree, conscious always of her grandmother's numerous and varied devices when she wanted to delude. She smiled to herself. Her grandmother could be so crafty sometimes. Yet Paula also sensed true vibrancy in Emma, a new energy and purpose. As she scrutinized her carefully she had to admit that Emma appeared to be her old self. Only more so, she thought, as if she has been totally rejuvenated.

She smiled at her grandmother and said gently, although a little reprovingly, "I know *you*, Grandy. You'll do far too much. You mustn't overtax yourself the first day."

Emma leaned back in her chair, thankful to be alive and on her feet again and capable of returning to her business. She was quite willing to acquiesce to anything at that moment. "Oh, I won't, darling," she said quickly. "I have a few phone calls to make and some dictation to give Gaye, and that's about it. I shall be easy on myself. I promise!"

"All right," Paula said slowly, wondering if she really meant what she said. Her grandmother could get caught up in the rush of the day's activities at the store without thinking. "I trust you to keep your promise," Paula added, a sober expression on her face. "Now I have to go to a meeting with the fashion buyer for the couture department. I'll pop in and see you later, Grandy."

"By the way, Paula, I thought I would go to Pennistone Royal the weekend after next. I hope you can come with me," Emma called to her across the room.

Paula stopped at the door and looked back. "Of course! I'd

love to," she cried, her eyes lighting up. "When do you intend to leave, Grandy?"

"A week from tomorrow. Early on Friday morning. But we'll discuss it later."

"Wonderful. After my meeting I'll clear my desk and cancel my appointments for that day. I have nothing on my schedule that is very important, so I can drive up with you."

"Good. Come and have tea with me this afternoon at four o'clock and we can make our plans."

Paula nodded and left the office, a radiant smile on her face as she thought of the prospects of a weekend in Yorkshire. She was also greatly relieved that her grandmother was being wise enough to prolong her recuperation by going to her country house in the North.

Emma was true to her word. She attended to some of her urgent correspondence, had a brief session with Gaye and also one with David Amory, Daisy's husband and Paula's father, who was also the joint managing director of the Harte chain of stores. David was a man Emma admired and trusted implicitly, and who carried the heavy burden of the day-to-day running of the stores. She was making her last telephone call of the afternoon when Paula came into the office carrying the tea tray. She hovered near the door and gave Emma an inquiring look, mouthing silently: "Can I come in?"

Emma nodded, motioned for her to enter with an impatient gesture of one hand, and went on talking. "Very well, it's settled then. You will arrive on Saturday. Good-bye." She hung up and walked across the room to the fireplace, where Paula was sitting in front of the low table pouring tea.

Emma leaned forward to warm her hands and said, "She's the most bolshy of them all and I wasn't certain she would accept. But she did." Her green eyes gleamed darkly in the firelight and the faint smile on her face was scornful. "She had no choice really," she murmured to herself as she sat down.

"Who, Grandy? Who were you talking to?" Paula asked, passing a cup of tea to her.

"Thank you, dear. Your Aunt Edwina. She wasn't sure at first whether or not she could rearrange her plans." Emma laughed cynically. "However, she thought better of it and decided to come to Pennistone Royal after all. It will be quite a family gathering. They're all coming."

Paula's head was bent over the tea tray. She lifted it quickly, a bright interested smile on her face. "Who, Grandy? What do you mean?" she asked, momentarily puzzled.

"Everybody's coming. Your aunts and uncles and cousins."

A shadow flitted across Paula's face, obliterating the smile. "Why?" she cried with surprise, sitting bolt upright in her chair. "Why do *they* all have to come? You know they will make trouble. They always do!" Her eyes opened widely and real horror registered on her face.

Emma was surprised at Paula's reaction. She regarded her calmly, but said in a sharp tone, "I doubt that! I'm quite positive, in fact, that they are all going to be on their best behavior." An expression resembling a smirk played briefly around Emma's mouth. She sat back, crossed her legs decisively, and sipped her tea, looking nonchalant and unconcerned. "Oh yes, I am absolutely *certain* of that, Paula," she finished firmly, the smirk expanding into a self-confident smile.

"Oh, Grandy, how could you!" Paula cried, and the look she gave Emma was reproving. "I thought we could look forward to a pleasant, restful weekend." She paused and bit her lip. "Now it's all spoiled," she went on in an accusatory tone. "I don't mind the cousins, but the others. Ugh! Kit and Robin and the rest of them are almost too much to bear all together." She shuddered and grimaced as she contemplated a weekend with her aunts and uncles.

"Please trust me, darling," Emma said in a soft voice which was also so convincing Paula's disquiet began to subside.

"Well, all right, if you are happy about it. But it's so soon after your illness. Do you think you can stand a house full of . . . of . . . people? . . ." Her voice trailed off lamely and she looked woebegone and suddenly helpless.

"They're not *people*, are they, darling? Surely not. We can't dismiss them like that. They are my family after all."

Paula had been staring at the teapot, vaguely disturbed. Now she flashed Emma a swift look, for she had detected that edge of cynicism in her voice. But Emma's face was bland and smiling, revealing nothing. She's concocting something, Paula thought with some alarm. But she quickly dismissed the idea, chiding herself for being so suspicious. She arranged a sunny smile on her face and said, "Well, I'm glad Mummy and Daddy are coming. I don't seem to have seen much of them for ages, with all my traveling." She hesitated, stared at Emma curiously, and then asked hurriedly, "Why have you invited all of the family, Grandmother?"

"I thought it would be pleasant to see all of my children and grandchildren after my illness. I don't see enough of them, darling," she suggested mildly and asked, "Now, do I?"

As Paula returned her grandmother's steady gaze she realized, with an unexpected shock, that in spite of her soft voice her grandmother's eyes were as cold and as hard as the great McGill emerald that glittered on her finger. A flick of real fear touched Paula's heart, for she recognized that look. It was obdurate, and also dangerous.

"No, I don't suppose you do see much of them, Grandy," Paula said, so quietly it was almost a whisper, not daring to probe further and also reluctant to have her suspicions confirmed. And there the conversation was terminated.

A week later, at dawn on Friday morning, they left London for Yorkshire, driving out of the city in a cold drizzling rain. But as the Rolls-Royce roared up the modern motorway that had replaced the old Great North Road they began hitting brighter weather. The rain had stopped and although the sky was dull and overcast the sun was beginning to filter through the gray clouds. Smithers, Emma's driver for some fifteen years, knew the road like the palm of his hand, anticipating the bad patches, the twists and the bumps, slowing when necessary, picking up speed when there was a clear smooth stretch of road before them. Emma and Paula chatted desultorily part of the way, but mostly Emma dozed and Paula worried about the forthcoming weekend, which, in spite of her grandmother's assurances to the contrary, loomed ahead like a nightmare. She gazed dully out of the window, troubled as she reflected on her aunts and uncles.

Kit. Pompous, patronizing and, to Paula, a devious, ambitious man whose ineffable hatred for her was thinly disguised beneath a veneer of assumed cordiality. And he would be accompanied by June, his cold and frigid wife, whom she and her cousin Alexander had gleefully nicknamed "December" when they were children. A chilly, utterly humorless woman who over the years had become an insipid reflection of Kit. And then there was Uncle Robin, a different kettle of fish indeed. Handsome, caustic, smooth-talking, and strangely decadent. She always thought of him as reptilian and dangerous and for all of his charm and polish he repelled her. She particularly disliked him because he treated his rather nice wife, Valerie, with an icy scorn, a contempt that bordered on real cruelty. Her Aunt Edwina was something of an unknown quantity to her, for Edwina spent most of her time knee deep in the bogs of Ireland with her horses. Paula remembered her as a forbidding woman, snobbish and dull and sour. Aunt Elizabeth was beautiful, and amusing in a brittle sort of way, yet she could be unpredictable and her skittishness grated on Paula's nerves.

Paula sighed and turned her thoughts away from her relatives, whom she found unpleasant for the most part and curiously threatening. They always seemed poised and armed and ready to strike, like a team of combatants. Except they weren't a team at all. There was too much dissension among them for that. She formed a picture of Pennistone Royal in her mind's eye, that lovely old house so full of beauty and warmth and which she loved as much as Emma did. She imagined herself riding her horse up on the moors in the brisk clean air and then quite unexpectedly she saw Jim Fairley's face. She closed her eyes and her heart clenched and there was an aching throbbing in her head. She dare not think of him. She must not think of him. She steeled herself against her emotions, those turbulent, distressing emotions that whipped through her whenever the memory of him came rushing back.

Paula opened her eyes and looked out of the window, determinedly closing her mind to Jim Fairley. Her love. Her only love. Forbidden to her because of her grandmother's past. A little later she glanced at her watch. They were already well beyond Grantham heading towards Doncaster, and were making excellent time. The traffic was relatively light because of the early hour. She settled back in her seat and closed her eyes. Smithers had turned on the radio and the soft music, combined with the motion of the car, began to lull Paula into a dozing state. Several times she was jolted awake and she looked at her grandmother, who seemed perfectly relaxed and comfortable, a gentle smile on her face, her eyes closed.

Half an hour later Emma stirred and sat up, wide awake and fresh. She moved slightly to look out of the window, smiling quietly to herself. She always knew when she was in

Yorkshire. This was where her roots were and her bones responded with that atavistic knowledge and sense of place. Her place. The one place where she truly belonged.

They drove quickly along the motorway, bypassing all the familiar towns. Doncaster, Wakefield, and Pontefract. And finally they were in Leeds. Gray, brooding Leeds, yet powerful and rich, pulsating with vibrant energy, one of the great industrial centers of England with its clothing factories, woolen mills, iron foundries, engineering companies, cement works, and great printing plants. Her city. The seat of her power, the foundation of her success and her great wealth. They passed buildings and factories she owned and the enormous department store that bore her name, slowing down as they threaded their way through the busy morning traffic in the city center, and then they were out on the open road again, heading towards the country.

Within the hour they were pulling up in the cobbled courtyard of Pennistone Royal. Emma practically leapt out of the car. It was bitterly cold and a penetrating wind was blowing down from the moors, yet the sun was a golden orb in a clear cobalt sky and, under the sweep of the wind, the early-March daffodils were rippling rafts of bright yellow against the clipped green lawns that rolled down to the lily pond far below the long flagged terrace. Emma drew in a breath of air. It was pungent with the peaty brackenish smell of the moors, the damp earth, and a budding greenness that heralded spring after a hard winter. It had rained the night before and, even though it was noon, dew still clung to the trees and the shrubs, giving them an iridescent quality in the cool northern light.

As she always did, Emma looked up at the house as she and Paula walked towards it. And once more she was deeply moved by its imposing beauty, a beauty that was singularly English, for nowhere else could such a house have flowered so magnificently and so attuned to the surrounding landscape. Its beginnings rooted in the seventeenth century, there was a majestic dignity to the mixture of Renaissance and Jacobean architecture, indestructible and everlasting with its ancient crenellated towers and mullioned leaded windows that glimmered darkly against the time-worn gray stones. But there was a softness to the grandeur and even the protruding gargoyles, weathered by the centuries, were now bereft of their frightening countenances. They did not linger long on the terrace. In spite of the clear bright radiance there was no warmth in the sun, and the wind that blew in across the Dales from the North Sea was tinged with rawness. For all its beauty and spring freshness it was a treacherous day. Emma and Paula moved quickly up the steps, past the topiary hedges silhouetted against the edge of the velvet lawns like proud sentinels from a bygone age.

Before they reached the great oak door, it was flung open. Hilda, the housekeeper, was on the stone steps, her face wreathed in smiles. "Oh, madame!" she cried excitedly, rushing forward to clasp Emma's outstretched hand. "We've been so worried about you. Thank goodness you're better. It's lovely to have you back. And you, too, Miss Paula." She broke into more smiles again and hurried them into the house. "Come in, come in, out of the cold."

"I can't tell you how glad I am to be home," Emma said as they went into the house. "How have you been, Hilda?"

"Very well, madame. Just worried about you. We all have. Everything is running smoothly here. I'm all prepared for the family. Is Smithers bringing the luggage, madame? I can send Joe down to the car if you think he needs help." Words tumbled out of her in her excitement.

"No, thank you, Hilda. I'm sure Smithers can manage," Emma replied. She walked into the middle of the great stone entrance hall and looked around, smiling to herself with pleasure. Her eyes rested on the fine old oak furniture, the tapestries that lined the walls, the huge copper bowl of daffodils and pussy willow on the refectory table.

"The house looks beautiful, Hilda," she said with a warm smile. "You've done a good job as always."

Hilda glowed. "I have coffee ready, madame, or I can make some tea. But perhaps you'd prefer a sherry before lunch," she volunteered. "I put your favorite out in the upstairs parlor, madame."

"That's a good idea, Hilda. We'll go up now. Lunch about one o'clock. Is that all right?" Emma asked, her foot already on the first step.

"Of course, madame." She hurried off to her duties in the kitchen, humming under her breath, and Paula followed Emma up the soaring staircase, marveling once more at her grandmother's vitality.

"I'll join you in a moment, Grandy," Paula said as they walked down the long corridor leading to various bedrooms and the upstairs parlor. "I'd like to freshen up before lunch."

Emma nodded. "So would I, darling. I'll see you shortly." She went into her own room and Paula continued down the corridor to hers. Later, after she had changed her traveling suit for a light wool dress and had attended to her face and hair, Emma went through into the parlor which adjoined her bedroom. This was her favorite room at Pennistone Royal. A fire blazed in the hearth and Hilda had turned on several of the silk-shaded lamps, so that the room was filled with soft light. Emma's swift glance was approving as she crossed to the fireplace to warm herself in her habitual way.

The upstairs parlor of this ancient house was distinguished by a gentle beauty, refinement, and good taste. It was understated and unpretentious, yet this very simplicity was deceptive to any but the most experienced eye. It was the kind of understatement that could only be achieved by great expenditure of money and the most patient and skillful acquisition of the very best in furniture and furnishings. The dark polished floor gleamed against the exquisite Savonnerie carpet that splashed faded pastel colors into the center of the room. The palest of yellows washed over the walls and gave the whole room a sunny, airy feeling and everywhere sparkling silver and crystal gleamed richly against the mellow patinas of the handsome Georgian tables, consoles, and cabinets and the large elegant desk.

Two long sofas, facing each other across a butler's tray table in front of the fireplace, were as enveloping and as comfortable as deep feather beds. They were covered in a romantic chintz ablaze with clear vivid flowers of bright pink, yellow, blue, and red entwined amongst trailing green vines on a white ground. The Pembroke tables and small consoles all held rare porcelain bowls and vases filled with fresh spring hyacinths, jonquils, tulips, daffodils, and imported mimosa. The warmth of the fire had opened them up so that the air was aromatic with their mingled scents. A Chippendale cabinet, of great elegance and beauty, was filled with matchless Rose Medallion china, whilst side tables held priceless crystal and carved jade lamps with pale cream shades of the finest silk. In front of one of the soaring leaded windows, a Georgian rent table held a selection of the very latest books and a library table behind one of the sofas was piled high with all the current newspapers and magazines.

The bleached oak fireplace, where Emma stood regarding the room, was ornately carved and upon it reposed lovely old silver candlesticks holding white candles and in the center rested a seventeenth-century carriage clock. The Turner landscape dominated the wall above the fireplace. Redolent with misty greens and clear blues, its romantic bucolic setting was evocative and poignant to Emma and it never failed to stir a nostalgic longing in her heart, as it did now as she turned to admire it.

Portraits of a young nobleman and his wife, by Reynolds, flanked the Chippendale cabinet and a collection of exquisitely rendered miniatures were grouped on the wall behind the desk. Emma's unerring eye for color and form and her skill at placing and arranging furniture was in evidence everywhere and yet this was not an overly feminine room, being devoid of useless clutter and bric-a-brac. It was a handsome and gracious parlor where a man could also feel at ease in the softly diffused beauty and great comfort.

When she felt warmed throughout, Emma went over to the small console that held a silver tray of drinks and crystal glasses. She poured out two sherries and carried them back to the fireplace. As she waited for Paula she glanced at the morning newspapers. Her own paper, the *Yorkshire Morning Gazette*, was looking much better since she had brought Jim Fairley in as managing editor. He had made a great number of changes, all of which had improved the paper. He had revamped the format and the layout looked brighter and more modern, as did her evening paper, the *Yorkshire Evening Standard*, which was also under Jim's control. Advertising revenue had increased, as had the circulation of both papers. He had done an excellent job and Emma was more than satisfied. Jim Fairley . . . Paula . . . She could no longer think of him without thinking of Paula, too. In Emma's mind the girl was always fatefully in his shadow. She sighed. The door opened and Emma turned away from her introspection. She looked at Paula with fondness as she walked across the room. "I have a sherry here for you, my dear," she said, gesturing towards the table.

Paula was smiling cheerfully, having decided in the privacy of her own room to be her most charming self to every one of her unpleasant relatives this weekend. It was the only thing she could do, and under the circumstances her grandmother needed as much support as she could get with the leeches around, as Paula called them, although this was mostly said to herself or her cousins Alexander and Emily, who shared her views.

"I thought I would go riding this afternoon, if you don't mind, Grandy," she said as she joined Emma by the fire. "It's such a beautiful day even though it is cold."

Emma nodded, delighted. She wanted to be alone after lunch and she had contemplated sending Paula into Leeds on some invented errand. Now that was not necessary. "Yes, you should, darling, It will do you good. But wrap up warmly. I intend to take it easy myself. I have to plan the seating arrangement for the family dinner tomorrow night and then I shall rest."

"When are the others coming?" Paula asked, keeping her voice purposely light and casual.

"I expect some of them will come tonight. The others tomorrow." Emma's tone was as mild as Paula's, for she had sensed the girl's unhappiness about the weekend and she did not want her to be more distressed than she already was.

"It will be quite a houseful, Grandy. We haven't all been gathered here for years."

"That's true."

"Is Aunt Elizabeth bringing her husband?"

"Does she have one at the moment?" Emma asked with not a little malice.

"Oh, you are terrible, Grandy!" Paula laughed, her eyes dancing. "You know very well she does. The Italian count. Gianni."

"Humph! He's as much a count as I'm the Pope," Emma retorted disparagingly. "More like an Italian waiter to my mind." She sipped her sherry. Her green eyes glittered above the glass.

"Grandy! You are awful! He's very nice. Much too nice to cope with Aunt Elizabeth."

"You're right! This one has lasted longer than the others, come to think of it. I'm surprised she hasn't done a bolt before now. Isn't it about time?"

Paula laughed again. "I don't know. Who does with her?

Anyway, perhaps this marriage will work better than the last."

"And all the others before the last," Emma commented dryly.

Paula was amused. "You've had several husbands yourself, Grandmother."

"Not as many as Elizabeth, and furthermore, I didn't divorce them one after the other. Nor did mine get younger and younger as I got older," Emma pointed out. But she had the good grace to laugh. "Poor Elizabeth. She has such an idealistic attitude towards love and marriage. She's as romantic now as she was when she was sixteen. I just wish she'd settle down."

"And grow up, Grandy. Anyway, I suppose she will bring Gianni and the twins with her. Emily was at the Bradford store this past week, so I guess she will drive over tonight."

"Yes, she's going to do that. I spoke to her yesterday and she . . ."

Hilda knocked on the door and bounced into the room, her cheery north-country face still aglow. "Lunch is ready, madame," she announced, and added proudly, "Cook has made all your favorite dishes, madame."

Emma smiled. "We'll be right down, Hilda." She was fond of the housekeeper who had been with her for thirty years and with whom, in all that time, she had never exchanged one cross word. Most of Hilda's life had been devoted to running Pennistone Royal, which she did unobtrusively and with great efficiency, pride, and love.

"What were you saying about Emily, Grandmother?" Paula asked as they followed Hilda out of the room.

"Oh, yes, I spoke to her yesterday and she said she would drive over in time to have dinner with us, and that perhaps Alexander would come with her. Otherwise he will drive over later."

Hilda was standing in the hall, outside the dining-room door. She held it open for them and followed them into the room. "Cook has made that fresh vegetable soup you like, madame, and done a lovely fried plaice." She bustled over to the sideboard to serve them, adding, "Chips, too. I know you said no more fried food because of your diet, but just this once won't hurt, madame," she said, ladling out the soup into Royal Worcester bowls.

"If you say so, Hilda." Emma laughed, and winked at Paula, who was so startled by this unexpected facial movement in her grandmother she almost dropped the glass of water she was holding.

That afternoon, whilst Paula went riding on the moors, Emma sat upstairs in her parlor, where she always worked, and went over all the legal documents which had been prepared by her solicitors before she was taken ill. She spent some time studying them thoughtfully and when she had finished she called Henry Rossiter in London.

She dispensed with the preliminary greetings quickly, as she always did, and said briskly, "Henry, where do we now stand on the liquidation of those personal assets of mine?"

"I have all the papers in front of me, Emma. I was just going over them," he replied, clearing his throat.

To Emma his voice sounded suddenly quavering and tired. My dear old friend is getting old, she thought sadly. I shall miss him when he retires. Emma herself had no intention of retiring. She would die upright, sitting behind her desk.

"Ah, yes. I have them all now, Emma. Everything has been sold and the prices were very good. Excellent, in fact. We realized just under nine million pounds. Not bad, eh?"

"That's marvelous, Henry! Where is the money?"

"Why, right here in the bank. Where did you think it was, my dear?" He sounded startled, even a little affronted, and Emma smiled to herself.

"I know it's in the bank, Henry, but which account is it deposited in?" she asked patiently.

"I placed it in your own private business account, E.H. Incorporated."

"Please transfer it today, Henry. To my current account. My *personal* current account."

It was obvious to Emma that Henry was astounded. There was silence for a few seconds and she heard him sucking in his breath. When he found his voice at last he said, "Emma, that's ridiculous! Nobody puts nearly nine million pounds in a personal current account. You've got about two hundred thousand pounds in that account anyway. Look here, I know you said you needed about six million pounds for some personal project, but the remainder of the money from the sales should be working for you."

"I don't want it working for me, Henry. I want it in my current account." She laughed and she could not resist teasing him a little. "I might want to go shopping, Henry."

"Shopping!" he exploded, not understanding that she was jesting. "Come now, Emma! Not even *you* can spend that amount shopping! That's the most ridiculous thing I've heard you say in all the years I've known you." He was furious.

"I certainly can spend that amount of money shopping, Henry, depending, of course, on what *exactly* I'm buying," Emma said acidly, thinking to herself that Henry's marvelous sense of humor always seemed to evaporate into thin air when he was discussing money. "Please, Henry, no more discussion. Deduct the bank's fee for handling the sales, and the taxes to be paid, and put the rest in my personal current account."

He sighed in exasperation. "Very well. I suppose you know what you're doing, And after all, it is your money, Emma."

You're damn right it is, Emma thought. But she was too much of a great lady to say it, for Henry would have been hurt and flustered by this kind of remark. Instead, she changed the subject and they chatted in a social vein for a few minutes, before hanging up their respective telephones.

Emma worked on her seating plan for the family dinner on Saturday night and prepared a suggested menu for Hilda. Then, after locking the legal documents in her briefcase, she went into her bedroom to rest. Once she was in bed Emma exhaled a wearisome sigh. It was going to be an extremely difficult weekend, of that she was absolutely sure. Yet she felt no apprehension or the slightest twinge of anxiety, simply a cold detachment and a natural distaste as she envisioned the scenes which were bound to ensue after the family dinner on Saturday night.

She had an abhorrence of scenes, which in their inherent violence and futility both repelled and irritated her, and she tried to avoid them at all cost, particularly with her children. In spite of her reassurances to Paula, she knew that a few altercations would be inevitable during the next few days. She accepted this fact with resignation and steeled herself in preparation. She was not sure whether any of her children, other than Daisy, had lately developed enough inner strength to help them withstand a sudden crisis with a degree of fortitude. If they had, it would be a staggering

surprise to her, but she would welcome this development
because it might conceivably alleviate some of the unpleas-
antness. At the same time, she did not have to speculate on
how they would at first respond to her news.

Emma understood all of them well enough to anticipate
and gauge their reactions. Apart from Daisy, who was not
involved, each one of them would, in turn, be shocked and
infuriated by the news she would impart, especially since
they were all rendered powerless when thrust against her
deadly will, her superior intelligence, and her well-seasoned
shrewdness. She realized she was going to strike a swift and
terrible blow, a blow which would affect all of their lives. But
she felt no disquiet or pity, for it would be a blow from the
sword they had forced her to take up and wield in defense,
through their own foolhardy actions engendered by their
self-interest and avariciousness.

Neither did she suffer feelings of guilt about the innumerable plans she had made for the future. And she certainly did
not have one iota of compassion for those who would be the
most badly affected. There was only a heartbreaking sadness
buried deeply inside her that at times felt like a constricting
steel band around her chest. It was a sadness that sprang
from her hurt and her disappointment in her children, and
from a chilling horror at the knowledge that they had cold-
bloodedly plotted against her. Years ago Emma had ceased to
expect their love and she no longer sought their approbation
but, in spite of that, she had never imagined she would have
reason to question their loyalty at any time. The devastating
implications of their scheming had at first left her thunderstruck, but this initial reaction had rapidly been replaced by a
numbing anger and finally she had felt only pure contempt.
She smiled grimly as she reflected on their duplicity, a duplicity so ill-conceived and lacking in skill and imagination
she had known about it from its very inception.

At least she could have had a degree of respect for them if
they had been less transparent and a little more adroit in
their plotting. Emma had always had the ability to stand back
and admire a strong and cunning adversary, however grudging
that admiration was. As far as her children were concerned,
she was appalled at their lack of judgment, and their ingenuousness, which had precipitated their reckless and fatal actions and which had apparently led them to underestimate her.

She frowned and turned her thoughts away from the dissident members of her family, focusing her love on Daisy, Paula, and all of her other grandchildren. Eventually the quiet calm was restored and she slept, a deep untroubled sleep.

Afternoon tea had been a ritual at Pennistone Royal for years. It was a ritual Emma enjoyed, but even if she had not, Hilda would have not permitted it to be abandoned. "Over my dead body, madame," she had cried when Emma had suggested forgoing it a few years ago. Emma had shrugged and laughed helplessly. Hilda was a local woman who had come to work for Emma just after she had bought and restored Pennistone Royal and she was more like a member of the family than a paid servant. She was devoted to Emma, whom she described to anyone who would listen as "a good simple woman, with no fancy ideas," adding with that typical Yorkshire bluntness, "and a real lady, whatever her beginnings were. More so than many who were born such, I can tell you!" Emma was already a legend in the area, not only because of her power and wealth but for the many charitable deeds she had performed, quietly, with no fanfare and no desire for accolades, as was her way. But whenever Hilda had the opportunity she would proudly enumerate all of Emma's good works yet again, like a litany, not forgetting to mention that her Madame had put *her* own son Peter through university and had created a series of scholarships for the talented children of Pennistone and Fairley. "And what about her Foundation?" she would continue with a sniff, arching her neck and narrowing her eyes shrewdly. "Now, the Foundation gives away more money than *I* care to mention. Millions! Yes, millions. There is nothing tight-fisted about Emma Harte, that's the truth. Which is more than I can say about some of the other rich folk around here. They wouldn't give a blind man a light on a rainy night, never mind part with a few coppers for the needy." And when she wasn't singing the praises of Emma she was proclaiming the virtues of Paula, whom she had helped to raise and whom she loved just as much as if she were her own daughter.

And so, promptly at four o'clock, Hilda came sailing into the parlor, carrying before her a great silver tea tray set with a beautiful Georgian silver tea service of exquisite design and delicate china which was translucent when held to the light.

Following in her wake was one of the two young maids who came daily to work at the house, who also carried another gargantuan tray, this one laden with food painstakingly prepared by the cook.

"Put that on the desk for a minute, Brenda," Hilda instructed, "and bring one of the small tables over here by the fire to hold it." She put her own tray down on the butler's table and, puffing and blowing from exertion, she paused to catch her breath, motioning to Brenda where to position the second table for convenience. The two women carefully arranged the trays in front of the fire and then Brenda slipped out of the room, leaving Hilda to make the finishing touches. She surveyed Cook's handiwork critically and then a smile of gratification slowly spread itself across her plump rosy face. There were hot buttered scones, thin slices of bread and butter, homemade strawberry jam, clotted cream, wafer-like sandwiches of cucumber, tomatoes, and smoked salmon, sweet biscuits, and a fruit cake decorated on the top with almonds. It was a real old-fashioned Yorkshire tea. Hilda carefully folded the fine lawn serviettes, put one on each plate with a small pearl-handled silver knife and fork, threw logs onto the fire, plumped the cushions, and then looked around. When she had reassured herself that everything was to her satisfaction she knocked on Emma's bedroom door.

"Are you awake, madame?"

"Yes, Hilda. Come in," Emma called.

Hilda opened the door and poked her head around it, smiling. "Tea is ready!" she announced. "And Miss Paula is back from her ride. She said to tell you she'll be here in a few minutes. She's changing out of her riding clothes."

"Thank you, Hilda. I'll be there shortly."

"Ring if you need anything, madame," Hilda added, and then went down to the kitchen to have her own tea and give a word of praise to Cook.

When Paula came in a little while later she stood in the doorway and caught her breath, unexpectedly moved by the beauty of the parlor. It was hushed and still, as if time had passed it by. The only sound was the crackling of the fire that burned in the huge hearth. Sunshine filtered in through the tall leaded windows, dusky and golden, bathing the furniture and paintings in a mellow light, and the air, heavy with the perfume of hyacinths and spring flowers, flowed around her, enveloping her in its heady fragrance. There was something poignant about this great old room, and her heart ached with a sudden wistfulness as memories stirred within her, faintly elusive and nostalgic. She glided silently across the floor, almost afraid to move within that stillness, fearful that the rustling of her dress might disrupt and destroy that gentle peace. She sank onto one of the sofas and her eyes roamed around the room, lingering on all the well-remembered things she had lived with all of her life. Here it was easy to forget that there was a world outside, a world full of pain and ugliness and despair. She drifted gently on the edge of memory, recalling her childhood in this ancient place, the happy times she had spent here with her mother and father, her cousins and her young friends. And Grandy. Always Grandy. Her grandmother was never far away, always there to wipe away her tears, laugh at her childish pranks, admire her small achievements and to scold and cosset and love her. Her grandmother had made her what she was. It was Grandy who had told her she was clever and beautiful and special. Unique, she had said. It was Grandy who had given her inner security and confidence and strength, who had taught her to face the truth without fear and with a courageous heart. . . .

She did not hear Emma come in, so soft was her step. Emma, too, paused to admire, but her attention was focused solely on Paula. How lovely she looks, Emma thought, like a figure from some old painting, remote and wistful, the maiden with the unicorn. Indeed, there was something faintly medieval about Paula's appearance, for she was wearing a dress with a high ruffled neck and long sleeves that widened at the cuffs and dipped down into deep folds around her delicate wrists. The dress was of the deepest violet and its vivid color intensified the violet lights in her eyes, which were as huge liquid pools in the alabaster face. Her blue-black hair was pulled back severely from her face, held at the nape of her neck by an antique tortoise-shell hair slide so that the widow's peak was emphasized more dramatically than ever. The only jewelry she wore was a pair of old pendant earrings made of amethysts and diamonds that dropped delicately from her ears and threw off prisms of dancing light in the bright sunshine.

"There you are, darling!" Emma exclaimed, moving gracefully across the room. "You're looking beautiful and refreshed after your ride."

Paula glanced up swiftly, momentarily startled. "Oh, Grandy, you made me jump. I was miles away."

As Emma seated herself opposite Paula her eyes lighted on the tea tray. "My goodness, look at all this food. Hilda is too much," she murmured, shaking her head in mild exasperation. "How can we eat all this! It's only a few hours to dinner."

Paula laughed. "I know! Perhaps she feels you need building up. You know how she fusses over you. But she's really gone to town today. It's like the nursery teas she used to make when I was small."

"I'm not hungry at all," Emma murmured, "and she's going to be so hurt if we don't eat anything."

"I'm ravenous, so don't worry," Paula remarked, picking up a sandwich. "It was cold up there on the moors and I rode for miles. It's given me quite an appetite." She bit into the sandwich as Emma looked on approvingly.

"I'm glad to see you eating for once. You always seem to pick at your food. No wonder you're so thin. . . ."

The telephone on Emma's desk rang, Paula jumped up. "Don't disturb yourself, darling," she said, dashing across the room, "it's probably only one of the family."

She picked up the phone. "Yes, Hilda, I'll take it. Hello? It's Paula. Do you want to speak to Grandmother?" She listened briefly and said, "Oh, all right. Yes. Fine. Goodbye." Paula came back to her place on the sofa. "It was Aunt Elizabeth. She's coming tomorrow morning and bringing the twins . . . and the husband!"

"So now we know," Emma remarked with a chuckle. The telephone rang again. "Oh dear, I do hope they're not all going to call and tell us when they are arriving. This could go on for the rest of the day," Emma exclaimed impatiently.

Paula hurried across the room and took the call, which as always was monitored first by Hilda. "Emily! How are you?" she cried when she heard her cousin's voice. They were close friends. "Yes, of course you can. She's right here." Paula put the phone down on the desk and motioned to Emma. "It's Emily, Grandy, she wants to talk to you."

"Knowing Emily, this could be quite an involved conversation," Emma said with a fond smile, and picking up her cup of tea, she took it with her to the desk. Sitting down, she lifted the phone and said briskly, "Hello, darling. How are . . ."

"I'm fine, Grandmother," Emily interrupted in her young breathy voice, in a tremendous rush as always. "I can't talk long! I'm in a frightful hurry! But I just wanted to tell you that Sarah is flying up from London this afternoon. I'm going to pick her up at Yeadon Airport at six-thirty, so we'll definitely be there for dinner. Oh, and Alexander said to tell you he might be late. Uncle Kit's being truculent about that machinery. He's had Alexander going over all the figures again. Alexander's furious! Well, anyway, he thinks he can be at Pennistone by eight o'clock, if that isn't too late. Also, Jonathan is taking the train up from London to Leeds. But he said not to send Smithers. He'll get a taxi."

All of this had issued forth in a steady uninterrupted stream, in Emily's typical fashion, which Emma was quite accustomed to. She sat back comfortably, an amused glint in her eyes, listening attentively, occasionally sipping her tea. Emily was always pressed for time, even more so than she was herself, and it often occurred to Emma that her voluble and volatile young granddaughter seemed to speak in a series of exclamation marks. Now she said teasingly, "For someone in a rush this seems to be a very long conversation, Emily dear."

"Grandy! Don't be mean! I can't help it if all your idiot grandchildren make me the repository of their messages. Ooh! I've one more. Philip is going to try and come with me; if not, he'll drive over with Alexander. Grandy dear . . ." Emily paused and her voice dropped, was suddenly soft and full of lilting charm. "Can I ask a favor?"

"Of course, darling," Emma replied, repressing an amused but loving smile. She knew that cajoling tone of Emily's only too well, adopted whenever she wanted something.

"Could I borrow one of your evening dresses, please? I only brought a few things when I came up to Bradford last week. I didn't know you would be giving a big family party. I've nothing to wear. I looked through the store here today and everything is so *dowdy!* And I simply don't have time to go over to the Leeds store."

Emma laughed. "If you think the clothes in the store are dowdy, I don't know what you'll find here, dear," she remarked, wondering what on earth a pretty twenty-one-year-old blond dynamo could possibly find suitable in *her* wardrobe.

"That red chiffon dress! The one from Paris! It fits me. So do the red silk shoes," Emily rushed on excitedly. "I knew you wouldn't mind me trying it on, so I did last weekend when I was at Pennistone. It looks super on me, Grandy. Please, can I borrow it? I'll be careful."

"I'd forgotten about that dress, Emily. Of course you can wear it, if you wish. I don't know why I ever bought it in the first place. Perhaps you'd like to keep it," Emma suggested generously.

Emily sucked in her breath in delighted surprise but said, "Oh, Grandy darling, I couldn't do that!" There was another little pause. "Don't you *want* it, Grandmother?"

Emma smiled to herself. "Not really, Emily. It's far too dashing for me. It's yours."

"Oh, Grandy! Goodness! Oh, thank you, darling! You're an angel. Grandy? . . ."

"Yes, Emily? What else?"

"Would it be an imposition to ask you to lend me your *old* diamond earrings? That dress needs a little . . . well . . . it needs a little something, doesn't it?" Emily cried enthusiastically. "It needs good jewelry, don't you think?"

Emma burst out laughing. "Really, Emily, you're so funny. I don't know what you mean by *old* diamond earrings. Do I have such a thing?"

"Yes! Those drops. The teardrops. You never wear them! Maybe you've forgotten them," Emily volunteered, her voice rising hopefully.

"Oh, those. Yes. You can wear them and anything else you want. In the meantime, how are things at the Bradford store?"

"Thank you, Grandy, for the earrings, I mean. And things here are very good. I'll tell you about some of the changes I've made when I see you. Otherwise it's all sort of quiet and dull."

"Well, you'll be in Leeds next week, which isn't so bad," Emma pointed out. "And we'll talk about your changes tonight. By the way, it doesn't matter if the boys are late. Hilda always makes a cold supper on Fridays," Emma explained, and went on, "Your mother just called. She's coming tomorrow wi . . ."

"Grandmother! Gosh! I forgot!" Emily broke in. "I wanted

to alert you to something *awful*. Mummy has had a furious row with the twins! Something about a statue they've made for you. They're insisting on bringing it and Mummy says it's simply hideous and won't fit into the car. But that's not surprising, with all the luggage *she* drags around with her. Anyway, there's been a terrible fuss and the twins are upset and they want to move in and live with you! I just thought *you* should know exactly what to *expect!*" She sighed dramatically. "What a family!"

"Thank you for telling me," Emma said thoughtfully. "But let's not worry about all that now. I'm sure by the time Elizabeth arrives the twins will be calm again. They can stay with me for a while if they wish. Is that all, Emily?" Emma asked patiently, although she was now anxious to terminate the conversation, as diverting as it was.

"Yes. Gosh! I must rush, Grandy. I'm way behind. Goodbye. See you tonight."

"Good-bye . . ." Emma stared at the telephone and then she laughed. Emily had already hung up. She leaned back in her chair and shook her head, still laughing. "It doesn't surprise me at all that the store managers tremble when Emily arrives on the scene. She's a whirlwind."

Paula smiled at Emma, nodding her head in agreement. "I know. But she's awfully good at her job, Grandy. I think you ought to consider sending her to the Paris store for a while. She would be terrific."

Emma raised an eyebrow in surprise. "But she doesn't speak French," she said, "otherwise I might consider it."

"She does, Grandy." Paula sat up and gave Emma a penetrating look. "She's been taking lessons," Paula explained, cautiously feeling her way. "She would love to go and I think she might be the answer you've been looking for."

"Well, I'll think about it," Emma remarked, rather pleased at Paula's information. Emily was diligent, she knew that. Perhaps it *was* the solution. Emily, like all of her other grandchildren who were old enough, worked within the Harte companies and had proved herself to be tireless and assiduous in her work. She would consider it later. Now she turned her mind to more immediate problems. "I have made the seating plan for dinner," Emma began, and poured herself another cup of tea.

Paula looked at her with interest, a smile playing around

her softly curving, gentle mouth. "Yes, you told me you were going to, Grandy." Paula waited expectantly.

Emma cleared her throat. "I think I have seated everyone appropriately. I've tried to separate the ones who don't get along too well, although, as I said, I am sure everyone will be on their best behavior." She put her hand in her pocket and her fingers curled around the paper. She was still reluctant to bring it out and show it to Paula.

"I hope so, Grandy! It's such a crowd and you know how difficult some of them can be." She laughed sardonically. "Impossible, wouldn't you say?"

"Oh yes, indeed," Emma replied. She leaned back against the sofa and stared at Paula intently, questioningly. "I suppose they all thought I was drawing my last breath these last few weeks, didn't they?"

The unexpected question surprised Paula and she threw a swift look at Emma, but, as always, her grandmother's face was inscrutable. "I don't know," she began thoughtfully. "Perhaps . . ." She hesitated and then her exasperation with her aunts and uncles got the better of her. "Oh, they're such leeches, Grandy!" she exclaimed angrily. "I don't know why you bother with them! I'm sorry. I know they're your children, but I just get furious every time I think of them."

"You don't have to apologize to me, dear. I know only too well what they are." Emma smiled thinly. "I don't delude myself that they are coming to see me out of concern. They accepted my invitation out of curiosity. Vultures come to regard the carcass. But I'm not dead yet and I have made no immediate plans for dying," she finished, a note of triumph in her voice.

Paula leaned forward quickly, staring at Emma fixedly. "Then why did you invite them, Grandy, if you know what they are?" she asked in a deliberate voice.

Emma smiled enigmatically and her eyes turned cold. "I wanted to see them all together for one last time."

"Don't say that, Grandy! You're better and we are going to take care of you properly this time. To hell with the stores and business," Paula cried passionately.

"By the 'last time,' I meant the last time I will invite them here for this kind of weekend," Emma declared. "I have a little family business to attend to, and as they are involved, they should be here. All of them. Together." Her mouth tightened into the familiar resolute line and her eyes gleamed darkly.

Concern clouded Paula's eyes. "You must promise me, you won't let them upset you," she said, noting the expression on Emma's face. "And you shouldn't be worrying about family business this weekend. Is it *so* important it can't wait?" she demanded fiercely.

"Oh, it's nothing all that vital," Emma said dismissively with a shrug. "Just a few details regarding the trust funds. It won't take long, and of course I won't let them disturb me." A half smile flickered across her face. "Actually, I'm rather looking forward to it."

"I'm not sure that I am," Paula said carefully. "May I see the seating plan?"

"Of course, darling." Emma moved her position slightly and put her hand in her pocket. She felt the paper and hesitated, and then, taking a deep breath, she pulled it out. "Here you are." She handed the paper to Paula, waiting expectantly, holding herself perfectly still, hardly daring now to breathe at all.

Paula's eyes traveled quickly over the paper. Emma was watching her intently. Paula's eyes stopped. Opened wide. Moved on. Returned again to the previous spot. A look of total disbelief spread itself across her face. "Why, Grandy? Why?" Her voice rose sharply in anger and the paper fluttered to the floor as she moved almost convulsively in the chair. Emma was silent, waiting for the initial surprise to disappear, for Paula to calm down.

"*Why?*" Paula demanded, jumping up, her face white, her mouth trembling. "Why have you done this, Grandmother? You have no right to invite Jim Fairley tomorrow night. He's not family. I don't want him here! I won't have him here! I won't! I won't! *How could you, Grandmother!*"

She ran to the window and Emma could see she was fighting to control herself. Her thin shoulders hunched over as she pressed her forehead against the pane of glass, her narrow shoulder blades sharp and protruding under the silk dress. Emma's heart ached with love for her and she felt her pain as deeply as if it were her own. "Come here and sit down. I want to talk to you, darling," Emma said softly.

Paula swung around quickly, her eyes now so dark they looked navy blue. "I don't want to talk to you, Grandmother.

At least not about Jim Fairley!" She stood poised by the
window, defiant, reproachful, filled with rage. She trembled
and clasped and unclasped her hands in agitation. How could
her grandmother have been so thoughtless? To ask Jim Fairley
to the dinner was cruel and unfair, and she had never known
her grandmother to be either of these things. She turned her
back on Emma and laid her head against the window again,
looking out at the green treetops yet seeing nothing, pushing
back the tears that rushed into her eyes.

To Emma she looked suddenly pathetically young and vulnerable and hurt. She is the one thing of value that I cherish,
Emma thought, her heart contracting with love. Of all my
grandchildren, she is the one I love the most. My hard and
terrible life has been worth it just for the joy of her. This girl.
This strong, dauntless, courageous, loyal girl who would put
my desires before her own happiness.

"Come here, darling. I have something I must tell you."

Paula stared at Emma abstractedly as if she were in shock.
With reluctance she came back to the fireplace, moving like a
sleepwalker, her face blank. She was still fuming, but the
shaking had ceased. Her eyes were flat and dull, like hard
stones of lapis lazuli in her ashen face. She sat down erect
and rigid on the sofa. There was something contained, unyielding about her that was frightening to Emma, who knew
she must quickly explain, so that look would leave her granddaughter forever. Emma had chosen an oblique way of in-
forming Paula that she had invited Jim Fairley to the dinner,
because she did not trust herself to do it verbally. But now
she must speak. Explain. Put the girl out of her terrible
torment.

"I have invited Jim Fairley tomorrow, Paula, because he is
indirectly involved in the family business matters I mentioned to you earlier." She paused and sucked in her breath
and then continued more firmly, looking at Paula closely.
"But that is not the only reason. I also invited him for you.
And I might add he was delighted to accept."

"W-w-w-what d-d-do you mean . . . f-f-for me?" Paula stuttered. She was transfixed, incredulous. A deep flush rose up
from her neck, filling her face with dark color and her mouth
shook again. "I don't understand . . . invited him for me
. . ." She was flustered and confused. Her hair had somehow
worked loose from the hair slide in her agitation and she

moved it away from her face impatiently. She shook her head in bewilderment. "What are you saying, Grandmother? You have always hated the Fairleys. I don't understand."

Emma pushed herself onto her feet and went and sat on the sofa. She took one of Paula's beautiful tapered hands in her own small sturdy ones. She gazed at Paula and her heart tightened when she looked into her eyes, vast caverns in the paleness of her face and full of pain. Emma touched that wan face, smiling gently, and then she said in a hoarse whisper, "I am an old woman, Paula. A tough old woman who has fought every inch of the way for everything I have. Strong, yes, but also tired. Bitter? Perhaps I was. But I have acquired *some* wisdom in my struggle with life, my struggle to survive, and I wondered to myself the other day why the silly pride of a tough old woman should stand in the way of the one person I love the most in the whole world. It struck me I was being selfish, and foolish, to let events of sixty years ago cloud my judgment now."

"I still don't understand," Paula murmured, bafflement in her eyes.

"I am trying to tell you that I no longer have any objections to you seeing Jim Fairley. I had a long conversation with him yesterday, during which I gathered he still feels the same way about you. That he has always had very serious intentions. I told him this afternoon that if he wishes to marry you, he not only has my permission, but my blessing as well. I bless both of you, with all my love."

Paula was speechless. Her mind would not accept her grandmother's words. For months she had cautioned herself not to think of Jim, had finally accepted that there was no possible future for them. She had been hard on herself, ruthlessly pushing aside all emotion, all feelings, pouring her energy into her work in her abject misery. Through the blur of her tears she saw Emma's face, that face she had seen and loved all of her life. That face she trusted. Emma was smiling fondly, waiting, and her eyes were wise and understanding and full of love. The tears slid silently down Paula's cheeks and she shook her head. "I can't believe you would change your mind," she said, her voice choked.

"I did."

These two simple words, uttered with firmness and conviction, finally penetrated Paula's aching brain, her battered

heart. Her containment cracked, as an ice floe cracks under
brilliant sun. She began to sob, her whole body heaving as
the smothered and pent-up emotions of months were released. She slumped forward, blindly reaching for Emma,
who cradled her in her arms like a child, stroking her hair
and murmuring softly to her in the way she had done when
she was a little girl. "It's all right. Hush, darling. It's all right.
I promise you it's all right."

Eventually the heaving sobs subsided and Paula looked up
at Emma, a tremulous smile on her face. Emma wiped the
tears from her face with one hand, stared intently at her and
said, "I never want to see you unhappy again as long as I live.
I've had enough unhappiness for both of us."

"I don't know what to say. I'm numb. I can't believe it,"
Paula replied quietly. Jim. *Jim!* Her heart leapt.

Emma nodded. "I know how you feel," she said, and her
tired eyes brightened. "Now, why don't you do me a favor?
Go and call Jim. He's still at the paper. He's waiting for you,
in fact. Invite him for dinner tonight, if you wish. Or better
still, drive into Leeds and have dinner with him alone. I'll
have Emily and Sarah for company, and perhaps Alexander
and the others will arrive in time for supper." She laughed
gaily, her eyes shining. "I do have other grandchildren, you
know." Paula hugged her and kissed her, and then she was
gone, flying out of the room without another word.

Wings on her feet, Emma thought, going to her love. She
sat for a while on the sofa, preoccupied with thoughts of
Paula and Jim and so many other things. Then she stood up
suddenly, abruptly, and walked to the window, stretching
her stiffened limbs, smoothing her dress with her hands,
patting her silver hair into place. She opened one of the
leaded windows and looked out.

Below her in the garden the trees glistened in the cool
night air, and everything was dark green and perfectly still.
Not a blade of grass, not a leaf stirred, and the birds were
silent. She could see the daffodils rapidly losing their brilliant
color, bleaching palely to white now that the sun had set, and
the topiary hedges were slowly turning black. She stood
there for a long time in the gloaming, watching the dusk
descend as the crystalline northern light faded behind the
low hump line of hills on the horizon. The mist was drifting
into the garden, wrapping everything before it in a vaporous,

opal-tinted shawl, rising suddenly to obscure the trees and the shrubs and the old flagged terrace, until all these images were fused together.

Emma shivered and closed the window, turning back into the welcoming warmth and comfort of the room. She walked across the faded Savonnerie carpet, still shivering slightly from the cold damp air that had blown in through the window. She picked up the poker and energetically pushed the burning logs around, throwing on more of them to build the huge roaring fire she loved.

She sat by the fireside staring into the flames, content and at peace, forgotten memories of her youth invading her mind as she waited for her other grandchildren to arrive. She thought of the Fairleys. All of them were gone now, except for James Arthur Fairley, the last of the line. "Why should he suffer, and Paula, for the mistakes of a dead generation?" she asked herself aloud, and then thought: I was right to do this. It is my gift to her. To both of them.

It was growing darker outside and in the dimly lit room the firelight cast its strange and mysterious shadows across the walls and the ceiling and in amongst them she saw so many old and familiar faces. Her friends. Her enemies. All of them dead long ago. Ghosts . . . just ghosts that could no longer touch her or hers.

Life is funny, she mused, it's like a circle. My life began with the Fairleys and it will end with them. The two points have now joined to make the full circle.

PART TWO

The Abyss
1904–1905

Long is the way
And hard, that out
of hell leads up to light.

—JOHN MILTON, *Paradise Lost*

PART TWO

FIVE

"Mam . . . Mam . . . Are yer awake?" Emma called softly from the doorway. There was no answer.

She hovered uncertainly near the door, her ears straining for the slightest sound, but the room was as still as the grave. Nervously she pulled the meager shawl more tightly around her slender shoulders, shivering in the thin nightgown in the bitter cold before the dawn, her pale face a ghostly beacon in the murky darkness.

"Mam! Mam!" she cried in an urgent whisper, and crept further into the room, moving cautiously, feeling her way around the few mean pieces of furniture, her eyes not yet adjusted to the gloom. She could scarcely breathe, so dank and stale was the malodorous air. She shuddered, momentarily repelled by the mingled odors of musty walls, soiled bedclothes, and cloying sweat. It was the unmistakable stench of poverty and sickness. She sucked in her breath and edged forward.

When she reached the iron bedstead her heart missed a beat as she peered down at the sick woman who lay inert underneath the bedclothes, which were thrown about in disarray. *Her mother was dying. Perhaps she was already dead.* Panic and fear sent shudders through her thin little body, so that she shook uncontrollably. She bent forward and pressed her face to her mother's body, straining towards that fragile form, as if to imbue it with renewed vigor, to give it life. She screwed her eyes tightly shut and uttered up a silent prayer, passionate and beseeching, every ounce of her concentration pouring into it. Please, God, don't let me mam die! I'll be good for the rest of me life. I'll do anything Yer want, God. I will, God, I will! Just don't let me mam die. Emma believed that God was good. Her mother had told her that God was Goodness. That He was understanding and forgiving. Emma did not believe in a wrathful God, the God of retribution and revenge that the Methodist minister warned about in his sermons on Sundays. Her mother had said God was Inconceivable Love and her mam knew best. Emma's God was compassionate. He *would* answer her prayer.

She opened her eyes and began to stroke the woman's feverish brow gently. "Mam! Mam! Can yer hear me? Are yer all right?" she asked again in a voice quavering with dread. There was still no visible response.

In the wavering light from the tiny candle flame the woman's face was clearly in focus. Usually pale, it had taken on an ashen cast and beads of sweat coated it with a glistening film that looked ghastly in the weak light. The once luxuriant brown hair fell in limp and listless fronds across the damp brow and lay in a tangled mass on the sodden pillow behind her. There was a sweetness in the face, which the pain and suffering had not completely obliterated, but all the traces of the gentle beauty of her youth had been dissipated by the ravages of grim poverty, by the years of punishing struggle for survival, and finally by this deadly and virulent sickness. An aureole of death was around Elizabeth Harte and she would not live to see these last few months of winter move forward into spring. She was suffering from the wasting disease which was consuming her little by little every day, leaving her a withered and wraith-like old woman. She was not quite thirty-four years old.

Hers was a grim sickroom, for it contained few elements of comfort or beauty, none of the amenities of life. The bed was the dominant piece of furniture and it took up most of the space under the sloping eaves. Apart from the bed there were few scant furnishings. The rickety table, made of bamboo, was wedged in the corner, between the bed and the small window, and upon this reposed a worn black Bible, a pottery mug, and the medicine Dr. Malcolm had prescribed. Near the door there was a crude wooden chest, whilst the mahogany washstand, with its cracked white marble top, rested against the wall on the far side of the window. The cottage was built into the side of the moorland and this made it cruelly damp and unhealthy through all the seasons of the year, but especially so in these harsh northern winters when rainsoaked gales and driving snow blew ferociously across the fells. Yet in spite of the dampness, the spartan frugality, and the dreary ambiance, the room was spotlessly clean. Freshly washed and starched cotton curtains hung at the window, and the few pieces of rustic furniture gleamed brightly with beeswax and Emma's constant care. Not a speck of dust marred the worn wooden floor, which was covered in part with clipped rugs, homemade from pieces of gaily colored rags hooked into sacking. Only the bed was unkempt and neglected, for Emma could change the bed linen but once a week, when she came home from Fairley Hall, where she was in service.

Elizabeth moved uneasily and with some agitation. "Is that our Emma?" The voice was so feeble with fatigue it was barely audible.

"Yes, Mam, it's me," the girl cried, clutching her mother's hand.

"What time is it, Emma?"

"Just turned four o'clock. Old Willy knocked us up early this morning. I'm sorry if I waked yer, Mam, but I wanted ter make sure yer were all right, afore I went up yonder ter the Hall."

Elizabeth sighed. "Aye, lass. I'm not so badly. Don't fret so. I'll get up later and—" She began to cough violently and pressed her fragile hands to her chest trying to contain the tremors that shook her. Emma poured medicine into the pot mug on the table and, slipping her arms around her mother, she propped her up so that she could drink from the pot. "Try this, Mam. It's the stuff from Dr. Mac, and it seems ter do yer good," she exclaimed, in the most cheerful voice she could summon. Elizabeth attempted to sip from the pot between bouts of the persistent coughing that wracked her body. Slowly the obstinate rattle in her chest abated and eventually she was able to take a long draught of the medicine. Although she was suffering from shortness of breath and exertion she managed to speak.

"Yer'd best go down and see ter yer father and the lads, luv. I'll rest a while and perhaps afore yer go ter work yer'll bring me up some tea." The febrile light in her eyes was dimming and she seemed more conscious of her surroundings, more aware of the girl who stood beside the bed.

Emma bent down and kissed the woman's lined cheek with tenderness and pulled the blankets up around the wasted shoulders protectively. "Aye, I will." She slipped out of the room and closed the door softly. As she ran down the narrow stone staircase, ignoring its high perilous slant in her haste, raised voices wafted up to meet her halfway. Emma stood quite still and drew in her breath sharply, her heart sinking into the pit of her stomach. A feeling of nausea swept over her as she envisioned the ugly scene awaiting her. Winston, her brother, and her father were quarreling again and the violence of their confrontation was only too evident from their angrily raised voices. The chilling thought that they would disturb her mother caused Emma to cry out involuntarily. She stifled the frightened half cry, pressing her roughened hands to her mouth, and sat down heavily on the cold stone steps, wondering helplessly how she could stop them fighting. If her mam heard them she would crawl out of bed to make peace between them, even if it took her last ounce of strength. Elizabeth Harte had always been the buffer between her son Winston and her husband. In these last few weeks she had been too debilitated to leave her bed, a virtual prisoner in the mean little room under the eaves. But when she heard their violent disagreements, she cried a lot and the fever accelerated and became more virulent and she coughed until she was worn out with coughing.

"Fools!" Emma said out loud. Grown men acting like bairns and them too selfish ter think of me poor mam. This thought galvanized her. She jumped up quickly, the sinking sickness replaced by a cold anger that grew in magnitude as Emma continued her descent down the staircase. She pushed open the kitchen door and stood rigid and tense on the threshold, her hand tightly gripping the doorframe. As she regarded the scene her green eyes took on a flinty look.

Unlike the damp and cheerless room upstairs, this was a cozy, heartwarming place. A fire blazed in the grate and a large iron kettle was hissing on the hob. The giant-sized cabbage roses on the wallpaper had long since lost their summer glory, but the smudged pink outlines left behind added a warming mellow cast to the walls. Pieces of polished horse brass gleamed around the fireplace, twinkling in the soft light with the luster of freshly minted gold sovereigns. Two comfortable high-backed wooden chairs stood on either side of the fireplace and there was a tall Welsh dresser opposite, filled with blue and white willow-patterned dishes. In the very center of the room, a large scrubbed wood table took pride of place and was surrounded by six rush-seated chairs. White lace curtains graced the windows and the red brick floor sparkled. The room had a robust, rosy glow, a

glow enhanced by the roaring fire that blazed up the chimney and the trembling flicker of the paraffin lamp that stood
on the mantelshelf.

It was a scene that Emma carried with her, especially
when she was at Fairley Hall, for it engendered a sense of
well-being within her and comforted her when she was alone.
Now her cherished image was shattered. Everything was in
its place, nothing had been moved, but the atmosphere was
charged, and ugly and angry words reverberated and bounced
off the walls. The two men, her father and her brother, faced
each other like animals, oblivious to her, oblivious to everything except this deadly hatred between them.

John "Big Jack" Harte was a large man, as his nickname
implied. Without his boots, in his stocking feet, he stood six
foot two and was ramrod straight. He had fought the Boers in
Africa in 1900, a sergeant in the Seaforth Highlanders, and it
was said of him that he could fell a man with one blow from
his massive fist. He had a powerfully built frame, a handsome
roughhewn face, a ruddy complexion, and a splendid head of
wavy hair the color of polished jet.

He stood towering over his son Winston, his fist raised in
anger and ready to come down hard on the boy. His face was
livid with volcanic wrath and his eyes flared dangerously.
"Thee's not going into no navy and that's the last I'll hear of it
in this house, me lad! Thee's under age and no permission will
thee get from me. Now drop it once and for all, our Winston,
or thee'll feel me strap across thee back. Thee's not too old
yet for a good hiding, me lad, and don't thee forget it!"

Winston glowered back at his father, his unusually beautiful face flushed and contorted with frustration and anger, his
blue eyes icy. "If I want ter go, I'll go," he screamed passionately. "Yer can't stop me if I runs away and run away I will,
out of this godforsaken hole, where there's nowt but misery
and poverty and dying—"

"Little monkey! Talk back ter me, would thee! We'll soon
see about that!"

The boy could not move for a split second and then, as the
bubble of rage burst in his head, he stepped forward and
lifted his arm as if to strike his father. But through the
dizzying haze of his blinding anger he saw something menacing in those eyes and he paled and backed away, faltering,
mortally afraid of his father's strength. Although he was not as

tall and as muscular as his father, Winston was well built and strong, but he was made of finer stuff, more like his mother. And he knew he was no physical match for Big Jack Harte. Winston had strong instincts for self-preservation and especially so when it applied to his person, for the fifteen-year-old boy was increasingly conscious of his striking looks and he knew them to be his most powerful asset.

"Don't think I didn't see that, our Winston! I'll teach thee ter raise thee hand ter me, lad! That I will. I'm going ter give thee a good hiding thee won't forget as long as thee lives. And it's long overdue!" As he spoke he began to unbuckle the black leather belt around his trousers, pulling it off hurriedly in his excitement. He wrapped it around his right hand, buckle first, moving towards Winston threateningly and with immense power.

"Ah, yer can't scare me, our dad!" Winston cried shrilly, nonetheless retreating to the Welsh dresser, putting the table safely between them. "Yer wouldn't dare hit *me!* Me mam won't never forgive yer, if yer puts that strap on me!" he warned, using the one threat he believed would influence his father.

But Big Jack Harte appeared not to hear. He moved forward rapidly and with agility, the black leather strap dangling ominously in his tightened fist. He lifted his arm and would have brought the strap down across the boy's head if Emma had not rushed across the room at this moment and jumped in front of her father. She grabbed his arm and held it with both hands, using all of her strength. Her face was gaunt in the firelight and she shook with rage. She stood before her father unflinchingly. She was the only one who dared defy him, who had the nerve to stand up to him. And she could usually quell his wrath, subdue him into docility.

Although her voice was quiet when she spoke, there was vehemence in her words. "Shut up, Dad! What's got in ter yer? Shouting and bawling at this hour and our mam lying badly upstairs. Yer should know better, our dad. And yer should be ashamed of yerself! Now sit down and drink yer tea, quiet like, or I'll be the one that runs away, and then where would yer all be, eh?" She held tightly on to his raised arm, which she could not move. "Come on, Dad," she cajoled in a softer tone, "don't be stubborn. Our Winston won't run off ter the navy. That's all big talk on his part."

"That's what yer think, is it, Miss Nosy Parker?" Winston interjected furiously from the safety of his corner on the other side of the room. "Well, yer wrong for once in yer short life, our Emma. I mean it. Yes, I do."

Emma swung around to face her brother. She strived to control herself. "Stop it, Winston," she hissed. "Yer'll have me mam downstairs next and her so poorly. And stop this stupid talk of joining the Royal Navy. Me dad's right, yer are too young. And yer'll break our mam's heart if yer runs away. So stop it. And now!"

Winston's eyes gleamed with unfamiliar resentment and hostility. "Miss Bossy Knickers, that's what yer are," he cried derisively. "Mind yer own business, Miss Bossy. Always interfering. Yer make me sick. Yer nowt but a slip of a lass and what do yer knows about owt, Emma Harte!" There was a tinge of venom in his voice, but he recoiled under her piercing gaze, which was full of coldness. Her expression was one of indifference as she turned her back on him with deliberateness. Winston was vaguely conscious that he was afraid of his sister. Not afraid in the sense that he was afraid of his father's brute force, but in another, wholly different way which he did not fully comprehend. As if to belie his feelings, he sucked in his breath and cried, "Too big for yer boots, Emma Harte. That's what yer are!" Emma ignored this last outburst and pressed her lips together, willing herself not to respond.

Jack had been dimly aware of this heated exchange between his two eldest children and he had used the few seconds to marshal his reeling senses, to cool his rage. Now he turned his leonine head slowly and regarded his son with penetrating intensity. "Enough's enough, Winston," he said in a voice still roughened with the residue of anger, yet controlled. "Leave thee sister alone. Thee's done plenty of damage for one day, and I won't be forgetting it for a hell of a long time, I can tell thee that, me lad!"

"She's always poking her nose inter me business—" Winston retorted, but stopped short when he saw the irate glint in his father's eyes, the flush rising on his neck to suffuse his face. Jack moved restlessly under Emma's loosening grip and Winston thought better of arousing his father again. He slid with catlike grace to the far end of the kitchen, towards their younger brother Frank, who had been cowering against the set pot shaking with fear and whimpering during the uproar.

Grimly, Emma followed Winston's movements across the room, her look cold and condemning. She was seething at his stupidity and inability to gauge their father's moods, to know when to hold his tongue. Watching him whispering to Frank and consoling him, she wished he *would* run away and then perhaps they would have some peace. This disloyal thought so paralyzed her she let go of her father's arm. Winston's presence had always been necessary to her and they were inseparable. He was her ally, her only friend, and as such she had considered him to be indispensable. The realization that perhaps he was not stunned her. She turned back quickly to her father, took his arm, and, somewhat shaken, said quietly, "Come on, Dad, sit down now."

For a moment Jack Harte would not yield under the determined but light pressure of her hands on his muscular body. He looked down at the girl and thought how thin she was and he knew how easy it would be to free himself from her grip. With a flick of his wrist he could send her frail body hurtling across the room. But he had never struck Emma and he never would. He relaxed and allowed her to maneuver him into the chair. He gazed at the pale face, usually so grave and thoughtful, which still slightly twitched with aggravation, and he was moved as only she, of all his children, could move him. And as he contemplated his daughter, the only one who dared to challenge him, Big Jack had a rare and sudden flash of insight. He recognized with great clarity of vision that he was facing implacable will. A will wrought of iron and, in one so young, frightening and shocking. That unyielding little countenance filled him with a mixture of emotions, new emotions for him, compounded of pride and fear. He was proud of Emma's strength, yet afraid for her because of it. It would get her into trouble one day, of that he felt sure. She was independent of spirit and there was no room for independent spirits in their world. Their class was inevitably ground under the heels of the bosses. Emma's fierce will would be broken and he dreaded that day. He prayed then that he would not be around to see it, for it would break his heart, just as surely as it would break hers.

As he continued to stare at her, he saw the girl clearly for the first time in years. He saw the undernourished body, the thin neck, and the scrawny shoulders underneath the shabby little nightgown. But he also saw something else. He saw the transparency of the skin, as white as the snow that lingered still on the highest fells. He saw the sparkling eyes full of emerald fire, twin reflections of his own. He saw the richness of the russet hair that came to a widow's peak above the proud brow. He saw in that undeveloped childish body the beginning of prettiness, but would it ever come to flower? His heart shifted and seemed to move imperceptibly with an unbearable ache and he was filled with profound anger and grief when he thought of the life of drudgery that lay ahead of her. She was a drudge already, here and at Fairley Hall, and she was so young.

Her light, girlish voice brought him out of his reverie. "Dad, Dad, don't yer feel well? Yer look funny like." She was bending over him.

"There's nowt wrong with me, lass. Have thee looked in on thee mam? How is she?"

"She was a bit poorly afore I came down, but she's resting easy like now. I'm going ter take her some tea in a minute."

She started to move away from him and he smiled at her, white teeth flashing, eyes loving, but she did not respond in her usual affectionate way, the way he had anticipated. She simply patted his arm and gave him a long careful look and he felt curiously reproached and shamed by his own child, as if he were the child and she the parent. And it bothered him enormously, for Emma was his favorite and he understood her and had the most profound love for her. He did not want to be diminished in her eyes. Her esteem was very necessary to him. Mechanically he leaned over and lifted his boots from the hearth. It was getting late and he would have to leave soon for the Fairley brickyard, where he and Winston worked. It was on the Pudsey road and it took them a full hour to walk there.

Emma crossed the kitchen with a burst of energy and renewed purpose. She wanted to dispel the mood, return things to normal, for although their thoughtlessness still rankled, she was not one to bear a grudge for long. She spied Frank at the set pot. He was calm again and with great concentration was preparing the sandwiches for their lunch and tea breaks, which they took to work with them in their jock boxes. She hurried over to join him, rolling up her sleeves purposefully, the air crackling with her vitality.

"Frank, lad, whatever do yer think yer doing!" she cried

when she reached the boy, her eyes widening in surprise, her head bobbing from side to side in her excitement. "Lathering that dripping on like there's no termorrow!" She grabbed the knife from the startled boy's hand and, clucking in mild irritation, she began to scrape some of the dripping off the bread. These scrapings she thriftily returned to the brown stone jar that stood on the wooden chopping board which covered the set pot opening. "We're not gentry yet, our Frank," she went on, and expertly finished making the sandwiches herself, folding the bread cakes over and cutting them in half decisively and with a little flourish.

Frank shrank from Emma, his lower lip trembling, his hazel eyes brimming with hot tears, his small face pinched and scared. Frank was twelve and small for his age. He had a head of fair hair as soft as duck's down, a milky skin, and a gentle face, almost girlish in its prettiness. Much to his humiliation, his sweet appearance had earned him the nicknames of "Sissy" and "Nancy" at the Fairley mill, where he worked as a bobbin ligger. Under Winston's expert tuition he had learned to fight back with his fists, but his preference was to walk away from the taunts and jibes, his head held high, ignoring them. And that was the way he would be all of his life, always sensitive and thin-skinned, but capable of turning the other cheek, proudly and with disdain.

His fair hair fell over his eyes and he pushed it away nervously, turning pathetically to Winston, his defender, who had just finished washing at the sink. "I didn't mean no harm, Winston," he said with a sob, and the tears slid down his freckled cheeks. "Emma's never said nowt afore, about me spreading the dripping too thick." Confusion and hurt brought forth fresh tears.

Winston had witnessed this scene at first with astonishment and then with amusement, aware that Emma's brisk manner was her way of reasserting her motherly authority over them, and also of restoring their usual morning routine. He knew that her clucking and spluttering about the dripping was harmless. He put down the towel he had been using and pulled the younger boy to him, holding him comfortingly in the crook of his arm.

"Well, I'll go ter hell and back!" he exclaimed, feigning horror, as he addressed his father. He bit his lip to hide a smile and continued, "I never thought I'd live ter see the day our Emma turned inter a nip scrape. I think some of old man Fairley's habits have rubbed off on yon lass." He spoke mildly, all the hostility washed out of his eyes, which now danced mischievously.

Emma whirled on them, her face flushed in the firelight that blazed up the chimney and filled her hair full of golden lights. She brandished the knife before her. "That's not fair! I'm not a nip scrape! Am I, Dad?" she appealed, and rushed on breathlessly before he could answer, "Anyway, old man Fairley's that well off he's bowlegged with brass and do yer all know why? Because he wouldn't nip a currant in two and give yer half. So there!" She spoke heatedly, although not with anger, and there was an embarrassed expression on her crimson face. Winston knew his teasing had hit its mark, for Emma loathed stinginess and it was the worst accusation anyone could level at her, even in jest. She was mortified.

Bridling and tossing her head, she said huffily, "That dripping was two inches thick. Yer couldn't have eaten them sandwiches. Yer would've been sick, that yer would."

The three of them gaped at the flustered girl, who was still shaking the knife at them, her cheeks as red as beets, and then suddenly Winston started to laugh, unable to suppress his amusement any longer. Jack threw him a startled glance, his thick black brows puckering together in a jagged line across his brow as he gazed at the boy mystified. But he saw at once that Winston's laughter was not malicious and he saw, too, Emma's increasing confusion and humiliation. As he looked from one to the other the boy's mirth infected him. He chuckled and slapped his knee.

Emma glared at them and slowly a sheepish grin spread itself across her face. She was laughing herself. "What a fuss over a ha'porth of dripping," she muttered through her laughter, shaking her head as she put down the knife. Frank looked in bewilderment at them all, at first uncomprehending, and as he realized their merriment was real he laughed, too, wiping away his tears on the sleeve of his gray shirt. Emma hugged him to her. "Don't take on so, Frank luv. I meant no harm, yer silly duck nut. And don't wipe yer nose on yer sleeve," she scolded gruffly as she stroked back his hair and kissed the top of his head with tenderness.

The laughter broke the tension which had been lingering in the room and a feeling of friendliness and genuine family

affection was miraculously restored. Emma sighed with relief
and began her managerial bustling again. "We'll all have ter
look sharp and get a move on, or we'll be late for work," she
cried, catching sight of the clock on the mantel. It had just
turned a quarter to five and her father and Winston had to
leave at five o'clock to reach the brickyard by six, when they
had to clock in. She felt the teapot under the cozy. The pot
was still hot. "Come on, Frank, take this tea up ter our mam
for me," she said, pouring tea into a mug and adding generous portions of milk and sugar. "And, Dad, mend the fire for
me, will yer, please. Bank it up so that it lasts till me Aunt
Lily comes in. And, Winston, wash the pots whilst I finish
making yer jock. And, Dad, don't forget the fireguard."

She handed the mug of tea to Frank and continued, "And
ask me mam if she wants some bread and jam, and hurry up
about it, me lad, there's still a lot of chores ter be done afore
I go ter the Hall." Frank took the tea carefully in both of his
small hands and hurried across the room, his boots ringing
hollowly on the brick floor as he headed for the staircase.
Whistling under his breath, Winston gathered the dirty mugs
and plates from the table and carried them over to the sink,
whilst Jack turned to the fireplace and began stacking on the
logs. Emma smiled to herself. Peace was restored. She moved
to the set pot and began to wrap the sandwiches in the cotton
serviettes her mother had so carefully hemmed, dampening
them first so that the sandwiches would stay fresh.

Jack devoted his attention to the fire, interspersing the logs
with treasured pieces of coal and then heaping on coal dust so
that the fire would last until his sister Lily came in to tend to
Elizabeth later in the morning. As he swung his great body
around to reach for the fireguard he glanced surreptitiously at
Winston, who was mechanically washing the pots at the kitchen
sink, and he regretted his outburst of anger earlier. There
was no deep-rooted hatred between them, only this irritation
that was increasingly difficult to repress in them both. He did
not even blame the boy for wanting to leave Fairley; nevertheless, he could not permit him to go. Dr. Malcolm had said
nothing specific about Elizabeth's health, but Jack did not
require a medical opinion to confirm what he already suspected. She was dying. Winston's departure at this time
would be the last nail in her coffin. He was her favorite child.
She loved all of her children, but Winston was special, being

the eldest and so like her in looks. Jack dare not let him leave
and yet he could not tell the boy his reasons. "And he always
picks the wrong time ter discuss it," Jack muttered to himself
as he put the fireguard around the grate. He rested for a
moment against the guard, staring into the fire, blinded by
searing grief and overwhelming despair. It was grief for Elizabeth, who had been so brutalized by life, despair for his
young children, who would be motherless before the last of
the snows melted into spring.

He felt a light touch on his arm and he knew it was Emma.
He swallowed hard, his throat constricted. He coughed hoarsely
and straightened himself to his full height, attempting a smile.
"Yes, luv, what is it?".

"Yer'll be late, Dad. Yer best go and see me mam now,
afore yer leave."

"Aye, lass. I'll just wash this coal dust off me hands." Jack
moved to the sink, where Winston was drying the pots. "Go
up and see thee mam, lad, and I'll be up in a minute. Thee
knows how upset she gets if we don't all see her afore we
leaves." Winston nodded, wiped the last of the mugs quickly,
and left the kitchen, still nervously whistling between his
teeth.

Jack looked over at Emma, who was standing at the set
pot, the tea caddy in her hands. She was measuring out their
mashings of tea and sugar into small pieces of paper, screwing
the ends together securely so nothing would be spilled. "Thee'll
be catching thee death in that nightgown, Emma, and there's
no warmth in that shawl. Thee best get dressed, lass, now
everything's in order down here."

"Yes, I will, Dad. I've finished putting up yer mashings,"
she said with a sunny smile that illuminated her serious face
with sudden radiance. Her eyes, so unusually deep and vividly
green, were bright and shining, and Jack knew that her
affection for him was intact. She ran across the kitchen to her
father. He was smiling down at her. Emma stood on tiptoe
and, putting her thin arms around his neck, she pulled his
face down to hers. She kissed his cheek and said, "I'll see yer
next Saturday, Dad." Jack held her for a brief moment longer,
his sinewy arms tightening around her protectively as a surge
of tenderness swept through him. "Aye, luv, and take care of
theeself up yonder at the Hall," he mumbled in a tight voice.
She was gone before he could catch his breath, slipping out of

his arms and streaking across the room like a flash of lightning, and Jack was alone in the kitchen.

He sighed and reached for his coat on the peg behind the door. He felt around in the pockets for the small leather straps he fastened around his corduroy trousers to prevent the dust from the bricks rising up his legs. He sat down at the table and buckled them on, wondering as he did whether he should tell Elizabeth he had given in his notice at the brickyard. He frowned, his large hands expertly tightening the straps until he had just the right pressure. It had been a hard decision for Jack to make, since jobs were scarce and so many men were out of work, and also he liked working in the fresh air, even though slinging wet clay up onto a gantry for ten hours a day was killing work for any man. He did not object to the hard work, he did object to the pay it brought him and he had said so to Stan, the gaffer, last Friday. "Eighteen shillings and tenpence is nowt much ter take home at the end of the week, Stan. And me a married man with three kids. I'm not blaming me kids on anybody but meself, mind thee, but bloody old man Fairley's paying starvation wages. That he is, Stan, and thee knows it," he had said with a quiet vehemence.

Stan had shaken his head, and even though he had spoken with some sympathy he had not been able to meet Jack's fixed stare. "Aye, Big Jack, there's summat in what thee says. It's a bloody crime, it is. But there's gaffers walking around that only get twenty bob a week. I don't get much more meself. Nowt I can do about it, though. Take it or leave it, lad." He had told Stan he would leave it, in no uncertain terms, and he had reluctantly gone to the Fairley mill on Saturday morning, cap in hand, swallowing his pride. He had seen Eddie, the foreman, his friend since boyhood, who had signed him on to start in a week's time at twenty shillings a week, which was an improvement if not much of one. He pondered the question of telling Elizabeth and abruptly decided against it. She knew he loathed mill work and it would only grieve her and aggravate her condition. No, he would not tell her until it was an accomplished fact, until he was already working at the mill next week. He had one consolation, small though it was. The mill was down at the bottom of the village, in the valley on the banks of the river Aire, and it was only ten minutes away from the cottage. He was close at hand if Elizabeth needed him, if there was an emergency, and this thought cheered him so enormously it made the mill work seem that much less unpalatable to him.

The church clock in the village struck five and he sprang up, striding across the room swiftly with that easy leonine grace many tall men have quite unconsciously. He took the stairs two at a time, his heavy hobnail boots hitting the stone steps with a harsh metallic ring that was an oddly mournful echo in the silence of the cottage.

Emma was dressed and standing with Winston and Frank by the side of the bed. They seemed a woebegone little trio in their drab and shabby clothes, which were also patched and darned. But these clothes were scrupulously clean and neat, as they were themselves with their scrubbed faces and carefully combed hair. And each child, as disparate as they were in appearance, had a sort of refinement that stood out so strikingly those poor, threadbare garments became insignificant. They had a curious dignity as they stood there so solemn-faced and quiet. The children parted and stepped back to make way for Jack as he bounded into the room, bristling with energy, a cheerful smile carefully arranged on his face.

Elizabeth lay back against the mound of pillows, pale and piteously depleted, but the feverish glaze on her face had vanished and she appeared more tranquil. Emma had washed her face and brushed her hair, and the blue shawl she had wrapped around her mother's shoulders intensified the blueness of Elizabeth's uncommonly lovely eyes, and her hair fanned out across the pillows like skeins of soft spun silk. Not a spot of color stained the whiteness of her face and to Jack, in the candlelight, it was like the carved ivory he had seen in Africa, the contours and planes sharp and finely chiseled, devoid of any crudity of form. She had the appearance of a small and very delicate figurine. Her face lit up when she saw Jack. She stretched out her thin arms weakly towards him and when he reached the bed he pulled her to him almost fiercely, holding her feeble body against his own strong virile one as if to never let her go.

"Thee looks worlds better, Elizabeth luv," he said in a voice so gentle it seemed to stroke the air delicately. And it was hardly recognizable as his own.

"I am, John," she asserted, a brave expression settling on

her face. "I'll be up tonight when yer gets home, and I'll have a good sheep'shead broth boiling for yer, luv, and dumplings, too, and fresh bread cakes."

He released her tenderly and placed her back on the pillows, and as he gazed at that pitifully wasted face he did not see it as it truly was at all. He saw only the beautiful girl he had known all of his life. She looked at him with such trust and adoration his heart clenched with sorrow and there was nothing he could do to save her. And that strange impulse came over him again, an impulse which was occurring with increasing frequency and compelling urgency, in reality a compulsion to pick her up bodily in his arms and take her out of this mean room and run with her to the top of the moors, which she longed for always. There on the high fells the air was pure and bracing and the sky was a vast reflection of her eyes, and he felt in some inexplicable and mysterious way that on that high ground this disease would be blown out of her, that she would be miraculously revived and filled with life.

But the lavender tints and pale vaporous mists of the long summer days were now swept away by northern gales. If only it was summer he *would* take her up there, the Top of the World she called it, and he would lay her down against a knoll of heather amongst green ferns and tender young bilberry leaves, and they would sit together in contentment in the shelter of Ramsden Crags, warmed by the sun, alone except for the linnets and larks fluttering by in the hazy golden light. It was not possible. The earth was hard with black February frost and the sweeping moorland was savage and desolate under a sky bleak and rain-filled.

"John luv, did yer hear what I said? I'll be up tonight and we can all have our suppers together, in front of the fire, like we used ter afore I sick." There was a new vividness in Elizabeth's voice, a trilling excitement unquestionably created by Jack's presence.

"Thee mustn't get out of bed, luv," he cautioned hoarsely. "Doctor says thee must have complete rest, Elizabeth. Our Lily will come in later and tend to thee, and make the supper for us. Now thee must promise me thee won't do owt foolish, lass. Now promise me."

"Oh, yer do fret so, John Harte. But I promise, if that's what pleases yer. I'll stay abed."

He leaned forward so that only she could hear. "I love thee, Elizabeth, I do that," he whispered.

She looked deeply into his eyes and she saw that love so clearly reflected, changeless and everlasting, and she said, "I love thee, too, John, till the day I die and even after that."

He kissed her quickly, hardly daring to look at her again, and as he got up off the bed his movements were jerky and disjointed, almost as if he had relinquished command of his great body. He crossed the bedroom in three quick strides. "Come on, Winston, kiss thee mam and let's be off. We're running late, lad," he called brusquely to hide his emotion.

Winston and Frank each kissed their mother and moved away from the bed to the door with the utmost quiet. Winston had not addressed a remark to Emma since his teasing in the kitchen earlier, and now he gave her one of his most charming and breezy smiles, and said from the top of the stairs, "See yer Saturday, Emma. Ta'rar, luv."

She waved and smiled. "Ta'rar, Winston," adding as an afterthought, "Frank, yer'd best finish getting ready for work. I'll be down right sharpish and we can leave together." Frank nodded his acquiescence, his little head bobbing up and down, his pale face serious. "Yes, Emma," he cried, and clattered noisily down the steps after Winston.

Emma sat down on the edge of the bed. "Do yer need owt afore I go, Mam?"

Elizabeth shook her head. "The tea was good, luv. It's all I need till yer Aunt Lily comes, and I'm not hungry."

She's never hungry. How will she ever be well if she never eats? Emma asked herself, and said with a cheerfulness she did not feel, "All right, Mam, but yer must eat the food me Aunt Lily brings when she comes. Yer must keep up yer strength."

Elizabeth smiled faintly. "I will, luv."

"Shall I blow out the candle?" Emma asked, preparing to leave.

Elizabeth looked lovingly at the girl. "Aye, yer can when yer go. I'll rest a while. Yer a good lass, Emma. I don't know what I'd do without yer. Now get yerself off ter the Hall. I don't want yer ter be late, when Mrs. Turner let yer come home ter see me in the middle of the week. And be a good lass. Mrs. Fairley's a real lady, that she is."

"Yes, Mam," Emma whispered, blinking back the tears.

She kissed her mother with great tenderness and rearranged the bedclothes, patting the pillows and straightening the sheet and quilt with her usual efficiency. As she pulled the bedclothes up around Elizabeth she said, "I'll try and find a sprig of heather on me way home on Saturday, Mam. Perhaps there's a bit the frost didn't get, under the crags."

SIX

J ack and Winston had gone to the brickyard and Frank was alone in the kitchen, which was now dimly lit, for Jack had turned out the paraffin lamp as he always did when he left for work. The only illumination came from a candle on the table and the fire, which occasionally flared and momentarily filled the room with a sudden lambent light. Dusky shadows lurked eerily on the perimeters of the kitchen and the air was hushed, except for the intermittent crackling of the logs, which hissed and spurted from time to time.

Frank sat in one of the high-backed chairs by the fireside and the chair dwarfed him, so enormous was it, and he appeared much smaller and more fragile than he actually was. The boy was small-boned and delicate, yet for all that he was surprisingly wiry and tough, like a little terrier.

This morning he seemed forlorn in his gray work shirt and baggy trousers, hand-me-downs from Winston, and his legs in their carefully darned gray socks, dangling over the edge of the chair, looked pathetic and far too weak to lift the great boots, which were too large and ugly and had also once belonged to Winston. But in reality, and in spite of his appearance, there was nothing forlorn about Frank Harte, for he occupied an inner world so filled with beautiful images and soaring dreams and expectations, it made his day-to-day existence seem totally inconsequential. And this perfect world protected him from the harshness of their poverty-stricken life, nourished him so completely he was, for the most part, quite oblivious to the deprivations and spartan conditions in which they lived.

Essentially Frank was a happy little boy, content to retreat into his imagination, one that was vivid and fertile, and the only time he had been truly dismayed and saddened was when he had left the church school in the village last summer. It was with a degree of resignation that he had stoically accepted the fact that he had to work in the mill with the other young boys, collecting empty yarn bobbins. His father had told him regretfully yet firmly that they needed the few shillings he would bring home every week and so he had left school when he had reached twelve years. He had been an astonishingly acute and avid pupil, soaking up knowledge with a rapidity and understanding that had utterly amazed the teacher. She thought he was unique and was distressed to discover his fate was to be the mill. She knew he was capable of so much more if only he was given the chance; she also knew he was doomed by the circumstances of his birth.

Although Frank no longer went to school, he continued his studies as best he could on his own. He read and reread the meager collection of threadbare books his mother owned and anything else he could get his hands on. Words were somehow awesome and yet magical to Frank, and he loved them with a deep intensity that bordered on veneration. He would form and re-form sentences in his head and continually wrote little snatches of prose on the precious bits of paper that Emma brought home for him from the Hall. He was constantly caught up in abstract ideas, although he did not yet comprehend they were abstract ideas, and these ideas puzzled and challenged him. For Frank Harte had a truly genuine intellect, one that was to develop with great brilliance later in his life.

Now he sat staring steadily into the fire, a mug of tea in his small hands, a rapt expression on his face, and his eyes, so dreamy and faraway, saw endless and incredible visions amongst the flickering flames. At one moment, a poetic thought, so fragile that it was almost intangible, utterly entranced him, and a look of joy flitted across his face, as his sensitive mouth moved into a curve of ecstasy.

The door creaked and startled him and he lifted his head sharply and looked about. Emma came into the room, silent and preoccupied. Frank began to sip his tea, his hazel eyes peering over the rim of the mug, following her progress around the room. She stopped at the window, moved the curtain, and, looking out, said, without turning to him, "It's still dark outside, but we don't have ter leave just yet. We can wait a bit longer until it's lighter and I'll run part of the way ter the Hall, so I won't be late."

Frank put the mug down on the hearth and said, "Me dad filled the teapot with hot water and he told me ter make yer a sandwich. It's there, on the set pot."

She eyed the sandwich warily, and noticing the expression on her face, Frank exclaimed defensively, "I didn't lather it with dripping. I put it on and scraped it off, just like yer said, our Emma." There was a hidden smile on Emma's face and her eyes crinkled with amusement as she poured herself a mug of tea and put the sandwich on the plate. She carried them both over to the fireplace and sat down opposite Frank. She munched on her sandwich abstractedly, still worrying about her mother.

Her little brother regarded her thoughtfully and with some curiosity, for he was extremely susceptible to Emma, whom he adored. He constantly sought her approbation, but in his anxiety to please he usually did something ridiculously foolish which irritated her and so incurred her disfavor. However, this was usually short-lived. There was not a little admiration in his pale eyes as he leaned forward and said confidingly, and with great solemnity, "I'm glad yer stopped 'em fighting. I'm scared when they shout. I am that, Emma."

She looked at him absently, lost in her thoughts, as she put the plate down on the hearth. "I knows. But it's always over nowt, lad."

"Well, it still scares me," he went on quickly, "that's why I was lathering the dripping on too thick afore, yer knows. I was nervous," he finished, trying to completely exonerate himself with her.

Emma laughed. "Oooh! What a whopper that is, our Frankie!" she chided.

The boy bristled. His thin body tensed and his mild eyes were suddenly fierce as he cried with unaccustomed passion, "Me mam says yer not ter call me Frankie, our Emma!"

Emma now viewed him with keener interest, faintly amused by this burst of temperament, which was quite unprecedented. She saw how serious he was and said with a smile, "Sorry, luv. Yer right, our mam does hate nicknames."

Frank straightened himself in the chair, assuming a dignified and important air. "Me mam says I'm a great lad and

Frankie is a baby name!" he exclaimed in his squeaky boy's voice, which nonetheless was surprisingly firm.

"That's true, yer are," Emma replied, giving him a loving smile. "Well, we'd best get ready." She took the dirty dishes they had been using to the sink, washed and dried them quickly, and then returned to the fireplace. Emma picked up her boots from the hearth, where her father had placed them to warm, and pulled them on decisively. As she was lacing up her boots, Emma stole a glance at Frank and she thought impatiently: There he is, daydreaming again. A lot of good his dreams will do him! *She* rarely had time to indulge herself in fantasies, but when she did they were unromantically solid and practical. Her dreams were the dreams of the pragmatist. She dreamed of warm coats for them all. Lots of beautiful black coal in the cellar. A larder stuffed to overflowing with smoked hams and wheels of cheese, hunks of beef, and row upon row of bottled fruits and vegetables, just like the pantry at the Hall. And gold sovereigns jingling in her purse, enough to buy all these necessities and luxuries for her mother and new boots for her father. She sighed. Frank dreamed of books and visiting London and riding in fine cabs and going to the theater, dreams that were fed by the illustrated magazines she sometimes brought home from the Hall. And Winston dreamed of joining the navy and sailing around the world and having an adventurous life in exotic places. Frank and Winston dreamed of pleasure and glory. Emma, when she had the time to dream, dreamed of survival.

She sighed again. She would willingly settle for a few extra shillings a week to help them along, never mind gold sovereigns. She stood up purposefully and went and put on her coat, calling to Frank, "Don't sit there gawping like a sucking duck, lad. Get yer coat on. It's twenty ter six and I'll be late if I don't hurry now."

She handed Frank his coat and scarf, which he tied around his neck. Emma, clucking and shaking her head, immediately untied the scarf and wrapped it around his small fair head, fastening it tightly under his chin. She picked up his flat cap and slapped it firmly on top of the scarf, ignoring his wriggling and his protestations.

"Oh, Emma, I don't like me scarf this way," he cried defiantly. "The other lads laugh at me and say I'm a sissy."

"It won't keep yer ears warm around yer neck and I've told

yer afore, Frank, don't pay no heed to what folks say. Now
come on and look sharp about it."

She tied on her own scarf, handed Frank his jock box,
glanced around the room once more, and then blew out the
candle. Gripping Frank's hand tightly in hers, she pulled him
out of the cottage.

They emerged into a black dawn and the cold hit them in
an icy blast, moisture-laden and full of frost. The two children
hurried down the flagged path, past the shriveled and frozen
elder and lilac bushes in the meager little garden, its bleak
inhospitable soil as hard and unrelenting as iron. The only
sound was the whining of the wind and the sharp slap of their
boots against the cold stones, as they made their way down
Top Fold. This small cul-de-sac of cottages where they lived
was set high up in Fairley Village. Behind it was the higher
background of the sweeping moors and it was an isolated
spot, desolate and uninviting, and only the pale lights that
gleamed in some of the cottage windows gave credence to the
idea that it was inhabited. When they finally reached the top
of the street, Frank lifted his cold little face to Emma and
said, "Shall I stop at me Aunt Lily's then?"

"Yes, luv. And tell her ter go ter see me mam early this
morning. Tell her she's been rambling a bit but was resting
quiet when we left. And don't stop chattering ter me Aunt
Lily for long. Yer knows the gaffer closes the mill gates at six
o'clock sharp. If yer gets locked out yer'll have ter wait til
eight o'clock and they'll dock yer wages. And be a good lad!"
She kissed his face and pulled his cap down more tightly on
his head.

"Will yer wait and watch me till I gets to Aunt Lily's?"
Frank asked tremulously, trying hard not to show that he was
frightened at this hour. Emma nodded. "Yes, luv. Go on
then."

Frank ran off into the mist, occasionally sliding on the
cobblestones, which were slippery and glazed over with hoary
frost. She watched his little figure streaking down the street
until he was just a faint outline in the murky light. But she
could hear his boots hitting the cobbles and when they stopped
she knew he had reached their aunt's house, a small cottage
on this main street that slanted down to the village and the
river Aire. His loud banging on the door with his tin jock box
reassured her that he had indeed reached his destination.

He'll waken the dead as well as me Aunt Lily, she thought
wryly, and then she wished she had not thought of the dead.
Emma shivered as she turned in the opposite direction and
headed towards the moors.

And she was a solitary yet gallant figure, in her long black
skirt and shabby coat, which was far too small, as she trudged
doggedly and bravely on towards Fairley Hall, her eyes occasionally lifting to scan the leaden sky and the bleak dark
moors that stretched in an unending line before her.

SEVEN

The hills that rise up in an undulating sweep to dominate
Fairley Village and the stretch of the Aire Valley below
it are always dark and brooding in the most clement of
weather. But when the winter sets in for its long and deadly
siege the landscape is brushstroked in grisaille beneath ashen
clouds and the moors take on a savage desolateness, the stark
fells and bare hillsides drained of all color and bereft of life.
The rain and snow drive down endlessly and the wind that
blows in from the North Sea is fierce and raw. These gritstone
hills, infinitely more somber than the green moors of the
nearby limestone dale country, sweep through vast silences
broken only by the mournful wailing of the wind, for even
the numerous little becks, those tumbling, dappled streams
that relieve the monotony in spring and summer, are frozen
and stilled.

This great plateau of moorland stretches across countless
untenanted miles towards Shipley and the vigorous industrial
city of Leeds beyond. It is amazingly featureless, except for
occasional soaring crags, a few blackened trees, shriveled
thorns, and abandoned ruined cottages that barely punctuate
its cold and empty spaces. Perpetual mists, pervasive and
thick, float over the rugged landscape, obscuring the highest
peaks and demolishing the foothills, so that land and sky
merge in an endless mass of gray that is dank and enveloping,
and everything is diffused, without motion, wrapped in unearthly solitude. There is little evidence here of humanity,

little to invite man into this inhospitable land at this time of year, and few venture out into its stark and lonely reaches.

But it was towards this harsh moorland that Emma so stoically marched on this icy February morning in 1904. The narrow winding road that snaked its way across the hills was the quickest route to Fairley Hall and Emma had to brave the moors in all seasons of the year and at all hours.

She shivered as she hurried along, and huddled further into her coat, which was a castoff from the Hall and offered as much protection as paper, threadbare and patched as it was. It had already been a sorry, worn-out bit of clothing when Cook had given it to her in the summer, but Emma had received it gratefully and she had patiently darned the holes and lengthened the hem and sewn on new buttons. She had outgrown it all too quickly, and it stretched across her back tightly and the sleeves were too short and her thin arms poked out pathetically in scarecrow fashion, exposing childish wrists to the elements. The wind bit treacherously through the meager coat and the damp air drenched her, penetrating into her bones, so that her legs felt numbed and without life. She pulled her scarf more securely around her head and then thrust her chapped hands back into her pockets quickly. Her teeth chattered and her eyes watered from the icy blasts and she fervently wished she was already at the Hall, as much as she disliked that place.

The howling wind tore at her skirts and buffeted her forward and drove the fog down around her in great whorls, making her slow her steps considerably. She looked up expectantly. Dawn would break soon.

By the time Emma reached the stone-walled field that led out to the moors she was breathless. She rested against the stile for a moment, her breathing still labored, her heart thundering in her chest. She looked down the steep road she had just traversed. Below her the fog was patchy, clearing in parts, and in the distance she could see the twinkling lights now burning brightly in all the cottages, as the village awakened. Beyond, in the valley, there was a faint dim glow that told her that the Fairley mill was preparing for its daily business. Soon the shrill mill whistle would start to hoot, breaking the silence with its strident tones, announcing the opening of the gates. In a short time, the men and women of Fairley would be hurrying down to clock in and start another day of drudgery, combing the raw wool, spinning the fine woolens and worsted cloths that were shipped all over the world.

Emma thought of her brother Frank, who would be amongst the workers. Frank, so small, so frail, and so ill-equipped to cope with the long hours of tedious toil, sorting and stacking the yarn bobbins, emptying the giant skips, sweeping the floors, and cleaning the machines. She worried constantly about Frank. It was such a terrible thing, such a wrong thing, that he had to work at the mill. He was only a little boy. When he wailed to their father about the acrid, oily smell of the wool making him feel sick, their father just turned away helplessly, saying nothing, a bewildered look in his eyes. Emma knew they needed the money Frank earned, miserable few coppers that it was, but she wished her father would find him a more congenial job, one which was not so arduous and which was in an atmosphere less debilitating than the mill. She considered their predicament and her father's acceptance of it, and his apathy, which was so terrible and frightening to Emma. She thought of her mother lying sick in the cottage in Top Fold, and momentary panic gripped her. She had been afraid to leave her mother this morning. But Emma knew she had had no choice. If she did not go to the Hall to work out the week she would not be paid.

She looked lingeringly at the village where her mother lay, and which was also the last sign of life until she reached the Hall, and then she turned abruptly. She had rested long enough and now she must hurry if she was to reach the Hall by six o'clock, which was when Cook expected her. Emma hitched up her skirts, climbed over the stile, and jumped down into the field with agility. The ground under her feet was unyielding with frost and the mist floated and rolled in front of her, obliterating the dead gorse bushes and the few paltry, frostbitten trees as it drifted over the landscape. Now and then banks of snow became visible, the fantastic glistening shapes illusory in the vaporous air, and to Emma there was something fearful, almost menacing about the moors at this hour. She shuddered but she pressed on bravely. She could hardly see the path, but she had been working at the Hall for two years now, and she knew it well, and her feet followed it with a degree of sureness. The crunching of her footsteps on the frosty earth was the only sound in the early-morning air.

Her thoughts returned to her father as she tramped along. Emma loved her father and understood the nature of him, but he had disturbed her not a little in the last few months. Her dad just wasn't the same since he had returned from the Boer War. It seemed to Emma that all the spirit had ebbed out of him, and he was given to quiet withdrawn moods, yet conversely, he would often erupt into sudden almost uncontrollable anger, when Winston, or anyone other than herself or her mother, exasperated him.

These inconsistencies in her father's behavior and his wildly contrasting moods baffled Emma, and when he stared at her vacantly he seemed like a lost child. Sometimes she wanted to grab hold of him and shake him vigorously, in an effort to rouse him to renewed life. She was too small and fragile for that, so instead she would attempt to shake him out of his dejection with her questions, badgering him about money, reminding him of her mother's sickness. His face always remained immobile and closed, but his eyes filled with pain. It was Elizabeth's sickness and his sorrow for his wife that had changed Jack Harte and petrified his spirit, and rendered him virtually useless; it was not the war which had wrought the drastic upheaval in his nature.

But Emma, in her youthful naïveté, did not fully comprehend this. Passionately devoted to one singular pursuit, that of changing the constrained circumstances in which they lived, she was solely concerned with their survival, and this blinded her to anything else. All she knew was that her dad had no answers for her, no solutions to their problems. In an effort to placate her he would resort to the same old phrase he employed so often lately. "Things'll get better soon, luv," he would say. Her brother Winston was always duped by this confident and optimistic mood of their father's and his eyes would instantly shine with anticipation of better days. He would ask excitedly, "When, Dad? When?" Emma's pragmatic brain would scream, "How, Dad? How?" although she never uttered a word. She was afraid to throw out this challenge when her father was attempting to reassure Winston and she also knew, unquestioningly and from past experience, that there would be no genuine response and that no practical ideas would be proffered. Emma, realist that she was, had

acknowledged this inevitability months ago and she had come
to accept it with resignation, since she did not know how to
combat her father's inertia and impotence, his procrastination
and his lack of enterprise.

"Nowt ever happens ter change our lot because me dad
never does owt ter change it!" Emma said aloud and with
vehemence, as she scrambled over the low wall and out onto
the moorland path beyond the field. She sighed with exasperation, yet she knew that her father could not help his attitude, although she was not sure why. Emma had not yet
come to understand that when hope is taken away from a man
he is left with nothing, sometimes not even the will to live.
And all the hope had been kicked out of Jack Harte long ago.

She blew on her frozen hands and then pushed them back
into her pockets, as she began her ascent up the lower slope
that would lead her to Ramsden Ghyll and then on upwards,
to the top of the moors and the road to Fairley Hall. Emma
had not mentioned money to her father lately, but it never
left her thoughts. She contemplated it now. They must have
more money if they were to survive, if her mother was to
regain her strength and her health. Emma knew that without
money you were nothing, just a powerless and oppressed
victim of the ruling class, a yoked and shackled beast of
burden destined to a life of mindless drudgery, and an existence so wretched and so without hope, so filled with terror
and despair that it was hardly worth the contemplation let
alone the living. Without money you were susceptible to all
the capricious whims and moods and fancies of the careless,
thoughtless rich, to all the vicissitudes of life. Without money
you were vulnerable to the world.

Since she had worked at Fairley Hall, Emma had come to
understand many things. Blessed with the faculty of acute
observation, she was also innately shrewd and amazingly
perceptive for her years. She had quickly seen and noted the
outrageous and monstrous discrepancies between life at Fairley
Hall and life in the village. The Fairleys lived in luxury, even
splendor, pampered and totally isolated from the harsh realities of the lives of the workers, whose pitiless and endless toil
financed their velvet-lined world of ease and privilege.

Perspicaciously observing the Fairleys and the way they
lived with her keen and intelligent eyes, Emma had begun to
comprehend that money did not only buy necessities, but so

much else as well. She had come to realize that the possessor
of money also possessed power, a most desirable asset to
Emma, because she knew now that power made you invulnerable. It made you safe. By the same token, Emma had
come to bitterly accept the fact that there was no justice or
liberty for the poor. But she suspected, in her shrewd way
and with the beginning of cynicism, that you could *buy* both
quite easily. Just as easily as you could buy the medicines and
nourishing food they needed for her mother, providing you
had the right amount of shillings to place on the counter. Yes,
she thought, money *is* the answer to everything.

There must be a way for me to earn more money, she
decided as she made her way up the path. There were poor
people and there were rich people in the world, and if some
people could be rich then obviously so could others, she
reasoned. Her father always said it was a question of birth
and of luck. Emma was scornful of these ready answers, for
she doubted their veracity, and so she refused to accept
them. If a person came up with a brilliant plan and worked
hard, harder than anyone else, then surely that person could
earn money. Lots of it. A fortune perhaps. Emma had kept
her eye on this goal for some time, never wavering, never
truly discouraged, for what she lacked in experience of life
she made up for with traits perhaps of greater value—intuition,
imagination, and ambition. Instinctively Emma understood
many things, and one of these was the cold hard fact that
money was not necessarily always inherited or acquired by
chance. She knew, in spite of what her father said, that there
were other ways to amass a fortune. She sighed. It seemed to
Emma, as she hurried along, chilled to the bone and full of
despair about her mother, that she was all alone and friend-
less, battling the world without a helping hand or an encouraging word from anyone. But she had determined months ago
that she would not let this defeat her. She would find a way
to make money, lots of it, for only then would they be safe.

Her feet followed the narrow path and in spite of the
denseness of the fog, she knew she was reaching the top of
the lower slope, for she was panting and her legs were aching
from climbing. She shivered under the rising wind that whis-
tled down from the high fells, and pulled up the collar of her
coat. Her hands were frozen stiff, but her feet were warm.
Her father had repaired her boots just the week before,

buying strong leather from the tannery and thick felt for the inner soles. She had stood by him and watched as he had cut the soles and hammered them firmly onto the worn uppers, cobbling the boots on the old iron last in the kitchen. She thought, too, of the steaming hot broth Cook would have waiting for her, and the warmth of the huge kitchen at the Hall, and these incentives made her hurry.

A few skeletal trees loomed up in front of her in the relentless environment, stark and spectral against the glassy green sky. Her heart began to pound rapidly, partially from exertion, but also from dread, for beyond these lone trees the path plummeted down into Ramsden Ghyll, a dell between the hills. The Ghyll was the spot Emma hated most on her journey to the Hall, for it was an eerie place, filled with grotesque rock formations and blasted tree stumps. The mist, trapped as it was between the twin peaks that soared above the dell, gathered and coagulated into heavy gray darkness that was almost impassable.

Emma was nervous of this place, but nonetheless she hurried on, chiding herself for her nervousness as she plunged down the path into the Ghyll. She was afraid of the beasties and the goblins and the specters of the moors which seemed to float vapor-like, yet so threateningly, amongst these great rocks formed of millstone grit. She was afraid, too, of the lost souls the villagers superstitiously said haunted the Ghyll. To block out the images of goblins and monsters and lost souls, she began to sing in her head. She never sang aloud at this hour on the moors, for fear of waking the dead. She did not know many songs, except for the few they had all learned at school, and she found these insipid and childish. So instead she sang "Onward, Christian Soldiers," forming the words silently and marching bravely along to the rhythmic beat that ran through her head.

She was halfway across the Ghyll when the words were suddenly swept away. Emma stopped tramping and stood perfectly still. She was transfixed, listening acutely. Just below the level of the wind she heard it, a low lumbering sound as if something huge and powerful, and propelled by immense force, was coming down the path from the other side of the Ghyll. She shrank back against a formation of rocks and held her breath, fear trickling through her like icy water. And then he was standing there before her, not an inchoate monster like a rock or a tree, but a wholly formed monster, a man, who was enormously tall and who peered down to stare at her through the swirling fog.

Emma sucked in her breath and clenched her fists in her pockets. She wondered frantically whether she should dart out in front of him and run back along the path, but she was so paralyzed with terror she could not move. And then the monster spoke and terrified her even more.

"Faith and if it's not me good fortune, to be sure, to be meeting a spry young colleen on these blasted moors at this ungodly hour. 'Tis the Divil's own place, I am thinking, and no fit land to be a-wandering in, on this cold morning."

Emma was speechless. She looked up at the man who towered above her, but she was unable to distinguish his features in the murky light. She pressed herself closer into a crevice between the rocks, wishing she could dissolve into it, her eyes starting out of her head in alarm.

The man spoke again, his voice ghostly and disembodied coming to her through the mist. "Ah, and 'tis afeared the little colleen is, and no wonder, a-startling ye like I did. But it's only a stupid man that I am to be sure, that has lost himself in this blasted fog on his way to Fairley Hall. Can ye be pointing me in the right direction and I'll be on me way?"

Her heart beat less frenziedly, but Emma was still trembling and afraid, for a stranger on these moors—and he was indeed a stranger—could be just as dangerous as any monster. Her father had warned her never to talk to anyone she did not know, who was not from the valley, and who was therefore a "foreigner" in these parts, and suspect. She flattened herself against the rocks, wishing he would go away, pressing her lips firmly together. Perhaps if she did not respond to his questions he would disappear as suddenly as he had appeared.

"Faith and I am thinking that the cat's got her tongue. Sure and that's it," the man continued, as if addressing a third person. Emma bit her lip and looked about her anxiously. There seemed to be no one else there, although it was hard to tell in the graying light.

"I won't be harming ye, little colleen," the strange voice went on. "Just show me the way to Fairley Hall and I'll be on me way, to be sure I will."

Emma still could not see the man's face, for it was lost in the mist that engulfed them both. She looked down. She could make out his great feet encased in hobnail boots and the bottoms of his trousers. He had not moved a fraction from the spot where he had first stopped, but had remained stationary, as if he sensed that any sudden movement on his part would send her scurrying out of her hiding place, such as it was, and off into the fog in terror.

He cleared his throat and said again, more softly, "I won't be a-harming ye, little one. Don't be afeared of me."

There was something in the tone of his voice that made Emma relax her taut muscles. Slowly the quivering in her limbs began to subside. He had a strange voice, but it was lovely, musical and lilting, and different from any voice she had ever heard before. And then Emma, listening acutely, and with all of her senses alerted in anticipation of trouble, realized how gentle his voice was, recognized with a sudden rush of clarity that it was filled with kindness and warmth. Still, he *was* a stranger. Then, much to her horror and with some surprise, Emma found herself asking involuntarily, "Why do yer want ter go ter the Hall then?" She was so angry with herself she could have bitten her tongue off.

"I be going there to repair the chimneys and the flues. It was himself who came to see me last week. Squire Fairley. Yes, indeed, himself came to visit me in Leeds and was kind enough and generous, too, he was, I might be adding, to be offering me the job."

Emma eyed the man suspiciously, lifting her damp face to peer at him through the mist. He was the tallest man she had ever seen and he was roughly dressed in workman's clothes and he had a sack slung over his shoulder.

"Are yer a navvy then?" she now asked with some caution, for she had just remembered that Cook had told her that a navvy had been engaged to do repair work and bricklaying at the Hall.

The man roared with laughter, a deep belly laugh that shook his whole vast frame. "I am that, to be sure. Shane O'Neill's the name, but the whole world calls me Blackie."

Emma squinted up at him again, trying to examine his face in the dim and vaporous air. "Yer not a blackamoor, are yer?" she asked tremulously, and then rebuked herself for her stupidity. O'Neill was an Irish name and that explained his singsong speech, which was so unfamiliar to her. But she had heard of the Irish brogue and surely this was it.

Her question seemed to tickle this giant even more and he laughed again, saying, "No, I'm not a blackamoor, little colleen. Not at all, at all! Just a black Irishman. And what might ye be called?"

She hesitated again. Emma believed that the less people knew about you, the better off you were, the safer you were, for if they knew nothing they could do you no harm. But to her fresh amazement she found herself telling him, "Emma. Emma Harte's me name."

"Pleased to be a-meeting ye, Emma Harte. Well then, now as we are acquainted, so to speak, will ye be kind enough to put me on the road to Fairley Hall, please?"

"It's the way yer came, back yonder," Emma said, shivering, now thoroughly chilled from lingering in the damp and icy dell. Then once again, much to her annoyance but before she could stop herself, she explained, "I'm going ter the Hall. Yer can walk with me if yer wants."

"Why, thank ye, Emma. So, let us be a-marching! 'Tis divilish cold and damp out here. Worse than the bogs of the ould sod in winter, sure and it is!" the man declared, stamping his feet on the frozen earth in an effort to warm them.

Emma slipped out from her hiding place amongst the rocks, and led the way up the track that would take them out of Ramsden Ghyll and onto the flat plateau of moors that stretched all the way to Fairley Hall. It was a narrow and somewhat precarious track, rising steeply upwards, and they had to walk in single file. Emma hurried in front of the Irishman, scrambling and sliding about in her haste to be out of the dell. They did not speak, for it was a steep hill and strenuous to traverse. Also, the path itself was rough, and scattered as it was with rocks and gnarled tree roots embedded in the frozen ground, it was exceedingly treacherous and dangerous in winter.

When they came up out of the Ghyll and onto the flat plateau the mist had dispersed, blown away by the gusting wind that roared down from the soaring fells. The morning air was tinged with opal and the livid sky was filling with incandescent light, a light that seemed to emanate from some hidden source below the horizon, a light peculiar to these northern climes that blazed with the most intense clarity. It was flooding the hump line of hills with sudden bright radiance, so that they were as burnished and shimmering as molten brass.

Emma stopped, panting for breath, and turned to look towards Ramsden Crags in the distance, as she always did. "Look at the horses," she said, pointing to the huge crags that were poised in solitary splendor against the horizon.

Blackie O'Neill followed her gaze and caught his breath. The girl was right. The rocks did look like great horses rearing up against the skyline, their roughhewn shapes suddenly taking on life, as if they were giant mythical steeds galloping across the heavens and glimmering like struck gold in the radiant light.

"Why, 'tis a beautiful sight. What is that place?" Blackie asked.

"Ramsden Crags, but the villagers sometimes call it Flying Horses. Me mam calls it the Top of the World," Emma confided.

'And indeed it looks as if it is just that, to be sure it does," Blackie murmured, dumping his sack on the ground and breathing deeply of the fresh air, now that they were out of the misty Ghyll.

Emma had not yet really looked fully at Blackie O'Neill. He had been behind her on the path leading out of the dell and he stood behind her now, at the edge of the Ghyll. Her mother had always instilled good manners in her, and had told her that it was rude to stare and scrutinize people, but now Emma's curiosity got the better of her and she permitted herself to turn slowly. She looked up at the man who had so scared her initially and she was startled to see that he was young, perhaps no more than eighteen. And he was quite the most extraordinary man she had ever set eyes upon.

Blackie returned her gaze, smiling broadly, and in a flash of insight the girl knew why she had so inexplicably lost her fear of him in the Ghyll. In spite of his size, and his roughness of dress, there was something ineffably gentle and fine about this man, both in his expression and in his general demeanor. His face was open, friendly, and quite guileless, and his wide smile was warm, and sunny, and somewhat mischievous, while his dark eyes were kind and understanding. Emma found herself smiling back at him unabashedly, warming to him in a way that was unprecedented for her, as wary and suspicious of strangers as she always was.

"Yer can't see the Hall from here," Emma explained, "but it's not far now, just over the crest of the moors yonder. Come on, I'll show yer the way, Blackie!" she cried enthusiastically, much taken with her new friend.

Blackie nodded, and, lifting the large sack, he slung it over one shoulder with apparent ease, as if it were a small and insignificant bundle in his large strong hands. He fell into step with Emma, who was already marching briskly along the top road, and began to whistle nonchalantly, his head thrown back, his vibrant curls blowing in the breeze.

From time to time, Emma looked up at him surreptitiously. She had never met anyone like him before and he fascinated her. Blackie, in turn, was not unconscious of this scrutiny; in fact, he was very much aware of it and it amused him. He had sized up the girl in a flash, for he was quick and intelligent and had a perceptive eye. He guessed she must be about fourteen, or thereabouts, and a local girl going on an errand to Fairley Hall. She was such a small sprite. No wonder he had frightened her in the fog. As they traversed the road together he smiled, admiring the stalwart way she stepped out, endeavoring to keep up with his long strides. He slowed down considerably when he saw how breathless she was becoming.

Shane Patrick Desmond O'Neill, commonly known to the world as Blackie, was about six feet three inches tall, but he appeared to be so much bigger in stature because of the largeness of his frame, his broad sweeping back and his powerful shoulders. He was brawny and well built, but there was no excess flesh on him. He was all muscle and sinew. He exuded virility, a ruddy health, and indomitable strength. He had long legs and a surprisingly narrow and well-defined waist below an expansive chest. It was easy to understand why the world called him Blackie. His thick and heavy hair, which flowed back in vital waves from a clear brow, was as black as ebony and just as shiny, and his eyes, of a brown so deep they also looked black, resembled great chunks of glittering coal. Set widely apart, under thick curving brows, these eyes were large and soft and very often wise, although they could gleam and flash with anger when Blackie's temper was aroused. Likewise they could just as easily turn mournful and tragic when his Celtic soul was troubled by melancholy thoughts. But, for the most part, they were filled with irrepressible merriment and bubbling fun.

His skin was dark, yet not swarthy; rather, it was a nut brown and tinged with ruddiness across his high cheekbones, a sort of light mahogany color that undoubtedly came from long exposure to the elements. His nose was straight and fairly narrow, although it broadened slightly at the tip, and his nostrils were flaring. His wide mouth and long Irish upper lip betrayed his Celtic origins. He had a cleft in his strongly molded chin and when he laughed, which was often, his cheeks dimpled and his face took on an amazing vitality.

Blackie O'Neill was, in fact, an exceptionally handsome young man with his laughing face, flashing teeth between red lips, and his striking and vital coloring. But it was his manner and his attitude that were most intriguing and which, in many ways, set Blackie apart from other men. He exuded liveliness and gaiety. His face was full of vivacity, and it had great mobility and not a little wit. An easy, careless charm was second nature to him, and he was buoyant of spirit, as if he accepted life for what it was, and was constantly entertained by it. There was a lighthearted self-confidence inherent in him, and to Emma, observing him, he seemed untouched by the weariness and the fear and the hopelessness that haunted the men of the village, bowing them down and aging them prematurely.

For the first time in her young life Emma had met someone with an unquenchable spirit and a soul that was joyous and without rancor, a man who loved his life and lived it to the fullest, and she had a vague glimmering of all this, and it intrigued and mystified and impressed her.

As she hurried along next to this handsome young giant her eyes turned to him often, and she found she was filled with an intense and voracious inquisitiveness about him. He was a cheerful companion, who in the oddest and most inexplicable way made her feel safe as he tramped by her side, saying little, smiling his vivid smile, sometimes whistling merrily, his bright eyes scanning the crest of the moors expectantly, anticipating the sight of the spires of Fairley Hall. And something of his light and genial good humor seemed to mysteriously transfer itself to Emma, and her face, so unremittingly stern and intent for one so young, was softened by a hint of hidden gaiety.

She was taken by surprise when Blackie opened his mouth and began to sing, his rich baritone filling the silent air with the most melodious sweet sounds that startled her, so beautiful were they. She listened with rapt attention, all other thoughts swept out of her head, as the lilting voice flowed all around her to touch her heart and hold it enthralled. Blackie's voice rang out true and clear and pure.

> "The Minstrel Boy to the war is gone,
> In the ranks of death you'll find him.
> His father's sword he has girded on,
> And his wild harp slung behind him. . . ."

As she listened to Blackie singing, Emma was filled with a swift and piercing pain, and tears rushed to her eyes, for she was touched in a way she had never been before. There was something hauntingly sad yet bittersweet about the words and the poignant melody, and her throat ached with the tears, so sudden, so unexpected, which she tried to choke back, afraid of appearing childish, and even a little foolish, to this man as he finished the ballad of the Minstrel Boy.

Blackie looked at her, and observing the glistening tears that trembled on her lashes, asked softly, "Did ye not like me song then, little one?"

Emma swallowed deeply and cleared her throat several times. Finally she was able to speak. "Oh yes, I did, Blackie. I really did. It's just that it's so sad, yer knows." She brushed her hand across her eyes, wiping away the tears quickly, and noting the look of concern clouding his face, she added hurriedly, "But yer have a luvely voice, yer do that." She smiled, hoping her tears had not offended him.

Blackie had been surprised by the girl's sensitive and emotional reaction to his singing, and he returned her smile and said with great gentleness, "Aye, 'tis a sad song to be sure, but a beautiful one, Emma. Still and all, 'tis only an old ballad. Ye must not be upset. And since ye are kind enough to say ye like me voice, such as it is, I'll be singing ye a song that will surely make ye laugh, I am thinking."

And he did. His rich and splendid voice formed the most merry sounds now, the lively words of an Irish jig tripping lightly from his facile tongue. He had purposely selected an amusing bit of nonsense, filled with tongue-twisting clan names, and soon Emma was laughing delightedly, the momentary sadness of the ballad forgotten in her newly found merriment.

When he had finished she cried gaily, "Thank yer, Blackie, ever so much. That *was* funny. Yer'll have ter sing it for Mrs. Turner, the cook at the Hall. She'll like it, I bet she will, and I bet it'll make her laugh."

"Sure and will I not be happy to, Emma," Blackie replied kindly, and then he said curiously, "And why are ye off to Fairley Hall so early in the day, might I be asking?"

"I'm in service there," Emma answered solemnly, returning his friendly gaze with unflickering, steady eyes, a sober expression washing over her face.

"Indeed ye are, are ye! And what can a little snippet of a colleen like ye do to earn ye keep?" he asked, and grinned broadly, apparently extremely amused, his manner teasing but not unkindly so.

"I'm the kitchen maid." Seeing her half-averted eyes, the downcast drooping of her mouth, and the grim expression that swept across her face, Blackie decided she did not savor her work at the Hall. She volunteered no more information, and retreated behind the mask-like expression which had settled on her small countenance. Sensing her discomfort, he did not question her further and they walked on in silence, something of the gaiety they had so recently shared washed away in the wake of her mood, which had so abruptly changed.

She was a funny little thing to Blackie, this colleen of the moors whom he had come upon so unexpectedly, a shabby starveling creature, all skin and bone. This Emma Harte looked to him as if she needed a good meal, several good meals, for many months to come. Indeed she did. She was a poverty-stricken child who should be at home and in bed, and not wandering these moors, so godforsaken and lifeless, at the crack of dawn in the midst of a bitter winter. Poor mavourneen, he thought, and his heart seemed to constrict for a second, full of compassion and sympathy for this girl who so singularly moved him.

In spite of her shabbiness, her clothes were tidy and neatly patched, and he could see that her face was scrubbed and shining clean. Not that too much of that face was visible, swathed as it was in the thick black woolen scarf. But her eyes, whenever she turned them on him, were of incredible beauty. They were large and luminous and vividly green, just about the greenest eyes he had ever seen. They reminded Blackie of the sea that lapped the shores of his native Ireland, and they were as deep and as ancient and as unfathomable.

Emma cut into Blackie's thoughts when she asked, "Yer said afore yer were a black Irishman. What's that, then?" Blackie turned to Emma and saw that the stark strained look had disappeared from her face.

His eyes held a mischievous glint as he said, "Well, mavourneen, not a blackamoor from Africa, as ye suspected, but a man with my coloring, the black hair and the black eyes—'tis said we inherited them from the Spanish."

She had been about to ask him what "mavourneen" meant, but this last statement so astounded her the question was swept out of her mind. "Spanish! There aren't no Spanish in Ireland. I knows better'n that!" Emma scoffed with a degree of fierceness, her eyes flashing. "I've been ter school, yer knows," she informed Blackie as an afterthought, and proudly, wondering if he thought she was a fool.

Blackie was amused by her reaction, but he kept a straight face. "Then, being as how ye are such an ejicated young colleen, ye must be a-knowing that King Philip of Spain sent a great Armada to invade England in the time of Queen Elizabeth. 'Tis said that some of the galleons foundered and sank off the coast of Ireland and that the survivors, Spaniards all, settled in the Emerald Isle. 'Tis them, they say, the black Irish are descended from, and maybe that's the God's truth, I am thinking."

"I knows about Spain and that Armada, but I didn't know owt about the Spaniards living in Ireland," said Emma, looking up at him carefully.

There was such skepticism in her eyes that Blackie slapped his leg and roared with laughter. "Faith and it's doubting me that she is! But 'tis the truth I be telling ye, Emma. On the heads of the Blessed Saints I do swear it's the truth I am speaking, mavourneen."

Emma now said challengingly, "Hey, what does that mean, that word 'mavourneen'? Yer keep calling me that, Blackie. I never did hear such a word afore. It's not rude, is it?"

Blackie shook his head, his vital curls rippling and dancing as he did, the perpetual laughter flickering in his eyes and across his wide mouth. "It's the Irish word for dear or darlin', Emma. Like the word 'luv' the Yorkshire folk are always

using. It ain't no rude word, little colleen. Affectionate is the
best way of describing it, I am thinking. Besides, who would
be rude to a spry young ejicated lady like ye?" he finished,
adopting his most serious voice, his most gallant manner.

"Oh, aye," Emma said, a flick of that hard Yorkshire skepticism noticeable in her voice.

There was a small silence and then, half turning and touching his arm impulsively, she asked, "Do yer live in Leeds
then, Blackie?" Her face was suddenly animated and interested and he sensed a new excitement in her.

"I do. I do. Sure and it's a grand town. Have ye ever been
there, Emma?"

Her face fell as disappointment registered on it. "No. But
I will go one day! Me dad promised ter take me on a day trip,
and I knows he will when he can spare the time like."

And the money for the fares, Blackie thought astutely. But
detecting the lack of conviction in her voice, and sensing her
dejection, he said vigorously and with some positiveness,
"Sure and he will, Emma! Faith and ye will find it the most
exciting place, mavourneen. Aye, 'tis exceedingly exciting.
And busy! A virtual metropolis, I am thinking. It has great
arcades with the most wondrous shops filled with grand finery
for the ladies, and the gents, too. Yes, finery like a queen
would wear, Emma. Silk and satin gowns beyond description.
Beautiful hats with great feathery plumes and veils, fancy
stockings and soft leather buttoned boots and parasols and
reticules. All ye little heart could be desiring. And silk cravats for the gents as can afford 'em. Aye, and diamond stick-
pins, too, and ebony walking canes with silver knobs and
sleek top hats. Such finery like ye never did see in ye whole
life, I am thinking, Emma."

Blackie paused, and then observing the wonderment in her
eyes, the vibrancy now illuminating her face, and acutely
aware of her eagerness to hear more, he continued his description of Leeds. "There are elegant restaurants serving the
most incredible delicacies to tempt ye palate, Emma. And
dance halls, and a music hall called the City Varieties and
plush theaters where they put on plays that come all the way
up from London town. Why, I've seen Vesta Tilley and Marie
Lloyd on the stage in Leeds meself, with me own eyes,
mavourneen. Then there are the new tramcars. Amazing
vehicles, to be sure, that run on tracks without the need for

horses to pull 'em anymore. They go from the Corn Exchange to all parts of town. I have ridden on one, sure and I have. I sat on the top deck, that's open to the world and the weather, viewing the town like a real gent. Faith and there are many wonders to see in Leeds, yes indeed."

Emma's eyes glowed, all the weariness and worry which had enveloped her earlier that morning miraculously dissipated, her imagination inflamed, and her emotions stirred most palpably by Blackie's recital. She attempted, as always, to contain herself, but in her anxiousness for further information about this most extraordinary place, her voice rose and became shrill. "Why did yer go ter live in Leeds then, Blackie? Tell me more about it!"

"I went to live in Leeds because there was no work in me native Ireland." His voice dropped, was low now and sad, yet there was no disgruntlement or rancor in it, only dim resignation.

"It was me Uncle Pat, settled in Leeds for this many a year, who did bid me come over to be a-working by his side as a navvy. Lots of work in Leeds, being as how it's a growing metropolis, as I told ye afore, Emma. When I saw all the new manufactures going up and the mills and the foundries, as well as the handsome carriages and the elegant houses of the gentry, I thought to meself: Sure and this is the place for a boyo like ye, Blackie O'Neill, a spalpeen that's not afeared of hard work, strong and brawny and a match for any man. This is indeed the place to be a-staying, faith and it is, for the streets are surely paved with gold! A man can make a fortune in Leeds, I was believing, so stay I did. That was five years ago. Now me Uncle Pat and me have our own business going. We do repair work and building for the millowners and the gentry. Doing well, sure and we are, little colleen. Small it is now, but I know it will be growing. Ye see, I aim to be rich one day. I am going to make meself a pile and be a millionaire!"

He tossed his head cockily and laughed, his face full of youthful optimism. He put his arm around her shoulders and said confidentially and with the utmost self-assurance, "I aim to get me a diamond stickpin and be an elegant gent, a real toff, that I do, mavourneen. On the Blessed Heads of the Saints, I swear I do!"

Emma had listened attentively. Blackie's account had been thrilling and it had held her spellbound, had aroused all manner of longings within her. But it was that magical word "fortune" that had made the most profound impact on her. Her razor-sharp mind seized on it, as thoughts of fancy clothes and theaters were swept away. Those things were insignificant in comparison to Blackie's revelations about the opportunities for making a fortune in Leeds. Here was someone after her own heart, who knew that money could be earned as well as inherited. Emma's heart was pounding so hard she thought her chest would burst, and now it took all of her strength for her to retain her composure. She felt she could not speak and then, at last, "Can a girl like *me* make a fortune in Leeds?" she asked in a strangled voice, breathless in her anticipation of his answer.

This was the last thing Blackie had expected. He was dumbfounded. He stared down at Emma and saw the starveling girl who reached only up to his chest, so fragile and wan and undernourished, and his heart clenched with feelings of pity and protectiveness. Poor little mavourneen, he thought, I should have held me tongue. Foolish boyo that I am, filling her head with dreams of a better life, a world she'll never see. He was about to answer her negatively when, with a terrible clarity, he recognized the gleam in her eyes for what it was—ambition, raw and inexorable. He took in the face, now suddenly stern in its fixity, the eyes blazing hard green light. It was the most implacable face he had ever seen and he was shocked by what he saw. Blackie felt a cold chill on the back of his neck and his Celtic intuition told him that she was in deadly earnest. He could not encourage the preposterous idea of her running off to Leeds, yet he must attempt to pacify her.

And so Blackie bit back the "no" he had been about to utter, drew in a deep breath, smiled, and said with all the gallantry he could summon, "Faith, and to be sure ye could. But not now, Emma. Ye are but a little colleen. Ye can't be going off to Leeds until ye are older, I am thinking. 'Tis a fine city, sure and it is, full of prospects, but awesome and dangerous, too, for a little snippet like ye."

Emma appeared not to hear this. At least she ignored it. "Where would I work to make this fortune?" she rushed on, undaunted. "What would I do?"

Blackie realized she was not going to be easily appeased. He pretended to consider the question seriously, for he was only humoring her, in spite of his initial response. She did not look as if she would make it to Fairley Hall, let alone Leeds, and had he not imagined that relentless expression on her face? Sure and he had! Anything was possible on these ghostly moors, at this hour, in the depth of winter.

"Well, let me be thinking this one out," he said cautiously. "Perhaps ye could work in one of the manufacturies making the fine dresses or maybe in one of the elegant shops selling the finery to the ladies. Many things there are ye could do, but as I said afore, I must be thinking on it careful. That's important, sure and it is. We must find ye the right occupation. That's the secret of success, ye knows, Emma. Least, so I've heard tell."

She nodded, realizing the truth of what he said, and debated whether to confide further in Blackie, but her Yorkshire canniness, that inbred wariness, made her hold her tongue. She decided she had said enough for the moment. But she did have one more question and it was of crucial importance to her. "If I comes ter Leeds one day, when I'm growed up like yer say I should be, will yer help ter show me the ropes like, Blackie?" She was gazing up at him and he saw that her face was the face of a child again and he breathed a sigh of relief, although he was not certain why.

"Faith and sure I will, Emma. It will be me pleasure. I live at Mrs. Riley's boardinghouse on the 'ham and shank,' but ye can always find me at the Mucky Duck."

"What's that then? The 'ham and shank'?" Her brows puckered in bewilderment.

He laughed, amused at her puzzlement. "What rhymes with 'ham and shank'?"

"Lots of things!" she exclaimed pithily, and threw him a scathing look.

"The Bank, that's what. Ham and shank. The Bank. See? It rhymes. Rhyming slang we calls it in Leeds. 'Tis the railway bank though, not the riverbank, near the Leylands. But that ain't such a good neighborhood, full of roughs and toughs it is! Not the place for a colleen to be a-wandering in alone, I am thinking. So if ye wants to find me, just go to the Mucky Duck in York Road and ask for Rosie. She's the barmaid and she'll know where I am, if I ain't in the pub. Ye see, I might be at the Golden Fleece in Briggate. Ye can be leaving a message with Rosie, to be sure ye can, mavourneen, and she'll get it to me or me Uncle Pat the same day."

"Thank yer, Blackie, ever so much," said Emma, mentally repeating with the greatest of care the names he had reeled off, so that she would remember them. For she did intend to go to Leeds and make her fortune.

Emma fell silent. They walked along not speaking, both of them lost in their own thoughts, yet it was a harmonious silence, without unease or awkwardness. Strangers though they were, they had taken to each other and a kind of understanding had sprung up between them, brief as their acquaintance was.

Blackie looked about him, thinking how grand it was to be alive, to have a job of work to do, a few shillings warming his pocket, and most importantly, the prospect of lots more to come. Even the moors had a strange compelling beauty now that he could see them properly. The fog had lifted long before and the air was no longer damp and moisture-laden. It was a brisk day, with a light wind that imbued the naked trees, so rigid and lifeless at this season, with a new and graceful mobility as they waved in the breeze. And the sky was no longer the color of dull lead. It leaked a hard metallic blue.

They had almost reached the end of the flat plateau of moorland, and Blackie was beginning to wonder when they would arrive at Fairley Hall, when Emma announced, "The Hall is yonder, Blackie," as if she had read his thoughts. She was pointing straight ahead.

His eyes followed the direction of her outstretched arm. He could see nothing but the empty moorland. "Where? I must be the blind one, Emma. I can't see no spires and chimneys, like himself described to me last week."

"Yer will when we gets ter the top of the ridge over yonder," she asserted, "then it's downhill all the way. In a couple of ticks we'll be in the Baptist Field and that's right next ter the Hall."

EIGHT

Emma and Blackie were now standing on top of the ridge she had indicated. Behind them, sweeping into the cloudless sky, were the high fells where the last of the snow shimmered here and there like uneven swatches of white satin rippling in the watery sunlight. Below them was a small valley, typical of the West Riding, cradled in the arms of the encircling moors that extended to the rim of the horizon.

And in this dun-colored valley, all dim grays, dusty charcoals, and earthy browns, stood Fairley Hall. Only the tops of the spires and the chimneys were visible to the eye from where they were standing, for the house itself was obscured by a copse of trees. Unlike the stunted trees that intermittently broke the barrenness of the moors, these trees were tall and stately oaks, their widely splayed branches intertwining to form an intricate pattern. Plumes of smoke from the chimneys twisted upward behind the trees, filling the chill blue sky with wispy gray question marks. Suddenly, a flock of rooks fluttered out of the copse, winding up and out in a long wavy line like a coil of thick black rope flung carelessly into the air. Otherwise there was no sign of life in this neat little valley which slumbered undisturbed at this early hour, serene and peaceful in the infinite silence.

Surprisingly, the ridge on which Emma and Blackie stood did not drop down precipitously as Blackie had anticipated, but fell away into a short gentle slope that rolled towards the edge of a small field. Drystone walls, built long ago by the crofters, surrounded this field and others in the distance, cutting out a patchwork design on the floor of the valley, a design that to Blackie seemed extraordinarily orderly and tidy, juxtaposed as it was against the wild and sprawling moors. It looked as though a giant hand had neatly carved up the land most precisely and then enclosed each portion with the old and rugged walls.

Emma ran ahead, calling to Blackie as she did, "Come on then, I'll race yer ter the gate!" She flew off down the slope at such a speed he was momentarily taken aback, both by her incredible swiftness and her unexpected burst of energy. She was wiry, this one. Gripping the sack tightly in one hand, Blackie leaped after her, at first at a goodly pace. With his great physical strength and long legs he could have outstripped her easily, but when he had almost caught up with her he fell back, slackening his speed, so that she could win her race.

Emma stood triumphantly by the gate. "Yer'll have ter look more sharpish and get a move on if yer wants ter beat *me*," she proclaimed with a small swagger. "I'm a good runner, yer knows," she added, panting.

Blackie grinned at this tiny display of vanity and then adopted an admiring attitude. "Indeed, so I can see, mavourneen! Ye are as fast as a greyhound at the dog tracks, I am thinking. I'd put me money on ye any day, sure and I would."

Emma bestowed a gratified smile on him and a gleam of satisfaction flicked across her face briefly. Then she turned quickly, unlatched the gate, pushed it slightly, and jumped onto the first rung, clinging to it fiercely as the gate swung forward into the field, carrying her with it. Glancing back at Blackie over her shoulder, she called, "I always have a swing on this gate here, even though I'm not supposed ter." When the gate groaned to a quivering standstill she stepped off briskly and pulled it back, apparently intending to repeat the operation, her face slightly flushed, her eyes merry.

Blackie threw down his sack. "Here, let me give ye a push, Emma. Sure and ye'll be having a better ride with a bit of force behind ye."

Nodding excitedly, she climbed onto the first rung again and clutched the gate tightly with her small chapped hands, as Blackie sent it flying into the field much faster than before. Her worn coat billowed out behind her and laughter washed over her face. Blackie watched her, enjoying her delight in this simple pleasure. Why, she's only a bairn at that, he thought, a rush of warmth filling his throat. How could I have imagined otherwise? Sure and it's stupid that I am.

Emma dropped off the gate and beckoned to him. "Come on! Let's be going. I'm ever so late and I'll be copping it from Mrs. Turner."

Blackie picked up his sack and joined her. He put his arm around her in a brotherly fashion and fell into step with her as they proceeded to the bottom of the field. "I have to be confessing to ye that I'm mighty curious about the folk at Fairley Hall. What are they like, mavourneen?"

There was a tiny silence.

"Yer'll see in a minute." Emma smiled oddly. "We're almost there now." Freeing herself from him, she ran ahead without another word.

Blackie looked after her, frowning, puzzled by that curious smile. She was such a small figure on the path in front of him, skipping along almost with a carefree air. He had to admit she baffled him. One minute she was a child, her face soft and laughing; the next she seemed like an old woman, her face cast in bronze. Yet they were all queer, these Yorkshire folk, with their flat harsh accents, their self-reliant characters, their dour and opinionated natures, their rabid suspicion of strangers, their shrewdness and lightning perception of character. And their veneration of money. Still, he had discovered they could be generous-spirited and hospitable, and they had a sense of humor, even if it was somewhat blunt and pithy at times. Indeed, they were funny folk, and perhaps the very peculiarities he had discerned in Emma were simply vestiges of these Yorkshire traits. Yes, that must be it, he thought, and he quickened his steps to catch up with her.

Emma was waiting for him at the copse of trees which skirted the end of the field. "There's the Hall, Blackie," she said in a voice totally devoid of emotion.

Blackie stopped dead in his tracks and let out a long low whistle in stunned astonishment. Fairley Hall was in their direct line of vision and it bore no resemblance to the images he had conjured up in his head after his recent talk with Squire Fairley in Leeds.

"Mary, Mother of Jesus!" he cried, his eyes opening widely in disbelief. "It's not possible, mavourneen. Nobody could have built a house like that!" He closed his eyes convulsively and when he opened them again he discovered he was not only disappointed in what he saw, but utterly appalled as well.

"The Hall's the grandest house for miles around. Nowt as big as it by here," Emma pointed out in the same toneless voice. "Me dad calls it Fairley's Folly." He did not notice the faint bitter smile on her lips.

"I can see why," Blackie murmured, thinking that it was the most grotesque house he had ever seen. As he stared at it, his jaw slack and his mouth dropping open, he recognized with dismay that it had no redeeming features at all. For Blackie O'Neill had an unusually accurate eye for perspective and line and, in fact, his one dream in life had been to study architecture. This had not been possible, but, encouraged by his parish priest, Father O'Donovan, when a boy, he had taught himself as much as he could from a few books, and because of his desire to learn and his very natural talent, he had become exceedingly knowledgeable about design and construction.

Now he scanned the house with keen and critical eyes. The closer they drew to it, the more Blackie perceived what a monstrosity it was. It appeared to crouch like an implacable monster amidst carefully planned yet oddly incongruous gardens, its blackened stone walls grim and unwelcoming. Gothic-like spires leapt up from the four corners of the central building, which was square and dominating and was crowned with a bizarre cupola. It struck him that this central building was the oldest part, probably dating back to the late 1790s, and if it had been left alone it would have had a semblance of dignity, perhaps even a touch of grandeur. But other wings had obviously been added over the years, seemingly with little thought, and they sprouted off on both sides without regard to form or design. He could now see that they were bastardized interpretations of Regency and Victorian styles, and all of them mingled together to create a chaotic effect.

In essence, Fairley Hall was a hodgepodge of diverse periods that competed with each other to create a façade that was without proportion, symmetry, or beauty. The house was large, solid, and rich, a veritable mansion, in fact, but its architectural inconsistencies made it hideous. Blackie sighed. He loved simplicity and he thought wistfully of the lovely old Georgian houses in Ireland, with their fluid lines and classical proportions that gave them such perfect balance. He had not expected to find such a house on these rough Yorkshire moors, but not unaware of the standing and importance of the Fairley family, and their great wealth, he had anticipated a structure that had more taste and refinement than this.

They had almost reached the house when Emma cut into

his thoughts as she said, "What do yer think ter it then?" She looked up at him curiously, tugging at his arm.

"Not much! 'Tis a Folly to be sure, just as ye dad says. It may be the grandest house in these parts, but it ain't to the tastes of a boyo like me."

"Won't yer have a house like the Hall then, when yer gets ter be this toff, this millionaire yer said yer'd be one day?" she probed, scrutinizing him shrewdly. "I thought *all* millionaires lived in grand houses like Fairley."

"True! True!" he said quickly. "They do live in grand houses, but not always ones as ugly as Fairley Hall, Emma. I would never want such a house for meself. It offends me eyes, sure and it does, for it has no beauty or harmony or style." Blackie glanced ahead and grimaced at the thought of occupying such a grotesque mausoleum.

That bitter smile played around Emma's mouth again and there was a tiny gleam of malicious satisfaction in her eyes. Although she lacked exposure to the world beyond the moors, and so had no basis for comparison, she had always instinctively known that the Hall was an eyesore without grace or beauty. Her dad and the villagers might sarcastically call it Fairley's Folly, but, nonetheless, they were still impressed. She laughed to herself, a little spitefully. Blackie had just confirmed her own opinions of Fairley Hall and this pleased her.

Now she turned to Blackie, who had risen even more in her esteem, and said inquisitively, "What kind of a house will yer live in then, when yer gets ter be this rich millionaire?"

The gloomy expression on his face lifted and was instantly replaced with a throbbing vibrancy. His black eyes shone as he exclaimed, "It will be in the Georgian style, built of pure white stone, with a handsome portico and great soaring columns and wide front steps. There will be many tall shining windows, looking out onto fine green lawns and gardens. It will have lots of spacious rooms, with lofty ceilings, and they will all be full of light and airiness. The floors will be made of polished oak and the fireplaces will all be in the Robert Adam style. In the entrance hall, which will be huge, I am going to have a floor made of white marble and a great curving staircase will lead to the upper floors. In every room I will use pastel colors, the light blues and pale greens that are soft and restful to the eyes, and I intend to purchase excellent furniture for all of these rooms. Yes, indeed! I shall select the best styles of Sheraton and Hepplewhite and maybe a little Chippendale. Paintings, too, I shall have, and many other fine and beautiful things. Ah, mavourneen, it will be a house to take yer breath away, faith and it will. I promise ye that. I aim to build it meself, to me own design, sure and I do!"

"Build it yerself, ter yer own design," she repeated in a hushed tone, her face full of wonder. "Do yer know how ter design houses then, Blackie?"

"Aye, to be sure I do, little colleen," he responded proudly. "I go to the night school in Leeds, to be learning draftsmanship, and that's the next best thing to architecture. Ye'll see, Emma, I'll build that house one day and ye'll come and visit me when ye are a grand lady."

Emma looked at Blackie in awe. "Can anybody go ter this night school ter learn things?" she asked, thinking of her brother Frank.

Blackie looked down at her expectant face, so filled with hope, and told her confidently, "Sure and they can. At the night school they teach ye everything ye might want to be learning."

His answer delighted Emma and she stored the information at the back of her mind to tell Frank later, and asked, with her usual avid curiosity, "Who's this Robert Adam then, and them others yer mentioned? Yer knows, Sheraton and Hepplewhite and Chippendale?"

Blackie's face glowed, for they were embarking on a subject close to his heart. "Robert Adam was the great architect of the eighteenth century, Emma. He built many grand and beautiful houses for the gentry that are wondrous to behold. Ah, but Adam was more than that, I am thinking, for he furnished them, too, with style and taste. Nobody has ever bettered him, mavourneen. The others I spoke about," he went on enthusiastically, "were the three greatest furniture makers of the Georgian period, sure and they were. Master craftsmen who made the furniture for the Quality folk."

He grinned and winked at her. "Ye see, I aim to have nothing but the best when I'm a rich boyo. For I often says to meself, 'What's the point of having money, Blackie O'Neill, if ye don't get the pleasure from it?' So I aim to be spending it. That's what it's for, I am thinking. Are ye not after agreeing with me?"

Emma regarded him soberly. Mostly when she thought of money it was in terms of the necessities of life. Blackie had presented new possibilities to her. "Aye, I suppose so," she said cautiously. "As long as yer've got enough money ter spare, ter buy all them fine things."

He roared with laughter. So much so that tears of merriment squeezed out of the corners of his eyes. "Ye are a canny Yorkshire colleen, I can see that," he said through his laughter. "But what's *enough*, Emma? I've heard tell of some men who never have enough money to satisfy them."

Like Squire Fairley, she thought sourly, but said, "And where will yer build yer beautiful house, Blackie? Will it be in Leeds then?"

He wiped his eyes on the back of his sleeve, his merriment subsiding, and shook his head. "No, I don't think it will. I am considering building it in Harrogate, where all the toffs live," he said importantly. "Aye, that will be the place, I am thinking," he continued, the certainty in his voice more pronounced. " 'Tis a fine town. A spa. Just the place for a spalpeen like me. Have ye heard of it, Emma?"

"Yes, me mam has been ter Harrogate, a long time ago, when she went ter visit her cousin Freda in Ripon. She told me about it once. She said it's a real posh place."

He laughed. "It is, it is! And tell me, Emma, do ye like the sound of me house, that I shall be building for meself one of these fine days?"

"Ooh, I do, Blackie! Yer house'll be luvely, I just knows it will. Not like this place. Yer should see this house at night. It frightens me more than when I have ter walk past the cemetery," she confided.

Blackie frowned and looked swiftly at her small face, which was childlike and trusting, and he smiled reassuringly. "Ah, 'tis only a house, little colleen. A house can't harm ye."

She did not respond to this comment but compressed her lips and quickened her steps, as they were suddenly engulfed by the giant bluegray shadows cast by Fairley Hall. Now that they were close to it, Blackie became conscious of another aspect of the house and it was one which instantly disturbed him. It seemed to Blackie, as he regarded it, that the great mansion was strangely brooding and hostile, as if it had never known life or laughter or gaiety. He had the oddest feeling that all those who crossed its threshold were held captive forever. He considered his reaction foolish, yet a chill ran through him as he attempted to shake off this morbid and irrational thought.

He looked up. Immense windows gazed down at them, heavily draped against the world, and to Blackie they were like the eyes of blind men, empty, hollow, and dead. A shaft of sunlight struck the blackened walls and those dim and mysterious windows, and this light, hard and full of clarity, appeared to emphasize the impregnability and bleakness of Fairley Hall. Blackie told himself he was being ridiculous and over-imaginative, but these emotions did not diminish as Emma led him around the corner of the house and out of the shadows. They headed across a cobbled stable yard, full of sunlight and blue sky, towards the servants' entrance. Automatically he put his arm around her shoulders and then he grinned at the absurdity of his action. She had been coming here far longer than he had and was surely without need of his protection. And protection against what? he wondered, mystified at himself.

Emma looked up at him and smiled, as if once again she had read his thoughts. But as they mounted the steps that smile faltered and the light in her eyes dulled. A watchful expression settled on her face as she turned the iron handle of the door and walked into the kitchen.

NINE

And what time do yer think this is then, ter be strolling in like there's no termorrow? And looking as if yer don't have a care in the world as well! Aay, lass, I'd about given thee up. I had that!"

The sharp voice echoing around the kitchen emanated from a little dumpling of a woman who was as broad of beam as she was short in stature. Birdlike brown eyes, peeping out above apple-rosy cheeks, flashed with indignation, and the starched white cap, perched like a crown on top of her graying auburn hair, bobbed about as she tossed her head.

"And don't stand there gawping at me like a sucking duck!" she went on crossly, waving the ladle at Emma. "Get a move

on with yer, now that yer are here, lass! We've no time ter be
wasting today."

"I'm ever so sorry, Mrs. Turner," Emma cried as she ran
across the room, pulling off her scarf and struggling out of her
coat. Bundling them up in a roll, she went on quickly in an
apologetic tone, "I set off in time, I did really, Mrs. Turner.
But it was ever so foggy on the moors and in the Ghyll
and—"

"Aye, and I expect yer stopped ter laik on yon gate as
usual," Cook interrupted with some impatience. "Yer'll be
copping it, lass, one of these fine days, yer will that!"

Emma had disappeared into a cupboard, under the stairs
which led up to the family's living quarters, and her voice
was muffled when she called out, "I'll catch up with me work,
Mrs. Turner. Yer knows I will."

"Yer'll have ter, that's a certainty," Cook retorted with
asperity. "I can see we'll have an uproar on our hands today.
What with Mrs. Hardcastle in Bradford and company coming
up from London town and Polly right badly." She shook her
head, sighed heavily at the thought of her burdens, adjusted
her cap, and banged the ladle down on the table. Then she
swung around and stared at Blackie, whom she had so far
ignored. Placing her hands on her hips, she looked him over
appraisingly, her beady eyes suspicious. "And what's this the
cat's dragged in then? Lochinvar," she said acidly.

Blackie took a step forward and opened his mouth, but
before he could speak, Emma's voice floated out from the
cupboard. "It's the navvy, Mrs. Turner. The one yer were
expecting ter mend the flues and all. His name's Shane
O'Neill, but the whole world calls him Blackie."

"Top of the morning to ye," Blackie cried, flashing her a
cheery smile and bowing elaborately.

Cook ignored this friendly greeting and said, "Irish, eh?
Well, I can't say as I hold that against yer. I can see yer a
strong lad. No room for weaklings in this house!" She paused
and her eyes now lighted on the sack he had placed on the
floor next to him, which was old and very grimy. "And what's
in that mucky *thing?*" she asked.

"Just me tools and a few er . . . er . . . personal items,"
Blackie said, shuffling his feet in embarrassment.

'Well, don't be dragging it over me clean floor!" she admonished. "Put it in that there corner, where it's out of the

way." She then marched to the stove, saying in a gentler tone, "Yer'd best come ter the fire and get yerself warm, lad."

Mrs. Turner bustled around the stove, clattering pan lids, peering at the contents of her bubbling pots, muttering under her breath. Her temper had abated. This was mostly irritation rather than real anger, and it was chiefly engendered by anxiety for Emma crossing the lonely moors rather than the girl's tardiness, which was not so important. What was half an hour, after all? She smiled to herself. Emma was a good lass, which was more than you could say for most in this dreadful day and age.

Blackie dumped his sack in the corner and loped over to the enormous fireplace that covered almost the whole of one wall. As he warmed his hands in front of the fire he became conscious of two things. He was frozen stiff and he was hungry. These sensations were precipitated by the steaming warmth of the room and the delicious smells pervading the air. He sniffed and his mouth watered as he inhaled the pungent smell of smoky country bacon frying, the warm, sweet fragrance of freshly baked bread, and wafting over these tempting odors he detected the rich savory tang of a vegetable broth boiling. His stomach growled and he licked his lips hungrily.

Slowly his body began to thaw and he stretched luxuriously like a great cat, his eyes sweeping quickly over the room, and what he saw cheered Blackie immensely, helped to dissipate his foreboding of earlier. For there was nothing brooding or menacing about this kitchen. It was a splendid, warming, cheerful place and spanking clean. All manner of copper pots and pans sparkled lustrously on the whitewashed walls, and the flagged stone floor shone whitely in the bright light of the gas jets and the crackling fire that leapt and roared up the big chimney. Strong oak furniture, highly waxed, gleamed softly in this roseate glow.

Blackie heard the click of a door and he looked up as Emma emerged from the cupboard. She had changed into a dark blue serge dress, obviously cut from the same cloth as Cook's, and she was fastening on a large blue-and-white-striped cotton apron. "Did yer say Polly was poorly again, Mrs. Turner?" she asked, moving hurriedly in the direction of the stove.

"Aye, lass. Bad cough she has. Summat terrible. I made
her stay abed this morning. Yer might look in on her later,
ter see if she wants owt." There was true warmth in Cook's
voice and her face softened as she regarded the girl. Blackie
looked at her and recognized there was no real animosity in
her. It was apparent, from the loving expression now flooding
her face, that Mrs. Turner was inordinately fond of Emma.

"Yes, I'll pop up after breakfast is served and take her some
broth," Emma agreed, trying not to look overly concerned
about Polly. Emma was convinced she had the same sickness
as her mother, for Emma had detected all the telltale signs:
the weakness, the fever, and the terrible coughing.

Mrs. Turner nodded. "Aye, that's a good lass." She frowned
and peered at Emma through the steam. "Yer'll have ter do
Polly's work today, as well as yer own, yer knows, luv. Can't
be helped! Murgatroyd tells me Mrs. Wainright arrives for a
visit this afternoon and with Mrs. Hardcastle still away we're
really shorthanded." She exhaled a loud sigh of exasperation
and banged the spoon against the side of the pot furiously.
"Aye, I wish I was the housekeeper here, I do that! It's a
right cushy job Nellie Hardcastle's got and no mistake. Always tripping off, that she is!"

Emma repressed a smile. This was an old bone of conten-
tion. "Yer right, Mrs. Turner, but we'll manage somehow,"
she said reassuringly. She liked Cook, who was the only one
who showed her any kindness at the Hall, and she always
tried to please her. Emma ran back to the cupboard under
the stairs and pulled out a large basket containing brushes,
cloths, polishes, and black lead, and headed for the staircase.
"I'll make a start," she called, beginning to mount the stairs,
waving to Blackie as she did.

Mrs. Turner's head jerked up quickly. "Nay, lass, I'm not
that heartless! Yer looks nithered ter death. Go ter the fire
and warm up, and drink a cup of this broth afore yer goes up
yonder." She lifted the lid off the large iron pot, stirred it
vigorously, clucked with satisfaction, and began to ladle broth
into a large mug. "Will yer have a cup, lad?" she called to
Blackie, already filling a second mug.

"To be sure I will and it's thanking ye I am," Blackie cried.

"Come on, lass, give Blackie this mug and take yer own,"
Cook said, and went on briskly, "And how about a bacon
buttie, lad? It goes down well with me broth."

"Thanks. I don't mind if I do. It's famished that I am."

"Can yer eat one, Emma luv?"

"No, thanks, Mrs. Turner," Emma replied as she took the mugs from Cook. "I'm not hungry." Cook gave her a sharp look. "Aay, lass, yer don't eat enough. Yer'll never get fat on broth and tea."

Emma carried the mugs carefully to the fireplace and handed one to Blackie without a word, but as she sat down on the other stool and looked up at him a sweet smile drifted over her face, the wariness abating. "Thank ye, mavourneen," he said, returning her smile, and then his eyes narrowed as he became aware of her for the first time since they had met on the moors.

As they sipped the broth in silence, Blackie regarded Emma surreptitiously, endeavoring to conceal the surprise he was feeling. He was stunned really. Now that she had removed the camouflaging scarf and shed the tight old coat, he could see her more clearly and he noted that the girl was not such a starveling creature as he had originally thought. He could not call her beautiful, if he was to measure her by the popular picture-postcard standards of the day. She was no typical Edwardian beauty, all pink marshmallow softness and swooning femininity; neither was she fluffily pretty or pert. But she was arresting and there was something indefinable about her that captured his imagination, held his attention, and made him catch his breath as he studied her. Her face was a perfect oval, with high, rather prominent cheekbones, a straight and slender nose, and a delicately curved mouth that dimpled at the corners when she smiled. Her teeth were small, even, and very white between her pale pink lips, which he noticed held a suggestion of sweetness and vulnerability when she was unguarded. If her smooth forehead was a little too broad it was by no means unattractive, and it was balanced by the widow's-peak hairline that cut into her clear skin so dramatically, and by the exquisitely shaped brows that were sweeping golden-brown arcs above her wide-set eyes. These eyes, which had struck him so forcibly earlier, were indeed as shining and as green as emeralds, set below thick and curling golden-brown lashes that cast gentle dusky shadows on her skin. This was like pale cream silk and as smooth, and without blemish. Her luxuriant russet-brown hair was simply dressed, pulled back smoothly to reveal her face most strikingly. The gleaming hair was plaited and then twisted into a bun that nestled at the nape of her neck and, in the dancing firelight, it seemed like a rich velvet cap threaded through with golden strands.

She is thin and still small, he thought. But he also knew she had some growing to do in the next few years. Blackie could tell from her build that she would be tall and slender when she matured into young womanhood. She was already beginning to flower, for he saw the swell of tender young breasts and shapely hips under the voluminous apron, and long legs that contributed much to her easy gracefulness.

Blackie's innate sense of beauty and fineness was not solely restricted to architecture, art, and artifacts, but extended to women and horses as well. His ardor for women was almost, but not quite, surpassed by his predilection for horses and the races, and he particularly prided himself on his ability to judge horseflesh and single out a thoroughbred when he saw one. Now as he looked at Emma more fully he thought: That's it! She has the look of a thoroughbred! He knew she was a poor girl from the working class, yet her face was that of an aristocrat, for it contained breeding and refinement. It was these aspects that combined to create that indefinable quality he had detected earlier. She was patrician and she had an inbred dignity that was unique. He saw only one feature that betrayed her station in life—her hands. They were small and sturdy, but also chapped and reddened, and the nails were broken and rough. He knew only too well that their ugly condition was caused by the hard work she performed.

He wondered what would become of Emma, and he was filled with a sadness alien to his nature as he contemplated her future. What was there for her in this house and this bleak mill village on the desolate moors? Perhaps she was right to want to try her luck in Leeds. Maybe there she had a chance of living and not merely surviving.

Mrs. Turner interrupted his musings as she bounced over to the fireplace and thrust a plate of sandwiches at him in her bustling manner. "Here's yer bacon butties, lad. Eat 'em now afore Murgatroyd comes down. He's a real nip scrape and likes ter keep us all on a starvation diet. Mean old bug—" She hit back the last word and looked with a degree of apprehension at the door at the top of the stairs.

Turning to Emma, she went on, "Yer don't have ter black-lead the grates this morning. They'll do till tomorrow. But light the fire in the morning room, dust the furniture, run the carpet sweeper over the rug, and set the table for breakfast, like Polly showed yer afore. Then come back and help me with the breakfast. Later yer can clean the dining room, the drawing room, and the library—oh! and pay attention when yer dust that there paneling in the library, lass, straight across with the duster and then down, so that the dust falls along the edge of the molding—and do all the carpets as well. Then yer'll have ter clean Mrs. Fairley's upstairs parlor. When yer've finished that it should be just the right time for yer ter take her breakfast up. Yer can make the beds afore lunch and dust the children's rooms. This afternoon yer can start on the remainder of the ironing. There's the silver ter polish and the best china ter wash . . ." Mrs. Turner paused, somewhat breathless, and drew a piece of crumpled paper from her pocket. She straightened it out and pursed her lips in concentration as she read it.

"Yes, Mrs. Turner," Emma murmured softly, and jumped off the stool. She smoothed down her large apron and waited for further instructions, wondering how she would cope with these multitudinous duties.

Blackie looked at Emma carefully, a small knot of anger twisting in his stomach. He had listened to Cook's recital at first with amusement, but now he was outraged. Nobody could do so much work in one day, least of all Emma, who was only a child. Yet Emma seemed unconcerned as she stood patiently at Mrs. Turner's side. Observing her more closely, Blackie realized that a certain geniality concealed the anxiety in her dark eyes, and her mouth had tightened unconsciously. He glanced quickly at Cook. He knew she was not trying to exploit Emma, for basically she was a kind woman, but he was still appalled. She was using Emma as a workhorse and this truly dismayed him, and he could not resist saying, "That's a heavy load for a little colleen, I am thinking."

Mrs. Turner stared at him with surprise, and flushed. "Aye, lad, it is. But Polly's right badly and there's nowt I can do about it, what with company coming and all. That reminds me, Emma," she went on hurriedly, looking embarrassed, "yer'll have ter prepare the guest room for Mrs. Wainright."

Emma turned to Mrs. Turner, who was studying the piece of paper attentively. "Shall I go upstairs, then?" she asked. Emma was no fool, and whilst she had listened to Cook's allocation of the work without complaint, she was, nonetheless, dismayed. She wouldn't have time to stop for breath if she was to finish by suppertime and she was anxious to get started on her chores.

"Aye, in a tick, lass," Cook said distractedly. "Just let me read these here menus. Maybe I can manage the breakfast meself, after all." She screwed up her eyes and peered at the paper. "Now, let's see. Scrambled eggs and bacon for Master Edwin. Kidneys, bacon, sausages, and fried potatoes for Master Gerald. A kipper for the Squire. Tea, toast, fresh bread, butter, jam, marmalade. That's it and it's enough!" Her head moved violently on her short plump neck and she grumbled, "I don't know why they can't all eat the same thing in this family!"

After a short pause, Mrs. Turner asserted, "Well, I believe I can cope with breakfast, luv. And lunch is simple. Just cold ham, Madeira sauce, mashed potatoes, and apple pie with custard." She turned the paper over and clucked to herself. "I'm thinking yer'll have ter give me a hand with dinner though, lass. Murgatroyd's got some menu suggested. Mmm! He has indeed. Clear chicken soup, saddle of mutton with caper sauce, roasted potatoes and cauliflower with a cheese sauce. Trifle. Wensleydale cheese and biscuits. And a Welsh rarebit for Master Gerald—" She stopped and blinked and glared at the paper. "A Welsh rarebit for Master Gerald indeed!" she repeated in disbelief. "As if he doesn't eat enough all day long as it is. He's getting to be a real little pig, our Master Gerald is. If there's owt I can't stand it's greediness!" she declared to the room at large. Bristling, she pushed the paper into her pocket. "Yer can go up then, luv, and be careful when yer dusting," she cautioned.

"Yes, Mrs. Turner," Emma said evenly, her face devoid of expression. "I expect I'll see yer later, Blackie," she cried, and flashed him a small smile.

"To be sure ye will, mavourneen, for I shall be here for a few days, I am thinking."

"Aye, that's true," Mrs. Turner interjected. "Squire has neglected things around here of late, what with Master Edwin sick since Christmas and the missis so frail these days—I'm glad Mrs. Wainright's coming, she always cheers things up around here—yes, the missis has been out of sorts—" Mrs. Turner stopped midsentence and clamped her mouth shut.

Blackie and Emma followed her gaze, which was directed towards the door at the top of the stairs. A man had entered and was ponderously descending the stairs. Blackie assumed it was the butler.

Murgatroyd was a tall, scrawny man. He had a cadaverous face etched with bitter lines which made his countenance forbidding. Small eyes, so pale they were almost colorless, were set closely together in deep hollow sockets. These porcine eyes appeared to be even smaller than they really were, since they were partially obscured by bushy black brows that sprouted like bristles in a heavy unbroken line across his forehead. He wore black trousers, a black-striped white shirt with a high collar, and a green baize butler's apron. His sleeves were rolled up to reveal long gangling arms, corded with bluish veins.

There was a mournful expression on his face and his eyes gleamed with hostility. "What's all this? What's all this?" he cried in a high-pitched voice as he paused at the bottom of the stairs. "No wonder we're behind today. Gabbing like a lot of magpies. I can see yer in dereliction of yer duty, Cook," he continued pompously. "That lazy, good-for-nowt lass should've been up yonder a good half hour ago, she should that! The Squire's not in the charity business, yer knows. She does little enough work as it is, for what she gets paid. Overly generous the Squire is. Three shillings a week indeed. A princely sum for doing nowt." He scowled at Emma, who was standing near the cupboard under the staircase. "What are yer waiting for? Get up yonder at once!" he snarled.

Emma nodded mutely and picked up the basket, the dustpan, and the carpet sweeper, and made for the stairs. As she edged past Murgatroyd some of the utensils fell out of the basket, including the black-lead powder. The tin rolled across the floor and the lid flew off, spilling the black powder at Murgatroyd's feet. Emma gasped with horror and bent to pick it up. As she did, Murgatroyd swung his arm and struck her hard across her head with the back of his hand.

"Yer stupid little sod!" he screamed. "Can't yer do owt right? Look at the mess yer've made on the clean floor."

Emma reeled from the unexpected and violent blow and

she staggered back, dropping the carpet sweeper and dust-pan. Blackie jumped off the stool in horror. Anger bub-bled up in him. He clenched his fists and stepped towards the butler menacingly. I'll kill him! he thought. I'll kill the bastard!

Cook was already halfway across the kitchen, and as she passed Blackie she pressed him back and shook her head warningly, hissing, "Yer'd best stay out of this, lad. Leave him ter me."

Mrs. Turner faced Murgatroyd like a bantam fighting cock. Her face was purple with rage and the look in her eyes was murderous. She raised her small fist and shook it at him, full of spunk. "Yer nasty bugger!" she cried passionately. "It was only an accident. The lass didn't do it on purpose." She regarded Murgatroyd through blazing eyes. "If I ever sees yer strike that lass again, yer life won't be worth living. I promise yer that. I won't go ter the Squire. Indeed I won't! I'll tell her bloody father! And yer knows what's in store for yer if Big Jack Harte gets his hands on yer. He'll make bloody mashed potatoes out of yer!"

Murgatroyd glowered at Mrs. Turner, but refrained from any response. Blackie, whose eyes had been riveted on Murgatroyd like a hawk's, detected sudden apprehension in him. Why, he's a coward, thought Blackie. He's a blustering poltroon, lily-livered, and full of hot air!

Cook swung away from Murgatroyd with disgust and turned to Emma, who was kneeling on the floor neatly replacing all the items which had fallen from the basket. "Are yer all right, luv?" she asked with concern.

Emma lifted her head and nodded slowly. Her face was like carved white marble and just as immobile. Only her malachite eyes had life, for they burned with an intense hatred for Murgatroyd. "I'll get a wet cloth and clean up the black lead," she said softly, sheathing her anger.

Murgatroyd now turned his attention to Blackie. He pro-ceeded into the room smoothly as if nothing had happened. "O'Neill, right? The navvy from Leeds. The Squire said ter expect yer this morning." He weighed Blackie with those cold eyes and nodded approvingly. "Well, yer looks like a strong bloke. I hopes yer not afraid of work, lad."

It was a considerable effort for Blackie to speak civilly to the butler, but he knew he had no alternative. He swallowed hard and said in the most matter-of-fact tone he could summon, "That's me, to be sure. If ye gives me the details of the work, I'll get to it."

Murgatroyd pulled a scrap of paper from his pocket and handed it to Blackie. "It's all written down here. Yer *can* read, I suppose?"

"I can that."

"Good. Now, as ter yer wages. Fifteen shillings for a week's work and yer board and lodgings while yer here. That's what the Squire instructed." His eyes were full of cunning.

Blackie bit back a knowing smile. Why, he's trying to swindle me, the crafty divil, he thought, but said, "No, sir! One guinea was the price that the Squire arranged with me in Leeds. And one guinea it is, *Mister* Murgatroyd."

The butler's eyes opened wide in surprise. "Yer don't expect me ter believe that the Squire himself came ter see yer, do yer, lad? His agent in Leeds always deals with such trifling matters," he declared.

Regarding Murgatroyd acutely, Blackie recognized immediately that the man's amazement was genuine. His handsome Irish face broke into a broad smile. "Faith and sure it was himself that came to see me and me Uncle Pat. We own a small building business, ye see. He engaged me to do the repairs here, and me Uncle Pat to work at the mills and the newspaper offices in Leeds. And I am certain about the price, to be sure I am. Perhaps ye should be after asking the Squire again. There's been a mistake, I am thinking." Blackie chuckled inwardly, for the butler was obviously not only flustered but vexed by the turn of events.

"Indeed, I will speak ter the Squire!" Murgatroyd snapped. "He must have forgotten what he arranged with yer. He's more important matters ter be thinking about! Well, get on with yer, lad. The yardman's in the stables. He'll show yer where everything is, and yer room above the stables, where yer'll be sleeping."

Murgatroyd dismissed Blackie with a curt nod and sat down at the kitchen table. "I'll be having me tea and a bacon buttie," he called to Cook, who threw him a nasty glance. She picked up the knife and began to attack the loaf of bread with great ferocity and from the expression on her face it was apparent that she wished it was Murgatroyd she was demolishing.

Blackie strode over to his sack and hoisted it on his shoulder. Emma was collecting her cleaning materials together at the foot of the stairs. "I'll see ye tonight, mavourneen," he said softly, and smiled.

"Aye, if I've finished me work by then," she responded glumly. Seeing the disturbed look that flashed onto his face, she smiled. "Oh, I'll be finished. Don't worry about me. Ta'rar, Blackie." He watched her disappear up the stairs before he opened the kitchen door and went out into the cold morning air, his mind full of disturbing thoughts about the occupants of Fairley Hall, and most especially Emma, who was so defenseless in this strange house.

Emma paused in the small upstairs lobby that adjoined the kitchen staircase and put down the cleaning utensils she was carrying. She eased the basket on her arm and leaned against the wall. Her face was drawn and her head ached from the stunning blow, and she was seething with resentment. Murgatroyd never lost an opportunity to mistreat her. It seemed to her that he enjoyed cuffing her, and even though he continually snarled at Polly, he was not as brutal with her. His reprehensible display of temper a few minutes ago had been nothing unusual and she knew he would have walloped her again if Cook had not interceded. He'll hit me once too often, she thought grimly, and then I'll show him.

She adjusted the heavy basket on her arm, picked up the other items, and walked slowly down the corridor, her senses alert, listening acutely for any untoward noises in the house. But there were no sounds, for the family was still asleep. The corridor was filled with murky light and smelled faintly of wax and dry dust and a peculiar mustiness that bespoke windows long shuttered and cloistered, airless rooms. She wished she was back in the kitchen, which was the only cheerful spot in Fairley Hall.

In spite of its grandness and rich furnishings, the house filled Emma with a nameless terror from which she wanted always to flee. There was something fearful and oppressive about the chill dark rooms with their lofty ceilings and heavy furniture, the immense halls, and the winding corridors that drifted endlessly through the house. It was a place of hushed silences, seclusion, and hidden mysteries, a secretive house redolent of unhappiness and decay. And yet for all that quiescence there was a sheathed turbulence everywhere, contained but ominous and stealthily waiting to break loose.

Emma was shivering as she glided across the rich Turkey carpet in the vast front entrance hall and pushed open the double doors of the morning room. She stood on the threshold and nervously glanced around. Meager fingers of gauzy sunlight fought their way into the room through the tall windows, heavily curtained in white silk and draped with thick blue velvet hangings. Dark portraits gazed down dolorously from the dim blue flocked-velvet walls and Emma imagined, absurdly, that their ancient eyes followed her as she crept towards the fireplace, squeezing past the many pieces of ponderous Victorian furniture made of a mahogany so dark they looked black in the gloomy light. The only sound was the plaintive ticking of the clock on the carved black marble mantelshelf.

Emma deposited the cleaning equipment on the floor and knelt down in front of the fireplace. She dusted off the traces of ash and filled it with the paper spills and chips of wood Murgatroyd had placed in a pile on the hearth, along with the matches. She lit the paper and when the chips took hold she opened the brass scuttle and lifted out small pieces of coal. These she gingerly placed on the burning wood. The coal did not catch light immediately, so she lifted her apron and fanned the fire until it began to blaze.

The monotonous ticking of the clock reminded Emma she had little time to waste. She cleaned the room with efficiency and speed, in spite of the cumbersome and cluttered arrangements of furniture. When she had accomplished this, she took a fine white Irish linen tablecloth from the sideboard drawer and placed it over the great circular table. She arranged four place settings of silver and ran back to the sideboard for the dishes. As she was taking out four blue-and-white Crown Derby plates she tensed and held herself very still. Her neck prickled and gooseflesh sprang up on her arms, for she knew she was no longer alone. She sensed rather than heard another presence in the room. She turned slowly on her haunches. Squire Fairley was standing in the doorway watching her intently.

She stood up quickly and dropped a small curtsy. "Good morning, Squire," she mumbled timorously, clutching the plates firmly to her breasts, so that they would not rattle in her trembling hands. Her legs shook, although more from surprise than fear.

"Morning. Where's Polly?"

"She's badly, Squire."

"I see," he said laconically.

His eyes bored into her as he regarded her with the utmost concentration. He frowned and a puzzled expression settled on his face. After a prolonged silence, during which Emma stared at him mesmerized, he nodded tersely, turned smartly on his heels, and left. The banging of the library door as he slammed it harshly behind him made her start in surprise. It was only then that she breathed with relief and finished setting the table for the family's breakfast.

TEN

Adam Fairley stood in the middle of the library and pressed his hands to his face. He was tired, exhausted, in fact, for he had slept badly yet again. His insomnia was nothing new. He seemed to be cursed with it these days, or rather, these interminable nights. Even when he resorted to drinking five, sometimes six large ports after dinner, and vintage port at that, the wine did not act as a sedative. He would sleep for several hours, a drugged and heavy stupor descending upon him, but then he would awaken suddenly in the early hours, perspiring or shivering, depending on his nightmares, his mind a turmoil of painfully dredged-up memories and analytical assessments of his life, which did not please him. It had not for a long time.

He walked up and down the room slowly, lost in contemplation, a compact, trimly built man of about six feet, with an attractive, intelligent face, well modeled and sensitive, which was pale and drawn today, and etched with fatigue. His fine eyes were grayish blue in color and intensely brilliant, almost incandescent, and extraordinarily lucid, filled with hidden depths and the suggestion of spirituality. But today they were red-rimmed and the light in them was dimmed. The most surprising feature in his somewhat ascetic face was his mouth, which was exceedingly sensual, although the sensuality was

generally repressed and disguised by the austere expression
that constantly played around his lips. His light brown hair
had a blondish cast to it, was straight and finely textured. He
wore it brushed loosely across his shapely head, slightly
longer than was the vogue. He had an aversion to the po-
maded hairstyles that were currently the mode for gentlemen
of fashion. Consequently, a forelock of hair continually fell
down over his wide brow, and he had developed a nervous
habit of pushing it back quickly. He did this now as he paced
the floor.

Oddly enough, this impatient gesture never seemed to
create dishevelment in him, for Adam Fairley was one of those
men who looked eternally well groomed, no matter what the
circumstance or whatever activity occupied him. His appearance was faultless. He was always superbly attired, befitting
the occasion, with the flair usually attributed to a dandy, and
yet he was not flashy in the least.

His Savile Row suits were so impeccably cut, so beautifully
styled and made with such perfect precision and unerring
tailoring, they were the envy of his cohorts in London and his
colleagues in the wool trade in Leeds and Bradford. For the
most part, they were of fine cloths from his own mills, or
from those of his friends—woolens and worsteds from the
great looms of Yorkshire, undisputed center of the world's
woolen business and of which Adam Fairley was the undisputed king. All in all, Adam Fairley was the quintessence of
sartorial elegance. He disliked anything shoddy or crude, and
his weakness for fine clothes was one of his few indulgences.
Conversely, it never occurred to him that the house in which
he lived was singularly lacking in beauty. He rarely noticed
it.

After a few minutes, he ceased pacing and walked across
the room to the enormous carved ebony desk. He sat down in
the dark wine-red leather chair and stared dully at his engagement diary. His eyes were scratchy and burning from
lack of sleep, his body ached, and his head was throbbing not
only from fatigue but from the wearisome thoughts that beset
him. He felt there was nothing in his life of any worth. No
joy, no love, no warmth, no companionship, not even any
interests into which he could channel his energies. There was
nothing . . . nothing but endless lonely days stretching slowly

and inexorably into endless lonelier nights, day after day, year after year.

As he reposed, all animation slipped away and his face took on gauntness. Violet smudges bruised his cheeks below his eyes, were strong evidence of the ravages of the night before, of the nocturnal festering of his soul, the countless hours he had paced his bedroom, racked with an anguish he found unendurable. And yet it was a boyish face, sorrowful and weary as it was, and Adam Fairley looked much younger than his forty-four years.

My life is a damnable mess, he thought with dissatisfaction. *What's the point of living? I have nothing to live for. I wish I had the courage to put a bullet through my head and end it all forever.*

This thought so shocked him he sat bolt upright in the chair and gripped its arms. He looked at his hands. They were shaking. Even in his worst moments, which had been not infrequent lately, he had never before thought of taking his own life. In the past he had always equated suicide with cowardice, yet now he admitted to himself that perhaps, in an oblique way, this act did take a kind of courage. It occurred to him, as he sat engulfed in melancholy introspection, that only the stupid never contemplated suicide. *Surely most men of intelligence have considered it at some time or other?* he asked himself. For he realized, with a sickening sense of futility, that knowledge of life and the human condition inevitably brought disillusionment and despair. For him it had also brought a sense of helplessness, which he found increasingly intolerable.

In spite of his wealth and position, Adam Fairley was a tormented man who had been bitterly disappointed in life. He no longer expected happiness, but he did crave contentment and, at the very least, peace of mind. And yet he could find no respite from his bitter loneliness and the desolation in his heart, all the more unbearable because it was, to a great extent, of his own creation. Adam's dissatisfaction and searing disillusionment sprang from his betrayal of himself, his ambitions, his dreams, and his ideals. It was the failure of intellect and of moral conviction.

Adam lifted his head wearily and looked around the library slowly, as if seeing it after a long journey. This was a baronial and impressive room, with its immense high-flung ceiling and grand proportions, its paneled walls of bleached oak, its collection of scholarly books, and its handsome antiques. Fine Persian rugs threw rafts of vibrant red and dark blue jewel tones across the polished wood floor, and a selection of rare hunting prints graced the walls not covered with the many bookshelves. A comfortable Chesterfield sofa, upholstered in a leather the color of tawny ruby wine, was positioned next to the intricately carved oak fireplace, along with several deep wing chairs of dark wine velvet. Nearby, an ebony library table was heaped with newspapers, journals, and illustrated magazines, and in one corner a black-walnut chest held a silver tray of crystal decanters filled with port, brandy, sherry, whiskey, and gin, as well as lead crystal Waterford glasses that glittered in the faint gray light.

The library had never been quite as ponderous as the other rooms in Fairley Hall, and Adam had always fought his wife's desire to overload it with bric-a-brac and "folderols," as he disdainfully called her other decorative trinkets. In consequence, the room had a degree of graciousness and dignity, albeit a dignity that was masculine. Like his bedroom, which was somewhat more austere, it perfectly reflected his character and his tastes. Adam spent most of his time in the library, unless they were entertaining guests, which was rare these days, and it had become his haven, where he thankfully retreated to read and meditate, undisturbed in his solitariness.

He took out his pocket watch and looked at the time. It was almost seven-thirty and he had seen no sign of the servants, except for the forlorn maid cleaning the morning room. Cursing the housekeeper's absence, he tugged on the bell pull and glared with irritation at the cold and empty grate. As he waited for Murgatroyd to appear, the photogravure of himself in the dress uniform of the Fourth Hussars caught his eye. He turned and bent to look at it more fully, pursing his lips as he scrutinized it intently. He smiled ruefully. What a face! So full of anticipation, expectation, and yes, even happiness. He hardly recognized it as himself. He laughed ironically, and thought: Oh, careless, foolish youth! How little do we know what's in store for us, when we set out so valiantly to conquer life. And that's probably just as well! he decided.

Murgatroyd knocked on the door and entered the room,

interrupting Adam's thoughts. "Good morning, Murgatroyd,"
he said in his cool and naturally resonant voice.

The butler advanced towards him smoothly, adjusting his
black jacket. "Good morning, Squire. I trust yer slept well,
sir. Fine day it is today, for yer journey ter Leeds. Sunny and
dry and hardly no wind at all. Cook'll be ready with yer
breakfast shortly. She's preparing yer a kipper, sir." This was
said with such obsequiousness Adam winced and averted his
face, so that Murgatroyd would not see the look of disgust in
his eyes.

When Adam made no response, the butler went on, "Is
there owt else yer'll be wanting, sir, besides the kipper, I
mean?"

Unctuous fool, Adam thought, now looking at Murgatroyd
fully. "A fire would be desirable, I think."

"Begging yer pardon, sir?" Murgatroyd seemed flustered.
He glanced swiftly at the empty grate and condemned Emma
under his breath.

"A fire, Murgatroyd!" Adam repeated. "It's cold enough in
here to freeze the balls off a brass monkey—" Adam stopped
and coughed behind his hand, a flicker of amusement touching his eyes as he noted Murgatroyd's discomfort. "Ahem!
Well, let me put it this way. The atmosphere in this room is
comparable only to the Arctic this morning. It seems to me
that I employ enough servants to run a battleship and yet it
appears that I cannot get a few simple amenities." Annoyed
as he was, this was said in Adam's usual self-contained way,
for he rarely displayed temperament with anyone, least of all
the servants.

Bloody hell! He's in a right proper mood this morning,
Murgatroyd thought, and said in an oily voice, "I'm ever so
sorry, sir, I am indeed. Polly's badly and the other lass was
late. I don't know, if I'm not standing over 'em every minute
of the day these lasses do nowt. I told yon lass ter light the
fire in here ages ago, I did th—"

"What's wrong with you, man? Are you crippled?" Adam
interjected softly, but his eyes were like icy pools.

A startled expression flashed across Murgatroyd's dolorous
face. "No! No, of course not, sir. I'll attend ter it right
sharpish, Squire," he said hurriedly, bowing subserviently
several times in a jerky fashion.

"Yes. Do!"

"Right away, Squire." He bowed again and backed out of the room.

"Oh, Murgatroyd!"

"Yes, sir?"

"Did the navvy arrive from Leeds? Young O'Neill."

"Yes, sir. Came by this morning, early, he did. I've given him the list of repairs."

"Good. See he has everything he needs to do the job right. And make sure he has the facilities of the kitchen. Plenty of food and the like."

Murgatroyd nodded, surprised at the Squire's concern about a mere laborer. It both baffled and interested him. "Yes, sir. Yer can rely on me, as always. I'll handle it. By the by, Squire, what shall I be paying him for his week's work?" His crafty eyes did not leave Adam's face.

Adam frowned. "I told you last night he was to receive one guinea for his work. Is your memory failing you, man?"

"No, sir. It must've slipped me mind, that's all."

"I see. Well, no harm done. In the meantime, I would appreciate it if you would attend to the fire immediately. I am rapidly turning into a block of ice. And I would like a cup of hot tea, Murgatroyd, if that's not too difficult to accomplish."

The sarcastic edge to Adam's voice did not go unnoticed by the butler. "Right away, sir," he said, bowing. He turned and scurried out, full of venom for Cook and the maids, and not so kindly disposed towards the Squire either. All that there tippling in the dead of night, that's what makes *him* liverish, he mumbled under his breath as he closed the door softly behind him.

Adam gazed at the door through narrowed eyes. Murgatroyd was developing a peculiar tendency to forget conversations about money, especially when related to wages for the outside workers who came to the Hall from time to time. The butler was too parsimonious by far and it bothered him. Also, Adam, who thought Murgatroyd was an ignorant man, suspected that the butler was a tyrant in his own domain downstairs.

He shook his head in bafflement and turned again to his youthful portrait. He did not need to see that face to be reminded of his abandoned military career. It had been much on his mind recently. He had come to believe that his life would have been so very different if he had followed his lodestar, and not turned away from it, out of loyalty to his father. It was too late for regrets, but, nevertheless, he had them.

As he stood there in the dark cold room a mental image of himself as a youth flashed into his mind's eye. He saw the thin intense boy he had been, home from Eton for the holidays, announcing to his father, with a fervency bordering on fanaticism, his intention of entering the army. His father had not only been flabbergasted but strongly, and vehemently, opposed to the idea, which he refused to countenance.

Adam recalled how unwavering his determination had been, how his dogged persistence and all manner of persuasive tactics had eventually convinced his father that he was sincere. The old Squire had finally succumbed and grudgingly agreed to let him take the entrance examination for Sandhurst, which he had passed with no problem. The old man really behaved quite decently, Adam now thought, and with a certain fondness, as he remembered his father.

The old Squire, Richard Fairley, had been a hearty, blustering Yorkshireman, one of the most powerful and richest industrialists in the North of England, with a gambler's instinct for the main chance, a shrewd eye for business, and a mind as sharp as a steel blade. Once Adam had proved himself to be an exemplary cadet at the military academy, he had thrown all of his power and money behind his son. When Adam expressed a desire to join a cavalry regiment, being an incomparable horseman, Richard Fairley had left no stone unturned to accomplish this end. Through his wealth and his political connections he had obtained a place for Adam in the Fourth Hussars. He could easily afford the expense of two hundred pounds a year a commission in the cavalry entailed, along with the cost and upkeep of two horses and a string of polo ponies, which he had bought for his younger son. Being an astute observer of human nature, the old Squire had come to recognize that Adam had all the natural attributes of character a soldier required. He was ideally suited to military life, for he had a keen mind, great discipline, a sense of honor, and courage. Something of a romantic, Adam thirsted for adventure in foreign parts and, as an imperialist devoted to the goals and ambitions of Queen Victoria, he longed to serve his country, and his Queen, in the rapidly expanding Empire.

Adam had just gained his commission in the Fourth Hussars when his elder brother Edward had been tragically drowned in a boating accident. The old Squire had been brokenhearted. He also believed that the touchstone of a man's character was dedication to duty. In no uncertain terms, and in spite of his understanding of Adam's basic temperament, he had informed his younger son that his duty was to return to Yorkshire and take Edward's place in the family business enterprises, which were huge.

This morning Adam could hear his father's voice echoing back to him through the passages of time. "No more galavanting around on horses in fancy uniforms, quelling the natives in godforsaken foreign regions," he had blustered, valiantly striving to subdue and disguise his raw grief for Edward. It was a grief that had been painfully apparent to Adam, who had been reluctantly compelled to resign his commission. He was bitterly disappointed, but he had behaved in the only way he knew how, as an officer and a gentleman, bound by codes of honor and obligation to family. He had accepted his filial duty with grace, not recognizing at the time that his ready acquiescence to his father's command was a mistake that was irrevocable. He knew it now. It was a fact that haunted him. As he walked back to his desk Murgatroyd knocked on the door and hurried in carrying a coal scuttle. "Yer tea'll be coming up in a minute, sir," he said.

"Thank you, Murgatroyd. I would appreciate it if you would light the lamps at that end of the room." As he spoke Adam struck a match and lit the lamp on his desk and then pulled his engagement diary towards him. He looked over his appointments with a disinterest that clearly reflected his ennui. He had a board meeting at the *Yorkshire Morning Gazette* in Leeds, the newspaper company of which he was the controlling shareholder. Later there was luncheon with a cloth buyer from London, one of his most important customers. Not such a heavy day after all. He would have time to stop at the mill in Fairley on his way to Leeds, to speak to Wilson, the manager, about his son Gerald's progress. He stifled a sigh. Business was beginning to pall on him. There were no challenges anymore. Now that he thought about it, there never had been really. He had no interest in the pursuit of money; in fact, he had never harbored any ambitions for great wealth or power. His success was his father's success, and his grandfather's before him, and he had only reaped the rewards. Certainly Adam Fairley had increased the fortune he had inherited, but to him it seemed as if this had happened through fortuitous accidents rather than any true brilliance on his part. In this he did himself an injustice, for he was not without a certain business acumen that, although it was less obvious than his father's, was, nonetheless, just as trenchant. He was known to be a tough negotiator in spite of his gentle soft-spoken manner, and some of his associates even considered him to be as calculating an opportunist as his father.

He pushed the diary away and ran his hand through his hair with his usual quick impatience. The fire was now burning brightly, and although its warmth had not yet fully permeated the vast room, the sight of the blazing flames flying up the chimney cheered him and the chilled feeling that had previously enveloped him was beginning to ebb away. The library had lost its shadowy gloominess. Although its style was basically severe and there was a paucity of bric-a-brac, the room had a comfortable ambiance that denoted masculinity, solidness, lineage, and old money rather than wealth newly acquired.

Murgatroyd had busied himself at the fireplace, then paused at Adam's desk. He cleared his throat. Adam looked up from the newspaper company's annual balance sheet he was perusing, "Yes, Murgatroyd, what is it?"

"I was wondering, sir, should I have the maid prepare the same room for Mrs. Wainright? The Gray Room in the main wing? She likes that there room, Squire, I knows that. And I always wants Mrs. Wainright ter be real comfortable like."

For once, the butler's fawning attitude failed to irritate Adam. He scarcely noticed it in his surprise. He stared at Murgatroyd, for a moment nonplussed. And then he remembered. In his preoccupation with his own problems he had completely forgotten that his sister-in-law was arriving this afternoon. "Yes, yes, that will be fine, Murgatroyd," Adam conceded, and added quickly, "And please find out what happened to my tea, and let me know when the children come down for breakfast. I will wait for them this morning." Adam dismissed the butler with a curt nod.

"Certainly, sir." A vengeful look settled on Murgatroyd's face the moment he left the library and hurried down to the kitchen to give Emma a piece of his mind and the back of his hand. She was undermining him, dillydallying with that tea.

Adam opened the center drawer of his desk and frantically

searched for Olivia's letter to Adele, realizing that this malaise of his spirits and his introspection were making him
extremely forgetful. He must pull himself out of his mental
dejection, which was becoming a permanent condition, or he
would drive himself insane. *As insane as that woman upstairs*.

Mostly, Adam resisted the temptation to conjecture about
his wife's mental stability, dismissing her odd behavior of the
last few years as a combination of female vapors, general
depression, hypochondria, and the peculiar vagueness that
had always been predominant in her character. She was full
of strange fears and delusions, but these, too, he had concluded to be mere female imaginings. He wondered now,
with a small stab of guilt, if his attitude had been engendered
by a sense of self-protection, for he never wanted to admit to
himself that Adele might conceivably be losing her mind. As
long as he did not think about it, he did not have to face that
reality.

Now he faced it, recognizing that at times she had been
like mad Ophelia, wandering dazedly around the upstairs
corridors in bewilderment, a glazed expression on her face,
her hair in disarray, the floating chiffon peignoir she favored
enveloping her like a nimbus. Some months ago, on a business trip to London, he had described her behavior to his
friend Andrew Melton, a doctor of some renown, who had
listened patiently, and had suggested that Adele be examined
by a doctor in Leeds or, better still, himself. Adam had been
prepared to take Adele to London at once. But on his return
to Fairley he had been astonished and relieved to find that
her strangeness had evaporated and she seemed perfectly
normal ever since. Frail, yes, but not suffering from delusions.
He broke out in a cold sweat, for he knew instinctively, and
with a crushing sense of dread, that the fragile cocoon of
sanity that surrounded her might shatter at any moment.

Now he obstinately pushed away this disturbing thought
and glanced at Olivia Wainright's letter. She would arrive at
Leeds station on the three-thirty train from London. He
would be able to meet her train immediately after his luncheon. He turned his attention to the balance sheet and
made a few notations on the side, and then went through
other business documents he had neglected and which needed
his immediate attention.

As he worked on the papers Adam was unaware that his

face had changed quite perceptibly. The haggard look had miraculously disappeared, and his eyes had brightened and held lambent lights. All Adam knew, as he worked, was that his spirits had lifted unexpectedly, and quite inexplicably. There was a diffident tapping on the door. Adam lifted his head and called, "Come in," shifting slightly in his chair to observe the door. It opened slowly and Emma entered. She was carrying a cup of tea on a small silver tray and she hesitated in the doorway.

"It's yer tea, Squire," she murmured. Her voice was hardly audible. She dropped a half curtsy as she spoke and almost spilled the tea. Her solemn green eyes regarded him steadily, but she made no move to bring him the tea and Adam thought she appeared afraid to approach the desk.

He smiled at her faintly. "Put it over there, on the table by the fireplace," he said quietly. She did as she was told, deposited the tray, and hurried back to the door. She dropped a curtsy again and turned to leave.

"Who told you to do that? To curtsy every time you see me."

Emma looked back at him, a startled expression crossing her face, and her eyes, widening, betrayed what seemed to him to be sheer fright.

She swallowed and said timidly, "Murgatroyd, Squire." She paused and looked at him with great directness and asked in a stronger voice, "Don't I do it proper like?"

He bit back a smile. "Yes, you do. But it irritates me enormously to have you all bobbing up and down constantly. You don't have to curtsy to me. I'm not King Edward, you know. I told Polly to refrain from doing it, and I assumed she had informed Murgatroyd of my wishes. Obviously she did not. You may tell Murgatroyd what I have said and don't do it again."

"Yes, Squire."

"What's your name, girl?"

"Emma, Squire."

He nodded thoughtfully. "You may go, Emma, and thank you again for the tea."

Emma started to curtsy automatically, but corrected herself quickly and flew out of the room. As she descended the stairs to the kitchen she laughed softly to herself, and it was a grim laugh. Did he think she was daft, trying to soft-soap her like that! Telling her she didn't have to curtsy. It was no skin off her nose either way and, whatever he did, she would never change her mind about him. Never. As long as she lived.

Adam crossed the floor to the fireplace and Emma's face stayed with him. It struck a chord in his memory, as it had done when he first noticed her earlier that morning, but one so hazy and nebulous he could not grasp it. She must be from the village, yet she did not resemble any of the villagers and he had known every family all of his life. The puzzled frown returned to his handsome face as he probed around in his mind, attempting to revive the memory to full consciousness. It remained fleeting and elusive. There was a purity and innocence and nobility in the girl's young face, and it was beautifully articulated, and those eyes, filled with a piercing and brilliant Arctic greenness, were the most dazzling eyes he had ever seen. He shook his head, vaguely irritated with himself. She reminded him of someone but he was damned if he could remember who it was.

He picked up the cup and saucer and drank the tea quickly before it became cold. He was warming himself in front of the fire when there was another knock on the door, the same light tapping as before, but this time it was much firmer. At his bidding the door opened and Emma was standing there once more. She seemed less hesitant, and Adam looked at her intently, as the memory became strangely alive again, yet still unformed.

For a brief instant their eyes met and locked and neither of them seemed able to look away, and Adam thought with amazement and sudden comprehension: Why, the girl's not afraid of me. She hates me! He recoiled from her gaze. Emma thought: He's a mean and wicked man, living off the toil of others, and her young and trembling heart hardened against him more resolutely.

Her voice was strong and cold as she said, "Murgatroyd said ter tell yer the children are waiting for yer in the morning room, Squire." She gripped the side of the door tightly to steady herself, for she was dizzy from the second punishing blow she had just received from Murgatroyd's cruel hand.

Adam nodded, aware that he had an inflexible enemy in this strange yet attractive girl, although he could not conceive why this should be so. She retreated quietly without another glance and Adam noticed that she had not had to correct herself from curtsying, The girl learned fast and she was unafraid, and with his lightning insight he recognized unequivocally, and without benefit of knowing her, that she had enormous pride and a fierce and determined will. As he dwelt on this revealing discovery, the evanescent memory returned, vague yet insistent, hovering like a transitory ghost on the edge of his consciousness. But as he tried to grasp it firmly, to bring it into focus, it slipped away. After a short time he shrugged with resignation and then dismissed it as unimportant. He had more urgent matters which needed his attention.

ELEVEN

A few moments later, Adam strode into the morning room, his manner brisk, his face composed. As he entered the room he collided with one of the fragile tables. He grabbed it, along with the Meissen shepherdess that reclined on its surface, just before both crashed to the floor, and as he righted them he swore under his breath with mingled irritation and frustration.

Glancing at the butler, who was standing by the sideboard waiting to serve them breakfast, he said in a quiet voice, "Please remove this table later, Murgatroyd. Find another place for it. I don't care where, just get it out of the way. I'm always tripping over it."

"Yes, sir," Murgatroyd said, arranging the lids on the numerous silver chafing dishes.

Adam sat down and regarded his two children, who were already seated. "Good morning," he said pleasantly. Gerald made a mumbled response, but Edwin pushed his chair back, stood up swiftly, and came to Adam's chair. He kissed him lightly on the cheek and said with the sunniest of smiles, "Good morning, Father."

Adam returned his younger son's smile and patted his shoulder affectionately. His disillusionment with his life and his marriage was equaled only by his disappointment in his children, although he did have a genuine fondness for Edwin, who was the nicer of the two. He also bore a striking physical resemblance to his father.

"How are you, old chap?" Adam asked gently. "Feeling better, I hope." Observing Edwin's pale face, he went on quickly, "But we have to get some color into those cheeks, Edwin. I think you should go riding this afternoon, or at least take a walk on the moors. Blow the cobwebs away. Right, old chap?"

"Yes, Father," Edwin said, sitting down and shaking out his linen serviette carefully. "I wanted to go out yesterday, but Mother said it was too cold for me." His face, surprisingly mature for a fifteen-year-old, lit up in anticipation. "Shall I tell Mother *you* said I could go out today?"

"Don't worry about that, Edwin. I will tell your mother myself," Adam answered crisply, thinking that Adele would turn the boy into a hypochondriac like herself if he did not watch her. Adam now felt he had been remiss of late, in neglecting Edwin as he had. He resolved to keep a tighter rein on him and remove the boy from his mother's sickly and sickening influence.

Murgatroyd meanwhile had carried a silver platter to the table. He was standing by Adam's side and he presented the kipper to him with an ostentatious and ridiculous flourish. "It looks right delicious, Squire. I'm sure yer'll enjoy it. Shall I serve it now, sir?"

Adam gave his assent and repressed a feeling of rising nausea as he looked at the platter. The strong odor of the smoked fish made his stomach lurch, and he regretted the port he had drunk so conscientiously the night before. While Murgatroyd served the fish, Adam picked up the silver teapot and poured himself a cup of tea, adding sugar and milk absently, hoping desperately the tea would quell his biliousness into submission. He turned to Murgatroyd. "Thank you. The boys can serve themselves this morning, since you are short of help. You can go about your other duties, Murgatroyd."

"Thank yer, Squire." The butler returned the platter to the sideboard and backed out of the room. Gerald scraped back his ornate Victorian chair unceremoniously and rushed to the sideboard, followed more slowly and sedately by Edwin, who displayed a decorousness at all times.

When they returned to the table Adam stared with enormous distaste at the large portions of food piled upon Gerald's plate, and the nausea swamped him again, so that he felt faint and slightly dizzy. Why, the boy had become a positive glutton. He decided to have a word with Gerald privately later. His seventeen-year-old son was far too gross, and his appearance, in combination with his crude and raucous manner, affronted Adam whenever he set eyes on him. For Gerald's body was a mass of blubber, totally devoid of any sharp contrasts or hard angles, a roly-poly body thickly covered with layer upon layer of fat, as dense as a whale's. A dollop of lard, thought Adam grimly. He corrected himself. A mountain of lard. He winced.

"How are you progressing at the mill, Gerald? Is it still going well?" Adam waited impatiently as his elder son masticated his food laboriously, eventually swallowing it in one gulp after what seemed like an interminable time to Adam.

Gerald wiped his epicene mouth on his serviette unhurriedly, and with great deliberation, and said finally, "Yes, it is, Father. Wilson is very pleased with my progress. He says I have a real aptitude for the wool business, and I'm enjoying it. He says there's no sense keeping me on the mill floor, learning all the different processes. He thinks I know enough and he's moving me into his office today," he finished in a conceited tone. Gerald's round ruddy face was bland enough, but his dark brown eyes betrayed a shifty cunning.

"That is good news, Gerald. I'm delighted," Adam said, although he was not especially surprised. Gerald had always been predisposed to entering the business and he had tremendous energy and a capacity for hard work, in spite of all that monstrous weight he carried around. He was also exceedingly avaricious, which Adam found deplorable. In fact, he had lately come to believe that money was Gerald's most consuming passion, even taking precedence over food. He considered both to be regrettable.

Adam cleared his throat and continued thoughtfully, "I shall be talking to Wilson myself later. I intend to stop at the mill on my way to Leeds. I have quite a few appointments to keep there today, before I meet your Aunt Olivia's train. You do know she is coming to stay with us for several months, don't you?"

"Yes, Father," Gerald said tonelessly, patently disinterested in his aunt's arrival. He attacked the remainder of his breakfast with renewed and unrestrained vigor.

But Edwin's face immediately lost the forlorn look which had so recently washed over it. "I'm so glad Aunt Olivia is coming to stay, Father," he announced excitedly. "She's such a good egg. A real sport!"

Adam smiled. He would not have chosen those particular terms to describe Olivia Wainright, but understanding what his son meant, he nodded in agreement. He picked up the *Times*, which was folded next to his plate, and opened it, the pages rustling as he began to read the day's news.

Silence descended upon the room. The only sounds were the crackling of the logs, the faintly hissing gas jets, and the gentle tinkling of silver against china as the boys ate their breakfasts. They knew better than to chatter needlessly when their father was engrossed in the *Times*. This presented no problems since Gerald had little in common with Edwin, who had long been alienated from him.

"A damnable mess! A damnable mess!" Adam suddenly exploded behind his paper, his resonant voice echoing around the room and breaking the silence. Unaccustomed to seeing their father angry, or hearing him raise his voice, his sons stared at him in startled surprise.

Finally Edwin ventured a question. "What's wrong, Father? Has something in the paper disturbed you?" he asked.

"The Free Trade Question! Parliament has only just reassembled and they are already off to a running start with that one. It's going to be a damnable mess, you mark my words. It will bring Balfour down, I am sure. And his government. Maybe not now, but certainly in the not too distant future, if this ridiculous nonsense continues."

Edwin cleared his throat. His light gray-blue eyes, so like his father's, were alive with intelligence in his gentle face. He said, "Yes, I think you are absolutely right, Father. I read in yesterday's paper that Winston Churchill is strongly opposed to the Free Trade Bill, and you know how shrewd he is. He is fighting it hard and I am sure it will be a troublesome time for the government, just as you say."

Adam's surprise was apparent. "I didn't know you were interested in politics, Edwin. This is something new, isn't it?"

Edwin opened his mouth to speak, but Gerald sniggered

and interjected scornfully, "Churchill! Who cares what he thinks? He's only Member for Oldham anyway. A Lancashire mill town. If he follows in his father's footsteps his political career will be as short-lived as Lord Randolph's. Churchill is a braggart and a flash in the pan!"

Adam coughed behind his hand. When he spoke his voice was cold but quiet as always. "I don't agree with you, Gerald. And I think Edwin is quite right. Winston Churchill is a keen young politician who knows what the issues are all about. You know, he made quite a name for himself in the South African war, with that escape of his from the Boers. Became a hero to the public, in fact, and when he entered politics his maiden speech was well received. He's been doing extremely well ever since, and I have a sneaking suspicion that we have not heard the last of young Winston. I believe he is going to be an important man in this country one day. But really, all that is irrelevant. You attacked Churchill in the most spurious way, but carefully ignored Edwin's actual point, which is that the government is going to be in serious trouble over the Free Trade Bill. Edwin was echoing my own sentiments."

Gerald, who had been listening acutely, looked as if he was about to make a caustic retort. But he thought better of it, stood up, and took his plate to the sideboard to serve himself more food. A malicious gleam entered his dark brown eyes and his posture was arrogant as he moved ponderously from dish to dish.

But Edwin's face was radiant as he turned his shining eyes on his father and smiled. He had been vindicated for once and he had found an unexpected ally in his father.

Adam smiled kindly at his younger son. "Do you understand what the Free Trade Question is all about, Edwin?" Adam asked.

"I think so, Father. Isn't it about taxing food and other goods?"

"Yes. But it's also a little more complicated than that. You see, the Protectionists, led by Chamberlain, are trying to persuade the government to abandon the system of Free Trade and cheap food which this country has thrived upon for so long. They want to impose tariffs and taxation on all goods to protect the English manufacturers against so-called foreign competition." Adam paused, and then continued. "It might make some sense if we were in a slump, but our industries

are enjoying a ruddy health right now. That's one reason why
Chamberlain's bill is preposterous, as a great majority of us
realize. It would be disastrous for the country. First of all,
everyone fears it would mean dearer food. That would not
affect us, of course, or people of our station in life. However,
it is a very real fear to the working-class housewife, who sees
the price of meat and bread increasing. Apart from this, there
is a general belief, especially among Liberals, that free trade
is the only way to preserve international peace and understanding. There's an old saying that comes to mind, Edwin,
'If goods do not cross frontiers, armies will.' Churchill understands these essential points. He has said time and time again
that the Protectionists are wrong in economics, wrong in
political conceptions, and most frighteningly wrong in their
estimate of public opinion. He's right, my boy."

"What will happen, Father?" Edwin queried.

"I think we are going to witness a bitter and bloody battle
between the Tariff Reform League, which supports Joe Chamberlain, and the Unionist Free Food League created by the
Unionist Free-Traders, who oppose him. The Duke of
Devonshire is the president of the latter group and he's
gathered many distinguished Conservatives around him, including Churchill."

"Do you think they will win? Churchill's group?"

"I certainly hope so, Edwin, for the sake of the country."

"But the House is divided, isn't it, Father?"

"Indeed it is. And the Tory Party. That's why I said I felt
trouble was brewing. Arthur Balfour is attempting to sit on
the fence, but that won't do him much good. He may well
find himself out of 10 Downing Street sooner than he expects."

Gerald returned to the table noisily and he sat down so
abruptly and so heavily the table rocked, the china and silver
rattled, and tea splashed out of his cup, staining the white
tablecloth with an ugly dark patch. Adam observed Gerald
with immense coldness, and glared at him, his annoyance
mounting. "Really, Gerald! Do try to be a little more man-
nerly at the table. And don't you think you ought to curb
yourself? This unrestrained gorging of food is not good for
your health. It's also perfectly disgusting!"

The boy chose to ignore this mild chastisement, reached
for the pepper pot, and generously seasoned his food. "Mother
says I have a normal appetite for a growing boy," he re-

marked smugly. Adam bit back an acerbic comment and sipped his tea.

As he ate, Gerald glanced at his father cagily. "To return to our earlier discussion, Father. I'm sure you'll agree that as gentlemen we can have differences of opinion without resorting to quarrels." Adam flinched at this pretentiousness as Gerald went on talking. "I just wanted to say that I still don't think much of Churchill, in spite of your comments to the contrary. After all, who does he represent? A lot of cotton spinners in clogs and shawls!"

"That's not strictly true, Gerald. And don't be too hasty to dismiss the working classes. Times are changing."

"You sound like one of the new socialists, Father. Bathtubs for the workers? You know they would only put coal in them."

"That's a snide and ridiculous story which has gone around lately, Gerald, put out by those antiquated diehards who are afraid of changes in this country," Adam said cuttingly. "But it is only a story and I'm dismayed you would give it dignity by repeating it. I had expected better of you, Gerald."

Gerald grinned fatuously, but his narrowed eyes were hostile. "Don't tell me you're intending to give the Fairley workers bathtubs, Father."

Adam looked at his son icily. "No, I'm not. But I've always tried to improve conditions at the mill, as you well know, and I shall certainly continue to do so."

"Well, don't bother," Gerald exclaimed heatedly. "The men are restless enough as it is. Keep 'em down and working hard and hungry. It keeps 'em out of trouble and under our control."

"That's not a very admirable motto, Gerald, or a very farsighted policy either," Adam snapped. "But we shall discuss the mill later. In the meantime, I would like to point out that you've a lot to learn about human nature and the workers, my boy. They've been treated abominably in the past. More reform has to come, and I hope it does so without too much bloodshed."

"You'd better not let your friends in the wool trade hear you talking like that, or they'll castigate you as a traitor to your class, sir," Gerald responded.

"Don't be impertinent!" his father exclaimed, his eyes flashing with chilly silvery lights. Adam, who rarely lost his temper, was in danger of doing so now. But he took control of himself and poured another cup of tea. Because of his fatigue and mental weariness his patience was worn threadbare, and his nerves were far too close to the surface for his own comfort.

Gerald grinned and winked at Edwin, who was gazing at him in astonishment after this exceptional display of insolence. He was horrified at Gerald's effrontery, and he looked from his father to Gerald, and then dropped his eyes.

Infuriated, but in command of himself, Adam opened the newspaper and was about to disappear behind it, when Edwin, conscious of his father's disquiet and in an effort to distract him, said, "Did you know Kitchener when you were in the army, Father?"

"No, I didn't, Edwin. Why do you ask?" Adam queried with impatience. He put the paper down, staring at Edwin curiously.

"I read a story yesterday about him clashing with Lord Curzon in India. Did you see the story in the *Times*, Father? I wondered exactly why they are always at loggerheads? Do you know, sir?"

"Yes, I did see the story, Edwin, and the chief reason those two are always arguing is because when Kitchener went to India as Commander in Chief of the British army he took it upon himself to redistribute the troops. He rapidly gained greater administrative control of the army and the Viceroy was opposed to that, and still opposes it, I might add. Curzon's met his match there, I'm afraid. Kitchener's not a man to be thwarted. He'll have his way, come hell or high water."

"You don't like Kitchener, do you, Father?" Edwin suggested.

"I wouldn't say that, my boy. But why do you assume such a thing?"

"You once told me, when I was little, that it was Kitchener's fault that Gordon was killed at Khartoum."

Adam gave Edwin a penetrating look. "You have a prodigious memory. But I didn't quite say that. If I recall correctly, I said that Kitchener's relief expedition arrived too late to save General Gordon. Khartoum had already been stormed by the Mahdists, who had brutally murdered Gordon. It wasn't Kitchener's fault exactly. In reality, it was Gladstone's, because he delayed in sending relief to Gordon for too long. It caused quite a furor at the time. In fact, public indignation at Gordon's abandonment actually contributed to the downfall of Gladstone's government. But no, I don't blame Kitchener for Gordon's death, to answer your question. And Kitchener's a good soldier, my boy, and devoted to duty."

"I see," Edwin said thoughtfully, vastly relieved that his father was calmer.

"Are you interested in the army, or is it going to be politics for you, Edwin? I can see you are interested in both," Adam said. Not one to remain irritated for long, his anger with Gerald was beginning to lessen.

"Oh no, Father. I think I would like to be a barrister." Edwin announced this with enthusiasm. But then his face fell as he noticed the fixed frown on Adam's face. "Do you not approve, Father?"

Adam smiled quickly, sensing his son's sudden disappointment. "Of course I approve. Anything you want, old chap. I was rather taken aback, that's all. It didn't occur to me that you would be interested in the law. However, I have always known you were not really cut out for the business. And anyway, Gerald seems to be at home at the mill." He threw a swift look at his elder son and his voice hardened as he went on. "Correct, Gerald?"

Gerald nodded and said, "Absolutely! I know Wilson will give you a good report on me." He paused and glanced at his brother slyly. "Anyway, Edwin would not like working in the mill and he's far too delicate in health for the harsh conditions. I thought at one time he might be interested in the newspaper, but since he's not, I heartily endorse his ambition to study law. And why not? It's quite a good idea to have a legal brain in the family."

This was uttered in the most dulcet of tones, the words artfully couched to hide Gerald's cunning. He was inordinately jealous of his younger brother and the last thing he wanted was Edwin interfering in the business. By rights it was his, as the eldest son and heir, and he aimed to keep it for himself and himself alone.

Adam was studying Gerald. He was not deceived. Gerald's guile was all too apparent to him, and under the circumstances it was probably fortuitous that Edwin did not nurture any ambitions to enter the family business. Adam suspected Gerald could be a ruthless adversary when necessary. "Well, that seems to be settled then, Edwin," he said slowly, drumming his fingers lightly on the table. "It appears you have Gerald's good wishes, too."

Edwin beamed, first at Gerald, and then at his father. "I'm so glad you approve and that I have your consent, Father," he cried jubilantly. "I thought you might object, sir."

"Of course I don't." Adam picked up the *Yorkshire Morning Gazette* and turned to the Bradford Wool Market. He perused the section quickly and said to Gerald, "Good. Wool prices are relatively steady and exports well up. We're still cornering the world market. England's cloth exports are averaging something like twenty-seven million running yards a year, the same as last year and the year before. Not bad at all."

Gerald's avaricious eyes glittered darkly in his flaccid face. "Wilson told me yesterday that we would have an excellent year ourselves. Business is booming. By the way, are you going to see that wool man from Australia this morning? Bruce McGill. You do know he's coming to the mill."

"Damnation! I'd forgotten," Adam exclaimed with exasperation. "I can't see him, I'm afraid. Wilson will have to deal with him."

"Yes, Father. Well, I'd better be going to the mill." Gerald rose and clattered out noisily.

Adam frowned at his retreating figure and then turned to Edwin. "I'll have a word with my solicitor about you, my boy, when I see him next week. Perhaps he will have some ideas about your further education after public school. We'll have to decide which university you will go to, Edwin."

"Yes, Father, and thank you so much. I do appreciate your interest in me, I really do, sir." This was said with steadfast earnestness. He loved and respected his father.

At this moment Emma knocked and came into the room, carrying a large tray. She stared at Adam coldly and then glanced away quickly, fixing her eyes on the silver teapot. "Murgatroyd sent me up ter start clearing away, if yer've finished, Squire," she said in a hard voice, clutching the tray tightly and holding herself very still.

"Yes, we have finished, thank you, Emma. You can take everything away, but leave the teapot. I may want another cup before I leave." Adam's eyes were gentle and he smiled at her kindly.

Emma, who had partially turned to listen to him, had averted her head again and she did not see the kindness and compassion that illuminated his sensitive face. "Yes, sir," she said stonily, and went to the sideboard. She propped the tray against it and returned to the table to collect the dirty dishes.

Adam sighed and continued his conversation with Edwin, who gave him his ardent attention.

Emma moved around the circular table quietly, gathering the used silver and the plates with as little fuss and noise as possible. This was protection in itself, for she believed the less people noticed your existence, the easier it was to get along without trouble. Unfortunately, and to her constant dismay, Master Gerald always noticed her and took great pleasure in picking on her, just as he had in the hall a few moments ago. He had jostled against her and pinched her viciously on the thigh, so that she had almost dropped the tray. Her heart filled with anger and humiliation at the remembrance.

She carried the dishes to the sideboard and began to stack them on the tray, wondering how long she could tolerate living in this house, and the terrible people who occupied it. She wished she could run away with Winston, but she knew that was not possible. They did not take girls in the Royal Navy and there was certainly no other place she could go. And anyway, her mam needed her, and her dad, and little Frankie. Panic gripped her and a fine sweat broke out on her forehead and ran down between her breasts. She must get away from this house. From Fairley. Before something dreadful happened. Her panic spiraled into sheer terror. It was a senseless terror she found incomprehensible. And then it came to her, in a sudden rush of icy clarity. She was powerless in this house, and she knew, with sinking dread, that all sorts of wicked acts could be committed against the poor by the rich. Money. She must get money. Not just a few extra shillings for sewing and mending clothes in the village, but lots of money. Yes, that was the answer. She had always known it was. She must find a way to make a fortune. But how? Where? It was then that she remembered Blackie O'Neill and his tales of Leeds, the city whose streets were paved with gold. That was the key, and there she would find the secret of making money, so much money she would never be afraid or powerless ever again. And then the tables would be turned on the Fairleys. Slowly the fear began to slip away.

The tray was filled to overflowing and Emma picked it up, almost staggering under its weight. She gritted her teeth and glided out of the room in silence, her head held high, a proud look on her face, rigid determination in the set of her shoulders. And for all of her youth and inexperience there was a certain regality in her carriage.

Edwin had begun to fidget in his chair. Eventually he said, "May I be excused, Father? I have to keep up with my schoolwork, otherwise I will be behind when I return to Worksop."

Adam's glance was approving. "Why, that's very diligent of you. Go ahead, old chap. But do get some fresh air this afternoon."

"Yes, sir." Edwin stood up and went to the door with his usual grace.

"Oh, Edwin."

"Yes, Father?" The boy stopped, his hand on the doorknob.

"I think it would be nice if you dined with your Aunt Olivia and myself this evening."

"Gosh! Thank you, sir. I'd enjoy that!" Excited by this unexpected invitation, Edwin forgot himself and exuberantly slammed the door behind him so hard the gas fixtures on the wall rattled and trembled precariously.

His father smiled. Edwin was growing up to be a nice boy and Adam was delighted he was beginning to show a little independence of spirit. Perhaps his mother's sickly influence had not been so damaging after all. Adele. He should go up and see her. He had many matters to discuss with her, which, as usual, he had been avoiding for weeks. If he was honest with himself he had to admit that he was avoiding it now. He thought of his wife. Fragile, pretty, vain, brittle Adele. Smiling her sweet smile. That perpetual smile that had begun to horrify him. Adele with her iridescent blond beauty that had so captivated him years ago. How quickly he had discovered it was a chilly beauty that camouflaged selfishness and a heart that was as cold as marble. It also apparently disguised mental instability as well. They had not had any real contact or communication for years. Ten years to be exact, when Adele had retreated gratefully into a shell of vaporish semi-invalidism. Smiling sweetly, as ingenuous as always, she had closed her bedroom door firmly, locking it pointedly against him. At the time Adam had been startled to find that he accepted her termination of her connubial duties with a resignation that bespoke his own profound relief.

Long ago, Adam Fairley had come to accept that his lifeless and loveless marriage was by no means unique. Many of his friends were bound in similar bleak and fruitless unions, although he doubted that they had to contend with disorders of the mind as well. With abandon, and without a second thought, his friends took solace in other comforting feminine arms. Adam's fastidiousness, and his innate sense of taste, precluded casual affairs with women of easy virtue. For in spite of his sensuous nature, Adam Fairley was not essentially carnal or given to fleshly pursuits, and he required other attributes in a woman as well as a beautiful face and body. And so, over the years, he had learned to accept celibacy as a permanent condition, and it bordered now on asceticism. He did not understand that this was a state of being that held its own attractions for the women he came into contact with socially, who found him irresistible. In his misery with his life he was blind to the flurry he created, and if he had noticed he would not have cared.

Adam went to the window, parted the curtains, and looked out. The dark rain clouds had scurried away, leaving a sky that was a vivid light blue, and so sharp and polished it was like the inside of an upturned enameled bowl, and the pale yet bright sun intensified the cold lucency of the northern light. The black hills were as stark and barren as always, but for Adam they held an overpowering and enigmatic beauty. They had been there for eons before he was born and they would be there long after he was dead. Always the land remained, changeless and everlasting, the source of the Fairleys' power and their strength. In the scheme of things, he was just a droplet in the vast universe and suddenly his problems seemed of little significance, and even petty, for he was just a transitory being on this rich and splendid earth and, being mortal like all men, he would die one day. And what would it matter then? What would it have all been about? And who would care?

His reflective mood was shattered by the sound of horses' hooves, as Gerald drove rapidly across the stable yard in the trap on his way to the mill. Adam thought then of Gerald and

Edwin. He had become aware of so many things this morning, not only about himself but also about his sons. By reason of primogeniture, Gerald would inherit the Fairley lands, the Hall, the mill, and all the other Fairley holdings, with the understanding that he would take care of his brother for his lifetime. But Edwin would receive nothing of real worth and would have to rely solely on the bounty of Gerald. Not a very pleasant prospect, Adam thought. He now recognized that it was imperative that he make proper provision for his younger son in his will. He determined to see his solicitor at the first opportunity. *He did not trust Gerald. No, he did not trust Gerald at all.*

TWELVE

The Fairley family fortune, now controlled by Adam Fairley, was founded on two sound principles—the acquisition of land and the making of cloth.

The land came first.

Adam Fairley could trace his lineage back to the twelfth century and one Hubert Fairley. A document drawn in 1155, and still in existence in the vault at Fairley Hall, states that Hubert was given the lands of Arkwith and Ramsden in the West Riding of Yorkshire by the Crown. The document was drawn in the presence of Henry II and signed by fourteen witnesses at Pontefract Castle, where the King used to stay on his visits to Yorkshire. With Hubert's continuing prosperity and growing renown as a "King's man," Arkwith eventually came to be known as Fairley. It was Hubert who built the original Fairley Manor on the site where the present Hall now stands.

Succeeding Fairleys received more land and favors from their grateful sovereigns. Staunchly Royalist, many of them took up arms in defense of their Crown and country and were admirably rewarded. It was Henry VIII who granted to John Fairley the adjoining land of Ramsden Moors at the time of the Dissolution of the Monasteries, for services to Henry during the King's ecclesiastical reforms. Later Henry's daughter Elizabeth Tudor sold "the valley of Kirkton on the banks of the river Aire to William Fairley, Squire of Fairley Manor and Hamlet." Elizabeth I, always desperately striving to replenish the royal coffers, had long resorted to selling off Crown lands. She looked with a degree of favor on William Fairley, for his son Robert was a sea captain who had sailed with Drake to the Indies. Later his ship was part of the great English fleet, led by the intrepid Drake, which sailed into Cádiz harbor and defeated the Armada in 1588. Consequently, the Queen sold the Kirkton land at a fair price. It was the procurement of this particular parcel of land on the river Aire that was a decisive factor in the development of the Fairley fortunes, for the river was to be the source of power for the original mill.

Robert's son Francis, named after Drake, had no seafaring or military ambitions and, in fact, from this time on there were no more military men in the family until Adam became, for a brief period, a cavalry officer in the Fourth Hussars. Francis, plodding, diligent, but not too imaginative by nature, at least had enough of the merchant's instinct to foresee the growing importance of so basic and essential a product as cloth. He started a small domestic industry for the weaving of wool at the end of the sixteenth century. The local villagers continued to spin and weave in their cottages, but what had formerly been woven for personal use was now made for sale. It was from this modest beginning that the great Fairley enterprises flowered; they were to make Francis' descendants not only rich but the most powerful woolen kings in the West Riding. By the beginning of the seventeenth century, Fairley was already a flourishing wool-manufacturing hamlet with a cropping shop, a fulling mill on the river, and a breached reservoir.

Francis Fairley had joined the cloth to the land.

But without the land there could have been no cloth. Fairley's location in the West Riding, its geology, and its climate all contributed greatly to the success of the family's wool-manufacturing business.

Fairley Village is situated in the foothills of the Pennine Chain, that great range of interlocking spurs of hills that roll down the center of England from the Cheviots on the Scottish border to the Peak in Derbyshire, and which is called "the backbone of England" by those who live in its regions. The geology of the Pennine Chain varies. In the north of Yorkshire the hills are of white limestone rock on which grows sweet grass. But there are few springs in limestone country, and these abound with limestone, and limestone water is particularly harsh to fibers. Further down the Chain there is a sudden break called the Aire Gap, through which the river Aire flows towards Leeds. It is just south of Skipton and the Aire Gap that the West Riding begins. Here the Pennine Hills are now composed of dark and hard millstone grit, with a fringe of coal measure and coatings of peat or clay. Very little grows on millstone grit. Oats and coarse grass are its only crops. However, these are the crops that short-haired sheep feed and thrive on best. Also, coal and grit country has numerous streams which rarely fail, for the moisture-heavy winds that sweep in across the hills from the Atlantic provide abundant rain the year round. The water in these rocky little becks contains no lime. It is soft and kind to fibers. Sheep's wool and soft water are the two necessities for the making of cloth, and both are plentiful in the West Riding.

And so with these natural elements in their favor the Fairleys' wool business grew, and especially so in the eighteenth century. But this amazing growth was also due to the enterprise and progressiveness of three Fairleys, father, son, and grandson—Joshua, Percival, and David. All were pioneers in the wool business and, being astute, they recognized the importance of the new inventions coming into being, which would help increase production in the most efficient manner. Whilst some rival manufacturers in the West Riding at first resisted these technological innovations that were to change the social and economic structure of England, the Fairleys did not. They enthusiastically purchased these "new-fangled machines," as they were scathingly called by less progressive cloth merchants, and at once put them to advantageous use.

Gerald, heir presumptive to the immense fortune presently in the hands of Adam Fairley, had inherited one singular trait from his forebears, a trait totally lacking in Adam. And this was their love for the wool business. It elicited in Gerald the same intense passion evoked by money and food. When Gerald was on the mill floor, amidst the clattering machinery, he too was in his natural element. He felt completely alive, was filled with a pulsating strength. The strident noise of the rattling machines, which deafened Adam, were not at all discordant to Gerald, who thought they made the most beautiful music he had ever heard. And the malodorous stink of the oily wool, so noxious to his father, was for Gerald an intoxicating perfume. When Gerald saw the great stacks of hundreds upon hundreds of bolts of Fairley cloth, he thrilled with an excitement incomparable to anything he had ever felt in the seventeen years of his young life.

This morning, as Gerald drove down the lower road that cut across the valley from the Hall, he was thinking about the mill; or, more precisely, his father and Edwin in relation to the mill. He did not see the landscape or notice the weather or feel the biting cold. He was lost in the labyrinths of his own convoluted thoughts. Edwin had been neatly disposed of at breakfast. Very neatly indeed. And more precipitously than he had ever imagined possible in his wildest and most exigent dreams. Not that Edwin was a real threat. After all, he, Gerald, was the heir and by birthright everything was his under the law. Yet it had often occurred to him recently that Edwin might conceivably want to enter the woolen business and that he could not have prevented. It would have been an unnecessary nuisance. Now there was no longer any need for him to worry about Edwin. His brother was rendered powerless, and of his own volition. As for his father . . . well! There was something corrupt in Gerald and he was riven by an immense hatred for his father. Insensitive as he was, Gerald had only a vague glimmering that this feeling sprang from a terrible and consuming envy. He constantly tried to diminish his father in his own mind. He picked on a few of Adam's traits, which in reality were insignificant and irrelevant, and blew them out of all proportion until they became damning and unforgivable faults. Parsimonious to a point of being miserly, narrow-minded, and parochial, Gerald fumed internally about the money his father spent on his clothes, his trips to London and abroad, and he became enraged and even violent when he contemplated the good hard cash his father was pouring into the newspaper.

Gerald was pondering on all of this as he drove down to the mill. Suddenly he laughed out loud as it struck him that his father's lack of interest in the business and his attitude in general paved the way for him, and sooner than he had anticipated.

Now that he thought about it, he really had no alternative

but to take matters into his own hands, considering the way his father was behaving. He determined to talk to the Australian wool man himself this morning. Wilson had told him yesterday that Bruce McGill wanted to sell them Australian wool. The way orders were pouring in for their cloth they might be in need of it and, in any event, it was surely worthwhile striking up a friendship with McGill, who was one of the most powerful and wealthiest sheep ranchers in Australia.

He also decided it would be a good idea to encourage his father's penchant for protracted absences, instead of fighting it. Those disappearing acts would suit his own ends now. He could not wait for the day his father retired. It would not be soon enough for him. In the meantime, he must start establishing his own prerogatives at the mill.

THIRTEEN

Adele Fairley's upstairs sitting room at Fairley Hall contained many individually beautiful objects, and yet, in spite of that, it was not a beautiful room. It was lifeless and oddly empty in feeling, a feeling that sprang from an all-pervading ambiance of bleakness, of utter desolation. Certainly this feeling did not emanate from a need for furnishings, for, on the contrary, it was teeming with possessions.

The sitting room was vast, large and square in its dimensions, with a vaulted ceiling that appeared to float up and beyond into infinity. This was lavishly embellished with plaster cornices and moldings, and panels inset with oval plaques and cherubim, and entwining flowers and acanthus leaves, the whole expanse painted a stark and pristine white and from the center of which dropped a gigantic and magnificent chandelier of shimmering crystal. Many windows, tall and majestic, intersected the walls, and an eighteenth-century Gothic fireplace of glacial white marble was an imposing counterpoint with its huge mantel and great carved columns and soaring proportions.

Almost everything in the room was blue: Pale blue damask sheathed the walls, rippled at the windows, slithered across the sofas and fragile gilt chairs, and even the antique carpet was a sweep of glistening blue on the dark oak floor. Mirrors, crystal ornaments, glass domes covering dried flowers and wax fruit, pieces of finely wrought silver, and priceless porcelain were all charged and glittered with cold reflected light that only served to underscore the icy sterility of the room. A fire blazed continually in the hearth, costly jade and porcelain lamps threw out rays of softening light, the antique furniture gleamed as pools of ripe dark color, yet these did nothing to diminish the gelid atmosphere, and there was a sense of abandonment hanging heavy in the air.

Weighted down as it was with possessions, it betrayed the pathetic efforts of a lonely and disturbed woman to find some solace in material wealth, an attempt to restore her damaged psyche by surrounding herself with things rather than people, as if they could give her the illusion of life. Few people who entered this room ever felt truly comfortable or at ease, and even Adele herself, the sole perpetrator of this monument of dubious taste, now seemed lost and adrift, a ghostly presence moving abstractedly through the multitudinous paraphernalia she had accumulated so acquisitively, so assiduously, and which she no longer seemed to notice.

This morning she came into the room tentatively, pausing cautiously on the threshold of her adjoining bedroom. Her lustrous silver eyes, large and beautiful but now filled with pinpoints of apprehension, flicked around the room hurriedly, and her aristocratic fingers clutched nervously at the silver-streaked white silk peignoir she was wearing. She pulled the filmy fabric closer to her body protectively, glancing around quickly, yet again, to reassure herself she was absolutely alone, that no servant was skulking in a dim corner, dusting or cleaning and intruding on her privacy.

Adele Fairley was tall and graceful, but so tempered of movement that at times she appeared to do everything in slow motion. This was the effect she gave now as she left the safety of the shadowy doorway and glided into the room. Her pale blond hair was almost silver in tone, and it fell about her face in soft curls and delicate tendrils, and cascaded down her back in undulating waves to blend into the silvered snowy silk enveloping her body, so that the two seemed almost indistinguishable. She paused at one of the windows and turned to gaze out across the valley, a remote unseeing look in her eyes. The landscape had changed in the past few weeks. The dusty grays and somber blacks had given way to the first signs of spring greenness. There had been a sudden softening of the bleak earth, and there was a sense of vibrancy and a throbbing renewal of life visible all over that harsh land. But Adele saw this only dimly, as if through a veil, lost as she was in her own thoughts and preoccupations. An inverted woman, isolated within herself, she lived quite separate and apart from the world around her, and she was curiously detached, curiously oblivious to externals. Her internal life had become her only reality.

As she stood, motionless, at the window, the sunlight struck her face, illuminating the smooth contours. In spite of her thirty-seven years there was a girlishness and a purity about Adele Fairley, but it was the purity of a perfectly sculptured marble statue that had been immured for years behind glass, and has never been warmed by love or pained by sorrow or moved to compassion at another's suffering,

Unexpectedly, and with an abruptness that was most unnatural for her, Adele swung away from the window, suddenly intent in her purpose. She glided swiftly to a display cabinet on the far wall, her eyes glittering. The cabinet, a French vitrine, contained many exquisite objects that Adele had collected on her travels with Adam over the years. These had once been Adele's pride, and she had found constant pleasure in them, but now they no longer interested her.

She stood in front of the cabinet and looked about her anxiously before taking a small key from her pocket. As she unlocked the cabinet her lovely eyes narrowed into cunning slits, and a sly and secretive expression slipped onto her face, distorting it into a baleful mask that blurred her stunning beauty. She reached inside the cabinet and carefully lifted out a decanter. This was of dark red Venetian glass, intricately chased with silver, very old and priceless. It glinted in the sun and threw off a myriad of fiery prisms, but Adele did not stop to admire it as she once had. Instead, she removed the stopper hastily and, with trembling hands, lifted the decanter to her pale cold lips. She drank urgently, greedily, like one dying of thirst, tossing back several swift draughts with a seasoned hand, and then, hugging the decanter to her possessively, she closed her eyes thankfully, breathing deeply. As the liquid trickled slowly through her, warming her, the profound terror that perpetually worked inside her began to subside, and the fundamental anxiety that was ever present when she first awakened to a new day gradually began to ebb away. A sense of well-being, of euphoria, washed over her as the alcohol permeated her system. She looked around the room. It now appeared less hostile and frightening to her and she became aware of the soft sunlight pouring in, of the brightly burning fire, of the spring flowers in the vases.

She smiled to herself and purposefully lifted the decanter to her lips again, and with avidity. Only a trickle of liquid touched her tongue and she held the decanter away from her, shaking it impatiently, glaring at it with anger and disbelief. It was empty.

"Damn! Damn! Damn!" she cried out vehemently, her voice fuming with rage. She looked at the decanter again. Her hands began to shake and her body was suddenly besieged by cold tremors. Did I drink so much last night? she asked herself. She was aghast to discover she could not remember. Then the rising panic truly took hold of her, and it was with an awful sense of dread that she comprehended her predicament. *There was no more alcohol in her suite of rooms*. This scared her to a point of paralysis. Even if she did not succumb to the temptation of taking another drink during the day, she always needed to know it was available, for her own sense of security. But there was not a drop left now.

Half staggering, she groped her way blindly to a chair and fell into it, her mind blank. Still clutching the decanter to her body, she wrapped her arms around herself and rocked to and fro, whimpering and moaning, held in the clutches of an unbearable anguish. Oh God! Oh God! What will I do? What will I do? She shivered, and closed her eyes, as always fleeing reality.

Her face, drained of its roseate tints, had paled to ashy white, and in repose, with her head thrown back limply against the chair and her hair hanging loosely over her shoulders, she looked wan and childlike. Despite her incredible beauty, and the exquisite and costly morning robe she was wearing, she was a sad and pathetic figure in that cavernous room, and there was an air of doom, of terrible tragedy, surrounding her.

Eventually she opened her eyes. "My sweet little baby," she said, gazing down at the object in her arms. "Sweet darling baby. Darling Gerald." She paused and stared down at her arms again, confusion registering on her face. "Or is it Edwin?" She nodded her head slowly. "Of course it's not Gerald. It *is* Edwin." She began to coo and murmur unintelligible words to herself as she rocked frantically in the chair.

About an hour later Adele Fairley underwent a transfiguration. The agitation that had held her in its grip fell away, and her demeanor became composed. Almost simultaneously, the delirious expression that had given her features a febrile glaze was replaced by one of tranquillity, and her eyes cleared and filled with lucidity, as the half-crazed gleam disappeared.

She glanced out of the window and noticed it was raining. Not the typical light shower so common in Yorkshire at this time of year, but a heavy downpour. Torrents of water, driven against the windows by the high wind that had sprung up, slashed furiously at the glass, which quivered and rattled under the onslaught. The trees lashed the air and the gardens appeared to vibrate under the force of the gale. Only the moors were unaffected by the tumult, implacable and somber, a line of black monoliths flung defiantly into the bleached-out sky. Adele shuddered as she gazed at them. They had always seemed grim to her southern eye, accustomed as it was to the bucolic green gentleness of her native Sussex, and she thought of them as an imprisoning wall that encompassed this house and the village, shutting her off from the world. She was an alien in this alien land.

She shivered. She was cold. Her hands and feet were like icicles. She pulled the thin robe closer to her, but it offered no warmth. She saw, with dismay, that the fire had dwindled down to a few burning embers. As she stood up and moved into the room her foot struck the decanter which had slipped unnoticed to the floor. Puzzled, she picked it up, wondering what it was doing there. Why was it on the floor? She examined it carefully for any cracks. Then it came to her. She had been looking for a drink earlier and had taken the decanter out of the vitrine. When was that? An hour, two hours ago? She could not remember. She did recall her behavior. She laughed softly. How foolish she had been, to become so panic-stricken. She was mistress of this house, and all she had to do was to ring for Murgatroyd and instruct him to bring her a bottle of whiskey, and one of brandy, surreptitiously, as he always did, so Adam would not know.

The clatter of china in the corridor outside the sitting room alerted her that the maid was approaching with her breakfast. Hastily, Adele returned the decanter to the vitrine, locked it, and swept out of the room with unusual swiftness, the silver-streaked white peignoir billowing out behind her like irides-cent wings, her hair streaming down her back in rivulets of silver.

She closed the bedroom door quietly and leaned back against it, a satisfied smile on her face. She must select a morning dress, a becoming one, and after breakfast she would attend to her hair and her face. Then she would send for Murgatroyd. As she went to the wardrobe she told herself she must try to remember that *she* was the mistress of Fairley Hall, and no one else. She must assert herself. This very day. Her sister Olivia had been kind in taking over so many managerial duties, since her arrival in February, but now she would have to relinquish them.

"I am well enough to assume them myself," Adele said aloud, and she truly believed her words. Yes, that will please Adam, she decided. And then her throat tightened at the thought of her husband. She frowned. But would it please him? He thought her a fool, and quite unlike her sister, whom he considered to be a paragon of every virtue under the sun. Lately she had come to think of Adam as a man surrounded by a wall of great reserve and he always seemed so distant. She shivered. In recent weeks she had also been frighteningly aware of the menace in his eyes. Not only that, he was always watching her with his pale eyes. So was Olivia. They didn't know it, but she watched them watching her avidly, and whispering together in corners. They were in league. They were plotting against her. As long as she was fully conscious of their plotting they could not harm her. She must be on guard against them at all times. Adam. Olivia. Her enemies.

She capitulated to her delusions. She began to pull out dress after dress, frenetically and with a superhuman energy, flinging them carelessly onto the floor. She was searching for one dress in particular. It was a special dress with special powers. Once she put it on she would automatically become mistress of this house again, of that she was quite certain. She knew the dress was there. It must be there . . . unless. . . unless Olivia had stolen it . . . just as she had stolen her role

as mistress of Fairley Hall. She continued to pull out dresses
and other clothes frantically, tossing them onto the floor until
the wardrobe was completely empty. She stared at it for a
prolonged moment, and then distractedly looked down at the
piles of silks and satins, georgettes and chiffons, and velvets
and wools that swirled in a mass of intense color at her feet.

Why were her peignoirs and morning dresses and day suits
and evening gowns lying on the floor? What had she been
looking for? She could not remember. She stepped over
them, and walked across the floor to the cheval mirror near
the window. She stood in front of it, playing with her hair
absently, lifting it above her head and then letting it fall
down slowly to catch the light, repeating the gesture time
after time. Her face was blank, utterly without emotion, but
her eyes blazed with delirium.

FOURTEEN

Emma entered Adele Fairley's sitting room so hurriedly
she was almost running. Her feet, in their new black
button boots that shone like glittering mirrors, barely seemed
to touch the floor, and the starched white petticoat underneath her long blue woolen dress crackled and rustled in the
silence. She gripped the heavy silver tray tightly in her
work-roughened hands, holding it out in front of her, and
high, to avoid contact with the furniture, and to prevent any
accidents.

Her face, just visible above the outsized tray, was scrubbed
to shining cleanliness and glowed with youthful health, as did
her green eyes that were vividly alive, and brilliant with
intelligence beneath the thick lashes. As always, her russet
hair, brushed and gleaming, was pulled back severely into a
thick bun at the nape of her neck, and today the widow's
peak was more pronounced than ever, accentuated as it was
by the maid's cap that framed her face like a little halo. This
was as glistening white and as stiffly starched as her large
apron and the collar and cuffs on her dress, all recently
purchased for her in Leeds by Olivia Wainright. The dress,
too, was new, but this Emma had made herself from a length

of cloth from the Fairley mill, which had also been given to her by Mrs. Wainright. Emma's delight in the new dress was surpassed only by her pride in Olivia Wainright's smiling approval of her dexterity with the scissors and her skill with a needle and thread.

These new clothes, simple though they were, not only helped to dispel the starveling appearance that had given Emma the downtrodden air which had so appalled Blackie, but they also considerably enhanced her naturally arresting good looks. The combination of blue and white was crisp and immaculate, and the tailored style of the uniform, and the smart little cap, brought her finely articulated features into focus and made her seem older than she really was. But more important than the clothes was the subtle change in her demeanor, which had occurred over the last two months. Although she was still internally apprehensive about being in such close proximity to some members of the Fairley family, and indeed of working at Fairley Hall at all, that apprehension was more controlled than it had ever been in her two years of service there. Also, her initial timidness about being suddenly propelled into the upstairs quarters had lessened. Her diffidence was now disguised by a rigid self-containment that manifested itself in an exterior composure so austere and so dignified it bordered on hauteur, and which in anyone else of her age would have seemed ridiculous yet was somehow perfectly natural in Emma. She was beginning to acquire a measure of self-confidence, and tentative as this still was, it gave her a kind of naïve poise.

This change in Emma's manner had been wrought by a number of circumstances, and the most obvious, although in reality of lesser consequence in the overall scheme of things, was the radical developments in the domestic scene at Fairley Hall, precipitated by Olivia Wainright's arrival. Olivia Wainright was a woman of impeccable character, high principles, and down-to-earth common sense. Although she was innately fine and good, had a well-developed moral sense of right and wrong, and was constantly infuriated and moved to compassion by the blatant lack of humanity in this Edwardian era, she was by no means a bleeding heart. Neither was she easily persuaded, or manipulated, by importuning or sentimental appeals to her charity, generosity, and intrinsic decency. In fact, she could be exceedingly severe with those

she considered to be malingerers or professional beggars, and
was sternly disapproving of certain so-called worthy charitable organizations which she considered did more harm than
good, and, as often as not, foolishly squandered the monetary
donations they received. Yet she had a fierce abhorrence of
injustice and mindless cruelty and brutality, most especially
when directed at those with no means of retaliation. If her
dealings with staff were exacting, strict, and firm, they were,
nevertheless, tempered by a quiet sympathy and a considered benevolence, for she recognized the dignity of honest
toil and respected it. Furthermore, she was a lady in the
truest sense of that word, educated, honorable, refined, well-
bred, dignified, and courteous to everyone, servants not
excluded.

Olivia's very presence in the house, her keen interest in all
aspects of its management, her daily involvement with the
servants, and her redoubtable character had all had the most
profound effect. The atmosphere at the Hall in general, and
especially downstairs, had improved vastly. It was less fraught
with antipathy and intrigue. Olivia had become, quite
automatically, a natural buffer between Murgatroyd and the
other servants, in particular Emma. From the first moment
she had become aware of the girl's existence, Olivia had
taken a most particular and uncommon liking to her, and had
shown her both kindness and consideration. Even though
Emma still worked hard, she was treated with less abuse and
in a more humane fashion. The butler continued to verbally
castigate her on occasion, but he had not struck her once
since the advent of Olivia, and Emma knew he would not
dare. Cook's threats to expose his mistreatment of her to her
father might not intimidate him for long, but certainly Olivia
Wainright did, of that Emma was positive.

Emma felt a degree of gratitude to Olivia Wainright, yet in
spite of that she was curiously ambivalent in her feelings
about the older woman. Suspicious, cautious, and wary though
she was with everyone, she sometimes found herself admiring of Olivia, much against her will. This emotion continually
surprised Emma and also vexed her, for her fundamental
distrust of the gentry, and the Fairleys in particular, had not
abated in the least. So she endeavored always to suppress the
rush of reluctant warmth and friendliness that surfaced whenever she came into contact with Mrs. Wainright. Being self-

protective to a point of coldness, she truly believed such
feelings were weak, perilous, and most foolhardy, since they
made you vulnerable and, even more dangerously, gave the
other person the advantage, which inevitably put you at their
mercy. And yet, because of Olivia Wainright's singular and
most apparent interest in her, Emma was taking a new pride
in her work, and much of the time she was less fearful and
not quite as resentful as she had been in the past.

Apart from this, when Polly became sick Emma had been
given Polly's duties of attending to Adele Fairley. This close
and more familiar contact with her mistress had, in itself,
been an influence on Emma, and had also helped to change
her life at the Hall to some extent, and for the better. As for
Adele, Emma found her spoiled, self-indulgent, and extremely
demanding of her time and attention, but her unfailing and
profound gentleness with the girl outweighed these other
characteristics, as far as Emma was concerned. Then again,
Adele's chronic vagueness, and her perverse disregard of the
stringent domestic rules quite common in such a large house,
gave Emma autonomy to care for Mrs. Fairley as they both
deemed fit, and without too much interference from anyone
else in the establishment. This new independence, meager as
it actually was, engendered in Emma a sense of freedom, and
even a degree of authority that she had not experienced at
the Hall before, and it certainly removed her from Murgatroyd's
jurisdiction and foul temper for much of the time.

If Emma looked up to Olivia Wainright, thought her the
more superior woman, and, against her volition, secretly
adored her, she could not help liking Adele Fairley in spite of
what she was. Mainly she felt sorry for her. To Emma she
could be forgiven her carelessness and her strange lapses,
since Emma considered her to be childlike and, oddly enough,
in need of protection in that strange household. Sometimes,
to her astonishment, Emma found herself actually excusing
Mrs. Fairley's patent obliviousness to the suffering of others
less fortunate, for Emma knew instinctively this was not
caused by conscious malice or cruelty, but simply emanated
from sheer thoughtlessness and lack of exposure to the lives
of the working class. Her attitude towards Mrs. Fairley was
much the same attitude she adopted at home. She took
charge. She was even a little bossy at times. But Adele did
not seem to notice this, and if she did, she apparently did not

mind. Emma alone now took care of her and attended to all
her daily needs and comforts. Adele had come to depend on
her, and she found Emma indispensable in much the same
way Murgatroyd was indispensable, because of the secret
supplies of drink he provided.

Between them the two sisters had, in their different ways,
shown Emma a degree of kindness and understanding. And
whilst this did not entirely assuage the hurt she felt at the
humiliations inflicted on her by other members of the family,
it made her life at the Hall all that more bearable. But it was
one other element, fundamental, cogent, and therefore of
crucial importance, that had done the most to bring about the
change in Emma's personality. And this was the consolidation
of several natural traits that were becoming the determinative
factors in her life—her fierce ambition and her formidable
will. Both had converged and hardened into a fanatical sense
of purpose that was the driving force behind everything she
did. Blackie's initial stories about Leeds had originally fired
her imagination, and on his subsequent visits to the Hall she
had assiduously questioned him, and minutely so, about prospects of work there. Constrained, circumspect, and even
negative as he was at times, he had unwittingly fostered her
youthful dreams of glory, of money, of a better life, and,
inevitably, of escape from the village.

And so Emma had come finally to the realization that her
life at Fairley Hall was just a brief sojourn to be patiently
endured, since it would end one day. She now believed, with
a sure and trusting knowledge that reached deep into her
soul, that she would leave when the time was right, and she
felt certain this was in the not too distant future. Until
then she was not merely marking time, but learning everything she could to prepare herself for the world outside,
which did not frighten her in the least.

Emma also had a secret she had shared with no one, not
even Blackie. It was a plan, really. But a plan so grand it left
no room for doubt, and it filled her days with that most
wonderful and desirous of all human feelings—hope. It was a
hope that foreshadowed all else in her cheerless young life. It
gave added meaning to her days and made every hour of
punishing toil totally irrelevant. It was this blind belief, this
absolute faith in herself and her future, that often put a lively

spring into her step, brought an occasional smile to her normally solemn young face, and sustained her at all times.

On this particular morning, filled with all that hope, wearing her new pristine uniform, and with her cheerfully shining face, she looked as bright and as sparkling as a brand-new penny, and was quite a different girl from the one Blackie had met on the moors. As she moved purposefully across the rich carpet she was like a gust of fresh spring air in that cloistered and overstuffed room, and even the dolorous atmosphere seemed to visibly diminish with her vivacious presence. Squeezing gingerly between a whatnot and a console overflowing with all that preposterous bric-a-brac, Emma shook her head in mock horror. All this blinking junk! she thought, and with mild exasperation, as she remembered how long it always took her to dust everything. Although she was not afraid of hard work, she hated dusting, and this room in particular.

"Half of it could be thrown out inter the midden and nobody'd miss owt," she exclaimed aloud, and then clamped her mouth tightly shut self-consciously and peered ahead, fully expecting to see Mrs. Fairley sitting in the wing chair she favored near the fireplace, for traces of her perfume permeated the air. But the room was deserted and Emma breathed a sigh of relief. She wrinkled her nose and sniffed several times, and with not a little pleasure. She had grown used to the pungent floral scent pervading the suite of rooms and had actually come to like it. In fact, somewhat to her surprise, for she was not one given to frivolities, Emma had discovered that she was most partial to the smell of expensive perfumes, the touch of good linens and supple silks, and the sparkle of brilliant jewels. She smiled secretively to herself. When she was a grand lady, like Blackie said she would be one day, and when she had made the fortune she intended to make, she would buy herself some of that perfume. Jasmine, it was. She had read the label on the bottle on Mrs. Fairley's dressing table. It came all the way from London, from a shop called Floris, where Mrs. Fairley bought all of her perfumes and soaps and potpourri for the bowls, and the little bags of lavender for the chests of drawers that held her delicate lawn and silk undergarments. Yes, she would have a bottle of that Jasmine scent and a bar of French Fern soap and even some little bags of lavender for her underclothes. And if she had enough money to spare they would be just as silky and as soft as Mrs. Fairley's fine garments.

But she did not have time to indulge herself in thoughts of such fanciful things right now, and she put them firmly out of her mind as she hurried to the fireplace with the tray. There was too much to be done this morning and she was already late. Cook had overloaded her with extra chores in the kitchen, which had delayed her considerably, and consequently she was irritated. Not so much about the extra chores, but about the delay they had caused. Punctuality had taken on a new and special significance to Emma and had become of major importance to her in the past few months. She hated to be late with Mrs. Fairley's breakfast, or with anything else for that matter, for since being elevated to the position of parlormaid she took her new responsibilities very seriously.

She placed the breakfast tray carefully on the small Queen Anne tea table next to the wing chair, in readiness for Mrs. Fairley, who liked to have her breakfast in front of the fire. She looked over the tray to be sure it was perfect, rearranged some of the china more attractively, plumped up the cushions on the wing chair, and turned her attention to the dying fire. She knelt in front of the fireplace and began to rekindle it with paper spills, chips of wood, and small pieces of coal, handling them cautiously with the fire tongs in an effort to keep her hands clean. She clucked impatiently. Mrs. Turner with her extra chores was a real nuisance sometimes! If she had been up to the sitting room on time she would not have been faced with the task of making the fire again. This annoyed her because it ate into her precious time, and Emma, so rigid and relentless with herself, hated any deviation from her normal routine. It put her out of sorts because it ruined her timetable for the entire day. This timetable, Emma's own recent creation, was her Bible and she lived by it. She knew that without it she would be hopelessly lost.

She picked up the bellows and worked them in front of the meager fire. Under the force of the small but strong gusts of air, the smoldering chips of wood spurted and spluttered, finally ignited and began to burn rapidly. In the sudden conflagration her face was illuminated. A small frown now creased her brow and her cheerful expression was obliterated, as she remembered with clarity and bitterness what her life had been like without that timetable.

On that day, early in February, when Polly had been struck down and forced to take to her bed, Emma had resignedly accepted the fact that she had to do Polly's work as well as her own. She knew she had no alternative. Strong of constitution and basically optimistic of nature, she had scurried about the Hall like a demon and with immense energy, telling herself that Polly would be up and about the next day and well enough to do her own work again. But this had not happened. Emma was suddenly burdened with the whole load of domestic chores, seemingly for an indefinite period. She soon became overwhelmed by her innumerable duties and acutely nervous about completing them efficiently.

Those first few days she had been bone tired at the end of every day, for she started working at six o'clock in the morning and barely stopped for breath, let alone a rest, until she finished at seven in the evening. By then she was almost always too weary to eat her supper and, in fact, it had usually taken a supreme effort of will and the last ounce of her strength to crawl up the attic stairs to her room. White and shaking and speechless with exhaustion, she had hardly had the energy to undress, and she invariably dropped onto the uncomfortable little bed in a dim and mindless stupor. She would fall into a heavy and stupefied sleep at once, and yet she never felt refreshed when she awakened the next day. Her back and shoulders still ached, her eyes were red-rimmed with fatigue, her arms and legs were like leaden weights, and her hands were sore and raw.

As she had shiveringly dressed in the cold attic room and washed in the icy water from the washbowl, she had seethed with a fulminating anger she found hard to quell. Yet she did not dare to complain for fear of reprisals from Murgatroyd or, even worse, dismissal. Daily, she dragged her weary body through that mausoleum of a house, up and down the many stairs, along the winding corridors, across the great halls and larger rooms, dusting, polishing, sweeping, black-leading grates, stoking fires, making beds, cleaning silver, ironing linens, and taking care of Adele Fairley's needs as well. And as she did, she often wondered how long she could continue without collapsing. This thought terrified her even more and made her grit her teeth and marshal her diminishing energies, for the money she earned was so desperately needed at home. She could not afford to collapse, for the sake of her family, and so she pushed herself almost beyond endurance, propelled by sheer force of will power and sustained by the icy terror of losing her job.

One morning, after about a week of this backbreaking toil, Emma was cleaning the carpet in the drawing room, rushing up and down and across the immense expanse of florid flowers and arabesques entwined in oriental convolutions, the carpet sweeper a dangerous weapon in her hands as she handled it with force and a certain abandon. As she had raced to and fro, a staggering thought entered her mind and it so amazed Emma it brought her to a standstill in the middle of a clump of purple rosettes. She leaned on the carpet sweeper, totally absorbed in her thoughts, and slowly a look of absolute comprehension crossed her face. Emma, pragmatist that she was, and intelligent and acutely observant, had just realized that the cleaning and care of Fairley Hall was difficult to manage because it not only was badly planned but was downright muddled, in fact. At that moment, it also struck her that this was due to Murgatroyd's poor organization and his haphazard distribution of the work. Lots of minor jobs were repeated daily, and unnecessarily so, and too much time was wasted on them because of Murgatroyd's pernickety fussing about trivialities. Then again, major jobs such as cleaning the silver, ironing the mountains of washing, and dusting the paneling in the library were all jammed together to be completed in one day. It was not possible for one person to accomplish all of this work properly, and also attend to the general chores which had to be done the same day. But there was a solution and it had come to Emma in a flash, as she had stood poised with the carpet sweeper in the center of the drawing-room floor. It was a solution so simple she was surprised no one else had ever thought of it. *The solution was planning*. She suddenly knew that if the work was planned properly and systematically, in a sensible way, and distributed more intelligently, it would be easier to manage. Of this she was absolutely confident, and the more she thought about it, the more convinced she had become.

In an effort to make some sense out of this muddled daily routine, Emma began to time herself at each job, and then scribbled down the amount of time each one took on a scrap of paper culled from the wastepaper basket in the library. She next made a list of all the daily chores, plus the major tasks for the entire week. For several nights thereafter, as exhausted as she was, Emma had forced herself to stay awake as she wrestled with the problem. She had studied her piece of paper assiduously, pondered over each chore and the time involved, and then she had set about creating her own special work plan. She first distributed the heavier work more evenly, staggering the jobs that were complicated or time-consuming over the whole week, so that they were easier to handle along with the daily routine. She also allocated a given amount of time to each specific chore, ruthlessly cutting corners with the less important ones for expediency's sake. Satisfied at last that she had made a semblance of sense out of what had previously been a hopeless muddle, she had copied her make-shift plan on a less grubby piece of paper and had hurried excitedly to show it to Cook, well pleased with herself and also vastly relieved. If the new routine was followed precisely the work could be accomplished in a more orderly and practical fashion, to the benefit of everyone.

To Emma's amazement Cook had not only been thunder-struck but had thrown a temperamental fit that was unprecedented, and had gone on to warn her, in the most dire terms, of Murgatroyd's most certain and deadly wrath at such unthinkable and unwarranted cheekiness, her plump red face clouded with worry and also alarm. Only then did Emma recognize the magnitude of what she was proposing and she had trembled at the thought of Murgatroyd's bellicose temper, his strident invectives and stinging blows.

But Mrs. Turner had not reckoned with that streak of stubbornness in Emma, that implacable will. Almost at once, both of these characteristics overcame the girl's initial misgivings and she firmly resolved, in her doggedly willful way, to be neither thwarted nor forestalled in her efforts to bring a little ease and orderliness to her work. As she listened impatiently to Mrs. Turner's continued and overly ominous rantings, it occurred to Emma, now coldly calculating, that she could not permit herself to be deterred by Cook, whom she had just decided was a fool. She determined there and then that the only way to accomplish her purpose was to circumvent Murgatroyd altogether.

"I'm going upstairs ter show this plan of mine ter Mrs. Wainright," Emma had announced in a hard, firm voice, her face sternly set, her relentless eyes blazing icy green. "We'll

see what she has ter say about it all. She's already been
planning them there menus since she's been here, and I bet
she's going ter start running this house afore long. And about
time somebody did!" she had finished defiantly, and, as was
later proven, quite prophetically. Without another word to
Cook she had turned and marched up the kitchen stairs,
before her nerve failed her, leaving Cook aghast at her temerity. For a split second, the usually verbose Mrs. Turner
was rendered speechless, flabbergasted at this unexpected
display of vociferous rebellion on the part of Emma, who was
normally so acquiescent and docile.

She finally found her voice. "Going up ter see Mrs. W.
won't be doing yer no good, lass," she had cried vehemently
as Emma continued to climb the stairs without looking back.
"Yer stepping out of yer station in life, my girl, and that'll get
yer nowt but the sack!" she continued as the door had banged
loudly behind a silent and determined Emma.

Emma had barely spoken more than two words to Olivia
Wainright in the short week she had been visiting at Fairley,
and she had felt shy and awkward as she had tapped on the
library door. At Olivia's bidding she had entered the room
and had stood nervously in the doorway, hesitating, her
hands clenched tightly at her sides, paralyzed by unanticipated
fright. Olivia Wainright was sitting behind Adam's desk, attending to the sadly neglected household accounts he had
asked her to look into, and which previously had been handled by Murgatroyd. In her tailored dark serge skirt and
white lace blouse, with its high neck and leg-of-mutton sleeves,
she looked the epitome of aristocratic elegance. A large and
exquisite cameo brooch relieved the severity of the high
neckline and a long strand of rosy pearls gleamed lustrously
against the guipure lace bodice, and there were matching
pearl studs at her ears. Her dark hair was swept up into an
elaborate pompadour and it gave her face a fragile appearance, like a lovely flower on a long and slender stem.

Emma, timorous and quaking, was rooted to the spot. She
gazed at Olivia, mesmerized by her beauty, grace, and sophisticated stylishness, and as she had continued to stare in
awe she became painfully conscious of her own old patched
blue dress and the stained and graying striped piny that had
seen better days. She ran her hands down her rumpled skirt
and across the creased pinafore in an effort to smooth out the

wrinkles, but it was a vain effort. She had looked down at her old boots with their worn cracked uppers and then flushed with embarrassment, and she felt shame for the first time in her life. It was a shame that made her heart clench achingly in a way she had not experienced before, and it filled her with the most intense feelings of inferiority and worthlessness, feelings she was not to forget as long as she lived. Emma knew that poverty was not a crime, even if the world treated it as such, yet she felt like a criminal as she hovered, shamefaced, anxious, and tongue-tied, on the edge of the luxurious carpet, acutely aware of the picture she made. Why should this rich and elegant lady take what she had to say seriously? she wondered.

But Emma, for all her intelligence and precocious perception, had no way of knowing that Olivia Wainright was an exceptional woman, understanding of heart and generous of spirit, who put great store in justice, fair play, and compassion, and was only too willing to help the deserving better themselves if they so desired. Nor did Emma realize that Olivia was not regarding her critically or with derision or the self-serving pity of the patronizing do-gooder, but with enormous curiosity and a most genuine interest. Preoccupied as she had been with her sister's poor health and Adam's depressed state since her arrival, she had not as yet had time to delve into the domestic situation at the Hall. And whilst she had noticed the little maid flitting about the house, this was the first opportunity she had had to observe her so closely. From the moment Emma had entered the library Olivia had been struck by her unique and refined good looks, which were not at all diminished or obscured by the disreputable uniform and the grimy cap that so dismayed Olivia, whose own servants were dressed attractively and decently, albeit in plain utilitarian attire. Returning Emma's steady gaze, she noticed that the girl's face and hair were scrupulously clean and she had an aura of neatness and grooming about her, in spite of that dreadful clothing, and this Olivia found commendable.

Emma meanwhile had become aware of the questioning look on Olivia's face, and knowing she could no longer procrastinate so uncertainly on the threshold, she had taken a diffident step forward. Her boots creaked horribly in the quiet room, much to her mortification, and she stopped, abashed and self-conscious, a look of discomfiture on her face.

Olivia had paid no attention to the squeaking, if she heard it at all, and had smiled kindly and said in a gentle voice, "What is it? Do you have a problem you wish to discuss with me?" Gracious and empathic, Olivia Wainright had been blessed since girlhood with an extraordinary ability to make everyone, and especially servants, feel comfortable in her presence. This inherent quality quite obviously transmitted itself to Emma, who now approached the desk more confidently, praying her boots wouldn't squeak again. They did. Emma winced and cleared her throat loudly, hoping to counteract the sound. She stood in front of Olivia, swallowed hard, remembered to curtsy, and said with a kind of shaking firmness, "Yes, I do have a problem, so ter speak, ma'am."

"First, tell me your name, child," said Olivia, smiling again.

"It's Emma, ma'am," said Emma nervously.

"Well then, Emma, what is this problem you have? The only way we will solve it is to talk about it. Isn't that so?" asked Olivia.

Emma had nodded, and in a voice that was almost a whisper, she had explained the domestic routine, its basic difficulties, and her own problems of coping with them because of the poor organization. Olivia had listened patiently, a warm smile on her calm and lovely face, a thoughtful expression in her lucent blue eyes. But as Emma continued her doleful recital, Olivia had become quietly enraged, and her blood had boiled at the inequity of the situation and the execrable management of her brother-in-law's home, an establishment of some standing and enormous wealth, where matters should not have been allowed to deteriorate so disgracefully, as they most apparently had, and nearly beyond redemption from the sound of it.

When Emma had finished speaking, Olivia studied her intently, somewhat surprised by the girl's sweet and melodious voice and her concise explanation. This had been perfectly lucid, despite her limited vocabulary and her idiomatic speech pattern, which fortunately was not so broad in dialect as Olivia had expected it to be. Olivia had instinctively perceived that the girl was neither exaggerating nor embellishing, and she knew she had listened to a veracious witness to the prevailing circumstances at the Hall, and she was shocked.

"Do you mean to tell me, Emma, that at this moment you are the only maid employed in this house?" Olivia had asked.

"Er, no, not exactly, ma'am," Emma had replied quickly. "There's a girl that sometimes helps Cook. And Polly. But she's still badly as I said afore. *She's* really the parlormaid."

"And since Polly's sickness you alone have been doing Polly's work as well as your own? Cleaning this entire house and looking after Mrs. Fairley as well? Am I correct, Emma?"

"Yes, ma'am," Emma said, shuffling her feet nervously.

"I see," Olivia had responded quietly, and she was further outraged. Olivia Wainright was accustomed to order and tranquillity in her own homes, and being an able and proficient administrator of her London house, her country estate, and her business affairs, she was, not unnaturally, astounded at the preposterousness of conditions at Fairley. "Inexcusable and utterly ridiculous," murmured Olivia, almost to herself, straightening up in the chair.

Misunderstanding these words and detecting the edge of annoyance in Olivia Wainright's voice, Emma became alarmed. "I'm not trying ter get out of owt I'm supposed ter do, ma'am," said Emma, fearful that she might be dismissed for her boldness and presumption, which conceivably could be taken for shirking. "I'm not afraid of hard work, I'm not that! It's just that Murgatroyd's got it—got it planned bad, ma'am."

"So it would appear, from what you tell me, Emma," Olivia had responded, the thoughtful expression lingering in her eyes. Emma looked at her carefully, and encouraged by the woman's outwardly tranquil appearance, she had finally pulled out the crumpled bit of paper and smoothed it out.

"I made this here plan, ma'am. Well, anyways, I think it'll be easier for me to do me chores this way. I worked it out proper like." Emma stepped closer to the desk and handed Olivia the paper. As she did, Olivia noticed the girl's terribly chapped and sore hands and was appalled. She looked into the solemn face hovering before her and saw the dark smudges under her enormous eyes, became aware of the tired droop of the painfully thin shoulders, and she was so unexpectedly moved her heart ached with the most genuine sorrow. Olivia was seized with a sudden sense of shame for Adam, even though she was perfectly sure that he was not cognizant of the facts. She sighed and looked down at the grubby bit of paper. Olivia studied it carefully and was both newly amazed and impressed. The girl was obviously above average intelligence and most certainly had an efficient and practical turn of mind. The household routine had been worked out precisely and in an organized manner, and Olivia decided she herself could not have improved upon it.

"Well, Emma, I see exactly what you mean. Seemingly you devoted a lot of thought to this timetable and I must compliment you. Indeed I must."

"Yer mean yer think it's more—more better my way?" asked Emma, relieved and not a little elated.

"More efficient, I believe you mean, Emma," Olivia had responded, suppressing a smile of amusement. "I think we should put your timetable into operation immediately, Emma. I certainly approve of it and I am confident Murgatroyd will recognize the sense of it as well," she had said, pronouncing the butler's name with coldness. Observing the worried expression that flickered in Emma's eyes, she had added reassuringly, "I will speak to him about it myself. I shall also instruct him to engage another girl from the village to assist you with the heavier work. It is still rather a lot for you to cope with single-handedly, Emma, in spite of your most practical timetable."

"Yes, ma'am. Thank yer, ma'am," said Emma, bobbing a curtsy and smiling for the first time in days.

"Well then, run along, Emma. And please tell Murgatroyd I wish to see him. At once," said Olivia, who was not especially enamored of the butler, and even less so at this moment.

"Yes, ma'am. Please, ma'am, can I have my plan back? Me *timetable*, I mean. So as I knows what I'm doing."

Olivia concealed another smile. "Of course. Here it is. By the way, Emma, is that the only uniform you have?" asked Olivia.

Emma flushed and bit her lip and looked down at the crumpled dress and pinafore with dismay and great embarrassment. "Yes, ma'am. For winter, that is. I've got a cotton one for summer," Emma had mumbled self-consciously.

"We must rectify that at once. If you tell me your size I shall attend to it myself, when I go to Leeds later this week," Olivia announced, and had added, "I shall buy you several uniforms, for winter and summer, Emma. One of each is simply not enough."

"Ooh! Thank yer, ma'am, ever so much!" cried Emma. A thought struck her and she had said respectfully, "Begging yer pardon, Mrs. Wainright, ma'am, but I could make 'em meself, if I had the cloth. Me mam taught me how ter sew, ever so good like."

"Did she indeed? That's excellent. I shall ask the Squire for some lengths of cloth from the mill and I shall purchase the cotton for the summer uniforms in Leeds. You may go now, Emma, and incidentally, I am glad you came to see me with your problems. You must always do that, for as long as I am staying here at Fairley."

"Yes, ma'am. Thank yer, ma'am. And I will come ter see yer if owt else bothers me," Emma had promised. She bobbed a curtsy and hurried out of the library, clutching her timetable as if it were the crown jewels. She did not see the look of compassion mingled with admiration on Olivia Wainright's face, nor was she aware that she had set in motion a chain of events that was to change everybody's life at Fairley Hall.

As was to be expected, there was no ugly uproar or altercation in the kitchen about Emma's unprecedented display of independence. Murgatroyd tactically ignored it, since it suited his own purpose admirably. In fact, he paid little attention to Emma's activities, and Emma knew this was because he was too preoccupied maintaining his own position in the household to care about her. Now that he was under the eagle eye of Mrs. Wainright he had to watch his step and, undoubtedly, whatever she had said to him had been effective. Observing Murgatroyd out of the corner of her eye, as he scurried to and fro, bowed and scraped, and pulled his weight in the household for once, Emma would often smile to herself and there was both irony and a flicker of smugness in the smile that flitted across her young face. Emma had begun to comprehend that Murgatroyd had met his match in Olivia Wainright. Gentle of manner though she was, and soft-spoken and most cordial, Emma knew that the courteous demeanor disguised a strong will and an exacting but fair nature.

However, as the weeks passed, the timetable and Emma's rigid adherence to it had begun to amuse Cook, who had long forgotten her own objections to it. She had never witnessed anything like it in all her years of service. It sent her into

Tazidime IM/IV ®
ceftazidime/Lilly

See prescribing information on back pages of pad.

Tazidime IM/IV ®
ceftazidime/Lilly

gales of loud, though kindly, laughter. She would slap her
pendulous thighs and shake her head and say, between gusting peals of mirth, "Aye, lass, yer a rum 'un, yer are that.
Whoever heard of a blinking timetable, 'cept at the railway
station? And yer tek yerself so serious, yer do that, Emma
lass. Yer run about this 'ere house like the Devil himself is
after yer, slaving yer fingers ter the bone. And where's it all
going ter get yer, when all's said and done? I'll tell yer
summat, and yer should mark me words, lass. The more yer
do in life, the less yer gets thought of. I knows, aye, that I
do."

At these raucous but genial outbursts, Emma would look at
Cook with large eyes, but say nothing. She did not have
time to explain her reasons. Time now meant money to
Emma, and she would not waste her precious time chattering. And anyway, Emma was sure Cook would not understand. How could she know that the timetable was, in a
sense, a kind of protection for her? It enabled her to work in
a more efficient and orderly manner. She could ease the work
load on various days and conserve her strength. Not only
that, because of it, Emma was able to steal a little time for
herself and this stolen time was of vital importance to her.
Several afternoons a week, and early most evenings, she
retreated to her attic room and worked on the dresses and
other clothes she altered or repaired for Mrs. Wainright and
Mrs. Fairley. She was paid separately for this work, at Olivia
Wainright's insistence, and her little tobacco box of shillings
and sixpences was slowly growing. Nothing was going to
deter her from making this money, her own secret money,
even if she had to occasionally skimp on some of her chores to
make time for the sewing. It was with a grim determination
that she sewed diligently into the middle of the night, by the
light of three candles, her eyes scratchy, her fingertips sore,
her shoulders aching as she hunched over the elaborate gowns
and blouses and skirts and dresses and fine undergarments,
plying her exquisite stitches..For the money she earned from
this sewing was being acquired, most methodically and religiously, to finance Emma's Plan, which she always thought of
with a capital *P*.

Cook knew about the sewing, but not about the late hours
Emma kept, and had she known she would have been annoyed, for she was fond of the girl and had her welfare at

heart. So Emma did not enlighten her about this either, preferring to keep her own counsel.

Although Mrs. Turner was a woman with a degree of native shrewdness, she was not blessed with great intelligence or perception, and she did not understand Emma's character in the least. Nor did she have the foresight to recognize that the girl was displaying the first youthful glimmering of an amazing organizing ability that was to prove formidable; or that her punctuality, diligence, and unrelenting efficiency were the first outward signs of an immense self-discipline and the driving ambition that would grow to monstrous proportions, and which would prove to be the very roots of her success later.

At this moment in her life, Emma certainly did not understand this either, and the future was far from her mind as she remembered the events of the past few months whilst attending to the fire. She sighed softly. Those days had been bad days, but they had passed now. She visibly brightened. Things *had* improved. Her timetable worked successfully and her life was a lot easier. Mrs. Wainright had kept her word and had hired another girl, Annie Stead, from the village, whom Emma was patiently, and sometimes vociferously, training as the betweenmaid. The domestic routine was running as smoothly as clockwork, so much so it was like a miracle and one that Emma prayed would last. But apart from this, and most importantly, Mrs. Wainright had increased Emma's wages by two shillings a week, a welcome addition to the family income.

Emma lifted a large log with the tongs and dropped it onto the fire, which was now burning merrily and throwing off so much heat Emma's face was warm and flushed. She stood up, smoothed her pinafore, adjusted her dainty cap, and straightened her cuffs, for she took exceptional pride in her appearance ever since Blackie had told her she looked "fetching" and was the prettiest colleen in the whole county of Yorkshire. She glanced around the sitting room and scowled. The thunderstorm had ceased as abruptly as it had begun, but the sky was still overcast and it filled the room with gloomy shadows. It's ever so dark in here, she said to herself, and turned up the lamps on the black lacquered chinoiserie tables flanking the fireplace. The room was immediately suffused with brighter light, warm and glowing, which counteracted the dismal atmosphere and the chilliness produced by the preponderance of blue furnishings.

Emma stepped back and regarded the mantelpiece, her head on one side, her eyes thoughtful as she appraised the objects aligned along the marble shelf. There were a pair of silver candlesticks, beautiful Georgian pieces holding white candles, an elaborate porcelain clock, supported in the paws of two lions rampant on either side, and which chimed like a tinkling bell on the half hour, and Dresden figurines of a lady and gentleman in old-fashioned dress. Emma, by herself, had rearranged all of these objects in a more harmonious way, as she had done with numerous other pieces elsewhere in the room. Sometimes she was sorely tempted to hide half of the bric-a-brac in various cupboards and drawers, since she considered it to be superfluous, but she did not dare go that far. Occasionally she wondered where she had found the courage to regroup most of it without permission, not that Mrs. Fairley seemed to notice, or anyone else for that matter. She was still contemplating the mantelpiece, congratulating herself on the attractive effect she had created, when a slight rustling sound caught her attention. She turned swiftly to see Adele Fairley standing in the doorway of her adjoining bedroom.

"Oh, Mrs. Fairley! Good morning, ma'am," Emma said, and dropped a curtsy. Although the Squire had told her weeks ago not to curtsy to him, because it annoyed him, Emma felt obliged to do so in the presence of her mistress and Mrs. Wainright.

Adele nodded and smiled weakly, and then she seemed to sway and stagger, as if she was ill, and she clutched at the doorjamb to steady herself, and closed her eyes.

Emma rushed across the room to her side. "Mrs. Fairley, are yer all right? Do yer feel badly?" Emma inquired solicitously, taking her arm.

Adele opened her eyes. "I felt faint for a moment. But it's nothing. I didn't sleep very well."

Emma scrutinized her through narrowed eyes. Mrs. Fairley looked paler than ever, and her hair, normally so beautifully groomed, was uncombed and she looked disheveled, which was also unusual. Emma noticed that Adele's eyes were red and swollen.

"Come ter the fire and get yerself warm, ma'am, and have

some of this nice hot tea," Emma said sympathetically, and led her firmly across the floor. Adele, swaying and leaning heavily on Emma, drifted into the room on a cloud of Jasmine scent that was momentarily overpowering, her silvered robe dragging limply behind her.

Emma settled her in the wing chair, glanced at her anxiously, and said briskly, "I made scrambled eggs for yer this morning, Mrs. Fairley. I knows yer enjoys 'em, and yer didn't eat much of yer dinner last night, I noticed." As she spoke she removed the lid from the silver dish and pushed it forward, drawing her mistress's attention to it.

Adele Fairley brought her distant gaze from the fire and looked at the eggs without interest, an absent expression on her face as pale as death. "Thank you, Polly," she said, and her voice was listless and without any emotion. She lifted her head slowly and stared at Emma, a puzzled expression flickering onto her face. She blinked in bewilderment and shook her head. "Oh, it's you, Emma. Of course, I'd forgotten, Polly is sick. Is she any better? When is she coming back to work?"

Emma was so completely unnerved by these remarks she stepped back involuntarily and stared with disbelief at Adele, her eyes widening, the silver lid in her hand poised in mid-air. In an effort to disguise her alarm, she plopped the lid back on the dish with a loud clatter and cleared her throat nervously. And then she said in a voice that quivered, "But, Mrs. Fairley, don't yer remember?" She paused and gulped and continued tremulously, "Polly's—Polly's—" She stopped again and then blurted out quickly, "Polly's dead, Mrs. Fairley. She died last week and they buried her on Thursday—" Her voice, so low now it was almost a whisper, trailed off, as she stared at Adele with growing disquietude.

Adele Fairley passed her hand over her brow wearily and covered her eyes and then, after a second, she forced herself to look directly at Emma. "Yes, I do remember, Emma. Forgive me. These headaches, you know. They are quite dreadful and leave me utterly exhausted. Sometimes I am inclined to be forgetful, I am afraid. Oh dear! Yes, poor Polly. So young." Adele's face, only briefly lucid, glazed over and she turned to the fire in a trance-like state and regarded the flames with sightless eyes.

Emma, who had grown accustomed to Adele's chronic absentmindedness, was, nevertheless, appalled at this partic-

ular lapse of memory, which was shocking to her, and unforgivable. How could Mrs. Fairley forget someone's death so
quickly and apparently with such ease? Emma asked herself,
horrified. Especially Polly, who had worked like a little Trojan for her for five years, and had been devoted. Until this
moment Emma had, for the most part, been able to excuse
Adele's heedless indifference to the troubled lives of others,
ascribing it to her pampered life and her unrealistic and even
childish view of the world. But this incident she found hard
to overlook. Emma did not attempt to conceal the contemp-
tuous expression that slid onto her face and her mouth tightened into a stern and unyielding line. Why, she's no different
than the rest, she thought condemningly. They're all the
same, the rich. We don't mean owt to 'em. Beasts of burden,
that's all we are, and no more important in their lives than
the muck under their feet. I bet if *I* died tomorrow she'd pay
no mind to it.

Emma looked at Adele staring so unconcernedly into the
fire and she was outraged and also disgusted, and it occurred
to her that Adele was not only shallow and selfish but heartless. In Emma's opinion, even Adele's gentleness no longer
seemed a redeeming characteristic. But after a long moment,
Emma pushed the anger down, controlling it with steely
determination until it was finally quelled into partial submission, for she knew it was a wasted emotion. Emma also knew
that it was ridiculous to dwell on the natures of the gentry.
Where would that get the likes of her in the long run? What
would it achieve? Nothing! Neither could she afford to squan-
der her valuable time trying to understand the rich, whose
ways were so mysterious to her. She needed her time and
energy to make things easier for her mam and dad and
Frankie, who was only just recovering from the whooping
cough.

Emma began to busy herself around the Queen Anne tea
table, concealing her feelings behind a show of efficiency, her
composure restored to its usual quiet containment, her face
so inscrutable it was like pale stone. But as she poured the
tea, buttered the toast, and served the eggs, Emma kept
seeing Polly's pathetically dwindled face and her dark eyes
burning feverishly in their hollow sockets and her heart lurched
with a terrible sadness, and the pity she had felt for Adele
only a short while before was diluted.

"Eat this afore it gets cold, Mrs. Fairley," said Emma stonily.

Adele looked up at Emma with her lustrous silvery eyes and smiled her deliquescent smile, that melting smile that lighted up her face, and it was as if the conversation about Polly had never taken place at all. Tranquillity dwelt in her face and her eyes were clear and comprehending.

"Thank you, Emma. I am a little hungry. And I must say, you do take good care of me." She sipped the tea and went on chattily, "How is your mother, Emma? Is she still improving in health?"

So sudden and incredible was the change in Adele, Emma was further nonplussed by her mistress's behavior and she stared at her in puzzlement. And then she said quickly, "Yes, ma'am, thank yer. She's not half as badly as she was, being as the weather's improved, and it's easier on me dad now that he's working down at yon mill."

Adele inclined her head. "The eggs are good, Emma," she said, finishing a forkful, and there was sudden disinterest in her voice, and dismissal.

Emma understood that the brief moment of friendly discourse was over and she reached into her pocket and fished around for the menu for dinner, which Cook had given to her. Although Adele had long ago relinquished her control of the household affairs to Murgatroyd, and more recently to her sister, Cook persisted in sending up the menus daily for her approval. Mrs. Turner had worked for Adele since she had come to Fairley as Adam's bride and she was always deferential to Adele, and would brook no interference with this ritual of the menus, and made no bones about the fact that, to her way of thinking, Mrs. Fairley was still the mistress of Fairley Hall, and nobody else. And so she treated her as such and with the utmost consideration and respect. It never occurred to the loyal Mrs. Turner that Adele paid little attention to the menus, nor did it seem to disturb her that no comment, favorable or otherwise, was ever forthcoming.

Emma pulled the menu from her pocket and held it out to Adele. "Cook says will yer please look over this here menu for dinner, Mrs. Fairley," she said.

Adele made a little moue and laughed lightly. "I can't be bothered with that this morning, Emma. You know very well

I trust Mrs. Hardcastle to plan suitable menus and she always does. I am quite sure today is no exception."

Emma shifted on her feet nervously, the paper fluttering in her hand. She gave Adele a curious look, and a troubled expression spread itself across her face, which had paled. What's wrong with Mrs. Fairley? she asked herself, her heart pounding unreasonably. She's worse this morning than she's ever been. Emma bit her lip, as a most disturbing thought struck her. Was Mrs. Fairley touched? It had not occurred to her before that the rich could be daft in the head. She had always thought that such a terrible affliction was the prerogative of the poor, but perhaps she was wrong. And Mrs. Fairley was acting so peculiar it was enough to make anybody wonder. First she had forgotten Polly was dead, and now she was talking about Mrs. Hardcastle as if she didn't know she had been relieved of her duties as housekeeper weeks ago.

Emma hesitated, uncertain how to respond. Mrs. Fairley might be offended if she kept referring to her forgetfulness. So she said slowly, choosing her words with care, "Didn't I tell yer afore, Mrs. Fairley, that Mrs. Hardcastle left? It must've slipped me mind. It was when yer were badly in bed. Mrs. Wainright gave her the sack. She said Mrs. Hardcastle had a bad habit of tekking a holiday when it wasn't no holiday."

Adele stared down at the breakfast tray. Of course! Olivia had sent Hardcastle packing in a flurry of disfavor. Olivia had stood here in this very room and told her she had let Hardcastle go. She had been infuriated at her sister's presumption, but she had been unable to countermand her orders. She had been too ill, and anyway, Adam had backed Olivia to the hilt and it would have been useless to oppose them. Now she must watch herself. Pay more attention to the things she said, even to Emma, otherwise the girl might become suspicious of her, just as Olivia and Adam were suspicious. Yes, she must be more careful. She lifted her head and smiled warmly, her face a picture of innocence.

There was a clever and deadly cunning in Adele. She had the uncanny ability to dissimulate, and to disguise her bizarre foibles when she so chose, slipping easily behind a façade that simulated rationality, and her behavior at times could appear very normal, as it did now.

"Perhaps you told me, Emma. I know Mrs. Wainright

mentioned it. But I *was* very sick and so worried about Master Edwin at the time, and it obviously did not register. Well, let us not worry about that now. And let me see the menu." She held out her hand and took the paper. She gave it only a cursory glance, as always, and handed it back to Emma.

"Excellent! A repast for royalty, I would say," declared Adele smilingly. And for once, she added, "Give Cook my compliments and tell her she has outdone herself, Emma."

"Yes, ma'am," said Emma, replacing the menu in her pocket, tactfully not bothering to point out that it was not Cook who had planned the menu but Olivia Wainright. "Here's the *Gazette*, Mrs. Fairley," Emma went on, passing the newspaper to her mistress. "I'll go and do the bedroom now," she finished, bobbing a small curtsy.

"Thank you, Emma. And when you have finished you can draw my bath, so that I can bathe and dress after breakfast."

"Yes, ma'am," Emma said, and hurried into the bedroom.

Emma stifled a cry of amazement when she entered the room and saw the clothes Adele had pulled out of the wardrobe strewn all over the floor in chaotic heaps. She clamped her hand over her mouth, horror-struck, and stood perfectly still, glaring at the dresses and gowns and robes and other beautiful garments lying in tangled disarray. "Whatever's got in ter her?" she muttered under her breath, gaping at the clothes incredulously, and then added inwardly: She might not be touched, but she's acting as daft as a brush, she is that! As she stepped carefully around the clothes, a feeling of anger mingled with acute frustration made a tight knot in Emma's stomach. She realized furiously it would take her some time to bring order to the clothes and return them to the wardrobe and their former neatness. Her timetable would really be ruined now! Methodically she began picking them up, slipping each garment onto a coat hanger and placing it in the wardrobe, working with efficiency and her usual swiftness, in a concentrated effort to save as much of her precious time as possible.

Meanwhile, Adele continued to peck at her breakfast delicately and after a few mouthfuls she pushed the plate away, feeling revolted by the food. She shook her head violently from side to side, as if to clear it of cobwebs. As she did, she told herself she must try to be more alert and cease her perpetual daydreaming; otherwise she would never reinstate herself as mistress of the house. She would ring for Murgatroyd later, who at least recognized her authority, and order him to bring her the whiskey.

There was a sharp knock on the door and it was flung open with a certain abruptness. Engrossed as she was in her musings about the butler, Adele half expected to see Murgatroyd standing there, and she opened her eyes, sat up smartly, and turned to the door, smiling her melting smile, ready to greet the butler. She was therefore astonished to meet the cool and contemplative gaze of her husband. The smile congealed and she froze in the chair. Her hands flew up to her throat agitatedly, like birds fluttering in sudden flight, and she nervously fingered the silvered lace that flowed around the neckline of her robe. Her mouth went dry. She opened it to speak but no words came out. She licked her lips anxiously, staring at Adam in stunned silence. Then she fell back limply in the chair, in an attitude of shrinking intimidation. She was also utterly astounded, for he rarely came to her room.

Adam noticed her fearful reaction and, although it dismayed him, he wisely disregarded it.

"Good morning, Adele. I trust you slept well," he said in his usual soft yet sonorous voice.

Adele looked at him carefully, filled with antagonism and the most virulent resentment. In her present disturbed state of mind, feelings of fear and doubt were paramount within her, and she viewed everything he said and did with unwarranted mistrust. Consequently, she had become guarded and self-protective with him.

Finally she spoke. "No, I did not sleep very well," she said coldly.

"I'm sorry to hear that, my dear. Perhaps you can take a rest this afternoon," he suggested kindly.

"Perhaps," said Adele, looking at him in stupefaction and with some consternation, wondering what had precipitated this unexpected visit.

Adam remained standing in the doorway, leaning against it with his usual inbred elegance. He had not crossed the threshold of this room in ten long years and he had no intention of doing so ever again. It had always appalled and embarrassed him, with its clutter and frigid blueness and delicacy and overriding femininity. Now it sickened him.

Of late, conversations with Adele were extraordinarily painful to Adam. He always started out with the kindest of intentions, but she invariably managed to brush him the wrong way, and he found himself growing irritated with her, and increasingly impatient. He was therefore anxious to conclude what he had come to say as peaceably and as swiftly as possible, and so he said quickly, "I want to talk to you about Edwin, Adele." He eyed her warily, for he fully recognized he was embarking on a sensitive subject.

She sat bolt upright in the chair and clutched the arms. "What about him?" she cried, her eyes flaring with apprehension. Edwin was her favorite, and she adored him.

Conscious of her growing alarm, he said gently, "It's time he went back to boarding school, wouldn't you say? Even though it is almost half term, I think he should return immediately. I would like him to have the next couple of weeks catching up with his studies. He has quite a lot of ground to cover, you know. After all, he has been at home since Christmas. Far too long, in my opinion."

"It's perfectly ridiculous to send him back now, it's hardly worth it! He can return after Easter!" cried Adele with growing perturbation. She paused and took several deep breaths to steady herself. "Anyway, he's still in delicate health, Adam," she added, adopting a more cajoling tone and giving him the benefit of her sweetest smile that no longer made any impression on him.

"Nonsense!" admonished Adam firmly. "His health is fine. He's a robust boy and he has quite recovered from the pneumonia. You pamper Edwin, Adele. It's not good for him. And however well-intentioned your motives are, you are smothering him. He should be with boys of his own age, in more disciplined and rigorous surroundings. You treat him like a baby."

"I do not!" exclaimed Adele defensively, her voice rising to a shriek, and the smoldering resentment against her husband turned into instant hatred.

"I have no intention of quarreling with you about this matter, Adele," said Adam icily. "I have quite made up my mind and nothing will persuade me to change it, most particularly your abnormal desire to cling to the boy. I have also spoken to Edwin and he wishes to return to school as soon as possible."

Adam looked at Adele pointedly. "At least *he* sees the sense of it. And I must say, he has been most diligent under the circumstances, trying to continue his studies on his own. But that's hardly good enough for me, Adele." Adam cleared his throat and softened his tone. "You must consider Edwin, my dear. He misses school and his friends, which is only natural. And so"—Adam hesitated and then went on softly— "and so, I came to inform you that I intend to drive him to Worksop myself. Tomorrow."

Adele smothered a small gasp. So soon, she thought, and tears sprang into her eyes and she turned her head so Adam would not see. Her hand shook as she brushed away the tears surreptitiously. Adam was doing this to thwart her. It was not for Edwin's sake at all. He was jealous that Edwin preferred to stay at home with her. She had a sudden physical compulsion to jump up and fly at him with her hands, to strike him, to tell him he was cruelly taking away the only person who loved her and whom she loved.

But she looked back at Adam and at once saw the implacability etched across his sternly handsome face and she knew then, with a sinking feeling, that she would not achieve anything by fighting him. He was inexorable. "Very well, Adam, whatever you say," said Adele, her voice still quavering and filled with incipient tears. Gathering a little more strength, she continued, "But I wish you to know that I am only agreeing to this—this—ridiculous decision of yours because you say Edwin himself has expressed a desire to return to school. Although I am not so sure he's such a reliable judge of his fitness to return so quickly. Personally, I think it's preposterous when half term is imminent. He'll hardly get there before it's time for him to come home. All that traveling back and forth is debilitating, especially to a little boy who has been so sick. I think you are very hard on Edwin, Adam. I really do."

Adam could not resist the impulse of retorting caustically, "Edwin's no longer a little boy. Furthermore, I don't want him growing up to be a sissy, Adele, and he will if he remains tied to his mother's apron strings. You've always tended to spoil and pamper him, and it's a miracle that he's turned out so well. So far."

Adele gasped and her pale face flushed with deep color. "You are most unfair, Adam. Edwin's never been tied to my apron strings, as you so vulgarly put it. How could he have been? You sent him away to school when he was only—" Her voice was so filled with emotion she could not continue, but after a moment she went on tearfully, "Only twelve. And if I've spoiled him a little it's simply because he is sensitive and has always been put upon by Gerald."

Adam stared at her, taken aback, and then he smiled sardonically. "Well, well, my dear, you are more observant than I believed you to be. I am glad to know you realize Gerald hectors him incessantly and behaves most churlishly towards poor Edwin. That's another reason I want him out of this house—to remove him from his brother's taunting. He will be much happier at school, until he's old enough to defend himself on Gerald's level. Although personally I hope he'll rise above it. Not a very admirable offspring, our eldest son," he finished softly, but with enormous scorn.

This comment went over Adele's head. A weary look settled on her face. She sighed deeply, and passed her hand over her brow. A rising feeling of nausea was making her dizzy and she fervently wished Adam would go away and leave her in peace. This effort to maintain her sense of balance and appear coherent was sapping what little vitality she had left. She felt enervated. "The matter is settled then, Adam," said Adele quietly, fighting the pressing need to retreat into her inner world where nothing could touch her. "I have a splitting headache," she whined, "and I'm sure you have other urgent matters to attend to yourself."

"Yes, I do." He scrutinized her thoughtfully, and a strange sadness enveloped him. There was sympathy in his voice as he said, "I hope you feel better, my dear. I am sorry this conversation has been painful for you, but you know I am only thinking of Edwin."

Considering the conversation to be concluded, Adam inclined his head courteously and turned on his heel. Something made him pause and he looked back at her, frowning, suddenly conscious of the obscure expression in her eyes, the glassy sheen coating her face.

"I can assume that you will be well enough to grace us with your company at dinner this evening, can't I? You know we are expecting guests," said Adam.

She sat up, startled. "Tonight!" said Adele shrilly.

"Yes, tonight. Don't tell me you have forgotten the dinner

party Olivia has planned for Bruce McGill, the Australian sheep rancher. She mentioned it to you earlier in the week," Adam said sharply, holding his irritation in check.

"But that is on Saturday, Adam. Olivia told me it was Saturday. I know she did. I wouldn't make a mistake like that," she cried peevishly.

Oh, wouldn't you, Adam thought, and stared at her with coldness. "Today *is* Saturday, Adele."

Flustered, she touched her forehead nervously. "Of course. How silly of me," she murmured hurriedly. "Yes, I am sure I will feel well enough to come down for dinner."

"Good." He half smiled. "Please excuse me, Adele. I have to see Wilson at the mill, and then I am going into Leeds. I look forward to seeing you this evening, my dear."

"Yes, Adam," Adele said, and fell back into the chair, feeling faint, and also great alarm at the prospect of facing people, and in particular a stranger.

Adam closed the door softly behind him. He was considerably surprised. It was a major achievement for him to have wrested Edwin from her clinging hands with so little opposition. In a way, even her momentary show of spirit had been a relief to him. Usually her entreaties to keep Edwin at her side were accompanied by floods of tears, vaporish swoonings, and the most irrational display of hysterics that he always found himself incapable of dealing with. The scenes in the past had been insupportable and had mortified him.

Emma, working in the bedroom, had not been able to avoid overhearing this conversation, even though she never consciously eavesdropped, as the other servants often did. She finished making the bed and pursed her lips and thought: Poor woman. He's such a bully, and so mean ter her. Like he is ter everybody.

Although Emma's hatred for Adam Fairley was unreasonable and without any foundation, it was quite real. So was her enormous dislike for Gerald, who never lost an opportunity to torment her. But she held no grudge against Edwin, who was always sweet with her, and she did respect Olivia Wainright. Now she wondered if she had been uncharitable about Mrs. Fairley earlier, and she paused, clutching a silk pillow to her chest, and thought hard about this. Perhaps it's him that makes her act queer, she said to herself. He gets her ever so flustered and upset. Maybe that's why she's always forgetting stuff and things, and walks around in a flipping daze. Emma replaced the silk pillow, smoothed it over, and pulled up the eau de Nile green coverlet made of heavy satin, her mind still lingering on Adele Fairley's strange ways. A rush of sympathy for Adele flowed through her and quenched the feelings of anger mixed with animosity she had been harboring, and for some reason, quite unknown to herself, Emma felt decidedly happier about this change of heart.

Emma was dusting the Venetian glass-and-mirrored dressing table in front of the oriel window, humming to herself, when Adele walked into the room. Her face was tense with concern and her cheekbones stood out starkly, sharp ridges under her eyes, which were clouded with misery. Her anxiety about the impending dinner party had forced her to push aside both the desperate desire to retreat into herself and her longing for the soothing whiskey. In his present unrelenting mood, Adam struck terror into her heart, and it was imperative that she make an appearance that evening and behave with decorum and dignity. Whatever it cost her in effort, she must be controlled and at ease and charming, and no one must have the slightest inkling of her emotional turmoil.

Then the cunning in Adele surfaced and she smiled to herself. She had a card up her sleeve and it was always a winning card. Her beauty. Adele knew that her incredible looks never failed to stun people. So much so that their attention was deflected from the idiosyncrasies of her personality, which otherwise might be quickly detected. She decided she must look absolutely breathtaking at the dinner. She would hide behind the façade of her beauty.

She hurried to the wardrobe, which Emma had just restored to order, and opened the huge double doors impatiently. Emma's heart sank into her boots. She had an instant picture of Adele scattering the clothes all over the room again, and she looked up and said quickly, "I put all yer clothes away, proper like, Mrs. Fairley. Is there summat yer looking for? Summat in particular like?" Startled, Adele turned around abruptly. She had forgotten Emma was in the bedroom. "Oh! Emma. Yes. I am wondering what to wear for the dinner party tonight. Quite important people have been invited, you know." She rustled through the gowns and went on in a querulous tone, "You will be here to help me dress, won't you, Emma? You know I can't possibly manage without you."

"Yes, ma'am. Mrs. Wainright asked me ter work over the weekend, 'stead of having me time off as usual, 'cos of the dinner," said Emma quietly.

"Thank goodness!" Adele cried with relief, and continued her search for an appropriate gown. The fact that Emma had been forced to forgo her weekend at home with her family failed to register or make the slightest impression on Adele. She was only concerned with herself. Finally her hands lighted on a gown and she pulled it out, holding it up to show Emma. Lately, Adele had found it difficult to make decisions without conferring with Emma, and she now elicited her advice about the dress she was holding.

"Do you think this is beautiful enough?" she asked, pressing the gown against her body. "I must look my best tonight—outstanding, in fact."

Emma moved away from the dressing table and stood in front of Adele. She cocked her head on one side and screwed up her eyes, looking at the dress carefully and critically. She knew the gown was expensive and that it had come from Worth. Mrs. Fairley had told her that before. And it was beautiful, all rippling white satin and delicate lace. Yet Emma did not really like it. She thought it was too fussy and not at all flattering to Mrs. Fairley.

After a few moments' thoughtful consideration, Emma said, "Well, it is beautiful, ma'am. But I think it's a bit—a bit pale for yer, if yer don't mind me saying so. Yes, that's it, Mrs. Fairley. It makes yer look ever so washed out, so ter speak, next ter yer pale skin and with yer blond hair."

The pleasant expression on Adele's face dissolved and she glared at Emma. "But what will I wear? This is a new gown, Emma. I have nothing else that is at all appropriate."

Emma smiled faintly. There must be at least a hundred gowns Adele could choose from and all of them very beautiful.

"What yer need is summat more—more—" Emma paused, searching her mind for a word. She thought of the illustrated magazines she had read that showed photographs of the latest fashions, and the word she needed instantly flashed into her mind. "Yer need summat more *elegant*, that'll make heads turn. Yes, that's it, Mrs. Fairley, and I knows just the right dress." She ran to the wardrobe and pulled out a gown made of black velvet. It was the ideal color to show off Adele's beautiful ivory complexion and the lustrous silvery-gold hair. Then Emma frowned as she looked at it again. It was trimmed with blood-red roses that swathed one shoulder and fell down the side of the gown in a long trail.

"This is the one," she exclaimed with absolute sureness, and added, "If I tek them there roses off."

Adele stared at her in horror and disbelief. "Remove the roses! You can't possibly do that. You'll ruin the dress. And anyway, without the roses it will look too drab."

"No, it won't, Mrs. Fairley, ma'am. Honest, it won't. It'll look more *elegant*. It will. I just knows it will. And yer can wear that luvely necklet, the sparkling one, and them there earbobs. And I'll put yer hair up in that pompadour style I copied for yer, from the picture in the magazine yer showed me last week. Oh, yer'll look ever so luvely in this dress, Mrs. Fairley, yer will really."

Adele seemed doubtful and sat down heavily on the green satin chaise, frowning and biting her lip. Emma flew to the dressing table, picked up a pair of nail scissors, and, undeterred by Adele's cry of protest, she expertly cut the stitches holding the roses in place.

"Look, now it's really *elegant*, Mrs. Fairley," exclaimed Emma excitedly, pulling off the roses unceremoniously. She held up the gown with a triumphant flourish.

Adele was furious. "You've ruined it!" she gasped, her voice shrill. "And it *is* drab! Just as I said it would be." For once she was angry with Emma and her eyes blazed.

"It won't be drab when yer gets it on, and with yer beautiful jewels," Emma said firmly, ignoring the small burst of anger. "And if yer wants, I'll sew them blinking roses back on later. But first we'll try it this way, Mrs. Fairley. Please," she pleaded.

Adele was silent, her face like a thundercloud, and she gave Emma a petulant look as she twisted her hands nervously together in her lap.

"I can put them roses back on in two shakes of a lamb's tail, when I helps yer ter get ready. So don't worry about it, Mrs. Fairley," said Emma reassuringly.

"Well—all right," said Adele reluctantly, somewhat pacified, although still pouting.

Emma smiled confidently. "I'll pop it back in the wardrobe

for now. Don't worry, Mrs. Fairley, yer'll look luvely tonight, yer will that. I promise. Now I'll go and draw yer bath for yer, ma'am."

"Thank you, Emma," said Adele dully, still worrying about the dinner. Emma returned the gown to the wardrobe and hurried into the bathroom.

Adele went to her dressing table and took out the red velvet case that contained her diamond necklace, bracelets, and matching earrings. She lifted out the necklace and held it up to her throat. Its shimmering brilliance caused her to draw in her breath in surprise. She had forgotten how magnificent it was and, now that she thought about it, the black velvet gown would set it off perfectly. Perhaps Emma had been right, after all, in her choice. Adele smiled with delight. She would look so ravishing tonight even Adam would be speechless.

FIFTEEN

Later that day, when Emma finished her general chores, she returned to the upstairs sitting room with afternoon tea for Adele Fairley. Adele had declined to come down for lunch, claiming a headache and fatigue, and so Emma had taken great care with the tea, being determined to make Mrs. Fairley eat something to keep up her strength for the important evening that lay ahead. Having overheard the conversation between Adele and Adam, and later witnessing Adele's concern over her gown, Emma had intuitively sensed her apprehension about the dinner party. She felt protective of Adele, now that her sympathetic feelings were restored, and she wanted to assuage Adele's nervousness as best she could. Pampering her a little was the only way Emma knew how to do this.

For these reasons, even though she was more overworked than usual because of the dinner party, Emma had painstakingly prepared some of the things Adele enjoyed for tea, hoping to tempt her jaded appetite. There were tiny cucumber sandwiches and others filled with egg, cream crackers spread with shrimp paste, hot buttered scones, homemade cherry jam, Cook's delicious shortbread biscuits and Eccles cakes. She had also made a huge pot of the tea Mrs. Fairley preferred, although Emma didn't know how she could drink it. To Emma it tasted funny, like smoky water, and not at all like real tea, even if it was expensive and was specially ordered from Fortnum and Mason in London. But there was no accounting for the tastes of the rich, Emma decided, as she trudged up the staircase with the tea tray. They ate and drank the strangest things, to her way of thinking. She liked good plain food herself, and didn't hold with fancy dishes and rich sauces and peculiar delicacies, which never tempted her. She also believed the gentry ate too many meals with too many courses. To Emma it was disgusting the way they gorged themselves gluttonously like ravenous pigs. No wonder they suffered from indigestion and were liverish and bad-tempered. It was all that food and drink that did it. Even when I make me fortune, I'll still eat simple, she commented dryly to herself as she went into Mrs. Fairley's suite of rooms.

Adele had been resting all afternoon. She was still lying in the great four-poster bed, propped up against the pile of pale green pillows, reading the *Yorkshire Morning Gazette*, when Emma entered the room and carried the tray over to the bed. Adele looked up from the newspaper and smiled sweetly.

"I'm glad you suggested I take a rest," said Adele, adjusting her position against the pillows. "I slept for quite a long time and I do feel more rested and refreshed for tonight, just as you said I would, Emma." She smiled again and there was a hint of gratitude in her eyes.

Emma stared at Adele intently. The tense lines that had etched her mouth with anxiousness that morning had vanished. Her face was relaxed and calm, and her eyes were so clear and bright they were almost merry. Even the badly swollen lids had lost their red puffiness and the deathly pallor had been replaced by a delicate glow that perfectly reflected the pale pink satin nightgown she wore.

Why, she looks ever so beautiful, Emma thought, and said, "I've brought yer summat ter eat, Mrs. Fairley. Yer must be right famished, seeing as how yer didn't have owt since breakfast. Try and get summat down yer, even if it's only a few mouthfuls." She placed the tray next to Adele on the bed and continued, "I even made that funny tea yer like."

Adele laughed and for once there was gaiety in her voice. "You mean the Lapsang Souchong, Emma. Thank you."

"Yes, that's it. Lapsang Souchong—" Emma repeated slowly, and hesitated. Then she said questioningly, "Do I say it proper like, ma'am?"

"You do indeed," asserted Adele, somewhat amused, as she poured a cup for herself.

Emma smiled slightly. She liked to learn things, for future reference. She would need to know a lot when she went to Leeds to make her fortune. Now she cleared her throat and said, "Begging yer pardon, Mrs. Fairley, but I'd like ter look at yer dress again, if yer don't mind. I wants ter be sure that there's nowt wrong with it. That there's nowt that needs fixing, I wants it ter be perfect for the dinner. Will I be in yer way?"

"Of course not, Emma. And if it does need anything done to it, you may stay here and work. You don't have to go up to your room. But I'm sure it's not damaged. I've hardly worn it, you know," said Adele.

Whilst Adele had her tea, Emma took out the black velvet gown and examined it minutely for any defects. It was in beautiful condition, except for a loose hook and few torn stitches on the hemline of the train where Mrs. Fairley had obviously caught her heel. Emma also noticed there were lots of dangling threads visible down the side of the gown, where she had cut off the roses. She would have to pull the threads out gently, she realized, in order not to damage the expensive black velvet.

Emma carried the gown to the chaise and began to work on it with great care, for she was a perfectionist and gave every task her undivided attention. She was glad to sit down for a while. She had been run off her feet all day and she was facing a long and arduous evening, since she was to help Murgatroyd serve the dinner. She relaxed as she worked and the tiredness she had been experiencing earlier gradually began to evaporate.

A certain kind of compatibility had developed between Emma and Mrs. Fairley in the last few months. Disparate as they were in background and age, they were curiously at ease with each other, and although this understanding was unexpressed, it was, nonetheless, valid. The girl intuitively sensed the elder woman's terrible anguish, and despite her youth and inexperience, she recognized the tragedy of Adele's life. Quite automatically and without much forethought, Emma knew how to behave properly around her and without underscoring or feeding Adele's extreme anxiety in any way. On her part, Adele had grown to like Emma, whom she found patient, kind, and unobtrusive when she worked in the suite of rooms. Adele also thought Emma was pretty and this pleased her, for she could not abide ugliness. And so an aura of peace enveloped them as they sat together in the room, the young girl passively sewing, the older woman partaking of her afternoon tea.

The bedroom was filled with the mellowest of lights that flooded through the tall windows, and the fire crackled and blazed in the grate, giving off a cheery glow that was both warming and comforting. The pale watery apple-green silk that covered the walls, swathed the windows, and fell down in rippling cascades from the four corners of the carved oak bed created a cool and restful effect, one that gave Emma a sense of tranquillity and, since the bedroom was not as cluttered with bric-a-brac as the adjoining sitting room, she also found it less overpowering and irritating to be in.

And it was certainly more restful than the kitchen she had just left, which was full of hot bustle, flying tempers, and all manner of frantic goings-on. Annie, the betweenmaid, was assisting Cook with the preparation of the food for the dinner, which was such an elaborate meal even Annie's mother had been engaged to help out for the evening. Mrs. Wainright had planned a wonderful menu, they all agreed on that, even though Cook kept grumbling that things were getting a little too fancy for her liking. Emma suspected that Mrs. Turner's little tantrums, temperamental outbursts, and complaining sprang from her extreme nervousness about coping with such an intricate meal. Although Mrs. Turner always claimed that good solid Yorkshire cooking was her great specialty, Emma had long comprehended that it was her entire repertoire.

As she pulled out the threads, Emma thought about that menu and laughed to herself quietly, as she recalled Mrs. Turner's face when she had read it that morning. Her eyes had stood out on stalks and she had huffed and puffed for a full hour. She could just imagine her flustered rantings and ravings downstairs right now. Poor Cook had never prepared a dinner quite like this in all her years at Fairley. The guests were first to be served chilled caviar garnished with chopped hard-boiled eggs, chopped raw onions, and wedges of lemon with melba toast. After that came the lobster soufflé with a lobster sauce, followed by turtle soup flavored with sherry. "Not too much sherry," Mrs. Wainright had warned, "just the right amount to add a dash of piquancy." Then there would be Dover sole cooked in a creamy white wine sauce containing slices of mushrooms and shallots. The main course was roast beef with horseradish sauce, potatoes roasted in the pan with the meat, carrots and peas, and a thick gravy made of the juices from the beef. There was to be a cheese board of Stilton, Cheshire, and Wensleydale cheeses with a selection of crackers and digestive biscuits. Finally, three desserts would be served as a finale to the meal, which Cook kept referring to as "a blinking banquet." These were a compote of mixed fruits, made from Cook's pantry supplies bottled last summer, and currently soaking in Kirsch, a fresh lemon pie with thick whipped cream, and a chocolate mousse, which Mrs. Wainright had said must be light and fluffy to be really perfect.

Emma knew that some of these dishes had definitely strained Cook's talents, which had never been put to such a test, and, in fact, Emma herself had been pressed into hurried service earlier. She had made the soup and the sauces for the fish and meat dishes, prepared the mousse, and covered the fruit compote with the liqueur, scrupulously following Mrs. Wainright's instructions.

Emma was decidedly happy to have escaped for a while. The hubbub had increased with great rapidity in the last hour and Cook was so harassed she was getting truculent with the maids, and Annie's mother as well. Emma smiled again. She knew only too well how easily rattled Cook became when there was any change in the kitchen routine. Not only that, this was the first big dinner party the Squire had given in several years and it had sent everyone into a flurry, except Mrs. Wainright. And me, Emma thought then, preening a little inside, remembering Mrs. Wainright's compliments about her cool head, her efficiency, and her light hand with the sauces and the mousse.

Although she had no taste for rich and elaborate dishes herself, Emma liked cooking and had begun to find it a challenge to prepare interesting meals. With Olivia's arrival, the menus in general had become a little fancier than was normal at Fairley, and Emma had been helping Mrs. Turner with the cooking lately. She was also learning a lot from Mrs. Wainright, who wrote out explicit instructions for every new dish and usually came down to the kitchen to supervise. Emma had kept the menus and the instructions and had pasted them into an old school exercise book. Her pragmatism and intuition had automatically told her they would come in useful one day. Now she reminded herself to copy down the name of the peculiar tea, Lapsang Souchong, in her book, and the names of the wines Mrs. Wainright had selected from the cellar with Murgatroyd, each one for a different dish. Emma had listened carefully to Mrs. Wainright that morning and had learned for the first time that red wine was always served with meat, white wine with fish, and champagne with dessert. The names on the bottles were funny. "Frenchy names," Mrs. Turner had told her with a huffy grimace. Murgatroyd had glared. "But the very best, you ignorant woman," he had snapped. "Vintage wines the old Squire himself put down years ago. Can't be bettered hereabouts, not even in fancy London town," he had finished pompously.

Yes, I must remember ter copy the wine names proper like, and ask Mrs. Turner for the dinner menu and them there recipes, Emma said to herself. She pulled off a length of black cotton from the reel, licked the end, threaded the needle, and began to sew the hemline of the dress, her mind on her exercise book. Everything that might be of some value went into it. She didn't know what information she might require in Leeds when she put her Plan with a capital P into operation, and she must be absolutely prepared in every way. The tattered old book contained menus for all kinds of meals, innumerable recipes, household hints, sewing instructions, little sketches for dresses and hats Emma had designed herself, and some of Mrs. Fairley's special and most secret beauty hints. Now it'll have a wine list, Emma thought, and was pleased. Emma sewed patiently, thinking her ambitious thoughts, glancing up from time to time to observe Mrs. Fairley. She must keep a close eye on her, to be sure she didn't get nervous or upset before the dinner, which was a long way off yet. The guests were coming at eight-fifteen and dinner was to be served at eighty-thirty sharp, Murgatroyd had told her, warning her in a snooty voice to be dressed and ready in a fresh uniform. As if she didn't know that.

In point of fact, Adele Fairley was unusually calm as she finished her tea, picked up the newspaper, and continued to read it. Sheer fear of Adam's wrath, if she appeared in any way strange that night, had made her control her impulse, her very need, to send for Murgatroyd and ask for the drink, the only thing that could blunt the sharp edges of her pain these days. She had resorted to alcohol as an anodyne for her ills only in the last year and was still able to resist it, when circumstances forced her to do so. As yet she was not sodden with it, nor had she become a confirmed alcoholic. That afternoon she had assiduously removed the temptation of drinking by taking to her bed. Cowardly though this stratagem was, it had served its purpose. Also, Adele had not realized just how worn out she was, and she had fallen into a numbed and exhausted sleep immediately. When she awakened she discovered she felt better, and more importantly, and much to her amazement, she was less riddled with anxiety.

She concentrated on the newspaper, another ruse to keep her mind occupied and prevent her from dwelling on either the need for a drink or the impending evening that loomed ominously ahead. She turned the page and glanced at the Court Circular, which gave items of news from Buckingham Palace. As her silvery eyes scanned the column of fine black print she learned that the Russian and French ambassadors had been received by King Edward yesterday; the Marquess of Londonderry had had an audience with His Majesty after the Council; the Queen and Princess Victoria had visited an exhibition of drawings. Bored, she rustled through the paper to the back pages. Her eyes caught the Bradford Market. She passed on hurriedly. That was all she needed! More about wool. She knew enough about that to last her a lifetime. As her eyes lighted on the advertisement for John Smith and Tadcaster ales, Adele thought longingly of the whiskey and her mouth felt suddenly dry. She moistened her lips and her eyes flew nervously to the other page. She folded the paper in half and began to wade through a long story about Lord Fitzwilliam's Hunt at Clifton near Doncaster. She concentrated all of her attention on this, attempting to block out the persistent image of the glass of amber liquid that floated

before her eyes and settled enticingly on the center of the
page.

The sound of clattering hooves, whinnying horses, and the
clamor of raised voices floated up from outside and broke the
gentle mood and silence of the bedroom.

"What on earth is that dreadful fuss? All that shouting?"
Adele cried, her eyes flaring with surprise, as the voices grew
more voluble and angry in tone.

Emma shook her head, equally mystified. She put down
the gown she was still working on and ran to the window. She
parted the curtains and looked down into the courtyard below.
"It's the children, ma'am," she said quietly, biting her lip,
and turning back to face Mrs. Fairley. "It's Master Gerald.
He's shouting and bawling at Master Edwin summat terrible
like." Emma hesitated, almost afraid to go on. Adele looked at
her expectantly. Emma gulped. "Mrs. Fairley, I think he's
crying, poor Master Edwin is."

"Edwin!" shrieked Adele, and she pushed aside the tray so
vigorously Emma thought there would be an accident. Adele
leapt out of the bed and flew across the room like a Valkyrie
in flight, her hair streaming down her back. She moved with
such unaccustomed velocity, Emma stepped aside hurriedly
when Adele reached the window and violently jerked the
white lace curtains apart and looked out. The scene being
enacted below made Adele's throat tighten and her face took
on a ghastly pallor.

The two boys were still mounted, after their ride, and
Gerald was berating Edwin, his blubbery face swollen and
red with temper. Edwin, in spite of his tears, was valiantly
trying to defend himself against this verbal onslaught. Adele
threw open the window with great force, about to intervene.
At this precise moment, Gerald moved his horse closer to
Edwin's, and Adele cringed, hardly daring to breathe. She
watched Gerald deliberately kick his booted foot into the
lower rib cage of Russet Dawn, Edwin's chestnut stallion. As
the boot struck, the startled horse reared up on its hind legs,
crazed and afraid, its nostrils flaring as it leapt forward violently. Edwin would have been thrown onto the rough cobblestones if he had not been an excellent equestrian like his
father. He kept his head, and consequently his seat, and with
superb horsemanship brought Russet Dawn under control.

Adele was so horrified, so sickened, so angered by this

malicious act, her whole body began to shake and for a moment her throat was constricted. Long ago Adele had admitted to herself she was actually afraid of Gerald. He was a bully. But now her terrible rage and her concern for Edwin enabled her to overcome this inherent and often paralyzing fear.

The courtyard was suddenly deathly quiet. Gerald did not appear at all chagrined by his actions and was actually grinning. Edwin was wiping his tear-stained cheeks with the back of his hand. Adele seized the moment. She leaned out of the window and cried in an uncommonly harsh tone, "What is the meaning of this commotion, Gerald? What is this dreadful altercation all about? You are behaving in the most deplorable manner, which I will not tolerate."

Gerald looked up and blinked, taken aback at his mother's unanticipated appearance at the window, and also by the firmness of her tone. Gerald had always despised his mother, even as a little boy. He thought her foolish and vain, and he sniggered at her behind her back.

Now he moved restlessly in the saddle and cleared his throat. "It's nothing of any importance, Mother. Your precious darling is perfectly capable of taking care of himself, even though he is a big baby, thanks to your pampering," he said with rude disdain. "Go back to bed, Mother. We don't want you interfering with us, or as an arbitrator, for that matter."

"How dare you speak to me with such insolence?" exclaimed Adele with enormous coldness, shocked at Gerald's audacity, which she found inexcusable. "I want, no, *demand*, an explanation about this matter or you will answer to your father. Come to the library at once. And remove your filthy riding boots before doing so!"

Gerald was so flabbergasted at this extraordinary reversal in his mother's mien, which was normally meek and abstracted, he gaped at her open-mouthed, his usual scornful retorts unuttered. Edwin was not at all surprised, but he was afraid for his mother, and a worried look flashed across his sensitive face.

"But there's nothi—" Gerald began.

"At once, I said!" Adele snapped, and closed the window in his face with a loud bang, a grim expression ringing her mouth. Then she began to tremble, almost convulsively, although this was more from anger than any other emotion. She clutched the green silk draperies to steady herself.

Emma moved closer to her and took her arm. "Oh, Mrs. Fairley, don't upset yerself so. Please. Remember the dinner. Yer must keep yerself calm for tonight. Pay no mind ter Master Gerald, Mrs. Fairley. Yer knows what boys are like, always bickering and squabbling amongst 'emselves."

Indeed I do know what boys are like, especially that horrid little monster, Adele thought, but said, rather shakily, "Yes, Emma, you are right to some extent. But occasionally children must be chastised when they have misbehaved, and taught the difference between right and wrong. Now, where is my dressing gown?"

"It's here, ma'am," said Emma, picking up the purple velvet robe faced and trimmed with pink satin that matched the nightgown, which was lying across the chair in front of the dressing table. "And here are yer slippers," she went on, reaching for the purple velvet mules decorated with pink osprey feathers. She took them to Adele.

"Thank you. Where is the Squire?" asked Adele as she struggled hurriedly into her dressing gown and slipped her feet into the mules.

"He went ter Leeds, Mrs. Fairley. And I knows he won't be back till six. I heard him telling Murgatroyd that," said Emma.

"I see. Where is Mrs. Wainright? Perhaps you can find her, Emma, and ask her to join me in the library," said Adele.

"She's not here either, ma'am. She went to the village ter see the Reverend Martin about summat to do with the church," Emma explained, wondering how Mrs. Fairley would cope with Gerald alone. He could be a real devil when he wanted, and mean. She knew that only too well.

Adele sighed heavily and looked at Emma, but made no comment, her silvery eyes thoughtful. Resolutely she pushed aside the panic that was beginning to take hold of her. For once in her life it seemed she would have to deal with an unpleasant situation on her own. She had resolved earlier to assert herself in the household, and now the opportunity had apparently presented itself. However difficult it might prove to be, she must handle it at all costs. That despicable little fiend is not going to get away with this as easily as he imagined, she decided. She took several deep breaths and then looked at herself in the ornate Venetian mirror on the dressing table. She wound her hair into a chignon and secured it with several tortoiseshell combs. Satisfied with her appearance, she threw her shoulders back and moved across the room with sureness, coldly imperious in her bearing.

But she faltered at the door and looked back at the speechless Emma, who was astonished at this quite phenomenal show of strength.

"Perhaps you had better accompany me to the library, Emma," said Adele softly. Though her heart was beating with great rapidity and she felt physically weak, her steely determination to confront Gerald was intact. Nevertheless, she believed Emma's reassuring presence would bolster her courage even more.

"Yes, Mrs. Fairley, ma'am, 'course I'll come with yer," said Emma, vastly relieved that she had been asked. If there was trouble she could always run for Murgatroyd. He might be a tyrant downstairs in the kitchen, but he was devoted to Mrs. Fairley.

SIXTEEN

Together they made their way down the long and dusky corridor and slowly descended the first flight of the grand staircase richly carpeted in red. Adele held on to the polished oak banister to steady herself and Emma supported her other arm under the elbow. When they reached the central landing, where the two upper left and right flights converged to join the main staircase, Adele paused to catch her breath, clinging tightly to the intricately carved newel post.

An immense stained-glass window floated high above this landing and the staircase, and it blazed with brilliant jewel colors and threw off rafts of awesome fiery light that washed over the white walls and spilled into the cavernous hall below. Emma glanced down and she shivered unexpectedly. The deserted hall looked gruesome, even frightening, in the unearthly bluish-red radiance that made crouching beasties and grotesqueries of the dark wood furniture and the huge potted palms. Once again terror trickled through her veins and she wanted, as always, to flee from this oppressive house full of secrets and concealed violence.

Don't be daft, she told herself firmly, but she held on to Mrs. Fairley's arm more tightly, as much to quell her own fears as give support to Adele.

When they finally reached the hall, Adele looked around swiftly and then she also shivered and drew her robe about her. It seemed she echoed Emma's own sentiments when she said, "It's awfully gloomy and unwelcoming in here, Emma. Please turn up the gaslights."

Emma did as she was bid and hastened after Adele, who was already sweeping grandly into the library, her back stiff, her head lifted proudly on her tense shoulders, her face as unmoving as white onyx. Murgatroyd was busy polishing the crystal glasses on the black-walnut chest, in readiness for the evening, when Adele entered with Emma close on her heels. He straightened up quickly and looked in some amazement at Mrs. Fairley, who rarely appeared downstairs during the day, if at all.

"Why, madame, how nice ter see yer looking so well. Can I get yer owt, Mrs. Fairley?" he asked deferentially.

"No, thank you, Murgatroyd," Adele said, trying to smile.

"There's nowt wrong, is there, Mrs. Fairley?" he asked, peering at her closely.

Adele, walking across the floor with Emma in her wake, said quickly, "No, no, of course not, Murgatroyd. I wish to speak to the children about a certain matter, that's all. But thank you for your concern."

"Not at all, madame," said Murgatroyd. His curiosity aroused, the butler hovered solicitously around Adele, who declined the chair he proffered and stood in front of the fireplace. Emma retreated into the background, her face grim, her eyes watchful.

Adele turned to him. "If I need anything I will ring for you, Murgatroyd," she said, dismissing him with a slight nod.

"Certainly, madame," said the butler, bowing servilely. He picked up his cloths and backed out of the room. As he left he threw an ugly look at Emma. "The way that lass has wormed her way in with the missis and Mrs. Wainright is summat ter fair tek yer breath away," he mumbled enviously. He closed the door sharply behind him.

Adele remained standing, one hand gripping the edge of the mantelpiece, the other in the pocket of her robe, clenched in such a tight ball her nails dug into the palm. Her instinct was to run upstairs and retreat behind locked doors. Only her solicitude for Edwin kept her firmly rooted to the spot and prepared to face Gerald, whom she knew to be vicious.

The door opened and Gerald came in, followed closely by Edwin, who took up a position next to his father's desk. His face was a picture of dismay, and he trembled.

Gerald rolled ponderously across the room, his obese body bulging in his tight riding jacket and breeches. The sly Gerald had just decided it was infinitely preferable to deal with his mother, rather than his father. In his opinion that vain and vacuous woman could easily be manipulated. He knew his father could not.

You stupid bitch, he thought, smiling at Adele lovingly. He came to a standstill and positioned himself directly in front of her. He arranged a bland look on his face and said ingratiatingly, and with unfamiliar pleasantness, "Mother, please excuse me for being so rude to you. It was quite unpardonable, I know. But we were a little excited, I'm afraid. However, I didn't mean to be impertinent or hurtful to you in any way. I hope you can forgive me, Mother dearest."

Having anticipated an angry and abusive display, or at the most, further insolence, Adele was momentarily startled. A little surge of relief flooded through her and she was about to relax her taut muscles. She instinctively checked herself. Despite Gerald's low opinion of her, she had more insight than he credited her with, and she knew what he was and she did not trust him. She also recognized that, like all bullies, he was a coward.

She held herself perfectly still and rigid. And she was unbending. She knew if she relented she would not only lose face but would expose Edwin to further mistreatment at Gerald's hands.

"You did behave with the most appalling rudeness, Gerald," said Adele. "I will overlook it this time, but I expect more respectful and gentlemanly conduct in future." Her voice was steady. She looked him right in the eye unflinchingly, and went on, "You will now give me an explanation of your abominable behavior in the courtyard. I wish to know why you—" Adele paused and glanced coldly at her son. "Why you were treating Edwin so unspeakably. I think it is quite reprehensible the way you continually pick on him. Your own brother, indeed. I will not permit it to continue, Gerald."

Gerald, shifting about impatiently, realized this was not going to be as simple as he had thought. Moreover, he was confounded by his mother's control. Now understanding that a mere apology would not suffice, as he had misguidedly imagined, he took a deep breath and began to explain, in a conciliatory tone. "It was really all a tempest in a teacup, Mother dear. Please believe me, that's the absolute truth. It was unfortunate I became so—er—er—ruffled." He paused and flashed her a falsely loving smile. "We were out riding on the moors, as you know. On our way back we came across a dog, probably from the village, caught in one of those traps Father has had put down for the rabbits and other vermin. Edwin became upset about this, excessively so, I would say, and actually wanted to release the dog. I wouldn't let him. We argued about this, Mother, mainly because I didn't want Edwin injuring himself. Those traps are extremely dangerous, you know. I persuaded Edwin to ride on, and for some reason, quite unknown to me, he became more tearful as we reached the house. That's all there is to it, Mother dearest."

"I see," said Adele thoughtfully. She gave Gerald a penetrating look. He flinched slightly under this fixed examination, but said blandly enough, "I have told you the truth, Mother. Ask Edwin."

"Oh, I fully intend to," said Adele grimly. Her legs had turned to water and a pulse in her temple was beginning to pound. Pitilessly she forced herself to continue, and she turned to regard Edwin. "I would now like you to tell me your side of this—this—ghastly tale, dear."

"Yes, Mother," Edwin said, joining her by the fireplace. His face was still chalk white and his alarm was patently obvious, although this was caused by consternation for his mother's health, rather than fear of his brother. In spite of his sensitive nature, Edwin could stand up to him most of the time.

He coughed behind his hand and then said softly, "Gerald did tell you the truth, Mummy. At least, most of it. He simply omitted the fact that the dog was still alive and writhing in the most terrible pain. When Gerald wouldn't let me attempt to release it, I suggested we send the yardman out to set it free. Or if that was not feasible, to shoot it and put it out of its suffering. That seemed to me to be the only merciful thing to do." Edwin stopped and stared accusingly at Gerald, who quickly averted his eyes.

Edwin's voice rose in anger. "But he laughed at me. Actually laughed, and said I was being childish and hysterical. Gerald even went so far as to suggest that it would be a waste of time and also of the bullet. That's why I became so heated." He pushed his hand through his fair hair agitatedly. "It was his cruelty that maddened me. And when I said I would tell Father about the dog Gerald became terribly abusive."

Adele swallowed, attempting to subdue the feeling of revulsion that swamped her. "How disgusting you are. To let a poor helpless animal suffer like that and not try to put it out of its torment. Why, you are not even—" Her furious gaze stabbed at Gerald, who did not budge but merely returned his mother's condemning gaze steadily.

"Please, Mother, don't *distress* yourself so. You'll make yourself ill again," said Gerald in a gentle voice that sheathed his deceitfulness. "The dog was on its last legs. It's probably dead by now, anyway." He shrugged. Gerald knew he must dispense with this matter before his father returned from Leeds, otherwise there would be an uproar of no small proportions. So he said, again with fraudulent gentleness, "What would you like me to do, Mother, to make amends? I do so hate to see you in such a disturbed state."

Adele had been staring right through the bulbous Gerald, an inscrutable look on her face. "I would like you to bring the yardman to me immediately, Gerald," said Adele.

Gerald blinked and his jaw dropped open stupidly. "You mean bring him here, into the house? Into Father's library?" he said, balking at this idea.

"Yes, Gerald, into the house. I certainly have no intention whatsoever of going to the stables."

"But, Mother, perhaps—"

"Don't argue, Gerald."

"Yes, Mother. As you wish," he said grudgingly, unable to conceal his disapproval.

Adele's eyes searched out Emma, who was standing in a

shadowy corner, her face as ashen and as perturbed as Edwin's. "Emma, please run down to the kitchen and get me a glass of water. This horrendous story has made me feel quite queasy."

"Yes, ma'am," said Emma, bobbing.

"And you, Edwin," Adele continued, "will be doing me a great service if you will be kind enough to get me the smelling salts from my bedroom. They're on the dressing table, dear." Edwin nodded and slipped out after Emma.

Adele now focused her blazing eyes and all of her attention on her elder son. He was edging towards the door. "Gerald, before you go for the yardman I wish to speak to you." Adele's voice was sweet and she smiled brilliantly.

Gerald was instantly confused by this radical change. "What about?" he said rudely.

"A matter of some importance. Come back here, Gerald." Adele beckoned.

Gerald reluctantly moved forward and it occurred to him too late that his mother's voice had not been sweet at all. It had oozed acid and that smile had been a dangerous smile. He wavered and, quailing, held back.

Adele took a sudden step forward and, in a lightning movement, grabbed the boy's wrist. They were only a few inches apart and Adele lifted her other hand and struck him savagely across the cheek.

Gerald recoiled and tried to break free. Adele held him in a vise-like grip that was surprisingly strong, and she leaned forward urgently. She stared deep into his eyes, and with loathing.

"If I see you endanger Edwin's life in any way, ever again, or hear that you have done so, I won't answer for the consequences!"

A quick denial sprang to Gerald's facile tongue, but when he saw the knowing gleam in his mother's eyes he thought better of it. For the first time in his life he was cowed by this woman who, in her towering rage, appeared more beautiful than she had ever been, and was awesome.

"I *saw* you kick Russet Dawn," Adele continued in the same venomous hiss. "And in the rib cage. You know as well as I do that when a highly strung hunter is struck unexpectedly, and with force, it is guaranteed to bolt. That's why you did it, of course! Edwin could easily have been killed. You know what they do to murderers in England, don't you, Gerald? They hang them by the neck until they are dead! Need I say more? Do you understand me?"

Gerald had blanched. His mother's long nails bit into his flesh and red weals were appearing on his blubbery face. "Yes, I understand you," he mumbled.

"Good. You are fortunate I have decided not to reveal your wickedness to your father. But I warn you now, I will do so if anything like this ever happens in the future." Adele regarded Gerald for a long moment and then released her hold, flinging her son's hand away violently, as if it were contaminated. "Get out of my sight! Now! Before I strike you again!" she shrieked. Gerald fled.

The door slammed and Adele covered her jerking mouth with her hands. She was shaking. This was the first time she had ever struck one of her children, or anyone else for that matter, and her own violence appalled her. Adele leaned back on the sofa and closed her eyes. After a short time she heard Emma's voice.

"Are yer feeling a bit faint, then, Mrs. Fairley? Here's the water." Opening her eyes, Adele saw Emma and Edwin standing before her. She drank the water gratefully and gave the empty glass back to Emma. "Thank you."

Edwin knelt down at his mother's feet and waved the smelling salts under her nose several times. Adele grimaced and drew back. "Thank you, dear. But that's quite enough. I'm perfectly recovered."

In spite of this assurance, Edwin continued to frown anxiously. "Are you certain, Mummy darling? You look frightfully pale."

"Yes, Edwin." Adele smiled at him and patted his head. "You're a good boy." She glanced at Emma. "But I would like another glass of water, please."

"Yes, ma'am. I brought a jug of it up." Emma ran to the walnut chest where she had left the water and poured a second glass.

"Perhaps you should take a brandy, Mother. It might give you a little strength."

"No!" cried Adele.

This was uttered with such fierceness, Edwin shrank back. He seemed hurt as he said, "I'm sorry, Mother. I just thought it would revive you."

"I know, dear, and at any other time I would take a small glass, for medicinal purposes only, of course. But I must keep a clear head for tonight's dinner party, Edwin. It will be a long evening and various wines will be served. I don't want to start drinking too early in the day." In fact, Adele needed a drink desperately, but she fought the desire. She threw him a tender look. "I didn't mean to sound so sharp. Do forgive me, my dearest."

"There's nothing to forgive," said Edwin, returning her loving glance. "I know how wearisome this has been for you. I'm sorry you had to get involved."

The door opened to admit Gerald, accompanied by the yardman. "On our way over from the stables I took the opportunity to explain about the poor trapped dog and your grave concern about it, Mother dearest," said Gerald with a hint of sarcasm, his cocky manner fully restored.

Adele rose and regarded them both with coldness. "I see." She eyed the yardman. "I assume you know how to handle these traps and can release the dog easily. I want you to go and do that immediately."

"Aay, I don't knows abart that," the man muttered. "T'maister won't think owt much o' this. Women laiking abart in t'men's business. Mind yer, I allos told 'im yon traps were right dangerous. I know'd there'd be trouble, I did that. I told t'maister summat bad'd 'appen. Newfangled junk, that's wot yon traps are."

"Quite so. But since you are apparently the only person here who can manipulate them, please go and do as I say. I will take full responsibility with the master," Adele said. "We cannot be certain the dog is dead. In fact, it is probably alive and suffering. Go and attend to the matter at once. If it is dead, bury it. Should it be alive, and if it has some chance of surviving, bring it back here and care for it. Otherwise, if the poor thing is beyond hope, shoot it and bury it out on the moors."

She glared at the man shuffling in the doorway. "What are you waiting for? Go at once! Master Gerald will accompany you, so that he can report back to me on his return," she snapped, her nerves jangling.

"But, Mother!" said Gerald fractiously. "There's no reason for me to go. He's perfectly capable of handling this by himself."

"Don't quibble! Do as I say," commanded Adele.

Seeing the obdurate look in his mother's eyes, Gerald shrugged and said, "Let's get on with it then, man." They left together, Gerald in a high dudgeon.

Adele sat down and stared into the fire. Although she was oddly oblivious to the suffering of people, paradoxically the thought of an animal injured and in pain always moved her.

Emma brought her the water. "They'll do as yer've told them," she said. "Don't worry so, Mrs. Fairley."

"Shall I assist you upstairs, Mother?" Edwin suggested. "You should rest for a while, before dressing for dinner."

"Yes, Edwin, that is a good idea," said Adele thankfully. She was drained. Dealing with Gerald had taken its toll and vitiated her energy. The impending evening would be a further strain, and she wanted to gather her diminishing strength in readiness for it. At this moment she fervently wished she could retreat to her comfortable enveloping bed with a bottle and lose herself in her inner world. She stood up abruptly and Edwin took her arm and led her out of the library.

They mounted the stairs slowly and Emma followed dutifully behind. As Edwin shepherded his mother into the bedroom with great gentleness, Emma caught Edwin's attention and motioned for him to follow her. He excused himself to his mother and hurried after Emma, who was waiting in the sitting room.

"What is it, Emma?" he asked with misgiving, conscious of the worried expression on her face.

"Don't leave yer mother alone, Master Edwin," Emma cautioned softly. "Can yer stop a bit and read ter her, or chat with her, till I changes me uniform and comes back ter help her get ready?"

"Why, of course I can, Emma. But wouldn't it be wiser if she slept for a while?" he asked. "Why shouldn't she be left alone?"

"Because she frets about things and she's ever so nervous about this blinking dinner party. And I knows she won't sleep, 'cos she had a long rest this afternoon. Just sit with her and keep her company. Help ter get her mind off the dinner. I'll be back in a tick, ter start doing her hair," said Emma.

Edwin nodded in agreement. "Yes, you are quite correct, Emma. She does worry and easily becomes distracted." He

reached out impulsively and touched Emma's arm lightly.
"Thank you so much, Emma, for taking care of my mother
with such kindness. I do appreciate it, really and truely I do,"
he said with warm sincerity, his eyes soft and gentle.

Emma looked up at Edwin, who was tall for his age,
surprised but delighted at this show of gratitude. "That's ever
so nice of yer ter say that, Master Edwin. I do me best, yer
knows," she answered sweetly, glowing with genuine pleasure. And then she smiled. It was the most dazzling of
smiles, one that illuminated her face with such radiance it
actually appeared to shimmer in the dying afternoon light,
and her eyes, widely open and tilted upward, were so spec-
tacularly green and brilliant they were breathtaking.

Why, she's beautiful, Edwin thought, momentarily staggered and blinded by her radiance and that beguiling smile
and those incredible emerald eyes full of vivid intelligence,
honesty, and innocence that gazed at him unwaveringly and
with perfect trust. How odd that I never noticed her beauty
before, he thought in wonderment, unable to tear his eyes
away from hers. Imperceptibly, Edwin's young heart shifted
and tightened and he was besieged by an overpowering emotion, one he had not previously ever felt and which he did
not understand. They continued to gaze at each other, as if
mesmerized, locked in a prolonged moment of silence so
intense the air seemed to vibrate around them, and they
were like two figures isolated and petrified by time. Edwin's
naked face was bleached, the bones stark and pronounced.
His limpid eyes were registering every plane and angle and
smooth contour of that face before him, as if he felt compelled to commit it to memory forever. A light flush began to
permeate Emma's neck and cheeks, and her pale pink lips
parted slightly. She was puzzled by that strained and staring
look in Edwin's eyes and concern flooded her face, extin-
guishing the radiance. It was then that Edwin recognized
obtusely, just below the level of his consciousness, that something of tremendous importance had happened to him, although
he was not sure what this was. He did not comprehend, in his
youthfulness, that he was now beholding the only woman he
would ever truly love. The woman who would tragically
haunt him for all the days of his life, and whose name he
would cry out, and with yearning, as he drew his last breath.

Quite unexpectedly tears pricked the back of Edwin's eyes

and he was forced to turn his head. He swallowed hard, coughing behind his hand with embarrassment, humbled and oddly shy in front of this girl who had wrought such sudden upheaval within him. "Excuse me," he said, coughing again, hardly daring to look at her, but he could not resist and his eyes swept back to hers. Emma smiled gently and with kindness, and her face was so exquisite, so fragile, so tender, Edwin had to curb the strongest impulse to reach out and take it between his hands and touch it reverently. Eventually he managed to say in a strangled voice, "You are a fine girl, Emma. And I *will* stay with Mother, as you suggest, until you can come back."

He turned on his heel and went towards the bedroom. As he crossed the floor, with that easy gracefulness inherited from his father, he experienced a peculiar sense of loss, a sensation of such profound loneliness it overwhelmed him and brought him to a standstill. Shaken, he swung around with involuntary force and Emma was startled. He stared at her with great intensity and his eyes were questioning and perplexed. Emma studied him gravely, and with a new understanding remarkably mature in its perception. She smiled faintly, and before he could say anything else she hastened out of the room with the tea tray, the dishes rattling noisily.

Miraculously, the hubbub in the kitchen had abated, and although Mrs. Turner was flushed and perspiring, she seemed less irritable and anxious about the dinner. She was presiding over the steaming pots and pans with a certain bombastic pride, a self-congratulatory smile on her plum-colored face, the ladle hooked onto her apron pocket, her hands on her hips.

Emma placed the tray near the sink and said, "If yer don't need me for owt, Mrs. Turner, I think I'd best go and get ready for tonight."

"Aye, luv, yer had, and right sharpish," responded Cook, looking at the clock on the mantel. "Everything's under control here. It's clear sailing from now on, I'd say." She bestowed a complacent smile on Emma. "There's nowt much ter them there fancy recipes, once yer get the hang of 'em," she continued in a satisfied tone. "Next time we have a big dinner, I'll be able ter do 'em with me eyes closed!"

Annie, who was polishing a large silver meat dish in the

corner, looked up and grinned. She winked at Emma, who turned away, bit back an amused smile, and said, "I'm sure yer will, Mrs. Turner. I'll see yer later."

Emma climbed the steep and twisting narrow stairs that led to her room in the attics. She shivered as she entered it. The window was wide open, and the blue curtains were billowing out wildly in the cool evening breeze from the moors. Emma ran to the window and closed it, and then quickly undressed. She stood at the washstand in front of the small leaded window and scrubbed her face with cold water and a flannel until it shone with rosy freshness. She brushed out her long hair, deftly twisted it into a thick bun, and then put on the evening uniform she had recently made. This was a black wool dress with long tight sleeves and a long straight skirt, and it was considerably more severe than her daytime uniform. But a white silk collar and cuffs relieved the starkness of the black, as did the frilled organdy apron she now tied around her slender waist.

Emma stared at her reflection in the mirror and was suddenly pleased with what she saw. She secured the jaunty white organdy cap on top of her head, smiling happily to herself. It had just occurred to her that she looked pretty. Blackie was always telling her that she was fetching, and Master Edwin obviously thought the same thing. She knew *that,* if only from the way he had looked at her earlier. She dwelt on Edwin. He was not a bit like the other Fairleys. She shuddered, thinking then of Gerald and the horrifying story of the dog. He was cruel and full of malice, whereas Edwin was kind and good. In fact, he did not seem to belong at Fairley Hall at all. She wondered if he had been stolen away from some other house by the gypsies, and sold to the Squire for a lot of money. She laughed out loud at her vivid imaginings which she knew were foolish. Things like that only happened in the tales her brother Frank made up on his bits of paper, and then read to her when she had the time to listen. She sighed suddenly. She would be sorry when Edwin returned to school. Tomorrow, she had heard the Squire say. She would miss his friendly smiles and his daily pleasantries and his thoughtfulness. His mother will miss him, too, she thought, overcome by a feeling of deep sadness for Adele. Intuitively Emma realized that Edwin was the only person who could give a measure of comfort to that troubled and haunted woman.

Now, in a hurry as always, Emma turned away from the mirror, hung up her day uniform on a peg behind the door, and hurried downstairs. She must help Mrs. Fairley to dress for dinner. The sitting room was empty and when Emma went through into the bedroom she was surprised to find Edwin alone. "Where's yer mother, Master Edwin?"

Edwin looked up from the book he was reading and stifled a small gasp at the sight of her. Emma was even more beautiful, if that was possible, and he gazed at her in entrancement. The black dress made her look much taller, and willowy, and it gave her a certain elegance that was striking. Also, the black enhanced her ivory complexion, which had taken on the appearance of lustrous porcelain, creamy and rich and tinted with the palest of apricots. The white cap, perched provocatively atop her shapely head, set off her tawny russet-brown hair, and her eyes glowed with intense color and were brilliantly alive. Cat's eyes, he thought. Yes, there was something decidedly feline about Emma at this moment and it was highly arresting.

"Excuse me, Master Edwin, but where's Mrs. Fairley?" Emma said with a hint of impatience mingled with concern.

Edwin was interrupted from his contemplation of her. "She's bathing, Emma," he answered quickly.

Emma frowned. "But she usually waits for me ter draw her bath for her," she said, biting her lip. She eyed the clock. "And I'm not late! It's only just six o'clock."

"Please don't worry, Emma. Mother's not upset. She simply wanted to start dressing earlier than usual. In fact, I went in and drew the bath for her," he explained.

"Yer should've rung for me, Master Edwin," Emma pointed out reprovingly, her mouth sternly set.

Edwin laughed gaily. "For heaven's sake, Emma, don't look so cross. No harm has been done. And don't you think you have enough to do tonight? It was no bother for me to run Mother's bath."

"If yer say so, Master Edwin. And thank yer," said Emma politely. She then asked quietly, "How is yer mam? She's not gone and got herself all worked up again, has she?"

"Not at all, Emma. I read to her, as you suggested, and we chatted for a while. I made her laugh, in fact, telling her about the boys at school and their antics. She's in good spirits, Emma, truly she is."

"Thank goodness for that," said Emma with some relief. She gave him a tentative smile and began to busy herself in the bedroom. As she continued her small tasks, Emma chatted unselfconsciously to Edwin, who was observing her every movement studiously and with admiration. "So what happened to the dog, then, Master Edwin? Did Master Gerald come back and report about it, as Mrs. Fairley told him ter do?"

"Yes, Emma. Gerald was here a little while ago. The dog was still alive. But the injuries were so bad there was little hope for it. They shot it and dug a grave out on the moors." He sighed heavily. "Well, now it's out of its suffering. That's the most important thing. I cannot abide cruelty, Emma," he finished on a confiding note.

"Aye, I knows that, Master Edwin," said Emma. "What a shame the poor little dog got caught," she murmured sympathetically. "Them traps are right dangerous, yer knows."

Before Edwin had a chance to comment further, Adele came into the bedroom, wrapped in a thick woolen bathrobe. "There you are, Emma." She glanced at Edwin. "Would you excuse me now, my dearest boy? I have to dress, you know."

"Yes, Mother," said Edwin, as respectful as always. He ran over and kissed her. "Have a lovely evening, Mummy darling," he added, smiling at her with his usual sweetness.

"Thank you, Edwin. I am sure I will," said Adele, not sure at all that she would. But she determined not to give one thought to the forthcoming evening, or she would become hysterical and quite incapable of leaving her room at all. After Adele had dressed herself in her underclothes, Emma laced her into her corset. "Tighter, Emma," cried Adele, with a small gasp, gripping the bedpost to steady herself.

"Nay, Mrs. Fairley, ma'am, if I makes the laces any tighter yer won't be able ter eat owt," Emma pointed out. "Come ter think of it, yer won't be able ter breathe either!"

"Of course I will! Don't be foolish, Emma," said Adele crisply. "I like a tiny waist."

"Well, tiny waist or no, yer don't want ter be fainting away at the dinner, now do yer, Mrs. Fairley?"

Adele paled slightly as she recognized the truth of this. It would be a catastrophe if she passed out during the evening.

Adam would never believe it was actually from lack of breath, and for no other reason. "Well, perhaps you are right," she conceded reluctantly. "Don't make the laces any tighter then, but don't loosen them either, Emma. They are perfect just as they are. And please tie them in a strong double bow, so they won't work open."

"Yes, ma'am," said Emma, finishing the task quickly. "Now we'd best start on yer hair, Mrs. Fairley. Yer knows it takes me ages."

Adele sat down at the glittering mirrored dressing table, studying her face admiringly and with loving self-absorption, whilst Emma brushed out the long shimmering hair and started the tortuous procedure of shaping it into a magnificent coiffure. This was an elegant pompadour, currently the height of fashion, which Adele had noticed in an illustrated magazine showing the latest London and Paris haute couture. The previous week, when Emma had copied it for Adele, she had taken a degree of license and had elaborated upon it, adding her own special touches and adapting the original style so that it was more flattering to Adele's fragile looks. To Adele's astonishment the finished results had been not only quite outstanding and distinctly original but extraordinarily professional as well.

Now Emma swept the masses of hair up and away from Adele's face, working the great lengths into the basic pompadour that was the foundation of the style. She rolled and folded the hair all around Adele's head, so that it framed her exquisite features dramatically, anchoring it securely with hairpins. Emma worked patiently and skillfully in silent concentration, and at one moment she actually stood back to admire her handiwork, nodding her head with satisfaction, her eyes glowing. She had almost finished when she realized she had exhausted her supply of hairpins.

Emma clucked to herself with annoyance. Adele stared at her through the mirror, frowning. "What is it? No problems, I hope, Emma! My hair must be beautifully dressed tonight."

"Oh, it will be, ma'am," Emma reassured her. "It is already. But I need a few more hairpins, for the top curls. I'll just pop along ter see Mrs. Wainright, and ask ter borrow some. Excuse me, ma'am." Emma put the silver, monogrammed hairbrush on the dressing table, bobbed a curtsy, and flitted out.

The corridor was gloomy and wreathed in amorphous shadows, and the pieces of ornate Victorian furniture that punctuated its long expanse were like nebulous phantoms in the cold murky light emanating from the gas fixtures on the walls. Emma had to traverse the entire length of the shadowy corridor to reach Olivia Wainright's room and, since it was deserted, she ran all the way, although this was prompted not so much by nervousness or fear as by her pressing need to save time, as usual. She was panting when she tapped on the door.

"Come in," Olivia called out in a light melodious voice. Emma opened the door and stood politely on the threshold, as always surveying the room with grudging approval. It was the only one that appealed to her at Fairley Hall, apart from the cheerful kitchen.

Olivia Wainright was sitting at the carved oak dressing table with her back to the door. She swiveled around quickly. "Yes, Emma, do you need me for something?" she asked with her usual courtesy.

Emma had taken a step forward, smiling in return, but she suddenly stiffened and stopped short. Olivia's face was unnaturally pale, denuded as it was of the French rouges and powders and the other cosmetics she normally favored. This intense pallor gave her a wan and exhausted look, as did her very white lips. Her aquamarine eyes were glittering and appeared larger and bluer in the paleness of her delicate face, their almost supernatural color emphasized even more by the sky-blue silk robe she wore. Her dark brown hair, usually beautifully groomed and upswept in a fashionable style, fell around her shoulders like a glossy velvet cowl in the refracted light from the dressing-table lamps.

Emma knew she was gaping at Olivia Wainright and that this was the height of rudeness. But she could not help herself, and she could not turn away, so stupefied was she. That pallor, the tumbling hair, those brilliant eyes, all merged to form a face that overflowed with gentleness and poignancy, a luminous, haunting face with which Emma was only too familiar.

Olivia, meanwhile, had immediately perceived Emma's strong reaction. She was mystified and regarded the girl at first curiously, and then with mounting nervousness, the powder puff dangling in her hand.

"Good gracious, Emma, whatever is it? Why, you look as if you have seen a ghost, child. Are you feeling ill?" she cried in a voice unusually vehement for her.

Emma shook her head. Finally she spoke. "No, no, Mrs. Wainright. Nowt's wrong. Please don't fret yerself, ma'am. Excuse me, if I looked a bit funny like—" Emma paused, uncertain of how to correctly explain her behavior, which she knew must have seemed queer and was also improper. She coughed behind her hand. "I felt a bit faint for a second," she lied, and continued more truthfully and in a stronger voice, "I ran ever so fast down the corridor. Yes, that was it."

Olivia relaxed, but she continued to frown. "You are always running, Emma. One of these days you will have an accident. But never mind that now. Are you sure you are perfectly all right? You are very white indeed. Perhaps you should lie down until the guests arrive," Olivia suggested with obvious concern.

"Thank yer, ever so much, ma'am. But I'm better. *Honest*. I was just puffed. And I can't rest now, Mrs. Wainright. I've got ter finish getting Mrs. Fairley ready. That's why I came. Ter borrow some hairpins, if yer can spare a few," Emma explained in a rush of words to camouflage her considerable embarrassment.

"Of course. You may have these," Olivia said, gathering up a handful.

Emma took them from her and attempted a smile. "Thank yer, Mrs. Wainright."

Olivia's perceptive eyes contemplated Emma thoughtfully. She was not at all certain she believed the girl's explanation. However, since she could not imagine any other logical reason for her ashen face and her apparent distress, she had no alternative but to accept it.

"You do look a little peaked to me, Emma," she said slowly. "After the guests have arrived, and when you have attended to the ladies' wraps, I want you to rest in the kitchen until it is time to serve dinner at eight-thirty. I don't want you collapsing from fatigue. Inform Murgatroyd that is my wish."

"Yes, ma'am. That's kind of yer," said Emma. She felt guilty and ashamed for pretending to feel faint, and also for having lied to Mrs. Wainright.

Olivia reached out and patted Emma's shoulder. She shook

her head in fond exasperation. "Sometimes I think you are much too diligent for your own good, Emma. You know I am more than satisfied with your work. Try and take things at a slower pace, child," she said with the utmost kindness.

Emma, staring up at her fixedly, felt her throat tighten with emotion and tears stung her eyes. She cleared her throat. "Yes, ma'am." She bobbed a curtsy and left the room as sedately as she could. Once she was safely in the corridor, Emma exhaled deeply and with enormous relief. She leaned against a small carved table to steady herself. Her legs felt wobbly and her heart was hammering. She looked back at the door, shaking her head from side to side in total disbelief. *Olivia Wainright looked like her own mother.* As incredible as that seemed, Emma had just seen it with her own eyes. "She's the spitting image of me mam," she whispered to herself with awe, and still disbelieving.

Emma then wondered why she had never noticed this likeness before. Instantly she understood. It was very simple really. In all of the time Olivia had been staying at Fairley Hall, Emma had never seen her so intimately revealed, undressed and ungroomed in the privacy of her room, until a few moments ago. Sitting at the dressing table in the diffused light, so informally attired, her face naked of cosmetics, she looked a different woman from the one Emma was accustomed to seeing move around the house so elegantly and with cool authority. In her naturalness Olivia was still stunningly lovely, but without the stylish clothes, the elaborate hairdos, and the other artifices of fashion, she appeared ingenuous and vulnerable, and there was a sweet simplicity about her that was girlish and even innocent.

And Emma was not mistaken. Olivia Wainright, stripped of the outer trappings of the chic society woman, did resemble Elizabeth Harte. In fact, the resemblance was so extraordinary as to be uncanny. They might have been created from the same mold, except that Elizabeth's beauty was now only a faint echo of Olivia's. Worn out as she was by the struggle to survive, riddled with consumption, undernourished, and in constant pain, her fine looks had blurred and slowly begun to fade. Yet Emma had seen in Olivia her mother's beauty as it had once been, and this had not only startled her but moved her as well. Emma was not the only one to have noticed the strong likeness between these two women from such different worlds. Another occupant of Fairley Hall had also detected it and, like Emma, had been rocked to the core at this discovery.

But Emma was unaware of this as she stood staring at Olivia Wainright's door, still shaking her head. She regained some of her composure and for once in her life she did not run. She walked down the corridor, and slowly, benumbed by this odd coincidence. As she made her way back to Adele's bedroom, it did not occur to Emma that perhaps she had unconsciously recognized the similarity earlier, and that this might partially explain her secret adoration of Olivia. Only years later did this thought strike her, and quite forcibly so.

In Emma's absence, Adele had attended to her face. For once she had decided it was necessary to resort to her jars of French cosmetics. She had applied a little rouge, just enough to highlight her cheekbones and dispel the paleness of her skin, and had also touched her lips with it. She was lightly powdering her nose when Emma entered.

"Here I am then, Mrs. Fairley," said Emma in a low voice, hurrying to the dressing table, and the waiting Adele.

Normally too preoccupied with self to be conscious of anyone else, Adele was particularly keyed up and alert tonight, in readiness for the important and perhaps trying evening that lay ahead. She was so acutely aware, in fact, she noticed the subdued note in Emma's voice, which was always so cheerful, and she gave her a piercing look.

"Did Mrs. Wainright give you the hairpins? Was there a problem?" she asked quickly.

"Oh no, ma'am," responded Emma, already starting to work on the remaining curls. "She had plenty ter spare."

"What is Mrs. Wainright wearing tonight, Emma?" Adele continued curiously, watching Emma carefully through the mirror.

"I didn't see her dress, Mrs. Fairley," said Emma quietly, her face closed and still.

Adele pursed her lips in frustration and disappointment. She had been longing to know which one of her many exquisite gowns Olivia had selected. Adele had always been highly competitive with her older sister, and this was now more pronounced and consuming than ever. Adele was filled with mortification, and infuriated by the fact that Olivia managed to appear elegant and arresting on every occasion. She smiled, and not a little smugly. *She* would outshine everyone tonight.

Olivia will be dowdy in comparison to me, she thought, and gloatingly.

"There we are, ma'am, all finished!" exclaimed Emma with a triumphant flourish of the brush, stepping back to regard Adele's hair. She gave Adele the small silver hand mirror. "See if yer like the back, Mrs. Fairley."

Adele moved and twisted and swiveled in the chair, viewing her pompadour from all angles. "Why, Emma, it's positively divine," she cried with delight. She laughed gaily. "It's a work of art. A masterpiece. And so flattering to me. You *are* a clever girl."

Adele put on her evening slippers and then stepped into the gown Emma was holding for her. She stood in front of the cheval mirror, and Emma patiently fastened the long line of buttons up the back, praying Adele wouldn't remember the roses she had removed earlier. They were ugly, and Emma was convinced they ruined the gown, which was elegant and dramatic in its basic simplicity. As she did up the last button, Emma said huriedly, hoping to divert her attention, "All we need for the finishing touch are yer jewels, Mrs. Fairley."

"In a moment, Emma," said Adele, stepping back to view herself. She was ecstatic at the vision she made. The black velvet gown stunningly emphasized her tall, lithesome figure and its excellent cut drew attention to her tiny waist. It had a low neckline that was draped adroitly across the shoulders, and a tightly molded bodice that hugged her figure deliciously. She decided it was her most becoming gown as, intoxicated with herself, she swirled around on her elegantly shod feet that peeped out beneath her skirt. Emma was quite right about the roses. They were ghastly, she thought, marveling that her young maid had such an innate sense of taste.

She sat down and took the diamond chandelier earrings out of the red velvet case and put them on. She added two bracelets and several rings, and then Emma placed the diamond necklace around her throat, securing it carefully. It was a glittering lacy web of brilliant, perfectly cut and mounted stones. The diamonds had such fire, such life, such matchless beauty, Emma gasped.

"It is exquisite, is it not?" remarked Adele. "The Squire gave it to me," she went on, and sighed. "He used to give me so many lovely jewels," she confided softly.

"It fair takes me breath away, Mrs. Fairley, it does that,"

Emma said in awe, wondering what it had cost. A fortune, no doubt. Bought from the toil of others, she thought with a stab of bitterness, thinking of Frankie and her dad laboring at the mill.

Adele did not see the scowl on Emma's face, and she threw her a gratified smile and opened another velvet case. She lifted out a large diamond brooch and commenced to pin it on the small draped sleeve that barely covered the top of her left arm.

Emma compressed her mouth. "Er—er—Mrs. Fairley, ma'am, I don't knows that yer needs that there brooch, if yer don't mind me saying so—"

"It was my mother's," said Adele peremptorily.

"Oh! Then please excuse me, Mrs. Fairley. I understand. Yer wants ter wear it for sentimental reasons," said Emma with the utmost politeness. But she was dismayed. The brooch was unnecessary, and it ruined the whole effect she had been striving for.

Sentimental reasons, repeated Adele inwardly, gazing into the mirror. Her eyes, narrowing perceptibly, were as cold and as glittering as the diamonds she wore. She looked down at the brooch absently and thought of her mother and then slowly lifted her head.

Vaguely, Adele removed the brooch and returned it to its case. She wanted no reminders of her mother. Nor did she want Olivia to be reminded either. Olivia thought she was mad, just like their mother had been mad. So did Adam. They were plotting against her. Oh yes, they were. Adam and Olivia. She saw them, whispering in corners of this hideous house.

Her eyes fixed on Emma, who was closing the jewel cases, and she grabbed hold of her arm tightly. Taken by surprise, Emma flinched. But noting the sudden glazed and febrile expression, she did not struggle or attempt to free herself. "Yes, Mrs. Fairley? What is it?" she asked gently.

"You must get away from this place, Emma! Away from this house. Before it's too late. It's pernicious," Adele whispered.

Emma looked at Adele, baffled by this statement. "Per—per—what? I don't know that word means, Mrs. Fairley."

Adele laughed her shrill laugh, and it sent an icy chill

through Emma. "It means wicked. Wicked! Wicked! Wicked!"
she shrieked, her voice almost a scream.

"Hush, hush, Mrs. Fairley," said Emma as calmly as she
could. She was shaking and gooseflesh made prickles up and
down her arms. What a queer thing for her ter say, she
thought fearfully. But she didn't have time to think about that
now. She had something more important to worry about:
Mrs. Fairley herself. Emma freed her arm carefully and
peered at the clock. Her heart sank. The guests would soon
be arriving, and in her present state Mrs. Fairley was hardly
in a fit condition to go downstairs and join them.

Emma looked around helplessly, considering the best course
of action to take, her face white and tense. She wondered if
she should run and fetch Mrs. Wainright, or perhaps Master
Edwin. And then some instinct warned her to avoid involving
them. She alone would have to pull Mrs. Fairley out of this
distracted mood. Emma knelt on the floor and took hold of
Adele's slender, aristocratic hands with her own small scarred
ones. They were as cold as death. Emma squeezed them so
tightly she thought they would snap in half from the pressure. "Mrs. Fairley! Mrs. Fairley! Listen ter me," Emma said
urgently, making her voice strong and compelling. "Yer *must*
listen ter me. The guests'll be here any minute. Yer *must*
pull yerself together and go down ter meet 'em. Yer must, for
yer own sake!" she exclaimed fiercely, passionate in her determination to reach Adele.

Adele appeared not to hear. Her opaque eyes regarded
Emma blindly. Emma tightened her grasp on Adele's hands,
even though ugly red marks were beginning to appear. She
gripped them so strenuously her own fingers hurt. "Please,
Mrs. Fairley! Get a hold of yerself. At once, do yer hear! *At
once!*" Emma's voice was now enormously cold, and commanding, and all of her stubborn will rose up in her. It
surfaced on her face, stern in its fixity of purpose, as she
forced Adele to listen to her. The older woman's expression
remained closed. Emma contemplated slapping her cheek, to
rouse her from this stupor. She changed her mind. She did
not dare. She was not afraid of the consequences. She simply
did not want to mar Adele's fragile skin.

Finally Adele's eyes flickered with a hint of life, and her
pale lips parted. Emma took a deep breath and gripped her
by the shoulders. "Yer must go downstairs, Mrs. Fairley.

Now! Afore it's too late! Yer're the Squire's wife. The mistress of this house. The Squire's waiting for yer, Mrs. Fairley."

Emma shook her more forcefully. "Look at me, Mrs. Fairley. *Look at me*." Emma's eyes blazed hard green light. "Yer must get control of yerself. If yer don't, there's bound ter be trouble. There'll be a right scandal, Mrs. Fairley!"

Adele heard her dimly, above the sound of splintering crystal that reverberated in her head. Slowly the shattering and tinkling began to ebb away, and she saw Emma more clearly as her eyes became focused and lost their cloudiness. Now Emma's voice was penetrating her tired mind. It was strong.

"I'll be there, if yer needs me, ma'am. All yer have ter do is signal me during dinner, if yer needs owt. Or ring for me later. I'll see yer all right. I will! I'll look after yer, Mrs. Fairley. I promise!" Emma said, her tone cajoling yet firm.

Adele blinked and sat up with an abruptness that was almost violent. What had Emma been saying? That she was the mistress of this house . . . the Squire's wife. Yes, that was what she had said. And it was true. Adele passed her hand over her brow and it was a gesture that bespoke her confusion and weariness and despair.

"Shall I fetch yer a drink of water, Mrs. Fairley?" asked Emma, relieved that a semblance of comprehension, of normality, was returning to Adele's face.

"No, thank you, Emma," Adele whispered, looking directly at her. "I don't know what happened. My head began to ache again. Yes, that was it, Emma. Another of my dreadful headaches. They are so debilitating, you know." She smiled faintly. "But it has passed, thank goodness."

"Are yer sure, ma'am?" Emma inquired solicitously, studying her closely.

"Yes, yes. And I must go downstairs!" She stood up shakily and moved to the cheval mirror. Emma hurried after her.

"Now just look at yerself, Mrs. Fairley. See how beautiful yer are," Emma pointed out, adopting an admiring and reassuring voice, in an effort to bolster Adele's self-confidence. "The Squire will be right proud of yer, ma'am. He will that."

Oh! My God! Adam! Adele trembled and fear was a sharp blade in her heart. She must go down there and conduct herself with propriety and dignity and grace and charm; otherwise Adam's wrath would come tumbling about her head, and that she could not survive. She regarded her own image in the glass, and suddenly she saw it objectively, as one views a stranger. That image was of a stunningly beautiful woman. Then she remembered. She was supposed to hide behind the mask of her beauty, so that everyone would be deluded, including Adam.

Her deliquescent smile wreathed her face with loveliness and her luminous eyes sparkled with silvery lights. She smoothed the skirt of her gown and swung around lightly. "I'm ready, Emma," she said sweetly.

"Shall I come with yer, Mrs. Fairley?"

"No, thank you. I can manage on my own," Adele answered with absolute sureness. She glided through the adjoining sitting room and out into the corridor, just as the porcelain lions' clock on the mantelshelf struck the hour.

SEVENTEEN

The dinner had been a tremendous success so far, much to Adam Fairley's profound relief and satisfaction. He leaned back in his chair at the head of the table, smiling inwardly, and surveyed his guests and the glittering scene that spread out before his eyes.

The dining room was a little overblown, yet there was something imposing about it, and it had a certain elegance that was singular. This was due in no small measure to the handsome antique Jacobean furniture, the good paintings, the Aubusson tapestries, and the armorial bearings that appeared throughout. The soaring walls were hung with red Spitalsfield silk, and the tall carved Jacobean chairs surrounding the long table were covered with rich red Genoa velvet, which also draped the windows. The stained glass in the central curved bay, Flemish in origin, depicted the pedigree of the Fairley family, and this was repeated in the family crest emblazoned on a heavy silk panel that hung above the great stone fireplace. A fine Wilton carpet, specially woven to fit the vast dimensions of the room, covered the floor, and its cut-velvet pile echoed the warm color of the silk on the walls. In the flickering light from the many candles the room had acquired a mellowness that softened its baronial overtones, and even the high-flung white ceiling, with its coffered panels, appeared less cavernous in the reflected rosy light bouncing off the walls.

The atmosphere was relaxed and friendly, almost jovial, and everyone appeared to be at ease. It had been a long time since Adam had heard the murmurous sounds of genial chatter and gaiety reverberating against these old walls, and it filled him with a sense of such gratification he was positively startled. At the beginning of the evening he had been suffering from extreme nervousness. It was not unnatural for Adam to feel apprehensive, in view of Adele's past performances, and whilst he had been able to conceal his fears, he had been uneasy, all of his senses alerted for trouble. But as the dinner progressed without incident, these feelings were lessening and he had started to unbend. From time to time he would marvel that the malaise of his spirit, which had slowly been diminishing in the last few weeks, had now, this night, miraculously disappeared. It was as if a great burden had been lifted from his shoulders and he felt unfettered and even carefree.

He lifted the crystal glass of champagne Murgatroyd had just refilled and sipped it slowly, savoring its sparkling iciness. The food had been delicious, the wines excellent, and Murgatroyd and Emma had executed their duties with aplomb, as though they were a seasoned team accustomed to handling such a complicated and elaborate dinner every night of the week. He realized this achievement was no accident. It had been accomplished only with Olivia's expert planning, and her perfect taste was apparent everywhere.

Adam looked down the long expanse of white linen, until Adele was in his direct line of vision. He had watched her closely all night and her behavior had astounded him. She was charming and attentive to their guests and, on the surface at least, she seemed like the woman she had been years ago. And she looked magnificent. She was flirting outrageously with Bruce McGill, who appeared to be fascinated, much to Adam's wry amusement. He suspected there was something of the actress in Adele. Certainly she had made a grand enough entrance. Bruce had arrived earlier than the other guests, in order to conclude their business, and they had been strolling across the hall when she had materialized at the top of the staircase. Aware that they had noticed her, she had paused histrionically at the central landing, clinging for a second to the newel post, and then she had floated down the main staircase like Aphrodite descending from the heavens. Bruce, his mouth slightly agape, had been momentarily speechless and, to Adam, he had looked like a moonstruck schoolboy. That expression still lingered on the Australian's face. Seated at Adele's left, he was giving his rapt attention to her and Adele's tinkling laughter drifted down to Adam on the warm air. He narrowed his eyes, observing her closely. For all of her beauty there was something oddly removed about her. The Snow Queen. Never to be touched.

Adam's eyes swiveled to Olivia, who was seated at the center of the table. She had that special self-assurance so often found in upper-class English women, who were always at ease and in command of themselves and the situation, whether seated on a horse or at a dinner table. She looked just as magnificent as Adele, but in a less brittle way. Her kingfisher-blue silk gown was elegant, and provocatively low-cut, although not quite as daringly so as Adele's. A choker of sapphires made a ring of blue fire around her neck, the same stones cascaded in linked drops from her small ears, and matching bracelets entwined those superb arms. She was listening quietly to her dinner partner, and in repose her face was serene. Sleeping Beauty. Waiting to be awakened, Adam said to himself, instantly astonished that such an extraordinary thought should have entered his mind. Feeling excessively hot and uncomfortable, Adam sipped the cold champagne and, as a distraction, regarded the other women guests over the rim of his glass. Certainly Adele and Olivia deserved most of the accolades for elegance and beauty, he decided.

He caught Olivia's eye. She was smiling at him warmly and she inclined her head towards the dining-room door. He nodded, understanding that she thought the meal should now be terminated.

Adam gestured to Murgatroyd, who hastened to his side. "I assume you have put out liqueurs and cigars in the library, Murgatroyd."

"Oh, yes, Squire. The best French cognacs, port, and Bénédictine. Also the usual Scotch and Irish. Mrs. Wainright instructed me to put a tray of drinks in the drawing room for the ladies as well."

"Excellent, Murgatroyd." Adam turned to the female guests seated nearest to him. "I know you will excuse us if we gentlemen leave you to your own devices for a short while," he said with a smile. He pushed back his chair and looked around the table. "Shall we adjourn, gentlemen?" he continued, standing up. With murmured assents the other men followed suit and filed out of the dining room, chatting amongst themselves.

Upon entering the library, Bruce McGill took a whiskey and soda from Murgatroyd and made his way to the fireside. Bruce was in his late forties, tall and spare, and with the rolling gait of a man who has spent all of his life on a horse. He had thick and curling brown hair above a craggy face, one that automatically inspired confidence, especially in women, and his eyes were merry. His manner was masculine and there was a dashing air about him that was most engaging.

He joined Adam and said, "Here's to your health, laddie, and a long and successful business relationship." He smiled broadly and his eyes twinkled. "I think it goes without saying that we will have a most rewarding friendship." He clinked glasses with Adam.

"And to you, too, Bruce." Adam had taken a strong liking to Bruce McGill, for all of his toughness and penchant for striking a hard bargain. The man was straightforward and honest, and Adam appreciated these qualities since they were also inherent in his own nature. Now he said, "So you're going up to town next week, now that you've finished your business in Yorkshire. How long will you be staying in London?"

"A fortnight. I sail for Sydney early in May." Bruce's face lit up eagerly. "Any chance of seeing you in town, Adam? Can you come up for a few days? We could dine, take in a few theaters, have a little fun. I have some very nice friends I am sure you would enjoy meeting." He paused and winked. "Delectable friends, in fact, even though I do say so myself."

Adam chuckled and shook his head. "As tempting as it sounds, I don't think I should be absent from the mill right now. We have a lot of pressing orders to fill, and I can't leave all of the administrative burdens to Wilson. He needs me. Sorry, but I must decline, Bruce. Next time you're here, perhaps."

"You have been a very good host to me, Adam, on my

various trips to Yorkshire in the last few months. And talking of hospitality, if I can't persuade you to be my guest in London, can I inveigle you into coming to Australia later in the year? I would really like you to visit Dunoon."

"That's very kind of you, old chap," said Adam. His eyes brightened at the idea. "I might just do that. Indeed I might."

"You would enjoy it. I promise you that. There's only me and my boy, Paul, out at the sheep station in Coonamble, except for the hands, of course. My wife died three years ago. But I have a good housekeeper, and we would make you very comfortable. We could also spend a wee while in Sydney. It's an interesting city, if not as sophisticated as London," he finished with a rueful laugh. Now he grasped Adam's arm as he said, "Look here, I have another idea. Why don't you consider buying land in Australia, Adam? You know, it would be a good investment. You might even think about starting a small sheep station of your own. I could find you the right hands, and I'd even supervise it in your absence. Become your own supplier, eh?"

Adam looked at Bruce speculatively. "You've got a good point there, Bruce. It's worth considering, and I will think seriously about taking the trip. I'll let you know about that later this year." Adam took out his pocket watch and glanced at it. "Let's have another drink and then perhaps we should join the ladies in the drawing room, before they get too restless."

"Good idea. Incidentally, I must compliment you on your wife, Adam. She is beautiful and most entertaining. You are a lucky man."

"Aren't I just," said Adam, smiling faintly. If only you knew. If only you knew, he thought with raw bitterness, as they made their way across the library.

EIGHTEEN

"Will there be owt else then, Squire?" Murgatroyd asked. The guests had long since departed, Adele and Olivia had retired, and Adam was alone in the library.

"No, thank you, Murgatroyd. Oh, and by the way, I must

commend you on the way you executed your duties tonight. I was most pleased, and also with Emma. Please tell her so, and give her my thanks."

Murgatroyd, who had absolutely no intention of doing this, said, "Right ho, Squire. That I will. And thank yer, sir, ever so much."

Adam picked up the brandy and soda Murgatroyd had just prepared for him, and with a friendly nod he left the butler to his late-night duties. When Adam entered his bedroom a few moments later he was delighted to see that the fire had been lit in the grate. Its blaze was cheerful, and he hurried over to it. Adam stood, as always, with his back to the fire, his long legs spread wide apart, enjoying the warmth from the rapidly burning logs. He stared ahead, somewhat absently, his face serious, the drink in his hand untouched, his mind awash with innumerable thoughts.

His bedroom was spartan in its austereness. The walls were white and unadorned, the high ceiling punctuated with dark beams, and the polished floor was bare. Apart from the heavy wine-colored draperies at the windows and the handsomely framed portrait of his father above the fireplace, it was devoid of luxury and the usual trappings of wealth. It had the character of an officer's quarters. The few personal items, such as the ivory brushes on the dressing table and the writing materials on the desk, were laid out with such military precision and neatness they looked as if they were awaiting inspection by a superior. Adam's only concession to comfort was the large black leather chair positioned next to the fireplace. However, it was this very simplicity that appealed to him, for it was a relief after the emphatically decorated rooms downstairs. Like his masculine-appointed library, he found his bedroom tranquil and relaxing, a quiet inner sanctum where he could shed the burdens of the day, undisturbed in his preferred solitude.

Yet, for some reason, tonight the room appeared alien to him and even desolate, in spite of the warm blaze of the firelight and the diffused glow from the old oil lamp on the table by his narrow bed. He peered about him fretfully, frowning intently. He was suddenly uncommonly restless. Adam began to pace the floor, keyed up in a way he had not been in years. He was beside himself and he did not know why. And he was now so damned warm. He pulled at the velvet cravat around his neck and hastily untied it. He strode backward and forward urgently, but after ten minutes of this frantic pacing, he paused finally at the fireplace, grabbed the glass, and drank down the brandy and soda in several swift gulps.

Adam looked around the room. He ran his hand through his hair distractedly. He was hemmed in, constrained by these four walls. He thought condemningly: But you were your own willing prisoner, Adam Fairley. Were you not? He laughed ironically. He had built his own sarcophagus. The walls appeared to advance on him menacingly. He experienced a choking sensation. He must escape. He leapt for the door and wrenched it open. He stepped out into the dimly lit corridor and proceeded swiftly down the staircase. He pushed open the door of the library. Moonlight was streaming into the room and it was so bright he did not bother to light a lamp. He hurried to the walnut chest and poured himself a large brandy. His hands shook. He drank the brandy neat, slopping some on his ruffled cuff in his haste. He poured another one. His hands continued to shake uncontrollably.

Adam stood by the walnut chest, endeavoring to calm himself. Eventually he started to breathe more normally, the pounding in his heart subsided, and the sense of oppression slowly began to lift. Why am I so agitated tonight? What in God's name is wrong with me? He felt unutterably lonely and despairing. He had a desperate need to talk to someone. To a friend who would understand. But he had no friends in this cheerless and godforsaken house. Except Olivia. Of course! Olivia! She was compassionate and wise. He would go and talk to her. She would listen to his troubles, intelligently and with patience. He would go to her at once. Now. Adam left the library. He took the stairs two at a time, bursting with renewed energy mingled with relief at the thought of talking to Olivia, of unburdening himself. He had reached the central landing when the grandfather clock in the hall struck twelve. It brought him to an abrupt standstill. "Fool," he muttered. He could not go to Olivia's room this late. It would be an unpardonable intrusion. She was probably in bed and asleep by now. He continued to mount the stairs more slowly. The spring had left his step and his shoulders sagged.

Adam paused at the door of his bedroom, his hand on the knob, and then, against his volition but with great deliberateness, he continued on down the corridor to Olivia's room, propelled by some force infinitely stronger than himself. A sliver of light showed under her door. His spirits lifted. It gave him the encouragement he needed. Before he could knock, the door flew open and a stream of light flooded out into the darkened corridor. Adam was momentarily startled and blinded, and he blinked several times. Olivia stood silhouetted against the bright radiance from the lamps behind her. Her slender body looked ethereal, almost unreal. He could not see the expression on her face, for she stood in her own shadow.

Adam stared at her, unable to speak.

Olivia opened the door wider, and, without uttering one word, she moved aside to let him pass. He took several long strides into the room and, in spite of his natural polish and inbred charm, Adam discovered, much to his chagrin, that he was utterly tongue-tied. He had no idea what he would say to her. All previous thoughts were swept entirely out of his head. Olivia closed the door softly behind her and leaned against it, a gentle expression on her face. Adam hovered nervously in the entrance, towering above her, his mouth dry. She looked up at him expectantly.

Finally Adam cleared his throat in embarrassment. "I'm sorry to intrude so late, Olivia," he began, wracking his brains for a plausible explanation. He took a deep breath. "But I—I—couldn't sleep, and so I went downstairs for a drink." He indicated the glass in his hand, smiling ruefully. "On my way back to my room, I remembered I had not thanked you for arranging the dinner party so beautifully. I do appreciate everything you did to make it such a tremendous success."

"Oh, Adam, please," Olivia exclaimed warmly. "You know how much I love entertaining. I enjoyed it enormously."

"Nevertheless, it would have been most ungrateful of me not to have expressed my appreciation to you," said Adam. He was beginning to breathe more easily. He was also vastly relieved to have handled this presumptuous invasion of her privacy with a degree of adeptness.

Olivia did not answer. She continued to look up at him questioningly. A tiny frown wrinkled her smooth brow, and her eyes, very blue and perceptive, did not leave his face. He's had a lot to drink, but he's not drunk, she thought. He's in absolute command of himself. The perfect gentleman, as always.

Under her steady gaze Adam became fully conscious of his dishevelment. He realized, to his considerable discomfiture, that he was not only without his coat, but his shirt was open halfway down his chest and his cravat dangled loosely around his neck. He was acutely embarrassed again, and he fumbled with the front of his shirt, attempting, unsuccessfully, to pull it together. He smiled weakly. "Well, I had better leave you, my dear. I don't want to disturb you further. I would not have ventured to intrude if I had not seen your light."

"I thought I heard someone outside in the corridor," she said, not adding she had known instinctively that it was he.

Adam took a tentative step towards the door. Olivia made no effort to open it. She remained leaning against it, her face tranquil, her outward composure intact, but her heart was fluttering and unaccustomed waves of panic shot through her. After a long moment of silence she looked up at him and said softly, "Don't go, Adam. Please stay and chat for a while. I am not at all tired. I was reading, as you can see." She gestured to the newspaper on the table near the sofa. "Your own illustrious journal at that," she added, hoping she sounded nonchalant enough. When he made no response, she said hastily, "Unless you want to retire yourself—"

"No. No. I don't," he interrupted peremptorily. Realizing his anxiety had made him excessively vehement, he softened his tone. "Actually, I would enjoy talking to you, Olivia. I'm wide awake myself. All that stimulating conversation tonight, I've no doubt," he muttered with a small nervous laugh. "Provided you are certain I am not keeping you out of bed."

"No, really you are not. Please, come to the fire, Adam, and make yourself comfortable," Olivia said, moving gracefully into the room, her panic subsiding. She brushed so close to him he caught the faintest whiff of her perfume, something light and evocative. Its name eluded him but the scent lingered in his nostrils tantalizingly.

Adam followed her to the fireplace slowly. Olivia sat down on the sofa in front of the fire. It would have been the most natural thing for Adam to have seated himself next to her, but he did not. He carefully avoided the sofa and lowered himself into a nearby chair.

Olivia settled back against the cushions, smoothed her

skirt, and then she looked across at Adam and smiled. It was such a loving smile Adam experienced a peculiar plunging sensation near his heart, and he stared at her transfixed. She had changed her evening gown for a soft and flowing blue silk robe of oriental design; otherwise she looked exactly the same as she had at the dinner. He had never seen her looking more beautiful in all of the twenty years he had known her.

He lowered his head as he became conscious he was staring at her far too intently. He compressed his mouth and peered into his drink, and then he lifted the glass to his mouth automatically. He was mortified to see that his hand trembled.

Observing him from her position on the sofa, Olivia thought: He is very nervous. If only I can make him feel relaxed, and at ease, perhaps he will stay. And so she said, "It was a lovely evening, Adam."

Adam stiffened. "What did you make of Adele tonight?" he asked rather brusquely, and went on in the same tone, "I was delighted to see her so controlled. But then it occurred to me, in the drawing room after dinner, that she was so normal she was—well—almost abnormal."

Olivia looked at Adam alertly. "I'm sure she was playing one of her roles, Adam. She sometimes does that, you know, when she is confronted with a situation she finds difficult. I think it's probably the only way she can deal with people. She retreats, in a sense, and dons a mask to conceal her real feelings."

Adam was thoughtful as he digested her words. "Why, I think you are right, Olivia," he said. "That's exactly it. And it's remarkably astute of you to recognize it."

A faint smile flickered in Olivia's eyes. "She is my sister, after all." She sighed and shook her head. Her face was tinged with sadness. She had long been aware of Adele's deep-seated inner conflicts, her inability to create a stable relationship with anyone, least of all Adam, and she sighed again. "I have really tried to help her since I have been at Fairley, but she is so wary and truculent at times it is quite a difficult task." Olivia leaned forward with some intensity and continued, "Do you know, Adam, as strange as this might sound, I feel she is suspicious of me."

"It doesn't seem strange at all. She is the same with me, these days," he said. "In a way, I am sorry I did not discuss

Adele's health with you when you first arrived in February. But I didn't want to worry you unduly. I must confess, though, I was a bit concerned about her last year. Her behavior was so extraordinary it was—"

Adam paused, seeking the appropriate word, and finally he said, "Her behavior was actually rather irrational. There is no other way of describing it. However, she has improved enormously in the past six months, and so I hesitated to alarm you unnecessarily." He smiled faintly, looking shamefaced. "And you have had your hands full with this mismanaged household since you arrived."

Olivia shifted her position on the sofa and crossed her legs. Her heart went out to him. He looked so boyish and vulnerable. "You could have spoken to me, Adam. A burden shared is often so much easier to carry," she said sympathetically. "Of course, I know Andrew Melton has been a great help to you. He told me you have discussed Adele with him, from time to time. When I last saw him he sounded most encouraged, and very optimistic about her—" Olivia's voice wavered, and stopped.

Adam's face had turned to stone and there was an enormously cold look in his light eyes. He lit a cigarette, staring ahead. He discovered he was unable to meet her gaze. He said, "When did you have occasion to see Andrew Melton?"

He spoke with such harshness, Olivia was further startled. "Why, he has been to a number of my dinner parties in London, and he has taken me to the opera and concerts on several occasions," she said quietly, baffled by his manner. "He naturally asked me about Adele. I hope you don't think Andrew betrayed a confidence." When he did not reply, she said in a more insistent tone, "You don't, do you?"

Adam ignored this question. The anger he was now experiencing was overwhelming. "So you have been seeing quite a lot of Andrew," he said at last in a tight voice.

"There is nothing improper in that, is there, Adam? My being friendly with Andrew? After all, you introduced us. Now you look most disapproving."

"No, of course there is nothing wrong in your seeing him. And I am not disapproving," he said, his voice low.

Oh, yes, you are, Olivia thought, although she still could not conceive the reason for his attitude. He and Andrew were the closest and oldest of friends. She sat back on the sofa and folded her hands in her lap, saying nothing. She did not want to upset him further.

Adam could no longer bear to keep his face averted. He was compelled to look at her. Their eyes met. He saw the questions in hers, the confusion and hurt on her face. Her lips parted as if to speak, but no words were forthcoming. She is so incredibly lovely, he thought. Yet there is something frail about her at this moment, something so very vulnerable. His heart shifted, and as he continued to look into her eyes, those eyes as blue as speedwells, the most curious longing swept through him. He ached to put his arms around her, to hold her close to him, to beg her forgiveness for his curtness, to expunge the sadness on her face with his kisses. *With his kisses*. He was appalled.

And then he knew. Adam Fairley recognized, with the most stunning clarity, what his agitation and tension and restlessness were all about. He stood up abruptly and gripped the mantelshelf. You bloody fool, he thought. You utter bloody fool. You are jealous. You were jealous of Bruce McGill earlier, when he was hovering around Olivia. And you are jealous of Andrew Melton because he is infinitely more eligible. You would be jealous of any man who so much as looked at her. *You are jealous because you want her for yourself*.

He felt the blood rushing up into his face. He had a sick feeling in the pit of his stomach and he thought he would never be able to look at her again without betraying his feelings. Staring broodingly into the grate he became aware of the glass in his hand. Dazedly he lifted it to his cold lips and tossed the brandy down in one gulp.

Although Adam's reactions to this sudden self-knowledge were violent, they were evolving internally. By exercising iron control he had managed to retain a self-possession that was quite remarkable under the circumstances. Nonetheless, Olivia was growing conscious of the silence between them, and she sensed, rather than saw, his disquiet, for his face was hidden from her. He has something on his mind, she said to herself. She attempted to hazard a guess, and failed. She sat very still, and waited, hoping he would confide in her. She glanced at him surreptitiously from the corner of her eyes, and she curbed the impulse to reach out and rest her hand on his arm comfortingly. He moved his head imperceptibly, and his face was starkly revealed to her. It was rigidly set and his lips were so pale they were almost white. He gripped the mantel with one hand, and a muscle in his face began to work.

"Adam! Adam! You look strange. What on earth's the matter?" she cried.

Vaguely he heard her voice. He shut his eyes tightly and then opened them quickly. "Nothing's wrong. I'm perfectly all right," he said curtly. He had to get out of here. At once. Before he behaved dishonorably. Disgraced his name. Made a fool of himself. He did not move, and he admitted to himself, with a terrible sinking feeling, that he could not move. Yet in all good conscience he had to leave. He could not abuse her position in his house, take advantage of her vulnerability under his roof. Like a sleepwalker he moved across the floor.

"Adam! Where are you going?" Olivia called after him. She stood up. Her face was ashen. Her voice shook as she cried, "Have I done something to offend you, Adam?"

Slowly he turned on his heels and looked directly at her. He noted the concern in her face, the alarm in her eyes, and he was moved in a way he had not been moved for years. How could you ever offend me, my love? he thought. Once more he had that crushing urge to reach out for her, to pull her into his arms. He swallowed hard. "You have not done or said anything to upset me, Olivia," he answered as evenly as possible, striving for normality.

He hesitated, and in that moment of hesitation he weakened. And Adam Fairley was undone.

"I was simply going down to the library to get myself another brandy and a cigar," he lied. As he spoke he knew he could not leave her. He could not leave her here alone as long as that look compounded of fright and perplexity remained in her eyes.

"I have a decanter of brandy here," she said, gesturing to the console table. "But no cigars, I'm afraid. There are plenty of cigarettes, of course." Without waiting for him to answer, Olivia picked up the glass he had left on the mantelshelf and took a step in the direction of the console in front of the window.

He strode across the room and took the glass from her. His hand brushed hers and he felt small shock waves running up his arm. "Please, Olivia, sit down. I will fix it myself," he said firmly. He pressed her gently onto the sofa. It seemed to him that her flesh burned his fingers through the thin silk of the robe she was wearing.

Adam stood at the console with his back to her, his hand clutching the neck of the crystal decanter. He closed his eyes. Oh, my God. My God. *I love her. I love her.* I've loved her for years, he thought. How could I not have realized that before? I want her. Oh God, how I want her. I want her more than I have ever wanted any other woman, his raging senses screamed. But you cannot have her, a small voice answered in the back of his mind. His hand tightened on the decanter. He must take command of himself and of his emotions. He must not embarrass her, or frighten her. He must behave as normally as he always had in her presence and as a gentleman of honor.

"Do you mind if I open the window, Olivia? It's frightfully hot in here," Adam said at last.

"No, please do," Olivia said quietly. Her panic had been allayed, but she was still bewildered by his behavior.

Olivia's eyes had followed Adam across the room, her gaze preoccupied, her face wreathed with concern. But suddenly her full attention was riveted on him. He was reaching across the table to open the window, and his body was at an oblique angle. The silk shirt stretched tautly across his broad back and shoulders and forearms, his exceptional physique apparent through the fine fabric, his muscles rippling as he moved with his usual litheness. My darling, she thought. My love. Her heart ached and the pain seeped into her eyes like dark ink, staining them to the deepest of blues.

Adam breathed deeply at the window. After several seconds he picked up the decanter and two glasses, and brought them back to the sofa. He looked down at Olivia and smiled. "I thought you might join me, Olivia," he said, his voice steady. "It's not much fun drinking alone." He poured two brandies, and handed her one.

"Thank you," she said, returning his smile.

"Forgive me for behaving so rudely before," Adam said, settling in the chair. "It was churlish of me to let my worries get the better of me, when you were putting up with me at this late hour." He stretched out his long and elegant legs and leaned back in the chair, relaxing. The hammering in his head had receded and the tight pain in his chest had all but disappeared. His only thought was to exonerate himself with her and put her at ease.

"You don't have to apologize, Adam. And if you need a shoulder to lean on, I'm always here," she said softly. She gazed at him with enormous gentleness.

"Yes, I know that, Olivia," he responded. He bent forward and picked up the drink from the table. His shirt sagged open to reveal his chest and the mat of fair hair that covered it. Olivia, regarding him keenly over the rim of her glass, felt herself flushing unexpectedly. Her heart missed a beat. She dropped her eyes quickly.

"Well, I'm certainly not going to bore you with my problems tonight," Adam went on quietly. "Especially after such a pleasant evening. You know, this house was getting to be a veritable tomb until tonight. No laughter, no fun, no gaiety anymore. Things are going to be different from now on," he exclaimed. He lit a cigarette, feeling unexpectedly elated.

Olivia observed him thoughtfully. She found in Adam every quality she most admired and respected. His intellect and his cultivation were a constant revelation. Her eyes lingered on his handsome face. He has such distinction and grace, she thought. And such beautiful eyes. Large and widely set and lucent. So different from her husband's eyes. His had been small, black, and deeply socketed. Charles had always been considered a handsome man. She herself had thought him too stockily built and glowering to be truly handsome. She had not loved Charles at all. Poor dead Charles. Her father had arranged the marriage.

"Penny for your thoughts," said Adam, watching her intently, fully conscious of her introspection.

Olivia jumped, startled from her reverie, and, taken off guard, she said, "I was thinking about Charles."

"Oh. I see." So that was it. Adam concentrated on the tip of his shoe, so she would not notice the expression on his face. If he were honest with himself he had to admit he had also been jealous of Charles.

Now he said in a gentle voice, "Are you happy, Olivia? I have often wondered about that lately."

"Of course I'm happy," she cried. Did he imagine—could he possibly believe she was grieving for Charles? "Why would you think I am not happy?"

A faint smile played on his lips. "I don't know, really. I

suppose because you are alone. No one wants to be alone. You are still a young woman, and a beautiful one at that. I'm sure you must have other suitors, as well as Andrew Melton." He tried to laugh. "Why, I saw a decided gleam in Bruce McGill's eye tonight, and I don't doubt there are other gentlemen with expectations."

Olivia sipped the brandy. Her eyes were brilliant and they did not leave his face. "Andrew is not a suitor," she said. "He is a good friend, that's all. Nor am I interested in Bruce McGill." She gave him a long look. "Actually, I'm not interested in any man," she exclaimed more strongly. And thought: Only in you, my darling, but you are my sister's husband and therefore you will never know.

Adam ran his hand through his hair impatiently. "Do you mean you have not considered the idea of remarrying?" he pressed.

"No, I haven't, because I have no intention of remarrying. Ever." Olivia hesitated and then said, "Adam, I am a little cold. Would you mind closing the window, please?"

"At once," he said, leaping up.

When he returned, Olivia edged to the end of the sofa. "Please sit here, by my side, Adam. There is something I must ask you."

He had no alternative but to lower himself on the sofa. He did this with a certain grimness, avoiding the merest contact with her.

"Yes, Olivia? What is it, my dear?"

"I am troubled because you are, or rather were, so upset earlier. I know you said you did not wish to talk about your problems tonight. But can't you confide in me?" She gave him the most tender of smiles. "It does help to talk to a friend on occasion, and I hate to see you distressed."

Adam wondered how to extricate himself. He certainly could not tell her the real reasons for his disquiet earlier. "There is nothing to discuss, Olivia," he said finally. "I suppose I worry about the children, the mill, and the newspaper. Just the usual everyday worries of a man in my position. But not too serious," he lied expertly.

"And you worry about Adele, don't you?" she prompted.

"To a certain degree," admitted Adam, reluctant to think about his wife.

"Please try to relax about her health. She *is* better. You

told me that yourself, and Andrew agrees. And I am here to help you. To make things easier for you," Olivia said in her most reassuring tone.

"But you will be leaving in a few months. You said you had to return to London in July."

"Oh, Adam, you know I will stay as long as I am needed."

"Will you really?" Adam felt his spirits lifting.

She smiled. "Yes. Was that worrying you? You know I love being here. And I am quite lonely in London, in spite of my busy life and all of my friends. Adele, the children, and you, why, you are the only family I have now." Impulsively, she reached out and placed her hand on his knee in a consoling way. "I will stay in Yorkshire as long as you think I am needed."

Adam could not answer. He could only stare down at her hand. It lay there on his knee, soft and cool and white, like an immobile dove. But it scorched through the cloth of his trousers like hot steel. He felt the flush rising on his neck to suffuse his face. His heart began to beat more rapidly and he had to bite his inner lip to control himself. He picked up her hand, intending to place it safely in her lap. But, as he held it, he found his fingers slowly tightening on hers and he felt her tremble. He looked into her face. Her eyes were so dark they were almost black. And they were filled with that strange sadness he had noticed so often lately.

Olivia returned his gaze steadily, and then, with a small shock, she became conscious of the naked desire on Adam's face, saw the sensuality on those partially opened lips, heard his rapid breathing, and she was afraid. Not of Adam Fairley. Of herself. She extracted her hand gently, and moved away from him slowly.

A look of suffering flashed into Adam's eyes, and, before he could stop himself, he reached out and took her hand and brought it up to his lips. He uncurled her fingers and kissed the palm, pressing it to his mouth. He closed his eyes. He thought he would explode.

He heard a strangled cry. He raised his eyes. Olivia's head lay back on the sofa and her mouth was quivering. A small muscle leapt on her slender white neck, and her breasts rose and fell under the silk robe. Adam moved closer to her. He looked deeply into her eyes, which hovered so close to his, and at last he recognized that sad expression for what it truly was. It was not sadness at all. It was an aching longing, an undisguised yearning—and it was for him. He knew this unquestionably. Joy surged through him. He bent over her and kissed her, crushing her mouth under his so fiercely her teeth grazed his lips. Her arms were around his neck. Her hands touched the back of his head, his shoulders, his spine, pressing him closer to her. Adam could hear her heart banging against his own and she trembled as violently as he did himself.

Olivia moved slightly within his arms and now he felt the cool insistent touch of her hands against his bare chest. He kissed her hair and her face and her throat, all the while murmuring her name, calling her his love, his darling, his only love, saying things to her he had never said to any woman. And she answered him with the same endearments, her voice vibrating with such love and desire it further thrilled him.

Abruptly, Adam pulled away from Olivia and stood up. He looked down at her. Her eyes were wide and questioning.

Olivia stared back at Adam. His face was congested, his eyes blazed, and his entire body throbbed with unbridled passion as he towered above her. Mesmerized, she was unable to tear her eyes away from him.

In the terrible grip of his own onrushing desire, pushed beyond endurance by the sensuality flaring in him after years of self-imposed celibacy, further aroused by Olivia's responsive ardor that fully matched his own, and inflamed by drink, Adam Fairley could no longer hold himself in check. Without uttering a word, he picked her up in his arms and carried her across the floor.

Olivia clung to him, her arms wound tightly around him, her face buried in the soft tendrils of hair that curled on the back of his neck. He smelled faintly of cigarettes and brandy and Guerlain's Impériale Cologne and raw masculinity. She could hear his heart thudding as loudly as her own. She tightened her grip on him.

At this moment the vestiges of her principles disintegrated and the stringent rules she had lived by were abandoned. All were swept away by the force of their passion and yearning for each other. Emotions repressed for years finally tore loose, for she no longer had the will to restrain them, and she could not think rationally any more. She was in the arms of the only man she had ever loved. The man to whom she had irrevocably belonged from the first day she had met him. And that was all that mattered now.

Adam's legs shook as he strode to the bed. I shouldn't be doing this, he thought. She is my wife's sister. It is against all the precepts of my religion, my upbringing, my code of honor. I should not be doing this. It's wrong, he told himself. And then he thought: *But I don't give a damn.*

Adam put Olivia down gently on the bed. She lay back against the pillows, looking up at him, her face still white and strained, her breathing hurried. Adam sat down on the edge of the bed and leaned over her. He put his hands around her neck and unclasped the necklace and carefully removed the sapphires from her ears. He placed them on the bedside table and took her face in his hands with great tenderness. He kissed her long and deeply. Then, half smiling, he stood up and walked swiftly to the bedroom door. He heard her gasp. He turned and looked back at her. He took in the pain and bewilderment on her face, the stark terror flooding her eyes.

"I've waited for you for twenty years," Olivia whispered in a voice so low it was a moan. "That's half my life, Adam Fairley. You're not going to leave me now?"

Adam shook his head. "No, I'm not going to leave you, my darling. Never. Ever again."

His eyes did not leave her face. With one hand he locked the door and with the other he began to unfasten the rest of the sapphire studs on his ruffled silk shirt.

NINETEEN

Emma sat at the table in the kitchen of Fairley Hall, sewing a white lace collar onto a silk blouse which Olivia Wainright had given to her as a gift, along with a dark green cotton dress and a thick woolen shawl of the brightest red. All were welcome additions to her meager wardrobe and, for once, Emma was unable to suppress her warm feelings for Olivia Wainright.

It was warm and snug in the large kitchen. The fire burned

merrily in the hearth, the sun poured in through the sparkling windows, and the whole room gleamed in the bright afternoon light, which bounced off the shining copper and polished brass and struck the flagstone floor sharply, so that this, too, looked golden. The atmosphere was exceptionally tranquil, it being Sunday. Murgatroyd had just departed for Pudsey to visit his sister, and Annie, the betweenmaid, was upstairs in the dining room, following Emma's instructions and setting the table for dinner. The roaring fire spurted and crackled almost in unison with the little whistles and snores that issued forth from Mrs. Turner's spherical body. The cook was sprawled in a chair, dozing in front of the fire, her cap askew, her ample bosom rising and falling contentedly as she slumbered on, dreaming her untroubled dreams. The only other sounds were the ticking of the clock and the occasional roar of the wind as it rattled against the windows. Although it was sunny, and the sky was a clear cerulean blue, it was a blustering April day outside.

Emma smoothed out the silk and held the blouse up in front of her, gazing at it appraisingly. With her innate sense of taste and her keen eyes she was quick to recognize its elegance. It was almost new, and such a lovely blue. Like the sky outside, Emma thought, glancing out of the window. Like me mam's eyes, she said to herself, and decided she would give it to her mother when she went home later in the week. The idea of being able to give her mother something so beautiful filled Emma with immense pleasure, and her usually sober face was suddenly illuminated by a most joyful smile. She picked up a lace cuff and started to stitch it neatly onto one of the long, full sleeves, her mind turning with thoughts of Leeds, and her Plan with a capital *P*.

Just then the outside kitchen door flew open so violently, and with such rattlings and bangings, Emma was startled. She looked at the door expectantly, and decided it had been blown open by the force of the gale which was raging outside. She was about to go and close it when a cheery face appeared around the doorjamb. Vibrant black curls blew in the wind, bright black eyes danced merrily above tanned cheeks, and the wide mouth broke into a mischievous grin.

"Sure and I hope ye won't be turning a cold spalpeen away on this bitter day." The voice was full of lilting brogue and laughter and love of life. "'Tis a cup of tea I hope ye'll be offering me."

"Blackie!" shrieked Emma, totally forgetting the sleeping Mrs. Turner in her delight, and she leapt up and ran across the room, her skirts swishing around her long legs, her face wreathed in smiles. Blackie eased his great frame through the door, and came down the steps in three swift jumps. He swept Emma up into his brawny arms, swung her around several times until the room whirled before her eyes, and then he put her down carefully. He steadied her gently and held her at arm's length, scrutinizing her intently.

"Ye get to look more fetching every time I be seeing ye, mavourneen," he exclaimed. "I do believe ye are the prettiest colleen in the whole of England, and that's the God's truth, I am thinking."

Emma blushed prettily. "Aay, Blackie, yer a real tease. Don't be so silly." This was said somewhat scathingly, but nevertheless she beamed with pleasure.

The noise and bustle and sudden flurry had awakened Cook, who sat up with a start and rubbed her eyes. She blinked, momentarily confused. "Now, lass, what's going on?" she shouted, glowering at Emma. "Yer making enough noise ter waken t'dead!"

Before Emma could announce the arrival of their unexpected visitor, Blackie was striding across the kitchen to pacify Cook. "Faith and are ye not a sight for sore eyes, Mrs. Turner me luv," Blackie said. "'Tis only me, come to pay me compliments and give ye this." He paused at her chair and, with a small flourish, pulled a brown paper bag out of his coat pocket, which he gave to her, bowing elaborately. Mrs. Turner's irascibility instantly evaporated at the sight of Blackie O'Neill, of whom she had grown very fond.

"Why, Blackie, aren't yer the one," said Cook, positively glowing. She peeped into the bag and her birdlike brown eyes lit up. "Ooh, Blackie, me favorite toffees and humbugs. Thank yer, lad. That's right thoughtful of yer. It is that. And have yer heard our news? We don't have ter worry no more about the likes of Murgatroyd. No, by gum, we don't." A gloating look settled on Cook's face as she confided, "He's had his wings clipped, Blackie lad. He has that. Things have changed around here since Mrs. Wainright came." Cook gave him the benefit of a gratified smile and went on, "Mrs.

Wainright is ever so good to us all. Yes, she is indeed. Why, that woman's an angel."

"From all I be hearing she must be an angel," said Blackie, his eyes merry. "And can I not see with me own eyes that things have improved, Mrs. Turner? To be sure they have, thank God." Blackie stole a quick look at Emma and was further impressed. She was blossoming into a truly lovely young woman. She looked cared for and beautiful, with her glowing face and silky hair, wearing her crisp blue dress and starched white apron.

"Yes, indeed, it warms the cockles of me heart to see the colleen so well fed, and dressed in a bit of decent clothing," Blackie added, nodding his head approvingly. Cook clucked her agreement and leaned back in the chair. She popped a humbug into her mouth and propped her feet up on the hearth, toasting her toes.

Now Blackie sat down at the table opposite Emma. He fished around inside his coat and brought out a small package. "And *this* is for ye, mavourneen," he said importantly, placing it on the table in front of her. His gay black eyes regarded her fondly.

Emma stared at the package and then she looked up at Blackie with large eyes. "What is it?" she asked, her voice hushed.

"Just a little bit o' nonsense. A birthday present for ye," said Blackie. His mouth twitched with pleasure as he observed her growing curiosity mingled with anticipation.

"But it's not me birthday till the end of April," said Emma. She picked up the package and turned it over in her hands, examining it with mounting interest. She had never received a present like this before. A present wrapped in silver paper and tied with a silver ribbon. Never in her whole life. It looked almost too beautiful to open.

"Yes, I know when it is," Blackie told her. "But me Uncle Pat's sending me to Harrogate, to do a big building job, and I'll be gone for three weeks or more. I didn't want to be missing the special occasion of ye birthday. That's why I brought it for ye today, me bonny mavourneen."

Emma looked down at the gift in her hands. Her face was flushed and her vivid eyes sparkled with shimmering green light. "Can I open it now then?" she asked, unable to contain her excitement. "I don't have ter wait, do I?"

"Sure and ye don't, Emma. Open it this minute," said Blackie, enjoying the scene enormously.

Emma untied the silver ribbon and removed the silver paper with the greatest of care. A small black box was revealed, which Emma stared at wide-eyed, her heart fluttering. Slowly she lifted the lid. "Oh, Blackie, it's lovely," she gasped, her eyes growing larger. With trembling hands she took out a small brooch designed in the shape of a bow and decorated with bright green stones. She held it up to the light. The cheap little brooch glittered with such radiance in the sunlight its tawdriness was diminished and, in her hands, it seemed to take on a special kind of beauty, and even Blackie was amazed.

"Look, Mrs. Turner," Emma shrieked, running to show her. Cook said, "Well, aren't you a lucky lass? That was right kind of Blackie ter remember yer fifteenth birthday."

"It's only glass," Blackie said in an apologetic tone. "But when I saw it in the shop in Leeds, in one of them grand arcades, I said to meself, 'Why, 'tis the color of Emma's emerald eyes, sure and it is.' So buy it I did, without another minute's hesitation." Blackie grinned in his engaging way. "When I'm a toff, that millionaire I'm planning to be one day, I shall be buying ye a brooch exactly like this one, mavourneen. But it will be made of the real emeralds, I can promise ye that," he announced with the utmost confidence.

"Yer don't have ter do that," Emma exclaimed quickly. "This is the most beautiful brooch I've ever seen. Why, I shall keep it *always*. I don't want no emeralds, Blackie. This is perfect. Thank yer, ever so much." She smiled at him radiantly and kissed him on the cheek.

He hugged her to him and said, "I am glad ye be liking it, Emma."

Emma sat down, the smile lingering on her face, and after a few seconds she returned the brooch safely to its box, but she left the lid off, so that she could admire it.

"Well now, how about a nice cup of tea, lad?" said Cook, heaving herself up out of the chair with a great deal of huffing and puffing. She straightened her cap, smoothed down her apron, and went on, "The kettle's on t'hob and I'll have a pot mashed in two shakes of a lamb's tail." As she spoke the cook padded over to the dresser, took down a brown pot and a tea caddy, and began to busy herself at the dresser.

"Thank ye, Mrs. Turner, I don't mind if I do," said Blackie, crossing his great legs and sitting back comfortably in the chair. He gave his full attention to Emma. "And what are ye doing here on Sunday, might I be asking?" he queried, frowning. "I thought ye would be having the day off, as ye always do. I was going to stop off at ye dad's and leave ye the present, after I'd dropped in for a little visit with Mrs. Turner here."

"The Squire gave a dinner party last night and Mrs. Wainright asked me ter work over the weekend, seeing as how there was a right lot of clearing up ter do," explained Emma. "I won't be going home till Thursday, but Mrs. Wainright's ever so kind, Blackie, and she's given me four whole days off. Two ter make up for this weekend, and next Saturday and Sunday as well."

"I am glad to be hearing that," said Blackie. "So, the Squire had a dinner party, did he? I bet it was real posh, Emma, eh? Lots of toffs here, I am thinking," Blackie grinned. "I've no doubt about that, at all, at all. Ah, yes, the money is a wonderful thing to be having."

Emma nodded solemnly, her eyes glittering. "Yer right, Blackie, anybody can be a toff with money." She eyed him appraisingly and continued, "Yer don't look so bad yerself. Is that a new suit, then?"

Blackie beamed and sat up straighter, smoothing down his somber black jacket made of good broadcloth. "It is indeed. And a new tie," he said, touching the dark blue cravat proudly. He winked. "Sure and I'm all in me Sunday best today. Ye don't think I'd come visiting an ejicated young lady in me working clothes, do ye now?"

Emma smiled and, ignoring this comment, said, "Yer should've seen Mrs. Fairley and Mrs. Wainright. They looked ever so beautiful. Like the pictures from the illustrated magazines. Real *elegant*."

"I can just imagine," said Blackie. He gazed at Emma affectionately and added, "And that's the way ye'll be looking one day, me spry young colleen, when ye are the grand lady."

Emma blushed. "Oh, I don't knows about that," she murmured, suddenly bashful. "But tell me, what's happening in Leeds? Tell me some more about Leeds, Blackie. What've yer been doing there lately?"

"Not much news," said Blackie cautiously, his eyes wary as he became conscious of that look on her face, that look which always appeared when she mentioned the city. "Things are just the same, I am thinking. I have nothing exciting to be telling ye, mavourneen, sure and that's the God's truth. And all I've been doing, since I last saw ye in March, is work hard. Me and me Uncle Pat, why, we've more jobs than we can handle these days. Thanks to the Squire. Sure and it is himself who has helped us to prosper. Giving us the recommendations and all." Now unable to conceal his jubilation, he added exuberantly, and without stopping to consider the effect it might have on her, "I not be telling ye a lie, Emma, when I say that business is booming in Leeds."

Emma looked at Blackie intently. She thought: Then I must go there soon, but said, "And what's in it for the Squire? Recommending yer for all this work?"

Blackie threw back his great head and roared with laughter. "There be nothing in it for himself," he said. "Whyever should ye be thinking such a thing, mavourneen?" Blackie pulled a red kerchief out of his pocket, wiped his eyes, and blew his nose.

"'Cos I knows the Squire, and *he* would never do owt for nowt," she said pithily, contempt curving her mouth. "Talk about hard-faced, yer could straighten nails on his."

Blackie laughed again and slapped his knee. "Emma! Emma! Not everybody's on the take or on the make," he remonstrated gently. "Especially a fine gent like the Squire. He recommends us because he is acquainted with our work. He knows we are good bricklayers and builders, me and me Uncle Pat. Sure and he does." He paused and said with a degree of certitude, "He also recommends us because he likes us, I am thinking."

"Oh, aye," remarked Emma dryly, her eyes doubtful. She found this hard to believe.

Blackie leaned forward across the table, and said confidingly, "Well, it is more than the *liking* of us. Ye see, mavourneen, me Uncle Pat saved the Squire's life three years ago, and himself has been grateful ever since."

"Saved the Squire's life," Emma echoed coldly. "And how did he do that, then?"

"The Squire was driving through Leeds in his gig, Down Briggate, I believe it was, and the horse bolted. Sure and it

did. Me Uncle Pat saw it happening, and with the great
presence of mind he leapt on the horse and brought it to a
standstill, after a great struggle, terrifying to behold, so I
understand," said Blackie, unconsciously throwing back his
shoulders. "He's a big man and strong, me Uncle Pat is, but
it took all of his great strength, indeed it did! The Squire
could have been killed, sure and he could, if it hadn't been
for me Uncle Pat. And mighty dangerous it was. Why, me
Uncle Pat was almost trampled under the horse and maimed
for life."

Blackie gave Emma a knowing look. "Anyway, mavourneen, the Squire was grateful, as I said, and impressed with
me Uncle Pat's bravery and he wanted to reward him—"
Blackie shook his head and went on scoffingly, "Me Uncle
Pat, well, *he* wouldn't be taking the money. 'Only a heathen
takes money for the saving of a man's life,' so says me Uncle
Pat to the Squire. So, the Squire, out of his eternal gratitude,
gives us the work and recommends us," Blackie finished
triumphantly, nodding his head. "And glad we are to be
getting it, mavourneen."

"Yer Uncle Pat *must* be very brave," said Emma. She
pondered for a moment and then her mouth compressed into
a thin line. "Well, I hope yer charge the Squire plenty, *and*
them that he recommends," she commented with acerbity.

"Why, Emma Harte! What a thing to be saying," cried
Blackie, feigning horror. He concealed his amusement and
exclaimed, "I can see ye are growing up to be a real hardheaded Yorkshire lass."

"The tea's ready," announced Cook, interrupting their conversation. "Emma, get out the best cups and saucers, and put
the best lace cloth on the table, being as it's Sunday and
we've got company." Cook waddled over with the tea tray.
"What can I do to be helping ye, Mrs. Turner?" asked
Blackie, standing up.

"Nowt, lad. Sit yerself down. We'll have it all ready in two
ticks." She bustled away, returning a few seconds later with
another tea tray laden with plates of thick ham sandwiches,
slices of delicious veal-and-ham pie, hot sausage rolls, small
dishes of pickled onions, beetroot, and piccalilli, warm buttered scones, blackberry jam, and a giant-sized caraway-seed
cake.

"I swear I've never set eyes on a tea party like this, Mrs.

Turner. Faith and that's the truth," said Blackie. "Ye have outdone yeself, Mrs. Turner, me darlin'. Sure and it's the finest spread I've ever seen."

"Sounds ter me as if yer kissed the Blarney stone afore yer left Ireland," said Cook, but her eyes were laughing and full of fun. She glanced at Blackie warmly and slapped him on the shoulder. "Aay, get on with yer, lad. There's nowt ter be gained from flattering an old body like me."

At this moment, Annie, the betweenmaid, came down the steps from the upstairs quarters. Tall and robust, with a creamy pink-and-white complexion, flaxen hair, and pale blue eyes, Annie looked for all the world like the typical buxom milkmaid and her manner was also decidedly bovine. Emma, putting out the cups and saucers, looked up. "Did yer finish upstairs, Annie? Is everything all right, luv?" Annie nodded slowly, but her usually placid expression had disappeared, which Emma noticed instantly. "Come ter the sink and wash yer hands then, luv, and we'll be having our teas," Emma went on hurriedly, maneuvering Annie across the kitchen, and out of Cook's earshot. "Did yer break summat, luv?" asked Emma.

"No, Emma. I was ever so careful, like yer told me ter be," said Annie.

"Well, what's wrong, then? Yer look worried ter death. I can see yer not yerself."

"It's Mrs. Fairley," Annie whispered conspiratorially. "She fair give me a right turn, she did that, Emma."

"What happened?" Emma turned on the tap and made a show of washing her hands to drown out their voices.

"I went up ter see the missis, like yer told me ter, after I'd finished setting the table. But when I knocked on her door she didn't answer. Anyroads, I went in ter the sitting room, and there she was, sitting in the dark, talking a mile a minute—"

"So what's wrong with that?" interrupted Emma impatiently.

"Yer don't understand, Emma! There was nobody there with her. She was talking ter the empty chair," whispered Annie, her eyes like saucers.

"Nay, Annie luv. That can't be so. Maybe Mrs. Wainright was there. Perhaps she was somewhere in the room and yer didn't notice," countered Emma with a deep frown, although she guessed, as she spoke, that this was probably not the case.

"Mrs. Wainright's not back from Kirkend," murmured Annie. "Anyroads, when Mrs. Fairley sees me, she stops talking ter the chair. I asked her if she wanted her tea, ever so polite like, as yer told me ter be. She said she didn't, but ter tell yer she'll have her dinner in her room later," said Annie. She began to breathe a little more easily, now that she was safely back in the kitchen.

"I'd best go up ter see her," said Emma worriedly.

"No, yer don't have ter, Emma. The missis told me she was tired, so I helped her ter bed. She laid herself down and was off in a few minutes—" Annie stopped and took hold of Emma's arm. "Emma—" she began hesitatingly, and paused again.

"Yes, luv, what is it now?" asked Emma.

"Mrs. Fairley smelled ever so funny. She smelled of *whiskey*. Least I think it was," confided Annie.

Emma's eyes narrowed, but she adopted a skeptical tone. "Oh, Annie, yer must be imagining things."

"No, I'm *not*. Honest, Emma!"

Emma glared at Annie. "First of all, how do yer knows what whiskey smells like, Annie Stead? All yer dad sups is beer." She gave Annie a penetrating look, and added protectively, "Mrs. Fairley has a special medicine that she takes. That's what yer smelled, Annie Stead."

"If yer say so," said Annie, for she was in awe of Emma, and also afraid of her. Nonetheless, she found the courage to add, "Still, the missis *was* talking ter herself. Make no mistake about that!"

Emma, who felt compelled to defend Adele Fairley, thought quickly, and said with a small, knowing smile, "Come ter think of it, Mrs. Fairley often reads aloud ter herself. That's probably what she was doing when yer went in ter see her. Yer just didn't notice the book, that's all." She gave Annie such a threatening look the girl blanched and shrank away. "But if yer that concerned, I'll go up and see her right now," remarked Emma coolly.

Annie shook her head. "No! No! Leave her be, Emma. She was fast asleep when I left her a few minutes ago."

"Now, there, lasses! What's all this 'ere whispering by the sink? Yer knows I don't like that sort of thing," cried Mrs. Turner crossly. She clapped her hands. "Emma! Annie! Come 'ere at once and get yer teas. I won't have that there whispering!"

"Don't say owt ter Cook," Emma cautioned. She turned off the tap, dried her hands, and attempted to look unconcerned. So Annie has smelled the drink, too, Emma thought with dismay. But, as she sat down at the table, she acknowledged to herself that there was no point in going upstairs, if Mrs. Fairley was sleeping. That's the best thing for her right now, Emma decided, with her usual common sense.

Under Blackie's ebullient influence Emma soon cheered up. He was a marvelous raconteur and he kept them laughing during tea with his amusing stories and teasings. Emma found she was able to put Adele Fairley out of her mind completely, and she began to enjoy herself as much as the others. She laughed a great deal, much to Blackie's satisfaction. In his opinion, Emma was always too serious by far, so that he derived great pleasure from her gaiety.

The atmosphere was frivolous, and the kitchen rang with Blackie's boisterous laughter, the girls' high-pitched giggles and squeals of delight, and Cook's occasional reprimands "ter keep the noise down," uttered good-naturedly enough through her own pealing laughter.

When they had finished eating, Emma said, "Sing us a song, Blackie. Will yer, please?"

"Sure and I will, mavourneen. And what will ye pleasure be?"

"Would yer sing 'Danny Boy,' Blackie? Mrs. Turner likes that t—" Emma broke off and looked at the kitchen door, which had burst open wildly and was swinging on its hinges in the wind. She was flabbergasted to see her brother Frank standing on the threshold. He banged the door shut furiously, and hurtled down the stone steps, his boots clattering loudly, his small face white and cold, his thin body shivering in his threadbare jacket.

"Good gracious me! What's all this, then?" cried Mrs. Turner, looking perturbed.

Emma jumped up and flew across the room. "Frank lad, what's wrong?" she asked, pulling him to her protectively. Frank was gasping for breath, his eyes were wide with fright, and the freckles stood out on his drawn face. Emma led him to the fire gently, clucking to him in her motherly way and patting his shoulder soothingly. The boy's breathing was labored, for he had run all the way from the village, and, as yet, he was unable to speak. Finally he managed to gasp,

"Me dad says yer've got ter come right sharpish, our Emma. Now!"

"Whatever's the matter?" said Emma, staring into his face with alarm, her mind racing. Frank's eyes filled with tears and before he spoke Emma knew instinctively exactly what he was going to say. She held her breath and prayed to God she was wrong.

"It's our mam, Emma. Me dad says ter tell yer she's right badly. And Dr. Mac's there. Come on!" he yelled, frantically tugging at her arm.

Emma's face went chalk white and fear darkened her eyes, so that they took on the color of malachite. She pulled off her apron, ran to the kitchen cupboard, and grabbed her coat and scarf without uttering a word. Blackie and Mrs. Turner exchanged worried glances. Mrs. Turner said, "Now, lass, I'm sure it's nowt serious. Don't be fretting yerself. Yer knows yer mam has been a lot better lately." Her tone was reassuring, but her plump face was the picture of concern.

Blackie had risen and solicitously helped Emma into her coat. He squeezed her arm and said consolingly, "Mrs. Turner's right. To be sure she is, Emma. Don't be afeared now. Ye mam's in good hands with the doctor." He paused and looked into her stricken face. "Would ye like me to come with ye?"

Emma looked up at him and shook her head. "But if Dr. Mac's with her it must be summat serious." Emma's voice quavered and her eyes brimmed with tears.

"Now, don't be jumping to the conclusions," Blackie said with great gentleness, endeavoring to calm her fears. "Ye mam will be fine, mavourneen. Sure and she will." Emma looked up at him sorrowfully and she did not answer. Blackie put his strong arms around her and hugged her to him. After a few seconds he released her and touched her face tenderly. "Ye must have faith," he whispered softly, gazing into her eyes.

"Yes, Blackie," she whispered, tying on her scarf. Then she grabbed Frank's hand and hurried him across the room. "I don't think I'll get back in time ter help yer with dinner, Mrs. Turner," she called, running up the steps. "But I'll try. Ta'rar." The door slammed behind Emma and Frank.

Mrs. Turner sat down heavily in the chair. "It seemed too good ter be true. The way her mam improved in the last few

weeks. The calm before the storm, if yer asks me," she
muttered dourly. "Poor bairn, and she was having such a
good time for once."

"Let's not look on the black side, Mrs. Turner. Her mam
might be having a small attack, that's all. It could be a false
alarm," said Blackie with a show of cheeriness, but his heart
was heavy and a melancholy look clouded his black eyes.

Once they were outside, Emma did not attempt to question Frank at all. She knew, deep in the marrow of her
bones, that it was imperative for her to get home as quickly
as possible, without wasting a minute of precious time. Her
father would not have sent for her unless her mother had
taken a turn for the worse. In spite of the confident reassurances Blackie and Mrs. Turner had given her, Emma was
quite positive of this, and she trembled as her alarm flared
into cold terror.

Hand in hand, Emma and Frank ran across the stable yard,
down the path by the copse of great oaks, and through the
Baptist Field. Together, they struggled up the small slope
rising to the plateau of moorland and the wide track that led
to the village. By this time, Frank was fighting for breath and
he found it difficult to keep up with Emma's increasing pace.
She gripped his hand tighter and pulled him along after her
relentlessly, ignoring his protestations and little gurgling cries.

He tripped and fell, but Emma did not stop, nor did she
pay any attention to him. With an almost superhuman strength
she dragged him along in her wake, his little body trailing
limply in the dirt behind her. His wailing cries and ear-
piercing screams finally registered, and pulled her up short.

"Frank! For heaven's sake," she yelled wildly, staring down
at him furiously. "Get up, lad! This minute!" She attempted
to pull him to his feet, but Frank lay inertly on the path.

"I can't keep up with yer, our Emma."

Emma, who was not a naturally cruel person, was now
disturbed almost to the point of hysteria. Her only thought
was to get home to her mother, who needed her. "Then yer'll
have ter follow me," she shouted with coldness.

Emma set off along the rough moorland track, her iron will
pushing her forward with a preternatural energy. She gathered speed as she ran, her skirts flying out behind her in the
wind. And one thought filled her mind as she ran: Don't let

me mam die. It was a prayer really, and she repeated it over and over again. *Please, God, don't let me mam die.*

When she reached Ramsden Ghyll, Emma stopped and looked back. She could see Frank following on behind. But she could not wait for him, and she plunged down into the Ghyll without slowing her pace. At one moment she stumbled and almost fell, but she recovered herself quickly, and flew on. It was dark in the Ghyll, where the overhanging rocks cast giant shadows and excluded all light, but Emma did not notice the eerieness or the gloom. She was soon scrambling up the path on the other side of the Ghyll, and out into the bright sunlight. She was panting excessively and her breathing was impaired. Yet she did not stop. She hurtled forward along the top path, stones and bits of dirt flying out behind her, until, sobbing and breathless, she staggered up to Ramsden Crags. She rested against a rock, trying to regain her breath. The sound of pounding horse's hooves thundering along the path suddenly broke the silence. Emma looked back, startled. She was surprised to see Blackie galloping towards her on one of the Squire's horses. He held Frank in front of him.

Blackie brought the horse to a standstill and Emma recognized Russet Dawn, Master Edwin's chestnut. Blackie leaned down and gave her his large hand. He stuck out his foot and said, "Jump up, Emma. Use me foot to mount." Emma did as he instructed and pulled herself up onto the horse behind him. "Hang on," he cried as they set off again at a brisk canter. Soon they were in sight of the church spire and within minutes they were pulling up at Top Fold.

TWENTY

The kitchen of the Harte cottage was deserted when Emma entered and closed the door softly behind her. It was gloomy in the late-afternoon light, and desolate. The fire had burned out and the grate was filled with cold ashes and there was a smell in the air of cabbage and fried onions and burnt pots. Me dad spoilt the Sunday dinner again, Emma thought absently, as she took off her coat and scarf and looked around. The cottage was ominously silent and Emma shivered as she crept up the stone steps to her mother's room, her heart beating rapidly as her alarm increased.

Her father was alone, bending over Elizabeth. He was gently wiping her sweating face with a flannel and he stroked her damp and tangled hair lovingly. He looked up as Emma tiptoed in. His eyes were dark and brooding and filled with sorrow, and his face was harshly set and the color of dull lead in the twilight.

"Me mam—what happened?" Emma whispered hoarsely.

Jack shook his head wearily. "Dr. Mac says it's a relapse. She's been growing weaker and weaker these last few days. She's no fight left in her," he mumbled in a strangled voice. "Doctor just left. No hope—" His voice cracked and he looked away swiftly, biting down his grief, swallowing hard on the incipient tears aching in his throat.

"Don't say that, Dad," Emma cried softly but with great vehemence. She glanced around. "Where's our Winston?"

"I sent him ter get Aunt Lily." Elizabeth stirred restlessly. Jack turned back to her quickly and sponged her face again, and with tenderness. "Thee can come over ter the bed, Emma. But don't make a noise. Thee mam must rest quiet like," Jack said, his voice low and sorrowing. He stepped back, so Emma could sit on the small stool, and he touched her shoulder gently. "Thee mam's been asking for thee," he murmured.

Emma took hold of her mother's wasted hand. It was icy and lifeless. Elizabeth opened her eyes slowly, as if the effort to lift her lids was almost too enormous. She stared blankly at Emma. "Mam, it's me," Emma said quietly, tears brimming into her eyes. Her mother's face was utterly without color and there was a peculiar sheen to it. Faint purple smudges stained the skin around her eyes, and her delicate lips were as white as the bedsheet. She continued to look at Emma dazedly. Emma clutched her mother's hand more tightly and fear rose in her like a fierce wave. She said again, and more insistently, "Mam! Mam! It's me, Emma."

Elizabeth smiled faintly and recognition illuminated her eyes, which suddenly lost their cloudiness and became more comprehending. "Emma luv," she said weakly. She attempted to touch her daughter's face, but she was too exhausted and her hand dropped limply onto the bed. "I waited for yer ter come, Emma." Her voice was a fluttering whisper. Her breath came in small, rapid pants, and she shivered under the blankets.

"Mam! Mam! Yer'll be all right, won't yer?" Emma said, her voice urgent with apprehension. "Yer'll get better, won't yer, Mam?"

"I am better, luv," Elizabeth said. A gentle smile played around her lips. She sighed deeply. "Yer a good lass, Emma." She paused and her breathing became belabored. "Promise me yer'll look after Winston and Frank. And yer dad." Her voice was now so faint it was hardly audible.

"Don't talk like that, Mam," cried Emma, her voice quavering.

"Promise me!" Elizabeth's eyes stretched widely with mute appeal.

"Yes, I promise, Mam," Emma said chokingly. The tears rolled down her cheeks silently. She leaned forward and touched her mother's dwindled face and kissed her lips, and laid her face next to her mother's. "Fetch yer dad," cried Elizabeth, with a little panting gasp, and the last of her rapidly diminishing strength.

Emma turned and motioned to her father, who was standing by the window. He strode over to the bed and sat down, and took Elizabeth in his arms and held her to him desperately. He felt as if a scythe was ripping at his insides, tearing out his heart. He did not know how he could endure the pain, the agony of her dying. She lay back on the pillows. Her face was waxy and turning gray. She opened her eyes and he saw they were filled with a new and radiant light. She tried to clutch at his arm, but she was far too weak and her hand fell away, trembling. He bent towards her. She whispered to him and he nodded, unable to speak in his searing grief.

Jack pulled back the bedclothes and lifted Elizabeth in his strong arms, carrying her carefully to the window. She was so light, as light as a fallen leaf, and she barely stirred in his arms. The window was open and the curtains billowed out in the evening breeze, and her dark hair was blown around her face. He looked down at her. She had the most rapturous expression on her face and her eyes were shining. She breathed deeply of the fresh air, and he felt her whole body stretch tautly in his arms as she lifted her head and looked out longingly towards the moors.

"The Top of the World," she said, and her voice was so clear and so strong and so young at that moment, he was momentarily startled. It echoed around the room with a vibrancy that was almost abnormal. She fell back in his arms. A tender smile flickered briefly on her lips. She sighed several times, long deep sighs that rippled through her whole body. And then she was still.

"Elizabeth!" Jack cried, his voice raw with emotion, and he cradled her body in his arms, rocking her to him, and his tears drenched her face.

"Me mam!" Emma screamed, and flew across the room. Jack turned and looked at Emma blindly, tears coursing down his cheeks. He shook his head. "She's gone, lass," he said, and he carried Elizabeth back to the bed and covered her body with the bedclothes. He crossed her hands on her breasts and smoothed her hair away from her face, so tranquil in death, and touched her eyelids. He bent down and kissed her icy lips, and his own shook with his pain and despair.

Emma was sobbing by his side. "Dad, oh, Dad," she cried, clinging to him. He straightened up and looked down into her streaming face. Then he put his arms around her and pulled her to him comfortingly. "She's free now, Emma. Free at last of the terrible suffering." He choked back his own sobs and held Emma closer to him. He stroked her hair and consoled her, and they were locked together for a long time in their mutual anguish.

At last Jack said, "It's God's will," and he sighed.

Emma moved away from him and lifted her tear-stained face. "God's will!" she repeated slowly, and her young voice was excessively harsh and unremitting. "There's no such thing as God!" she cried, her eyes blazing. "I knows that now. Because if there was a God, He wouldn't have let me mam suffer all these years, and He wouldn't have let her die!"

Jack stared at her aghast and before he could respond she was running out of the bedroom. He heard her feet hammering on the stairs and the front door banging behind her. He turned wearily, his great body sagging, and he looked down at his dead wife and a sob rose in him again, and he was engulfed by a terrible darkness. He stumbled like a sleepwalker to the window and looked out. Dimly, through his pain, he saw Emma running up Top Fold towards the moors. The sky was saffron bleeding into scarlet as the sun fluttered down below the bleak hills. Its last shimmering rays were streaking across Ramsden Crags, just visible in the gloaming.

"If Elizabeth is anywhere, that's where she is now," he said. "At the Top of the World."

TWENTY-ONE

When Adam Fairley returned from Worksop, early on Sunday evening, he found Olivia sitting alone in the library. He hurried over to her, smiling with delight, his eyes lighting up with love. He was still overwhelmed by the emotions of the night before, and this showed in his glowing face, which had lost its ascetic gauntness, in the buoyancy of his step, in the joyfulness of his whole demeanor.

But when Olivia looked up at him, he drew in his breath sharply and stared at her, his intelligent eyes sweeping over her face swiftly. She was excessively pale and she seemed burdened by a certain weariness, and he saw at once, and to his enormous dismay, that she was greatly disturbed.

Adam took hold of her hands and pulled her up from the chesterfield, without speaking. He kissed her cheek and took her into his arms, embracing her warmly. She clung to him and buried her head on his shoulder, and he felt her body trembling against his own. After a few seconds she drew away gently, and looked up at him. Her gaze was penetrating, and in her lovely aquamarine eyes Adam detected confusion and misery.

"What is it, Olivia?" he asked softly. "You are troubled and that sorely grieves me."

Olivia shook her head and sat down. Her face was etched with sadness and her shoulders drooped dejectedly. She folded her hands in her lap, staring at them studiously, and still she did not speak. Adam joined her on the sofa and picked up one of her hands. He held it tightly in both of his own, pressing it lovingly.

"Come, come, my dear, this won't do," he exclaimed in a falsely cheerful voice. "Did something happen to upset you?" Adam knew, as he spoke, that this was the most ridiculous question. She was obviously disturbed about the development in their relationship, and this both alarmed and frightened him.

Olivia cleared her throat and finally lifted her head slowly. Her eyes shone with tears. "I think I must leave here, Adam. At once. Tomorrow, in fact."

Adam's heart sank into the pit of his stomach and he was filled with dread. "But why?" he cried, leaning closer. He tightened his grip on her hand.

"You *know* why, Adam. I cannot remain here after—after last night. I am in an untenable position."

"But you said you loved me," he protested.

Olivia smiled faintly. "I do love you. I've loved you for years. And I will always love you. But I cannot stay here, Adam, in the same house as my sister, your wife, and conduct a clandestine love affair. I cannot!"

"Olivia, Olivia, let us not be hasty. Surely, if we are discreet—"

"It's not only that," she interrupted quickly. "What we did last night was wrong. We committed a terrible sin."

Adam said, almost roughly, "Because I committed adultery. Is that what you're saying, Olivia? It was not you, but I, who committed a sin, in the eyes of the law. That is a matter for my conscience, not yours. So let me worry about that."

"We both committed a sin—in the eyes of God," she answered very softly.

Observing the grave look on her face, he knew, with an awful sense of foreboding, that she was in deadly earnest. He did not want her conscience to drive her away from him. He could not let her go. Not now. Not ever again. Not when they had found each other at last, after all the years of loneliness and unhappiness they had both endured, trapped in their worthless marriages.

Adam spoke urgently. "Olivia, I understand the way you feel. Believe me, I do. You are a good and honest person. Duplicity and intrigue are not in your nature. I know, too, that you have a strong sense of personal honor. As I do myself. I fought my emotions, my desire for you, very hard last night."

He paused and gazed deeply into her eyes. He touched her face tenderly. "I suppose it *was* wrong, in a way. But we didn't hurt anyone, least of all Adele. And I certainly don't feel any remorse or guilt. You shouldn't either. That would be pointless, for we cannot undo what we did, nor can we alter the fact that we love each other. And I do love you. More than I have ever loved any other woman."

"I know," she murmured sadly. "Nevertheless, we cannot think of ourselves, selfishly. We must put duty first." Her eyes filled with the tears she had been trying to withhold, and her face overflowed with her love for him. "I know it is not in you to behave shoddily, Adam."

"Everything you say is true, of course. But I cannot live the rest of my life without you, my love." He shook his head. "I cannot!" His luminous eyes implored her. "Please stay with me, at least until July, as you planned, and as you promised last night. For my part, I promise I will never intrude on you, or force myself upon you." Adam took her hands in his again. "Such a thing would be irremissible, in view of the circumstances and your feelings about Adele, and your position in this house. But please, Olivia, stay with me for a few months," he beseeched her, his voice low and hoarse with his desperation. "I *swear* I will not attempt to make love to you. Please, please don't abandon me to life in this mausoleum. To life alone in this loveless house."

Olivia's heart went out to him. She did love him, so very much, and life had dealt him a cruel blow, saddling him with her sick and disturbed sister. He who was so vital, so full of life, and so fine and good. As she studied that strained and suffering face before her, Olivia felt her resolution wavering, her determination to leave Yorkshire dissolving. Slowly she began to weaken, for she found it hard to deny him. And what he asked was really not all that unreasonable. "All right, I will stay," she said at last, in the gentlest of voices. "But it must be on the conditions you have just mentioned." She moved closer to him on the sofa, took his agonized face in her hands, and kissed his cheek. "It's not that I don't desire you, my darling. Because I do," she murmured. "However, we cannot be lovers in this house."

Adam exhaled a long and deep sigh. "Thank God!" he exclaimed. That deadening coldness that had afflicted his body gradually seeped out of him, and his sense of relief was so enormous it was almost euphoric. Now he took her in his arms and pressed her head against his shoulder, stroking her hair. "I need you so very much, my love. Your presence is as vital to me as breathing. But I swear I will not lay a finger on

you, or compromise you in any way. I am happy just to be
with you, to have your companionship, to know you love me.
You feel the same way, don't you?"

"Yes, I do," Olivia responded. "We must be discreet,
though, and not display our affection for each other so readily, or so openly." She looked into his face, so close to hers,
and smiled for the first time. "Like this. It would be most
embarrassing if Gerald, or one of the servants, walked in
now." As she finished speaking she extracted herself from his
embrace.

"Quite right," Adam remarked with a small dry laugh. He
was ready to acquiesce to anything she wanted, if it meant
keeping her by his side. "Well, my love, if we are going to be
circumspect, perhaps we had better have a sherry, and sit on
opposite sides of the room, and chat about inconsequential
things." He made his voice light and he was able, at last, to
laugh. "Would you like a drink before dinner, my sweet?"

"Yes, that would be lovely, Adam. And most natural-looking,
wouldn't you say, should we be surprised by any member of
the household." Her eyes were suddenly merry and she
found herself laughing with him.

Adam grinned at her and stood up. Her eyes followed him
across the room. She felt an unexpected ache in the region of
her heart, and she wondered if they would have the strength
to control their emotions, to deny each other. *We must*, she
said firmly to herself.

Adam returned with the sherries. He handed her one,
clinking her glass. "Cheers, my dear." He smiled wryly and,
very pointedly, sat in the chair opposite. "Is this a discreet
enough distance?" he asked, his eyes twinkling.

"I should say so," she said, laughing again. She sat back on
the chesterfield and relaxed, her usual equanimity fully restored. She trusted Adam implicitly. He would keep his
word, and his distance, and that in itself would give her the
necessary strength to do the same thing.

"There is just one thing more," Adam began cautiously.
"You said we could not be lovers in this house. However, if I
saw you in London, might it—could it be—different? We
would be free there," he asserted.

Olivia's pretty mouth curved into a small smile. "Oh, Adam,
darling, you are impossible," she said, shaking her head.
Then her eyes became quiet and grave. "I don't know how to

answer that. We would still be committing a sin, wouldn't we?" She blushed and dropped her eyes. "I don't know what to say. I must think."

"Please, don't get upset again, my love," Adam cried, conscious of her discomfiture. "We will not discuss that side of our relationship again. Not until you wish to discuss it. Could I ask one favor of you, though?"

"Of course, Adam," said Olivia.

"When I am in town, you will dine with me, won't you? And accompany me to the theater? You will *see* me, won't you?" he asked, his desperation again apparent in his voice.

"You know very well I will. We have always spent time together when you have been in London. Why should it change now, Adam? We have even more reason to see each other—socially," she declared in a positive voice that was also calm.

This reassured him. "Good. Then it's all settled." Adam stood up and threw a log onto the fire, pushing back the memory of their mutual passion of the night before.

"Was Edwin glad to be back at school?" Olivia asked.

Adam was lighting a cigarette. He drew on it and said, "Yes, he was delighted to be back. Poor Edwin has been quite frustrated, cooped up with Adele all these months." He sighed. "She does coddle him so." Adam rested an arm on the mantelshelf and lifted one of his highly polished brown boots onto the hearth. He threw Olivia a swift glance, and, leaning closer to her, went on, in a lower voice, "I do hope you are aware that Adele and I have not lived together as man and wife for over ten years."

"Yes, I had assumed that," said Olivia. She stood up and went to him. She kissed his face and stroked his hair. "Everything will be all right. I know it will. Now, let me get you another sherry."

She took the glass from him, and he smiled at her, thankful she was with him, and that now she intended to stay at Fairley through the summer. He watched her gliding across the floor of the library, graceful and elegant and self-assured, and he realized, with a sudden flash of perception, that without her his life would sink into darkness again. She *was* his life, and he resolved never to be apart from her ever again, as long as he lived.

TWENTY-TWO

"**I** just don't understand how our Winston could do a thing like that," Big Jack Harte said to Emma. "Running away so soon after thee mam died, without so much as a ta'rar."

"But he did leave yer a note, Dad," Emma said quickly. When he made no response, she went on, "Don't worry, Dad. He'll come ter no harm in the navy. He's a big lad, and he can take care of himself." She leaned across the table and squeezed his arm in a reassuring way.

"Aye, I knows that, lass. Still an' all, it was right deceitful of him ter do a moonlight flit, packing his stuff and creeping out in t'middle of t'night. It weren't like our Winston at all," Jack grumbled, his disgruntlement obvious. He shook his head. "And there's summat else—*I'd* like ter know how he managed ter get inter the Royal Navy without me signature on his papers. He's under age, thee knows, Emma, and he would've had to have me signature on 'em."

Emma sighed. This conversation had been going on endlessly and repetitively for the last three days, since she had come home from the Hall, and it was beginning to irritate her.

But before she could answer, Frank piped up, "He forged yer signature, Dad. Yes, I *bet* that's what he did! He had ter do that, ter get the recruiting officer ter accept him."

Emma threw Frank the most furious glance, and said harshly, "Hush up, Frank. Yer just a little tiddler. Yer don't know owt about such things."

Frank was sitting at the other side of the kitchen, scribbling away, as was usual these days. He said, in a matter-of-fact tone, "I knows all sorts of things, our Emma. From them there illustrated magazines and newspapers yer brings home from the Hall. I reads every line, yer knows."

"Then I'll have ter stop bringing 'em," she snapped, "if they're going ter make yer so big-headed and cheeky. Yer getting ter be a right know-it-all, our Frank."

"Oh, Emma, leave the bairn alone," Jack muttered. He

sucked on his pipe, engrossed in his thoughts, and then he said, "Frank's right, yer knows. Our Winston must've forged me signature. No two ways about it, that's what he did. Sure as eggs is eggs."

"I expect he did," said Emma, "since that's the only way he could've joined up. But what's done is done, and there's nowt we can do about it now. He's more than likely well on his way—to wherever they're sending him."

"Aye, lass," Jack said, settling back in the chair.

Emma was silent. She regarded her father intently, a worried frown slicing across her smooth wide brow. Her mother had been dead almost five months, and whilst Jack strived always to conceal his agonizing grief, Emma knew it was eating away at him inside. He had lost weight, for he hardly ate, and his great and powerful body seemed to have shrunk. He was frighteningly contained, and, sometimes, when he was unaware of Emma's close scrutiny, his eyes would fill with tears, and his sorrow was most shockingly revealed on his drawn face. Emma would turn away helplessly, her own grief rising up in her so rapidly she found it hard to conquer. But she had to control herself. Someone had to hold the family together, and that apathy which had assailed her father months before her mother's death was even more apparent. Emma feared for her dad, and as the days went by her worry increased. Now this fresh problem of Winston's stealthy departure last week had imbued in Jack a new despondency.

Emma sighed. She had temporarily postponed her Plan with a capital *P*. She could not bring herself to leave for Leeds just yet, in view of Winston's scarpering off, even though she had saved quite a lot of shillings. She had over five pounds, a princely sum with which to finance the initial stages of her plan to make her fortune. But now was not the time to leave. And anyway, she had promised her mam she would look after the family. It was a promise that Emma felt honorbound to keep. For the moment.

She picked up one of Olivia Wainright's recipes, coated the back of it with the paste she had made from flour and water, and stuck it carefully into her exercise book for future reference. She looked at Olivia Wainright's handwriting. It was so beautiful. Rounded and elegant and flowing. Emma was striving to copy it. She was also paying strict attention to the way Olivia spoke, for she was endeavoring to imitate the way she pronounced her words. Blackie kept telling Emma she would be a grand lady one day, and she knew grand ladies had to speak proper like. She corrected herself silently. You didn't say "proper like." You said "properly," or "correctly."

Suddenly, the silence in the small kitchen was broken, as Frank cried excitedly, "Hey, Dad, I just thought of summat. If our Winston forged yer signature, then his papers aren't legal like, are they?"

Jack looked startled at this mature comment from Frank, which he himself had not even thought of. He contemplated his youngest child in wonderment. Frank continually amazed him these days. Eventually, Big Jack said, "There's summat in that, Frank. Aye, there is, lad." He was nothing short of impressed, for Frank was becoming a fountain of information, and all manner of intelligent comments fell from his lips when Jack least expected them.

"So what?" said Emma, glaring at Frank with open hostility, which was unparalleled for her, as protective as she was of Frank. But she wanted the subject of Winston's running away dropped. She knew that prolonging the discussion would only upset her dad further.

"If the papers aren't legal, our Emma, then me dad can get him out of the navy. Don't yer understand? They'd have ter—ter—discharge him! For falsifying the papers. Yes, that's it," shouted the triumphant Frank, delighted with his shrewd deduction.

"He's right, Emma," Jack said, his voice more positive, quite visibly cheering up.

"Our Frank might be right, but how are yer going ter go about getting Winston out, Dad?" Emma asked with her usual bluntness. "Are yer going ter write ter the Royal Navy then? And who would yer write ter, anyroads?" She frowned at Frank, who had a pleased smile on his pale, freckled face. The boy was intelligent, Emma could not deny that, but he annoyed her when he created additional unrest in the house with his comments, which were sometimes far too clever for her liking.

"Yer could ask the Squire what ter do, Dad," suggested Frank.

Jack mused on this, but Emma shrieked, "Ask the Squire what ter do? I wouldn't ask him for owt. Why, he wouldn't give yer ha'porth of spit without charging yer for it!" Her voice was icy and dripped scorn.

Jack ignored her remarks, and now said, "Well, I could go inter Leeds and call at the recruiting office, and ask about our Winston. Find out where they sent him. What barracks he was shipped ter. They must've got records. And I could tell 'em what he did. Thee knows—forging me signature an' all."

Emma sat bolt upright in the chair, her face formidable, and said in her firmest tone, "Now listen ter me, our Dad. Yer not going ter do owt. Our Winston's always wanted ter go inter the Royal Navy, and now he's gone and done it. And think on one thing, our Dad. Winston's better off in the navy than slogging long hours at the Fairley brickyard, working in all that dust and muck. Leave him be, Dad."

She paused and gave her father a long look that was also loving, and she softened her voice considerably. "He'll write, our Winston will, when he gets settled in. So just leave him be, as I said afore."

Jack nodded, for he respected Emma's judgment. "Yes, luv, there's common sense in what thee says. He always did want ter get away from Fairley." Jack sighed. "I can't say as I blame him for that, mind thee. It was just the way he did it, sneaking off like."

Emma couldn't help smiling, "Well, Dad, I expect he knew if he asked yer permission yer'd have said no, and that's why he ran off, afore yer could stop him." She stood up and went over and hugged her father. "Come on, Dad luv, cheer up. Why don't yer go ter the pub, and have yerself a pint, and enjoy a bit of company with the lads," she suggested. Fully expecting him to dismiss this suggestion, as he always did of late, she was amazed when he said, "Aye, I thinks I will, lass."

Later, after her father had left for the White Horse, Emma turned to Frank. "I wish yer hadn't said that, Frank, about Winston forging me dad's signature and it not being legal, and getting Winston out of the navy. It only upsets our dad more. Now listen ter me, luvey—" She shook her forefinger at Frank, her face grave. "I don't want no more talk about our Winston when I've gone back ter the Hall. Do yer hear, our Frankie?"

"Yes, Emma," said Frank, biting his lip. "I'm sorry, Emma.

I didn't mean owt wrong. I didn't think owt of it. Don't be cross with me."

"I'm not, luv. But just think on what I said, when yer alone with our dad."

"I will. And, Emma?"

"Yes, luvey?"

"Please don't call me Frankie."

Emma concealed a smile of amusement. He was so serious and adopting such a grown-up air. "All right, *Frank*. Now, I thinks yer'd best be getting yerself ready for bed. It's eight o'clock and we all have ter be up early for work tomorrow. And don't sit up half the night reading yer newspapers and books." She clucked and shook her head. "No wonder we never have any candles! Off yer go, lad. And I'll be up in a minute ter tuck yer in. And I'll bring yer a glass of milk, and an apple, as a special treat."

He scowled at her. "What do yer think I am, Emma Harte? A big baby? I don't wants yer ter tuck me in," he cried as he picked up his notebook and newspapers. He turned when he went out of the kitchen door. "But I'd like the apple," he said with a small grin.

After she had washed up the dirty supper dishes stacked in the sink, Emma went upstairs. Frank was sitting up in bed, writing in his notebook. Emma put the apple and the milk on the table and sat down on the bed. "And what's this yer writing now, our Frank?" she asked curiously. Like her father, she was constantly astonished by Frank's superior intelligence and his fertile brain. He also had an amazingly retentive memory.

"It's a g-g-h-o-s-t s-t-o-r-y," he told her in a moaning voice. He looked at her solemnly and made his eyes large. "A ghost story! All about haunted houses, and the spirits of the dead rising from their graves, and walking around. Ooooooohhh!" he whispered, his voice low and ominous. He fluttered the sheet at her. "Shall I read it for yer, our Emma? It'll scare yer ter death," he warned.

"No! Thanks very much! And don't be so daft," she cried, straightening the sheet. Then she shivered involuntarily, at the same time chiding herself for being foolish, for she knew Frank was teasing her. But the grim superstitions of the North were ingrained in her, and gooseflesh rose on her arms. Emma cleared her throat and assumed a superior expression. "And where's all this scribbling going ter get yer, our Frank? It's a waste of the good paper I brings home from the Hall, if yer asks me. Yer can't make no money, scribbling this junk."

"Yes, yer can!" he cried with such extraordinary violence she was startled. "And I'll tell yer where it's going ter get me. Onto a newspaper when I'm a big lad. Maybe even the *Yorkshire Morning Gazette.* That's what!" He outstared her, and finished, "Stick that in yer pipe and smoke it, Emma Harte."

Laughter bubbled in Emma's throat, but comprehending he was in earnest, she kept her face straight. "I see," she remarked coolly. "But not till yer grown up. In a few years perhaps we'll think about it."

"Yes, Emma," he said, and bit into the apple. "Ooh, Emma, this is luvely. Thank yer."

Emma smiled and smoothed his rumpled hair and kissed him in her motherly fashion. His small skinny arms went around her neck and he nuzzled against her affectionately, and with yearning. "I luv yer, Emma. Ever so much," he whispered.

"I luv yer, too, Frankie," she answered, hugging him tightly. And on this occasion he did not reprimand her for using the diminutive.

"Don't stay up all night now, luv," Emma told him as she quietly closed the door of his room.

"No, I won't. I promise, Emma."

It was dark on the cold stone-flagged landing, and Emma edged her way into her own bedroom and carefully felt her way to the stand by the narrow bed. She groped for the matches and lit the stub of candle in the brass candle holder. The wick flickered tenuously, illuminating the blackness with a pale light. The tiny room was so frugally furnished it was virtually empty, but, like the rest of the cottage, it was scrupulously clean. Emma carried the candle over to a large wooden trunk in one corner of the room. She placed it on the window ledge nearby, and, kneeling down, she lifted the heavy lid of the trunk. A strong odor of camphor balls and dried lavender floated up out of the trunk. This had belonged to her mother and all of the things in it were Emma's now. Her dad had told her that had been her mother's wish. Emma had only looked once in the trunk, and hurriedly at that, since

her mother's death. Until tonight she had been too emotional
and grief-stricken to sort through her mother's treasured
possessions.

She lifted out a black silk dress, old but hardly ever worn,
and therefore still in good condition. She would try it on next
weekend. She was quite sure it would fit her, with a few
alterations. Underneath the black dress was her mother's
simple white wedding gown. Emma touched it tenderly. The
lace on it was yellowed with age. Wrapped in a piece of faded
blue silk she found a small bouquet of flowers, dried and
withered and falling apart. They had that sweet and sickly
smell of dead roses. She wondered why her mother had kept
them, what significance they had. But she would never know
the answer to that now. There were some pieces of fine lawn
underwear, obviously part of her mother's meager trousseau,
a black shawl embroidered with red roses, and a straw bonnet
trimmed with flowers.

At the very bottom of the trunk was a small wooden box.
Emma had seen the box many times before, when her mother
had taken it out to select a piece of jewelry on very special
and important occasions. Emma opened it with the small key
sticking out of the lock. There was not very much jewelry in
the box, and what there was had practically no value at all.
She took out the garnet brooch and earrings her mother had
always worn at Christmas and weddings and christenings, and
on other such special days. It occurred to Emma, as she
looked at them lying in her hands, that the stones were like
dark rubies shimmering in the candlelight. Her mother had
favored the garnets above everything else she owned.

"I'll never part with these," Emma said aloud, swallowing
hard as her eyes misted over. She laid them on the floor and
poked around in the box. There was a small cameo brooch
and a silver ring, both of which she examined with interest.
She tried on the ring. It fitted her perfectly. Her hand went
back into the box and her fingers lighted on the gold cross
and chain her mother had almost always worn. Emma grimaced. She wanted no reminders of God, who no longer
existed for her. That was why she refused to go to Sunday
school, even though her truancy annoyed her dad. She dropped
the cross and chain on the floor next to the garnets, and lifted
out a string of amber beads that were large and cool to her
touch. They glowed with a deep golden color, and to Emma's

eye they had distinction. They had been a gift from a very
grand lady, so her mam had told her several years ago.

After studying her new possessions for a few minutes longer,
Emma began to replace them in the wooden box. It was at
this moment that she felt something lumpy underneath the
velvet which lined the bottom. She ran her fingers around
the edge of the box. The velvet was loose and she was able to
lift it up very easily. Its removal revealed a locket and a pin.
Emma took out the locket and looked at it with curiosity. She
did not remember ever noticing her mother wearing it. In
fact, she had never seen it before. It was old, and beautifully
worked, and made of real gold that glinted brightly in the
light. She tried to open it, without success. She stood up, and
hurried to find the scissors in her sewing box. After a few
seconds, and with a little pressure, she was able to prize it
open. There was a photograph of her mother on one side,
taken when she was a girl. The other side was empty. Or was
it? Emma looked more closely and saw that in place of a
photograph there was a small lock of fair hair.

I wonder whose hair it is, she thought, trying to lift the
glass covering it. But this was so firmly embedded in the
locket she knew that if she pried at it too hard with the
scissors it could easily shatter. Emma closed the locket and
turned it over in her hands inquisitively. It was then that she
saw the engraving on the back. It was indistinct and almost
worn away by time. She could hardly make it out. She looked
at it again, screwing up her eyes. Finally she brought the
candle over to the trunk, and held the locket under the
flickering flame.

The letters were very faint indeed. Slowly she read aloud,
"A to E—1885." Emma repeated the date to herself. That
was nineteen years ago. Her mother had been fifteen in 1885.
Did E stand for Elizabeth? It must, she decided. And who
was A? She could not remember her mother ever mentioning
anyone in the family with a name beginning with A. She
decided she would ask her father when he came back from
the pub later. Emma now placed the gold locket most carefully on top of the black dress, and fingered the pin, peering
at it closely. How odd that her mother should have owned
such a pin. She frowned. This was the kind of stickpin a
gentleman wore in his cravat or stock, most probably with
riding clothes, since it depicted a miniature riding crop with

a tiny horseshoe set in the center. It was also made of gold, she could tell that, and it was obviously valuable. It had certainly never belonged to her father.

Emma shook her head and sighed, rather mystified, and she automatically placed the locket and pin where they had reposed before, covered them with the velvet lining, and then put the remainder of the jewelry away in the wooden box. Methodically she returned all of the other items to the trunk and closed the lid, still shaking her head in bafflement. There was no doubt in Emma's sharp mind that the locket and the pin had been hidden by her mother, for some unknown reason, and this both puzzled and intrigued her. She decided then not to mention them to her father after all, although she was not quite sure what prompted this decision. She picked up her sewing box, blew out the candle, and went downstairs.

The kitchen was shadowy in the dim light emanating from the two candles on the table. Emma lit the paraffin lamps on the mantelshelf and the dresser, and carried the basket of mending she had brought home from the Hall over to the table, where she sat down to do her sewing. She worked first on a blouse belonging to Mrs. Wainright, and then began to repair the hem on a petticoat of Mrs. Fairley's. Poor Mrs. Fairley, Emma thought, as she plied her stitches, she's as strange as ever. Quiet and sullen one minute, gay and chattering away the next. Emma would be relieved when Mrs. Wainright returned from Scotland, where she was visiting friends. She had only been away for a fortnight, but it seemed like months. The Hall was not the same without her presence, and a peculiar nervousness was beginning to invade Emma with increasing regularity, and it bothered her not a little, since she found this acute edginess incomprehensible.

The Squire had also gone away, for the grouse shooting, so Cook had told her. He wouldn't be returning until the end of the week, far too soon to suit Emma's tastes. Things were quiet enough at the Hall, and, with Mrs. Wainright and the Squire absent, Emma's duties had lessened. That was why Mrs. Turner had let her have Friday off, as well as Saturday and Sunday. "Spend a bit of time with yer dad, luv," Mrs. Turner had said, adding sympathetically, "He needs yer right now, Emma." And so she had spent three whole days at home this weekend, cleaning and washing and cooking for her dad and Frank. The only thing that had spoiled it was the fuss about Winston's disappearance earlier in the week. In Emma's mind, the interminable discussions were ridiculous, since there was no apparent solution to the problem.

Emma smiled suddenly to herself. Because there was less supervision at the Hall, she had been able to slip up to the moors on some sunny afternoons, to sit under the crags at the Top of the World, with Master Edwin. They had become firm friends during his summer holidays from boarding school.

Emma had become the recipient of many of Edwin's confidences. He told her all sorts of things, about his school, and the family, and most of them were special secrets she had promised never to reveal to a single soul. When Edwin had walked her across the moors on Thursday afternoon, he had told her that a great friend of his father's was arriving in a week's time, as a weekend guest. He was coming all the way from London, and he was a very important man, according to Edwin. A Dr. Andrew Melton. Edwin was excited about the impending visit, because the doctor had just returned from America, and Edwin wanted to know all about New York. Not even Cook had been informed yet, or even Murgatroyd. Edwin had made her swear not to tell, and she had even had to say, "Cross me heart and hope ter die," as a reassurance to Edwin, making the appropriate gestures as well, crossing her heart and raising her right hand solemnly.

Emma's thoughts of Fairley Hall, and, more particularly, of Edwin, ceased abruptly as her father came in from the pub, just as the church clock was striking ten o'clock. She recognized at once that he had been drinking more than usual. He was unsteady on his feet, and his eyes were glazed. When he took off his jacket to hang it on the peg behind the front door he missed the peg, and the jacket dropped to the floor.

"I'll get it, Dad. Come and sit down, and I'll make yer some tea," Emma said, putting aside the petticoat and rising quickly.

Jack picked up the coat himself, and this time he managed to hook it onto the peg. "I don't want owt," he mumbled, turning into the room. He took several jerky steps towards Emma and stopped. He stared at her for a long moment, astonishment flickering onto his face. "Thee has such a look of thee mam sometimes," he muttered.

Emma was surprised by this unexpected remark. She did

not think she looked like her mother at all. "I do?" she said questioningly. "But me mam had blue eyes and darker hair—"

"Thee mother didn't have no widow's peak either, like thee does," Jack interjected. "That thee inherited from me mother, thee grandma. But still an' all, thee bears a striking resemblance ter thee mam, right this minute. When she was a girl. It's the shape of thee face, and thee features mostly. And thee mouth. Aye, thee's getting ter look powerfully like thee mam as thee gets older. Thee is that, lass."

"But me mam was beautiful," Emma began, and hesitated.

Jack steadied himself against the chair. "Aye, she was that. Most beautiful lass by here thee ever did see. Weren't a man in Fairley didn't have his eye on thee mam at one time or t'other. Bar none. Aye, thee'd be right surprised if thee knew—" He bit off the rest of this sentence, and mumbled something unintelligible under his breath.

"What did yer say, Dad? I didn't hear yer?"

"Nowt, lass. Nowt that matters now." Jack regarded Emma through his bleary eyes, which were, nonetheless, still quite discerning, and he half smiled "Thee's also beautiful. Like thee mam was. But, thank God, thee's made of sterner stuff. Elizabeth was very delicate. Not strong like thee." He shook his head sadly and moved uncertainly across the floor. He kissed her on the forehead and muttered his goodnight, and then he mounted the stone stairs, looking so much more pathetically diminished in size Emma wondered if he would be called *Big* Jack ever again. She sat down on the chair, gazing absently at the candle flame that flared so brightly before her eyes. She wondered what would become of her father. He was like a lost soul without her mother, and she knew he would never be the same. This realization filled her with a terrible sadness, for she was also aware there was nothing she could do to ease his acute pain, or the burden of his grief, which was total. He would mourn her mother until the day he himself died.

Eventually Emma roused herself from her reflections, picked up the petticoat, and continued sewing. She worked late into the night, doggedly determined to finish the repairs and alterations of the clothes from the Hall. Mrs. Wainright paid her extra for this work, and Emma's crucial need for money enabled her to ignore her tired eyes, her aching fingers, and the general fatigue that gradually settled over her as the hours ticked by. It was well turned one o'clock in the morning when she folded away the last of the garments and crept upstairs to bed, avidly calculating the exact amount of money Mrs. Wainright now owed her.

Once a year the grim and savage moors of the West Riding lose their blackened and colorless aspects. At the end of August a momentary transformation takes place practically overnight, when the heather blooms in such a burst of riotous color the dun-tinted hills blaze with a sudden and glorious splendor. Wave upon wave of purple and magenta roll across the Pennines, crowning the dark industrial valleys below with a stunning beauty that is breathtaking even to the most jaundiced eye.

The vast plateau of moorland that sweeps up above Fairley village, and which is part of that great Pennine Chain, is no exception. Here, too, the somber harshness is obliterated through September and into October. It is almost as if an immense bolt of local cloth has been flung generously across the hills, the weft and the warp of the weave a mixture of royal purple and blues and twists of green. For on the heathery slopes grow harebells and fern and bilberry, and even the scant gnarled trees are agleam with the freshest and smallest of fluttering leaves.

Larks and linnets glide up into the lucent air, and the sky, so often weighted down with rain-filled clouds, is dazzlingly blue and blazing with that incredible clarity of light so peculiar to the North of England. Not only is the relentless environment gentled and softened at this time of year, but the awesome silence of the winter is suddenly broken by the liveliest of sounds. The hillsides are all seamed by deep and narrow valleys and dells, each with its own tumbling little beck of clear water rushing down over polished brown stones, or sparkling with shimmering waterfalls that drop, unexpectedly, from the perilous rocky crags. Consequently, the sound of falling water is ever present on the Yorkshire moors in the summer months, accompanied by the sweet piercing trilling of the birds, the scurrying of the rabbits amongst the bilberry and bracken, the occasional bleat of the sheep that wander aimlessly over the heather-colored hills seeking sustenance.

Emma Harte had a particular love of the moors, even in those grim and bitter winters when they became so brutal and frightening. Like her mother before her, she was at home there, up in that solitary hill country where, in her stark solitude, she never felt lonely or alone. She found in their vastness, in their very emptiness, a certain solace for whatever ailed her, drew a strange yet reassuring comfort from that imposing landscape. To Emma it was always beautiful through the everchanging seasons, and most especially so in the late summer when the heather bloomed so profusely and with incredible brilliance.

On this Monday morning in August her spirits lifted considerably as she climbed over the stile into the long meadow, vividly green and speckled with daisies. She hurried along the narrow path, occasionally looking up, her deep-green eyes scanning the rising hills, lilac-tinted and running into purple beneath a sky that was china blue and without a single cloud. The sun was already seeping through the faint bluish haze on the horizon, staining it to golden, and she knew it would be another scorching hot day, as it had been all month.

For once she was glad to leave the cottage in Top Fold. Her father's distress about Winston's rapid departure had depressed her all weekend, and it was with a sense of relief that she had closed the cottage door and headed for the Top of the World. In that powerful and compelling wilderness, up there in that bright air, so purely bracing at this early hour, she felt free and unfettered, for Emma was a true child of the moors. Born and bred among them, it was as though their very characteristics had long ago penetrated her own soul, for she was as untamable and as relentless, and they were as much a part of her nature as the very breath she drew.

As a small child she had run unchecked over the high ridges and through the narrow valleys and little dells, her only companions the birds and the small timid creatures that inhabited the region. There was not a spot she did not know, and know well. She had her favorite places, well-guarded secret places, hidden in the crevices of the rocks and the folds of those wild hills, where all manner of pretty flowers blossomed when least expected and larks made their nests and crystal water tumbled over rocky slopes, scintillating icily in the sunlight, cool to drink and paddle in barefooted, toes curling deliciously on the dappled stones.

Now, as Emma escaped to her beloved moors, the oppressed feeling she had experienced for the last few days was

lessening rapidly. She quickened her steps, following the
familiar winding path that snaked upward, and she thought of
Winston as she climbed on steadily. She would miss him, for
they had always been close and dear companions, but she was
happy for him. He had found the necessary courage to leave,
to escape from the village and the Fairley brickyard, before it
was too late. Her only regret was that her brother had been
afraid to confide in her, believing, quite mistakenly, that she
would tell their father or, at worst, attempt to persuade him
to change his mind. She smiled to herself. How faulty Winston's judgment of her was. She would have readily encouraged him to pursue his dream, for she understood the nature
of him, knew only too well how hemmed in and frustrated he
had grown, with nothing much to look forward to in Fairley,
except drudgery and boredom, and nights of drinking at the
pub with his cloddish mates.

Emma paused to catch her breath as she came up onto the
crest of the first ridge. She fanned her face, and took several
deep breaths, before commencing her ascent of the slope to
Ramsden Crags. They reared above her, huge granite horses
dramatically outlined against the sky, ringed in sunshine,
rivulets of which trickled down over their dark and ancient
surfaces like running liquid gold. In winter, coated with ice
and snow and sleet, their ghastly sheen could appall, but now
in the soft summer air they appeared quite benign and welcoming. Emma looked about her, devouring the scenery with
her eyes, as always drawing strength from those familiar
surroundings. The haze was evaporating and, in spite of the
gentle breeze blowing down from the high fells, she was
already beginning to feel the heat. She was thankful she was
wearing the dark green cotton dress Mrs. Wainright had
given her. It was light and cool against her bare legs.

Within minutes Emma was under the shadow of Ramsden
Crags. She put down the heavy basket of clothes she was
carrying, and seated herself on a flat rock. These days she
always lingered for a moment at the Top of the World, for
here she felt her mother's presence more assuredly than she
did in the little cottage. To Emma, her mother still lived and
breathed in this quiet sheltered spot, so well loved by them
both. Emma saw her adored face in the pale shadows and
vaporous moorland tints, heard her tinkling laughter echoing
around the timeworn crags, communed with her in the gentle

silence that was unbroken, except for the occasional bird call or the faint buzzing of a bee.

Emma rested her head against the rocks behind her and closed her eyes, conjuring up her mother's face. She opened them almost immediately and it seemed to her that her mother stood before her, radiant and smiling, the beloved image wholly formed. "Oh, Mam, Mam, I do miss yer," she said aloud, and she was filled with a longing, a yearning that was almost unbearable and brought an ache to her throat. She held out her arms, straining towards that nebulous image, which quickly faded. Emma sat quite still for a little while longer, leaning against the cool rocks, her eyes closed, pushing down the sadness that was still so near to the surface, and then, when she was contained, she picked up the basket and set off resolutely in the direction of Ramsden Ghyll.

Hurrying now, she shifted the heavy basket onto her other arm and descended into the Ghyll, all green darkness, shadowy and cool, where only thimblefuls of sunlight trickled in through the overhanging rocky ledges and ancient trees, whose crooked boughs knotted together like an old man's rheumatic gnarly fingers. A rabbit skittered across her path and disappeared behind a soaring boulder coated with mats of moss that were dark and velvety in the dim light. When she reached the middle of the dell, where all sunlight was totally obliterated, she began to sing, as she always did here, her light soprano echoing sweetly in the perfect stillness. "Oh, Danny Boy, the pipes, the pipes are calling. From glen to glen, and down the mountainside. The summer's gone, and all the roses falling. It's you, it's you must go, and I must bide."

She stopped singing and smiled to herself, thinking warmly of Blackie. That was his favorite song and he had taught her the words. He had not been to the Hall for over a month. He had finished all of his work there for the moment. But sometimes he stopped by to see her, when he was in the district, and she wondered when he would be coming back. She missed him. Within minutes Emma was up and out of the chilly dell and in the bright air again, under the wide and shining sky, heading for the ridge that dropped down to the Hall. She began to walk more swiftly, to make up time, for she was later than usual this morning, well over an hour late, and Cook would already be grousing about her tardiness, of that she was certain. She ran down the slope and opened the old rickety wooden gate at the edge of the Baptist Field, closing it carefully behind her, dropping the heavy iron latch into place.

Emma no longer swung on the gate. She thought she was too grownup to indulge in such a childish game. After all, she was fifteen and four months, already in her sixteenth year. A young lady almost, and young ladies, who intended to be grand ladies one day, did not do such frivolous things.

Entering the cobbled stable yard, Emma was somewhat taken aback to see Dr. Malcolm's horse and trap tethered at the mounting block. The yard was deserted and unnaturally quiet, and there was no sign of Tom Hardy, the stableboy, who normally was busily currying the Squire's horses and polishing the brass on the harnesses at this hour. She frowned, wondering why Dr. Mac was visiting the Hall at seven o'clock in the morning. Somebody must be badly, she surmised, and immediately thought of Edwin, who had taken a chill the week before. He was prone to chest colds, so Mrs. Fairley had told her. Emma's feet flew up the stone steps leading to the back door, but not so quickly that her keen eyes did not notice the steps had not yet been scoured. That there Annie's getting neglectful of her duties, she thought with a flash of irritation.

The moment she entered the house Emma knew that something was dreadfully amiss. She quietly closed the door behind her and went down into the kitchen. The fire blazed as always, the copper kettle hissed on the hob, but the delicious smell of breakfast cooking was noticeably absent. Cook sat in her chair near the fireplace, rocking to and fro, stifling her sobs and wiping her streaming eyes with the end of her apron, which was already sodden with her copious tears. Annie appeared to be reasonably controlled, and Emma strode rapidly across the flagged floor to her, hoping to elicit some information. But she perceived at once that Annie was as distraught as Cook, and she sat so rigidly in the chair she might have turned to a pillar of salt. Like Lot's wife, Emma thought.

Emma flung the basket down on the floor hastily. "What's wrong?" she cried, looking from one to the other. "Why is Dr. Mac here? It's Master Edwin, isn't it? He's sick!" Neither Cook nor Annie appeared to hear her words. Certainly they paid no attention to her. And the dysphoria and apprehension in the air instantly communicated itself to Emma, and so sharply she quaked inside. The overwrought Mrs. Turner now looked up, an anguished expression on her apple-dumpling face, her eyes red-rimmed. She gazed at Emma mutely, obviously unable to speak, and then she burst into further paroxysms of tears, rocking herself more violently than ever, moaning loudly between her sobs.

Emma was frantic. She reached out and touched Annie gently on the shoulder. The petrified girl jumped nervously, as if Emma's fingers had scourged her. She returned Emma's questioning look with a mindless stare. Annie blinked several times, very rapidly, and her mouth jerked, but she remained silent. And then she began to quiver. Emma took hold of her firmly with her small strong hands, attempting to calm her, filled with a mixture of impatience, and the beginnings of real panic.

Emma now realized she must go and find Murgatroyd immediately, but at that very moment the butler appeared at the top of the stairs leading to the family's living quarters. Emma's eyes flew urgently to his face. It was more dolorous than ever. He was wearing his black butler's coat, which was also unprecedented at this hour, when he was generally in his shirt sleeves and green baize apron, engaged in his pantry chores. On reaching the bottom of the stairs he leaned against the newel post and passed his hand over his brow in a futile gesture. His arrogant manner had been replaced by a deflated air, and this also registered most forcibly with Emma.

The bewildered girl took a few steps closer to him. "Summat serious has happened. It's Master Edwin, isn't it?" she whispered. It was a statement rather than a question.

Murgatroyd looked down at her mournfully. "No, it's the missis," he said.

"She's badly then, is she? That's why Dr. Mac's here—"

"She's dead," interrupted Murgatroyd roughly, in a low harsh voice.

Emma took an involuntary step backward. She felt as if she had been struck across her face with great force. It seemed to her that all of the blood was draining out of her, and her legs trembled. Her voice was unsteady as she cried, "Dead!"

"Aye, dead as a doornail," Murgatroyd muttered tersely, his darkening face revealing his distress, which was most genuine.

For a split second Emma lost all power of speech. Her mouth opened and closed stupidly in her extreme nervousness and shock. Finally, she managed to say, "But she wasn't badly when I left on Thursday afternoon."

"No, and she weren't poorly yesterday either," intoned Murgatroyd in a woebegone voice. He looked at Emma with gravity, and for once there was no hostility in his manner towards her. "She tummeled down t'stairs during t'night. Broke her neck, so Dr. Mac says."

Emma gasped, and, reeling, she gripped the edge of the table to steady herself. Her eyes, wide and dazed, were riveted on the butler.

Murgatroyd inclined his head in Annie's direction. "Yon lass found her at five-thirty this morning, when she went up ter take t'ashes out of the grates. Stiff as a board the missis was. Lying at the bottom of the front staircase in the entrance hall. That she was, and in her nightclothes. Fair scared the living daylights out of yon Annie, who come running ter fetch me like the Divil himself was after her."

"It just can't be so," Emma groaned, pressing her knuckles to her blanched mouth. Her eyes welled with tears.

"Aye, horrible it was, ter see her lying there, her eyes wide and open and all starey like, and glazed. And her head dangling loose like a broken doll's. I knows when I touched her she'd been dead for hours. Cold as marble, she was."

Murgatroyd paused in his harrowing litany, and then went on, "I carried her upstairs, fair gentle like, and laid her on her bed. And she might not have been dead at all. She looked ever so beautiful, just like she always was, with all that golden hair strewn about the pillow. Except for her staring eyes. I tried ter close 'em. But they just wouldn't shut. I had ter put two pennies on 'em, till Dr. Mac got here. The poor, poor missis."

The shaken and stupefied Emma dropped heavily into one of the chairs at the table. Tears were rolling down her cheeks, and she fished around in her pocket for the bit of clean rag that served as a handkerchief, and wiped her face. She hunched in the chair, so stunned and appalled she could hardly think. But gradually her composure returned, and it was then that she recognized she had grown extremely fond of Adele Fairley. She was doomed, Emma said to herself. And then she thought:

I knew summat awful would happen here, in this terrible house, one day.

The silence in the sun-filled kitchen was leaden, broken only by the muffled sobs of the weeping Cook. After a few minutes, the butler emerged from his pantry and said, with sour bluntness, "All this 'ere weeping and wailing like a lot of banshees has ter stop, yer knows." He spoke to the room at large, his eyes sweeping over them all. "We have our duties ter attend ter. There's the family ter consider."

Emma looked at him alertly, thinking compassionately of Edwin and the grief he must be experiencing at the news of his mother's untimely and shocking death. "The children," she said, through her subsiding tears, and blew her nose. "Do they know?"

"Dr. Mac's talking ter Master Edwin in the library right this minute," Murgatroyd informed her. "I told Master Gerald meself, after I'd got the missis upstairs ter her room, and afore I sent Tom ter the village for the doctor. Master Gerald waited for Dr. Mac, who dispatched him posthaste ter Newby Hall ter fetch the Squire home."

"What about Mrs. Wainright?" Emma ventured.

Margatroyd threw her a scathing look. "Do yer think I'm a gormless fool, lass? I already thought of that. Dr. Mac wrote out a telegram, and Master Gerald is ter send it ter her in Scotland, from t'first post office he comes ter that's open." The butler cleared his throat, and went on, "Now, lass, let's get a move on down 'ere. For a start, mash a pot of tea. The doctor needs a cup—" He glanced around the room and his beady eyes settled on Mrs. Turner. "So does Cook, by the looks of it."

Emma nodded, and hurried off to do as he had told her. Murgatroyd now addressed Cook in a louder voice. "Come on, Mrs. Turner. Pull yerself together, woman. There's a lot ter be done. We can't all collapse, yer knows."

Cook lifted her sorrowful face and regarded Murgatroyd fretfully. Her ample bosom was still heaving, but her sobbing had ceased. She pushed herself up out of the chair, nodding her head. "Aye, there's the bairns ter think about, and the Squire." She wiped her damp and streaked face on her apron again, and then looked down at it, still shaking her head. "Let me change me piny, and then I'll start on breakfast. Not that I thinks anybody'll want owt."

"Dr. Mac might want a bite," Murgatroyd said. "I'm off up ter see him now. And ter draw the curtains. We must show the proper respect for the dead."

Cook, who was changing her pinafore, said quickly, "Did yer send Tom ter the village ter get Mrs. Stead? Ter lay the missis out? She's the best by here for that job."

"Aye, I did that."

At the mention of her mother's name a flicker of comprehension entered Annie's deadened eyes. "Yer've sent for me mam," she said slowly, rousing herself from the stupor that had enveloped her for the last few hours.

"I did, Annie," Murgatroyd asserted. "She should be here any minute, and yer'd best look a bit more lively, afore she does arrive. She's got enough on her hands with the laying out. She don't needs ter be worrying about thee, lass."

The cook shuffled over to Annie and put her arms around her, looking down into the girl's pale face. "Do yer feel a bit better, luv?" she asked solicitously.

"Aye, I thinks so," Annie mumbled. "It gave me a right fright," she gasped, "finding the missis like that." Her shaky voice cracked with emotion, and finally the tears suppressed by shock flowed unchecked.

"Have a good cry, luv. Get it out of yer system, afore yer mam gets here. Yer don't want ter be upsetting her, now do yer, luv?" Annie buried her head against Cook's comforting body, sobbing softly. Mrs. Turner patted her shoulder and stroked her hair, murmuring kindly to her, and with motherly concern.

Satisfied that a degree of order had been restored, Murgatroyd turned on his heels and swiftly mounted the stairs. First he would consult with Dr. Mac, to see if he had any further instructions, and then he must go around the house, drawing all the curtains, shutting out the light until after the funeral, as was the custom in the North after a death in the family.

Emma made the tea and they sat drinking it in silence, all of them subdued and sorrowing. It was Annie who finally spoke first. She looked at Emma across the table and said, "I wish yer'd been here this weekend, Emma. Then yer'd have found the missis instead of me." Annie's eyes widened. "I'll never forget that look on the missis's face. Like she'd seen summat horrible afore she fell."

Emma stared at Annie through narrowed eyes. "What on earth do yer mean?"

Annie gulped. "It was like she'd seen—seen one of them there abominations me mam says walks over t'moors at night," Annie said, dropping her voice.

"Now, Annie, shut thee gob, lass. By gum, I won't have no fanciful talk about the spirits of the dead in this 'ere house," Mrs. Turner snapped. "All them silly village superstitions. Stuff and nonsense, if yer asks me."

Emma scowled. "I wonder what Mrs. Fairley was doing? Coming downstairs in the middle of the night. Murgatroyd said she'd been dead for hours. She must've been wandering around at two or three o'clock in the morning."

Annie volunteered quietly, "I knows what she was doing."

Both Mrs. Turner and Emma stared at her in surprise, and with expectancy. "And *how* do yer knows, Annie Stead?" asked Cook imperiously. "Unless I'm mistaken, yer were fast asleep in yer room in the attic. Or yer should've been."

"Aye, I was. But it *was* me that found her. And there was broken glass all around her body. From one of the best wine goblets, it was. She was still clutching part of t'stem, and there was dried blood on her hand, like rust, where she'd cut herself." Annie shivered at the remembrance, and whispered, "I bet she was coming down ter the library ter get herself a nip, 'cos I've sme—"

"Murgatroyd didn't mention no broken goblet ter me," interjected Cook peremptorily, glaring at Annie.

"No, *he* wouldn't. But I saw him sweeping it up, ever so quick like," Annie replied. "He thought I hadn't seen it 'cos I was scared stiff."

Cook continued to glare at Annie speechlessly, but Emma sucked in her breath, recognizing instantly the veracity of everything Annie had said. It was the most obvious explanation. "Yer not ter repeat that ter anybody, Annie. Yer hear what I say? Not even ter the Squire," Emma cautioned gravely. "What's done is done, and the less said, the better."

"Emma's right, luv," said Cook, recovering herself. "We don't wants no nasty gossip in the village. Let the poor missis rest in peace."

Annie nodded. "I promise not ter tell owt."

Emma sighed and was thoughtful. Then she looked pointedly at Cook and said, "It's right funny, when yer think about it. First Polly died, then me mam, and now Mrs. Fairley. All in just a few months of each other."

Cook returned Emma's concentrated stare. "It's said, in these parts, that everything goes in threes."

The funeral of Adele Fairley took place later that week. The Fairley mill was closed for the day, and all of the workers were in attendance, along with the servants from the Hall. The small cemetery adjoining Fairley Church overflowed with the villagers, the local gentry, and friends of the family from all over the county.

Two days after the funeral, Olivia Wainright left for London, accompanied by Edwin. Exactly one week later Adam Fairley departed himself, journeying south to join his youngest son at his sister-in-law's Mayfair town house.

Ernest Wilson was left in charge of the mill, much to Gerald Fairley's secret delight. For the callous, brainless, and irresponsible Gerald, quite unmoved by his mother's death, thought only of the infinite opportunities which now presented themselves. He fully intended to assert himself at the mill, and stringently so, in his father's absence, which he fervently hoped would be prolonged.

TWENTY-THREE

On a warm Sunday afternoon, in June of the following year, Edwin Fairley set out from Fairley Hall for the moors. He carried a picnic basket in one hand, laden with all sorts of delicious tidbits from Cook's groaning pantry, and in the other a sack containing some gardening implements and a few necessary items.

He and Emma had some hard work to do at Ramsden Crags, a task they had been planning for several weeks. Because of the inclement and frequently rainy weather, they had had to postpone this venture several times. On Friday, when Emma went home for her weekend off, Edwin had walked with her as far as the Crags. They had made an assignation to meet there at three o'clock today, the weather permitting.

And the weather does permit, Edwin thought. He glanced up. The pale sun was continually flitting in and out from behind the patchwork of gray and white clouds that littered the powder-blue sky, but there was no hint of rain. Even the light wind barely rustled the trees and the translucent air was so mild it was almost balmy.

Edwin purposely avoided the stables. A few minutes earlier, when he had gone down to the kitchen to collect the picnic basket, he had observed Annie Stead and Tom Hardy chatting and laughing together in the yard. They were courting, so Emma had informed him, and it was more than likely they would have paid no attention to him whatsoever, as immersed in each other as they appeared to be. On the other hand, he did not want to put them to the test, for he had no particular desire to arouse even their mildest curiosity. Not that it was unusual for him to picnic on the moors, but the sack might create a flicker of interest. He walked swiftly through the walled rose garden and out under the clump of old oaks. In a short time he was across the Baptist Field and mounting the slope rising onto the flat plateau of moorland and the narrow track that ran all the way to the Ghyll, and Ramsden Crags beyond.

Edwin breathed deeply, filling his lungs with the pure air, which was so much more bracing on this higher ground. His health was now fully restored and he felt vital again. At the beginning of May he had caught a summer cold, which had settled on his chest and developed into a bronchial condition. After two weeks in the school sanatorium he had been sent home to recuperate at the insistence of the school doctor.

Tom Hardy had driven the carriage over to Worksop to collect him, since his father was away, not an unusual circumstance these days. As far as Edwin could ascertain, his father made only periodic trips to Fairley, when absolutely necessary, and was often in London, or traveling on the Continent attending to unspecified business. However, his father had engaged a tutor for him, so that he would not fall behind in his studies. Although Edwin was a disciplined student, and perfectly capable of working alone, his father had wanted to be certain he sustained his brilliant scholastic record. It had been decided he would go to Cambridge when he was eighteen, to study for the bar under the Downing Professor of English Law at Downing College. Edwin and the tutor were alone at the Hall, except for Gerald and the servants. Edwin did not mind. Actually, he rather relished it. He was pretty much left to his own devices, except for the mornings of intense study with the tutor. Gerald ignored his existence, and barely addressed a remark to him. *He* was far too busy. Because the mill in Fairley, and the other two in Stanningley Bottom and Armley, took up most of Gerald's time, the two brothers only saw each other at meals, and not always then. Sometimes Gerald took one of Cook's packed lunches to the Fairley mill and ate there, an idea so unpalatable to Edwin it positively nauseated him.

Edwin began to whistle merrily as he headed along the ridge to Ramsden Crags, striding out at a brisk pace, his fair hair blowing in the breeze. He was looking forward to seeing Emma, and also to their impending project. Emma had challenged a theory he had about the Crags, and for some reason he felt compelled to prove his point. He wondered if he was being juvenile. Perhaps.

Edwin Fairley, who had just celebrated his seventeenth birthday, now considered himself to be quite grown-up, and he did appear much older than his actual years. This was due, not unnaturally, to the events that had taken place in the past year, not the least of which was his mother's death, so sudden and tragic. Her passing away had had a more profound effect on him than on his brother, for he had been so much closer and more intimately involved with his mother than Gerald. Edwin's sorrow was, at first, overwhelming, but being of a scholastic nature and a voracious reader like his father, he had inevitably buried himself in his studies. This intense dedication to learning prevented him from dwelling morbidly on her death, and its appalling circumstances. He had thrown himself, and with a vengeance, into innumerable other school activities, and all manner of sports, and these too had helped him to assuage his grief. They kept him busy from early morning until late at night. Eventually he had been enabled to adopt a more philosophical attitude, and now, finally, he accepted her loss with considerably less heartbreak.

Olivia Wainright had also played a crucial role in Edwin's development, albeit indirectly but, nonetheless, most effectively. When he visited her in London, for a portion of the school holidays, he was exposed to a wide circle of her friends—politicians, writers, journalists, and artists, many of them celebrated and outstanding men in their fields. These privileged encounters, in a society that was gay, pleasure-loving, and sophisticated, always had a tremendous impact on him. Olivia, aware of his charming manners and acutely attuned to his intelligent mind, made a point of including him at many of her soirées, which he thoroughly enjoyed and at which he executed himself admirably. Consequently, he had matured and had acquired a measure of polish and self-confidence. In certain subtle ways he was quite a different boy from the pampered "mummy's darling" he had been when Adele was alive.

But, apart from the changes in his personality and atti-tudes, Edwin had also undergone an amazing physical trans-formation, due in no small measure to his newly acquired interest in sports. He had grown in height and filled out, and he was a strikingly handsome youth whose marked resem-blance to his father was becoming more pronounced. He had inherited Adam Fairley's expressive bluish-gray eyes, his sensitive mouth with its hint of sensuality, and his intelligent, well-articulated face, although Edwin's was much less ascetic than his father's. He was now almost as tall and as broad as Adam. His physique, which was already quite splendid, and his rather classically handsome face, had earned him the nickname of "Adonis" at Worksop, much to his irritation. He was constantly embarrassed by the flurry his looks created with the sisters and cousins of his school friends.

Edwin considered them twittering, insipid, and callow crea-tures. He loathed their vapid attentions, which flustered him. He much preferred to be in the company of Emma, who had been such a consolation to him during his bereavement. Not one of those young ladies of Quality, or the rich debutantes his father foisted on him, could compare to *his* Emma in beauty and grace, wit and spirit. And by God, she was beautiful. Every time he returned to Fairley she delighted him even more. At sixteen she was fully and exquisitely devel-oped. Her shapely and feminine figure was that of a young woman and her face was sublime.

Edwin smiled happily. It would be grand to be with Emma, away from the prying eyes of the other servants. She made him laugh with her quick wit and her penchant for striking at the heart of the matter. He chuckled to himself. Murgatroyd came in for a great deal of her acerbity. She called him

"Frozen Face" behind his back, but only to Edwin. His brother Gerald had been dubbed "Skinny Ribs," which made him laugh uproariously, since the obese Gerald was disgustingly fatter. These thoughts of Emma made him increase his pace and he was soon at the Crags. He put down the picnic basket and the sack and, stepping forward, he shaded his eyes with his hand, scanning the landscape.

Emma, climbing up over the last crest, saw Edwin before he saw her. She began to run. The heath and bracken brushed against her feet, the wind caught at her long skirts so that they billowed out like puffy clouds, and her hair was a stream of russet-brown silk ribbons flying behind her as she ran. The sky was as blue as speedwells and the larks wheeled and turned against the face of the sun. She could see Edwin quite clearly now, standing by the huge rocks just under the shadow of the Crags above Ramsden Ghyll. When he saw her he waved, and began to climb upwards towards the ledge where they always sat protected from the wind, surveying the world far below. He did not look back, but went on climbing.

"Edwin! Edwin! Wait for me," she called, but her voice was blown away by the wind and he did not hear. When she reached Ramsden Crags she was out of breath and her usually pale face was flushed from exertion.

"I ran so hard I thought I would die," she gasped as he helped her up onto the ledge.

He smiled at her. "You will never die, Emma. We are both going to live forever and ever at the Top of the World."

Emma glanced at him out of the corner of her eye, and laughed. Then she looked down and said, "I see yer brought the sack."

"Of course. And a picnic, too, for later."

"I thinks we'll be needing it, after all the hard work we've got ter do."

"It's not going to be as difficult as you think, Emma, and I'll be doing most of the work." He scrambled down over the small boulders that were like roughhewn steppingstones, and dropped to the ground. He opened the sack, removed a hammer, a chisel, and a large nail. These he stowed away in his pocket.

Looking up at Emma on the ledge above him, Edwin said, "I'm going to prove to you that this central rock is not part of the actual formation of the Crags, but is quite separate. And also that it can be moved." As he spoke, Edwin kicked the base of a rock about four feet high and two feet wide. This was wedged between the larger boulders that soared up well beyond the ledge and into the sky.

"Well, maybe it can," Emma said, glancing down at him. "But I still thinks that even if yer moves it yer won't find owt behind it. Only more rocks."

Edwin shook his head. "No, Emma, I disagree. I am convinced there is a hollow space behind the rock." He climbed back up onto the ledge, edged past her carefully, and positioned himself next to the peak of the rock in question. This was adjacent to the ledge, but a few inches lower, and it protruded slightly. Edwin knelt down on the ledge and took out the hammer and chisel. He moved closer to the rock and leaned over it.

"What are yer going ter do, Edwin?" Emma asked curiously, and cautioned quickly, "Be careful yer don't topple over."

"I'm quite safe," he responded, and went on, "You remember the crevice where I lost that shilling weeks ago? I heard it rattling as it fell, even though you say *you* didn't. I am going to make this crevice larger, into a hole, so that I can look down and see what's there, below the rock."

"Yer'll see nowt but more rocks," she said bluntly.

Edwin chuckled, and began to chip away at the crevice. Emma watched him patiently, shaking her head. She was quite certain Edwin was wasting his time, but she had decided to humor him when he had first lost his shilling. After ten minutes of constant chipping he had made a hole in the crevice about two inches in diameter. He lowered his head and pressed one eye to the hole, gripping the sides of the rock to balance himself.

"Can yer see owt, then?" asked Emma.

Edwin straightened up and shook his head. "No, it's all black." He pulled the nail out of his pocket, and half turned his head so he could see Emma. "Edge closer to me, Emma, and listen very carefully." She did as he told her, shuffling along the ledge and squeezing up to him. They both bent towards the hole and he dropped the nail into it. There was no sound at all for a few seconds and then they heard a distinct tinkle as it landed.

"Now! Did you hear that, Emma?"

"Yes, I did. But it might have dropped on another rock, that's all."

"No, I don't think it did. It took too long to fall. It's on the ground," Edwin cried firmly. He returned the implements to his jacket pocket. "Move back along the ledge and climb down, but go slowly, so you don't slip. I'll follow you."

Emma lowered herself onto the boulders below the ledge, backed down them cautiously, and jumped to the ground. Edwin was right behind her. He took off his jacket, threw it carelessly on one side, and rolled up his sleeves. Emma stood watching him as he fished around in the sack, a skeptical look on her face. "What are yer going ter do now?" she asked.

"I'm going to remove all the moss and bits of heath and weeds growing here," he exclaimed, indicating the base and lower sides of the rock. "And you can help me." He handed her a garden trowel and took up a small spade himself. "You work at that side, and I'll work here."

Emma thought this whole idea was a waste of time and energy; nevertheless, she began to work vigorously, digging out clumps of heath and moss which had crusted the rock for years. After a while she began to perspire. She put down the trowel, rolled up her sleeves, and opened the collar of her dress. Feeling more comfortable, she began to dig again. After about twenty minutes of hard toil they had accomplished a remarkable job of cleaning up the face and base of the rock.

Edwin stepped back and regarded it thoughtfully. "Look, Emma," he said. He took hold of her hand and pulled her to him. He pointed to the rock. "Do you see how the rock itself is more clearly outlined, now that we've removed all the overgrowth. It's not part of the entire formation of the Crags at all. See how it has been wedged in between the great boulders. No rock could fall so accurately, Emma. I am certain it was placed there."

Emma nodded her head. She had to agree. He was right, and she said so, adding, "But, Edwin, it's still a fair size. How do yer think we're going ter shift it?"

He strode over to the rock and said, with absolute self-confidence, "I am going to make this crevice here larger." He tapped the central rock, and pointed out a small space at the base, between the rock itself and the soaring Crags rising up behind it. "Then I am going to use a crowbar and a wedge to push the rock away from the Crags."

"It'll never work, Edwin. And yer might hurt yerself."

"No, I won't, Emma. And I've thought it all out very carefully."

Working with the hammer and chisel, Edwin had soon made the space big enough to take the crowbar. He put the crowbar into the hole and wedged a small but strong log behind it, placing this on the ground to the left of the rock. "Stand back, Emma," he warned, "go over there by the trees. The rock will fall forward, and I don't want you standing in its path." Using all of his strength, Edwin pressed on the crowbar, pushing the protruding end of it onto the log, using it as a lever to force the rock away from the Crags. But it did not move. Edwin began to sweat profusely, and his arms ached, but he forced himself against the crowbar determinedly.

Emma held her breath, clasping her hands together. Edwin was wrong. It would not work. She had no sooner thought this than she saw it moving.

"Edwin! Edwin! I think I saw it coming away," she shouted.

"I know," he gasped, "I felt it myself." With a final thrust of energy he pressed against the crowbar, and, as he did, the rock toppled forward as he had predicted it would. A small aperture on the face of Ramsden Crags was revealed. This was about eighteen inches wide and two feet high. Edwin could not conceal his excitement. He swung around.

"Look, Emma! There's a hole here," he cried triumphantly. He knelt down and peered into it, and then he inched his head inside. "It's like a little tunnel. And here's the shilling and the nail!" He picked them up and pulled back. He held them out to show her, his face wreathed in smiles.

"Where do yer think it goes?" Emma asked, running to join him at the aperture.

"I don't know. Under the Crags, I suspect. They do stretch back for miles, you know. I'm going in."

"Oh, Edwin, do yer think yer should?" A worried look settled on her face. "It might be dangerous. What if yer started a rockslide and got stuck in there?"

Edwin stood up and pulled out his handkerchief. He mopped his damp face and brushed his hair back. "I'll only go in a little way. And I brought candles and matches. They're in the sack. Would you get them for me, Emma, and that length of rope, please?"

"Yes, 'course I will." She brought him the items he had requested. "I'm going in with yer," she announced.

He stared at her and frowned. "I don't think so. Not at first. Let me go and investigate, and then I'll come back for you."

She compressed her lips and said stoutly, "I'm not afraid, yer knows."

"Yes, I know that. But I think you should stay here, just in case I need something." As he spoke Edwin tied the rope around his waist. He handed her the other end. "Hold on to this. There could be a labyrinth of tunnels in there. I've been reading up on rock climbing and potholing, and potholers always tie a rope around themselves, for safety."

Emma, who was now visibly impressed that Edwin's deductions had been accurate, immediately saw the sense of this. "Well, just be careful—" She looked at Edwin, so tall and muscular, and then at the aperture. "How are yer going ter get in there? That's what I wants ter knows. It's ever so tiny."

"I'll have to squeeze in, and then crawl along."

"Yer'll get yerself all mucky, Edwin Fairley. Cook'll wonder what yer've been up ter. Yer'll cop it!"

Edwin's mouth twitched and he burst out laughing. "Emma, do stop worrying so much, and about trivialities. Cook's not going to say anything. We've come this far. Let's at least complete the project."

Emma sighed. "All right. But go ever so slow like, and if yer needs me, tug on the rope. Promise?"

"I promise."

It was with a certain amount of trepidation that Emma watched Edwin disappear into the aperture. Slowly the length of rope unwound itself, as he moved further into the tunnel, until she was finally clinging to the very end of it, straining against the outer wall of the Crags. A flicker of anxiety crossed her face, and she lowered her head and called into the tunnel. "Edwin! Are yer safe?"

"Yes," came back his voice, echoing hollowly as if from a long distance.

"Yer've used up all the rope," she cried, her voice rising shrilly.

"I know. Let go of it."

"No! I won't!"

"Emma, let go of it!" he shouted in a commanding tone. She did so, much against her better judgment, and knelt down, looking into the aperture, suddenly afraid for Edwin. It seemed ominous in there.

But within minutes she heard a small scuffling sound, and to her great relief she saw the top of Edwin's fair head. She moved away from the opening so that he could squeeze out. His shirt and trousers were covered with dirt and his face was smudged with grime. He straightened up, grinning broadly. "What's in there?" she asked, with mounting curiosity.

"A cave, Emma! A fantastic cave!" he cried, his light eyes shining. "You see, I was right after all. Come on, I'll show you. And we don't need the rope. The tunnel is fairly straight and leads right into the cave."

"A real cave. Fancy that!" Emma said, and then she smiled a little shamefacedly. "I'm sorry I was doubting yer, Edwin."

He laughed. "That doesn't matter. If you hadn't doubted me I might not have felt obliged to prove myself right. Come on. Let's go." He collected additional candles, and continued, "You follow me. Keep your head down at first. The tunnel is very low at the outset."

Edwin entered the hole and Emma wriggled in behind him, blinking her eyes as she adjusted to the darkness after the bright sunlight. They crawled along at first, but the deeper they went the higher and wider the tunnel became and they were able to walk in a crouching fashion the rest of the way. Soon Emma could see the faint flickering of the candle Edwin had left in the cave, and a few seconds later he was helping her to her feet in the cave itself.

Edwin began to light the extra candles and arrange them neatly in a line along a narrow ledge near the entrance. Whilst he was engaged in this task, Emma looked around with enormous interest. As the candles flared and illuminated the darkness, she saw that the cave was indeed fantastic, as Edwin had said. It was a large cavern with a ceiling that soared up into a weird conical shape. There were flat little ledges extending out from some of the rocky walls, while other portions had great indentations juxtaposed next to flat areas that were so perfectly smooth they looked as if they had been polished by a giant hand. There was a breathtaking grandeur about this ancient and spectacular interior, which was as old as time itself perhaps. It was cool and dry and absolutely silent. Emma felt a sense of awe.

Edwin handed her a candle and took one himself. "Let's investigate," he announced. He moved ahead and his foot struck something on the floor of the cave. He looked down, lowering the candle so that he could see better. "Emma, look at this! It's the remnants of a fire!" He kicked the blackened and charred wood, which instantly crumbled. "For heaven's sake, somebody discovered the cave before we did."

"Yer right," Emma asserted, staring at the charred wood. Then she caught a glimpse of what looked like a heap of sacks in the far corner. "Over there, Edwin. Sacks, I thinks."

He followed the direction of her pointing finger and strode rapidly across the cave. "They are, indeed. And on this ledge above them there is an old piece of tallow candle. Oh, come on! Let's see what else we can find. You go around that side, and I'll poke about here," he finished, his voice vibrating with eagerness.

Emma walked slowly, holding the candle out in front of her. She looked from side to side alertly as she moved, glancing down at the hard earth floor, scanning the high-flung walls. To her immense disappointment the far side of the cavern appeared to be quite empty. She was about to turn back and rejoin Edwin when the frail light from the candle illuminated a patch of smooth wall. She was certain she could make out faint markings on the wall, like writing scratched onto the surface. She ran over and held the candle close to it. It *was* writing. How interesting.

And then Emma sucked in her breath in amazement, for the first word she read was *Elizabeth*. She moved the candle. Written underneath was *Elizabetta*. And below, *Isabella*. Slowly, Emma's eyes followed the column running down the wall of the cave. *Lilibeth. Beth. Betty. Bess. Eliza. Liza. Lisa*. Next to this column was one single word, carved in giant capital letters. *ADAM*. She swallowed. Under the name was a small heart with an arrow piercing it, and inside the heart were the simple initials A E.

Emma's eyes were pinned to the wall and those initials. A coldness settled over her, as she remembered the locket she had found in her mother's wooden box. Not me mam and *him!*

"Emma! Emma! Where are you? Cooee! Cooee!"

She pulled herself together as Edwin's footsteps drew closer, echoing on the hard ground. She opened her mouth and closed it at once, for a moment not trusting herself to speak coherently. Finally she called, "Over here."

"What did you find?" Edwin asked, rushing to her side. She pointed to the writing on the wall mutely. Edwin's eyes lighted on his father's name at once. "Adam!" he read wonderingly, staring at the giant letters. "Why, my father must have found this cave years ago!" He sounded jubilant. "And look, here's every derivation of the name Elizabeth, even in Italian and Spanish. This is very intriguing, indeed. Who do you think Elizabeth was, or is?"

Emma was silent. Edwin appeared not to notice her lack of response, or her utter stillness, for she was as rigid as stone standing next to him. "Well, I don't suppose I can very well ask Father. However, let's search around a bit more." Edwin was buoyed up with enthusiasm. He left Emma standing in front of the scratchings on the wall, still staggered at their dreadful implications.

"Come here, Emma. I've found something else," Edwin shouted after a few seconds had elapsed. Emma stifled the desire to run out of the cavern and it was with considerable reluctance that she joined him in the corner where the sacks were stacked. Edwin was holding a flat oval pebble, about three inches long and two inches wide. He handed it to her and held the candle over it. "Do you see, Emma? The pebble has been painted on. It's a miniature, in oils, of a woman. See! I think it's Aunt Olivia. Yes, I'm positive it's her."

Emma said nothing, but thought grimly: *No, it's not. It's me mam.*

"Don't you think it's Aunt Olivia?"

"Yes," Emma responded dully.

Edwin put the stone in his pocket. "I think I shall keep this," he said.

Emma shivered and the candle wavered about in her hand. Edwin did not fail to notice this. "Emma, you're cold." He clucked sympathetically, and put his arm around her. Emma tried hard not to shrink away from him.

"Yes, I am. Let's get out of here. It's warmer in the sun." Without waiting for him to reply, she extracted herself and ran to the opening of the cave. She blew out the candle and placed it on the ledge, and crouching, and then crawling, she moved with incredible speed along the tunnel until she was out in the fresh air. She heaved a sigh of relief. She would never go back in there. Never.

Edwin emerged a few moments later. His eyes sought out Emma. She stood under the shadow of Ramsden Crags, shaking her dress free of the dirt and dust, her hair blowing about her in the wind, her face inscrutable. As he continued to gaze at her he recognized that the strange coldness which sometimes invaded her face had crept back onto it. Sensitive as he was by nature, and especially to Emma, he at once detected a change in her mood, and a change that was radical. It distressed him.

He walked over to her and took her arm. "Emma, is something wrong?" She did not answer, and averted her face. "Is something wrong?" he said again, and more loudly.

She shook his hand off. "No, nowt's wrong."

"But you look peculiar. And you fled like a frightened rabbit out of the cave."

"No, I didn't. I was cold, that's all."

Edwin turned away, realizing he would not make any headway with her at this moment. He brushed the dirt off his trousers, and began to busy himself collecting the tools. He felt suddenly deflated. Emma had seated herself on the flat rock where she always sat. He watched her as she lifted her long hair and moved it back over her shoulders gracefully. Then she folded her hands in her lap and sat staring ahead, looking out across the moors, and to the valley far beyond. He smiled to himself. She looked so prim and curiously dignified. No, regal, he told himself; it's the way she holds her head so high, and keeps her back so straight.

He wandered over to Emma, attempting a show of casualness. He sat down on the ground at her feet and looked up at her. "Do you feel better now? Out here in the sunshine," he ventured gently.

"Yes, thanks," Emma said quietly, without so much as glancing at him.

Edwin winced. She sounded so cold and remote. He rested his head against the flat rock and closed his eyes, wondering why she was adopting this stern attitude. She had shut him out most purposefully, he recognized that. He felt a twinge in his chest, and that sense of loss he had experienced before.

Meanwhile, Emma's fertile brain was racing. How could her sweet and gentle mother have been friendly with Adam Fairley? *That terrible man.* And anyway, her mother had spent part of her girlhood in Ripon with Cousin Freda. It struck her then, and quite forcibly, that Elizabeth was not a very unusual name. Might it not be some other Elizabeth whose name was carved on the wall? A girl from the gentry perhaps, who had known Adam Fairley when he was young. There was more likelihood of *him* being friends with a girl of Quality than with one from the working class. But there was the stone Edwin had found. Still, that might really be a painting of Olivia Wainright, just as Edwin believed. It certainly looked like her. She thought then of the locket. Yet even that didn't mean anything significant. Lots of people had names beginning with an A. Anybody could have given it to her mother. Emma now found all of these conclusions quite irresistible. And because the idea of a friendship between her mother and Adam Fairley was intolerable and unacceptable to her, for it would besmirch her mother's memory, Emma slowly convinced herself that her mother was not the Elizabeth of the cave.

In no time at all she felt more cheerful. She looked down at Edwin resting peacefully at her feet. Poor Edwin. She had been mean to him and unfair, when he was always so nice to her. She tapped him lightly on the shoulder, almost playfully.

Edwin opened his eyes and glanced up, not without apprehension, uncertain of her mood. To his delight Emma was smiling at him, that lovely and most radiant smile, and her emerald eyes danced with the brightest of lights.

"I feel like it's teatime. Are yer hungry, Edwin?"

"I'm absolutely famished!" He was overjoyed to see her good humor fully restored. He jumped up and strode over to his jacket. He pulled out his small gold pocket watch. "Why, Emma, it's already four-thirty. I'll unpack the picnic basket at once."

Emma began to laugh, shaking her head. Edwin stared at her nonplussed. "What is it?" he asked.

"I wish yer could see yerself, Edwin Fairley. Yer looks like a chimney sweep. Yer face is all mucky, and yer hands, and just look at mine." She held up her hands, palms outward, to show him. He joined in her laughter.

"I'll race yer ter the beck down yonder," she cried. She

leapt up and flew down the adjacent hillside. Edwin raced after her. He caught up with her and snatched at her belt. She laughed and struggled, but he held on to the belt tightly. They tripped and fell, and rolled down over the moorland, still laughing with hilarity. They landed at the edge of the beck, and Emma would have fallen in if Edwin had not held her tightly in his arms.

"Now look what yer've gone and done, Edwin Fairley," Emma remonstrated with mock annoyance through her laughter. "Yer've got me frock all wet in the beck."

Edwin released his grip on her and sat up, impatiently pushing the lock of hair away from his forehead "I am sorry, Emma. But it's only the hem. It will dry quickly in the sun."

"Aye, I hopes it will."

"You mean, 'yes, I hope it will,' Emma," Edwin corrected her.

She threw him a knowing look and said in a mimicking tone, "Yes, Edwin, you are quite right. I was not speaking properly." She pronounced the words very carefully and her voice, always sweet and melodious, was now so cultivated he gaped.

Emma poked him in the ribs. "I can speak like you if I want to," she said, and then confided, "I used to listen to your aunt. She has a lovely voice."

"So do you, Emma, when you pronounce your words correctly and don't lapse into the Yorkshire dialect." He smiled at her fondly. "I hope you don't mind when I point out mistakes in your speech. But you did ask me to do that."

"Yes, I did. And I am grateful." She smiled to herself. She knew she had surprised him and this tickled her tremendously. She leaned over and washed the dirt off her hands in the beck, then cupped them and splashed water onto her face.

Edwin took out his handkerchief and gave it to her with a boyishly gallant gesture. "Dry yourself on this."

When Emma had finished her toilet, Edwin also washed himself, and then they sat at the edge of the beck that tumbled down over the rocky hillside, talking happily, enjoying being together as they always did. Edwin chattered enthusiastically about going to Cambridge to study for the bar, and explained in great detail what a barrister actually was. In turn, Emma spoke proudly of Winston and how handsome he had looked in his uniform, when he had come home on leave from the Royal Navy.

"He's been back ter Fairley twice now," Emma said, "and me dad's much better. More settled about Winston being away—" She sat up abruptly and looked at the sky. "That's funny, I just felt a splash of rain."

Edwin lifted his head. "But the sky's blue and there are only a few gray clouds."

"We'd best get the picnic basket and hurry back ter the Hall," Emma announced quickly.

"Oh, don't be silly. It's only a summer shower. It will pass in a few minutes."

But as he spoke the pale sun was doused by bloated clouds moving up over the rim of the moors with gathering speed. There was a loud blast of thunder. It appeared to crack the sky wide open, releasing searing blades of brilliant white lightning and then an eerie grayness that flooded out swiftly, staining the sky as effectively as black dye colors cloth, and obliterating the light.

"Come on!" Edwin cried. He pulled Emma up to her feet and with urgency. "The weather is so unpredictable on these wretched moors. You never know when a storm will blow up."

Together they scrambled up the hill. The rain came down in lashing torrents. It was heavy driving rain that fell like a relentless waterfall. By the time they reached Ramsden Crags almost all of the light had vanished and the only illumination came from the staccato flashes of lightning charging the sky with electricity, and the thunder boomed, echoing and reverberating against the towering structure of Ramsden Crags. Edwin and Emma were drenched to the skin, their clothes, faces, and hair streaming with water.

Edwin grabbed the sack and his wet jacket and tossed them over to Emma. "Take these," he shouted, and pushed her towards the opening of the cave.

"Don't yer think we should make a dash in for the Hall?" she protested.

"We'll never make it, Emma. We're in for a real thunderstorm. Look at the sky. It's as black as night. Don't argue! Into the cave, my girl. We'll be safe there, and dry."

Although Emma was decidedly disinclined to return to the cave, she had to admit that Edwin's suggestion was sound.

They had no alternative, really. The moors could be extremely dangerous in this kind of stormy weather. She clutched the sack and his jacket to her, and, with her lips grimly tightening, she crawled into the aperture. Edwin followed, pushing the picnic basket in front of him.

Once they were inside the cave, Emma stood at the entrance, trying to get her bearings. Edwin pulled out his handkerchief, wiped his hands, and gave it to Emma. Then he immediately took charge, and with such a burst of energy and efficiency Emma was momentarily startled. He lit the candles on the ledge at the entrance and opened the picnic basket.

"Here's the Sunday *Gazette*," he called. "I brought it to read, in case you were late. Good thing, too. Make some paper spills with it." He dropped it at her feet, and went on, "I saw a pile of logs and twigs over by the sacks earlier. They were perfectly dry. We'll soon have a fire going." He picked up a candle, took Emma by the hand, and led her to a far corner.

"We'll make the fire about here," Edwin said, scuffing the earth with the toe of his boot. "It's about the best spot, since it gets the cross ventilation from the tunnel to the outside and that one back there." He gestured to another aperture Emma had not noticed before.

"Where does that go, Edwin?"

"I'm not really sure. It was too small for me to crawl into when I investigated earlier. But there are currents of air coming in from the moors. Now, come on, Emma. Let's hurry. Then we can sit on the sacks and attempt to dry ourselves. I'm freezing, and I'm sure you are."

"Yes, I am."

It did not take them long to get the fire started. The paper and the twigs caught hold at once, and when they were burning Edwin placed a couple of small logs on top of them. He began to busy himself with the empty sacks. There were about a dozen of them and some he arranged on the floor, rolling others into bolster-like shapes which he propped against the wall. "It will be quite comfortable, Emma," he said, turning and smiling at her reassuringly.

Emma was standing by the fire, shivering and shaking with cold. Her face still glistened with water and her wet hair streamed down her back. She was trying to wring out her dress, which was thoroughly soaked.

Edwin hurried to the fire, shivering himself. He began to cough. Emma looked across the flames at him and frowned. "Oh, Edwin, I hopes yer don't catch another cold, just when yer better."

"So do I," he gasped, coughing behind his hand. After a moment the rasping subsided, and he said, "I think you had better take off your dress, Emma. We can then spread it out to dry."

She stared at him askance. "Take me frock off!" she echoed disbelievingly. "Oh, Edwin, I couldn't do that."

"Don't be so ridiculous. You're wearing petticoats and—and—*things* underneath, are you not?"

"Yes," she muttered between her teeth, which were now chattering.

"So, please do as I say," he insisted in a brisk tone. "I am going to take my shirt off. It's absolutely sopping, and if we sit around in our wet clothes we will *both* catch pneumonia."

"I suppose yer right," she replied grudgingly. Emma turned her back to him and began to unbutton her dress, feeling shy and awkward.

"Give me the dress," Edwin ordered in the same firm voice, after she had stepped out of it. She handed it to him behind her back, without looking around. It was then that she decided she was being silly. After all, she *was* wearing a petticoat and a camisole top which completely covered her body, except for her arms.

She peeped over her shoulder and then slowly wheeled. Edwin was hanging her frock on a ledge, next to his shirt and undervest, anchoring them down with some small stones he had obviously found on the floor of the cave. Adopting a nonchalant air, Emma returned to the fire. She warmed her hands and face in front of the flames, and then tried to dry her long hair, squeezing the rain out of it and rubbing it between her hands. Edwin, who seemed quite oblivious to her state of partial undress, and also unperturbed, picked up the picnic basket and carried it over to the sacks. He knelt down and lifted out the stone jug of elderberry wine, and unpacked all of the food, which Cook had carefully wrapped in serviettes. Suddenly he let out a long low whistle of surprise.

Emma glanced at him. "What is it?"

"Good old Mrs. Turner," he exclaimed with a wide grin as he continued to rummage about in the bottom of the basket.

"By Jove, she thinks of everything. She not only put in a serviette and tablecloth for my picnic, but a carriage blanket as well. What luck. The blanket, at least, will help to keep us warm." He looked up, showing them to her triumphantly, and then his face fell. Water was dripping from her petticoat, making a puddle under her feet. "Good Lord, Emma. You're really quite thoroughly soaked and still shivering. Don't you feel warmer?"

"A bit. But me legs are cold from me petticoat. It's as wet as me dress was." She stepped nearer to the fire. Her boots squelched. She began to wring out the hem of the petticoat, striving to control her shivering.

Edwin stood up and looked down at his trousers, frowning. "I am afraid my pants are in the same condition." He grimaced and joined her at the fire and they hovered together in front of the flames, hoping to dry their clothes. But this was to no avail, since the fire was really quite meager and was therefore throwing off insufficient heat, and the atmosphere in the immense cavern was cold.

"This is futile!" Edwin declared after a short while. His legs were turning into blocks of ice and the coldness was now beginning to permeate his whole system. He began to cough, almost convulsively.

Emma looked at him with alarm, thinking how prone he was to taking chills. "Are yer all right?"

"I'm freezing. I hope I don't come down with bronchitis again." He shivered. "It's these wet clothes." He hesitated. "I'm afraid there's only one thing to do, Emma. I think I must take off my trousers, and you must take off your petticoat and—"

"Take off all our clothes!" she gasped, shrinking back against the wall of the cave, a look of horror on her face. "Edwin! We can't! It wouldn't be proper like," she finished, and with fierceness.

A faint half smile glanced across his lips. He shrugged. "Well, you may do as you wish, Miss Harte. But I have decided to undress, and hang my trousers and underclothes on the ledge to dry out. I am not going to catch my death because of any false modesty on my part."

Emma positively glared at him. "I thinks that would be very rude of yer, Edwin," she said tartly. "By gum, I do. It wouldn't be—be—gentlemanly."

Chagrin crossed his face. "Emma, I don't mean to offend you." He thought hard, wondering what to do, fully understanding her feelings. His eye caught the tartan carriage rug and a solution instantly occurred to him. "I have an idea. I shall wrap the carriage blanket around myself—like a kilt. It will cover me completely," he reassured her. "But I do think I must remove these wet things. We could be in here for hours."

Emma bit her lip. What he said was sensible, but it did not diminish her embarrassment at the thought of him undressing in front of her. On the other hand, she did not want to be responsible for him getting sick. It also struck her that she herself did not necessarily have to take her clothes off. She could still try to dry herself in front of the fire. After a moment, she said slowly, "Well, afore yer do take yer trousers off, crawl back ter the opening and see what the weather's like," she insisted, and sharply. "Maybe the storm's passed over and we can leave."

"That is a possibility," Edwin agreed, and hurried off to follow her instructions. Arriving at the end of the tunnel, Edwin was utterly dismayed when he poked his head out through the aperture. The rain was still falling in a deluge. A gale had blown up and was acting as a powerful lash against the rain. This was being driven in sheets onto the Crags. Bolts of lightning ripped through the blackened sky and thunder rolled down the hilly slopes like unceasing cannon fire. They were undoubtedly in for a long siege. He pulled his head back in quickly. It was then Edwin realized, and to his fury, that to return along the tunnel he would have to either crawl outside and re-enter, or shuffle backwards. He decided the former was the most feasible way and he edged himself out of the opening. He turned quickly on his knees and pushed back through the aperture, but not without getting drenched. When he finally crawled back into the cave he was shaking with cold and dripping rain.

Emma looked at him aghast. "Now why did yer go outside?" she demanded. "That was a daft thing ter do!"

He sighed, and explained. He picked up the serviette and dried his face and hair. Then he took the blanket and strode to the far side of the cave. He turned. "My apologies, Emma. But my trousers are wetter than ever. I have no alternative but to take them off now."

During Edwin's absence, Emma had put another small log onto the fire and sat huddled in front of it, continuing to squeeze the water from her petticoat, her face set in obdurate lines. And she was resolute in her determination not to undress, even though she was feeling the cold more intensely. Within a few seconds, Edwin was hanging up his trousers, underpants, and socks on the ledge, weighting them down with more small stones. Then he carried his boots over to the fire, where he deposited them to dry. Emma kept her face down, unable to look at him.

Observing her closely, Edwin began to laugh at the ridiculousness of the situation. "It's all right, Emma. I am quite decent. I can assure you of that."

Slowly, but with some unwillingness, Emma raised her head and she couldn't help smiling. Edwin had wrapped the carriage blanket around his waist and knotted it. It fell well below his knees, revealing only his bare ankles. "It does look a bit like a kilt," she said, adding with relief, "and it does cover yer proper like."

Edwin lowered himself next to her, and picked up the bottom of her petticoat, shaking his head sadly. "You are being foolish. You'll take a chill, Emma. Why, you've only managed to dry the hem of this. The rest is soaking." He dropped the skirt with an impatient gesture. Suddenly his face brightened and he reached for the tablecloth.

"Look here, Emma. You can wrap this around you. Like the saris the Indian maharanees wear." He jumped up and shook it out. "See, it's quite large." Edwin gave her a small demonstration. He wound the tablecloth around his chest and knotted the two ends together. Then he slipped his left arm down under the cloth, pulling the knotted ends up onto his left shoulder. "It does work remarkably well!" He smiled, glancing down at himself. "Of course, I think it's more like a Roman toga than a sari," he conceded in a serious voice.

"But it's one of Cook's best tablecloths!" Emma cried with consternation. "I'd really cop it if I messed it up. I would that!"

Edwin concealed an amused smile. "Under the circumstances, I don't think that is a matter worthy of our consideration. Now, is it?" He stretched out his hand to her. "Come along, you silly girl," he continued in a gentler tone, pulling her to her feet. "Go to the other side of the cave and do as I say." He shrugged himself out of the tablecloth and handed it to her.

Emma took it from him in a tentative way, and with such a show of nervousness her manner brought a smile to Edwin's face. He watched her as she scrutinized it carefully, a diffident expression flickering into her eyes.

Now laughter bubbled up in Edwin. "Emma, you are behaving so fearfully I do believe you think I am some scurrilous reprobate who has dishonorable intentions," he said, still laughing, and continued, "and that I am endeavoring to maneuver you into a situation, so that I can take advantage of you. Please be reassured I have no lascivious motives."

"I don't think that at all," said Emma, scowling darkly, not truly understanding all of his long words, yet intuitively grasping what he meant. "I knows yer wouldn't do owt—owt wrong, Edwin. I knows yer'd never harm me."

He patted her shoulder and looked down at her, smiling with tenderness. "Of course I wouldn't, Emma. Why, you are my best friend. My dearest friend, in fact."

"Am I really?" she cried, her eyes lighting up with pleasure.

"Yes, you are. Now, run along and change into the"—Edwin paused and chuckled—"the sari, such as it is. There are plenty of stones over there, and you can hang your things up to dry with mine. Meanwhile, I will prepare our picnic." Edwin watched her retreating figure and thought: She is so sweet and so very endearing. She *is* my best friend. I am truly most fond of her. It did not occur to him that he actually loved her.

The candles on the ledge in the corner had burned down and Edwin took two more out of the sack. As he lit them he was thankful he had had the foresight to bring a plentiful supply. He was arranging the food on the serviettes when Emma returned to the fire. She dropped her boots next to his.

Looking up, Edwin saw at once that she approached the corner somewhat timidly, with an air of bashfulness and extreme modesty and rectitude. The tablecloth surrounded her like swaddling clothes and she held it tightly to her, arms crisscrossed over her breasts. It draped her lithe body more than adequately, but he was startled to see that it came only to her knees, revealing shapely calves and the slenderest of ankles. He had not known she had such long legs or such pretty feet. Still hugging the tablecloth to her, Emma sat down and looked up shyly, not speaking.

"Don't you feel better, being out of your wet underclothes?" he asked, his manner purposely insouciant, which he hoped would alleviate her timorousness, as well as the awkwardness he knew she was feeling.

"Yes, I do," she muttered with a certain nervousness. She half smiled and glanced at the food spread out before them. "I'm ever so hungry," she announced, attempting to sound normal.

"So am I. I'm sorry there's only one plate and one mug. We'll have to share them." He poured some of the elderberry wine and handed it to her.

"Thank yer, Edwin."

"Now we're drier and warmer, this is quite a lark, isn't it?"

"Yes," she responded softly, sipping the elderberry wine. "My goodness, Cook did yer right proud!" Her eyes swept over the appetizing selection of sandwiches and other food. "She must think yer've now got an appetite like 'Skinny Ribs,' packing up all this stuff."

"Well, you know what Cook is like. Flapping around me like a mother hen. She thinks I need building up." He gestured to the food. "Take your pick first, Emma. There's bacon and egg pie, crab and tomato sandwiches, fruit cake and apples."

Emma selected a piece of the pie, which she herself had made. But she did not bother to mention this. They munched hungrily on the food, sharing the mug of elderberry wine, which Edwin kept refilling. He chattered gaily to her and gradually Emma's embarrassment began to slip away. Edwin seemed unaware of her semi-naked state, much to her intense relief. In point of fact, he was diligently ignoring it. When they had finished eating they sat back against the rolled sacks, warming their feet in front of the fire. Emma said carefully, without looking at Edwin, "What do yer think ter the writing on the wall, then? Do yer think yer dad made the carvings of the names?"

Edwin nodded his head vigorously. "Yes, I do. In fact, I've been giving some considerable thought to the matter, particularly to all those derivations of the name Elizabeth, and I do believe I've guessed the identity of the lady in question." He looked at her, his eyes brightly gleaming in the firelight. Emma held her breath. He continued, "It occurred to me that it must be Lord Sydney's sister. Her name was Elizabeth, and my father and the Sydneys grew up together. I am certain they all played up here as children."

"I didn't know Lord Sydney had a sister," Emma said, with a little intake of breath. Her eyes fastened on Edwin's face. "I've never seen her hereabouts, or heard mention of her."

"She died about ten years ago in India, where her husband was in the Diplomatic Service. I have heard Father speak of her with great affection, on many occasions. She was about his age. The more I think about it, I am sure that's the truth."

There was such a lessening of tension in Emma, such an alleviation of the painful thoughts in her troubled mind, her body sagged. How misguided she had been, jumping to such an unworthy conclusion about her mother and *him*. Of course Edwin was right, as he always was.

"That's got to be it!" she exclaimed, and smiled. After a small silence she said, "I wonder what time it is."

"I'll look at my watch." Edwin went to the entrance, where he had carelessly thrown his jacket when they had rushed in from the storm. "It's six o'clock," he called, carrying the jacket back to the fire. "This is very damp. I'd better spread it out on the floor to dry." He glanced at her, a concerned look crossing his face as he said, "Will your father be worrying about you, Emma?"

She shook her head. "No. He knew Cook wanted me ter come back this afternoon, instead of termorrow, ter help her with the jam making. She expected me at five-thirty."

"Oh dear, then *she* must be worrying about you," Edwin cried.

"She probably thinks I'm still at home, what with the storm and all. She knows me dad wouldn't let me come over the moors in this weather," Emma explained. "But I bet she's fretting about yer, Edwin. Wondering where yer are."

"Most probably. But she may conceivably think I made a dash for the village, which is closer than the house." He sighed. "Oh, well, it can't be helped."

"Do yer think it's stopped raining yet, Edwin?"

"Would you like me to crawl along the tunnel and see?"

"Yes, perhaps yer'd better. But don't go outside and get yerself all wet again!" said Emma a little dictatorially.

He picked up a candle and left. He was back in a matter of seconds. "It's still pouring and the thunder is cracking and booming," he announced as he deposited the candle on the ledge. "We can't leave just yet." He sat down cross-legged on the sacks, carefully covering his knees with the carriage blanket. "You know what these thunderstorms are like, Emma. They can last for hours."

"Aye, I knows." She stood up. "I'd best see if our clothes are dry, so that we can get dressed."

Emma glided lightly across the floor of the cave in her bare feet, her hair flowing down her back. She felt the clothes in her expert way, and said in a distraught voice, "Oh, Edwin, they're still ever so damp. We'll have ter leave 'em a bit longer." She swung around as she spoke and stared at him with the utmost dismay.

"We have to stay in here until the deluge subsides anyway," he answered. "Perhaps in half an hour they will be drier and by then the storm might have passed."

"I hopes so," she said, hurrying back.

They sat in the corner shivering, for the air in the huge cavern was now considerably colder and the fire was low. Edwin threw on another log and told her, "The supplies are diminishing. We must be frugal with these last few logs." They huddled together, attempting to draw warmth from each other. Edwin put his arm around her and pulled her closer to him. Emma looked up, her eyes wide. "Yer don't think we'll get trapped in here, do yer?" she asked tremulously.

He smiled reassuringly and his light eyes were soft and filled with the tenderest lights. "Of course not! Don't be silly," he exclaimed cheerfully. "And don't be afraid. I am here to protect you, Emma. Look, as soon as the clothes are in a better condition, we'll get dressed and see what it's like outside. If necessary we'll just have to brave the weather, depending on the time. We can't get back too late."

"All right, Edwin," she said, crouching closer to him.

Edwin put his other arm around Emma and began to rub one hand up and down her arm briskly, trying to warm her. "There, is that better?" he asked gently.

"Yes, thank yer, Edwin."

It all began perfectly innocently on Edwin's part. Slowly

the brisk rubbing turned to slower stroking, the stroking into languorous caressing of her face and neck and shoulders. Emma did not demur. It was only when Edwin's hand accidentally brushed against her breast that she flinched and drew back, staring at him with surprise tinged with apprehension. She quickly moved away from his embrace and settled herself against the rolled-up sacks, putting distance between them.

"I'm sorry, Emma. I really didn't do that on purpose. Truly. Come back here. You'll soon be shivering over there," he warned, irritated with himself and his carelessness, and also worried about her.

"I'm all right here. Thank yer," she said coolly, leaning back and adopting a dignified posture that repudiated him.

"Please yourself," Edwin muttered in dismay, drawing his legs up to his chest and wrapping his arms around his knees.

A long silence developed between them. Emma gazed into the fire, striving to control her shaking limbs, hoping he would not notice how cold she was growing. Edwin rested his head on his knees and stole a surreptitious look at her. At this precise moment the log blazed into sudden flames and his eyes started open in surprise. In the brighter firelight her figure was extraordinarily revealed to him. He had not realized before how flimsy the cotton tablecloth was, since she had hitherto hugged it so tightly to her. He could now clearly see her firm and voluptuous breasts pressing tautly against the fabric, the outline of her thighs, the long column of her legs, and that triangular smudge, faintly dark, just above them. He could not tear his eyes away from her. As he gazed at her with yearning, he felt a thrill rushing through him.

This was not the first time Edwin had been excited. Like most youths of his age, he had been sexually stimulated before, in the usual boyish ways. But he had never actually been aroused by a girl in such a potent manner, for he had never seen one in dishabille and been in such close proximity to one so scantily dressed. Consequently, he was shaken by the intensity of his emotions. He was breathless, almost panting, and his throat felt tight. After a few seconds he managed to drag his spellbound eyes away from her tantalizing figure, staring at the wall in front of him. Flickering shadows floated about there in the soft firelight, creating amorphous little shapes, resembling animals and trees. There's a rabbit and that's a great old oak, he told himself, inventing living forms for those dancing images. He concentrated hard on that wall, pushing his desire down, turning his mind away from Emma, striving to ignore his throbbing excitement.

It was Emma who broke the silence. Eventually she said in a small voice, "Edwin, I'm ever so cold." Immediately he swung his head to look at her. She was curled up, shuddering uncontrollably and her teeth were beginning to chatter.

"Shall I come over there and help to keep you warm, Emma?" he asked diffidently, almost afraid of suggesting this for fear of her anger or her rejection.

To his surprise she whispered, "Yes, please." She looked at him shyly through her thick lashes and added, "I'm sorry I got cross with yer, Edwin."

Without answering he scrambled over to her. He wrapped his arms around her and, with one hand, pushed down her knees. Very gently he eased her onto the sacks until they were both supine and reclining on them full length. He partially covered her shivering slender body with his own broader one.

"This is the only way we'll keep warm," he said. She edged closer to him, drawing comfort from him, cradled like a small child in his arms. "Yes, I knows," she murmured softly.

"Look at the dancing shadows," he pointed out, "and all the strange shapes they make. Animals and trees and mountains."

Emma smiled, following his gaze. Miraculously, the cave had been transformed before her eyes. She was no longer intimidated by it and she no longer associated it with her mother and Adam Fairley. It had become a magical and wondrous place. Their very special enchanted, secret place. Hers and Edwin's.

Edwin began to rub her arm and shoulders, which were icy. Soon the goose pimples began to disappear and it seemed to him that her skin now felt like the smoothest of satins. It was not long before the caressing started afresh, for Edwin could not resist the feel of her. Emma looked up at him, her large eyes spilling green fire, her pink lips slightly parted so that he could see her small white teeth. He moved his hand up and brushed the russet-brown hair away from her face, running his fingers lightly over her rounded cheeks and down her throat so whitely vulnerable in the candles' glow.

"You are so beautiful, Emma," he said in a low hoarse voice echoing with awe. "Please let me kiss you. Just once. Please," he begged.

She did not reply, but continued to gaze up at him. And there was so much trust and innocence and undisguised love in that pure face he was excessively moved. He bent towards her. He thought he would drown in the shimmering greenness of her eyes. His lips touched hers lightly. Her mouth was moist and sweet and so inviting one kiss did not suffice for Edwin Fairley. He kissed Emma again and again and again, with mounting intensity, allowing her no opportunity to protest.

When Edwin finally raised his head and looked down at her he saw that her eyes were closed. He stroked her face and her shoulders and his hand traveled down lingeringly until it was covering her breast. Only then did her eyes fly open wildly. "Oh, Edwin, no! You mustn't!"

"Please, Emma. I won't do anything wrong. Just let me hold you for a moment," he implored.

She hesitated, and he pressed his mouth to hers before she could refuse him, and he continued to fondle and stroke her. Almost without his conscious knowledge and quite unable to control himself, Edwin slipped his hand under the tablecloth which was draping her. He ran his fingers over her satin-smooth skin, his touch delicate but lightly quivering in his spiraling excitement. Emma pulled away from him with a small cry, a blush rising on her face, but he took hold of her and lovingly enfolded her in his arms, kissing her forehead.

"I love you, Emma," he whispered, his face close to hers.

"But it's not right, ter be together like this," she whispered back, trembling and afraid, her mind awash with dire thoughts of wickedness and temptations of the flesh that sent you to hell.

"Hush, my sweet Emma," Edwin said consolingly, his voice reassuring. "I am not going to do anything improper. I only want to feel you close to me. I won't harm you in any way. One never harms the person one loves the most in the whole world."

His words filled her with sudden joy and she drew closer to him, searching his face hovering above hers, that sensitive face she knew so well. It appeared to shine with radiance in the candlelight. His eyes were widely open and full of adoration.

"Do yer really luv me, Edwin?" she asked in the softest of voices.

"I *do*, Emma. Oh, how I love you! Don't you love me?"

"Yes, Edwin. Oh, yes!"

Emma sighed, aware of his hands fluttering over her again, smoothing and patting and feeling every part of her, but so soothingly she began to relax, enjoying his warm and affectionate caresses. Suddenly his fingers touched that most forbidden place of all, insistent but as light as a feather. She was hardly conscious of what he was doing at first. And she could no longer protest or stop him, for she was overwhelmed by unexpected and strange but delicious sensations that sent small tremors through her, and made her heart pound. His mouth, his hands, his body, all enveloped her and he drew her closer and closer until she felt as if she was melting into Edwin. A lassitude settled over her as he continued to fondle her, arousing her to the pitch he himself was aroused to.

Edwin paused and looked at Emma. Her eyes were closed and he saw that she trembled slightly. He slipped out of the carriage blanket and, with the lightest of movements, he parted the tablecloth that still half covered her. She did not stir, although her eyelids fluttered and her eyes opened, became wider, as she stared at him kneeling over her. Edwin Fairley's not a boy, he's a man, she thought, with a flash of amazement, and a trickle of fear, for that masculinity was now fully revealed. Edwin sucked in his breath, gazing at her wonderingly, filled with a yearning desire to possess her completely. And he marveled at her loveliness. Her skin had a floral pallor to it, but it was dappled golden, here and there, from the candlelight and the fire's rosy glow. She resembled a perfectly sculptured marble statue.

Slowly and with great tenderness and delicacy Edwin helped Emma to overcome her terror, her reticence, and her inherent shyness. In spite of their mutual virginity, Edwin began to make love to Emma, and eventually she to him, under his softly whispered guidance. His desire flared into a passion he could no longer check, and it was this passion that imbued in him a finesse that was unconscious yet remarkable in its expertise. Only once did she stiffen, and he heard a small cry strangled in her throat as she bit it back. But he was so

exquisitely gentle with her and adoring, this moment instantly passed, and soon he was carrying her along with him
on a mounting wave of ecstasy. They were clinging together,
moving now in perfect unison, engulfed by the sweet warmness
of their fresh young bodies. Emma thought she was slowly
dissolving under Edwin, becoming part of him. Becoming
him. They were one person now. She *was* Edwin. She moaned
and moved her hands down to the small of his back which
vibrated under her touch. It was then that Edwin experienced such a sensation of joy he thought he would scream out
loud. As he rushed headlong into the very core of her he did
not know that he shouted her name and begged her never to
leave him.

TWENTY-FOUR

Some hours later the thunderstorm died as instantly as it
had erupted into life, the torrential rain easing into a
light drizzle that finally ceased with an eerie abruptness. The
gusting high-powered gale that had ventilated those quiet hills
had dropped away and an awesome stillness suffused the air.

The remote and cloudless sky was a darkling bitter green,
almost black in its depth of color, yet glassy and clear and
filled with a curious luminosity, as if lit from within. A full
moon was out, hard in its metallic whiteness, a perfect orb
pitched high in the cold wide sky, illuminating the moors and
the fellsides with the clarity and brilliance of a noonday sun.
Its sharp radiance fell upon the terrible devastation, bringing
it into stark focus. The fulminating storm had ravaged the
landscape.

The immense fells, poised in precarious leaning angles
above the moorland, were towering precipitous cliffs and
from them the unceasing torrents of rain had rushed down in
streaming cataracts, inflating the natural waterfalls so that
they had become liquid avalanches, bloating the becks and
streams until they were swollen and spilling over their banks,
which were already bursting under the pressure. The cloudburst had swept over the moors like a gigantic tidal wave, its
force and speed uprooting trees and shrubs and heath, dis-

lodging rocks and boulders, hurling all before it on its relentless downward journey. The small glens and hollows between the hills that punctuated sections of the moorland were completely flooded. Animal life not swift enough to escape had been trapped in the onslaught. Stray sheep had been drowned in the flood, their stiffened bodies floating grotesquely in the murky waters of these newly made but unnatural ponds. Battered birds littered the ground, mangled bits of broken bones and bloodied feathers, their trilling songs stilled forever.

And lightning had left its stamp everywhere. It had struck trees, slicing them apart sharply and cleanly, and charring their scant foliage to blackened ashes. A horse tethered in the long meadow near Top Fold had been knocked down by a bolt, dying instantaneously before its owner could reach it, mane singed, gray coat dappled red and black. Not even the village was unscarred. Slates had been ripped off roofs, windows broken, plaster torn from interior walls, flaking off like minute sprinkles of snow, and one cottage was almost completely wrecked. A stained-glass window in Fairley Church had been shattered into hundreds of rainbow-tinted slivers. It was the memorial window recently endowed by Adam Fairley in commemoration of Adele Fairley's death.

Up at Ramsden Crags, water sluiced over the great elevation of rocks and the ground was so muddy it was like running oil, a veritable bog, mucid and slippery. The two lone trees that had stood there for years, solitary sentinels to the left of the Crags, had toppled over in toy-soldier fashion, also demolished by the incessant flashes of violent lightning. Edwin crept out of the cave first and gave his hand to Emma, who was closely following him. They ducked away from the water that tumbled unchecked from the Crags relatively close to the aperture, their feet sinking ankle deep into the mire that oozed under them. Edwin placed the picnic basket on a boulder and helped Emma up onto the drier rocks, swiftly climbing after her. They gasped, almost in unison, and exchanged alarmed glances, dismay washing over their faces as they viewed the destruction so appalling to behold.

"We were lucky to find the cave when we did," said Edwin to the gaping Emma by his side. He looked about him, shaken by the riven and shattered landscape. "Do you realize we could have been killed out here! Either by lightning or by drowning in the flood!" Emma nodded and shuddered at their narrow escape, not speaking.

"Look at the waterfall up on Dimerton Fell," Edwin then exclaimed. "I've never seen it so full or raging before. It's incredible."

Emma followed the direction his finger pointed, and caught her breath. The usually gentle waterfall, clearly visible in the moonlight and icily shimmering, had been transformed into a phenomenal spumescent cascade that was magnificent yet uncanny in its magnitude. Emma had to admit it was beautiful and said so, but her worry about returning to Fairley Hall was increasing by the minute. "Edwin, don't yer think we should try and make it back ter the Hall. Cook's going ter play pop with yer, and me as well."

"Yes, I do believe we should make tracks immediately," Edwin agreed. "Thank goodness the moon is so bright. At least we can see where we're walking. Shall we go?"

He made to leave and Emma tugged at his arm. "But what about the opening ter the cave?" She inclined her head towards the aperture. "The rock that covered it up before looks ter me as if it's sunk right inter the mud."

"You're right, it has." Edwin swung around, his eyes searching. He spotted the ruptured trees. "I'll use some of those branches to cover the hole, and come back another day to put the rock in place." He left the rocks, plodding through the slime doggedly, and dragged one of the trees over to the cavern's entrance. He stuck it deeply and securely into the muddy earth. The gnarled branches camouflaged the opening effectively.

Uncertain of what other disasters awaited them, they nonetheless set off bravely, their feet sinking into the glutinous mud, boots squelching, as they hurried away from the Top of the World, heading directly for Ramsden Ghyll. Emma slipped once as they scrambled over a ridge, slithering on the sodden ground. Edwin caught her immediately, and put his arm around her protectively, helping her to maintain her balance until they reached the narrow track. They had to maneuver their way with deliberation, stepping over disrupted rocks and splintered branches that had been flung haphazardly onto the path during one of the landslides. Upon reaching the Ghyll they stood hovering at the edge, staring in stupefaction. The bright moonlight illuminated part of the deep gully,

enough for them to see that it was brimming with bubbling
water seemingly about to seep over the top at any moment.
Dead birds, rabbits, and a sheep wobbled misshapenly among
the debris on its ghastly black surface, gruesome reminders of
the fury so recently unleashed. Emma shuddered and pressed
her face against Edwin's broad shoulder.

Edwin, holding her comfortingly, turned away. "I should
have realized the Ghyll would fill up. We'll have to turn back
and go down over the ridge to the beck, cross it, and make
for the lower road to the Hall."

"But won't the beck be flooded as well?" Emma suggested,
biting her lip.

"Most probably. But at least it's a bit narrower and not a
ravine like the Ghyll. It shouldn't be too deep. We can swim
across."

"I can't swim," Emma wailed.

"Don't worry. I'll look after you, Emma. I told you before,
you will always be safe with me. I'll never let any harm come
to you. Ever." He hugged her to him affectionately, hoping
to allay her nervousness, took her by the hand, led her back
along the track and down an incline, reassuring her gently all
the way. Unfortunately, Emma's prediction was correct. The
little beck, where they had washed earlier that afternoon, had
become a fully fledged and gushing stream, water spewing
over the rocky hillside with remarkable swiftness, an eddying
whirlpool foaming whitely against the banks. Edwin threw
the picnic basket on the ground, gritted his teeth, and lowered himself cautiously down the bank and into the whirling
depths. The water rose up to his chest. "Leave the sack,
Emma," he shouted, "and get onto my back. Put your arms
around my neck, and hang on for dear life. I'll swim us both
across."

Emma hesitated. This girl, who was not, in reality, afraid
of anything, had a strange and incomprehensible fear of water. Even as a small child, when her mother had washed her
hair, she had always screamed, "Don't get the water on me
face, Mam," the panic rising in her inexplicably.

"Emma, come along!" Edwin called. "This water's freezing."

Quelling her apprehension, Emma followed his instructions and tremblingly climbed onto his back. Edwin struck
out across the beck, but he had misjudged the force of the
water and several times he thought they would be dragged

downstream, as if there were a rapid current sucking at his legs like a vortex. Yet he knew this could not be so. They went under once, but he valiantly struggled to the surface, spluttering, and pushed forward, swimming with all of his strength. It was an exhausting battle for Edwin, and a terrorizing experience for Emma, who clung to him tenaciously. Finally they reached the opposite bank. Edwin panted and gasped and spit out water, catching hold of a small shrub miraculously intact on the side of the bank. He paused to regain his breath, grasping the roots of the shrub, and then he hauled them both up out of the swirling beck, stumbling and sliding in the process. They fell onto the ground and lay there for several minutes, chests heaving, coughing and rasping and wiping the water from their faces.

At last Emma said, "Thank yer, Edwin. I thought we'd drown once. I did, really. But yer a good swimmer."

Edwin's chest was congested and tight, and he was unable to speak, but he gave her a lopsided smile and shook his head wearily.

"Do yer feel all right?" Emma regarded him with some misgiving. In the moonlight he looked extraordinarily pale and depleted, and he shivered more violently than she herself did.

"Yes." He groaned, sitting up. "Let's get going. It's cold, Emma." He grinned ruefully as he looked at her dripping hair and face and clothes. "We're like a couple of drowned rats again."

"But we're safe and we'll soon be at the Hall," she responded, adopting a cheerful tone.

The lower road had turned to mire and was also strewn here and there with rocks and branches. In spite of its slimy surface, and the various obstructions, they managed to walk at a brisk pace, and once Edwin's breathing was more normally restored they began to run, holding hands tightly, only slowing their pace when they had to skirt boulders and dismembered trees, arriving at the main entrance to Fairley Hall much sooner than they had anticipated. One of the great iron gates, bearing the Fairley family crest in polished bronze, had been half ripped off its hinges, and dangled precariously from the high brick wall surrounding the grounds. Walking up the gravel path, they saw that even here the storm had wreaked its havoc. Flower beds had been flattened, bushes

shredded, hedges crushed, and some of the box and yew
topiary specimens, clipped into fantastic shapes, had been
smashed beyond recognition.

To Edwin's immense distress one of the great oaks had
been struck by lightning, split asunder, a monument to time
finally felled by God's wrath and nature's unpredictability. It
was here that Edwin paused and took Emma in his arms. He
pushed back her dripping hair and gazed down into her face,
its loveliness unmarred by the water and mud streaking it,
palely gleaming in the moonlight shafting through the bower
of green oak leaves drifting above them. He bent down and
kissed her fully on the mouth and with passion, but it was a
passion tempered now by tenderness. They clung together,
swaying gently. After a moment of silent communion, Edwin
said, "I love you, Emma. You love me, too, don't you?"

Her green eyes, iridescent with light and glittering catlike
in the darkness, swept over his face, and a swift pain shot
through her, piercing and poignant and she was filled with a
strange emotion she had not experienced before. It was a
sweet emotion, yet one tinged with sadness and a vague and
curious yearning she did not understand. "Yes, I do," she
answered softly.

He touched her face lightly, returning that penetrating
look concentrated so ardently upon him. "Then you will meet
me up at the cave at the Top of the World, later in the week
when the weather has improved, won't you?"

She was silent. Up until this moment Edwin had not
contemplated the possibility that she might refuse, but now
the idea struck him so forcibly he was filled with panic.
"Please, please say you will," he entreated, conscious of the
protracted silence, her hesitation. He pressed his body closer
to hers and cajoled, "We can have a picnic again."

Still she remained silent. "Oh, Emma, please, please don't
spurn me." His whisper was hoarse and a new desperation
had crept into his voice. Edwin held her away from him and
examined her face, so pale and inscrutable. There was a look
in her eyes that baffled him, one he was quite incapable of
interpreting. "You're not upset about—about—what happened?
What we did, are you?" he asked gently, wondering with
rising alarm if this was indeed the reason for her unexpected
and sudden unresponsiveness to him. Then in the faint moonlight sifting through the trees he saw the deep flush rising to

her neck to flood her face with dark color, and his heart sank. She *was* angry with him.

Emma turned away. But Edwin's harsh breathing stabbed at her and she quickly brought her face back to his, peering deeply into his bluish-gray eyes, and what she saw there made her heart lift on a crest that was joyous and it overwhelmed her. His eyes were full of love and longing but, hovering behind these mingled feelings so clearly apparent, she saw a flicker of fear. Emma knew then with the utmost certainty that Edwin Fairley did truly love her, just as he had said he did. And she loved him. He was part of her now. She marveled that this one person in the whole world could suddenly mean so much to her, could have become, within a few hours, so necessary, taking precedence above all else. It was a possibility she had neither anticipated nor bargained for. She could no longer bear to witness the pain in his eyes. "Yes, Edwin, I will meet yer up at the cave, and I'm not angry about what we did." She smiled and it was that same smile that always suffused her face with radiance.

Edwin's facial muscles, tight and intense with apprehension, relaxed, and he too smiled, taking her into his arms with a rush of relief and happiness. "Oh, Emma, Emma, my sweet Emma. You're everything to me."

Poised under the old oaks, locked in an embrace that was further sealing their destinies, they were oblivious to their dripping clothes, their shivering limbs, the cold night air. They were conscious only of each other and their fierce and flaring emotions, not realizing, in their euphoria, that emotions could wreak devastation as horrendous as the ripped and shattered landscape surrounding them. Eventually they drew apart, searching each other's face for confirmation of their love. Edwin nodded, his eyes awash with tender lights, and Emma smiled, and then silently they went up to the house, hand in hand. Edwin was jaunty and seemingly untroubled, but Emma, pragmatist that she was, had suddenly begun to consider the welcome they would receive. She was patently aware that it would be far from cordial and certainly one of furious reprimands.

When they turned into the cobbled stable yard they saw that the kitchen door was wide open, spilling light. Standing in this corridor of light was a distraught Mrs. Turner. She was perfectly still, watching, waiting, her arms akimbo, her plump face a stony mask, yet she gave the impression, in her very quietness, of wringing hands and doom and dire consequences. Emma slipped her hand out of Edwin's and hung back, allowing him to walk ahead of her.

Mrs. Turner was utterly relieved and overjoyed to see Edwin, but her anxiety had been so pronounced, and she had been so overwrought for hours, this relief quickly manifested itself in a flash of intense anger. It was only because Edwin was the young master of the house, and therefore entitled to proper respect, that Cook controlled that anger, but her voice was shrill as she stared down at him.

"Master Edwin! Where have yer been? Yer gave me a right turn when yer didn't come home. Why, it's almost ten o'clock. I thought yer were lost on the moors, or dead, with this raging storm. Aye, I did that!" She shook her head energetically and her eyes sparked. "By gum, Master Edwin, it's a good job the Squire's away, and Master Gerald is in Bradford for the weekend, or yer'd be copping it, yer would indeed. Scared me half ter death, yer did. Why, I've had Tom out twice with the lantern searching for yer up yonder!"

The cook heaved a great sigh that rippled her vast bosom. "Well, young man, don't dawdle about there, come inter the kitchen at once!" She turned and hurried inside, followed by Edwin, who was mounting the stone steps. She had not noticed Emma, who was reluctantly loitering in the shadows. Edwin stopped at the kitchen door and beckoned. "Come on, it's all right, Emma. I'll handle Mrs. Turner," he whispered.

"I've got water boiling in the set pot in the washhouse," Cook announced from the center of the kitchen, her eyes roving swiftly over Edwin's filthy clothes that dripped water, and his mud-splattered face. "Well, aren't yer a right sight, Master Edwin!" she snorted. "Yer look as if yer've been dragged through a hedge backwards, yer do that."

It was then that Mrs. Turner saw Emma slipping through the door and down the kitchen stairs. She was incredulous and her jaw sagged. "Aay, lass, what are yer doing here? I thought yer were safe at home with yer dad. I never dreamt yer were out in this weather."

Emma did not answer. Mrs. Turner looked from Emma to Edwin, staring at them open-mouthed. Her voice was brusque when she found it. "Yer haven't told me yet what yer doing trailing in at this hour, with Master Edwin, looking like a drowned rat. Come on, lass, speak up!" She glared at Emma, and tapped her foot impatiently, hands on her hips.

Before Emma could reply, Edwin stepped forward and said with a show of self-confidence, and just enough superiority to remind Cook who he was, "I came across Emma on the moors, during the storm, Mrs. Turner. She told me she was due back this afternoon, to help you with the jam making, or some such other domestic task. We tried to make it back together, but *I* decided the thunderstorm was too dangerous. We sheltered up at Ramsden Crags as best we could, waiting for the tempest to abate." He paused and fixed his cool eyes on the roiling cook. "It was rather difficult getting back, even when the rain ceased. The Ghyll is flooded and the beck by the lower road is dangerously high. But, here we are, safe, if a little bedraggled." He smiled engagingly, displaying that irresistible charm of his father's, which was so inherent in him.

"Bedraggled! I thinks that's the blinking understatement of the year, Master Edwin, I do that!" Mrs. Turner cried scathingly. "Yer looks like a couple of mudlarks, nay, guttersnipes!" Her head rolled again and her eyes flew open. "Thank heaven Murgatroyd's in Shipley. He wouldn't take kindly ter the fuss yer disappearance has caused around here, Master Edwin. Mark my words, he wouldn't."

"I didn't disappear, Mrs. Turner," Edwin responded quietly but with firmness. "I got stranded on those wretched moors, through no fault of my own."

"Aye, what yer say is true enough," she muttered. She glared at them suddenly. "Look at yer both, dripping mucky water and mud all over me clean floor. Upstairs at once, Master Edwin, and inter the bathtub. I don't want yer getting badly again. And take yer filthy boots off. I can't be having yer tracking mud all over t'carpet upstairs," she admonished, but not unkindly.

Mrs. Turner turned to Annie, who had remained silent but wide-eyed and agog with curiosity during this discourse. "Annie, run ter the washhouse and get two big pails of water, and hurry upstairs ter Master Edwin's bathroom with 'em. And then bring two buckets in here for Emma."

Cook now gave Emma her total attention. "Yer shouldn't have stayed up on the moors, lass, with Master Edwin. Yer should've turned back. Fact is, yer could have both made it back ter the village in no time at all," she remonstrated, her irascibility in evidence. She shook her head and looked from one to the other penetratingly. "I thought yer'd have had more sense than that, lass, and Master Edwin as well. Anyroads, inter the servants' bathroom, me lass. Yer need a hot tub afore yer catch yer death."

Emma forced a smile onto her face. "Yes, Mrs. Turner." She hurried to the servants' bathroom behind the kitchen without looking at Edwin.

Edwin had removed his boots and went up the stairs. He swung around at the top and said sweetly, with a warm smile, "I do apologize, Mrs. Turner, for causing you grief and worry. It was not intentional, you know."

"Aye, Master Edwin, I knows."

"Oh, by the way, I'm afraid I had to abandon the picnic basket. But I'll retrieve it for you another day."

"Aye, I expects yer will, if there's owt left of it," she mumbled. There was such chagrin on his face she softened, for Edwin was her favorite. "When yer've had yer bath, get straight inter yer bed, and I'll bring yer up a nice plate of cold lamb and some bubble-and-squeak. I knows how much yer enjoys that," she said, indicating the pan of leftover vegetables frying gently on the stove. "I've kept the bubble-and-squeak warm for hours for yer, Master Edwin."

"Thank you, Mrs. Turner." He smiled and was gone.

Cook gazed after his retreating figure and then sat down with a loud thump in the chair, her face creased with worry. She had seen the two of them, whispering and laughing together in corners of the house, when they were unaware of her keen but silent observation. She had also noticed them in the garden together, too many times for her liking of late. She pondered on Edwin's story, for a moment doubting it. She frowned. Yet it had a ring of truth to it, and she had never caught Master Edwin out in lies, or deceitfulness, since the day he was born. He wasn't like Gerald, who was cunning and devious.

Still . . . small suspicions crept into her mind, which was now awash with perplexed and troubled thoughts. It's not right, servants and gentry mixing, she said inwardly. Stepping out of her class, that lass is. She pondered further on this. "That's bad. It makes for real trouble. We have ter know our place," she said aloud to the empty room. Elsie Turner shuddered unexpectedly and goose pimples ran up her fat arms, as long-forgotten memories rushed back, so clear and vividly alive they brought her up in her chair with a start. Not again, she thought, and shivered. It can't be happening again.

TWENTY-FIVE

Emma walked across the terrace and down the path leading to the rose garden, carrying the flower basket on her arm, the garden shears in her hand. Lord and Lady Sydney were coming to luncheon, and Cook had sent her out to cut some blooms for the Waterford crystal vases in the dining and drawing rooms. Emma had a great love of flowers, in particular roses, and this garden was devoted to them, as its name implied. It was her favorite spot in the whole of the vast grounds of Fairley Hall and, to Emma, it seemed oddly out of character with the house, which she found ugly and depressing, for the garden was filled with an enveloping tranquillity that gave her a sense of peacefulness, and its beauty enriched her soul.

The lovely old garden was surrounded on all sides by stone walls hundreds of years old, covered with climbers that had been diligently trained over them, and which also scrambled up into two ancient trees at the far end, their blossoms shining amongst the darker foliage of the branches like fragile fragments of spun silk of the purest white. Wide borders under the walls flourished with floribunda roses, chosen especially for their large flowers and long blooming period, and they washed the garden with rafts of flaming color the summer through. They were planted in large blocks, thickly clustered together, each one of a different variety, a riotous mingling of candescent hues. Blood red faded into deep coral, which in turn edged into blush and paler dusty pinks, with white and yellow adding their delicately fresh tints to this lavish interplay of roseate shades, coils of velvet set amidst the verdant leaves.

In the center, surrounded by gravel paths, was the display area of the garden. This parterre, with its ornamental arrangement of flower beds of different shapes and sizes, was a stunning formal counterpoint to those wild and abundant borders rambling naturally in their informality, but which had been precisely planned for this striking contrasting effect. In the parterre, the rose beds of hybrid tea varieties were encircled by box, cut in triangles and diamonds and squares, the box clipped flat-topped, resembling molded slabs as though meticulously carved out of polished stone. Like the rest of the grounds, the rose garden had suffered severe damage in the violent storm that had torn up the district in June. But Adam Faírley had brought in expert gardeners, including a rose specialist and a landscape artist, to assist his own gardener, and with an enormous expenditure of money and time, and superb skill, they had miraculously restored it to its former glory.

In the shining stillness of this blazing August morning, the garden had an enthralling and poignant beauty that caused Emma to catch her breath and pause to admire its exquisiteness. The sun floated high in a cloudless cornflower sky and the air was limpid and heavy with the heady scent of the fragrant roses that drifted all around her. Not a leaf moved and the only sound was the faint flutter of rushing wings as a lone bird soared up into the pellucid light, its warbling a faintly retreating echo. Emma sighed, marveling at the loveliness all around her, and then moved on, intent in her purpose.

Since the roses in the parterre were never cut, Emma headed for the wilder borders under the walls. She perspired a little as she hurried down the gravel path and was grateful to reach the trees whose lush bowers, thickly green and low-hanging, offered cool refreshing shade. She knelt down and began to clip the stems, moving from shrub to shrub, selecting her blossoms carefully. The gardener had taught her how to cut only a few blooms from each bush, so that the overall appearance of the magnificent floribunda was never ruined by bare patches. She handled the roses gently, for their heads were fully opened, almost overblown, paying infinite attention to color and variety, filling the basket slowly.

Emma smiled to herself as she worked. Edwin had returned to Fairley last night with the Squire, who always came back to Yorkshire for the start of the grouse-shooting season. Edwin had been visiting Olivia Wainright at her country house in the South for the last two weeks. To Emma it seemed like two years. The Hall was a desolate place at the best of times, but especially so with only Gerald Fairley in residence, and it had begun to oppress her even more than usual. The lofty rooms, so vast and shadowy, were lifeless and eerily silent, and she always fled from them as soon as her work was finished. Now Edwin had returned, everything would be different. She had missed his smiles, his tender endearments and his adoration, and their picnics on the moors, which had continued through June into July until he had left.

Sometimes Emma had gone up to the Top of the World and sat alone on her flat rock under the shadow of Ramsden Crags, daydreaming, lost in a multitude of thoughts. She never went into the cave without Edwin. Before he had departed for his holidays he had instructed her firmly never to attempt to move the rock without him, for it would be dangerous and she might easily hurt herself.

But now he was back and her loneliness had already been dispelled. Earlier that morning, when they had bumped into each other in the upstairs corridor, they had whisperingly arranged to meet in the rose garden for a few minutes before he went riding. She could hardly bear the agony of waiting for him. She fervently wished he would hurry. Her basket was filled to overflowing; also, Cook would be wondering where she was. A few moments later Emma heard his footsteps crunching on the gravel and looked up expectantly. She felt a quickening of her heart, unreasonably so, and a rush of happiness surged through her, bringing that vibrant light into her eyes, a smile to her face.

Edwin strode swiftly down the path with a nonchalant and carefree air, blithely swinging his crop in his hand. He was wearing a white shirt with a yellow silk ascot at his throat, buff breeches, and highly polished brown riding boots that glinted in the sunlight. He looked taller, broader, more grown-up than ever. How handsome he is, thought Emma, and her throat tightened. She felt a sharp stab of pain, and she recognized it fully as the bittersweet pain of love.

Edwin's face lit up when he saw her and he increased his pace. Then he was standing over her, smiling widely, his grayish-blue eyes reflecting his own obvious delight at being back again. Emma thought her heart would burst. He stretched out his hand and helped her up, walking her to a corner out of view of the house. He seized her in his arms and kissed her passionately, running a suntanned hand down her back caressingly. Then he stood away, his strong fingers gripping her shoulders, and he gazed deeply into her face as if seeing it for the first time. By God, she is a beauty, he thought, excitement trickling through him.

"I've missed you, Emma," he said vehemently, his ardor apparent on his face. "I couldn't wait to get back. Did you miss me?"

"Oh, yes, Edwin, I did. It was lonely with yer gone." She smiled. "Did yer enjoy yer holidays, then?"

He laughed and made a face. "Well, yes, in some ways. But it was all a little too social for my liking. Aunt Olivia had tons of other guests coming and going interminably. She also gave two dances, which I could well have done without. Those silly debutante daughters of her friends do so get on my nerves."

Emma held herself very still under his hands gripping her so tightly. Jealousy flicked into her mind at the thought of Edwin holding other girls in his arms, if only to dance with them. She found herself quite unable to speak.

Observing the pained look which crossed her face, he chided himself for his thoughtlessness, and then he grinned engagingly. "I much prefer to be with you, Emma, my sweet one. Surely you know that." He relaxed his hold. "Let's go and sit over there," he suggested, nodding to the old rustic seat made of knotted branches resting under a shady tree in a dim far corner of the garden.

He carried the flower basket for her, and when they were settled on the seat he said, "Can we meet at the Top of the World on Sunday for a picnic? It is your weekend off, is it not?"

"Yes, it's me weekend off," said Emma.

"You will meet me then, won't you?"

Emma looked at him, her eyes serious as they searched his face, now so dear to her and rarely out of her mind's eye, day or night.

Edwin smiled lovingly. "You look very pensive all of a sudden. Don't tell me you've changed your mind about our trysts? It can't be that you don't love me anymore."

"Of course I love yer," she exclaimed. "Edwin—" Emma hesitated and swallowed. The words she knew must be said were lodged in her throat.

Edwin touched her shoulder fondly. "Well then, why are you hesitating about meeting me?"

"Edwin, I'm going ter have a baby!" she blurted out harshly, not knowing how to tell him more gently, no longer able to carry this worrisome burden alone.

As Emma spoke her eyes did not leave his face, and she clasped her hands together to stop them trembling. In that tortuous moment of silence that hung between them like a lead curtain Emma's heart dropped. She was acutely aware of the stiffening of Edwin's body, the imperceptible drawing away from her, the look of disbelief that wiped the smile off his face, the dawning horror that followed swiftly and settled there, a frozen mask that bespoke his shock.

"Oh, my God!" he cried, slumping back against the bench. He gaped at her, his face now pale and twitching. Edwin felt as if he had been dealt a violent and crippling blow in his stomach. He was utterly devastated. He vainly endeavored to still the shaking sensation that seized him, but with little success. At last he managed to speak. "Emma, are you absolutely certain of this?"

She bit her lip, eyeing him, trying to assess his attitude. "Yes, Edwin, I am."

"Jesus bloody Christ!" he cried, forgetting his manners in his anxiety. He gazed into space, a spasm working on his face. A smothering feeling enveloped him. He thought he couldn't breathe. Eventually he turned and stared at her, his eyes wide with apprehension. "My father will kill me," he gasped, envisioning his father's towering wrath.

Emma threw him a swift and knowing glance. "If yours doesn't, mine will," she informed him bluntly, her voice low and hoarse.

"What in God's name are you going to do?" he asked.

"Don't yer mean what are *we* going ter do, Edwin?" This was asked mildly enough, but Emma was conscious of the alarm rising up into her already constricted throat. Not for one moment in the past few weeks had she anticipated such a reaction from him. She had known he would be disturbed and upset and worried at her news, just as she was herself. But she had not thought he would act as if this was her responsibility, and hers alone. It frightened her.

"Yes, of course I mean *we*," he answered hastily. "Emma, are you really and truly certain? Couldn't you just be—be—late?"

"No, Edwin. I'm positive."

Edwin was silent, his mind floundering, a thousand thoughts pounding in his head. He had never contemplated this eventuality in his entrancement with her beauty, and the flaring passion she aroused in him. What an imbecile he had been not to have considered such an inevitability, the most obvious and natural consequence of their lovemaking.

Emma broke the silence. "*Please*, Edwin, talk ter me! Help me! I've been ever so worried while yer've been away, knowing about the baby, not knowing what ter do. I couldn't tell anybody else. It's been summat terrible for me, it really has, waiting for yer ter get back ter Fairley."

Edwin racked his brains. Eventually he cleared his throat, somewhat nervously. His voice was shaky. "Look, Emma, I've heard there are doctors—doctors who take care of such matters, in the early stages of pregnancy, for a goodly sum of money. Maybe there would be one willing to do it. In Leeds or Bradford. Perhaps we can find one. I could sell my watch."

Emma was flabbergasted. His words were like daggers plunging into her flesh. Their very cold-bloodedness was so shocking and repugnant to her she went cold all over. "Go ter some quack!" she cried angrily and with increasing amazement, her eyes widening. "Some charlatan who'll butcher me up with a knife and maybe kill me! Is that what yer are suggesting, Edwin?" Her eyes were now immensely cold and darkly green and watchful. She could hardly believe he had uttered those dreadful words.

"But, Emma, I don't know what else to suggest! This is an absolute disaster. A catastrophe. You can't have the baby."

Edwin continued to gaze at her in stupefaction, his mind in chaos. The decent thing to do would be to marry her. They could elope. To Gretna Green in Scotland. He had read about couples being married there. It was legal if you resided twenty-one days. He opened his mouth, about to say this, and then clamped it shut. But then what? The thought of his father's fury paralyzed him. Of course, his father wouldn't kill him. He would do much worse. He would disown him. Cut him off with nothing. Edwin thought then of Cambridge, his future as a barrister. He couldn't be saddled with a wife now, at his age, at this most crucial time of his life. His eyes roved over her. She *was* a beautiful girl. This morning her russet-brown hair was swept up and away from her face, plaits forming a circle on top of her shapely head like a crown. The oval face, paler than usual, was like gleaming porcelain, exquisite and refined. The widow's peak protruding onto her wide brow, and those large emerald eyes lifted her beauty out of the ordinary. She was startling, there was no question about that. The right clothes . . . elocution lessons . . . an invented background. Such things were possible, and the proper tutoring could work miracles. Perhaps there was a way to solve this. *No, there is not. It would never work,* a small voice insisted at the back of his mind. He would be ruined. He could clearly evaluate his father's reaction. He would be infuriated to a point of madness. She was a girl from the village. Edwin's eyes rested on Emma and he thought of her with calculated objectivity, and for a split second her beauty dimmed. *She was a servant, after all.* The class differences between them were too enormous to be bridged.

And so Edwin swallowed hard and remained silent, biting back the words he had originally been ready to utter. And that was a mistake he would live to regret, for had he spoken up, claimed her as his own, braved his father and the world, Edwin's life would have been so very different.

Emma now saw with unmistakable clarity the renunciation on his face, was bitterly aware of the repudiation in his eyes. She straightened her back and her head flew up sharply on her slender neck. It took all of her self-control to speak normally, for she was shaking and her anger, hurt, and disgust were living organisms in her heart. "I won't go ter one of them doctors, and yer silence tells me that yer not prepared ter marry me, Edwin." She laughed lightly, but it was a cynical laugh. "It wouldn't be proper, would it, *Master* Edwin? The gentry and the working class going so far as ter actually *marry,*" she pointed out with her usual stringent perception, her voice icily biting.

Edwin flinched. He had the peculiar sensation that she had just read his mind, and he flushed deeply. "Emma, it's not that. It's not that I don't love you. But we're too young to marry," he equivocated. "I'm about to go to Cambridge. My father—"

"Aye, I knows," she cut in, "he'll kill yer." Her brilliant eyes narrowed as she spoke, resting on his face with great intensity.

Edwin recoiled, and he knew then that he would never forget that piercing stare which condemned him so ferociously and with such loathing. He would never be able to eradicate it from his mind.

"Emma, I—I—I'm s-s-sorry," he stammered, becoming scarlet, "but it—"

She interrupted him again and with stinging sharpness. "I shall have ter leave Fairley. I can't stay here. I can't answer for what me dad would do. He couldn't stand the shame, for one thing, and he has a real violent temper."

"When will you go?" he asked awkwardly, not meeting her eyes.

A look of total disdain slipped onto Emma's face. He couldn't wait for her to leave. That was most patently obvious to her. Her disillusionment was complete. "As soon as I can," she snapped.

Edwin dropped his head into his hands, pondering on what she had just said. Perhaps that was the ideal solution. For her to run away. He felt a little surge of relief and looked up. "Do you have any money?" he asked.

Emma was reeling with nausea. The shock of Edwin's betrayal, of his weak and contemptible behavior had stunned her. She thought she was going to keel over and fall off the seat onto the ground. Pain bent against pain, twisting together to form an iron band so crushing it was almost unbearable. Hurt, anger, humiliation, disappointment, and sudden panic merged into one immense heartbreaking ache that suffused her whole body. The scent of the roses lifted on the air in suffocating waves, overwhelmingly sweet and cloying, and it made her feel faint. Their perfume was choking her. She wanted to run far away from this garden, from him. Finally she said in a small, toneless voice, "Yes, I have a bit of money saved up."

"Well, I only have five pounds to my name. But naturally I will give it to you. It will be of some help, Emma."

Emma's fierce pride rose up in her, commanding her not to accept, to refuse his offer, but for some reason, unknown to her at that precise instant, she changed her mind. "Thank yer, Edwin." She fixed him with that penetrating glare. "There's one other thing yer can do for me."

"Yes, Emma, anything. You know I'll do anything to help."

Anything, she thought wonderingly. But he wouldn't do *anything*, only whatever was convenient for him, only what would absolve him of his responsibility in this matter.

"I'll be needing a suitcase," she returned coldly, unable to conceal her bitterness.

"I'll put one in your room this afternoon, with the five pounds inside."

"Thank you, Edwin. That is very kind of you."

He did not miss the acidity, or the cultured tone she had unexpectedly adopted. He winced. "Emma, please, please try to understand."

"Oh, I do, Edwin. Oh, *how* I do!"

He stood up, shifting nervously on his feet, flustered and obviously anxious to be gone, to be done with all this. She looked at him standing there, so tall and handsome, the epitome of a gentleman on the outside. But what was he inside? she asked herself. A weakling. A terrified boy with only the physical attributes of a man. That was all. He was nothing. He was less than the dirt under her feet.

Emma herself now stood up and lifted the flower basket onto her arm. The strong fragrance of the roses invaded her nostrils, making her dizzy and sick again. She stared at him, poised near the bench.

"I won't be able to return the suitcase, since I won't ever be seeing you again, Edwin Fairley. Never, as long as I live."

She walked away slowly, erect and proud and with great dignity, a dignity that masked the terrible desolation in her soul. The silence in the garden was a tangible thing she could reach out and touch. Everything looked unreal, attenuated and fading, then piercingly brilliant, stabbing at her eyes aching in their sockets. The air went dark around her and her eyes misted over. It was as if the clinging fog that shrouded the moors had descended. A deadening coldness seeped into her and her insides were shriveling into nothing. Eroding. Eroding. Her heart fluttered in a rapid burst and then was still. And it hardened into stone. She placed one foot before the other, automatically moving them. They were like dead weights. She wondered if she had really expected Edwin to marry her. She was not sure. But she did know she had not expected him to behave with such a lack of concern for her predicament, her well-being, and also with such an abject display of cringing fear it was despicable. He had not even shown any concern for the child she was expecting. His child. What a pitiful specimen of humanity he was. She smiled with irony. Imagine him only having five pounds to

his name. She had more than that herself. Fifteen pounds, to
be exact. Plus her iron will. And her resoluteness.

Edwin watched her retreating figure soberly and with increasing unease, and then on an impulse he went after her.
"Emma," he called. She ignored him. "Emma, please wait,"
he called again. She stopped and he held his breath, hoping
she would turn back. But he realized she had paused because
she had caught her dress on a shrub. She disentangled
herself and went on up the steps to the terrace, without once
looking back.

Edwin stood rigidly on the gravel path, clutching his riding
crop so tightly his knuckles were sharp and pointed in the
brilliant sunshine. Panic assailed him as she disappeared into
the house. His legs were watery, his mind was swimming
with confusion, and then the oddest sensation took hold of
him, settling in the pit of his stomach. He felt as though
something vital was draining out of him, and a strange aching
emptiness engulfed him, sweeping away all other emotions.
Standing there in that ancient rose garden, Edwin Fairley, at
seventeen, did not know that this sickening, all-enveloping
emptiness, this hollowness in his heart and soul, was a feeling
which would never desert him as long as he lived. He would
take it with him to his grave.

Emma carried the roses into the plant room next to the
greenhouse and put the basket down on the table. She latched
the door behind her firmly and rushed to the sink. She
retched until she thought she would die, her eyes watering,
her insides heaving. After a few seconds the nausea subsided
and she wiped her face with her hands, resting against the
old zinc sink, breathing deeply. Then she turned automatically
to the roses and began to clip off some of the leaves, arranging the blooms carefully in the crystal vases, concentrating all
of her attention on them. She could not stand the scent of the
roses now. In fact, she would detest their pervasive perfume
forever, but she did have her work to do and this diligent
effort on her part helped to calm her troubled mind, her
quivering limbs.

It occurred to her, as she worked, that Edwin had not even
asked her where she was going. Only when. Where would
she go? She was not certain. But she would leave tomorrow.
Her father and Frank worked at the mill on Saturday mornings, as did some of the other workers who wanted to make

overtime. As soon as they had departed she herself would disappear. She would leave her father a note, just as Winston had done. She did not know what she would say in that note. She would think about that later.

Emma cursed herself under her breath as she worked. What a fool she had been. She felt no remorse or even regrets about their trysts at the cave. What had been done could not be undone, and to have regrets was a waste of valuable time. She was a fool for a different reason: She had allowed Edwin to distract her from her purpose, to interfere with her Plan with a capital *P*, in the same way she had permitted her mother's death, Winston's scarpering off, and her father's desperate need of her to make her waver in her determination to leave Fairley.

A faint hollow echo of a voice came back to her from the past. They were words said to her over a year ago, that night of the dinner party, that night before her mother's death, words long forgotten but remembered now. It was Adele Fairley's voice saying to her, "You must get away from this place, Emma. Away from this house. Before it's too late." Mrs. Fairley was not as daft as everybody thought, Emma said to herself. *She* had known. Somehow *she* had known that doom and disorder and danger lurked within these walls.

Emma paused in her work and stood perfectly still, lost in thought. She gripped the table as a sudden tremor swept through her, and closed her eyes, concentrating on her thoughts. After a few moments she opened her eyes, staring blindly at the roses. Emma did not realize that a wholly new and dangerous light had entered those remarkable emerald eyes. It was a terrible awareness compounded of her bitter comprehension and the most unremitting calculation. It was then that she made a vow to herself, a vow intensely pledged with every fiber of her being, every ounce of her strength. *It would never happen again.* She would never allow anyone or anything to dissuade her from her course, to stand in her way, to thwart her, or weaken her determination. She would, from this day on, be single-minded of purpose to the exclusion of all else. The purpose: Money. Vast amounts of it. For money was power. She would become so rich and powerful she would be invulnerable to the world. And after that? Revenge. She smiled and it was a smile that was both unyielding and vindictive.

Emma unlatched the door and picked up one of the vases, carrying it through into the dining room. She must get through her work today without the slightest show of emotion or panic, and she must avoid Edwin at all costs. She could never look on that face again, for her contempt had turned to bitter hatred; a hatred so consuming, so virulent it filled her mind absolutely, obliterating all else. She did not even think of the child she was carrying or the overwhelming problems facing her. This deadly hatred for Edwin Fairley, born in her that day, only served to reinforce the loathing she had always held for Adam Fairley, and it was a dreadful living force within her, lingering in her heart for almost all the days of her life. In essence it became a motivating factor, coalescing with her inherent ambition, her drive, her energy, and her shrewdness to propel her to heights not even she, at that moment, dreamed possible.

TWENTY-SIX

The following morning Edwin Fairley strolled across the mill yard, a disconsolate expression on his face. From time to time he glanced up at the village on the hill, wondering miserably about Emma.

He knew she would leave Fairley this weekend, if she had not already gone. He was quite positive about that. Very late last night, unable to sleep, beset by worry and twinges of guilt, he had crept up to her attic room. The suitcase he had deposited there that afternoon had disappeared, along with her clothes from the closet and the other small and pitiful things she kept at the Hall, such as the small vase of dried heather on the windowsill and bits of jewelry, including her prized possession, a horrid little green-glass brooch.

Edwin sighed. He was feeling wretched. He had behaved like an unspeakable cad. If only she had told him less abruptly, had waited until his head had cleared after the terrible shock of her disastrous news. Perhaps then he would have been able to think more intelligently, could have been more helpful. How? nagged a small voice. If he were honest with himself he had to admit he would not have married her.

That was out of the question. But—Oh, God, stop driving yourself crazy, he told himself furiously, unable to cope with the turbulent thoughts racing through his head.

Emma had gone. And that was that. Under the circumstances, maybe she had been wise to leave immediately. Had she stayed she might have dragged him into the situation, albeit unwittingly, and there would have been a scandal the likes of which he did not dare to contemplate. That's unfair and unworthy of you to think that, Edwin Fairley, he chided himself with a stab of shame and a flash of rare insight into himself and Emma. She would never have claimed him as the father of her child. He knew her well enough to recognize that somehow she would have protected him. Sickeningly, he wondered how she would manage on her own, what she would do, where she had gone, or was going. In his state of panic, and stunned disbelief yesterday, he had not even bothered to find out her intended destination and now it haunted him.

He stopped his pacing when he reached the horses tethered near the mill gates. He stroked Russet Dawn, trying to still those distressing feelings so paramount within him. A brisk ride over the moors would do him good. He looked up. Not that it was a very good day. It was excessively gloomy. The sky was overcast and heavy and there was a strong wind. On the other hand, the visit to Kirkend would certainly preoccupy his mind and might conceivably prevent him from dwelling on the problem of Emma, and also alleviate the discomfort he was feeling within himself.

Edwin stared into space, his eyes vacant, and so at first he did not notice the little trickles of smoke eddying out from under the doors of the great warehouse nearby. It was only when Russet Dawn suddenly whinnied and pranced that he looked about quickly and spotted the smoke, which was becoming increasingly more obvious. Edwin caught his breath, soothed the horses, and ran towards the warehouse apprehensively.

As Edwin sped across the yard Jack Harte was coming around the corner from the weaving shed, carrying a pile of empty sacks. The side window of the warehouse was in his direct line of vision and his eyes flared open as he saw the red glow inside. He also saw Edwin Fairley tugging at the latch on the heavy wooden doors. Jack started to run, fear flickering across his face, calling to Edwin to get away from the doors. "Don't open 'em, lad," he screamed, "it's the worst thing thee can do. Get away from there, lad!" Edwin glanced at him, but ignored his words and continued his fumbling efforts to open the doors. He finally managed this and went inside, just as Jack reached the warehouse. Jack dumped the sacks on the ground and rushed in after Edwin, still crying out his warnings of imminent danger.

At the far end of the vast warehouse several wooden skips used for transporting the wool and the bobbins had somehow caught fire. Flying embers from these had embedded themselves in the bales of raw wool packed in sacks, and which were stacked on top of each other. They were blazing furiously, other stacks adjacent to them catching light in rapid succession. The warehouse itself, as well as the enormous quantities of wool stored there, was going up in flames like a tinder box, sparks and embers flying, smoke billowing, beams and wooden walls cracking and splintering away as tongues of fire rose up to the ceiling and spread out in all directions. In a few minutes it would be a conflagration of terrifying proportions, for the wind coming in through the open doors was fanning the flames into a molten furnace and the heat was sweltering, the smoke overpowering.

"Get out of 'ere, Master Edwin," Big Jack yelled above the roar of the flames devouring the wooden building.

"We must do something at once!" gasped Edwin, who was staring at the blazing scene as if mesmerized.

"Aye, I knows that, lad. But this is no fit place for thee!" Jack grabbed his arm with a show of force and pulled him away. "Come on, out of 'ere this minute. We'll have ter get the steam engine and the pumps going right fast if we're ter stop this spreading."

They turned together, Jack leading the way through the heavy smoke swirling like a maelstrom in the warehouse, choking and blinking their watering eyes as they groped their way outside. Because of the density of the smoke, which was increasing by the second, Edwin did not see the iron ring attached to a trapdoor in the floor and he caught his foot in it, falling flat on his face. He tried to free himself, shouting to Jack, who was ahead of him. Jack pivoted swifty and ran back. Dismay flashed across his face when he saw the toe of Edwin's riding boot wedged in the ring. He knelt down, endeavoring to release it.

"Can thee get thee leg out of thee boot, lad?" Jack cried.

"Not in this position," Nevertheless, he wriggled and twisted his leg, but to no avail.

"This ring's a bit loose. I'll try and wrench it out of t'floor," Jack spluttered, coughing harshly and wafting the smoke out of his face. Using all of his strength, he pulled on the iron ring and to his relief, after several strong tugs, it began to tear away from the wooden trapdoor.

At this moment, the wide platform running around the warehouse, just below ceiling level, began to glow as the fire rolled along it unchecked, a river of white-hot roaring flames. Bales of burning wool were being released as the platform sagged, disintegrated, and collapsed. Jack looked up with horror, a cry strangled in his throat. Huge bales were plummeting haphazardly from the platform just above them, like fiery meteors intent on destruction, and Edwin was trapped immediately below. Without hesitation or thought for himself, Jack threw himself on top of the boy protectively, shielding Edwin's body with his own. One of the flaming bales landed on top of Jack's back. Jack bit down on the scream that bubbled in his throat. Pain tore through him from the crushing weight of the bale and the fire that immediately ignited his clothes and began to sear his flesh. He struggled violently to throw off the bale, heaving his great shoulders and kicking with his legs. With a burst of energy he managed to thrust it partially away from his shoulders, and with one final desperate heave that took all of his diminishing strength it rolled over to one side. Jack leapt up, choking on the smoke he had inhaled. He ignored his excruciating pain and his burning clothes, and wrenched again on the ring with both of his powerful hands. Mercifully, because he had managed to loosen it before, it came away at once, and Edwin scrambled to his feet, his face livid with fear as well as distress for the man who had so selflessly and valiantly saved him.

Coughing and spluttering, the two of them stumbled out of the warehouse as a central portion of the roof crumbled. Jack staggered and fell convulsively onto the ground, twisting and writhing in agony, chest heaving, unable to breathe. Coughing himself, but inhaling the fresher air, Edwin ripped off his jacket and began to beat out Jack's burning clothes with it.

Adam Fairley was racing across the yard with Wilson, shouting orders to the couple of dozen mill hands close on his heels. He was aghast when he saw Jack Harte's blazing clothes and Edwin's vain efforts to smother the flames. Shrugging out of his jacket, he cried to Wilson, "Bring buckets of water and get me those sacks over there."

With speed and efficiency and great presence of mind, Adam threw his jacket onto Jack's burning shirt, grabbed Edwin's jacket from him and wrapped it around Jack's legs. He added the sacks Wilson had flung to him and rolled Jack on the ground in them, unconscious of the flames which singed his own hands. Wilson panted up with two buckets of water, followed by other workers carrying extra pails. Adam and Wilson threw water over Jack to cool the heat and deaden the flames until they were entirely extinguished, leaving behind charred clothes and sacks clinging to Jack, who lay inert and seemingly lifeless.

Adam knelt down and felt Jack's pulse. It was faint but there was a beat. Jack looked up at Adam, a glazed expression in his bloodshot eyes. He blinked. A small groan escaped his lips before he passed out from shock and the pains of his extensive burns.

Adam stood up, shaking his head worriedly. "Carry him into my office, and gently!" Adam barked at two of the workers. He glanced swiftly at Edwin hovering by his side. "Are you hurt?"

"No, Father. My clothes are a bit scorched," Edwin answered between the coughing that wracked him, "and I'm full of this rotten smoke. But that's all."

"Then you're fit enough to ride up to Clive Malcolm's. Tell him Jack Harte has been badly burned. Tell him to get here at once!"

Edwin was rooted to the spot. He gaped at his father speechlessly, sudden comprehension trickling into his mind.

"Confound it, Edwin! Don't stand there like an idiot!" Adam screamed angrily. "Get going, boy. The man's life is in danger. He needs medical attention at once."

"Yes, Father." He stared at Adam again and then his eyes swiveled after Jack's body being carried into the offices. "He saved my life," he said quietly. "The bale would have fallen on me if he hadn't thrown himself over me."

"All right, Edwin, all right! I understand!" Adam snapped

impatiently. "I *understand* what you're saying. But we'll discuss that later. Now, for God's sake, do as I say. Go for Clive and ride like the very devil. Time is of the essence. Tell Clive this is extremely urgent."

"Yes, Father." Edwin swung himself up into the saddle and galloped out of the mill yard, one thought piercing into his brain with the most penetrating clarity: Emma's father had saved his life.

Adam now turned his attention to the burning warehouse. Fortunately, he had had the foresight to buy one of the new small steampowered fire engines several years before, for just such an emergency. Ten of the men had already dragged it out of the shed where it was stored. The coal to power it was burning and the men were expertly coupling two hoses to the hydrants. Other mill hands from one of the back buildings were swelling into the yard, including the bully boys and little bobbin liggers. Amongst them was Frank Harte, who had not witnessed his father's accident in the fire. Under Wilson's organization, this group was formed into a chain between the mill yard and the river Aire, passing the brimming buckets of water up to their mates, returning the empty ones down the line to be filled and refilled again and again, until their arms ached. Issuing orders, fully in command of the situation, Adam worked alongside the mill hands grateful for these tough and hardy Yorkshiremen who were going about their duties with cool heads and extraordinary courage in this unexpected and dangerous emergency.

Suddenly the wind shifted. Adam sighed with relief and then he groaned, dismay flooding his face when he saw that part of the burning roof had toppled onto a patch of shrubs adjoining a small copse of trees which edged right up to the main street of the village. Now, with the change in the direction of the wind, the copse was in danger.

"Wilson, send some of the other men over to me," Adam yelled. "They've got to handle that copse at once! The trees will go next, if we're not careful. The wind's blowing the fire that way."

"But the mill itself—" Wilson began.

"Damn it, man! Do as I say. I can always rebuild the mill. But there are women and children in those cottages. If the trees catch, the fire will spread up into the village itself in no time at all."

Wilson dispatched five men to consult with Adam, who took them aside urgently. He spoke rapidly but concisely. "Grab some axes from the shed and get over to the copse. Chop down small trees and bushes in front of those shrubs burning at the edge of the copse. Cut right down to the soil, clearing a narrow strip in front of the fire, so that any embers flying as it encroaches will fall into the strip and can be quickly extinguished. Then get buckets of water and start dousing all of the trees. We must prevent the fire taking hold in the copse at all costs."

The five men nodded their understanding and silently scattered to fetch the axes and buckets of water. They set to work in the copse at once. Meanwhile, Adam hurried back to Wilson, who was supervising the spraying of the warehouse. Under the force of the water from the hoses and the buckets the fire was beginning to die down, and with the change in the wind it was now relatively well under control.

Adam took out his handkerchief and wiped his sweating, smoke-streaked face. Then he swung around as he heard wheels turning into the yard. Clive Malcolm leapt out with his bag almost before the trap drew to a standstill. He threw the reins to his wife, Violet, who had accompanied him. Edwin cantered into the yard, just behind the trap.

Adam pointed grimly at the offices. "Harte's in a bad way, Clive. Do the best you can."

"Any other casualties?" Clive cried as he raced across the yard.

"A few men have small burns and one was struck by a piece of falling roof. But nothing too serious, as far as I can ascertain. Get to Harte first. Edwin, go along with the doctor and Mrs. Malcolm. See if there is anything you can do to assist them."

Adam coughed. His lungs were filled with smoke and he felt nauseous from it. He looked over at the copse anxiously. The men had already made progress and were preventing the fire from spreading and, although the shrubs were still burning, the trees leading up to the village were unharmed. Embers flying up into the air were falling into the narrow strip which had been cleared, just as Adam had predicted they would. They were being rapidly dampened and put out with water from the continuous supply of buckets being passed along.

As he looked about him, surveying the damage to the warehouse, Adam slowly became conscious that the wind had dropped unexpectedly. He looked up at the sky. Damnation, why doesn't it rain? he muttered. He glanced yet again at the overcast sky, praying silently. Wilson hurried to him. "I thinks we've about got it under control, Squire. I don't believe the mill's in any danger now." As he spoke, Wilson stared at Adam and a smile spread itself across his grimy face. "By God, sir, I thinks it's going ter rain. Do yer knows, I just felt a drop."

And Wilson was right. Rain it did. For once in his life, Adam Fairley welcomed the deluge that began to pour out of the sky, rippling down in heavy sheets, drenching them all and slaking the smoldering warehouse and the bushes in the copse. The mill hands stopped working and all of them turned to Adam, their voices rising in one single triumphant cheer.

"We're allus grumbling and grousing abart the blinking weather on t'moors, Squire, but this bloody rain's a gift from 'eaven," shouted Eddie, one of the foremen.

Adam grinned. "I couldn't have said it better myself, Eddie."

Eddie now approached Adam standing with Wilson. "Do yer mind if I goes up ter see me mate, Jack Harte, sir? There just might be summat I can do for t'doctor."

"Yes, Eddie, please do so. I'm coming in myself." Adam rested his hand on Wilson's shoulder. "I think you can manage down here now. By the look of the sky this is no light summer shower."

"I agree, sir. I'll get the men organized with grappling hooks and ladders. We can start clearing up a bit of this mess." Wilson glanced at the blackened and charred ruins of the warehouse, still smoldering and steaming under the rain falling in torrents. "We was lucky, Squire. We was that!"

Adam nodded. "I'll talk to you later about this, Wilson." His eyes narrowed. "It baffles me how the damn thing started in the first place." Wilson returned Adam's steely gaze but was silent.

Before he went into the offices Adam called the men together in front of the wreckage. "I want to thank you, lads, for pitching in the way you did, with such efficiency and coolness. And also with such bravery. There will be bonuses for all of you in your pay next week, as an expression of my very sincere gratitude. You saved the mill, and incidentally, the village as well. I won't forget this."

Some of the men grinned, others touched their foreheads with brief little salutes, yet others nodded. All murmured their thanks. One of the men stepped forward and said, "There weren't owt else we could do, Squire, now was there? It being our mill as well, so ter speak like. And yer didn't do so bad yerself, Squire, if yer don't mind me saying so. I thinks I speak for all t'lads when I say yer were a right trooper, sir."

A half smile flickered in Adam's eyes. "Thank you, Alfie." He nodded cordially and left. Adam found Clive Malcolm in his office attending to Jack Harte. Eddie was standing near the window, talking quietly to Edwin.

"How is he?" Adam asked from the doorway. Clive looked around and frowned. "Not good. But I think he's going to be all right, Adam. He's suffering from shock, of course, and bad burns on his back, shoulders, and thighs. Third-degree burns. I'm trying to make him as comfortable as possible, and then I must move him down to the valley hospital as quickly as possible. I shall need your big carriage, Adam, so I can keep him flat. I thought Edwin could ride up to the Hall and send Tom Hardy back with it right away. This is a real emergency with Harte. I just don't have the equipment and the medicines I need to treat him efficiently. I've got to get him into that hospital."

"I'll send Edwin at once." Adam inclined his head towards his son. "Off you go, my boy, and make it fast. We have no time to lose apparently."

"Yes, sir," Edwin said, and left.

"Where are the other men, Clive? And how are they?"

"Violet's patching them up in Wilson's office. They're not too badly hurt. First-degree burns, that's all. They will all be fine in a day or so."

"Will Jack Harte live?" asked Adam, sitting down behind his desk wearily, a serious expression clouding his face.

"Yes, I think so. But to be honest with you, Adam, it's hard to tell. I don't know if there are any internal injuries yet. Edwin told me that one of the large bales fell on Harte. He also inhaled a lot of smoke and the heat from that scorches the lungs. I think one lung has possibly already collapsed."

"Oh, my God!" Adam exclaimed, and passed his hand over his eyes. "You don't sound too hopeful."

"He's a strong man, Adam. I'm hoping we can pull him through." Clive gave Adam a sympathetic smile. "Try not to worry, old chap. After all, it wasn't your fault. You're lucky the casualties are so few."

Adam sighed. "I know. But that could easily have been Edwin lying there in that condition, Clive. He did save Edwin's life, you know. And at the risk of his own. Jack Harte performed an act of such dauntless courage I'll never forget it. He was fearless and unselfish." Adam's gray-blue eyes narrowed, and he shook his head. "You don't find many men like Jack Harte in this world."

Clive straightened up and his gaze rested on Adam, quietly intense. "I know. He was always a bit different, wasn't he? But we'll fight for him, Adam. I promise you that."

"All medical bills to me, Clive, for Harte and the other men. And instruct the hospital he has to have the very best of care. Spare no expense and don't put him in a general ward. I want a private room for him, and whatever else he needs he's to have."

There was a light tapping on the door. "Come in," Adam called. The door opened and one of the bobbin liggers, covered in grime and dirt, stood in the entrance nervously. Adam looked at him in surprise.

"Yes, son, what is it?"

The boy hesitated. "It's about me dad," he said, looking over at Jack, his lips trembling. "Is he—is he—?" he began tremulously, tears brimming into his eyes.

Adam leapt up and strode across the floor. He brought the boy into the room gently, putting his arm around his shoulders.

"It's Frank, Jack's son, sir," Eddie volunteered from his stance at the window.

"Come along, Frank," Adam said softly, his arm still encircling the boy's shoulder. Tears rolled down Frank's face as he stood staring at his father. "Is he dead?" he finally managed to say in a choked voice.

"Of course he isn't, Frank," Adam reassured him with the utmost gentleness. "He has been badly injured, I won't lie to you about that. But Dr. Mac has made him comfortable and as soon as my carriage arrives we are going to transport him to the hospital in the valley. He will get the very best of medical care there."

Adam pulled out his handkerchief and wiped the tears from Frank's face. "Now, you must be a brave boy, and you mustn't worry. Your father will be better in no time at all."

Frank looked up at Adam anxiously. "Are yer sure, Squire? Yer wouldn't fib ter me, would yer?"

Adam smiled kindly. "No, I wouldn't, Frank. I am telling you the truth, son."

"Your father is resting comfortably," Clive interjected, "and as soon as I get him to the hospital we'll be able to treat him properly."

Frank looked from Adam to Clive doubtfully, sniffing and suppressing his tears. He was silent and thoughtful for a moment and then he addressed Eddie. "He will get better, Eddie, won't he?" he whispered.

Eddie stepped forward, forcing a cheerful smile onto his drawn face. "Aye, lad, he will that! Yer father's a strong 'un. Now, don't yer fret yerself, lad. Come on, I'll take yer ter yer Aunt Lily's." Eddie threw a swift glance at Adam, who nodded acquiescently. Adam patted Frank's shoulder. "Run along with Eddie, Frank. And the doctor will stop by to see you later." Adam's eyes examined Frank, sudden concern in them. "Are you all right, son? You weren't hurt, were you?"

"No, Squire," said Frank, still sniffling.

"All right, then, off you go. And thank you, Eddie, for all your help. I appreciate it."

"I just did me best, sir," said Eddie, smiling briefly. "I'll be taking the lad ter his aunt's. She'll look after him." Eddie grasped Frank's hand, squeezing it reassuringly, and the two of them left, Eddie murmuring consoling words to Frank.

"I think I had better go into Wilson's office and see the other men, Clive. I want to thank them and make sure they are comfortable," Adam remarked.

"Let Violet take a look at those hands of yours, Adam," Clive ordered firmly. "They look a little raw to me."

Later that afternoon Adam strode up and down the library at Fairley Hall, a brandy and soda in his bandaged hand, a thoughtful expression on his face. Wilson, who had just arrived, sat on the chesterfield, watching him closely, quietly nursing his whiskey.

Adam finally stopped his incessant pacing and sat down in the chair opposite. He lit a cigarette, drew on it, and said,

"How do you think the fire started in the warehouse, Wilson? It went up very suddenly and burned rather too rapidly for my liking. I questioned Edwin earlier, and he said the wooden skips were blazing furiously when he opened the door, and that the first stack of bales was already flaring. I suppose the flying embers could have ignited the wool, and the draft from the door obviously fanned the flames, but it's still a mystery to me. Any ideas?"

Wilson was silent, his mouth tight and drawn, his face a picture of gravity. He sighed and looked directly at Adam. "I could hazard a guess, Squire, but it's not a very palatable one."

Adam leaned forward and stared at Wilson, fixing him intently. "Speak up, Wilson. You've obviously given this some thought, just as I have myself all afternoon."

Wilson scowled. "Arson, maybe."

"Arson!" Adam was so flabbergasted he sat up with a start and banged his drink down on the table with a crash. "Oh, come, come, Wilson, that's not possible. Surely it isn't!"

"Well, sir, raw wool doesn't burn that easily. But wood does. I also spoke ter Master Edwin and he told me the same thing—them there skips were going like wildfire. A bit of paraffin on one of the bales, soaking through the sacking inter the wool—" Wilson stopped and looked down into his drink, sighing. "Yer knows, Squire, that could have been a bloody holocaust down there this morning, but for the wind changing and the rain starting when it did. We only had the fire in the warehouse partially under control, yer knows."

"But why?" Adam demanded, still stunned and aghast at Wilson's words.

Wilson hesitated and sipped his whiskey. Then he looked Adam squarely in the eye. "Retaliation."

"Retaliation! Retaliation for what? Against whom? I've been more than decent with the men in the last few years, for God's sake. You can't be serious, man."

Wilson, who had been pondering on the cause of the fire for several hours, picked his words with care. He knew what had to be said, but he felt he must couch his opinions in the most diplomatic terms possible. He cleared his throat. "Yer haven't been at yon mill much in the past year, sir, what with yer traveling an' all. The men are a bit out of touch with yer, so ter speak. And when yer have been 'ere, yer visits have been brief—"

"Get to the point, Wilson. You said retaliation. I want to know what you mean by that," Adam snapped.

Wilson drew in his breath. "I thinks the fire might have been started on purpose like, because of Master Gerald."

Adam stiffened, his eyes widening, "Master Gerald! What's he been up to in my absence? By God, Wilson, I'll have his hide if he's responsible for this. I'll skin him alive!"

Wilson cleared his throat nervously. "Look, Squire, Master Gerald's a hard worker. I'm the first ter say that. And he luvs the mill, like yer father did. But Master Gerald—well, sir, he just doesn't know how ter handle the men. Most of 'em just grin and turn away like, pay no attention ter him and get on with their work. But there's a little extremist group down at yon mill. Troublemakers ter some extent, yer might say. Laborites, yer knows, Squire. Well, they have come ter resent Master Gerald's way of dealing with 'em."

"Out with it all, Wilson," Adam said sternly, his anger most apparent.

"It's his manner, like I said," Wilson replied, lighting a Woodbine. "He's allus pushing the lads around, goading 'em on, cracking t'whip like. And when they come ter him for a few simple concessions, like a longer tea break for one thing, he just wafts 'em away—"

"You can't be serious! You don't expect me to believe a fire was started simply because Master Gerald refused to give the men a longer tea break. That's preposterous and damned ridiculous, Wilson!" Adam exploded, his usual self-control slipping momentarily.

"No, Squire, not for that one thing only, but for lots of things that have mounted up like, over these last months. Small things, admittedly, but I knows some of the lads have been boiling lately at Master Gerald's harshness, his bullying, his temper an' all—" Wilson's voice trailed off.

Adam sighed heavily and leaned back in the chair, his eyes resting on Wilson contemplatively. "And so you think some of them started a fire to get even." Adam now moved forward, his gaze more penetrating than ever. "But that's a futile gesture, Wilson, since the mill itself could have gone up, and they would have been laid off for weeks on half pay."

"Aye, I knows. I've considered that fact meself," Wilson conceded wearily. "But I thinks a small fire was started ter make a point like. I don't think them as might have started it expected it ter get out of hand the way it did. I don't, really. Yer knows what I'm getting at, sir. Start a little blaze, destroy a few bales of wool. As I said, make a point. Slow down preduction, cause a bit of trouble. Make us sit up and take notice."

"The culprits?" Adam demanded, glaring at Wilson.

"That's it, Squire, I can't be pointing any fingers. That group of men I mentioned were all at t'mill this morning, and they all pitched in like hell, that they did." Wilson refrained from adding that three of the most violent agitators against Gerald Fairley were, in fact, noticeably and fortuitously absent that day. He himself would deal with them later. For he did believe arson was involved and he was fairly certain the absentees were the arsonists. He would put the fear of God into them. He prayed Adam Fairley would do the same with his son.

Adam was thoughtful, reflecting on Wilson's words, and then he said, "What you're saying doesn't really make any sense. Why would they start a fire and then expose themselves to it? That would be most foolhardy."

"I told yer, sir, I thinks them as started it intended it as a bit of a scare, that's all, never expecting it ter blaze the way it did, ter get out of control."

Now Adam was silent, his wrath with Gerald fulminating inside him. He attempted to calm himself, to think clearly. What Wilson said did make sense—to a degree. Raw wool, because it was oily, smoldered rather than blazed at first. Conceivably, paraffin might well have been poured over one of the bales. Whoever had started the fire probably thought only a portion of the warehouse and a few bales would be damaged. Fools, he thought angrily. The stupid bloody fools. The warehouse was highly inflammable because it was built of wood. They had not considered that aspect or the ultimate consequences of their irresponsible actions. They had not realized the danger to all the mill buildings and the village.

"Very well, Wilson, I accept your explanation. You could be correct in your assumptions," Adam said at last, his face tensely set. "And, since the members of that radical group you mentioned were working this morning, we cannot make any accusations, I suppose, can we?"

"No, sir!" responded Wilson vehemently. "We can't. *We daren't.* We've no evidence for one thing, and the way the men worked ter help extinguish the fire—by God, sir, they'd take right exception ter it, they would that. Also, the men'd stick together. We'd have a strike on our hands, I guarantee that, if we start talking about arson." Wilson nodded gravely and cleared his throat "Perhaps yer could have a word with Master Gerald when he gets back from Shipley tomorrow, sir, if yer don't mind me suggesting it. Caution him ter temper his manner, his rough ways with the lads."

"Oh, I intend to, Wilson. In fact, he'll get a dressing down the likes of which he's never had. Believe me, he will!" Adam declared, his fury rising to the surface again. "I never dreamt he would so willfully defy my instructions about treating the men decently." After a short pause he softened his tone. "In the meantime, we have a vital problem to contend with—supplies. All the bales in the warehouse were totally destroyed, as you know. How much raw wool do we have in the other warehouse?"

"Enough ter carry us through this month, I'd say, sir," Wilson responded, his mind working rapidly, evaluating their supplies and their orders. He puffed on his Woodbine. "We've got a shipment due in from McGill, from Australia, in two or three weeks, thank God. I thinks we'll be able ter manage till then."

"Do your best, Wilson. Get onto it first thing on Monday morning. I will come in early myself and we can make our assessments. And you had better build a new warehouse immediately. Use bricks, not wood. And also order another small fire engine. I don't anticipate a repetition of this disaster, but it's always wise to be prepared for any contingencies. As you said, we were lucky this time because of the change in the weather."

"No, I don't expect it will happen again, Squire," Wilson said, so sharply and with such conviction Adam glanced at him swiftly but made no comment. Wilson did not miss Adam's reaction and went on in a more even voice, "But yer right, it's allus best ter have plenty of fire-fighting apparatus on 'and, just in case. I was thinking, sir, if yer likes I'll go down ter yon mill termorrow and start taking stock. It'll save time."

"That's an excellent thought, Wilson, if you don't mind working on Sunday. I shall be there myself and we can do it together."

"Right ho, sir." Wilson paused, his eyes glinting shrewdly behind his steel spectacles. "And yer will have a talk ter Master Gerald, won't yer?" he pressed.

"Rest assured I will, and in no uncertain terms." Adam stood up. "Let me freshen your drink, Wilson."

"Thank yer, Squire. I wouldn't say no ter one for t'road."

As Adam poured the whiskey a sudden thought struck him most cogently: Wilson knew who the guilty parties were, but he was obviously not prepared to reveal their identities, for his own reasons, undoubtedly very sound reasons. So be it, Adam said to himself. He trusted Wilson to deal with them appropriately. He would deal with Gerald. His mouth tightened as he considered his elder son. The young idiot, he's undone all the good I strove so hard to achieve. Antagonizing the men was not only a rank display of poor judgment, it was an act of sheer folly. But it's also my fault, he admitted. I've given him far too much rope and my continuing absences have not helped. I shall have to spend more time in Fairley, he decided. But there was Olivia. He found it intolerable to be apart from her. She had become the whole reason for his existence. The rock on which his life was built. It was with sadness that he then acknowledged he had to pay more attention to the mills. That was, without question, an imperative taking precedence over everything else. Perhaps he could persuade Olivia to come to Fairley. She would understand. Damn that boy! A look of utter distaste crossed his face as he contemplated Gerald and the measures he would have to take with him. Gerald was a bully and therefore a coward. He would toe the line. *By God, he will*, Adam muttered under his breath.

He composed himself and carried the drinks back to Wilson. "I wish Dr. Mac would get here. I am extremely worried about Jack Harte," Adam said, handing Wilson the glass of whiskey.

"Aye, Squire, so am I. But Harte's a fighter. He'll pull through. He's got them bairns ter think about, yer knows."

Adam sighed. "I hope you're right, Wilson. I sincerely do. I can never repay the debt I owe him for saving Edwin's life."

PART THREE

The Slope
1905–1910

'Tis a common proof,
That lowliness is young ambition's ladder,
Whereto the climber-upward turns
his face . . .

—WILLIAM SHAKESPEARE, *Julius Caesar*

TWENTY-SEVEN

"There's the Mucky Duck, luv," said the tinker, drawing his horse and cart to a standstill in York Road and pointing a stubby and none-too-clean finger at the public house.

"But it says 'Black Swan,' " exclaimed Emma, reading the name on the sign swinging in the breeze. Confirming the lettering was a picture of a white pond upon which floated a somewhat primitive painting of an ebony swan, neck arched in such an ungainly fashion it was hardly a lifelike rendition of that elegant bird.

The tinker's wife, all Romany-dark curls and wrinkled tanned face, cackled uproariously at Emma's astonishment. "Aye, lass, that's wot they calls the Black Swan in Leeds. The Mucky Duck. Don't yer get it?" She cackled again, displaying several gold teeth that glittered as brightly as the golden rings looped through her ears and which dropped below the red-and-white-checkered scarf draped on top of her gypsy hair.

"Yes, I do," said Emma with an amused smile. She clutched her reticule to her and climbed down carefully from the cart. The tinker handed her the large leather suitcase which Edwin had deposited in her room yesterday with the five pounds. She looked up at the tinker and his gypsy wife and said gravely, and with enormous politeness, "Thank you very much for giving me the ride all the way from Shipley. It was very kind of you."

"Nay, lass, it weren't no trouble," said the tinker kindly. "Glad ter be of service ter a fine young lady like thee." He flicked the reins and the dilapidated cart moved off, pots and pans strung on the sides rattling and banging merrily as the old wheels turned in rickety rhythm. The tinker's wife looked back, shouting, "Lots o' luck in Leeds, me pretty 'un."

"Thank you," Emma called, waving at the retreating cart. She stood outside the pub for a moment and then picked up the suitcase, took a deep breath, and pushed open the swinging doors made of heavy wood, the upper panels inset with opaque glass embellished with engraved lilies and swans. She immediately found herself in a narrow and gloomy passage that smelled strongly of stale beer, tobacco smoke, and the faint reek of gas from the jets on the walls. The latter were lined with a dull brown wallpaper that only reinforced the forbidding atmosphere, which prevailed in spite of the burning gas jets and was not very inviting.

Emma looked about curiously. There was a carefully printed notice pinned on one wall which declared in large letters: *Women in shawls not allowed in here!* It seemed to her like an ominous warning. The opposite wall sported a repulsive painting of a charging bull in an equally ugly ornate gilt frame. Emma shuddered, her critical eye offended by its hideousness. Ahead of her was another set of double swinging doors, also inset with opaque glass, and she hurried forward and went through them. Emma stood in the entrance of what was obviously the main bar. It was brightly illuminated and infinitely more cheerful, with its colorful wallpaper and attractive sepia prints, and there was a piano in one corner. The bar was empty, except for two men leaning against the back wall drinking their frothing pints and chatting amiably together. Emma's sharp eyes scanned the surroundings, missing nothing. Two other rooms opened off the main bar. The sign hanging above the archway leading into one proclaimed it to be the Saloon Bar, while the other was labeled Tap Room. In the Tap Room she could see a lone workman playing darts, and two old men were seated at a table absorbed in a game of dominoes, clay pipes firmly clenched between their individual sets of nicotine-stained teeth, smoke swirling fuggily around them.

Emma now glanced towards the bar itself. Several large mirrors hung on the wall behind it, each one extolling the virtues of Tetley's pale ale and other local beers in black and gold lettering. There were innumerable bottles of spirits glittering against the mirrored backdrop and below them great kegs of beer. The long and expansive mahogany counter was polished to a sheen as glassy and almost as shimmering a surface as the mirrors themselves, and just visible above the mahogany bar was a mop of blond hair. Emma walked sedately across the room, her boots tip-tapping lightly on the wooden floor. Out of the corner of her eye she was aware of the two men regarding her, but she paid no attention and kept her glance fixed unwaveringly ahead.

When she reached the bar she put down the suitcase, but gripped the reticule in her hands. The blond head bobbed about below the bar. Emma cleared her throat. "Excuse me," she said.

The blond head swiveled to reveal a cheerful face that was open and honest. It was a pink and white face, and extremely pretty, with full cheeks and dimples and merry brown eyes that danced under shapely blond brows. "Yes, luv?" said the blond lady, rising slowly and somewhat ponderously from her crouching position, holding a glass tankard and a cloth in her hands.

Emma had to stifle a gasp, for that face, so sweet and dimpling and extraordinarily pretty, and that blond head with its array of elaborately dressed curls, sat atop an enormously fat body that was also amazingly tall. Her incredible body was tightly encased in a bright yellow cotton dress with a low square neckline and short puffed sleeves. Gargantuan bosom, portions of wide shoulders, and long plumpish arms were in striking evidence and were also white and pinkly tinted and soft.

The lady was looking at her questioningly and Emma said courteously, "I'm looking for a Miss Rosie. I was told she was the barmaid here."

The pink face broke into a wide and friendly smile that was also highly engaging and full of the most natural charm. "Well, yer've found her, luv. That's me. I'm Rosie. What can I do for yer, miss?"

Emma's taut body relaxed and she found herself automatically smiling back at the beaming Rosie. "I'm a friend of Blackie O'Neill's. He told me that you would take a message for him. Get it to him quickly, or to his Uncle Pat."

Ho! Ho! thought Rosie, concealing a knowing look. So Blackie was up to his tricks again with the lasses, was he! Well, he certainly knows how ter pick 'em, commented Rosie to herself. This one's a real looker. Rosie planted the glass and the cloth on the bar and said, "Yes, luv, I can get a message ter Blackie. Trouble is, it won't do yer any good. He's not in Leeds, yer see. He went off yesterday. Yer've just missed him. Aye, he went ter Liverpool ter get the boat ter Ireland. Summat about going ter see an old priest who was very badly, mebbe dying, so Blackie was telling me afore he left."

"Oh, dear," said Emma and distress registered on her face so acutely Rosie could not fail to notice it. The Junoesque barmaid stretched out her plump arm and rested plump fingers on Emma's hand gently. "Are yer all right, luv? Yer look a bit faintish ter me. How about a brandy, or a rum and pep, mebbe? Do yer good, yer knows."

Emma shook her head, endeavoring to quell the anxiety flaring within her. "No, thank you, Miss Rosie. I don't drink spirits," she murmured. The possibility that Blackie would be away had never occurred to her. She was so shaken she found it difficult to speak.

"Then how about a nice glass of lemon pop?" went on Rosie, regarding Emma carefully. "It's refreshing and yer looks ever so peaked ter me." Without waiting for a response, Rosie uncorked a bottle of lemonade and poured a glass. Emma did not want to spend the money for the lemon drink. Every penny was precious to her; yet, then again, she did not want to offend Rosie either, who was being so kind and friendly.

"Thank you," Emma said softly, and opened her handbag. "How much is it, please?"

"Nay, lass, it's nowt. This one's on the 'ouse. On Rosie," she said, placing the brimming glass in front of Emma. "Go on, 'ave a sip. It won't kill yer," she added jocularly, and laughed. Then her merry face sobered. The girl had turned as white as chalk and Rosie immediately noticed that the small hand in the white crocheted glove trembled as it picked up the glass.

" 'Ere, 'Arry! Fetch me one of them there stools from out of the Tap Room, will yer, please?" called Rosie to one of the men at the far end of the bar. "This 'ere young lady looks a bit wobbly on her pins ter me."

"Right, Rosie," said the man named Harry. He returned instantly, carrying a tall stool. " 'Ere yer are, luv, sit yerself down," he said, and gave Emma a warm smile before he rejoined his mate.

"Thank you." Emma perched on the stool gratefully. She felt weak and her head was swimming at the alarming news Rosie had imparted about Blackie.

Rosie leaned her elbows on the bar and looked at Emma

intently, a concerned expression on her face, her jolliness dissipated. "Look, luv, I knows it's none of me business, but do yer have troubles? Yer seems ever so upset ter me."

Emma hesitated. Distrustful by nature, she also firmly believed in the old north-country adage, "a still tongue and a wise head," and she was therefore not given to confiding anything in anyone. Now her mind worked rapidly and with its usual shrewdness. She was in a strange place. An enormous city. She did not know her way around. With Blackie in Ireland she had no one to turn to for help. And so she came to a swift decision. She would trust Rosie—but only to a certain extent. She had no choice, really. But first she had one other question and it was of vital importance.

She returned Rosie's steady gaze and instead of spilling out her troubles, as the barmaid probably expected, she said, "What about Blackie's Uncle Pat? Could I go and see him and perhaps find out when Blackie is returning? He is, isn't he?"

"Oh, yes, luv. Blackie'll be back in a couple of weeks or so. A fortnight he said he was going for. But it won't do yer any good going ter see Pat either. He's in Doncaster doing a right big building job. He's gone for a bit, I expects."

Emma sighed and stared fixedly at the lemonade. Rosie waited patiently, not wanting to appear nosy but, riddled with curiosity, she insisted, "Why don't yer tell me yer troubles, luv? Perhaps I can help."

After only a moment's further hesitation, Emma said, "Yes, I do have a problem. I have to find a place to stay. A boardinghouse. Perhaps you can advise me, Miss Rosie. That's why I wanted to see Blackie."

" 'Ere, lass, what's all this *Miss* Rosie? We don't stand on ceremony around 'ere. Everybody calls me Rosie. Just Rosie, plain and simple like. And why don't yer tell me yer name, being as how yer a friend of a friend."

Emma thought of her father and the possibility of him searching for her. But from the note she had left he would believe she had gone to Bradford and he did not know about the Mucky Duck or Blackie's last name. She was safe. "It's Emma Harte," she said, and added, to her own amazement, "Mrs. Harte."

Rosie's eyes widened. "Are yer married, then?" she asked, thinking: And where's the husband? but refrained from prying. Emma nodded, not trusting herself to say anything else for the moment. She had surprised herself more than she had surprised Rosie.

"Well, seeing as we're properly acquainted, so ter speak, and now that I knows yer problem, let's get down ter brass tacks. Yer looking for a place ter park yerself. Mmmmm. Let me think on that." Rosie frowned, her eyes thoughtful.

"What about that boardinghouse where Blackie lives? Couldn't I go there?" Emma volunteered. She was feeling a little calmer, thinking more clearly.

"By gum, no, lass!" exclaimed Rosie with such vehemence Emma was startled. "I couldn't be letting a luvely young lady like thee go down there, ter the blinking 'ham and shank' —that's the Bank, yer knows, near the Leylands. Full of toughs, it is. No, luv, that wouldn't be fitting like." Rosie scowled and seriously pondered this problem, wanting to help the girl. After a moment her face resumed its usual jolly expression and she smiled. "I 'ave it. Yer can go ter see Mrs. Daniel. She rents out rooms in her 'ouse. It's not far from 'ere. Yer can walk it easy. I'll write down the address for yer. Tell her Rosie from the Mucky Duck sent yer. Yer'll be safe there. She's a bit of a gruff 'un, Mrs. Daniel is, but kindly enough."

"How much will a room cost?" Emma asked quietly.

Rosie looked at her sharply. "Don't yer have much brass, luv?" she probed but not without sympathy. The girl looked visibly troubled again and her consternation at not finding Blackie had been more than apparent. What's that young boyo been up ter? Rosie wondered, staring at Emma. Yet the girl had said she was married. Still, there's more ter this than meets the eye, decided the shrewd Rosie.

Emma was conscious of Rosie's scrutiny. She cleared her throat and adopted a calm expression. "Oh, yes, I do have a few pounds," she said confidently, quite unconsciously tightening her grip on the bag, which had not left her hands since she had departed from Fairley early that morning. It contained every penny she had and her few bits of jewelry.

Rosie flashed Emma a reassuring smile. "Well, then, that's not so bad, is it! And Mrs. Daniel is fair and square like. She won't sting yer. I expects she'll charge yer a few shillings a week for a room, that's all. I don't thinks she gives yer any grub for that. But yer can buy yer own. There's a fish-and-chip shop at the end of her street, and there's allus a man with a cart selling pies and peas and roamin' around by her."

"I'll manage," said Emma, swallowing hard again. The mere thought of food nauseated her these days. The sickness she was now experiencing every morning seemed to last all day sometimes. She said, "I'm grateful, Rosie, for your help. Really I am. And I'm sure Mrs. Daniel's room will be fine."

"Aye, it will, luv. And she's clean and honest. Look, sit and rest yerself. I'll go ter the back parlor and get a bit of paper and write down Mrs. Daniel's address for yer." Rosie paused and added, "Yer a stranger in Leeds, aren't yer, Emma?"

"Yes, I am, Rosie."

"Then I'll put it all down for yer. How ter get there like. I'll only be a tick."

"Thank you, Rosie, you are kind."

Rosie bustled off to the parlor, numerous thoughts running through her head. She was much taken with this girl who had appeared from nowhere. In point of fact, she was intrigued by her. Emma Harte had such— Rosie paused in the middle of the parlor, seeking the appropriate word to describe Emma. Dignity! Yes, that was it. She was good-looking, too. That face! thought Rosie with not a little wonder. Why, she had never seen so striking a face in all her life before. She was a beauty, really, even if it was a different sort of beauty. Uncommon like.

"This is no ordinary girl, or a lass from the working class. And that's a certainty!" Rosie announced aloud to the empty room. Rosie Miller, who considered herself to be a sound judge of people, since she came into contact with all types and classes in the pub, knew *she* could never be deceived by anybody. Aye, she's a real lady, Rosie decided. There was the way Emma spoke, for instance. No dialect or local slang in her speech and only the faintest hint of a Yorkshire accent in her cultured voice. Not only that, there was her bearing and fine manners. Breeding, said Rosie knowingly. And her clothes, thought the barmaid, as she searched for a piece of paper and a pencil. Well, the black dress was a bit old-fashioned, Rosie had to admit, but it was made of good stuff and was elegantly cut. And the cream bonnet was definitely real Leghorn straw and the flowers trimming it were of pure silk. Rosie knew things about clothes. She did indeed, and she had only ever seen Quality ladies wearing a bonnet like

that one. London town it was. And what about the crocheted
gloves and the smart leather bag with its tortoiseshell frame?
Those were certainly the possessions of a proper lady, as
were the amber beads. Rosie considered the suitcase she had
observed on the floor. Costly, it was, and made of *real*
leather. Yes, she's gentry all right, Rosie concluded. She
licked the pencil and began to carefully print Mrs. Daniel's
address. As Rosie wrote she became further intrigued, considering that this Emma Harte had come seeking out Blackie
O'Neill, the Irish navvy. He was a handsome hunk of a man,
no doubt about that. Still, he was a common laborer. Now
what can the connection between them be? Rosie asked
herself, mystified.

" 'Ere I am," exclaimed Rosie, sailing up behind the bar.
She looks ever so sad, thought Rosie, glancing at Emma.
Emma jumped. She had been lost in her thoughts. "This is
the address, and I've wrote down the directions as ter how
yer get ter Mrs. Daniel's 'ouse," Rosie went on, handing the
paper to Emma.

"Thank you, Rosie." Emma read the paper. The directions
were quite clear.

Rosie leaned over the bar, adopting a more confidential air.
"I said afore, I don't want ter seem like a Nosy Parker, but
yer still seem upset, luv. Can I help yer in any other way?
Blackie's been a right good friend ter me. I'd like ter repay
his kindness by helping a friend of his, 'specially a friend in
need, so ter speak."

Emma remained silent. She had no intention of confiding
her real troubles to Rosie; on the other hand, she was a
kindhearted woman and was evidently a native of Leeds. It
occurred to Emma she might be able to offer some advice on
another matter. Emma turned her eyes on Rosie. "Yes, I do
have one other problem. I have to find a job," Emma explained.

"Ooh, luv, I don't know where a fine young lady like thee
could get work in Leeds." Rosie leaned closer and dropped
her voice and she could not resist asking, "Where's yer
husband, luv?"

Emma was not caught unawares. She had prepared herself
for this obvious question during Rosie's absence, since she
had told her she was married. "He's in the Royal Navy. At
the moment he's on Mediterranean duty. For the next six

months." This was said so coolly, with such sureness and confidence Rosie believed her.

"And don't yer have any other family, then?"

"No, I don't," Emma lied.

"But where were yer living afore?" Rosie questioned, keen eyes peering.

Fully conscious of Rosie's growing interest in her, Emma said, "With his grandmother. Near Ripon. My husband is an orphan, as I am. His grandmother died recently and now I am alone, since Winston is away at sea. That is, I'm alone until he comes home on leave." Although she had embarked upon a pack of lies, unintentionally and somewhat to her chagrin, Emma was endeavoring to stick to the truth as much as possible. It was simpler and, more importantly, easier to remember in the future.

"I see," said Rosie, nodding. "And how did yer meet Blackie, then?" She was no longer able to control her avid curiosity.

"Blackie came to do some work for—for my husband's grandmother," Emma improvised swiftly. "He was always kind, doing extra jobs for us, for very little money. He liked the old lady, you see. He also knew she was not long for this world. I had told him that when she died I wanted to come to Leeds to find work. Blackie said I should look him up." Emma paused and sipped the lemonade to gain time. She was rather astounded at her aptitude for deception, and also her suavity at telling such a tall tale. On the other hand, she must now continue and make it convincing. "Blackie suggested I might find work in one of the new shops, selling finery to the ladies. He thought a well-educated person like me would be useful in a shop. I can also sew and do alterations."

"Aye, that's an idea," said Rosie, feeling extremely pleased with herself. She had been right about this girl coming from Quality folk. It had been patently obvious to her all along that Emma could only have met Blackie in his capacity as a workman, doing repairs at her home. Impoverished gentry, that's what this Emma Harte was. "I'll tell yer what yer should do, luv," went on Rosie helpfully. "Monday morning, bright and early, pop along ter Briggate. Yer'll find it easy enough. It's a big street. There are lots of new shops in them there fancy arcades. Yer might find just the right opening—"

Rosie stopped short. A group of men had entered the pub and were heading towards the bar. She sighed and then smiled kindly at Emma. "Sit a while, if yer wants, Emma. But it's going ter get busy now. I won't be having much time ter chat with yer, luv."

"Thank you, but I had better go and see Mrs. Daniel and settle the matter about the room." Emma stood up. She smiled brightly. "Thank you again, Rosie, for all your help. I appreciate it."

Rosie nodded. "Aay, lass, I've done nowt, really. Hey, keep in touch with me, yer hear! Let me know if yer moves from Mrs. Daniel's 'ouse. So as I can tell Blackie where yer are. And pop in and see me, if yer gets lonely, or if yer needs owt else, luv."

"Yes, I will, Rosie. Thank you again. Good-bye." Emma picked up the suitcase and with another flashing smile she left the pub.

Rosie's soft doe-like eyes followed her thoughtfully. By gum, I hopes she's all right, she said to herself. Such a luvely girl. And all alone in the world. It's a right shame, it is, really. Rosie hoped she would see her again. There was something special about Emma Harte.

Once she was outside the pub Emma studied the paper Rosie had given her, pushed it into her pocket, and set off determinedly to find Mrs. Daniel's house. There were, in actuality, many rooms for rent in the vicinity of the Mucky Duck, but Rosie had purposely selected Mrs. Daniel's boardinghouse for Emma, even though it was much farther away than she had indicated. Rosie had wanted the girl out of this dreadful area of Leeds, for York Road was bordered on all sides by tough neighborhoods where grown men were not safe, let alone a defenseless girl. And so Rosie's own fear of the district had reached out like a protective arm to shield Emma.

Most of the streets stretching beyond and away from these devastating slum areas were safe, but they were narrow and ugly, with dark, mean-looking back-to-back houses pressing against each other, a cruel inheritance from the Victorian era, wretched dwellings for the working classes. Emma concentrated on the street names, hurrying as fast as she could, for this great city, full of bustling people, carts and horses, carriages and tramcars, was confusing and strange to her after the quietness of Fairley Village. Yet, conversely, she was not intimidated. However, she did not stop to consider these new and diverse sights, or gaze at them in wonder. Emma occupied herself fundamentally with one problem at a time, and at this very moment her aim was to install herself in a room, find a job, and wait for Blackie's return, in that order. She dare not think of anything else, and most especially the baby. She kept her eyes ahead but alert, noting the names as she sped along, one hand clutching her reticule in a fierce grip, the other grasping the leather suitcase.

After thirty minutes of fast walking, without a pause for breath, she sighed with relief. There in front of her was the street where Mrs. Daniel's house was located. Rosie's directions had been explicit. Now, for the first time, Emma stopped and put down the suitcase and pulled the paper from her pocket—Mrs. Daniel's house was number five. This street, too, was dark, with a poverty-stricken air, but Emma cheered considerably when she reached number five. It was a taller house than she had expected, and narrow, wedged in between others, its Victorian walls blackened by factory soot and years of industrial grime. But the lace curtains at the sparkling windows were crisp and white and the door knocker gleamed brightly in the faint afternoon sunlight. The three steps in front of the house had been scrubbed to silvery whiteness over the years and the edges were brightly yellow from the scouring stone obviously used daily to outline the worn rims.

Emma practically flew up the steps and banged the brass knocker several times. After a short delay the door was opened. A thin woman with gray hair and a sour expression on her lined and sallow face glared down at Emma.

"Yes, what do yer want?" she asked peremptorily.

"I would like to speak to Mrs. Daniel, please?"

"That's me," said the woman curtly.

The indomitable Emma was neither unnerved nor daunted by the woman's nasty tone and inhospitable manner. She had to get a room here at all costs. Today. She did not have time to roam Leeds looking any further. And so she smiled her most radiant smile and instinctively adopted a charming manner, one which she herself had not known she possessed until that very instant. "I'm pleased to meet you, Mrs. Daniel. My name is Emma Harte. Rosie from the Mucky Duck sent me

to see you. She thought you would be willing to rent a room
to me."

"I only takes gentlemen boarders," snapped Mrs. Daniel,
"less trouble. Besides, I'm full."

"Oh, dear me," said Emma softly, riveting her enormous
eyes on the woman. "And Rosie was so sure you would have a
room available. Even a small one would do." Emma glanced
up. "It's quite a large house, isn't it?"

"Aye, it is, but me two best bedrooms are let. There's only
the second attic and I never rents that."

Emma's heart sank but the smile did not waver. "Perhaps
you might consider renting that other attic to me, Mrs.
Daniel. And I certainly wouldn't be any trouble. Rosie will
give me a reference if—"

"It's not that," the woman interrupted in a snappish tone.
"I'm full up, as I said." She glared at Emma. "I can only cope
with two lodgers and I've got them already." She made to
close the door.

Emma smiled again, and winsomely. "Please, Mrs. Daniel,
don't be hasty. It would be a great help to me if you would
rent me the attic for a few weeks. Just as long as it is
convenient for you. It would give me a chance to find somewhere else. Rosie was so sure you would be obliging. She
spoke so well of you and recommended you highly. She told
me you ran a clean and proper house, and that I would be
safe here. Rosie said you were a good and honest woman."

Mrs. Daniel made no comment, but she was listening
intently. "You see, I'm not from Leeds," Emma rushed on,
determined to keep the woman engaged. She also wanted to
convince her that she would be no trouble and dispel the
apparent hostility the landlady had for women boarders. "I
was living near Ripon, with my husband's grandmother, and
she died recently." Emma noted the look of amazement on
Mrs. Daniel's face at the mention of a husband, but before
she had a chance to say anything, Emma explained, "My
husband is in the Royal Navy. On the high seas for six
months. I would be grateful if I could stay with you, for only
a few weeks. It would give me time to find a place of our
own, for when my dear husband comes back on leave."

The woman was silent, obviously ruminating on Emma's
story. Emma's mind raced. Persuasion, flattery, and charm
were having no effect at all. Perhaps she should appeal to her

greed. "I can pay you a month in advance, Mrs. Daniel. After all, a little extra money is always useful, isn't it? For that attic you never rent," Emma said pointedly, and began to open her purse.

Gertrude Daniel, widow woman and childless, was not as surly as she appeared on the surface. In fact, her dour manner and grim face actually belied a rather kind heart and a pithy sense of humor. However, she had the strongest desire to close the door in the girl's face. She wasn't interested in the money. And she didn't like women boarders. Trouble-makers, they were. Yet there was something about this particular girl that held her attention, and she *had* said she was married. Involuntarily, and to her enormous astonishment, she found herself saying, "We'd best go inside. I don't want ter be discussing this on the front steps, with all the neighbors watching from behind their blinking curtains. Not that I can rent yer the attic, mind yer. But perhaps I can suggest another place yer can try."

With this statement she opened the door wider and admitted Emma into the tiny hall and led the way to the front parlor. Gertrude Daniel was now considerably confused. She did not know for the life of her why she had let the girl into the house. Broken her own rule, she had. Her husband, Bert, had run off with their woman boarder years before. Still, Bert was kicking up daisies now. Nevertheless, she had never rented a room to a woman since then, and she had no intention of doing so now.

The front parlor was a shrine to Victorian bad taste. It was bursting with black horsehair sofas and chairs and mahogany whatnots. Purple chenille cloths covered a table, a piano, and a large stand. There were potted aspidistras on various other surfaces not crowded with bric-a-brac and the most revolting copies of famous oil paintings virtually jumped off the walls, which in turn were covered with bright red flocked-velvet wallpaper that stung the eyes.

"Sit down, then," said Mrs. Daniel, her voice still harsh.

Emma placed the suitcase on the violent red-and-purple Turkey carpet, and perched on the edge of a horsehair chair, clutching her bag. She was desperately trying to think of something infinitely more persuasive and ingratiating to say, when Mrs. Daniel cut into her thoughts.

"This is the best parlor," said the landlady, preening. "Nice, isn't it?"

"Oh, yes, indeed. It's beautiful," responded Emma swiftly, adopting her most sincere tone, whilst thinking how horrid it was.

"Do yer really like it?" asked Mrs. Daniel, her voice suddenly an octave gentler.

"I do! *Very much.*" Emma glanced around. "Why, it's one of the most elegant rooms I've ever seen. It's superb. You have excellent taste, Mrs. Daniel," gushed Emma, remembering words she had heard Olivia Wainright use so often in the past. She bestowed a glowing and admiring smile on Mrs. Daniel.

"Well, fancy that. Thank yer very much." Mrs. Daniel was inordinately proud of her front parlor and for the first time her face softened.

Emma did not fail to notice this and grasped the opportunity. She opened her bag deliberately. "Mrs. Daniel, won't you rent me the attic, please? I said I would pay in advance. If you're worried about the money I—"

"No, that's not it," interjected Mrs. Daniel. "If Rosie recommended yer, I knows yer all right for the brass—" Gertrude Daniel now hesitated, her eyes resting appraisingly on Emma. She had been scrutinizing her from the moment she had opened the door. Like Rosie earlier, she had noticed the girl's clothes at once. The frock was a bit dated, but good. She had also become increasingly aware of the girl's manners, her air of rectitude and refinement, her cultivated voice. This is Quality, she thought, and before she could stop herself, she said, "Well, I don't know whether me second attic would be suitable for yer, seeing as how yer such a fine young lady. But, since yer've nowhere ter go at the minute, I'll show it ter yer. Mind yer, it can only be for a few weeks."

Emma wanted to fling her arms around the woman's neck from sheer relief, but she kept herself perfectly still. "That is very kind of you, Mrs. Daniel. I do appreciate it," she said in her most dignified voice, imitating Olivia Wainright yet again.

"Let's go up, then," said the landlady, rising. She turned and threw Emma a quizzical look, eyebrows arched. "And how come a fine young lady like thee knows Rosie at the Mucky Duck?" she asked, suddenly puzzled by the odd association.

Stick to the truth, such as it is, a small voice warned

Emma. She said, without the slightest hesitation, "A workman, who used to come to Grandmother's to do repairs to the house, knew she was not long for this world. I had explained to him I hoped to come to Leeds one day, to make a home for Winston, that's my dear husband, and myself, and perhaps find work in one of the shops. He was a friendly sort and he told me to visit Rosie when I did come to Leeds. He felt she would be helpful."

Gertrude Daniel had listened attentively, assessing the girl's story. She spoke so sincerely and with such directness it was certainly a truthful statement. And it did make sense. She nodded, satisfied the girl was aboveboard. "Yes, I understand. And Rosie's a good lass. Help anybody, she would that. Providing they was worthy like." She nodded again and motioned for Emma to follow her.

The attic was indeed small, but it was neatly furnished with a few simple pieces, including a single bed, a wardrobe, a washstand under the tiny window in the eaves, a chest, a chair, and a small table. It was also spotlessly clean. Emma could see that from the most cursory of glances. "I'll take it," she said.

"It's three shillings a week," intoned Mrs. Daniel defensively. "It might seem a lot, but it's the fairest price I can give yer."

"Yes, it *is* fair," Emma agreed, and opened her reticule. She counted out a month's rent. She wanted to be certain she had a roof over her head until Blackie returned to Leeds.

Mrs. Daniel looked at the money Emma had placed on the table. She saw immediately that the girl had paid a full month in advance. She was not sure she wanted her here in the house for that length of time. It was almost against her volition that she picked up the twelve shillings and pocketed them. "Thank yer. I'll go and get yer case."

"Oh, please, don't bother. I'll bring it up—" Emma began.

"No trouble," said Mrs. Daniel, already thumping down the stairs. She returned almost immediately with the suitcase and placed it inside the attic. She had recognized that it was made of real leather and, in fact, she had examined it carefully and another thought had struck her as she had climbed the stairs.

Now she fixed Emma with a fierce stare and said, "There's one other thing I forgot ter tell yer. Since I can only manage

ter take care of the two gentlemen's rooms, yer'll have ter
make yer own bed and clean the attic." Her eyes swept over
Emma standing in front of her, so tall and beautiful and
refined in appearance. Her eyes narrowed. "Yer looks ter me
like yer've led a lady's life, an easy life, since the day yer was
born, if yer don't mind me saying so. Do yer knows how ter
do housework?"

Emma kept her face straight. "I can easily learn," she
remarked, not trusting herself to say another word for fear of
laughter breaking loose.

"I'm glad ter hear that," said the landlady bluntly. "And by
the by, I don't provide grub, yer knows. Not for only three
shillings a week, prices being what they are these days." Mrs.
Daniel continued to study the silent girl who was surrounded
by an aura of calm and dignity and, for some reason she could
not fathom, she added, "But yer can use me kitchen if yer
wants, as long as yer clean up after yerself. And I'll find a
spot in one of me cupboards, so yer can store yer groceries if
yer wants."

"Thank you," said Emma, almost choking with the suppressed laughter.

"Well then, I'll leave yer be, Mrs. Harte, so yer can
unpack." Mrs. Daniel nodded more cordially and closed the
door behind her.

Emma pressed her hand to her mouth, listening to Mrs.
Daniel's thudding footsteps retreating until they finally ceased.
She flew across the attic to the bed and pushed her face into
the pillow, now permitting herself to laugh unchecked, until
the tears rolled down her cheeks. *Do I know how to do
housework!* she kept thinking, and the peals of laughter would
start all over again. But eventually her merriment subsided
and she sat up, wiping her eyes. She pulled off her crocheted
gloves. She looked down at her hands and grinned with
amusement. They might not be as work-roughened red as
they used to be, but they were hardly the hands of a lady.
Not yet. *It's a good thing I kept my gloves on all day,* she
thought, *or my hands would have probably given me away.*

Now Emma stood up and walked over to the washstand.
She stared at her reflection in the swingback mirror. The
black dress and the cream bonnet were discards from Olivia
Wainright's wardrobe and their quality was unmistakable.
Her punctilious mimicry of Olivia's voice had not been diffi-

cult to accomplish, once she had commenced. In point of fact, speaking in a genteel fashion had come quite naturally to her, for she had a good ear and had practiced with Edwin. The tinker and his gypsy wife, Rosie, and Mrs. Daniel all believed her to be a fine young lady of Quality, albeit a trifle impoverished. And it was no accident. This was the precise impression she had strived to create, had hoped to establish immediately.

Before leaving Fairley, Emma had determined to start out in Leeds as she intended to continue—as a young lady who would become a grand lady. And a rich one. She smiled again, but now the smile was cynical and her eyes, turning dark with calculation, seemed, for a moment, as hard as the emeralds they so strikingly resembled. She would *show* the Fairleys but she could not dwell on that now. Her time was precious and must be planned with exactitude and used to the fullest. Every minute must be made to count. She would work eighteen hours a day, seven days a week, if necessary, to achieve her goal—to become somebody. To become a woman of substance.

Abruptly she turned away from the mirror, untied her bonnet, placed it on the chest, and hurried to the bed. Emma had such an abhorrence of dirt it was almost an obsession, and whilst the room itself appeared to be meticulously clean, she was impelled to examine the bed linen. The quilt was old but not badly worn. She pulled it off and looked at the sheets with her keen eyes. They were not new; in fact, they were neatly darned in places, but they were spotless and freshly laundered. To pacify herself completely, she stripped the bed down to the mattress, scrutinized it closely, turned it over, and with a sigh of satisfaction she remade the bed swiftly and with her usual expertise.

As tired as she was, she unpacked her suitcase and put her clothes neatly away in the wardrobe and the chest. In the bottom drawer of the chest she found two clean face towels. As she took them out her eyes lighted on several books lying in the drawer. Her curiosity aroused, she picked one up. It was a volume of poems by William Blake, bound in dark red leather and beautifully illustrated with engravings. She opened it and looked at the flyleaf. Slowly she read out loud, "Albert H. Daniel. His book." She put it back and regarded the other volumes, also expensively bound. Her mouth formed the

unfamiliar names: "Spinoza. Plato. Aristotle." She returned
them carefully to the drawer, wondering who Albert H.
Daniel was, and thinking how much Frank would love to get
his hands on books like these.

Frank. Little Frankie. She caught her breath and sat down
heavily on the chair, her heart beating rapidly. She thought
of her father and she was filled with sorrow tinged with a
deep yearning, and then a feeling of guilt flooded through
her, leaving her weak and vitiated. She sagged against the
back of the chair. That morning she had left him a note,
telling him she had gone to Bradford to look for a better
position in one of the big mansions. She had explained she
had a few savings to keep herself for several weeks. She had
urged him not to worry and had promised to return quickly,
if she did not find a suitable post, adding that should she be
fortunate enough to secure a good place she would write to
him with her address.

And what will I write? she asked herself worriedly. She did
not know. And she had more important things to think about
for the next few days. Survival. That above all else.

TWENTY-EIGHT

Emma had been in Leeds for almost a week and so far had
been unable to find work. For the past four days she had
diligently visited every shop in Briggate and the adjoining
streets, seeking any kind of position, prepared to take even
the most menial. But to her growing dismay and alarm there
were no openings at all. Doggedly, from early morning until
dusk, she tramped the pavements, those pavements Blackie
had said were paved with gold, but which seemed to her to
get harder and dustier by the minute.

In these four days Emma had come to know the central
areas of the city well, for she had a remarkable memory and a
good sense of direction. In spite of an occasional attack of
severe anxiety that would momentarily hold her in its grip,
she found Leeds exciting, thrilling, in fact. She had also
discovered, much to her own astonishment, that she had no
fear of this enormous metropolis, so accurately described to

her by Blackie well over a year ago. The great buildings, awesome in their incredible proportions, had seemed slightly overpowering on Monday morning when she had valiantly set out from Mrs. Daniel's boardinghouse, intent and relentless in her determination to secure a job. But she had quickly adjusted to the surroundings, which might easily have struck terror into one of weaker character, for Emma saw those immense structures for what they truly were: institutions of industry and progress, symbols of money and, inevitably, of power. And her staunch heart invariably quickened at the opportunities they offered, and her burning ambition was reinforced in her imaginative and optimistic mind, for Emma truly believed anything was possible.

The stores and factories, warehouses and iron foundries, printing works and office buildings towering above her, grim of architecture and pitted and blackened by the city's dirt, reminded her, in a curious way, of the moors, for these monoliths to commerce were just as implacable and indomitable and everlasting. As she had drawn an inexplicable and uncommon strength from those wild hills, so now she drew encouragement and hope from the soaring edifices starkly outlined against the skyline of Leeds, which was the fifth-largest city in England. Instinctively she recognized that here her future lay. In her youthfulness, she was determined it would be one of untold wealth, plus that irresistible power she longed so desperately to seize and hold forever in her own small but tenacious hands.

This morning as she trudged along, Emma unexpectedly found herself in front of Leeds Town Hall and stopped to stare at it, gasping at its austere grandeur. Many wide steps led up to the imposing south façade, where four giant-sized white stone lions guarded its portals in front of Corinthian columns that floated up to dizzying heights. It was a square building, surmounted by a most amazing tower supported by additional columns echoing those on the south façade. There were clocks on four sides and the tower itself was topped by a strange bold cupola. It was a massive building of great weightiness, black and Victorian, and Gothic in its inspiration, yet it was not ugly. Emma decided it had a handsome and even graceful exterior and it was undoubtedly the most astounding landmark she had seen in Leeds so far. As she gaped at it, her eyes flaring open with wonder, it was not possible for Emma to know that its architect, Cuthbert Broderick, had also been in love with money and power, and his Town Hall, opened by Queen Victoria in 1858, had been the ultimate expression of that love. However, with her rare perception, Emma intuitively understood it was a personification of all the city stood for. As she continued to regard the Town Hall a most vivid and compelling thought flitted into her mind: *This city can either conquer you, or you can conquer it*. With her usual self-confidence she decided at once, and with no hesitation whatsoever, that it would be the latter.

Emma walked away from the Town Hall, glancing up at other structures and thinking: They are only buildings after all, filled with people just like you. She immediately corrected herself. No, not like you, Emma Harte. *You* are different. And *you* will be *very* different. *You* will be somebody of importance one day, and so fervently did she believe this it sustained her, fortified her courage, and spurred her on.

She ventured into a few more stores, only to be told the same thing time and again—no vacancies. Sighing to herself, she walked along Boar Lane, occasionally pausing to gaze into some of the windows, continually fascinated by the array of finery on display: dresses and bonnets, shoes, reticules and jewelry, furniture and ornaments, and so many other necessities as well as luxuries. And as she viewed these elegant establishments, her plan with a capital *P* to make her fortune began to evolve. Always a potent idea, it had hitherto been vague, nebulous, undefined. Now suddenly she knew with great certainty what she would eventually do—what that Plan with a capital *P* would be. *She would have a shop*. Her own shop. A shop selling those essentials which people needed in their daily lives. That was it. Trade! She would go into trade. Obviously it would have to be a small shop at first. But it would grow. She would ensure that. She became excited. She would have more than one shop, two, maybe three, and she would be rich. Buoyed up by this idea, she increased her pace, propelled by her decision. Her perspicacious, inventive, and fertile brain raced, planning and scheming for the future tirelessly, as it always would.

Leeds was then, and still is, a lusty and vital city, and the streets on this busy Friday were, as usual, crowded with people rushing about their business. Tramcars rumbled out from the Corn Exchange to all parts of the town and outlying districts. Fine carriages with prancing horses carried elegant ladies and gentlemen of distinction to their destinations. Prosperity, that sense of self-help and independence, nonconformity, hardheaded Yorkshire shrewdness and industriousness, were endemic, were communicated most vibrantly to Emma, so that she was instantly infected. And the rhythm and power of the city only served to consolidate and buttress these very same characteristics so intrinsic in her, for with her energy, tenacity, and zest, her obstinate will and driving ambition, she was, without knowing it, the very embodiment of Leeds. This was undoubtedly the place for her. She had always felt that to be true and now she was absolutely convinced.

She made her way decisively to Leeds Market in Kirkgate, an enormous, sprawling covered hall composed of an incredible conglomeration of stalls selling all manner of merchandise imaginable—pots and pans, kitchen utensils, china, fabrics, clothes, foodstuffs to be bought and taken home or eaten there, including jellied eels, meat pies, mussels, cockles, cartloads of fruit, fancy cakes, and toffee apples. She stopped at the Marks and Spencer Penny Bazaar, her attention riveted on the sign: *Don't ask the price, it's a penny!* Her eyes roved over the goods on display, so easy to view, open to inspection, so well organized in categories and so cheaply priced. She tucked the information at the back of her mind, her eyes keenly thoughtful. The idea of this Penny Bazaar is simple, yet it is exceedingly clever, she said to herself. Emma lingered for a moment longer, inspecting the goods, which included almost everything from wax candles and cleaning products to toys, stationery, and haberdashery, and then, still reflecting about the bazaar, she moved on. It was well turned two o'clock and she was conscious of a growing hunger gnawing at her. She bought a plate of winkles and mussels from the fishman's stall, lavished them with vinegar and pepper, ate them with her fingers, dried her hands on her handkerchief, and set out for North Street, where the tailoring shops were located. That morning one of the salesgirls in a dress shop in Thornton's Arcade had suggested she try her luck there. "But go when it's daylight. It's a bit of a tough neighborhood," the girl had cautioned.

It was a boiling hot day. The sky was sullen and there

seemed to be no air in the muggy, crowded streets. Emma
fanned her face and opened the collar of her green cotton
dress, feeling hot and overcome by the intense heat bouncing
up in waves from the pavement. She leaned against a building in the shade, and when she was a little cooler she set out
again. She had to find a job to support herself until the baby
was born. After that she would work night and day if necessary, to get the money for the first shop. She smiled and with
a degree of unfamiliar exultation. Her tired feet were forgotten, the exhaustion dissipated, and she stepped out surely
and with confidence, secure in the knowledge that she would
succeed. She had no alternative. She could not afford to fail.

Before long, following the salesgirl's instructions, she was
entering North Street. The tailoring shops, in reality small
factories, were not too difficult to find, their names being
clearly indicated on the outside. Three sorties into three
shops and three turndowns. "Try Cohen's," one of the men in
the last workshop called after her. "It's in a side alley, off the
top of North Street." Emma thanked him and left. She found
Cohen's within minutes, but again was told, "Sorry, luv, no
openings." She paused at the end of this alley and looked
back down North Street. She decided to keep walking straight
ahead until she came to York Road. It was now getting late
and she felt it would be wiser to return to Mrs. Daniel's
house as quickly as possible. She would rest tonight and start
all over again tomorrow, looking for that job which was so
crucial.

Panting, Emma continued up the street, which was rather
steeply built. She was almost at the top when she felt something sharp strike her shoulder blade and a stone dropped at
her feet. She turned swiftly, startled. Farther down the street
two scruffy-looking youths were grinning at her inanely. She
shook her fist at them. "Wicked boys!" she shouted. They
laughed derisively and picked up handfuls of stones. Stiffening, Emma was poised to flee, but she instantly realized that
the stones were not intended for her, were not being aimed
in her direction. To Emma's immense horror she saw the
boys bombarding a middle-aged man who had slipped and
fallen. He attempted to rise, but stumbled, and then under
the onslaught he huddled against the wall of a building,
making a vain effort to shield his face. The louts were whooping
and yelling and pitching stones furiously and in an unending

stream. The man's parcel had rolled away, his spectacles were on the ground, and Emma could see that his cheek was bloodied where it had been struck by one of the stones.

Emma was outraged and revolted by this despicable display of needless cruelty and she leapt forward and ran down the street, her anger a raging force within her, and her face was grim and unremitting.

"Get going or I'll fetch a bobby!" she yelled, shaking her fist again. She was totally without fear in her fury. "Little hooligans!" she continued, her voice rising sharply. "Go on, get off with you, or I *will* fetch a policeman! The law will know how to deal with the likes of you, and it won't be very kindly."

The two boys laughed at her insolently and stuck out their tongues, making ugly grimaces and shouting foul words, but at least their attention was diverted from the man. Emma, who was dauntless at all times, was now so completely enraged she was invincible. She picked up a rock and said threateningly, "How about a bit of your own medicine?" She raised her arm and was about to hurl the rock when to her surprise, and considerable relief, the boys backed off, thumbing their noses at her as they slunk away, their vile curses echoing in the air. Emma ran across to the man, who was struggling to his knees. She took hold of his arm reassuringly and helped him up. He was a small, spry man, sturdily built and wiry. He had wavy black hair graying at the temples and receding on top, sharply defined features, and bright black eyes.

Compassion had eradicated her grim expression and Emma said with concern, "Are you hurt, sir?"

He shook his head, pulled a handkerchief from his pocket, and wiped the blood from his grazed cheek. "No, I am not hurt," he answered, blinking. "Thank you, young lady. You have been very kind." He blinked again and peered hard at the ground. "Do you see my spectacles? They fell off in this unfortunate little skirmish."

Emma found his glasses, examined them carefully, and handed them to him. "Well, at least they're not broken," she informed him with an encouraging smile.

The man thanked her and put on his spectacles. "There, that is much better. Now I can see," he said.

Emma bent down and picked up his parcel, actually a large paper bag. A loaf of bread had fallen out of it and rolled in the dirt. Emma held it away from her and blew on it, and tried to clean it with her hands, dusting off the dirt. "It's not too grimy," she explained, putting the loaf into the paper bag, which contained a number of other items, and giving it to him.

The man had retrieved a small black skullcap which he placed on his head and now he regarded Emma thoughtfully and with increasing interest. His voice was full of gratitude as he said, "Thank you once again, young lady. It was brave of you to come to my defense. To my rescue." He smiled and his eyes shone with appreciation. "Not many men would intervene in these parts, let alone a young lady like you. Yes, indeed, you are of the good heart and the great courage. Quite a remarkable feat you performed. Very commendable!" He gazed at her with undisguised admiration, not a little impressed.

Even though the man spoke the most precise English and enunciated his words clearly, Emma detected a slight accent she could not place. He must certainly be from foreign parts, she decided, and then said, with a frown, "Why were those horrid boys throwing stones at you?"

"Because I am a Jew."

Emma was not actually sure what a Jew was but, always reluctant to display her ignorance on any matter, she chose to disregard his explanation, repeating again, "But why would that make them want to throw stones at you?"

The man returned her questioning look steadily. "Because people are always afraid of what they do not know, what they do not understand, the unfamiliar or the different, and that fear invariably turns to hate. Unreasoned hatred that makes no sense. In these parts the Jews are hated and defiled." He shook his head. "Ah, the human condition is strange, is it not? There are some people who hate for no reason at all. They just simply hate. They do not realize that their unjustified hatred inevitably turns inward to destroy them. Yes, it is self-destructive in the long run."

His words, spoken so sadly and without rancor, pierced Emma's brain and touched her so profoundly she felt a sharp stab of pain near her heart. Was her hatred for Edwin wrong? No, a small voice insisted. It is not unreasoned hatred, the kind this man speaks about. You have every reason to feel the way you do. Edwin Fairley was treacherous and he betrayed you. She cleared her throat and touched the man's arm lightly. "I am sorry people hate you and try to hurt you. How terrible for you to have to live with such—such—" She stopped, searching for the right word.

"Persecution," the man volunteered. His dark eyes were clouded briefly by a haunting sorrow that was ancient, and then a faint and rueful smile touched his generous mouth. "Ah, but then this little flurry was nothing in comparison to some of the debacles that occur. When the roughs and toughs really run amok they become excessively violent. Unmerciful. Attacking us and our homes. We suffer not only sneers, but blows and broken windows and many cruelties." He shook his head wearily and then his face brightened. "But then, these are not your problems, young lady. I must not burden you with them."

Emma was aghast and perturbed by the things he had said and she was also baffled by his oddly calm acceptance of such a terrible situation. "But can't the bobbies—the police—do anything to stop it?" she cried, her voice unaccustomedly harsh with anger.

The man smiled wryly. "Not really. Occasionally they try to stop it, but mostly they turn a blind eye. Leeds is not such a law-abiding city in this day and age. We fend for ourselves, as best we can. Keep to ourselves. Go about our business quietly. Avoid confrontations that could easily provoke dangerous incidents." He was becoming patently aware of the growing expression of horror in the girl's eyes and also of the bewilderment etched on her face, and with sudden insight he said, "You do not know what a Jew is, young lady, do you?"

"Not exactly," Emma began, and hesitated self-consciously, acutely ashamed of seeming so uninformed.

Observing her embarrassment, the man said softly, "Would you like to know?"

"Yes, please. I like to know of many things."

"Then I shall tell you," he announced with a gentle smile. "The Jews are a people descended from the Hebrews and the Israelites, from the tribes of Israel. Our religion is called Judaism. It is founded on the Old Testament and the Torah both." Emma was listening intently and the man beheld the quickening interest on her face, the intelligence in her fine eyes. He was also fully conscious of her sympathetic attitude and so he continued patiently, "Do you know your Bible, young lady?"

"Some of it," said Emma.

"Then you have perhaps read the Book of Exodus. You certainly must know the Ten Commandments?" She nodded affirmatively, and he expounded further: "The Ten Commandments were given to our people by Moses, when he led us out of Egypt and created the Jewish nation. Christianity itself is based on Judaism. Did you not know that?"

Although she loathed to appear illiterate, Emma had to say in all truthfulness, "No, I didn't."

The man's bright black eyes searched hers thoughtfully. "Jesus Christ was a Jew, and Jesus, too, was persecuted." He sighed and it was a long, wearisome sigh. "I suppose we Jews seem strange to some people, because our customs and dietary laws and form of worship are not the same as the Gentile ways." He smiled to himself and remarked so softly it was practically a whisper, "But perhaps we are not so different after all, when you stop to think."

"Of course you are not! But people can be stupid and ignorant," Emma exclaimed with some vehemence, recognizing the sense of what he said, and instantly comparing the rabid class differences in England that also bred cruelty and terrible inequities. She gave him a swift look. "So you come from the land of the Jews, do you, sir?" she asked, thinking of the accent that tinged his speech.

"No, I do not. You see, the Jews scattered throughout the world over the centuries. To Spain, Germany, Russia, Poland, and many other countries. I myself come from Kiev, in Russia. Most of the Jews in Leeds also come from Russia, or from Poland. We came here to escape the terror and harassment of the pogroms directed against us. I had my baptism of fire in my own country and so, as difficult as things here can be sometimes, they are not as terrible as they were in Russia. It is good to be in England. We have freedom here, thank God."

The man was mindful of her listening to his recital so seriously and with infinite patience and another thought struck him. "You cannot be from Leeds, or you would know that there are many Jewish immigrants such as myself living here, and that we are despised by most."

"I didn't know," said Emma, adding, "I come from Ripon."

"Ah, from the rural area. That explains it!" He chuckled and his sad eyes unexpectedly twinkled. "Well, young lady, I will not detain you any longer with my discourse on the Jews. My most grateful thanks again to you. And may the good Lord bless and protect you all of the days of your life."

Emma flinched inside at this reference to the God she no longer acknowledged or believed in but, knowing the man meant well, she returned his friendly smile. "It was nothing. Really it wasn't. I was glad to help you, sir."

The man inclined his head courteously and started to walk away. However, after only a few steps he faltered and staggered against the wall, clutching his chest. Emma ran to him immediately. "Are you all right?" She noticed his face was now as white as cotton, and drawn, and his lips were faintly blue and perspiration had broken out on his forehead.

"Yes, I am perfectly well," he answered in a strangled voice, struggling for breath. After a moment he whispered, "It was only a twinge. The indigestion maybe."

Emma did not like the look of him. He appeared to be quite ill and in considerable discomfort. "Do you live far away from here?" she asked urgently. "I will take you to your home."

"No! No! You have already done enough for me. Please. Please. I am all right. Do not worry yourself."

"Where do you live?" Emma insisted firmly.

"In Imperial Street." He could not resist smiling through his pain. "A most unfortunate name for that poor little street, considering it is hardly royal in any sense of that word. It's located in the Leylands, about ten minutes away from here."

Emma's heart dropped at the mention of this area, since she had heard it was dangerous, the ghetto, but nevertheless, she kept her face calm and endeavored to appear untroubled. "Come along! I shall take you home. I don't think you are well at all, and besides, you might need me to protect you against another assault," she pointed out. The man was utterly amazed at her consideration and her willingness to assist him yet again, and not wanting to be a nuisance, he tried hard to dissuade her, but in spite of his protestations Emma took command purposefully. Clutching her reticule tightly, she relieved him of his parcel, gripped his arm, and together they walked slowly up the street.

The man's acute chest pains were diminishing and as his

breathing improved he began to feel better. He scrutinized the girl who was being so solicitous of him, helping him along so generously. Such kindness from a stranger he had never received. He coughed, pushing down the rush of emotion, saying quietly, "You are being most thoughtful and kind. I do appreciate it." He stopped, turned to her, and thrust out his hand. "My name is Abraham Kallinski. May I have the honor of knowing yours?"

Emma tucked the parcel under her arm and took his hand. His grip was firm. "It's Emma Harte." He noticed the silver ring on her left hand. "Mrs. Harte, I assume?" Emma nodded, but did not elucidate. Being a courteous and civilized man, Abraham Kallinski respected the privacy of others and he therefore refrained from asking any more questions.

They walked at a steady, even pace, Emma supporting Abraham Kallinski under his elbow, and as they walked he told her more about himself, for he was gregarious, an outgoing and articulate individual. Emma, with her inquiring mind and fierce desire to learn, listened alertly, giving him her full attention. She soon discovered he had left Kiev in 1880, making his way to Rotterdam and thence to Hull, Yorkshire's greatest seaport. "Like many of the other Jews from Russia and Poland, I came to Leeds intending to go to Liverpool and from there across to America," he explained. "However, I had to stay in Leeds for a period, to make the money for my ticket to America. Where Jews are, other Jews must go, and when I arrived I came immediately to the Leylands, where most of the Jewish immigrants live, seeking a *Landsmann*, that is, a man from my own country who spoke my language. I found work easily, for there is kinship and charity amongst Jews. We try to help each other." He laughed as he reminisced. "Ach, but I was young then. Twenty years old. When I was twenty-one I had the good fortune to meet the young lady who was to become my wife. She was born in Leeds. Her parents had fled Russia years before. And so, Mrs. Harte, I stayed in Leeds. I never did go to America in the end. Well, here we are!" he gestured to the surroundings. "This is where I have lived for the past twenty-five years, although not always in the same house."

Emma looked about, her eyes darting from side to side with unconcealed curiosity as they entered the Leylands. It was a huddle of mean streets, dark courtyards, and sly alleys, the houses clustered together as if seeking protection from each other. Emma shuddered inside at the obvious signs of wretchedness and poverty as they wended their way through Byron Street and into the heart of the ghetto. A group of barefooted children in patched clothing were playing in the middle of Imperial Street and several men were hurrying home, their steps purposeful, their heads bent, eyes furtive. They are strange-looking men, Emma thought, with their beards and large round hats and long coats. They are quite different in appearance from Mr. Kallinski, who seems so English. Emma smiled at this thought, having just been told he was Russian-born.

Abraham Kallinski stopped in front of a house at the far end of Imperial Street. To Emma's surprise it was larger and a bit grander than the others and was extremely well kept, with starched white curtains at the windows which were flanked by wooden shutters. "This is my home," he said, his face suddenly illuminated with such an expression of joy Emma was touched. His shoulders went back and there was pride in his voice.

"Then you will be all right now," said Emma. "I enjoyed listening to you, Mr. Kallinski. It was very interesting. I do hope you feel better. Good-bye, Mr. Kallinski." She handed him his parcel, the smile still lingering on her face.

Abraham Kallinski stared at this lovely girl, this Gentile girl, who had been so helpful and who had devoted so much of her time to him and with a compassion that was rare, and he put out his hand and clutched her arm, detaining her. "Please, please, come in for a moment. I wish my wife to meet you, Mrs. Harte. She will want to thank you. She will be most grateful for the aid you have given me today and so selfessly. Please!"

"Oh, really, Mr. Kallinski, that's not necessary. And I should be getting along."

"Please, just for a moment," he begged, his eyes soft and imploring. "It is hot. You are tired. Let us offer you a little hospitality. A glass of tea perhaps. A short rest."

Emma did feel tired and thirsty, but she did not wish to intrude. Furthermore, she did not relish the idea of being stranded in the Leylands alone, especially in the late afternoon. "Well, I really shouldn't," Emma began, wavering. She was longing for a glass of water.

Aware of her hesitation, Abraham Kallinski was the one who now took charge. He maneuvered Emma towards the door and opened it. "Come. We will go inside," he persisted, "a little refreshment will indeed fortify you."

Abraham Kallinski led her inside the house, which opened directly into a large kitchen that also seemed to Emma to be an all-purpose room. The woman standing at the stove turned as the door opened. Her eyes widened. "Abraham! Abraham! Whatever has happened to you?" she cried, rushing across the floor, the spoon she had been using still clutched in her hand. "Your clothes are all dirty, and look at your face! Oh, Abraham, you have been hurt!" She took his arm, her face a picture of distress mingled with fear.

"Now, Janessa, don't get excited," he said in his most gentle voice and with a tender look, for Abraham adored his wife. "I am not hurt. Just a little disheveled. A small incident, that is all. I stumbled and fell in North Street and two young hooligans threw stones at me. You know how they are." He brought Emma forward, his arm under her elbow. "This is Mrs. Harte, Janessa. Emma Harte. She came to my rescue. Sent the boys scurrying off with their tails between their legs and then she kindly brought me home. She insisted, in fact."

Janessa Kallinski put down the spoon and grasped both of Emma's hands in her own, squeezing them tightly. "I am delighted to meet you, Mrs. Harte. Thank you! Thank you for helping my husband! That was most charitable of you and courageous. You could easily have been hurt yourself." She smiled at Emma with genuine gratefulness and went on in a warm tone, "Please, come! Sit down. Let me offer you some refreshment. You look tired and hot."

"I am happy to meet you, too," Emma said politely. "And thank you, Mrs. Kallinski, I would appreciate a glass of water, please." Janessa led Emma to a chair and pressed her into it. "The water you can have with pleasure. But also you must take a glass of lemon tea with us. Now, please, rest yourself."

Mrs. Kallinski was back in a second with the water, which Emma accepted eagerly, and she was suddenly quite relieved to be seated after her long day tramping the streets. She had not fully realized just how tired and depleted she was beginning to feel.

Abraham followed his wife to the other side of the kitchen, where she had been preparing the evening meal. He gave her the parcel. "Here is the challah, Janessa. I am afraid it fell in the street, when I fell, but I do not think it is damaged." His eyes twinkled. "Not even bruised." He looked at Emma. "Please, excuse me for a moment." He inclined his head with that grave courtesy of his and went upstairs.

Emma's eyes scanned the kitchen. It was large and pleasant and more than adequately furnished with a sofa and several comfortable chairs, a sideboard, and a large table surrounded by six chairs. The table was covered with a fresh white cloth that gleamed brightly in the fading afternoon light and was set for four people. The wallpaper was attractive and conservative and the rug on the floor was of good quality, as were the other appointments. Emma now observed Janessa as she made the tea and filled the glasses. She was taller than her husband and slender, with an attractive figure. Her fresh-complexioned face was handsome rather than pretty, wide and Slavic in its features, and her mouth was full and soft. Her glossy straight black hair was pulled back and coiled on her neck and she had large pale blue eyes under well-defined black brows. She wore a black cotton dress and a crisp white apron that added to the rather stately and even regal impression she gave. Emma guessed she must be in her late thirties.

Within minutes Mr. Kallinski returned. He had removed the dust from his trousers, changed his jacket, brushed his hair, and attended to his bruised cheek. He washed his hands at the sink and then he spoke to his wife quietly before joining Emma. Janessa followed with the tea on a small tray. She handed a glass to Emma. "I know this will revive you more than the water did, Mrs. Harte," she murmured and sat down opposite Emma.

Emma thanked her and sipped the tea. It was delicious. Lemon-flavored with a piece of lemon floating in it, and it was sweet and hot. Emma had never had lemon tea before, but she refrained from mentioning this, as always wanting to appear both experienced and a young lady of Quality.

Mrs. Kallinski gave her undivided attention to her husband. "Are you sure you feel all right, Abraham? No twinges? No pains in your chest again?" She was unable to conceal her worry.

Mr. Kallinski threw Emma a warning glance and said quickly,

"No! No! Nothing like that, Janessa. Please do not worry. I am completely recovered from the fall."

Janessa looked doubtful, a frown scoring her brow, but she appeared to accept his statement in good faith. Abraham took a sip of tea and then regarded Emma. "Do you live far from the Leylands, Mrs. Harte?"

"Quite a little way. Do you know where the Mucky Duck is in York Road?" asked Emma. Mr. Kallinski nodded. "Well, I live about half an hour's walk from there, at the other end of York Road, in the opposite direction from the Leylands."

"Ah, I see," responded Mr. Kallinski. He peered at the clock. "It is getting later than I realized. When my sons return, which should be very soon, I will have them escort you home. It is not safe, this area, for a young lady alone."

Emma was about to decline this offer, but immediately saw the common sense of it. She did not want to be exposed to danger in the ghetto and the adjoining districts, and so she said, "Thank you. "I think that *would* be a good idea."

"It is the least we can do," interjected Mrs. Kallinski. "We don't want your husband worrying about you, now do we?" Then she continued in her good-hearted way, "And no doubt you are anxious to be getting home, to prepare your evening meal."

Emma cleared her throat, not responding, forever cautious about confiding in strangers, but under Mrs. Kallinski's affable gaze, she found herself saying, "No, I don't have to prepare supper for my husband. He is in the Royal Navy. When he is at sea, as he is at present, I live alone."

"Alone!" cried Mrs. Kallinski, her dismay dousing the lambent light in her eyes. "Do you not have any family?" The thought of this young girl being on her own in Leeds appalled Janessa, who came from a large, close-knit, and loving clan who were always there to protect and help each other.

Emma shook her head. "No, my husband's grandmother died recently. We have no one else between us." She saw the grieved expression on Mrs. Kallinski's face and remarked hurriedly, "Except each other, of course. But I am all right. Really. I live in a nice boardinghouse in a decent area, with a good woman, who rents me a room."

The Kallinskis exchanged swift and percipient glances. Abraham nodded his head in answer to his wife's unspoken question, which in her usual way she had communicated to him with her expressive eyes. Mrs. Kallinski now leaned forward, clasping her hands together, her wide face shining with benevolence. "If you do not have to go home immediately, if you have no other pressing reason to leave, will you not stay and partake of our Sabbath dinner with us? It would be our very great pleasure to welcome you."

"Oh, no, I couldn't. Really, I couldn't," Emma protested. "It's very kind of you. But I just couldn't." She flushed, wondering if the Kallinskis thought she had been trying to wangle an invitation to stay. "Thank you. It's very kind of you. But I couldn't intrude."

"Nonsense!" exclaimed Abraham. "You would not be intruding. Good gracious, after what you did for me today!" He lifted his hands in the air, palms outward, and made several small upward gestures and went on, "How can we ever thank you enough? Now, please, stay for the Sabbath dinner. It will be an honor to have you." Seeing the baffled look on Emma's face, he explained, "*Our* Sabbath day is on Saturday. It commences at sundown on Friday, when we always celebrate the beginning of the holy day with the Friday dinner."

"I see," Emma said. A worried glint crept into her eyes and they wandered to the clock on the mantelpiece. Abraham followed her glance and nodded, understanding at once what was in her mind. "Don't worry! Don't worry! Our sons will escort you home after supper." His voice was reassuring. "You will be safe with them, even if it is dark."

"But I—" Emma began.

"It is settled, Mrs. Harte," Janessa interrupted graciously yet with an air of decision. "You look tired, undoubtedly because of the trouble with those hooligans. The food will nourish you. Give you strength. You will enjoy it." She reached over and patted Emma's arm. "We have plenty. More than enough for an extra person, an honored guest. Please, relax, and when David and Victor arrive they, too, will welcome you. And thank you for assisting their father today. Yes, they will be delighted to have you share our Sabbath dinner."

Emma gave in under Mrs. Kallinski's persuasive and good-natured pressure. Also, she was feeling hungry again and she had nothing very appetizing to eat at Mrs. Daniel's, and the pots bubbling on the stove were emitting deliciously tempting odors. "Thank you. I will be happy to join you, as long as it is no trouble."

The Kallinskis beamed and Janessa leapt up, gliding to the stove to attend to the boiling pans. She spoke to Emma as she peeped at their contents. "You have not eaten Jewish food before, I think, but you will like it." She turned, the pan lid in her hand, and nodded positively. "Yes, I know you will enjoy it. First we will have the chicken soup with matzo balls—those are similar to Yorkshire dumplings but smaller—and then a crisply roasted chicken all golden brown and moist, with carrots and other vegetables from the soup. We will finish with honey cakes and lemon tea. Yes, it is good, you will see—" Janessa stopped midsentence and swung around. The door had opened, and her face lit up with pleasure and pride as her two sons entered the house. Seeing Emma seated near the fireplace, they both paused and looked at her with interest and considerable surprise.

"David! Victor! Come, meet our guest. An honored guest, for she helped your father out of trouble in the most admirable way today. A fine girl," said Janessa, plopping the lid back onto the pan. She wiped her hands on a tea towel and hurried over to her two sons, drawing them into the room. "Come along, boys, this is Emma Harte. Mrs. Harte." She led them to Emma, her face radiant. "This is David," she said, introducing the taller boy, "and this is Victor." The Kallinski boys shook hands with Emma, extended their greetings, and thanked her for coming to their father's aid. They crossed the room to the sofa and sat down together.

It was David who addressed Abraham, his eyes narrowing as he noticed the ugly black-and-blue bruise now most obvious on his father's cheek, which was puffy and swollen. "What happened, Father?" he asked quietly and with deference, but there was a fierce glint in his eyes and he was striving to control his flaring anger. He knew it was the work of the Jew-baiters again.

Slowly Abraham explained about the incident, not leaving out the minutest detail and extolling Emma's brave participation in the matter in the most glowing terms. As he spoke, Emma looked at the boys with growing interest, endeavoring to evaluate them.

David and Victor Kallinski were as different in every way as two brothers could be. David, who was the elder at nineteen, was tall like his mother and well built. He had been blessed with her lovely blue eyes, although his were much deeper in tone, and his face, handsome and open, had a suggestion of her Slavic bone structure in its width and overall shape. He had the same head of black wavy hair his father had once had and he had also inherited the older man's outgoing manner, yet essentially David Kallinski was even more gregarious, vital, and energetic than Abraham. David was a mover, a doer, ambitious, clever and driven. If there was a faint hint of cynicism in his alert blue eyes it was somewhat counteracted by the generosity of his wide mouth and his friendly demeanor. David was intelligent, intuitive, and excessively motivated towards one goal: success. And, as he knew only too well the true nature of man, he therefore lived by one rule and one rule alone—the survival of the fittest. He not only intended to survive, but to survive in style and with wealth.

Victor, who was sixteen, was small, almost birdlike, and in this he resembled his father to some extent. He had his mother's straight shiny black hair, but otherwise he did not appear to physically favor either of them. His large eyes were soft and hazel in color and his face was smooth and bland without any emphatic features, but he was pleasant-looking. His sober face mirrored his character, for Victor Kallinski was a gentle and reflective boy; and in one way his temperament was similar to his father's, in that Victor had, as did Abraham, a great forbearance and a deep understanding of human frailties, an understanding that was mature and remarkable in one so young. He was a thinker and a dreamer, and he had the soul of a poet. Victor was happiest when he was alone reading, or gazing at great paintings in the museum, or listening to the music of Mahler and Beethoven. He was reserved of nature to a point of shyness and not given to conversing easily with anyone, especially strangers. Victor was looking at Emma surreptitiously from under his long dark lashes, a quiet smile playing around his mouth, thinking what a compassionate girl she must be, and how her actions today only reinforced his inherent belief that essentially mankind was good. Like his father, Victor was utterly without bitterness.

David, the bolder and more self-assured of the two brothers, spoke to Emma first. "That was very spunky of you, to stand up to those boys and help my father. And you're not even Jewish, are you?" he commented with his usual forth-rightness. His piercing blue eyes swept over her in a quick, all-encompassing inspection and he was impressed with the image she made, sitting there in the chair, her hands calmly folded in her lap.

"No, I am not Jewish," said Emma. "But I fail to see what difference that makes. I would help anyone in distress, and certainly somebody being assaulted the way your father was."

David nodded. "Not many people would, though," he re-marked succinctly, wondering what a refined girl was doing in the neighborhood anyway. He opened his mouth to ask, when Janessa said, "Mrs. Harte, come and wash your hands, before the boys clean up, and then we will eat. It is almost sundown." Janessa swept across the floor and set another place for Emma at the table, hovering near it until Emma and then the boys had completed their toilets.

They all stood around the large table, which was beauti-fully arranged, the four Kallinskis and Emma. "Mother will bless the candles first," David whispered. Emma stood per-fectly still and watched and listened carefully, taking every-thing in. Janessa lit the two white candles and murmured a prayer over them in a strange language Emma did not under-stand, then they all sat down, David courteously pulling the chair out for Emma, Victor for his mother. Noting that all of the Kallinskis were bowing their heads, Emma followed suit. Out of the corner of her eye she saw Abraham bless the red wine in a small cup, again in that curious foreign tongue which she did not know was Hebrew. He took a sip of the wine and said another prayer over the twisted loaf of bread she herself had rescued from the street.

"Father just recited the kiddush and now we can eat, after the breaking of the bread," David further informed her. The bread was broken by Abraham Kallinski and passed around, and Janessa brought steaming bowls of soup to the table that smelled delicious, and so the meal commenced. As she ate, Emma became aware of the harmony and immeasurable love that existed in this family. She began to relax, for the atmosphere was warm and congenial and she was made to feel so at ease and so welcome she was overwhelmed with gratitude at one moment, and her throat thickened with unexpected emotion. And she kept thinking: *Why are the Jews hated? They are loving and gentle people and kind and considerate. It is despicable the way they are treated.* And this was the way Emma Harte was to feel all of her life, staunchly defending her Jewish friends, constantly shocked and grieved by the excesses of naked racism that infected Leeds like the blight for many years.

The roasted chicken, like the soup before it, was cooked to perfection and was delectable, and for the first time since she had left Fairley, Emma felt both nourished and replete. She realized she had eaten very little in the week she had been in Leeds. She decided to correct that, for she was wise enough to understand that she must keep up her strength.

There was much conversation at the table, about many diverse subjects which fascinated Emma, most of it conducted by the garrulous David and his slightly less garrulous father. Janessa would make a quiet comment occasionally and nod in agreement or shake her head at Emma, all the time smiling benignly, content to be in her home with those she loved, basking in the palpable love that flowed around her, and the festive mood of the Friday-evening dinner. Victor hardly volunteered a word, but he smiled sometimes at Emma, his hazel eyes soft and shyly friendly. A short while later, when she served the honey cakes and tea, Janessa looked down at Emma, her blue eyes twinkling. "I think you enjoyed our Jewish food, didn't you, Mrs. Harte?"

Emma's own eyes were dancing. "Oh, yes, I did, Mrs. Kallinski. It was delicious. And please, call me Emma." Her glance swept around the entire table. "I would like everyone to call me Emma." The Kallinski family nodded in unison and returned her smiles. "We would be honored," said Abraham in his gravely courteous way.

They were drinking their tea when David's eyes swiveled to Emma sitting by his side. Like the others, David had noticed Emma's well-bred air, her good manners, and the quality of her dress, for even though it was cotton it was well cut. He was curious about her. Now he said, "I don't want to seem nosy or rude, but what on earth were *you* doing in North Street this afternoon? Thank goodness you were, mind you. But it's not such a nice area for anyone to be wandering around in."

Emma returned his piercing glance with one equally brilliant. "I was looking for a job," she said calmly.

Total silence descended and four pairs of Kallinski eyes centered on Emma. It was Janessa who broke that silence. "A girl like you! Looking for work in that terrible district!" she gasped, utterly thunderstruck.

"Yes," said Emma softly. Since they were all gazing at her in amazement, she felt obliged to explain and she embarked on the same story she had invented for Rosie and repeated to Mrs. Daniel, finishing, "And in the past week I have been to every fancy store in Leeds, looking for work as a salesgirl without any success. So today I decided to try my luck in North Street, at the tailoring shops. But I didn't find anything there either. I had just been to Cohen's and was making my way home when I saw the boys assaulting Mr. Kallinski."

Three pairs of Kallinski eyes immediately swung away from Emma and lighted on Abraham, and again it was Janessa who spoke. "Abraham! Abraham! *You* must do something for Emma."

"Of course I must and I will," he replied, beaming at Emma sitting next to him. He patted her arm. "You do not have to worry about looking further. On Monday morning, at eight o'clock sharp, come to my tailoring shop and I will give you a job, Emma. I am sure we can find something suitable." He glanced at David. "Don't you agree, son?"

"Yes, Dad. We can start Emma off as a buttonholer. That's not so hard," responded David.

Emma was so surprised she was almost rendered speechless, but she quickly found her voice. "Why, thank you, Mr. Kallinski! That would be wonderful." She gave him an intent look. "I learn very fast and I will work hard." She paused and shook her head. "I didn't know you had a tailoring shop."

Abraham chuckled. "How could you have known? Anyway, it is in Rockingham Street near Camp Road. David will write down the exact address for you. It is not a very large workshop. We have about twenty people. But we do well enough, making up."

"What does 'making up' mean?" asked Emma, baffled by this expression but, as always, anxious to clarify anything she did not understand.

Abraham gave her an avuncular smile. "Ah, yes, of course you are not familiar with the term, since you do not know the tailoring trade. It means that we do work for larger clothiers, like Barran's and others, as do most of the Jewish tailoring shops in Leeds. We are an outside contractor."

"I see," said Emma. "So you make suits for the big clothiers and they go and sell them. Am I right?"

"Not exactly, but I will let David explain. He is the one who lives, breathes, eats, and sleeps the tailoring trade in this family."

David laughed engagingly. "That's not quite true, Dad." He leaned back in his chair and partially turned to Emma. "We don't turn out an entire suit. We 'make up' a particular section of a suit, maybe the sleeves, or jacket fronts and lapels, or the jacket backs, or sometimes trousers. We 'make up' whatever the big factories decide to send us any given week."

Emma, alert as usual, said, "But why? That seems a funny way to do it. Isn't it more complicated than just making the whole suit in one place?"

David grinned. "No, strangely enough, it isn't, because it's very well organized. It's also cheaper and faster. The big manufacturers can produce more finished suits by utilizing this method. They simply assemble all of the different parts at their own factories. It was an idea conceived by a little Jewish tailor called Herman Friend. It revolutionized the ready-made clothing industry and helped to put Leeds on the map as the biggest center of ready-made clothing in the world. And the trade is growing more enormous every year." An excited gleam entered his eyes. "I tell you, Emma, the tailoring trade is going to make Leeds even more famous one day and immensely rich. It is indeed and I intend to be part of it all."

"Such ideas he has, this son of mine," murmured Abraham, shaking his head wonderingly, a hint of disbelief in his eyes.

Emma was vastly intrigued, as she always was at the mention of money and new ideas. "This man, this Herman Friend, where did he get such an idea? Tell me more about him, David."

"Who knows what gave him the idea?" he said with a shrug. "But it was certainly an idea that worked. Anyway, Herman Friend had his own little workshop and was 'making up' for the John Barran factory, the first ready-made clothiers to start in Leeds after Singer invented the sewing machine. They're the biggest, and also non-Jewish, by the way. Friend invented the method of the divisional labor system when he was an outside contractor for Barran's, dividing the making of one single suit into five or six different operations. This immediately reduced the cost of producing ready-made suits and, as I said before, increased output. It also meant that Barran's, and the other big clothiers who adopted the system, could sell the suits at cheaper prices. Volume was the key and it put the price of a suit within the reach of the working man. Friend started to give out work to other small Jewish tailoring shops and the whole idea just snowballed."

Emma said, "A simple idea, but like so many simple ideas, it was very clever."

David nodded his agreement, somewhat taken aback by this observation. He was even further surprised when Emma continued, "Like the Marks and Spencer Penny Bazaar in Leeds Market. Now that is also a brilliant idea. Putting all the goods in different sections, showing them off so everyone can see them easily, examine them, and help themselves. And pricing them so cheaply. Don't you think *that* is clever, David?"

"I certainly do!" He smiled. "Did you know that Michael Marks is also a Jewish immigrant who came to Leeds from Poland? He started with that one stall in Leeds Market ten years ago. He recently went into partnership with Tom Spencer and now they have Penny Bazaars all over Leeds, and are expanding to other cities. They'll be a national chain one day. You'll see."

Emma's eyes were fixed on David, her mouth slightly open with amazement, excitement bringing a flush to her pale face. She *was* right. Leeds *was* the place to make a fortune. Now she said, "I believe anything is possible, if you have a good idea and are prepared to work hard."

"You're absolutely correct, Emma," responded David. He launched into another success story, which Emma ate up.

David and Emma could have talked all night, for they were both bursting with ambition, drive, and, most surprisingly, had an incredible vision quite remarkable for their years; and they intuitively began to recognize this and were drawn to each other instinctively. But Abraham glanced at the clock at this precise moment and said, "I think it is time for you boys to escort Emma home. I am enjoying her company, too, but it is getting late and I do not like the idea of you being on the streets when the public houses are turning out. Dangerous, I think."

"Yes, I must be getting along," Emma said, pushing back her chair. "But first I must help Mrs. Kallinski to clear the table and wash the dishes."

"No, no, that is not necessary, Emma. My husband is right. The boys must take you home immediately. David, don't forget to write out the address of the workshop for Emma, and then you must leave," said Janessa.

Emma thanked the elder Kallinskis for their hospitality and the lovely dinner, and even more profusely for the job, which was so vital to her survival. She promised to be at the workshop on Monday morning at eight o'clock, and carefully tucked the paper into her handbag.

It was a relatively long walk back to Mrs. Daniel's house, but Emma felt safe, flanked on either side by the silent Victor and the voluble David. They did not run into any street gangs, and for Emma the time passed quickly with David chattering about all manner of things, but mostly about the tailoring trade. They insisted on taking her right to Mrs. Daniel's front door. In the gaslight from the streetlamp a few. feet away, David and Victor were clearly illuminated. Emma looked from the solemn Victor to the laughing David and thought: They are so different but they are both very genuine. She gave her hand to Victor. "Thank you for bringing me home. Good-bye," she said.

Victor gripped her hand with firmness. "Good night, Emma. And thank you for helping Father. It was good of you."

"Yes, it was!" exclaimed David, who now grasped her hand in his. "See you Monday morning, bright and early. Good night, Emma."

They turned and began to walk away as she fitted the door key into the lock, but David stopped abruptly and ran back. "We think alike, Emma," he said, his voice vibrating confidently in the stillness. "I know we are going to be friends. Good friends."

Emma's face was serious and she believed him. She nodded. "I think so, too, David." He opened the door for her, and when she was safely inside he ran lightly down the steps and raced after Victor, who was waiting for him at the end of the street.

He was not aware of it then, but never had David Kallinski made a more prophetic pronouncement. They were indeed alike, for both were imbued with the will to succeed. And on

that hot August night in 1905 a friendship had begun that was
to last over half a century. Together they would climb, in
their own individualistic ways, struggling up out of grim
poverty, fighting all manner of prejudices, reaching for bigger
and better things, and in their rising and their reaching they
would carry the city with them. They would put their indel-
ible imprint on Leeds, not only in their outstanding achievements as business magnates, but in their vast philanthropies.
It was Emma Harte and David Kallinski, plus a handful of
other conscientious, driven, and visionary Jews and Gentiles,
who were to give birth to a city's greatness.

TWENTY-NINE

The days slipped into weeks. August became September
and then suddenly September had vanished. It was
already the middle of October and Blackie had not returned
to Leeds.

Emma constantly wondered what was detaining him in
Ireland, worrying excessively when she was alone in the
solitude of her little attic room, hoping he was not in some
kind of trouble. She longed for Blackie to return because he
was her closest friend and, although she was not aware of it,
because he was associated with her past. Blackie O'Neill was
the only emotional link to her background and so to her
family, whom she loved and sorely missed. But essentially,
the worry she periodically experienced was sincere concern
for Blackie's well-being, rather than her own, for she was not
given to self-pity. And she was managing reasonably well by
herself. She had her job at Kallinski's tailoring shop and her
room at Mrs. Daniel's house and, tentative and even tenuous
as these were, they gave her a certain degree of security that
was comforting.

The landlady, growing less fractious and more cordial every
day, had announced unexpectedly that Emma could continue
to rent the room indefinitely. It had not taken the sharp-eyed
Mrs. Daniel long to note that Emma was fastidious, honest,
and quietly reserved. She kept to herself, merely nodding
politely to the two gentlemen boarders when she ran into

them in the hall, moving swiftly upstairs to her own room in well-bred dignity. She was not a troublemaker, Gertrude Daniel had decided, and had told Emma, "Yer can stay as long as yer want ter, lass. Yer no bother. None at all," and with this utterance Mrs. Daniel's dour face had broken into a beaming smile and she had patted Emma's arm almost affectionately.

Emma was earning enough money at Kallinski's to keep herself adequately and, most importantly, without having to dip into her precious savings. She was careful with her money to a point of frugality, spending it only for necessities, walking everywhere even when she was dropping from exhaustion and tempted to take a tramcar. But thrifty as she was, she did buy nourishing food. She was sensible enough to recognize she must fortify her strength and preserve her energy at all costs. If she neglected herself she might easily get sick and be unable to work, a thought that filled her with dread. There was the baby to think about, after all.

The job at the little workshop kept her busy from eight in the morning until six, sometimes seven o'clock, at night. Emma actually enjoyed working there and had done so since the first day. Abraham Kallinski ran his Rockingham Street tailoring shop with efficiency, but he was no tyrant, and because he was just, no one ever thought of abusing his kindness. The workers did not have to clock in and there were no stringent rules about talking, or the length of time taken for tea and lunch breaks. The employees were paid by the piece and it was up to them to make a living wage; and providing Abraham met his obligations to the big clothiers on time, he was satisfied, and he did not believe in cracking the whip on principle.

The girls were mostly Gentiles, but all of the men were Jewish. There was a wonderful feeling of camaraderie in the air, with much friendly bantering rising above the clack-clack-clacking of the treadle sewing machines. Emma sat at the long wooden worktable, up to her calves in clippings and bits of padding, working nimbly and at a pace that astounded the most seasoned of the girls. They were a gregarious bunch, all of them Leeds born and bred, blunt, pithily humorous but kindly. They spoke in the odd vernacular particular to Leeds, abbreviating words, slurring others together, dropping *h*'s and adding them where they should not have been. Emma understood the girls easily enough, for the patois of Leeds was basically a bastardization of the Yorkshire dialect spoken in the rural areas. She herself continued to speak correctly, always conscious of Olivia Wainright's melodious voice, always parroting it, never permitting herself to fall into the rough speech patterns of her fellow workers. Emma knew that bad habits were easy to acquire and hard to break. At first the girls had teased her about her cultivated voice. "Talking like cut glass," they called it. Emma simply smiled and took their ribbing in such a good-natured way they soon ceased and accepted her as one of them. But none of the girls at Kallinski's ever quite became accustomed to her beauty or her air of breeding. They were forever stealing looks at her and they stood in awe of her, although she did not know this.

Abraham kept a watchful eye on Emma, for he would never forget her compassion and rare courage, but he did so without showing her any favoritism, even though he was inordinately fond of her. Emma was always aware of Victor's hovering presence, particularly when she hit a small problem with her work. Her involvement so preoccupied her she never once noticed the adoration that shone in his gentle eyes whenever they lighted on her. David was her champion. He had taken her under his wing that first Monday morning when he had set her to buttonholing. He was not surprised when she mastered this technique within a few days and became one of the speediest and most adept workers. Conscious of her superior intelligence and her amazing facility for learning with rapidity, he started her cutting sleeves one day when a regular cutter was absent. David had rolled out the long bolt of fine Yorkshire cloth on the wooden trestle table, chalking on the pattern from a paper form and wielding the scissors with a dexterity that was enviable, explaining in detail to Emma as he went along.

Under David's training Emma soon learned to cut sleeves, lapels, then jacket fronts and backs, and finally trousers, always willing to pitch in and help when they were running behind with orders. By the middle of September she could easily have cut and sewn an entire suit on her own, without assistance from David. Abraham was stunned at her enormous capacity for work and impressed by her quick understanding of all aspects of tailoring. In fact, he was speechless at her skill, her single-mindedness, and her unflagging en-

ergy. Victor was silently admiring. David simply grinned like
a Cheshire cat. He had perceived the nature of her character
at their first meeting, an occasion he would always consider
auspicious, if not indeed fortuitous. Emma Harte was a girl
who was going places. He would bet his last shilling on that.
He had his plans and she was part of them.

Janessa Kallinski continually extended invitations to Friday-
night Sabbath dinner, for she had also grown fond of Emma
and was as captivated as the rest of the family. Emma regu-
lated her visits scrupulously, displaying an innate sense of
social grace. She enjoyed her evenings in this warm and
loving Jewish home, but she did not want to take advantage
of their hospitality or appear to be forward and opportunistic.
And when she did accept an invitation she always arrived
with a small gift. A bunch of flowers bought in Leeds Market,
a pot of jam she had made in Mrs. Daniel's kitchen, and once
a chocolate mousse, painstakingly prepared from Olivia
Wainright's recipe and carried most carefully to the house in
the Leylands in one of Mrs. Daniel's best cut-glass bowls. The
mousse had been a triumph and had sent the whole of the
Kallinski family into gurglings of delight; and they were lavish
with their praise of her culinary expertise, which Mrs. Daniel
had also commented on favorably.

Mostly, however, Emma's free time was spent alone. She
was not always tired at the end of the working day but, since
she had no friends in Leeds, other than the Kallinskis, she
made her supper in the back kitchen and then retired to her
attic. Sometimes she sewed at night, spending endless hours
patiently altering the castoffs from Olivia Wainright's wardrobe. These had been given to her before Mrs. Wainright
had departed for London, following Adele Fairley's funeral. If
the clothing had seen better days, none of it was so badly
worn that it could not be fixed by Emma's ingenuity and her
deftness with a needle. The basic quality and elegance of the
clothes was unmistakable, and so she turned frayed cuffs and
collars, patched and darned holes, and let out seams. She
worked on a gray woolen suit, a red silk dress, various skirts
and blouses, and a black woolen coat, as well as the black
dress that had been her mother's, constantly endeavoring to
keep her limited wardrobe in the best of condition and neat.
She had no intention of buying anything new the next few
years. Occasionally she read the books she had found in the

bottom drawer of the chest. She did not always understand the philosophical works, but they intrigued her and she would read sentences over and over again, digesting the words with thoughtfulness, filled with an immense gratification when the true meaning of the books became clear to her. She had a thirst for learning and acquiring knowledge and one of her few purchases had been a dictionary. But her favorite book of all was the volume of William Blake's poems and she pored over this regularly, reciting the verses aloud, enunciating the difficult words precisely, making a supreme effort to develop and perfect her speaking voice. In point of fact, Emma Harte never wasted a minute of her time, continually striving to better herself.

The first few weeks she had been in Leeds she had lain awake almost every night fretting about the baby. One day it struck her most forcibly that worrying about an event not due to take place until the following March was perfecty ridiculous. Also, it was a waste of time, that most precious of all commodities to Emma. She would think about the baby the day it was born and not before. Then, and only then, would she decide what her next step would be. Emma hoped the baby would be a girl. She was afraid that if it was a boy it would look like Edwin Fairley and that she would hate it for this reason. The poor baby isn't to blame, she would think, and every day she said to herself: I *know* it will be a girl, and this invariably cheered her up.

Emma had been to visit Rosie at the Mucky Duck twice, and on the last occasion she had left a note sealed in an envelope for Blackie, telling him where she lived and worked. She had also written to her father. She had told him she had not found a suitable position in Bradford, but that she was staying on in the hopes of doing so. She promised to be in touch soon. The letter had been most purposefully posted in Bradford. Although Emma begrudged spending the money for the railway ticket, she was too terrified to post the letter in Leeds for fear of discovery. And so, with that sense of self-preservation uppermost in her mind, she had trailed all the way to Bradford, posted the letter at the main post office, and taken the next train back to Leeds.

Now, on a Saturday morning in October, Emma sat at the table in the attic penning another note in her meticulously neat handwriting. For obvious reasons, this letter had to be full of lies; lies that at first bothered her enormously, until she told herself they were really white lies; and because they were meant to protect her father from knowing the terrible truth, which would shame him, and were intended to assuage his anxiety, they did not actually count. However, she decided to keep her story as simple as possible.

Emma wrote carefully: *Dear Dad: I am sorry I have not written since September. I have been looking hard for work. I am glad to tell you I have obtained a position with . . .* Emma stopped, conjuring up a name that was so common it would therefore be difficult to isolate and trace, continuing: *a Mrs. John Smith. I am to be her personal maid. We are leaving for London today, returning in one month. When I get back to Bradford I will come and see you. Don't worry about me, Dad. I am fine. Love to you and Frank and Winston. Always your loving daughter, Emma.* She added a postscript. *P.S. Here's a pound to help out.* Emma wrapped the pound note inside the letter, put it in the envelope, sealed it firmly, addressed it, and stuck on the stamp.

She hurried to get dressed, selecting the black frock that had been her evening uniform at Fairley Hall and which now boasted a frothy white lace collar and cuffs. She had wondered whether she ought to take her uniforms when she had left Fairley Hall. Wasn't that stealing? she had asked herself. But in the end she had had no compunction about packing them in Edwin's suitcase. The Fairleys had had their pound of flesh and the uniforms certainly wouldn't fit the bovine Annie.

Once she was outside the house Emma's spirits lifted. It was an Indian-summer day, with a polished blue sky, white candy-floss clouds, and radiant sunshine. It's a shimmering sort of day, Emma decided, breathing in the fresh air that was balmy for October. She walked smartly to City Square and crossed it to reach City Station, where she bought a ticket for Bradford. Luckily the train was standing on the platform and she boarded it immediately. When the train eventually chugged into Bradford, Emma leapt out of the carriage, dashed to the post office and back to the railway station with such speed she was able to catch the return train to Leeds.

Emma felt easier now that the letter to her father had been mailed, and she relaxed against the carriage seat as the train rumbled along the tracks. She did not have to write to her father again for a month. That gave her sufficient time to think up another story. Although there was no natural deceit in her character, Emma knew she must resort to subterfuge to appease her father, until after the baby was born. He might still worry about her, but not as much as he would if there was total silence on her part. She must be in touch with him on a regular basis and then perhaps he would not attempt to find her. He did not know where to look anyway. He believed her to be in Bradford, and there must be hundreds of Mrs. John Smiths in that city. As always, she felt a sharp twinge of guilt when she thought of her father.

The trip to Bradford and back to Leeds had taken several hours and Emma was assailed by hunger pains when she stepped off the train in City Station. In fact, the hunger was so acute it was making her feel dizzy. She went directly to Leeds Market, where she bought herself a large portion of mussels and drowned them in pepper and vinegar, having lately developed a craving for spicy things. When these had been devoured with relish, she went to the pie stand and bought a meat pie, all fluffy, flaky pastry and piping hot and deliciously moist and tender inside. She strolled around the market for a short while, eating the pie unself-consciously and looking at the diverse stalls, and then she wended her way to Briggate. On Saturday afternoons Emma made a point of wandering around the main streets of Leeds, gazing in the store windows, making mental notes of displays and the type of merchandise on sale. She went into several of the fine shops, eyeing the interior displays and observing what people were buying, conscious of that thrilling sensation growing inside her, as it always did when she entered a shop. She loved the bustle, the bright colors, the array of merchandise and its often ingenious presentation, the clink of the cash registers, the interesting faces of the shoppers, the elegant women in their smart clothes. She could not wait until she had her own shop. *Shops*, she corrected herself, as she stared at a collection of winter bonnets, none of which was to her taste; nor did she like the way they were presented.

After several hours of browsing, Emma decided she ought to go home. She had mending and other tasks to do and her feet ached. She had barely walked in through the front door when Mrs. Daniel was upon her, sweeping down the narrow corridor from the back kitchen. Her eyes glinted sharply in the dim light and she threw Emma a quizzical look as she exclaimed, "Yer've had a gentleman caller!"

Emma stood stock-still, her heart pounding unreasonably. Her father? Winston? They had somehow managed to find her! Don't be stupid, she told herself firmly. It was more than likely David Kallinski. He had been once before, delivering a message from his mother, but Mrs. Daniel had been out and so she had never met him. Yes, it must have been David, Emma decided. She kept her voice steady. "Oh, really. Did he leave his name, Mrs. Daniel?"

"No, but he left yer this." Mrs. Daniel pulled an envelope out of her apron pocket.

"Thank you, Mrs. Daniel," said Emma, placing one foot on the stairs purposefully.

"Aren't yer going ter open it, then?" Mrs. Daniel asked, her disappointment registering so apparently Emma was amused.

"Yes, of course I am," Emma replied with a cool smile. She inclined her head to the landlady graciously. "Please excuse me, Mrs. Daniel." Without giving her another glance, Emma mounted the stairs, her heart lifting. She had recognized the handwriting. It was Blackie's, and she certainly wasn't going to give Mrs. Daniel the satisfaction of seeing her jubilation at receiving a note from a man who was obviously not her "husband" of Royal Navy fame, the much-talked-about Winston.

Once she was in her room, Emma tore open the envelope with trembling fingers, her eyes seeking the signature immediately. It *was* from Blackie. He would be waiting for her at the Mucky Duck at five o'clock today. Emma dropped onto the bed and leaned her head against the pillow, closing her eyes, filled with the most overwhelming sense of relief and happiness.

At exactly four, when the grandfather clock in the front hall struck the hour, Emma sailed downstairs and out of the house before Mrs. Daniel could waylay her with her prying questions and unconcealed curiosity. Outwardly, she was as contained as always, but inside she was bursting with a breathless anticipation at the idea of seeing Blackie O'Neill again. Oh, how she had missed him! It was only now that Emma realized the amount of discipline and self-control she had exercised, so as not to become depressed or feel utterly alone in Leeds, and she was astonished that she had been able to command her emotions so successfully.

So intent was Emma on reaching her destination, so involved was she with these inner thoughts, she was quite oblivious to the heads, both male and female, that turned to look after her as she swept along the pavement, heading for York Road and the Mucky Duck. She cut quite a swath in the gray woolen suit which she had skillfully repaired so that the worn parts would not show. It was of excellent cut and elegant in its basic simplicity. The long skirt was straight to the calf and from there it fell to her ankles in a small flare on either side. Topping the skirt was a tailored jacket, tightly fitted over the bodice, with rounded shoulders and narrow sleeves. Deep revers and a peplum from the waist to just below the hip gave it an undeniable chic not commonly seen in the neighborhood; it was five years old and dated for London, but not for Leeds, and it *was* by Worth. With it Emma wore the blue silk blouse discarded long ago by Olivia Wainright, and its dainty white lace collar and cuffs were just visible. She had pinned Blackie's green-glass brooch onto one of the lapels, but this was her only piece of jewelry, other than her mother's plain silver ring on the third finger of her left hand. The white crocheted gloves and the black leather reticule with the tortoiseshell frame completed her outfit.

Emma was now five months pregnant. She herself was conscious of a thickening around her waist and hips, but her condition was not yet obvious to anyone else. The suit emphasized her willowy figure and enhanced her natural gracefulness. Her burnished hair, full of golden lights in the late-afternoon sunshine, was swept back from her oval face and brought the striking widow's peak into focus. That afternoon she had piled those glossy tresses on top of her head in a modified pompadour, experimenting with a style she had not previously worn, and it not only made her appear taller than her five feet six inches but also gave her a sophisticated air. There was a decided spring to her light step. She was feeling revitalized and her exhilaration was apparent to every passer-by.

Emma knew she had set out far too soon. She slowed her pace, not wanting to reach the pub before Blackie did. On arriving in Leeds in August, she had already worked out the story she would tell him. At this time in her life there was little duplicity in Emma. However, now that she was pregnant she was more self-protective than ever and her inbred wariness was increasing daily. The last thing she wanted was her father or Adam Fairley swooping down on her, a situation quite likely to arise if Blackie knew the facts and sprang gallantly to her defense. And so, with a degree of artifice, she had concocted a story within the realm of truth yet deceptive enough to dupe Blackie whilst being eminently plausible. She rehearsed the story as she walked, although she had committed it to memory weeks ago.

A small troop of Salvation Army ladies, resplendent in their long black uniforms, their bonnets bobbing, were marching down York Road from the opposite direction, singing lustily and thumping a drum. Rather than hang around outside and expose herself to the ritualistic Saturday-night dissertation on the evils of drink, Emma went immediately into the public house. She could always chat with Rosie if Blackie was not already there. She pushed open the heavy front doors and moved along the narrow corridor rank with the smell of stale beer and smoke. She paused briefly before going through the inner swinging doors. Blackie had beat her to it. His voice was distinguishable over the hum of the noise inside. Emma stepped through the doors and stood to one side.

There he was in all his glorious Irish splendor, vibrant black curls rippling back from tanned face, black eyes dancing, white teeth flashing between rosy lips, his superb looks prominently highlighted in the glare from the burning gas lamps. The pianist was banging out "Danny Boy," and Blackie stood next to him, erect and proud, one hand on the piano top, his marvelous baritone ringing out above the clink of glasses and the subdued murmur of conversation. Emma put a gloved hand to her mouth to hide the laughter springing automatically to her lips. She had never seen *this* Blackie O'Neill before. But then she had never seen him in a pub either. What a performance he's giving, she thought in amazement, mesmerized by his theatrical stance.

In point of fact, Blackie O'Neill would have made a splendid actor. He certainly had all the necessary attributes required for that histrionic art—outstanding looks, natural charm, an instinctive sense of timing, emotional depth, and an animal magnetism that was spellbinding when projected to the fullest, and it was being decidedly projected at this very moment. There was not a little of the ham in Blackie and he was now playing outrageously to the crowd, who were electrified. He had come to the last verse of the old Irish air, and he stepped away from the piano, leaned forward, almost bowing, and then drew himself up to his full height of six feet three inches, expanding his broad chest. One great arm swept out and he finished triumphantly:

"And I shall hear, though soft ye tread above me,
And all my grave will warmer, sweeter be,
And you will bend and tell me that you love me,
And I shall sleep in peace until ye come to me!"

His voice struck at Emma's heart as it always did, and as the fading echoes of it washed over her in all-enveloping waves, her throat became tight with that bittersweet sadness she experienced whenever he sang. She blinked and looked around. There wasn't a dry eye in the place and she saw the flutter of white as handkerchiefs came out to wipe other moist eyes. The crowd was clapping spontaneously and she heard diverse voices shouting out requests: "Give us another, Blackie, lad!" . . . "How about 'The Minstrel Boy'!" . . . "Sing us 'Cockles and Mussels,' lad!" Blackie was bowing and grinning and bowing again, obviously enjoying every minute of the approval. He seemed about to oblige with another rendition when he spotted Emma.

"Later, mates," he cried above the din, and crossed the floor in several quick strides, pushing his way through the group surrounding the piano. Emma stood shyly near the door, clutching her reticule. Blackie was towering above her, his eyes sweeping over her in one swift but appraising glance. His surprise at the radical change in her appearance was evident, even though he tried to conceal it. He recovered instantly and said, with his usual enthusiasm, "Emma! It's wonderful to see ye, sure and it is, mavourneen."

Blackie pulled her into his arms and hugged her. Then he stood her away, as was his habit, still holding her arms and gazing into her upturned face. "Why, ye be looking more fetching than I ever did see ye, Emma. And quite the young lady. Yes, indeed!"

Emma laughed. "Thank you, Blackie, and it's lovely to see you, too."

He grinned at her, his delight as obvious as hers. "Come on, mavourneen. Let's be going into the Saloon Bar. It will be quieter in there, I am thinking, and we can talk better. It is also a more *suitable* spot for a fine young lady like ye." He winked as he said this and asked, "And what will yer be having to drink?"

"A lemonade, please," she responded.

"Wait here," Blackie ordered, and headed for the bar. Emma's eyes followed him. She had not seen him since the spring, almost nine months, and he, too, had changed. He seemed somehow more mature and, in spite of that natural exuberance that always bubbled to the surface, there was an air of containment about him, and she thought she also detected a certain sadness. Rosie, her vast body encased in startling orange satin, was beaming from ear to ear and waving at Emma, who returned her greeting. Blackie was back within seconds, carrying the drinks. "Follow me," he said, shouldering his way through the throng that filled the main room.

The Saloon Bar was relatively empty and certainly quieter, and Emma at once felt less uncomfortable here than in the public bar. She glanced around curiously. It was quite sedate, in fact rather elegant for a pub. Blackie found them a table in the corner, put down the drinks, pulled out a chair for her with a gentlemanly flourish, and seated himself opposite. He took a sip of the frothing pint and regarded her over the rim of the glass attentively. Then he placed it on the table and, leaning forward, said in a sober tone, "And what's all this about, then? What are ye doing in Leeds? A little snippet like ye. I thought I told ye a long time ago this was no place for ye, until ye were older. Sure and I did, Emma Harte."

Emma threw him a quick glance. "I'm doing all right."

"Aye, so I can see, by the looks of ye. But ye might not have been so lucky, I am thinking. Come on, out with it! What made ye leave Fairley?"

Emma was not ready to confide in him just yet and she ignored the question. "Yes, I *was* lucky," she conceded and, changing the subject, continued, "I didn't know you would be away. I missed you, Blackie. Why were you in Ireland so long? I thought you were never coming back."

His face became sorrowful. "Ah, mavourneen, mavourneen," he said through a deep sigh. "It was me good friend Father O'Donovan, who was dying. An old priest I truly loved, who taught me everything I know. That is, what bit of learning I do have. I stayed with him till the end. Sad it was, oh, very sad indeed." He shook his head and his Celtic soul seemed to be mourning afresh, for his eyes were dimming at the memory.

Emma stretched out her small hand and patted his arm. "I am sorry, Blackie. Really very sorry. I know how upset you must be." She was silent for a moment, commiserating with him, and then she murmured softly, "So that's why you stayed in Ireland all these months."

"No, mavourneen. Father O'Donovan, God rest his soul, died within a couple of weeks. But I did stay on for a bit of a holiday with me cousins, Michael and Siobhan, who I hadn't seen in many a year. Then me Uncle Pat did write to me and told me I must get meself back to England quick like. I got back to Leeds yesterday. Naturally, it being Friday night, I came in for a pint. And what a surprise I did get when Rosie gave me ye letter. I was thunderstruck, if the truth be known." He looked at her quizzically and finished, "Out with it, colleen. Why did ye decide to leave Fairley?"

Emma eyed him a little charily and said quietly, "Before I tell you the reason, Blackie, you must promise me something."

Blackie stared at her, amazed more by the seriousness of her tone rather than her request. "And what might that be?"

Emma met his direct gaze calmly. "You must promise me you won't tell my father, or *anyone*, where I am."

"And why all the secrecy?" Blackie demanded. "Does not ye dad know where ye be?"

"He thinks I'm working in Bradford," Emma explained.

"Ah, Emma, that's not right. Now why would ye not be telling ye dad where ye are?"

"Blackie, you haven't promised me yet," she insisted in her coolest voice.

He sighed. "All right, then, if that's the way ye be wanting it. I swear on the heads of the Blessed Saints that I won't be telling a living soul where ye be."

"Thank you, Blackie." There was a dignified expression on her face and she was not at all nervous or apprehensive as she said, "I had to leave Fairley because I am going to have a baby!"

"Jaysus!" Blackie exploded in stunned disbelief. "A baby!" he repeated, mouthing the word as if it were foreign to his tongue.

"Yes, in March," Emma informed him calmly, "and I had to leave because the boy, that is the father, well, he let me down."

"He did what!" Blackie bellowed, his face growing scarlet. "By God, I'll thrash the living daylights out of him! I will that. We will go to Fairley tomorrow and see ye dad and his dad. And by God he'll marry ye if I've got to beat him to a pulp to get him to the church!"

"Hush, Blackie," Emma said. She could see he was in the grip of a terrible fury. "It's no use, Blackie. When I told the boy the way it was, he said he *would* marry me. That I shouldn't worry. But then do you know what he did, that very night?"

"No, mavourneen, I cannot be imagining," muttered Blackie through clenched teeth. For the first time in his life he felt the desire to kill. The idea that anyone would abuse Emma enraged him to a point of madness.

Emma had been watching Blackie very carefully and she said softly, "He did a terrible thing, Blackie. *He ran away*. To join the Royal Navy. Fancy that!" Her eyes were large and her voice was low. "He took a leaf out of my *own* brother's notebook," she went on, "he copied Winston and did a moonlight flit. Just like that. When he didn't come to the Hall to see me, as he had promised, I went down to the village to see him. It was then his dad told me that he had run off. He even showed me the note the boy had left." She shook her head. "What could I do, Blackie? I couldn't tell his dad. And I certainly couldn't tell mine. So I ran away to Leeds."

"But perhaps ye dad would be understanding—" Blackie began, endeavoring to keep his voice steady.

"No, he wouldn't!" Emma cried with alarm, her face paling. She had known he might take this attitude and she must convince him she had to stay in Leeds. "He would be angry and hurt! It would kill him, coming on top of my mother's death. I don't want to take any trouble to my father's doorstep. It's better this way." Emma now softened her voice. "Honestly, Blackie, it is. I *know* my father. He has a terrible temper and there would be a dreadful scandal in the village.

It would ruin my life and the baby's. And my dad's, too. It's best he doesn't know. He couldn't stand the shame."

"Aye, mavourneen, I can see ye point." He stared at her, his face thoughtful. As she had so accurately assessed, he was not at all shocked by her revelation. Surprised, of course. And infuriated with the cowardice of the boy who had got her into trouble and then deserted her. But Blackie was familiar with human weaknesses, especially of the flesh, and he was not one to pass judgment. And yet, as he continued to observe her, he was immensely disturbed. It occurred to him that her story did not sit too well on his shoulders. His native intuition told him there was something terribly wrong with it, although he was not exactly sure what this was. He gave her the most penetrating look. There seemed to be no deception in her face. She was regarding him openly, her eyes innocent, and her lovely face overflowed with sweetness. Blackie pushed back the feelings of disquiet he was experiencing and said, in a controlled tone, "And what will ye do when the baby comes? What will ye do with the baby, Emma?"

"I don't know yet, Blackie. I'll think of something. For the moment I must protect my father—let him continue to believe that I ran away to better myself, that I'm working in Bradford. After the baby's born, of course I shall go and see him, so that he knows I'm really all right. In the meantime I will keep writing to him, and then he won't worry so much." Before Blackie had a chance to make any comment, Emma rushed on to explain about the letters she had sent from Bradford, and also told him everything else that had happened to her in Leeds. She painted a picture that was a trifle rosier than reality.

He gave her all of his attention and, as he listened, Blackie O'Neill began to realize that the change in her ran deeper than her outward appearance. Indefinable and subtle though this difference was, it *was* there, and it had not been wrought simply by the sophisticated upswept hairdo and the elegant clothes, undoubtedly castoffs from the Hall. There was a profound alteration in Emma herself. But that's to be expected, he decided. She's about to become a mother and her experiences of the last few months most certainly would affect her. Then it hit him. Emma was no longer the starveling child of the moors. She was a young woman and a beautiful one at that, and somehow she had managed to transform herself into a lady overnight. No, not overnight. It had been happening gradually over the past year and a half. He recognized that now. He himself had detected the thoroughbred strain in her the day they had met and now it was apparent for all to see. He smiled wryly. That explained Rosie's glowing description of her.

Her musical voice intruded on his thoughts. "The Kallinskis are very nice, and so kind, Blackie. I hope you'll meet them. And I like working in the tailoring trade. I'm doing very well, you know," Emma was saying. "I will be fine in Leeds, Blackie. I know I will."

"Yes, I suppose ye will, Emma. But ye are not looking ahead," he pointed out. "How will ye look after the baby and work as well?" he demanded with fierceness.

Emma gave him a sharp look. "I told you before, I'll think about that problem later! Right now, I have to make money. To keep myself and to save up for the baby coming." She leaned forward and took his hand, squeezing it, hoping to reassure him. "Please don't worry. There's always a solution to everything," she said in a positive voice.

She smiled and her face, so close to his, bewitched him, and once again he became conscious of her as a woman, and his heart beat all the faster. He saw her in a different light than he had ever seen her before.

Without a second thought Blackie said urgently, "I have a solution, Emma! Marry me! Then ye will be safe and secure. I'll take care of ye and the baby, too. Marry me, mavourneen!"

Emma was utterly astounded. She stared at Blackie, quite unable to speak, and for the first time since she had left Fairley she broke down, so moved was she by this loving and unselfish gesture on his part. She lowered her head and the tears spilled down her cheeks and dropped onto her hands fumbling in her bag for her handkerchief. She wiped her eyes and, through her tears, she said tremulously, "Oh, Blackie, how wonderful of you to ask me to marry you! What a *lovely* thing for you to do." She paused and gazed into his burning eyes. "But I couldn't do that. It just wouldn't be fair to hamstring you with a wife, and another man's child. You have your plans, after all. You're going to be that toff, that millionaire. You don't need the responsibility of a family. I couldn't do that to you, Blackie."

Blackie had spoken impulsively, not even certain of his real emotions or his true feelings for Emma, and yet, although he recognized the veracity of what she said, he felt a peculiar stab of disappointment at her refusal. "But ye cannot be by yeself," he persisted, grasping her small hand in his. "Ye would be better off with me, mavourneen. Sure and ye would."

"And what about you, Blackie O'Neill? Would you be better off with me?" She smiled a little timorously, the tears still glistening on her lashes. "No, I think not. I won't do that to you, Blackie. The answer is no. I won't marry you. But thank you anyway. I'm honored and flattered that you would ask me. Really I am, Blackie."

He could see that she was adamant and he was not fully certain whether he was relieved or not. He was filled with a variety of emotions. Nevertheless, he felt compelled to say, "Very well, mavourneen, we won't be discussing it further. At least for the time being. Let's just say me offer is open—indefinitely!"

Emma could not help laughing through her subsiding tears. She shook her head. "Oh, Blackie, what will I do with you!"

His anger was slowly dissipating, his doubts about her story were temporarily forgotten, and he joined in her laughter. After a few moments he said, "I'll tell ye what ye'll do with me, mavourneen mine. Ye'll come and have a bite of supper with me, at one of them fancy cafés I told ye about, and then I'll be taking ye to the City Variéties. Vesta Tilley is appearing tonight and ye'll enjoy the show, I am thinking. Would ye be liking that, Emma? Sure and it'll be grand to be having a bit of fun for a change. What do ye say? Will ye be accepting me invitation, then?"

"Yes, I'd love to come with you. Thank you. Blackie—I—" Emma hesitated and then confessed almost shyly, "I'm glad you're back in Leeds. I feel ever so much better knowing you're around, knowing you're my friend."

Blackie's long Irish upper lip drew back in a warm smile and his white teeth gleamed. "Aye, I am ye friend, Emma," he asserted. "And I'm glad ye confided in me. Now that I be knowing what ye are facing in the next few months I can do a bit of planning, make sure to be around when ye need me. But we won't be talking about ye problems any more tonight. Sure, and we'll face things one by one, as they come along.

Now we are going out on the town! I aim to be showing ye off, Emma, me darlin'."

Emma smiled up at him, her face animated. Thankfully her problems were miraculously retreating now that she was with Blackie. She had felt safe with him from the very first day they had met on the moors and she knew instinctively he would always protect her.

Blackie followed her out of the Saloon Bar and into the main room, which was teeming with people. He could hardly help noticing the masculine heads swiveling to stare, the admiring glances thrown in her direction. He drew himself up to his full height and lifted his head higher. She's a looker, all right, he thought. Why, there isn't a man breathing that wouldn't be proud and delighted to have her by his side. Sure and that's the truth, Blackie decided.

Then Blackie O'Neill stopped dead in his tracks, staring fixedly at her straight back, her delicately tilted head. With a sudden flash of comprehension he perceived why her story had so bothered him earlier. This transformed Emma Harte, gliding ahead of him so gracefully, would never have become involved with one of the loutish boys from the village. *Never*. Such an idea was not only inconceivable but preposterous. Then who is the father of her child? he wondered, completely baffled. He realized it would be unwise to question her tonight. Pushing this new and disturbing thought out of his mind, Blackie arranged a pleasant smile on his face and caught up with Emma. He took her arm and shepherded her out into the street, chatting to her in his vivacious way, striving for a semblance of normality. But his eyes held a reflective light.

THIRTY

Blackie and Emma sat on the tramcar going to Armley. It was a bitter-cold Sunday afternoon early in January of 1906. Emma was huddled in the corner of her seat, her altogether beautiful profile turned to him in chilly silence.

Jesus, Mary, and Joseph! Blackie thought in exasperation. She's so stubborn at times she's positively rigid. He glanced at her out of the corner of his eye and turned away, further dismayed by the obdurate look on her face. He knew better than to utter one word. She had been obstinate in her refusal to take this trip from the first day he had mentioned it two weeks ago. It had taken all of his powers of persuasion and his smooth Irish tongue to get her to agree, and then her acquiescence had been grudging. Sometimes he did not understand Emma at all, and he had long realized that she was an extremely complex young woman with the most pertinacious will it had ever been his misfortune to encounter. On the other hand, he had to acknowledge that she was amazingly intelligent, even brilliant, and gifted in so many ways. And in most instances she was flexible and open to suggestions, thank the Almighty Lord.

Blackie peered at her again. Surprisingly, that stern expression did nothing to mar her beauty. In fact, it seemed to give her a curiously imperious air that was arresting. Today her hair was drawn back and plaited, the plaits forming loops that hung low on her neck, anchored by a large black taffeta bow at the nape. She wore the green-and-black tartan tam-o'-shanter and the matching scarf he had given her for Christmas; the tam-o'-shanter was perched at a jaunty angle, the long scarf wound around her neck and thrown casually over the shoulders of her black wool coat. Her hands, as always clinging tightly to the black reticule, were encased in bottle-green mittens knitted for her by the devoted Rosie. The dark green tones of the scarf and hat suited her admirably and brought out the greenness of her incredible eyes and the alabaster pallor of her flawless complexion. There was no doubt about it. Emma, in these last months of her pregnancy, looked extraordinarily healthy and well cared for, and as immaculately groomed as always.

The tram rumbled out of the city center, heading for Whingate Junction in Armley, a picturesque village perched on a hill, about half an hour's ride away. Blackie sat lost in contemplation, patiently waiting for Emma's mood to change, praying that it would do so before they reached their destination. He would be glad when the baby was born and she could visit Fairley. Although she accepted her pregnancy philosophically and with little visible show of anxiety, Blackie knew she worried excessively about her father and Frank. She had even pressed him into service with the mailing of

. . . just don't

. . . wavering and he grabbed the oppor-
. . . in a positive tone, "Look, all I be asking is that
. . . carefully, and that ye weigh all the odds before
. . . sty decision not to move in with Laura." He took
. . . sturdy hand and squeezed it. "And please be nice
. . . Laura. She's a good friend and I don't want ye to be
acting rude or stuck-up."

Emma flushed and glared at him. "Rude! I'm never rude to
anyone! You know better than that. And I'm not stuck-up
either, Blackie O'Neill."

He realized his mistake too late and, hoping to rectify it,
Blackie said in the suavest of voices, "I know ye don't mean
to be snooty, Emma, me darlin'. But sometimes—well, sometimes ye do give the impression of being—let's say, a bit
hoity-toity."

"I do?" she said wonderingly, frowning and biting her lip.
Emma was flabbergasted at this statement, for she truly did
not know she could be formidable at times. Invariably her
distant manner was engendered by her total preoccupation
with her problems and her numerous plans, and nothing else.
She remained silent, ruminating on what he had said, feeling
mortified.

Sensing that she might be hurt, Blackie remarked gently,
"Ye'll be liking Laura. She's a sweet girl, that she is indeed.

Blackie ~~~~~ her mind. "It see~~~~
dryly. To this remark she had not dergn~~~~
conversation had been terminated.

Blackie stole another look at her, moved close~~~
arm around her shoulders, easing himself up t~~~
seat. "I hope ye'll consider moving to Armley," he~~~
fully, steeling himself for her strong reaction, which,~~~
ingly, was not forthcoming. She remained perfectly still, her
face staring ahead.

Encouraged, Blackie went on, "Ye'll be happier living with
Laura Spencer. Sure and ye will, mavourneen. Now that her
widowed mother is dead she is looking for a paying guest,
someone to share the expense of the house with her. A nice
house it is, too. Small, of course, but cozy and well set up.
Her late father was a foreman at the printing works, and her
mother was a weaver. They had a bit of money and a decent
going-on. It shows in the house, the furnishings and all, and
Laura keeps it beautifully." He paused and searched her face,
proceeding in a cheery tone, "Ye'll be real comfortable there.
And as I told ye afore, Laura can get ye a job at Thompson's
mill in Armley, where she works. I don't know why ye are
being so stubborn about it, Emma."

She swung her head unexpectedly and looked at him intensely, her green eyes flashing. "Because I don't like being
uprooted! I've just learned the tailoring trade and now you

those all-important letters to her dad, badgering him to seek out any of his friends who might be going to London. She was determined to keep up the pretense that she was traveling with her nonexistent Mrs. John Smith, which readily explained her absence from Bradford. As luck would have it, he had been able to oblige her in November and December, when some of his mates from the pub were going south to find work on London's East End docks. They had willingly agreed to post Emma's letters to her father, without asking any embarrassing questions. Blackie had commented to Emma, though. "Ye dad will be wondering why ye don't give him an address, so he's can write to ye," he had pointed out.

"No, he won't," Emma had asserted sharply. "In the November letter I told him I was going to Paris with my lady, and in the December letter I told him I was accompanying her to Italy. As long as he hears from *me*, that's all that matters."

_____ eved her, utterly astonished at the machinations of

_____ ms ye've thought of everything," he said

_____ deigned to respond and the

_____, and put his

_____ to her on the

_____ said care-

_____ surpris-

want me to leave Kallinski's and start working at the mill, learning to weave. It doesn't make sense, Blackie. And besides, I like it at Mrs. Daniel's. She is very kindly these days and I do have the use of her kitchen."

Blackie groaned. "But, Emma, ye'll be having a whole house to share with Laura. Not only that, she lives just ten minutes away from Thompson's mill. At present ye spend three quarters of an hour walking to Kallinski's in the morning and the same amount of time to be getting home at night. It's a lot of walking in this raw weather. Even the Kallinskis see the sense of what I be suggesting, and David told me the other day that they will be happy to take ye back, after the bairn is born. So what do ye have to lose? Nothing, I am thinking." He sighed wearily. "Ye are a willful, headstrong girl, Emma, and all I am wanting is what's best for ye."

Emma recognized the practicality of what he was suggesting, but for once in her life she was indecisive. "I know—"

Blackie now saw th_____ tunity, saying _____ ye *consider* it_____ ye make a ha_____ hold of he_____ with L_____

And I know she will be liking ye, Emma. Sure and she will, mavourneen."

"*I'm* not so sure about that, in view of what you've just said," Emma countered.

Blackie laughed a little shamefacedly. "Now let's be forgetting that. All ye have to be doing is exercise a bit of that remarkable charm ye be possessing in such abundance, and everything will be fine." He squeezed her hand again and went on, "Armley is a grand little spot and very safe. 'Tis especially pretty in summer when the trees and flowers are blooming. There's Armley Park where the brass band plays every Sunday and other pleasant lanes and thoroughfares where ye can be taking a stroll. Also, St. Mary's Hospital is nearby, and ye could be having the bairn there, when ye time comes. And there are plenty of shops, so ye won't be having to venture into Leeds for owt. Why, ye have everything ye be needing in Armley."

Emma looked at him alertly. "Shops," she said thoughtfully. "But I thought Armley was a tiny village. There can't be *that* many shops, Blackie."

"Oh, aye, there are, mavourneen. Ye see, Armley is spread out, so to speak. It be quite large really. There are a lot of fine homes. Mansions, in fact, where the posh folk live. Millowners and the like. There are a number of good shops in Town Street catering to the Quality trade. I've seen 'em, when I've been visiting Laura afore. Ye'll have a chance to look at 'em yeself, when we walk down the main street to get to Laura's house."

"What sort of shops?" Emma pressed, her eyes turned on him with fierce interest.

Aware that he had now captured her complete attention and observing the change in her attitude, Blackie spoke excitedly, hoping to sway her further. "Well, let me be thinking. There be grocers, butchers, and greengrocers, all on Town Street, along with a pork butcher's shop, an off-license, a fishmonger's, Keene's dairy, a chemist, and a newsagent. I've also noticed a draper's, a haberdasher's, a shoe store, and a fine ladies' dress establishment as well, mavourneen. It is quite an active thoroughfare, almost as busy as Briggate, indeed it is. Why, I think there are shops selling practically everything, Emma."

Emma had listened carefully and she was rapidly reversing

her preconceived ideas about sharing Laura Spencer's house. "Tell me more about the village," she said. "For instance, how big is it? How many people live there?"

"Ah, Emma, me love, now ye have me. I must be confessing I don't know its exact size, or how many people reside in Armley. But it must be a goodly number, I am thinking, for the shops do a brisk business. Then again, there are several churches and chapels and quite a few schools, so there must be plenty of folk in the vicinity. Yes, it is a thriving place, sure and it is. Laura told me there is a public library and Liberal, Conservative, and Workingmen's clubs. Why, there is even a jail in Armley. Horrible dungeon of a place, it is, by the looks of it." Blackie winked at her. "There are lots of pubs, too. I meself know at least six personally."

Emma laughed for the first time since they had set out. "*You* would know that."

"And what's wrong with a young spalpeen liking a pint of bitter now and then and an occasional noggin of good Irish?" Blackie asked jestingly, adopting an injured air. Then he tugged on her arm urgently. "Come on, mavourneen! Here we are. Ye can be seeing Armley for yeself."

The tram had stopped at the terminus halfway up the hill. Blackie jumped down agilely and helped Emma to alight. "Careful now, love. It's pretty bad underfoot. I don't want ye to be having a spill and upsetting Tinker Bell," he said, clasping her hands tightly in his.

"Tinker Bell?"

"Aye, Tinker Bell. That's what I be calling the baby, to meself of course. Ye know, after Tinker Bell in *Peter Pan*. Don't ye approve of me name for her?"

She laughed. "Yes, I do, Blackie. But how do you *know* it will be a girl?"

"Because ye keep telling me it will be." Blackie tucked her arm through his, pushed his hands into the pockets of his new navy-blue overcoat, and said, "That's the Towers up there, where the rich folk live." He inclined his head toward a splendid driveway lined with trees. "And Town Street is just ahead of us. Now watch ye step. It's slippery today."

"Yes, I will, Blackie." She drew closer to him, shivering. The north wind gusting down the hill was laden with frost and biting. Emma looked up. The sky was a frozen canopy soaring above them, icily white, and the pale winter sun was hardly visible, a tiny silver coin thrown negligently up into the far corner of that vast and hollow firmament. It was oddly silent now that the tram had stopped, for there were no carriages out or people abroad on this bleak and cheerless Sunday.

"There's Charley Cake Park," Blackie informed her, his head swiveling to the triangular-shaped plot on the opposite side of the road. "It'll be a nice little place for ye to sit in the summer with Tinker Bell, watching the passers-by."

"I won't have any time to sit anywhere with any Tinker Bell," Emma retorted, although this was said in a mild tone. She looked up at him skeptically. "Charley Cake Park! What kind of name is that? I bet you made it up."

"Now, why is it ye always challenge everything I be saying? I shall have to call ye Doubting Emma if ye are not careful, me lass. Anyway, that's the name, sure and it is. Laura told me that years ago a man called Charley hawked cakes there and that's how it—"

"Got its name," Emma finished for him, her eyes full of merriment. "I believe you, Blackie. Nobody could invent a name like that."

He grinned, but said nothing, and they walked on in silence. Emma glanced about her with considerable interest. They were now passing a neat row of houses facing onto Town Street. It reminded her of a scene from a fairy tale. Immense pie-like wedges of powdery snow slid across the red rooftops and hung precariously at the edges, and dripping from the gutters were countless icicles, shimmering scintillas of spun sugar in that pellucid air. Magically, the snow and ice had turned the mundane little dwellings into quaint gingerbread houses. The fences and the gates and the bare black trees were also encrusted with frozen snowflakes that, to Emma, resembled the silvery decorations on top of a magnificent Christmas cake. Paraffin lamps and firelight glowed through the windows and eddying whiffs of smoke drifted out of the chimneys, but these were the only signs of life on Town Street. The houses looked snug and inviting, and Emma imagined a happy family in each one; parents lazily warming themselves in front of the lambent flames, rosy-cheeked children at their feet, eating apples and oranges and roasting chestnuts, all of them laughing and enjoying a peaceful afternoon together, surrounded by love. She thought with a terrible yearning of her father and Frank and she wished with fervency that she was sitting with them in front of the fire in the little cottage in Fairley.

"Now, Emma, here are the first of the shops," Blackie announced, his voice booming out in the stillness. "They go all the way down Town Street to Branch Road. Look, mavourneen, did I not tell ye the truth?"

Emma followed the direction of his gaze, her eyes wide with excitement, her sadness pushed to one side. "Yes, you did," she conceded. They passed the fishmonger's, the haberdasher's, the chemist's, and the grand ladies' dress establishment, and Emma recognized that this was indeed a fine shopping area. She was enormously intrigued and an idea was germinating. It will be easier to get a shop here. Rents will be cheaper than in Leeds, she reasoned logically. Maybe I can open my first shop in Armley, after the baby comes. And it would be a start. She was so enthusiastic about this idea that by the time they reached the street where Laura Spencer lived she already had the shop and was envisioning its diverse merchandise. Blackie might call her Doubting Emma, but she certainly had no doubts about one thing—her ultimate success. Her first shop *would* be in Armley and she would assiduously court the carriage trade. That was where the money was. Blackie had said so himself.

They walked along the street of terrace houses, all of them neat and respectable with their green painted doors, shining windows, trim gardens, and black iron gates. Just before they reached Laura Spencer's house a thought struck Emma. She stopped and grabbed Blackie's arm. "What have you told Laura about me?" she asked.

Blackie gazed down at her, a faintly surprised look on his face. "Why, exactly what ye told me to tell her," he responded quietly. "The same story ye told everybody, right down to the last detail, *Mrs.* Harte, sailor's wife, expectant mother, dear friend of Blackie O'Neill." Emma smiled with relief and nodded, and they went up the garden path together. She wondered what Laura was like, but in a sense that hardly mattered to her. The important thing was that *she* made a good impression on Laura.

Emma now realized that Blackie had confided very little about his friend and she did not know what to expect as they stood on the front step. She certainly wasn't prepared for the girl who opened the door and greeted them so charmingly, and with undisguised delight. Laura Spencer had the shining and tranquil face of a Madonna, and there was an expression of such trust in her eyes, and her smile was so loving, and so sweet, it was at once apparent to Emma that she was confronting someone who was unquestionably different from anyone else she had ever met.

Laura ushered them into the house, exclaiming on the rawness of the weather, sympathizing about the long cold journey they had just endured, her genuine concern for their well-being obvious. She took their coats, scarves, and Emma's tam-o'-shanter and hung them on the hatstand near the door, and then drew them into the parlor, moving with infinite grace as she led them to chairs grouped around a roaring fire.

Now Laura took hold of Emma's hands as she said, "I'm so happy to meet you, Emma. Blackie has told me such lovely things about you. Goodness, your hands are cold! Sit here and get the chill out of your bones, dear."

Emma said, "I'm glad to meet you, too, Laura." Without appearing to rudely scrutinize the room Emma swiftly took in the subdued blue-and-white-striped wallpaper, the heavy blue velvet curtains at the windows, the few pieces of mahogany furniture, scant but gleaming with beeswax, and the attractiveness of the other furnishings. The room was small but neat, and not at all cluttered like Mrs. Daniel's hideous front parlor. An air of solidness and comfort prevailed.

Laura said to them both apologetically, "I am so sorry I wasn't all prepared for you, but I had to visit a sick friend and I was delayed longer than I anticipated. I just got in a little while before you arrived. Anyway, the tea will be ready shortly, and the kettle's boiling."

Blackie said, "That's all right, Laura. Don't fuss yeself. We're in no hurry, so take ye time, love." This was uttered so softly and so temperately Emma's eyes flew to Blackie with quickening interest. She discerned a marked difference in his demeanor, which was restrained, and there was a look of mingled gentleness and respect on his face. This did not surprise Emma. She had already perceived that Laura's refined manner was bound to bring out the best in other people.

"Please excuse me for a moment or two," Laura continued in her soft voice, placing the remainder of the china on the table. "I have a few last-minute things to do in the kitchen."

Blackie and Emma murmured their assent and Blackie said, "Do ye mind if I smoke me pipe, Laura?" She was halfway across the floor and she turned and shook her head, her eyes filling with laughter. "No, of course not. Please make yourself at home, and you too, Emma."

From her vantage point near the fireplace, Emma could see Laura in the small kitchen that adjoined the parlor. She was wearing a pale blue woolen dress with a full skirt, long sleeves, and a large white Quaker collar, and although the dress was a little worn and darned in places, its simplicity and pristine colors added to the impression of immaculateness and virtue she conveyed. She's beautiful, Emma thought, intrigued by the tall, slender girl who appeared to be surrounded by an aura of spirituality.

Laura Spencer's features were so classically drawn, so fragile, and the bones were so fine, her face seemed attenuated at times. There were those, who were undiscerning, who considered her plain and faded and they would not have agreed with Emma at all. But Emma saw the Dresden china-like delicacy of the features that contributed so much to her exquisiteness, saw the golden lights in her honey-colored hair that gave it a shimmering iridescence, saw the tenderness and wisdom that filled the enormous hazel eyes with a radiant luminosity. And she recognized Laura's loveliness for what it truly was—an outward reflection of purity.

Emma was not wrong in these assessments. There *was* indeed something special about Laura Spencer. Very simply, she refused to countenance evil. Laura was a Roman Catholic and unwavering in her faith; her religion, which she never discussed or inflicted on her friends, was the mainspring of her life. To Laura, God was neither nebulous nor remote. His presence was constant, eternal and everlasting.

Sitting there in that cozy parlor, listening to Laura's light voice echoing out from the kitchen, Emma was not yet entirely aware of all of this. But somehow, in some curious fashion, Laura's inner grace had mysteriously communicated itself to her, and she was experiencing a sense of peace so profound she was startled. Emma continued to gaze at Laura and she thought: *I want her to be my friend. I want her to like me. I want to share this house with her.*

"Ye are very quiet, mavourneen," Blackie said. "That's a

bit unusual for ye, I am thinking. Ye are generally such a chatterbox."

Emma jumped. He had startled her. "I was just thinking," she responded. Blackie smiled and puffed on his pipe. Emma was just as captivated by Laura as he had anticipated, and he was delighted.

"Could you bring the kettle into the kitchen, please, Blackie," Laura called, "so I can mash the tea."

"Sure and I can, mavourneen," he exclaimed. He lifted the steaming copper kettle off the hob and strode across the room, a towering bulk in that small space.

"Can I do anything?" Emma inquired eagerly, also rising.

Laura looked around the kitchen door. "No, thank you, Emma. It's all ready now." Within seconds she came into the parlor carrying a large tray containing plates of food and Blackie followed with the teapot.

As she sat down, Emma thought how nicely Laura had arranged the table. "You are very artistic, Laura. The table looks lovely," Emma volunteered. She smiled at Laura, who seemed pleased at this shyly offered compliment.

"Aye, 'tis a feast fit for kings, sure and it is," Blackie said, also regarding the table. "But ye shouldn't have made such a spread or gone to all this trouble, Laura. Ye have enough to do with all ye church work and charities."

"It was no bother, Blackie. You know I like cooking. And I enjoy having visitors. Now, come along. Help yourselves. You must both be hungry after that chilly trip from Leeds. I'm sure you've worked up an appetite, Blackie."

"Aye, I have that," he responded, and helped himself to a sandwich. Something of Blackie's natural exuberance flowed to the surface during the tea and he kept the girls giggling at his stories, as was his artful way when he wanted to be entertaining. The actor in him could never be suppressed for long, and he became so volatile neither Emma nor Laura could get a word in edgewise. Laura, however, did respond swiftly to some of his more outrageous pronouncements, and Emma realized this gentle girl was blessed with a sense of humor in spite of her basic seriousness, and that mild manner belied a stringent wit.

For her part, Laura Spencer was impressed with Emma. She had been initially startled by her striking beauty, but while she had prepared the tea, Laura had observed her discreetly, and she had quickly become aware of the younger girl's pleasant yet dignified manner. She had also detected the intelligence in those matchless green eyes and the refinement in the oval face. Blackie had told her that Emma lived in a small uncomfortable attic and spent hours walking to and from work. He was worried about her health. And no wonder, Laura thought. She needs a little mothering at a time like this: seven months pregnant and utterly alone. She was filled with a rush of sisterly warmth for Emma.

As the tea progressed, Blackie pondered about the two girls who flanked him at the tea table. He loved them both, albeit in wholly different ways, and he was gratified that they had taken a liking to each other. He had known they would, even though they were exact opposites physically, and in temperament. He stole a look at Laura, who was wiping her vulnerable mouth with her serviette. There she was, all porcelain fragility, retiring, spiritual Laura, who was utterly selfless in so many ways. He glanced at Emma out of the corner of his eye. Next to Laura's gentle loveliness, Emma's beauty seemed fierce and wild; there was something frightening about her, and he had long suspected she might turn out to be ruthless and expedient, if that was ever necessary. And yet, in spite of their intrinsic difference, they shared several common traits—integrity, courage, and compassion. Perhaps those things will bind them in friendship, he thought. Also, even though Laura, at twenty-one, was only a few years older than Emma, Blackie believed she would look after her in an affectionate and motherly way. Likewise, he sensed that Emma's spirited and vivacious presence in the house would help to assuage the loneliness Laura had felt since her mother's death four months ago. He hoped so.

Emma was talking enthusiastically to Laura about the tailoring trade and Kallinski's workshop, and her vibrant voice caught his attention. Blackie turned to look at Emma. In the roseate glow of the parlor her animated face blazed with life. Her looks would blind any man, he said to himself. Then he wondered, as he had so often lately, who it was she had blinded seven or eight months ago. He still had not dared to ask her who the father of her child really was. He crushed down on that disturbing thought and turned his attention to the matter at hand—how to broach the subject of Emma moving in with Laura, and going to work at Thompson's mill.

Almost as if she had read his mind, he heard Laura say, "You sound as if you really love the tailoring trade, Emma. And you've certainly mastered it quickly, from what I hear. I'm sure you would have no trouble learning to weave—" Laura paused, as always not wanting to appear presumptuous or forward.

"Is weaving very difficult?" Emma asked cautiously.

"No, not really. Not when you've got the hang of it and understand the process. I don't think *you* would find it hard, Emma. Honestly I don't."

Emma glanced swiftly at Blackie and then turned back to Laura and said, "Can you get me a job at Thompson's? Are you *sure?*"

"Yes, I am positive!" Laura exclaimed. "I spoke to the foreman the other day, and you can start any time you want. They are looking for new girls to train. You'd go on the looms right away, as a learner, of course."

Emma pondered this for a split second and made up her mind. She plunged right in. "Would you be willing to let me share the house with you, Laura? I won't be any trouble and I'll pay my way." Her gaze did not stray from Laura.

Laura's angelic face broke into a delighted smile and her fine hazel eyes lit up. "Of course, Emma. I would love to have you. Anyway, I can't really afford to keep this house on alone, but I am reluctant to give it up. I've lived here most of my life. Apart from that, you would be wonderful company for me. I've been looking for someone congenial and pleasant like you." She leaned forward and squeezed Emma's arm affectionately, and in a reassuring way. "And also, I think you would be better off here with me, what with the baby due in two months. I can look after you, Emma. And I know Blackie agrees—"

"I do that!" interjected Blackie, pleased with the turn of events.

"Do let me show you the rest of the house, and the room you would have, Emma," Laura suggested. She led the way up the steep and narrow staircase. Laura opened a door on the landing. "This would be yours, Emma," she announced with a bright smile. She swept in ahead of them and lighted a candle on the dresser.

"Now, isn't this nice and comfy!" Blackie stated, hovering in the doorway. He pushed Emma forward.

Emma looked back at him. "Yes, it is," she said. Taking up most of the space was a large brass bed covered with a patchwork quilt. The walls were white, and there was even a clipped rug on the floor by the bed.

"This was my parents' room," Laura said. She then added, rather shyly, "I thought you would like it, Emma. Since it's large, and has a double bed, your husband could stay here when he's home on leave." Emma opened her mouth and instantly shut it when she saw Blackie's face.

Blackie said, "Er—er—well, he's not due to come home for a long while yet. A *very* long while. He's at sea. So, we don't have to be worrying about that!" He looked around, desperately wondering how to change the subject, and continued rapidly, in a rush of words, "Now, Emma, do ye not see that space over there by the window? Between the wardrobe and the washstand? Ye could be fixing up a sewing table there and making the dresses for the ladies, like ye said ye wanted to. Laura wouldn't be minding. Would ye, Laura, me love?" He hoped he had managed to avert an awkward discussion about that damned imaginary husband of Emma's.

"No, not at all. It won't disturb me." Laura glanced at Emma, who was surveying the room, a crease still puckering her smooth brow. Laura thought with dismay: Oh, dear. She doesn't like the house. But being unwilling to influence Emma in any way, she was prompted to say, "It's a bit cold up here. Shall we go downstairs? You can let me know later, Emma. You don't have to make up your mind now."

Emma saw the flicker of consternation on Laura's face and she grasped her arm. "I like the room! Really I do! I would love to share the house with you. That is, if I can afford it, Laura."

The three of them trooped back to the parlor. Blackie threw logs onto the fire and Laura got out her housekeeping accounts book. She joined Blackie and Emma in front of the hearth. "The rent is four shillings a week, so your half would be two shillings, Emma. Then there is the cost of the logs and the coal in winter and the paraffin for the lamps. If you could split that with me I would be most grateful. Altogether, it will come to about five shillings a week in winter. But it will be less in summer."

"Five shillings!" Emma exclaimed.

Laura stared at her, a worried expression flooding her eyes again. "Oh, dear. Is that too much? Perhaps I can—"

"No, it's not too much," Emma interrupted. "I expected it to be more. It's certainly very fair. Why, I pay three shillings a week for the attic at Mrs. Daniel's."

Laura looked at Emma askance, and Blackie roared, "I always told ye that bloody woman was robbing ye blind, and ye wouldn't pay no mind to me! Ah, Emma! Ye should have moved in with Laura weeks ago, like I was begging ye to."

"Hush, Blackie. Don't get so excited," Laura said lightly but with firmness. She handed the housekeeping book to Emma. "You can see all the figures for yourself. I want you to know what everything costs."

Emma did not want to take the book, but Laura forced it on her. She gave it the most cursory of glances, for she knew this girl would not attempt to make money out of her. After a moment she handed it back. "Laura, please! I don't have to go through all these figures. I know you are scrupulous. In fact, maybe you are not charging me enough. I don't want you to be out of pocket."

Laura said, "Yes, it is enough. Really it is." She returned the accounts book to the sideboard drawer and went on, "Did Blackie tell you that you're not paid for the first month, while you are learning to weave?" Emma nodded. Laura cleared her throat and looked at Emma carefully, then she said, "Well, for that first month you don't have to pay me anything."

"No, I can't do that. It wouldn't be right," Emma cried.

Laura was adamant. "I will not take money from you when you're not earning, Emma." The older girl saw the immense pride flaring on Emma's face and, understanding that she did not want to accept charity, and not wishing to embarrass her further, Laura remarked quietly, "Just give me the two shillings for the rent. That's a happy medium." Emma reluctantly agreed, so as not to offend Laura, although she was determined to pay her the whole of the five shillings. She would take it out of her savings.

"It's all settled, then. Emma will move in next Saturday. I shall bring her meself, sure and I will!" declared Blackie, now taking charge. He beamed at them both. "Ye see, I was right all along. I knew it would work out and that ye would be liking each other."

Emma smiled but made no comment. She was happy she

had made the decision to move to Armley, to share Laura Spencer's house. A strange pervading sense of peace settled over her again, and she relaxed in the chair, feeling suddenly at ease and more sure of the future than she had been for a long time. Everything was going to be all right. She knew that now. Emma was not aware of it at that moment, but she was never to forget that first encounter with Laura Spencer as long as she lived. Over the years she grew to realize that Laura was the only truly good person she had ever known, and she loved her deeply.

The following Friday Emma said a sad farewell to her fellow workers at the tailoring shop, who were sorry to see her leave, and to all of the Kallinskis, with whom she had Sabbath dinner at Janessa's insistence. After dinner Janessa took Emma to one side. "I want you to promise me that you will come to me if you need anything in the next few months," she said. "Armley is not so far away and I can soon be there."

"Oh, Mrs. Kallinski, that's lovely of you. Thank you. I promise I will."

It was a tearful parting and only David seemed undismayed. He knew their paths would cross again. He intended to make sure of that. Emma gave him her address in Armley and he extracted a faithful promise from her to write as soon as she was settled. Even Mrs. Daniel had tears in her eyes when Emma left and she, too, asked her to stay in touch.

On Monday morning Laura took her to Thompson's mill. From the moment she entered it, Emma hated that place as fiercely as she had loved Abraham Kallinski's little factory. No camaraderie here. No jokes and laughter. Rigid discipline reigned, and the gaffers were harsh and demanding as they walked up and down between the looms. Emma instantly loathed the stench of the oily raw wool and was deafened by the unceasing rattling of the shuttles; on her third day there she was totally unnerved when she witnessed a shuttle fly off and strike a girl in the face, scarring her for life, an accident that was not unusual.

Laura was a good teacher, patient and explicit in her instructions; nevertheless, Emma found the weaving process difficult and she was terrified of getting a "trap," which occurred when a hundred or so threads broke on the loom. A "trap" took hours to repair. These were precious hours lost, and the weaver had to work furiously to make up the lost time. But Emma was careful and she never did have a "trap" as long as she worked at the mill.

In her diligent way she persevered, for she was determined that nothing was going to get the better of her; she also knew she had no alternative but to prove herself a competent weaver in order to earn a living. With her single-mindedness, her fast mind and nimble fingers, she mastered the craft of weaving within the month, as Laura had predicted she would. Her self-confidence grew as her expertise increased, yet she still disliked working in that cheerless and rigidly controlled environment.

She and Laura started at six o'clock in the morning and finished at six at night, interminable and dreary days to Emma. As the weeks dragged on she grew heavier with child and increasingly weary and exhausted. To her dismay, her legs continually swelled up from standing long hours at the loom, and she often thought that the baby would be born right there at her feet on the mill floor. However, Laura was a great comfort to her and Emma constantly marveled at her good humor, and she never ceased to wonder what she would have done without Laura's staunch support and her devotion.

One Tuesday evening, towards the end of March, Emma knew the baby was coming and Laura took her into St. Mary's Hospital at Hill Top. After ten hours in labor she gave birth to her child, exactly one month to the day before her own seventeenth birthday. To Emma's joy it was a girl.

THIRTY-ONE

Emma sat in front of the fire in the parlor of Laura's house, staring morosely into space, her mind weighted down with a problem; a problem that pushed all else to one side. She had lived with it for the last few days, ever since the baby had been born. Now she knew it must be solved, and imminently. Emma had many imperatives, but taking precedence was her concern for her child. It was essential that she make a decision about the baby's immediate future. She could not afford to procrastinate.

Emma shivered, suddenly aware of a coldness in her legs, a numbing aching in her bones. She bestirred herself heavily, not as swift of movement as usual, picked up the poker and drove it into the logs in the fireplace, angrily, as if to "vent" her sense of helplessness. The logs fell apart, spurted, and flooded the room with the brightest of lights that illuminated its shining neatness, its cozy comfort.

The light glanced across the child lying at her feet in the makeshift cot, which Laura had fashioned out of a drawer and had lined with thick blankets and downy pillows. The baby lay on her side, her fluff of silver-blond hair shimmering in the firelight, her round pink face turned to Emma, her tiny hand curled in a miniature fist next to her delicate mouth. She slept in perfect peace. This child was hers. *Part of her*. How could she ever give her up? Quite unexpectedly, a fierce sense of protectiveness invaded Emma and that single-mindedness of purpose to succeed, to rise above her circumstances, was strongly reinforced. "I won't let anything happen to you!" she whispered softly but with vehemence to the sleeping child. "I won't! And you'll have the best that money can buy. I promise you that!"

Emma continued to observe her daughter, now four days old, for a few moments longer and then she turned back to the fire. *No sacrifice she could ever make would be too great if it ensured the security and well-being of her baby*. Eventually she picked up the flannel nightgown she was making, determined not to dwell on the future. She began to sew. One step at a time. One day at a time. Slowly. Slowly. Building as you go along. That is the only way.

As she continued to ply her perfect stitches, an aura of total dejection, abnormal for Emma, enveloped her. She knew she could not keep the baby with her, even though she longed to do so. She had to work at the mill to earn a living and there was no one available to care for the child during the day. Emma would not countenance the idea of adoption or an orphanage. There was only one other solution. Emma was not particularly happy about this alternative; however, she had come to the realization, after several sleepless nights, that she really had no choice. She turned the problem of the baby over in her mind yet again, wrestling with the advantages and disadvantages of the scheme she had concocted, diverse thoughts racing through her head as swiftly as her needle flew along the hem of the nightgown.

"Hello! Hello! Anybody home?"

Startled, Emma looked up quickly. The door had opened to admit Blackie O'Neill. It was a brisk March day outside and the wind had whipped the rosiest of tints into his perennially tanned cheeks and ruffled his black hair into a mass of dancing curls. He had a happy-go-lucky air about him and, to Emma, he seemed considerably pleased with himself. He was carrying several packages.

"Blackie! I didn't expect you so soon!" Emma exclaimed in surprise. She put down the sewing and stood up, automatically smoothing her immaculate hair.

Blackie grinned and deposited the parcels on the table. He pulled Emma to him and wrapped his huge arms around her, hugging her tightly, and with a show of great affection. "Well, ye be looking the picture of health and beauty after ye confinement," he remarked, staring at her appraisingly. Emma forced a smile, attempting to conceal her disquiet, but she said nothing. Seemingly unconscious of her dispirited mood, Blackie went on enthusiastically, "I brought a few presents for the bairn. Trifles ye might be liking," He indicated the items on the table.

"Oh, Blackie, you're too generous! You *mustn't* spend all your money on the baby. You bought the shawl only the other week."

"That's what money is for, I am thinking. To be spent." He shrugged out of his topcoat and went to hang it on the stand in the doorway. "Me and me Uncle Pat are doing better than ever. We got three important jobs this week, and we'll be having to take on more men. Aye, success is in the air for the O'Neills." He turned and winked at Emma. "Anyway, I had a bit of a windfall yesterday, so to speak. Backed the winner at Doncaster races. That I did, mavourneen. I had a pound each way, at twenty to one, and made quite a bundle. So, this morning, I thought to meself: Since ye are a flush boyo this week, with a bit of extra money in ye pocket, Blackie O'Neill, ye must be sharing ye good fortune with Emma. And I took meself off at once to Briggate and bought a few things for me darlin' Tinker Bell."

"I'm glad you won, Blackie. But shouldn't you be saving

your money so you can build that grand house you're always talking about?" suggested the pragmatic Emma.

Blackie was amused. He shrugged. "I'll be having me Georgian house one day, Emma. And the few shillings I've spent today won't be making all that much difference." He lowered his enormous frame and knelt on the floor next to the cot. He peeped at the baby. "And isn't she the most darlin' thing!" He smoothed the cot blanket with infinite care. "A little cherub, sure and she is." The baby moved and opened her eyes, blinking her long silvery lashes. She gurgled and kicked her legs under the coverlet. Blackie's eyes lit up. "Look, mavourneen! I do believe she be recognizing her Uncle Blackie already. Sure and she does!"

"It seems she does. And she is a sweet baby, Blackie, and good, too. She hasn't cried at all since I've been home from St. Mary's Hospital." Emma now glanced at the table. "Thank you for the presents, Blackie."

"Hush!" cried Blackie, straightening up. "Come on, Emma. Open them. Start with this." He handed her the largest package. Emma sat down in the chair and unwrapped it. "Why, Blackie, this is just lovely," she exclaimed, lifting out a pink knitted coat trimmed with pink ribbons.

Blackie beamed. "Here's the bonnet and a pair of booties to match," he said, offering her another parcel. "I hope they will all be fitting her. I had to be guessing the size, since I'm not accustomed to buying things for such a wee mite." He looked at Emma anxiously. "Do you think they are all right, then?"

"They are perfect. *Really perfect*. Thank you, Blackie."

"Unwrap this. It's the last," he said "Not as practical as the coat and bonnet, I am thinking. But necessary, in a way. Tinker Bell has to have a few toys, ye know, mavourneen."

Emma pulled the paper off excitedly and held up the fluffy white lamb which sported a large pink bow and a bell at its neck. "Oh, isn't it sweet! And you bought a rattle as well." She shook the polished bone ring, which also had a bell attached, and then placed the lamb and the rattle in the cot next to the baby. She stood up and kissed Blackie. "Thank you, Blackie. You're so good to us." Emma was touched by his thoughtfulness and the obvious care he had taken in selecting the clothes and the toys.

"Aay, it's nothing at all, me love," he said, and glanced around. "And where might Laura be?"

"There's a jumble sale at the Catholic church this afternoon and she's looking after one of the stalls. She'll be back in time for tea. You are staying, aren't you? We expected you to."

"Sure and I am." He settled himself in the chair opposite Emma and fished around in his pocket for his cigarettes. After he had lit one he said, "And when do ye have to go back to the mill, mavourneen?"

Emma did not answer for a moment and then she lifted her head slowly. "I can please myself. The foreman told Laura I could have the whole week off, after I came out of hospital. We're not so busy right now, and it doesn't matter to the mill either way, since I'm paid by the piece. They don't have to pay my wage when I'm not working."

"Are ye going to take next week off? I think ye should," Blackie remarked, eyeing her closely.

"So does Laura. She worries about my health. But I feel very well. I do really, Blackie. I could go back on Monday but—" Her voice trailed off and she examined the sewing, finishing thoughtfully, "I don't think I will, though. I've things to do next week." Emma dropped her eyes, not elucidating further. Blackie did not want to pry, knowing this would irritate her. Emma was not always given to making confidences, and he had learned not to question her unduly.

After a moment Emma said, "So business is good, is it?"

"Aye, it is, colleen! And do ye know, I am drawing up me first plans for me first house, one of me own design." He laughed wryly. "Well, it's not a *whole* house, just a wing we are to build onto an existing house for a customer in Headingley. The gentleman that owns it, a real toff I might be adding, liked me ideas, and he told me to go ahead and to be making me plans. Them night-school classes in draftsmanship are going to be paying off. Ye'll see, mavourneen."

"That's wonderful, Blackie."

This was said somewhat listlessly, and Blackie was at once aware of her closed face, her obvious lack of interest. He studied her carefully and saw the dark glint in her green eyes, the grim expression on her lips. No, not grim. Miserable, he decided. He wondered what was disturbing her, but again refrained from asking any questions. As he continued to expound about the wing of the house he was to design and build, Blackie continued to watch her out of the corner of his eye. Finally he could not prevent himself saying, "Why are ye looking so gloomy, me love? That's not like ye." She did not respond. "Nay, Emma, ye've got a face like a wet week. What's upsetting ye?"

"Oh, nothing, really—" She hesitated and then blurted out against her will, "I'm a bit concerned about the baby not being christened."

Blackie was flabbergasted. He stared at her uncomprehendingly and threw back his head and roared with laughter. Emma looked hurt, but he could not help it. "Concerned about the baby not being christened!" he echoed, trying to swallow the last of his merriment. "I can't believe me own ears, Emma. Why should that matter to ye? After all, ye've been telling me for months that ye are an atheist."

"I am! I haven't changed my mind about *that*," Emma cried. "But I don't feel right about it. Not having her christened. The baby might believe in God when she grows up, and then she might hold it against me if she ever finds out she wasn't baptized."

He could see she was in real earnest and so he said, "Why don't ye go to see the vicar of Christ Church and arrange—"

"Oh, I couldn't do that," Emma interjected harshly, fixing him with a cold stare. "The vicar would want her birth certificate, that's customary, and he'd see straightaway that the baby is—is—illegitimate, and then he wouldn't do it. Besides, I don't want him, or anyone else, knowing my business."

"Well, Emma, if ye don't go to Christ Church, I don't know what ye can do. There's no solution I can think of. Ye can't have her christened, and that's that!"

"Yes, I know. I wouldn't have mentioned it to you if you hadn't asked me why I was gloomy. And you're right, there's nothing to be done. I shall just have to hope the baby isn't angry with me one day."

If the child's ever angry it will be about her illegitimacy and not her baptism, or rather, lack of it, Blackie thought. But he said, "Ye are such a contradiction, mavourneen mine. But look here, Emma, if it's that important to ye, why don't we take the baby to a church in another part of Leeds? One where ye are not likely to be knowing anybody, and have her christened there. Then it won't matter about anybody seeing the birth certificate."

"No! No! I don't want a soul to know she's illegitimate," Emma snapped.

Suddenly an idea occurred to Blackie. A marvelous idea. "I've got it! We'll have our own christening! Right here and now!" He leapt up and strode purposefully to the sink in the kitchen. "Leeds Corporation water is as good as any for a baptism, I am thinking," he shouted gaily. "Bring me a bowl."

"What do you mean by 'have our own christening?' I don't understand." Her brow puckered into a frown.

"Since ye are so troubled about the bairn not being baptized, I meself am going to do it. *Now*. Bring her over to the sink. Come on," he urged, standing in the kitchen doorway.

Total disbelief flickered onto Emma's face. "You do it! But would it be proper? Would it be a *real* christening, I mean?"

"Sure and it would. Do as I say," Blackie commanded. "I can do just as good a job as a vicar, or a priest, for that matter. Even though I am a lapsed Catholic I still believe in God, ye know. I might not be going to the church, Emma, but I never lost me faith. *Never*. Be sure of that. And God lives within all of us. That is my true belief. I feel Him in me heart, and that's what's most important. To feel His love and His presence eternally with us."

Although Emma was astonished, she knew that he meant every word he said.

Blackie continued in a tender voice, "I don't think He will be angry that I am taking matters into me own hands, in this emergency. And He will accept her as one of His blessed children, Emma. Sure and He will. His own son, Jesus, said, 'Suffer little children to come unto me, and forbid them not; for of such is the kingdom of God.' Please, believe me, it's the baptism and the spirit of love behind it that counts, and not the man that does it, or where it's done. We need neither a church nor a font, Emma."

"I believe you, Blackie. I want you to christen the baby."

"That's my Emma," said Blackie. "Now, pick up the baby and bring her over here." Blackie occupied himself at the sink, preparing the bowl of tepid water, and then he hurried across to the sideboard and pulled open a drawer, searching for a towel.

Emma now lifted the baby out of the makeshift cot and cradled her in her arms, stroking her small face and cooing to her. "Oh, my sweet little girl," Emma exclaimed, entranced with the child. Unexpectedly Edwin Fairley's face flashed

before her eyes. If only Edwin had not been so cruel. If only
Edwin could see the baby now, he would love her as I do. To
her horror, Emma found she could not expunge his face, or
his name. She had not thought of him for weeks and then
only with the most intense hatred. He had barely crossed her
mind when the baby was born. Emma was so involved with
these unparalleled thoughts of Edwin Fairley that she became distracted and her guard was lowered.

Blackie was calling from the other side of the room, "And
what will ye be calling Tinker Bell, then? Have ye thought of
a name?"

So preoccupied was Emma, she did not think twice. Edwin's name was on the tip of her tongue and she said automatically, thoughtlessly, "Edwina—" As that name fell from
her lips Emma froze by the sink, so aghast was she at her
own carelessness. What made me say that name? she wondered, furious with herself. She had never had any intention
of calling the baby after Edwin. She had decided to name the
baby Laura weeks ago. Emma felt as if the blood was draining
out of her.

Blackie's jaw had dropped open and he was staring at her
back. He could see that she held herself tensely and her
shoulder blades were protruding through the thin silk of the
white blouse she was wearing. He repeated the name Edwina
to himself and then, without having to give it a second
thought, he knew who the father of her child was. Edwin
Fairley. There was no doubt in his mind about that. Everything fell neatly into place. Why had he not thought of Edwin
before? It was so obvious. And he had been suspicious of her
story for months, convinced that the fastidious Emma would
not have entangled herself with a village yokel. Blackie's
heart ached for Emma and he longed to console her. But he
held himself in check. Although her face was turned away
from him, Blackie was now acutely conscious of her embarrassment and he guessed that she had just made a dreadful
slip of the tongue. He was positive she had never meant to
call the child Edwina. Why would she so blatantly spell it out
for him? No, the canny Emma would never do that. It had
been a mistake she could not now gracefully correct.

And so Blackie adopted an unconcerned tone and said,
with a show of gaiety, "And where did ye find such an *elegant*
name, mavourneen? In one of them illustrated magazines, I

am thinking. Sure and it is real fancy, but very fitting for me darlin' Tinker Bell. I like it. Sure and I do."

Emma nodded, not trusting herself to speak. Blackie fussed with the towel, draping it over his arm, and then he tested the water, taking his time so that she could regain her composure. "Now then, I'm ready," he said with a bright smile. "Hold the the babe forward, Emma. . . . Yes, that's right. Good, mavourneen." .

Somewhat recovered, Emma said, "Her full name is to be Ed—Edwina." She almost faltered, then swallowed and went on more steadily, "Laura Shane—"

"Shane!" interrupted Blackie, his surprise evident.

"Yes, after you. I can't very well call her Desmond or Patrick, and Blackie would seem odd, now wouldn't it?"

Blackie chuckled. "True! True! Well, 'tis flattered that I am and right pleased, Emma. So, let's commence." He dipped his fingers in the bowl of water with a flourish and made the sign of the cross on the baby's forehead.

"Wait a minute," Emma exclaimed, her eyes stretching widely. "I'm not a Roman Catholic and neither is the baby. In the Church of England the vicar just sprinkles the water on in drips. He doesn't make a cross. We must do it properly. Start again, please."

Blackie bit back a smile. For a so-called atheist she was being mighty particular. "Sure and I understand, Emma." He wiped the cross off the baby's brow with the towel and resumed. Once again he dipped his large brown fingers in the water and ceremoniously sprinkled a few drops on the child, who stared up at him unblinkingly.

"I christen thee Edwina Laura Shane Harte. In the name of God the Father, the Son, and the Holy Ghost." Blackie crossed himself and then he bent down and kissed the baby. He smiled at Emma, and kissed her, too. "There ye are, mavourneen. The baby is christened. Does that make ye feel happier?"

"Yes, Blackie. Thank you. It was beautiful. And just look at the baby. She's smiling again and she didn't even cry when you dropped the water on her. I'm going to make sure she has a good life. The best of everything, Blackie." She turned her face to his and her gaze was solemn. "She'll have the most beautiful clothes and go to the best schools and she'll be a real lady. I'm going to make sure of that. Nothing is going to stop me." The serious expression eased into a tender smile. "I wonder what she'll look like when she's older, Blackie. What do you think?"

A Fairley, that's a certainty, Blackie mused, regarding the child objectively. The signs were already there, as young as she was. He said, "She'll be lovely, Emma. Aye, she will indeed. But put her back in the cot, and get out Laura's bottle of port wine. I think the least we can do is to be drinking a toast to the baby."

"Oh, Blackie, do you think that's all right? Laura might be annoyed if we dip into her—"

"Don't be silly, Emma," Blackie cried through his laughter. "She won't care. And anyway, I'll go out later to the off-license and buy another bottle. We have to be toasting Edwina, ye know. It's the custom."

Emma nodded and did as he asked. They toasted the baby with the ruby port, which Emma had poured into two small glasses. "May she be healthy, wealthy, and wise," pronounced Blackie, taking a sip, "and I won't be adding beautiful, for we know she'll be taking after her mother!"

Emma smiled at him with great fondness, and they sat down in front of the fire, drinking the wine, lost in their own thoughts. After a short while Emma said, "We can't tell Laura about the christening. She wouldn't approve. She wouldn't think it proper. She'd also wonder why I didn't go to the church."

Blackie nodded and frowned. "Aye, ye are right about that. Still, what are ye going to be telling her, Emma? After all, she doesn't know the truth. She'll be thinking it funny if ye don't have the bairn baptized."

"I'll tell her I'm having it done in Ripon," said Emma, recognizing as she spoke that she had finally made her decision about the baby's immediate future.

"Ripon! Why there?" Blackie threw her a curious glance.

Emma looked at him carefully, cleared her throat, and said softly, "Because that's where I'm going next week with the baby. I'm taking her to my cousin Freda's." Blackie seemed baffled and Emma explained quickly, "She will live there with my cousin. You know I can't keep the baby with me when I have to work. You said that yourself months ago."

Blackie's eyes narrowed. "Have ye been in touch with ye cousin, then? Has she agreed to take Edwina in?"

"No. I was afraid to write, in case she turned me down. But if I arrive there with the baby I know she won't do that," Emma said, speaking in the most assured voice she could summon. "Freda's a good woman, Blackie, and she was very close to my mother, even though she is much younger. She's a motherly sort and she loves children. She has two little ones of her own. I just know she won't refuse me when she sees the baby. And I shall pay her for looking after Edwina."

Blackie sighed. "Aye, I see the practical side of the idea, but won't ye be missing the child, Emma?"

"Oh yes, I will, Blackie. I will! But as soon as I'm on my feet, I shall bring Edwina back to live with me. In the meantime, I shall go to see her once or twice a month."

Blackie shook his head, looking sorrowful, and his Celtic soul ached that she had to be separated from her child. But he said cheerfully, "And when do ye intend to be going to Ripon?"

Emma bit her lip. "I shall take the baby over there next week, before I go back to work. On Thursday. I'll stay with Freda that night and all day on Friday, to be with the baby a bit longer." She saw the dismay on his face and cried, "I have to do it! I have no choice!" Tears were imminent and her voice shook.

"I know, Emma, I know. Don't be getting yeself upset," Blackie responded sympathetically. He leaned forward and squeezed her arm. "It's the wisest course under the circumstances."

"At least she will be with a member of my family and she'll be in the fresh country air," Emma pointed out firmly, as if to convince herself, as well as Blackie, of the wisdom of her decision.

Blackie said, "But what about ye dad? Won't ye cousin be telling him about the baby?"

"No, she won't, if I ask her not to," Emma countered in a confident tone, hoping she was right. "She knows what he's like, and she'll protect me for my mother's sake. They were like sisters." Emma looked him right in the eye and went on, "I shall tell her the whole truth, Blackie, about the boy from the village letting me down and running off to the navy. I'll have to."

"Aye, I expect ye will," remarked Blackie, now convinced that the truth had been slightly bent. Then another thought struck him forcibly, and he reflected for a minute before saying, "Emma, ye mentioned the birth certificate before. Ye will have to go and register the bairn's birth with the registrar in Leeds, to get the certificate. And ye'll have to give the father's name. It's the law."

Emma's face darkened with distress. She had already thought of this herself and it bothered her not a little. She held herself very still, not answering.

"I can guess what ye are thinking, mavourneen. When the registrar asks ye for the name, ye are going to say 'father unknown,' are ye not?"

"Yes," she acknowledged softly.

"Aye, I knew it. Well, I think ye should be putting *me* down as the father," he said emphatically.

Emma was thunderstruck. "Oh, Blackie, I can't! I won't! Why should you have that responsibility?"

His piercing stare was unwavering. "Do ye want to give the name of the *real* father, Emma?" he asked pointedly.

"No!" she exclaimed, her eyes flaring.

"Well, then, wouldn't it be better to have *my* name on the certificate? The paper will still show that she's illegitimate, I realize that. But at least a name, such as it is, would look better than 'father unknown.' Think on that one, mavourneen."

"But, Blackie—"

He held up his hand to silence her and there was a reproving look on his face. "Do ye know how often ye say 'But, Blackie'? Always disagreeing with me, ye are. It's settled," he announced in a voice that forbade argument. "And I shall come with ye to the registrar's office, just to make sure ye be doing as I say." He stretched out his hand and patted her arm again. "Ye'll see, it will be fine, Emma. And I am happy to take the responsibility, as ye call it, for Tinker Bell." He grinned crookedly. "I mean Edwina Laura Shane. Me darlin' godchild, so to speak."

Emma's eyes filled up. She fumbled for her handkerchief and blew her nose, striving to curb her emotions. "You're so good, Blackie. I don't know why you do so much for me."

"Because I care about ye, Emma, and the wee one. Somebody's got to look out for ye both in this hard world, I am thinking," he remarked softly, his affection reflected in his bright black eyes.

"You might regret it later. I mean, regret putting your name on the birth certificate."

Blackie laughed dismissively. "I never regret anything I be doing, mavourneen mine. I've found regrets to be a sinful waste of time."

A brief smile touched Emma's lips. She knew it was fruitless to attempt to dissuade him once his mind was made up. He, too, could be very stubborn. She stared into the fire reflectively. "I must keep the birth certificate in a safe place. Locked up. Laura must never see it," she said. Her voice was so quiet it was almost inaudible.

Blackie was not certain he had heard correctly. He leaned forward and asked, "What was that?"

She gave him the benefit of a long knowing look. "I said, Laura must never see the birth certificate. Because *your* name will be on it."

"I don't care about that," exclaimed Blackie. "But she shouldn't see it, for the simple reason that she'd know then ye are single, and that the babe's illegitimate. Did I not tell Laura ye were married to a sailor called Winston Harte? Pack of lies I told that poor girl. Ye are forgetting things, Emma." He sighed heavily. "That's the trouble with lying."

Emma flushed. "They were only white lies. I told them for the baby's sake, and you agreed all along that I was right," she retorted fiercely. "And I'm not forgetting anything. I was only thinking that I must protect *you*. And I don't want Laura to be hurt. She would be, if she saw your name on the birth certificate. She might believe you really were the father."

"So what?" Blackie demanded, further bewildered.

"Laura loves you, Blackie."

"Loves me! Laura! That's a lot of cod's wallop, mavourneen." He burst out laughing and shook his head disbelievingly. "Hell could freeze over before Laura would look at *me* twice. I don't have to tell ye that she's a staunch Roman Catholic, and devout, and she knows I'm lapsed. Come on, Emma. That's a daft idea. Loves me, indeed! On the heads of the Blessed Saints, I do swear ye have lost ye mind."

Emma threw him a fond but impatient look. "You are a great fool, Blackie O'Neill. You can't see what's staring you in the face. Of course she loves you. Very much."

"Did she tell ye that?" he cried, his glance quizzical.

"No, she didn't. But I know she does." Observing his

skeptical expression, Emma added vehemently, "I just *know*, deep down inside, that she does!"

Blackie could not help laughing again. "Ye are very imaginative, Emma. Sure and ye are. I don't believe it at all, at all."

Emma shrugged resignedly. "You don't have to, but it's true," she asserted strongly. "I can tell by the way she looks at you, and talks about you sometimes. I bet if you asked her, she'd marry you."

Blackie was stunned. A peculiar look settled on his face, one Emma could not read. Emma said hurriedly, "You mustn't tell her I've said anything, though. She'd be upset if she thought we'd been talking about her, behind her back. And anyway, she's never actually *told* me she loves you. That's just my opinion."

Still Blackie did not answer. Emma rose and went over to him. She touched his massive shoulder lightly and he looked up at her, his eyes suddenly twinkling. "Promise me you won't mention it to Laura, Blackie. *Please*."

"I promise I won't mention it to a living breathing soul," he said, patting the small hand resting on his shoulder. Satisfied that he would keep his word, Emma nodded and glided into the kitchen. "I've got to start preparing things for tea," she called over her shoulder.

"Aye, mavourneen," he said, and threw another log on the fire. Blackie settled comfortably in the wing chair and lit a cigarette, chuckling to himself from time to time, vastly amused at Emma's words and not at all convinced of their veracity. 'Tis romantic girlish notions Emma is harboring, he thought, and drew deeply on his Woodbine. Nonetheless, he discovered she had given him something disturbing to think about. He sat dwelling on the possibility of Laura loving him; an idea that previously had never entered his mind and one so staggering he was shaken. Slowly, numerous things Laura had said and done in the past few years came back to him with vividness; things he had considered irrelevant but which now assumed significance in the light of Emma's comments. Was Emma correct in her conjectures about Laura's involvement with him? For the life of him he did not know. Yet Emma was nobody's fool. She was perceptive and, in fact, he had often been startled at her insight into people. Bemused, he ruminated on Laura Spencer and he discovered he found it quite difficult to gauge the depth and extent of his own feelings for her. Oh, he loved her. There was no doubt about that. It was virtually impossible not to love that gentle and tenderhearted girl. But how did he love her? Was he in love with her? Did he want her for his wife, as the mother of his children?

Did he want to share the rest of his life, and his bed, with her? Was it she who was the object of his masculine desire and passion? He shook his head, nonplussed, unable to isolate and understand his true feelings for Laura. And what about Emma? He loved her, too. He had always believed this had been merely a fraternal interest; now he wondered if he had unconsciously deluded himself. He remembered the night in the Mucky Duck when he had asked her to marry him, out of a sense of protectiveness; yet that night he had seen that she was a highly alluring young woman. Blackie found he was jolted into annoyance with himself. Could it be, was it conceivable, that he actually loved Emma in the way a virile man loves a woman, with all his heart and his very soul? He strove to examine, with objectivity, his emotional involvement with both girls, only to find that he was even more perplexed and confused than ever, on the horns of a dilemma. How can a man love two women at the same time? he asked himself with mounting irritation. He ran his hand through his hair distractedly. This is a fine kettle of fish, Blackie O'Neill, he said to himself. The gaze in his black and brilliant eyes was inward and contemplative, as he endeavored to answer these disquieting questions which Emma's conversation had posed. But the answers eluded him maddeningly, and they would continue to do so for some considerable length of time.

THIRTY-TWO

The main street of Fairley village was deserted, it being two o'clock on Sunday afternoon. It was a cool April day and, as was normal at this time of year, the sky was heavy with cinereous clouds that rolled in a gathering mass along the crest of those black implacable moors which stretched in eerie silence towards the smudged horizon. The watery sun

had retreated hours ago and the village looked inhospitable,
the gray stone walls and slate rooftops of the cottages fusing
into the forbidding semi-industrial landscape, an unrelieved
etching of monotones beneath that sullen metallic sky. The
wind blowing in from the nearby limestone dale country was
tinged with North Sea rain and a shower was imminent. It
had already poured earlier, and the roofs and cobblestones
held a silvery sheen that was glassy and stark in the dismal
environment.

To Emma, climbing the steep hill, the village appeared
smaller than she remembered, oddly diminished, but she had
broader comparisons to draw upon now, and she recognized
that her eyes had become accustomed to the imposing buildings of Leeds, the fine establishments of Armley. The depressing aspects of her surroundings were dimmed, became
irrelevant, for she was filled with happiness. She smiled to
herself. She was looking forward to seeing her father and
Frank, and this reunion, so yearningly longed for, was uppermost in her thoughts, as it had been for days. They did not
know she was coming today; she had not written to announce
her impending visit, wanting to give them a lovely surprise.
Her anticipation was fully revealed on her eager and shining
face. Frank must have grown in the past ten months, she
thought. She wondered how they would look, little Frank,
now thirteen, and her father. She herself had taken great
pains with her appearance, before setting out that morning,
determined to look her very best. This was partially prompted
by her sense of pride, but also to prove to her father that she
had been successful out on her own in the world. She was
wearing the red silk dress and the black wool coat which had
formerly belonged to Olivia Wainright, and new black button
boots purchased only last week. The shopping bag she carried
contained thoughtfully selected presents; socks, a shirt, and a
tie for her dad, plus his favorite pipe tobacco; socks, a shirt,
and writing materials for Frank, along with an edition of
David Copperfield. And, carefully placed on top of these
things, there was a bunch of spring flowers for her mother's
grave. She had dipped into her precious savings to buy
everything, but she had done so joyfully and with love; and in
her black reticule there were three crisp pound notes for her
father, to help with the family expenses.

The hill was steep, but Emma climbed it easily. There was

a decided bounce to her step and she felt wonderfully alive. Optimistic as she was by nature, Emma was now inordinately confident of the future.

The baby was comfortably settled with her cousin Freda in Ripon. As Emma had predicted to Blackie, Freda had been more than willing to take Edwina in, and for as long as Emma wished. If she had been surprised at Emma's unexpected arrival on her doorstep, or shocked at her story, the loving and compassionate Freda had not betrayed this at all. She had taken everything in her stride. Her welcome had been genuine and she had fussed over Emma and commented ecstatically on Edwina's prettiness and her docile temper. She had promised to care for the child as if she were her own, and had faithfully pledged to keep Emma's circumstances a secret from Jack Harte, with whom she was not on very good terms, and whom, she explained, she had not heard from since Elizabeth's death in 1904. When Emma had left Ripon to return to Armley she was in a calmer frame of mind and, although she was saddened to leave the child, her confidence in Freda, who was so like her mother, had helped to assuage her wistfulness considerably. She knew Edwina was in capable hands, and that she would be looked after and cherished with complete devotion.

Now, as she passed the White Horse halfway up the hill, Emma quickened her steps, not wishing to encounter any of the men or boys from the village, those perennial stragglers who indulged in a last pint and never left the pub before two o'clock. They might appear at any moment on their way home for a late Sunday lunch. She was only a few steps past the pub when she heard the door open and the sound of raucous voices echoing in the chilly air, as a handful of men staggered out into the street, vociferously merry with the vast amounts of beer they had consumed. Emma hurried faster.

"Emma!"

Her heart dropped and she had the urge to run, reluctant to become embroiled in a conversation or to expose herself to curious questions from the locals. She increased her pace, without looking back. Drunken louts, she thought disdainfully.

"Emma! For God's sake wait. It's *me. Winston!*"

She stopped abruptly and swung around, her face lighting up. Her elder brother, resplendent in his naval uniform, was chasing up the street after her, waving his white sailor hat in his hand, his mates forgotten. They were staring after Winston, mouths agape, ogling Emma poised on the hill. Winston panted up to her. He threw his arms around her and hugged her to him, showering her face and her hair with kisses. A warm flush of happiness swept through her and she clung to him tightly, her love for him as fierce and as real as ever. With a sharp stab she realized how much she had missed him.

After a few seconds clutched in this tight embrace, they pulled away and automatically stared at each other, their eyes searching, questioning. Emma caught her breath as she looked up at Winston. His face had always been beautiful, but in an almost girlish way. Now it was extraordinarily and staggeringly handsome. Since she had last seen him he had matured. The high cheekbones, the wide brow, the straight nose, the generous mouth, and the well-shaped chin were all as finely drawn as ever, and yet they appeared much less delicate. There was strength in his face that bespoke his enormous masculinity. And those cornflower-blue eyes, widely set below the arched black brows and fringed with thick and curling black lashes, were brighter than she remembered, positively blinding in the cold northern light. His black hair was blowing in the breeze and his perfect white teeth flashed in his fresh-complexioned face as he smiled at her. He had grown and filled out. He was practically as tall as their father, and wide-shouldered and muscular. He's too handsome for his own good, Emma thought. Women must adore him but men must surely hate him, she decided, and then wondered how many girls had already fallen at his feet, how many broken hearts lay scattered in his ports of call. He would be irresistible to the opposite sex, she saw that only too clearly. She marveled to herself that this incredible specimen of manhood was her brother; the skinny, hot-tempered boy who had teased her unmercifully, pulled her hair, quarreled with her and fought her, but who had always been her staunch ally when necessary, and whom she had never ceased to secretly worship.

Winston, gazing back at Emma, was thinking: She's changed enormously. There's something very different about her. She's more self-assured, even worldly. By God, she's a stunning girl. He corrected himself. No, Emma is a woman now, and ripe for the plucking. A feeling of jealous possessiveness raced through him, was so powerful, so searing he was shaken at the intensity of his feelings. The brightest man breathing is not good enough for my sister. And he recognized then that he truly adored her. In point of fact, that was to be the major problem all of his life. No other woman would ever measure up to his sister in his eyes.

"You look wonderful," Emma said at last, breaking the silence, her eyes overflowing with the tenderest of lights.

"So do you, little sister," Winston said. "Quite grown-up, too." He smiled at her lovingly and with pride, and then the smile congealed. His joy was dampened when he remembered how poor little Frank had grieved for Emma, was still grieving for her, and a furious glint entered those startling eyes. He grabbed her arm roughly. "Hey, our Emma, where the hell have you been all these months? We've been worried to death! How could you run off like that?"

There was a hidden smile on Emma's face. "Oh, the pot's calling the kettle black, is it?"

Winston glared. "I'm a man. That's different. You'd no business sneaking off that way. You were needed at home."

"Don't shout, Winston," said Emma. "Dad knows where I've been. I've written to him regularly, and sent him money."

Winston was scrutinizing her closely and scowling darkly. "Yes, but you never put an address on those letters—where we could write back. That was wrong of you, Emma."

"Dad knows I've been traveling with my lady, Mrs. John Smith of Bradford. Please, Winston, don't look so angry, and let go of my arm. You're hurting me."

"Sorry," Winston muttered, and released his powerful grip. He took hold of her hand. "Come on, don't let's stand here, making a spectacle of ourselves. I can see half a dozen lace curtains twitching." He almost dragged her up to Top Fold.

"I expect you have a ship now, don't you, Winston?" asked Emma warmly, hoping to dispel her brother's belligerent mood.

"Yes," said the laconic Winston.

Undismayed by his curtness, Emma persisted, "Where are you stationed, Winston?"

"Scapa Flow."

"Well, you must give me your address, so that I can write to you every week. Would you like me to?"

"If you want."

"Yes, I do. And I'll give you my address. You'll write back to me, won't you, Winston?"

"Yes."

Emma sighed inside. However, she knew him well enough not to be discouraged by his gruff answers. The evasiveness in her letters about her whereabouts over the past months obviously still rankled with him. She hoped her father would not have the same attitude, that *he* was not harboring any grudges. Now she said gaily, "It must be exciting, being in the navy. Seeing different places. I'm ever so glad you joined up, Winston, really I am. Why, you can see the world, just like you always dreamed about doing when you were little." He did not respond, but Emma saw a softening on his face, and she pressed, "It *is* exciting, isn't it?"

Winston was incapable of remaining angry with his beloved Emma for long. Also, he knew his brusqueness with her was really caused by his own growing apprehension. He must not upset her unduly. Not now when within minutes she was about to suffer a terrible shock. And so he adopted a cheeriness he did not feel, and said, "Yes, you're right. It is exciting. I love the navy, Emma. I'm learning a lot. Not just about life at sea, but many other things, educational things. It's fascinating. I aim to do well in the navy, Emma."

His last statement filled her with pleasure. She opened her mouth, but before she could comment, he rushed on, "I'll tell you something I've never told anybody else, Emma. I was a bit scared at first."

Emma's eyes flew open. "*You* scared? I don't believe it."

Winston was relieved he had managed to divert her from asking any trying questions about the family. He cleared his throat. "Well, I was," he confided, a wry smile playing on his mouth. "It was the night I boarded my ship for the first time. It was a cold night, and dark and raining, and they moved us from Shotley Barracks, opposite Harwich, to Sheerness. The picket boat drew up to the battleship, and I was going up the accommodation ladder to the quarterdeck when I saw these giant brass letters on the bulkhead shining in the faint light. 'Fear God, Honour the King,' they said. I got a funny sensation in the pit of my stomach. I was awed, Emma, and fearful. Those words were so—so—meaningful, so serious. Powerful, really. I suddenly understood about the great traditions of the British navy and all they stood for. The honor, the courage, and the glory inherited from men like Drake and Raleigh and Nelson. I realized I was in the service of my King and country. I felt a pride, a sense of duty. That night I think I began to take the navy seriously. It was no longer simply an escape route from Fairley, or a lark."

Emma was both impressed and moved by his words. "I'm proud of you, Winston. I bet Dad is, too."

This remark wiped the smile off his face. "Hurry up," he said, striding out.

Emma had to run to keep up with him. "Well, Dad is, isn't he?" she asked cheerfully, ignoring his glum expression, smiling widely.

"I don't know," mumbled Winston, and he kept his head averted.

"Did you tell him all that? About the traditions of the navy and the way you felt? It would please him, Winston. It really would. He was a good soldier himself when he was in the Boer War and he's very patriotic, you know."

Attempting to circumvent any discussion about their father, Winston said, "And what about you, Emma? How have you been? I notice you are talking very fancy, for one thing."

Amused, she peeked at him out of the corner of her eye and said in a jocular tone, "So are you, Winston Harte. Do you think I'm deaf?"

"No, I don't. I've been paying attention to myself, Emma. In every way. And I don't just mean speaking properly either. I'm going in for a commission," he announced. "You don't think I want to stay a rating, do you? I'm moving up the ladder. I'll be an able seaman next, then a leading seaman. Eventually, I intend to be a petty officer, maybe even a chief petty officer one day."

"Not an admiral?" Emma teased.

"I know my limitations," he retorted, but his voice was kind. He put his arm around her shoulder protectively, in the way he had done when they were children. She was immediately aware of his unspoken love. Emma smiled inside, thinking how wonderful it was to be with Winston again, and in a few seconds she would be hugging her father, and little Frank, and it would be like old times.

They hurried down Top Fold in silence, and when they reached the garden gate leading to the cottage Emma's heart lifted with happiness and she extracted herself from Winston's embrace and flew up the flagged path, propelled by her mounting excitement. She did not see the heartsick expression clouding Winston's face.

Frank had his back to the door, and he was peering into the oven set to one side of the fireplace, when Emma walked in. "Yer late again, our Winston. Me Aunty Lily'll play pop if she knows. I've tried ter keep yer dinner warm, but it looks a bit funny now. Still, here it is, Winston." The younger boy straightened up and swung around. He almost dropped the plate he was holding the moment he saw Emma. His mouth sagged and his eyes became so huge they filled his narrow face like liquid pools of gray light. He was dumbfounded. Then he banged the plate down onto the table negligently and sped across the room. He flung himself into Emma's outstretched arms with such velocity he almost knocked her over. She held him close to her, stroking his hair. He began to cry, sobbing as if his heart would break. She was at once startled and baffled, and she tried to soothe him.

"Frank, lovey, don't cry so. I'm here, safe and well, and with presents for you, too. Presents you'll like, Frank."

He raised his freckled and damp face to hers and said, with a snuffle, "I've missed yer, Emma. Ever so much. I thought yer'd never come back. Never ever again."

"Don't be silly. I'll always come back to see you. I've missed you, too, Frank. Now, come along, stop crying and let me take off my coat."

Winston had thrown his cap onto a chair and, unable to look at Emma in his anxiety, he stared with distaste at the food on the plate. It had long ago coagulated into a mass of limp Yorkshire pudding, frizzled roast beef, mashed potatoes, and brussels sprouts, all running together in a rapidly drying gravy. "I don't feel very hungry," he muttered in a low voice. Winston discovered to his dismay that he had lost his nerve. How could he tell her? All the right words had fled, leaving his mind empty.

"Me Aunt Lily'll be mad if yer don't eat yer dinner," warned Frank.

Emma hung up her coat behind the door and returned to the fireplace with the shopping bag. She placed the flowers in the sink and pulled out the presents for Frank, hoping to bring a smile to that cheerless little lace. "These are for you, love," she said with a bright smile, and then addressed her

older brother. "I'm sorry, Winston, I didn't bring you anything. I didn't know you'd be home on leave. But never
mind, this will come in useful, I'm sure." As she spoke she
opened her reticule and took out one of the new pound
notes. "Take this, Winston. You can buy yourself some cigarettes and a pint or two."

She carried the presents over to Frank, who accepted them
from her silently. Then his eyes lit up. "Thank yer, Emma.
Just what I needed." His pleasure was undisguised.

Now Emma busied herself at the Welsh dresser, taking out
the other items. "These are for Dad," she said, her voice
light. "Where is he?" She glanced from Winston to Frank, a
look of joyous expectation on her face.

Winston put the knife and fork down on the plate with a
loud clatter, and Frank stood gazing at her vacantly, clutching his presents. Neither of them spoke.

"Where's our dad?" asked Emma. They still did not reply
and Winston dropped his eyes again but looked up quickly,
flashing a warning to Frank, who had blanched.

"What's wrong? Why are you both so quiet?" This was a
fierce demand and fear began to trickle through her veins.
She grabbed hold of Winston's arm urgently and brought her
face closer to his, peering into his eyes, "Where is he, Winston?"

Winston cleared his throat nervously. "He's with our mam,
Emma."

Emma experienced a little burst of relief. "Oh, you mean
he's gone to visit her grave. I wish I'd been a bit sooner and I
could have gone with him. I think I'll run up there now, and
catch him before he—"

"No, Emma, you can't do that," Winston cried, jumping
up. He put his arm around her and led her to a chair. "Sit
down a minute, Emma."

Winston lowered himself into the chair opposite her. He
took her hand in his and held it tightly. "You didn't understand me, love," Winston began in a tiny voice that was so
faint she could hardly hear it. "I didn't mean our dad had
gone to visit Mam's grave. I meant he was there with her.
Lying next to her in the graveyard."

Winston watched her attentively, ready to move towards
her if necessary, the desire to insulate her pain uppermost in
his mind. But she seemed uncomprehending.

"Our dad's dead," said Frank, with his usual childlike bluntness. His voice was leaden with sorrow.

"Dead," whispered Emma, incredulous. "He can't be dead. It's not possible. I would have known if he had died. I would have known inside. In my heart. I just know I would." As she uttered these words she realized from their grim expressions that it was true. Emma's face crumpled. Tears welled into her eyes and spilled out over the rims and rolled down her cheeks silently, falling onto the front of the red silk dress in small splashes.

Winston's eyes were blurred and he wept as he had wept when his father had died. Now his tears were for Emma. She had been so much closer to their father than either he or Frank. He brushed his hand across his eyes resolutely, resolving to be stalwart. He must try to console her, to alleviate her grief. He knelt at Emma's feet and wrapped his arms around her body. She fell against him, sobs wracking her. "Oh, Winston! Oh, Winston! I never saw him again. I never saw him again!" she wailed.

"There, there, love," Winston said, stroking her hair, murmuring softly to her, pressing her to his chest, comforting and tender. After a long time her sobbing began to diminish and slowly subsided altogether.

Frank was making tea at the sink, swallowing his own tears. He had to be brave, a big boy. Winston had told him that. But Emma's terrible distress had infected him and his shoulders jerked in silent misery. Winston became conscious of the boy's wretchedness and he beckoned to Frank, stretching out one arm. Frank skittered across the floor and buried his head against Winston, who encircled his sister and brother in his arms, lovingly, and with great devotion. He was the head of the family now and responsible for them both. The three of them stayed huddled together in silent commiseration, drawing solace from their closeness, until eventually all of their tears were used up.

The kitchen was full of gently shifting shadows, the graying light outside intruding bleakly through the glass panes, the flames in the grate meager as the logs burned low. There was no sound except the sibilant hissing of the kettle on the hob, the murmurous ticking of the old clock, the pattering of spring rain as it hit the windows. Winston's voice sounded hollow in this dolorous silence. "It's just the three of us now. We've got to stick together. We've got to be a family. That's what Dad and Mam would want. We must look after each other. Emma, Frank, do you both hear me?"

"Yes, Winston," whispered Frank.

Dazed and sorrowing, Emma drew herself up and wiped her face with one hand. She was white with anguish. Her eyes were swollen and red-rimmed, and her mouth quivered, but she took steely control of herself, smiling at Winston weakly. She nodded her understanding of his words. She could not speak.

"Frank, please bring the tea over to the table," Winston said, rising wearily. He sat in the chair opposite Emma and took out a cigarette. He looked at the packet of Woodbines and remembered, with a nostalgic twinge of sadness, how his father had always complained about his tab ends.

Emma pulled herself fully upright. She faced Winston. "Why didn't you tell me straightaway, when I ran into you outside the White Horse?" she murmured.

"How could I, Emma? In the middle of the village street. I was so relieved to see you, I could only think how glad I was that you were safe and well. I was happy for a split second. And then I became afraid. That's why I chattered on about the navy, and rushed you home the way I did. I knew you'd break down. I wanted you here, in this house, when you heard the bad news."

"Yes, you were right. You did the best thing. When did—did—our dad—" She pressed her handkerchief to her face and endeavored to suppress the sobs. She had been grief-stricken at her mother's death, yet in a sense that had been anticipated for months. The news of her father's passing away had been so unexpected she was devastated, in a state of awful shock.

"He died five days after you left, last August," said Winston dully, dragging on his cigarette, his face a picture of despondency.

Emma turned a ghastly putty color and her face was so rigid, so unmoving it might have been cut from stone. I never knew, she thought. All these months I've been writing to him. Writing terrible lies. And all the time he was dead, and buried in the cold earth. She clapped her hand over her mouth, choking back a sob, heaving in silence.

Winston eventually calmed her down again and Frank

brought the tea. She took hold of the cup. Her hand shook so
badly she had to put it down. She stared into space and
finally managed to ask, "How did he die?" Her voice was
drained. She looked at Frank and then at Winston.

"There was an accident," Winston said. "I was in Scapa
Flow. Aunt Lily sent me a telegram and they let me come
home on compassionate leave. We didn't know where to find
you, Emma. We kept thinking you'd be back in a few days.
Hoping against hope. But—"

Emma was silent. She had no excuses. A sick dismay
lodged in her stomach, and guilt mingled with her grief,
which was absolute. After a few seconds she asked tremulously, "What kind of accident?" She was determined to know
everything now, however heartrending it was. She turned to
Frank, who had seated himself next to her. "You were here
before Winston arrived. Can you explain it to me? Would it
be too hard for you, Frankie? Too painful, lovey?"

"No, Emma. I can tell you." He gulped. "Winston said I
have to be brave and strong and accept life's hard knocks," he
intoned in that serious voice he sometimes adopted. Her
heart went out to him. He was such a little boy and he was
trying to be so courageous.

"You're a good, brave boy, Frank. Tell me all about it. But
take your time." She squeezed his hand reassuringly.

"Well, yer see, Emma, that Saturday yer left, me and me
dad was working at t'mill, as yer knows. Anyways, there was
a fire and me dad got burned. On his back and his shoulders
and legs. Third-degree burns, so Dr. Mac said. And he
breathed a lot of smoke."

Emma's blood ran cold as he was speaking. She shuddered,
and her heart tightened as she imagined her father's pain, the
suffering he must undoubtedly have endured from his tortur-
ous injuries. She tried to steady herself, not wishing to disturb Frank, who was on the verge of tears again.

"Are yer all right, our Emma?" he asked solicitously.

"Yes, Frank. Finish telling me."

Speaking gravely, he gave her the precise details of the
injuries their father had sustained, the care and attention he
had received, the concern of Adam Fairley, the devotion of
Dr. Mac and his wife, and the doctors at the valley hospital.
When he had finished, Emma said in a choked voice,

"How horrible for Dad to die like that, in such pain. I can't bear to think about it. How awful it must have been for him."

Frank eyed her carefully. "Me Aunty Lily said he didn't want to live anymore." His tone was hushed and his face was all bone and freckles, and he looked like a little old man to Emma.

She stared at him stupefied, her brows puckering. "What a weird and terrible thing for her to say about our dad. What did she mean, lovey?"

Frank looked at Winston, who nodded his assent. "We went ter see me dad every day," Frank explained. "Tom Hardy took us in the Squire's carriage. Me dad didn't seem ter get any better, Emma. On the Wednesday after the accident, when we was there, me Aunt Lily said ter him, 'Now, Jack, yer can't go on like this yer knows, lad. Yer've got ter make an effort. Or yer'll be where poor Elizabeth is, in the cemetery.' And me dad, well, he stared at her ever so funny like, with a faraway look in his eyes. Then he said, 'I wish I *was* with Elizabeth, Lily.' And when we was leaving, I kissed him and he said, 'Good-bye, Frankie. Always be a good lad.' Just like that. Final like. And when he kissed Winston—" Frank's eyes flew to his brother. "Tell her what he said ter yer, Winston."

Winston ran his hand through his hair. "Dad said to me, 'Look after the young 'uns, Winston. Stick together. And when Emma comes back from Bradford, tell her ter pick a sprig of heather for me and thee mam, up at the Top of the World, and keep it by her always for remembrance.' And then—" Winston's voice cracked at the memory. He took a deep breath, and continued softly, "Dad tried to get hold of my hand, Emma, but his were all burned and bandaged, so I brought my face down to his and he kissed me again, and he said, 'I love thee all, Winston. But I love Elizabeth the best and I can't live without her.' I began to cry, but Dad just smiled, and he had such a bright light in his eyes. They were as vivid as yours, Emma, and he looked happy. Really happy. He said I shouldn't be sad, because he had me mam to go to. I thought he was a bit delirious, to tell you the truth. The doctor came in then and asked us to leave. It was on the way back to Fairley that Aunt Lily said he'd die of a broken heart and not his burns. That he'd never stopped grieving for our mam. He died that same night, Emma. Peacefully, in his sleep. It was as if he had wanted to die, like Aunt Lily said."

Emma said, with a strangled sob, "Did he understand that I hadn't returned from Bradford, and that's why I wasn't there, Winston?"

Her brother nodded. "Yes, and he wasn't upset, Emma. He said he didn't have to see you, because you were locked in his heart forever."

Emma closed her burning eyes and leaned back against the chair. My father needed me and I wasn't here, she thought. If only I had waited a few days longer. She dreaded to hear more, but she could not stop herself probing for additional details. "It must have been a terrible fire. Obviously you weren't hurt, Frank, thank heaven. Were many of the men injured? Who else died?"

"No, I wasn't hurt at all," Frank reassured her. "A few of the men had minor burns, but not serious. Only me dad died, Emma."

Emma looked at him in puzzlement. "But if there was a fire at the mill, surely—"

"The fire wasn't in the mill building. It was in the big warehouse," Frank interrupted. "Me dad was crossing the yard and he spotted the flames raging. If he hadn't gone inter the warehouse he wouldn't have been hurt at all. Yer see, Master Edwin was down in the mill yard that day, and he was struggling ter open the door of the warehouse. He went inside. Me dad ran in after him, warning him it was ever so dangerous. A blazing bale was falling from the gantry, near Master Edwin. Me dad threw himself on top of Master Edwin, ter protect him. The bale hit me dad, and he saved Master Edwin's life, and with selfless courage, so the Squire said."

Emma went icy cold all over. "My father saved Edwin Fairley's life!" she cried with such ferocity even Winston was brought up sharply, aghast at her tone. "He died to save a Fairley! My father sacrificed himself for one of *them!*" She spat out the words venomously. "I can't believe it!" she shouted. She began to laugh hysterically, and her bitterness rose up in her.

Her brothers were gaping at her incredulously. Frank cringed and drew away from her. Winston said, "But, Emma, anybody would have done the same thing—"

"Would they really!" she stormed, leaping out of the chair. She stood in the center of the kitchen, her volcanic rage a stupendous force in her slender body. "Would *Squire* Fairley? Or *Master* Gerald? Or *Master* Edwin?" Again she spat out the names and with a complete and virulent loathing. "Would they have risked their lives to save our father's? Never. Never, I tell you. Not in a million years. Oh God! I can't stand it," she screamed, and her whole body vibrated with her fulminating fury.

"Calm down. Calm down, Emma. You'll make yourself sick. It happened, and nothing will change that," Winston said, shaken at her violent reaction, and afraid for her.

"The Squire has been ever so decent," interposed Frank, also trying to mollify her. "He pays us me dad's wages. A pound a week, we get. And he's going to pay it until I'm fifteen—"

"That's mighty big of him!" snarled Emma, her eyes threatening and ugly. "That's forty-eight pounds a year." She laughed caustically. "He's paid it for the past ten months, I suppose. And he'll pay it for another two years. Very decent of him indeed!" Her tone dripped acid. "Is that all my father's life was worth to the Fairleys? Approximately one hundred and fifty pounds, give or take a few shillings. It's a joke. A disgusting joke!" She caught her breath, her chest heaving. *"Is that all he was worth?"* she demanded once more.

Winston cleared his throat and said in his gentlest voice, "Well, he does a bit more than that. The Squire, I mean. He moved Frank into the mill offices and he's being trained as a clerk. And every Sunday Aunt Lily goes up to the Hall and Cook gives her a basket of food. Enough for the whole week. For her and Frank. You see, Aunt Lily moved in here, Emma, to look after Frank. She gave up her cottage when Dad died. She's gone up to the Hall now, Emma, to get the food. It helps a lot."

"A basket of food," she repeated scathingly, and laughed nastily. "Well, well, well. The Squire is being generous." She swung her head sharply and glowered at Frank. "I'm surprised you don't choke on it, our Frank. I know I would!"

She turned on her heels and walked across the room, her head held high. Frank and Winston gazed at her stiff back and they exchanged worried glances. She put on her coat and took the flowers from the sink. She paused in the doorway and looked around. "I'm going to the cemetery," she said, her voice steely. "And then I shall go up to the Top of the World. I doubt there's any heather there at this time of year, but I shall look. Anyway, I want to be by myself for a bit. I'll be back later, and we can talk some more. Make some plans for Frank's future. I'd like to see Aunty Lily as well."

"I'll come with you," said Winston. "We'll both come, won't we, Frank?" The younger boy nodded his acquiescence.

"No!" exclaimed Emma. "I told you I want to be alone. To think for a while."

She closed the door softly behind her, before they had a chance to protest. She walked slowly up Top Fold, her feet dragging, a feeling of exhaustion swamping her. She headed for the small graveyard next to the church, aware of nothing except her overwhelming grief. Her face tightened and darkened, and there was a chilly light in her eyes as she looked ahead unwaveringly. And then her consummate hatred for the Fairleys, so close to the surface, rose up again and took hold of her, jostling against the grief for prominence in her mind. Was there no end to the pain that family would cause her? Was she to be cursed with them all the days of her life? Damn the Fairleys. All of them. Damn them! Damn them! Damn them! May they rot in hell!

THIRTY-THREE

And so it began: the most relentless pursuit of money ever embarked upon, the most grinding and merciless work schedule ever conceived and willingly undertaken by a seventeen-year-old girl.

By day, Emma worked at the mill; at night, after a hastily eaten light tea, she retreated to her bedroom at Laura's and designed and cut and sewed clothes for a rapidly increasing clientele, local women informed by the devoted Laura of her flair with a needle, and her reasonable prices.

On Sundays, Emma baked fruit pies, bacon-and-egg pies, meat pies, and all manner of fancy pastries and cakes; she cooked mousses, jellies, custards, and trifles, using Olivia Wainright's recipes, catering parties and special occasions for the neighbors and, before long, the local gentry. When she was not engaged in her culinary endeavors for her growing number of customers, she bottled fresh fruits and vegetables; pickled onions, red cabbage, and walnuts; made chutneys and relishes and jams, which were all painstakingly labeled and dated in her meticulous script, supplies being hoarded in Laura's cellar to be sold later in her shop. Emma scrupulously lived on the weekly wage she earned at the mill as a weaver, and every penny she made from her dressmaking and catering was poured back into "the business," as she called it, to purchase the necessary sewing materials and foodstuffs.

This worried Laura, but Emma pointed out, "You've got to spend money to make money," and she refused to listen to warnings about "getting in over your head." However, it was not long before Emma began to show a small profit, much to her satisfaction, and Laura's great relief.

Emma was dogged, ruthless with herself, scraping, saving, and working seven days a week and seven nights as well. She had no time to lose now. Her first goal—the first shop. And after that, more shops until she had a chain of shops just as Michael Marks had a chain of Penny Bazaars. But hers would be elegant stores which would cater to the carriage trade. That was where the real money was, where great quantities of money could be made by an astute retailer. To get that first shop Emma herself needed money. Money for the rent. Money for the fixtures and fittings and display stands. Money to purchase the stocks. Somehow she had to get that money and she determined that nothing and nobody would stop her. Emma had no doubts about her ultimate success. "Failure" and "defeat" were words now entirely erased from her vocabulary, for her belief in herself was absolute, and she knew, also, that she had one essential and most vital characteristic—an enormous capacity for work.

For a whole year, after she had learned of her father's death, Emma took no time off whatsoever, except to visit Edwina one day every month. She regretted she did not have time to go to Ripon more often, as she had promised Freda, but she assuaged her terrible feelings of guilt and worry by reminding herself she was working for Edwina's future.

Emma made only one trip to Fairley to see Frank during this time, and that was when Winston was home on leave again. They had decided, she and her elder brother, on that devastating April Sunday, that Frank should remain in Fairley with their Aunty Lily. It seemed to them both to be the best solution. He would continue to work in the mill offices until he was fifteen. At that time, they agreed, Frank could determine for himself whether or not he wished to pursue a writing career. If he did, Emma and Winston would somehow find a way for him to do this; perhaps working in Leeds, as a copy boy on one of the newspapers, learning the journalistic profession and attending night school; or perhaps they would have enough money between them to send him away to school.

"Frank has been given a brain, Winston. A marvelous brain. And he has a talent for words. It's a gift, really. It must not be wasted," Emma had proclaimed. "We must give him every chance, no matter what." Winston had nodded his concurrence. Emma had also made another decision that afternoon. She had informed Winston, and in no uncertain terms, that he must send Frank writing materials on a continuing basis. "Even if you have to forgo a few pints and cigarettes," she had ordered. She herself would undertake to supply Frank with a good dictionary and other books of her choice. He ought to be exposed to literature, such as the plays of Shakespeare, the novels of Dickens, Trollope, and Thackeray, philosophical works and histories. Victor Kallinski knew all about books and he would help her to select the most appropriate ones. Frank had been given his orders, too. He must study diligently, reading every night and in all of his free time, in order to further his education on his own. Aunt Lily was instructed to enforce this program.

"There will be no shirking, Frank, since Winston and I are making a special effort for you," Emma had warned in her sternest tone. Frank had been only too delighted to accept her offer, and he was not at all appalled by the rigid timetable she had worked out for him. He could not wait for the first books to arrive and he knew, too, that he would not change his mind about writing.

Emma had told Winston, Frank, and her Aunt Lily only partial truths when she had given them her address in Armley. She had explained that she called herself *Mrs.* Harte and had invented a husband in the navy, simply as protection against unwanted and bothersome young men who might otherwise come courting, Winston had smiled at this ruse. He had actually congratulated her on her sense of self-preservation and told her she was being practical. Emma did not breathe a word about Edwina.

With Winston's career in the navy progressing, Frank's future temporarily settled, and Edwina safe in Ripon, Emma felt she was free to embark on her Plan with a capital *P* and devote herself solely to her own ambitions. She was unflagging and intensely involved in her work schedule, one that would have felled anyone else. She was oblivious to the passing of the days, her surroundings, and anything else that would intrude on the average girl's thoughts.

Sometimes Emma was even oblivious to her friends. At first, Blackie had believed Emma would not be able to sustain the exhausting grind, and so he had quietly cautioned Laura not to interfere. But as the months dragged on and Emma persisted in her endless toil, they both became concerned. In particular, David Kallinski was worried to such an extent that one night he sought out Blackie at the Mucky Duck.

David had been tense, and without preamble had launched into the reason for his visit. "Emma won't listen to me, Blackie. When I last spoke to her I suggested she should be a little kinder to herself, that she should only work during the week, like everyone else with any sense, and take the weekends off. I said something about doing everything in moderation, and do you know what she replied?"

Blackie had shaken his head, his own worry a reflection of David's. "I've no idea, lad. She comes out with all sorts of strange remarks these days."

"She said to me, 'In my opinion, moderation is a vastly overrated virtue, particularly when applied to work, David.' Can you believe it?"

"Aye, I can. She's stubborn, Emma is, David. And what ye be telling me doesn't surprise me. I've tried talking to her meself lately, without success. She just won't pay no mind to anybody," Blackie had grumbled.

"Try talking to her again, Blackie. *Please*," David had implored. "Get her to take this Sunday off. I'll come up to Armley, and we'll go for a walk in the park, and listen to the band. Blackie, promise me you'll at least *try*."

"By God, I'm going to do it, David! I shall be real forceful

with her. I shall tell her how she is worrying us all. That
ought to do the trick, I bet. I'm going to bring Emma to the
park with Laura and me, even if I have to drag her there by
the scruff of her neck!"

Now on the designated Sunday, a brilliantly sunny July
afternoon, David Kallinski walked along Stanningley Road to
the entrance of Armley park. He was dressed in his best blue
suit and a sparkling white shirt, set off by a deep wine-
colored cravat neatly knotted above his waistcoat, and fastened with an imitation-pearl pin. With his carefully pressed
clothes, and his black boots shined to perfection, he had a
well-groomed immaculate look about him. His thick black
hair gleamed like jet and his handsome face, freshly barbered
and smelling faintly of bay rum, was vibrant with pleasure at
the thought of seeing Emma.

He entered the park through handsome iron gates, surmounted by the city's coat of arms, and strolled down the
principal approach, a wide carriageway leading to a large
classically designed fountain. He stood at ease, his hands in
his pockets, watching the soaring jets of water being discharged high into the air and cascading back down into the
fountain, scintillating like hundreds of strings of tiny diamonds as they caught and held the sunlight. Fascinated by
the intricately constructed fountain, he moved closer and read
the inscription.

Erected by William Gott of Armley House
In Commemoration of the Sixtieth Year of
the Reign of Her Majesty Queen Victoria
1837 to 1897

The Gott family were immensely wealthy millowners and
had endowed many statues to the city of Leeds. When he
could afford it, David decided, he would make philanthropic
donations that would help people, rather than building statues and fountains, which, however beautiful, were essentially
useless.

He turned away and traversed the exquisitely landscaped
gardens, laid out in Italian style and flanked by pathways
avenued by young limes and elms and poplars, all offering
shade on this scorching day. The gardens blazed with glorious

color. Stylized flower beds were awash with the abundant reds and pinks of the gay geranium, the deep purples and sharp yellows of the velvet-petaled pansy, the whites and pinks and mauves of the tall and graceful foxglove. Variated greens, lushly inviting, sloped away into the distance and were highlighted with patches of pink and white thrifts, and the cheerful little nasturtium leapt like fire alongside the cool blues of the iris. Skirting the gardens were all manner of shrubs and trees, for Armley Park contained more specimens than any other park in Leeds; various hollies moved darkly polished branches towards the softer weigela with its apple-like blossoms, while copper beeches, their leaves trembling with a burnished radiance in the warm breeze, towered majestically above mock orange blossom trees, festooned and dripping with the palest of blush pinks. Rockeried paths and open spaces of grass, as smooth as emerald satin, were enclosed by additional shrubs and trees, and richly planted borders of the vivid zinnia ranged down the flagged and graveled walks.

Along these pathways moved starchly uniformed nannies pushing perambulators; courting couples; prettily gowned ladies accompanied by stiffly tailored hubands. David mingled amongst them, thinking how idyllic the scene was on this splendid day. He was glad to be alive with his future ahead of him and so many things to see and do, so much to achieve. Success beckoned and he was as positive as Emma that his own business enterprises would prosper.

And why not? This was the year of 1907, when King Edward's reign was at its zenith and his popularity with his people unchallenged; a year when society flirted and danced and hunted and sailed and laughed away the days under King Bertie's outgoing and benevolent rule; a year when the aristocracy made pleasure the god and gave no thought to the grim realities of life, or of war, for the African debacle was forgotten and peace in Europe was assured. In short, 1907 was a year when the ruling classes lived their carefree lives to the full, not considering the stony-faced world beyond the shores of their glorious and invincible England. And every Englishman, David Kallinski included, was lulled into a sense of false security by their debonair example. The years ahead were full of promise. Change was ripe in the air. Things could only get better. The future, for all, was bright with hope.

Consequently, David's step was lively as he headed for the bandstand. This pagoda-like structure, a dubious tribute to England's far-flung empire, added a touch of the exotic and the oriental to this typical English park, and appeared oddly incongruous in that peaceful and gentle setting. Particularly so this afternoon, since it housed the visiting military band of the Grenadier Guards, bedazzling in their magnificent uniforms and shining from head to toe with the proverbial "spit and polish" of the British army, and curiously out of place in that somewhat outlandish and whimsical replica of a mandarin's teahouse.

He scanned the seats in front of the bandstand and, seeing no sight of his friends, settled himself in one of the small wrought-iron chairs. The band finished warming up and, after a few flourishes, they commenced their program with the national anthem. As the concert continued thoughts of Emma drifted into David's head and took complete hold of him. She was rarely out of his mind these days, and he realized his interest in her was not solely as a business associate, but as a woman. The tender but also passionate feelings he now harbored for her had crept up on him so stealthily he had been taken by surprise. And how did she feel about him? he wondered. Anything at all, other than affection and friendship? Was she too preoccupied with her work to give him a solitary thought? And she was married, a circumstance he had to face. The prospects were bleak for any man who had the bad luck to fall in love with a married woman. But love her he did. Where is that damned husband of hers? David asked himself. The missing husband had not appeared on the scene at all, not even when the baby was born. Sailors came home on leave, didn't they? It was a mystery, but David had not, as yet, ventured to ask Emma about her husband, or whether she still loved him. David suspected that she did not. Emma never mentioned him, nor did she appear to miss him. David sighed. He had to admit that his hands were tied. He could not, in all conscience, proclaim himself to her, in view of her marital status.

David, lost in his reverie, was startled by Blackie's voice at his shoulder. "There ye are, me boyo!" David looked up quickly and was disappointed to see that only Laura Spencer accompanied Blackie. David stood up and took Blackie's outstretched hand. He bent down and kissed Laura affection-

ately on the cheek, and flashed her a gay smile that belied his
real feelings. However, he was unable to keep the dejection
out of his voice when he asked, "What happened to Emma?
Where is she?"

"Ah, David, 'tis sorry I am to be telling ye that Emma
declined the invitation. I tried, sure and I did, to persuade
her to join us. But she was obstinate as always. She's finishing
a blasted frock for a lady at the Towers, and she wouldn't
budge an inch," explained Blackie with a little grimace. "Still
an' all, she did say she'd be right delighted to see ye for
supper at Laura's later." Blackie continued in a cheery tone,
"Now, me lad, don't look so downcast! We'll go back to the
house in a few hours. She'll be finished by then." He swung
his head to Laura. "And what about ye, love? What would ye
like to be doing?"

"Let's go for a walk, if David doesn't mind," Laura murmured softly.

"Yes, let's do that," David said.

The three of them wandered away from the bandstand and
the rousing strains of "Land of Hope and Glory." David
glanced at Laura. She looked radiant. She was wearing a
simple dress made of an inexpensive muslin of the palest
yellow, patterned with daisies and sprigs of green, and the
gauzy fabric floated around her like a cloud of hazy sunny
color, emphasizing her willowy figure and her grace of movement. A large-brimmed straw hat, trimmed with yellow and
pink tea roses, shaded her face and there was something
ethereal about her today. Under the brim of the hat her face
looked incandescent, framed by her golden hair and illuminated by her liquid eyes.

"You *are* looking lovely, Laura," David said gallantly. "And
I like your dress. It's very becoming to you, love."

"Thank you, David," she said. "Emma made it for me. She
also trimmed this old hat and turned it into a brand-new one.
She's so talented, isn't she?"

David nodded and Blackie grunted. "Aye, but her talent
won't be doing her much good in the graveyard, I am thinking."

"Blackie! What a terrible thing to say!" Laura cried. She
gave David a lightning glance. He was silent, but she noticed
then that he was biting his lip and looked worried. Laura
wisely made no further remarks, but she threw a rather cold
glare at Blackie, who had the grace to look chagrined.

They walked around the park slowly. Blackie and Laura talked amiably together about things in general; the usually gregarious David was silent and brooding. Eventually they found themselves at the top of a steep ridge where steps led down to the river Aire. Laura complained of the heat, and so they sat down on a bench under the shade of a weeping willow. David gazed morosely across the river, his eyes resting reflectively on the ruins of the grand Cistercian Abbey of Kirkstall on the opposite shore. Then they flitted across the tranquil scenery that stretched towards the horizon, taking in Horsforth Woods beyond the ruins, which were capped further by Rawdon Village and Wharfedale's Reach. He sighed and took out his packet of cigarettes. He offered one to Blackie, who accepted it and murmured his thanks. Finally, David could not hold back any longer. He faced Blackie and said, "I don't understand it, Blackie. What is it that drives Emma so hard?"

"Hatred, pure and simple," Blackie replied automatically, and he could have bitten off his tongue. Furious with himself, he turned away.

Laura gasped and covered her mouth with her hand. She said, "Oh, Blackie, surely not!"

David was equally disturbed by this statement. "Hatred!" he said sharply. "Not Emma. She is loving and sweet. And hatred for who?"

Blackie did not answer for a moment. He cursed himself instead. He was a big-mouthed fool. A stupid boyo. He was that, indeed. In Blackie's opinion Emma's hatred was for the Fairleys. But he was not about to divulge this to David or Laura.

"Come on, Blackie. Give me an answer," David pressed. "Don't sit there looking so mysterious."

Blackie roused himself. "I don't really know, David. I shouldn't have spoken so rashly, lad. But ye know what the Irish are like, always blabbering on. Anyroads, I didn't mean anybody specific." Blackie paused, his face a picture of assumed innocence. "I think perhaps it is hatred for the circumstances of her life," he suggested, trying to cover his error. "And hatred for poverty. That's what drives Emma. Her terrible need for money."

David looked a bit skeptical and he frowned. "*I* know Emma wants money. But then, so do you, Blackie. So do I.

On the other hand, we don't devote our lives to its accumulation to the exclusion of all else."

Blackie leaned forward, his black eyes intense. "Aye, lad, but we be wanting money for different reasons than Emma. It occurs to me ye be desirous of it to buy yeself a better life. Sure and why so? 'Tis the fine house ye be wanting, David, and the smart carriage and the elegant clothes. A few of the beautiful things, I am thinking, just like me. And a bit of security for the future, eh?"

David nodded, for Blackie did indeed speak the truth. "But you said Emma wants money for a different reason. What does she want it for?"

Blackie smiled a small, odd smile. "As a weapon."

"A weapon! Against whom?" Laura demanded.

Blackie took her hand gently. "Don't be upsetting yeself, Laura. Ye be misunderstanding me, love." He regretted having embarked on this discussion and he was loath to continue, but they had him cornered. Two pairs of questioning eyes pinned him down. He had to explain his statements as best he could. Blackie cleared his throat. "I mean that Emma *herself* believes that money is a weapon—"

"Against who?" David cried, interrupting him abruptly. "You still haven't answered Laura."

"Not *against* anyone in particular, David." He shrugged. "Maybe against the world. Yes, I am thinking she will use her money, when she has it, against the world. Or rather, them in it that might try to do her wrong. Ye see, Emma wants money to protect herself and Edwina. She aims to build a fortress around herself and that child, so that nothing can hurt them. Ever. That's all I meant, lad."

David was not only disbelieving but shocked. "You are painting a very strange picture, Blackie. That's not the Emma I know."

"Aye, lad, but I know her better than ye and for much longer. And I think I understand what drives her," Blackie murmured, remembering that exigent look in Emma's eyes the first day they had met on the moors. "I know for a fact she won't rest until she gets that shop. And then it'll be another shop, and another, and another. Emma aims to be a very rich woman one day. You know something, David? She'll succeed. Sure and she will."

"But at what cost?" asked David. "Look at her now. She's

as thin as a rail and worn out. She has black rings under her eyes far too often these days." His eyes rested on Laura. "You live with her. You must admit I'm right."

Laura confessed, "Yes, you are correct to some extent, David, but, in all fairness to Emma, she does eat properly and takes care of herself."

"Except that she never sleeps."

"Oh, she does, David!" Laura countered in defense of her friend. "At least five hours. She doesn't seem to need as much rest as other people. But, of course, to be truthful, I am worried about her, too." Laura touched Blackie's arm lightly. "Maybe you should speak to her again. I mean, about taking it more easily."

"How little ye be knowing her, Laura, if ye think anything I say would do any good. She won't listen," said Blackie regretfully.

"You mean we just have to stand by and watch her kill herself with work!" cried David heatedly.

Blackie could not resist chortling. "Don't let Emma hear ye say that," he said through his laughter. "She doesn't believe hard work killed anybody. Sloth, maybe. And ye know yeself what she said about moderation, David." Blackie shook his head, his eyes still merry. "Aye, she's unique, Emma is."

David gazed at him for a moment and then he turned away and sat puffing on his cigarette, attempting to evaluate Blackie's words.

"You know, I thought Emma's idea about having a shop was foolish at first, Blackie," Laura ventured, "but now I am beginning to think it might be the best thing. It would get her out of the mill. She hates that place."

David said, "I had hoped she would come into partnership with me. By this time next year I will have saved up enough to start my own factory. I intend to make a line of women's clothes, as well as take on outside contracting, like my father does. Emma has already designed a line for me." His face lit up. "Have you seen it, Laura?"

"Yes, Emma showed me her sketches. Her ideas are marvelous, I think. Why, that coat with the detachable cape, and the reversible jacket are brilliant, and her maternity clothes—well—they are revolutionary, wouldn't you say? I don't know of anyone making those wraparound skirts, blouses, and dresses that expand to fit the figure as it gets larger. Do you, David?"

"No. She's far ahead of her time as far as styling is concerned."

"I can't argue with ye about that," interjected Blackie. "Listen, both of ye, don't let's be looking on the black side. Emma will be all right in the long run. She's a real survivor. But if it makes ye both feel better, why don't we *all* talk to her tonight. Careful like, so we don't upset her. Perhaps we can get her to slow down for a bit. The three of us together might be able to make some headway." Blackie was not convinced Emma would pay any attention to them, but he wanted to alleviate their worry, Laura's in particular.

"Yes, let's do that," agreed David. He now looked at Blackie guardedly before commencing in a cautious voice, "Look here, Blackie, I know this is none of my business, but where the hell is that husband of Emma's? It seems a bit queer to me that he hasn't been home on leave. Emma came to work for Dad in August of 1905. That's almost two years ago and her husband has been noticeably absent all that time."

Blackie had been anticipating this question, dreading it, in fact, for months. He had warned Emma time and again to prepare a plausible story. Last week she had told him she was soon going to announce that her sailor husband had deserted her. Taking a deep breath, Blackie now decided to save her the trouble. "Ah, David, I'm glad ye asked me, sure and I am." He turned swiftly to Laura and took her hand in his. "And ye might as well be knowing, too, me love. Emma has been a trifle embarrassed, not knowing how to be telling ye both her news. Ye see, that bleeding husband—" He stopped short and squeezed Laura's hand apologetically. "Sorry, love, I know ye don't like me to be swearing. Anyroads, that rascally husband of hers has done a bunk, ye might say. He deserted Emma some time ago." Blackie, praying he was being convincing, went on, "Seems he wants a big naval career, sure and he does. He told Emma he didn't want to be tied down by a wife. I don't expect we'll see hide nor hair of him in these parts. No, he won't ever be back. That's my guess."

"Oh, Blackie, how terrible for poor Emma and the baby," Laura cried, and he felt her hand tremble in his.

Blackie put his arm around her. "Now, mavourneen, there's no reason for ye to be getting all worked up. Emma isn't that bothered, not at all, at all. 'Tis glad, she is, I am thinking.

Sure and did she not say to me, 'Good riddance,' after she be telling me all the details," he lied smoothly.

David was utterly still, but his heart was beating rapidly and a tingling excitement surged through his veins. "I'm sorry to hear that," he remarked in an even voice that did not betray the jubilance he was feeling. "Still, if Emma is not unhappy, then perhaps it is for the best." He wondered, as he spoke, how much a divorce cost.

Blackie nodded. "Aye, ye are right."

David sprang up. His despondency had vanished. "Shall we make our way back and then listen to the music for a while, before going on to the house?"

"Sure and why not," agreed Blackie. He helped Laura up off the bench and they walked slowly in the direction of the bandstand. And Blackie thought: I must warn Emma I've neatly disposed of that sailor husband of hers.

Whilst these discussions had been taking place in Armley park, Emma was not at home sewing, as her friends believed. She was on her way to see Joe Lowther, who lived in another part of Armley.

The minute Laura and Blackie had departed, Emma had quickly changed into her black silk dress, donned her Leghorn straw bonnet, and taken sixty pounds out of the black tin box that contained her savings. She had rushed out of the house, close on the heels of her friends, a look of resolve on her face.

Quite by accident, when she had been shopping for groceries yesterday, she had seen *it*. The shop. *Her shop*. It was one of three that adjoined each other in a small block that fronted onto Town Street, and it was vacant. Emma had stopped abruptly, gazing at it hypnotized. It appeared exactly right for her in every way. The timing was perfect; she now had the money required for the rent and the stocks. The large empty window had been whitewashed, but there was a small clear space in the center, where a notice had been neatly stuck on the inside. TO LET, it had read, and underneath was printed the name of the landlord, Mr. Joe Lowther, and his address. Emma had memorized the details and hurried home late on Saturday afternoon, determined to be the first applicant the following day. She did not care that this was Sunday, a day when business was not normally conducted, since she was prepared to do business any day of the week.

Now as she walked briskly through the labyrinth of streets, almost breathless with mounting excitement, she half regretted selecting the black dress. It was really too warm for this scorching day. But in spite of the heat and the warmth of the dress, Emma did not slow her pace, and within fifteen minutes she was approaching the street where Joe Lowther lived. She found the house and marched up the stone steps resolutely. She knocked soundly three times and waited. A few moments elapsed before the door was opened by a tall, sturdily built young man. He was fair, with large gray eyes and light brown hair, and his pleasant face was open and honest. He was in his shirt sleeves and his hair was rumpled.

He stared down at Emma, obviously surprised to see a visitor. "Yes, miss, what can I do for you?" he asked gruffly.

"I'd like to see your father, please," Emma said politely, and proffered a tentative smile.

"My father? I think you must have the wrong house, miss. My father's been dead these past six years."

"Oh dear, perhaps I've made a mistake. I was looking for the home of a Mr. Joe Lowther."

"Then you've found it, miss. I'm Joe Lowther."

Emma was surprised. "Oh! Well, please excuse me, but I thought you seemed a bit young to be the landlord of the shop on Town Street. The shop that's to let," Emma said with her usual forthrightness. She saw at once that the young man was bristling and she rushed on, "Are *you* that Mr. Lowther?"

"That's me, all right," said the young man. His eyes narrowed. "Are you interested in the shop, then? For your *mother*?"

"No," Emma said, faintly amused. He was apparently stinging from her reference to his youthful appearance, and so she smiled that radiant smile and her unwavering green gaze, warm and self-assured, did not leave his face. "Actually, I want to rent the shop for myself."

Joe Lowther said, "Oh, you do, do you! Aren't you a bit *young*? What experience of retailing do you have, miss?"

Emma considered this to be none of his business, but refrained from telling him so, being canny enough not to brush him the wrong way again. Instead she said, "I have some experience, and I've also done a lot of dressmaking and catering here in Armley. I have a nice business going, and now I want a shop so I can conduct it from there." Her voice vibrated with enormous confidence as she added, "And I'm certainly not too young, Mr. Lowther."

Joe shook his head. "No. No. It wouldn't work. I can't say I'd be willing to rent the shop to you, miss," he said with a certain brusqueness.

Emma ignored his blunt retort. "But I am willing to take the shop off your hands now, Mr. Lowther. At once. Today." Emma climbed up two steps until she was on a level with Joe Lowther. She stared at him, exercising all of her considerable charm, smiling beguilingly. "Can't we go inside and discuss this, Mr. Lowther?" she asked in a voice as smooth as silk.

"I can't see the sense in that, since I won't change my mind," he declared stubbornly. Her proximity was distracting him and as he looked into her face, only a few inches away from his, Joe felt himself growing hot around the collar.

Emma opened her purse, resorting to the one stratagem in which she had absolute belief. "I can pay in advance, Mr. Lowther."

Joe reluctantly brought his gaze up to meet Emma's and he discovered he was mesmerized by those brilliant eyes observing him with such cool concentration. Whatever will the neighbors think if I invite her in? he asked himself. But since he was not generally discourteous, Joe was now ashamed of his rudeness and he found himself saying in a kinder voice, "Well, you're right about one thing, we had better go inside." This was really prompted by his concern for the gossips in the street and, so she would not think he had changed his mind about the shop, Joe felt obliged to add, "It's not very fitting to discuss business on the doorstep at the best of times, and especially on Sunday. I don't usually do business on *Sundays*, miss."

"Well, there's always a first time for everything, Mr. Lowther," said Emma, eyeing him with amusement from under her thick lashes. She was aware that Joe was ill at ease and she intended to use this to her advantage.

Why, she's as bold as brass, Joe thought, seething with combined annoyance and exasperation. Nevertheless, he opened the door wider and ushered her into the house. He showed her into the parlor. "Excuse me. I'll be back in a

minute. Please sit down," said Joe. He closed the door behind him and retreated.

Emma stood in the middle of the room, blinking in the dim
light. She grimaced as her eyes adjusted to the dolorous
gloom. The room reminded her of Mrs. Daniel's front parlor,
all Victorian folderols and a preponderance of overstuffed
furniture. But the furniture is good, she thought. There's just
too much of it. She seated herself on an uncomfortable horsehair chair to wait.

Emma had discovered three important things since she had
been in Leeds: Money talked in the most persuasive voice.
Put cold hard cash down on a table and few people could
resist picking it up; payment in advance was another irresistible temptation and the more advance you paid, the stronger
you were; and finally, opportunity had to be seized firmly the
instant it presented itself, because it did not come knocking
on the same door twice in one week. Emma considered all of
these things, but mostly she wondered if Joe Lowther could
be swayed by money. For some reason she was not positive
of this. She frowned, ruminating on Joe, endeavoring to
assess him. He was certainly bashful. She also knew she had
unnerved him on the doorstep and, in her shrewd opinion,
this gave her the upper hand. Still, that did not mean he
would agree to rent her the shop. Apparently he believed her
youth to be a disadvantage, and yet he did not appear to be
much older than she was. He was perhaps twenty or twenty-
one. Nonetheless, it was imperative that she convince him
she was capable and experienced at retailing, and that she
would therefore be a responsible tenant. Perhaps three months'
rent would be a suitable inducement. It would not only
reassure him of her serious intentions, but would also illus-
trate her business acumen over the past year. It then struck
Emma that she must be her most charming self. Joe Lowther
would succumb to sweetness. Sweetness and money. An
unbeatable combination. Emma smoothed her dress, feeling
calm as the door opened.

Joe had put on his tie and jacket and his hair was now
combed back neatly. Emma could see the water glistening on
it. She dropped her head quickly so he would not detect the
smile on her face. Joe Lowther had become quite transparent
to her. There would be a bit of a tussle between them, but
the shop would be hers when she left this house.

Joe sat down opposite Emma and, adopting his brusquest tone, he commenced, "Now, about the shop, miss. I've been thinking it over, and I have definitely decided I can't rent it to you."

"Whyever not?" Emma asked in her most dulcet voice.

"Because two people have failed in it this year, and they'd had a lot more experience than *you*. I don't want to sound harsh, miss, but you must understand I can't take a chance on renting to somebody who's a novice. I'm seeking a tenant that really knows retailing, who'll make a go of the shop, so I don't have to be worrying about it being vacant half the time. I've better things to do than play nursemaid."

Emma gave Joe a smile that would have melted half the ice in the Arctic Circle and made her eyes wide but serious. "Oh, I do realize that, Mr. Lowther," she answered. "And, in some ways, I understand your reluctance because of my youth. However, it's not really of great consequence when you consider that I have been running a business from my home. I have been dealing with people, *selling* to them. My business has been highly profitable. I've made a lot of money with my dressmaking and homemade foodstuffs. I have good steady customers, mostly the carriage trade, and they would certainly give me their patronage if I had a shop." Emma paused and flashed a brilliant smile. "Why, they have assured me of that," she fibbed adroitly. "So you see, I'm not really as inexperienced as you believe, and I do have expectations."

"Carriage trade, you say," remarked Joe, not unimpressed. "And how long have you been running this little business from your home?"

"About a year," said Emma, leaning forward, eagerness washing over her face. "And it's not so *little* either."

Joe regarded her intently. She was direct and sounded businesslike and certainly she was not lacking in assurance. In fact, he had never met a girl as self-possessed as she was. Her spirit and enthusiasm were refreshing, almost infectious, and his doubts about her youth and ability were rapidly diminishing. However, she disconcerted him, but then he had always been awkward around girls and one as beautiful as she was bound to make him feel insecure. Still, she only wanted to rent a shop from him and that was all. "Well, I don't really know what to say," he began hesitatingly.

Conscious that he was wavering, Emma held up her hand.

"Just a minute, Mr. Lowther," she said authoritatively. "I said earlier I would pay you in advance." She opened her black reticule and brought out a thick roll of bank notes. "As you can see, Mr. Lowther, I don't make idle claims. I am a woman of some substance, albeit a young one, and indeed I can pay you *well* in advance. I know I can make a go of the shop, Mr. Lowther. I expect to be a success within *six months*."

Joe stared at her incredulously. "Oh, come on! That's a bit farfetched. Do you think I fell off a banana boat? I'm not green, you know."

Emma decided these comments were unworthy of a reply. Instead she stretched out her hand. "I have been so rude, Mr. Lowther. I haven't introduced myself. My name is Emma Harte."

He took her hand tentatively. He felt its dry coolness through the crocheted glove and her grip was firm, strong like a man's. "Pleased to meet you, Miss Harte," he said.

"It's *Mrs.* Harte," said Emma.

"Oh, excuse me," said Joe, assailed by unexpected disappointment.

Emma grabbed the moment to drive her point home. "I don't know what the rent is, Mr. Lowther, but I would be prepared to pay you several months in advance." She must make the offer so tempting he would not be able to refuse. "Shall we say *six months* in advance? Surely that shows you my good faith and also my belief in myself."

Joe was floundering, his resolve crumbling under the force of her compelling and winning personality. He recognized he was drawn to her. Dangerously attracted to her. The unworldly Joe was horrified. A married woman! Then it came to him in a rush. That was the real reason he did not want her as a tenant. He was afraid of falling under her spell.

Emma knew she was holding all the cards and she made her final move. She leaned forward and touched his arm gently. Joe jumped as if bitten by a snake. "Look here, Mr. Lowther," Emma said firmly. "I have another idea. Apart from paying you the rent in advance, I'm also prepared to give you a letter of agreement stating that should my business fail I will not vacate the premises until you find another tenant. In other words, I will guarantee to give you sufficient

warning before leaving. Shall we say three months' notice?"
she suggested in a guileless voice.

Joe found it impossible to argue with this girl. Not only
were her terms sound, they were all in his favor. He would
look like an imbecile if he refused such an offer. "Well," he
said at last, "you are certainly confident of your success in the
shop, Mrs. Harte. Otherwise you wouldn't suggest such an
arrangement. But it's fair enough, I suppose. Don't you want
to look the shop over first, before going into this venture?"

"I know the shop, Mr. Lowther," Emma said with an airy
wave of her hand. "I went into it several times. Your previous
tenant was badly organized, the stock was shoddy and far too
expensive for its quality, and she was obviously not a very
clever buyer. Not only that, she didn't know her customers!"

"Oh," said Joe, dumbfounded.

"I presume it's settled, Mr. Lowther," said Emma briskly.

"Er, yes, of course. I'll rent the shop to you," he said. "For
a guinea a week. That makes it four guineas a month. There
are living quarters attached to the shop. A large kitchen-
parlor, a bedroom, and a huge cellar for storage. You could
live there, behind the shop, and very comfortably, if you had
a mind to."

Emma nodded. "Yes, I probably will live there. It makes
sense. Now, four guineas a month is around forty-eight guineas a year, give or take a few shillings, isn't it?" She began to
peel off the notes, doing some fast mental arithmetic. "Could
I have a receipt, please?" she asked politely, handing over
the cash.

"Naturally," said Joe. "And I will get you the key and the
rent book. I'll mark the book paid for six months. Should it be
in your name or your husband's?"

"Mine, please. My husband is in the navy, Mr. Lowther.
In foreign parts."

"Is he really!" said Joe.

Emma nodded and went on, "I'll write you the letter of
agreement about the three months' notice. I'll bring it around
tomorrow evening. Is that convenient? You can show it to
your solicitor, if you want."

"No. No. That's not necessary. And tomorrow night is
perfectly convenient," said Joe. He stood up. "I'll go and get
the key and the rent book. I'll be back in a jiffy."

"Aren't you going to count the money?" Emma asked, nodding at the pounds in his hand.

"I trust you," Joe said. "Please excuse me, Mrs. Harte."

Emma heard him whistling as he went through into the kitchen. A wide smile of self-congratulation mingled with exultation flew onto her face. She could hardly contain herself. She now had her first shop.

THIRTY-FOUR

Joe Lowther shrugged into his black overcoat and dug his hands into his pockets, shivering as he strode along at a brisk pace. A fierce wind was whistling down the lane and it blew the sleet and snow against his body in swirling flurries. He was drenched again, as he had been every night this week. December had ushered in the foulest weather, which now at the end of the first week appeared to have settled in for a long siege. He was later than ever tonight. Once again he had been inveigled into staying at the foundry to finish the books as a special favor to Mr. Ramsbotham, who had lately acquired the annoying habit of piling extra work on him. His tardiness irritated him for another, more significant reason. Usually on Friday evening, after his supper, he went to Emma Harte's to look over the books for her. Tonight he would not be able to get there until almost ten o'clock, and Joe, the product of a lower-middle-class upbringing, was rigid in his observance of the proprieties. It did not seem correct to go calling on a young woman who lived alone at such a late hour. Still, he had promised and he felt honor-bound to keep his word.

Joe had taught Emma bookkeeping, and supervising her ledgers was a practice he considered unnecessary these days. Nevertheless, it was one he did willingly and, if he was honest with himself, he looked forward to doing it. Emma had a staggering aptitude for figures and kept meticulous books. It had struck him recently that she actually enjoyed toiling over those endless columns of figures in a way he did not. If the truth be known, he did not like bookkeeping at all. It was hardly his vocation. However, he had been appren-

ticed in the accounting office at the foundry when he was
fifteen, and after nine years it had become a way of life for
him. It never occurred to Joe to seek a more congenial
employer. He was too set in his ways and, since he was not
ambitious and lacked the drive to strike out in new directions, he remained shackled to Ramsbotham's dreary books.
Nor did it ever occur to the stolid Joe that he did not have to
work at all, if he chose not to. He detested idleness and,
more importantly, he harbored a palpable fear of boredom.
His job at the foundry filled his days and helped to counteract
the empty evenings of solitude that yawned inexorably before
him month after month, year after year.

But Joe Lowther could have stopped working when his
mother had died four years ago. It was then that Frederick
Ainsley, the family solicitor, had sent for him to hear the will
read and Joe had discovered, to his profound astonishment,
that his mother had left him not only in comfortable circumstances but extremely well off. "It is An Inheritance, my
boy," Mr. Ainsley had said, speaking in capitals as befitted
the occasion and the size of the estate. "A tribute to your
poor departed mother's prodigious and most commendable
efforts over the years, and to your grandmother's before her,"
the solicitor had intoned. Frederick Ainsley had then gone on
to enumerate the number of properties Joe now owned,
thanks to the unflagging industriousness of those two women
on the maternal side of the family. The Inheritance, which
Joe immediately felt obliged to think of in Mr. Ainsley's large
letters, included eight shops in Town Street, a row of cottages in Armley, several terrace houses in nearby Wortley,
and, to Joe's further incredulity, two large plots of land near
St. Paul's Street in Leeds itself. "Better hang on to those,
Joe," Ainsley had instructed. "They will increase in value.
Lots of building going on in Leeds. When you do sell it
should be for a high price." Finally, the speechless Joe had
learned that his mother had left him fifty-five thousand pounds
in cash in the Midland Bank. Joe had staggered out of the
solicitor's office reeling from shock on that awesome day.
Later, sitting on the tram on his way home to Armley, a cold
anger had settled over him. His mother had never ceased her
querulous warnings of financial disaster looming on the horizon. His sweet-tempered and henpecked father had been
mercilessly driven into an early grave from overwork and lack

of nourishing food and proper medical attention. Why had his mother been so cruel when they had had so much? he had asked himself, and his resentment of her had not lessened with time.

Joe had not touched that capital during these past few years. He had simply added to it, paying the revenue from the properties into the bank every month. Unlike his avaricious mother, there was little cupidity in Joe and as long as he had sufficient for his daily needs that was good enough for him. Most of the time money never crossed his mind at all.

However, he thought about it this night as he trudged through the dark wet streets. Two weeks earlier Emma had mentioned that she was investing in David Kallinski's first clothing factory in York Road. She had already designed a line of ladies' clothes for David and her enthusiasm was infectious. When Emma had suggested David might let him invest as well, Joe had been surprised. "Money should be made to work, Joe," Emma had pronounced, and she informed him that she hoped to double her money in no time at all.

Although Joe was cautious by nature, this was chiefly engendered by shyness, rather than any particular canniness. His laissez-faire attitude about finances had prompted him to shrug nonchalantly and agree to invest, if David wanted him to do so. Emma had said she would arrange it. "I think two thousand pounds would be just the right amount," she had gone on. "If you can afford it. As a financial man, you should know, without me telling you, that money is a tool to be used to make more money, Joe. What good is it doing in the bank?"

I don't really need to make more money, Joe now said to himself. He was settled for life. On the other hand, he did not particularly want to lose two thousand pounds. He dismissed this negative thought. Joe had an infallible belief in Emma's innate shrewdness, having witnessed it at first hand, and he had long recognized her brilliance in business matters, amazing for a twenty-year-old girl. He trusted her judgment. Also, Joe was intelligent enough to acknowledge that he was really investing in the clothing factory for the fun of it. He liked David and Emma, and because he had few friends and was miserably lonely, he longed to be involved in their lives, to be part of this exciting venture.

So caught up was he in his diverse thoughts Joe found

himself on his own doorstep in no time at all. He knocked the snow off his boots as he climbed the steps. Delicious aromas of food cooking greeted him, and the warmth of the sparkling kitchen dispelled his lonely feelings.

Mrs. Hewitt was setting the table for his supper. "There yer are, Joe," she cried, her face beaming, "By gum, yer look nithered ter death, luvey. Come ter the fire and get yersel warmed up."

"Hello, Mrs. Hewitt," Joe said, taking off his cap and struggling out of his coat. He hurried over to the sink, rubbing his hands to dispel their iciness. He dried his hair and face, washed his hands, and then sat down by the fire. "It's a blustery night, Mrs. Hewitt, and very cold. I think there'll be a hard frost."

Mrs. Hewitt nodded. "Aye, yer probably right, lad." She glanced at him and frowned, "Nay, Joe, don't sit there in yer wet boots, luv. Take 'em off at once. That's how yer get toothache, yer knows, luvey, sitting in wet boots."

Joe smiled at this old wives' tale, but he unlaced his boots and placed them on the hearth to please her. She was a nice old body and looked after him far better than his mother ever had, and three nights a week she helped to transform this depressing house into a home.

"Look at this custard flan," Mrs. Hewitt exclaimed, pointing to the dessert on the table. "Have yer ever seen owt a luvely? I bought it as pudding for yer, at Mrs. Harte's. By gum, Joe, no wonder she does a roaring trade. And the way she's trained them two lasses of Mrs. Long's to be her helpers, why, it fair takes me breath away."

Joe smiled at her. "I never thought she'd make such a go of it when she took that first shop. But she proved *me* wrong and a lot of others as well."

"Aye, lad, she's a right good tenant for yer," Mrs. Hewitt conceded.

"What's for supper?" Joe asked, warming his hands. "It smells good."

"I can't be taking no credit for yer dinner tonight, Joe," the old woman replied. "I bought yer a steak-and-kidney pie from Mrs. Harte's, being as how yer liked the last one."

"It sounds grand, Mrs. Hewitt."

"I was talking to Laura Spencer today, in the haberdashery, and do yer know, that wedding dress they're making for me cousin's lass is one of Mrs. Harte's own designs. Miss Spencer told me that Mrs. Harte is going to be designing clothes for one of them big factory places in Leeds."

"So I understand," said Joe.

"Fancy that and yer never told me, Joe."

"It didn't occur to me, Mrs. Hewitt. Is it so important?"

"Of course it is, Joe. Anything ter do with Emma Harte is important. Why, everybody thinks she's a right luvely young woman. So polite and dignified. The talk of Town Street with her fancy shops. And such a bonny lass." She carried the bowl of turnips to the oven and continued, "Would yer like a beer, Joe? I've got one cooling on the cellar head."

"I wouldn't say no, Mrs. Hewitt. Thank you." Joe lit his pipe and settled back in the chair, warming his damp feet.

"Well, it's all ready now, Joe," Mrs. Hewitt proclaimed. "I've finished the pots and yer supper'll stay nice and warm in the oven, luvey. Drink yer beer first, and then yer can help yerself later. I'll have ter be off. Ta'rar."

Later, after he had read the paper, Joe took out the meat pie and vegetables and settled down to his supper. He had just finished eating when a loud banging on the door brought him up with a start. The door burst open to admit a flurry of snowflakes along with Mrs. Minton, one of his tenants. Her face was purple and from the furious glint in her eyes Joe knew this was not caused by the icy wind but rather by her roiling temper.

"Good heavens, Mrs. Minton—" he began.

"Don't Mrs. Minton me, Joe Lowther!" she yelled. "It's a crime! A bloody crime. *I just knew it!* Ever since she moved in I knew she was after me shop. And when yer rented her that other one on t'corner I told me husband it wouldn't be long before she had me out. There I am, plonk in the middle, between her food shop and her haberdashery, and she's aiming ter squeeze and squeeze till she get's me out inter the middle of Town Street. Yer can't deny I'm right!" The enraged Mrs. Minton paused for breath, her hands on her hips, her stance defiant.

"Please, Mrs. Minton, calm down. I don't know what on earth you're talking about."

"I'm talking about Emma Harte, that's what! She wants me shop! I don't need a crystal bloody ball ter tell me that. She wants ter expand inter me shop. The shop I've had for ten years. The commercial travelers think she's no good, hoity-toity stuck-up Mrs. Harte. Lady Muck, they calls her. Cutting 'em out, she is, going ter the manufacturers and warehouses herself and buying directly, instead of from the travelers. Then she slashes her prices so's nobody else in Town Street can get a sale in edgewise. Aye, she's a crafty cunning bitch, that Emma Harte is."

"Mrs. Minton!" Joe bellowed. "Emma Harte is a nice girl and she works hard. She isn't trying to squeeze you out. She's simply running her shops in a businesslike manner." Joe stared with distaste at the slovenly woman in her filthy coat and grimy scarf. She was a living reflection of her dirty shop which was a triumph of confusion and run in the most slipshod manner imaginable.

"Aye, I bloody expected yer ter defend her," Mrs. Minton shouted. "I told me husband I wouldn't be getting nowheres with yer. Stands ter reason yer'd watch out for yer fancy woman! Aye, and don't look like that. We all knows what's going on between the both of yer!" She took a step nearer to Joe and peered into his face, hissing, "Yer fancy woman that's what Emma bloody Harte is, and she a married woman. I'm surprised yer haven't put a bun in her oven already. But time will tell, me lad."

Joe had blanched. "Why, you foul-mouthed, despicable old woman. There is nothing between Mrs. Harte and myself other than a business relationship. And you'd better watch your words, Mrs. Minton, or you'll find yourself the recipient of a writ for libel. I will not tolerate this kind of disgusting talk!"

Mrs. Minton leaned forward and waved the rent book she was clutching under his nose. Joe thought she was going to strike him with it. "I think you had better leave, Mrs. Minton," he said icily. "Before I really lose my temper. I've just about had enough of you."

With a toss of her head she swung on her heels and marched to the door. She looked back, her eyes blazing with animosity, and she shouted, "Well, she's not going ter have the satisfaction of squeezing me out, because I'm leaving on me own account! And yer can take yer bloody rent book and shove it!" She flung the rent book across the room at Joe and it landed in the custard flan.

The door banged behind her. Joe stared at the rent book

floating in the custard, fished it out, and carried it to the sink,
wiping it clean with the dishcloth. He looked inside. Miserable old battle-ax, he thought, she owes me a month's rent.
He knew he would have to whistle for that. He did not care.

Joe was horrified at the things Mrs. Minton had said about
Emma and himself. Surely they must have been uttered out
of her consuming spite. Or did everyone in the neighborhood
really believe there was something between them? "Fancy
woman" was not a prestigious name to pin on a woman. It
was just another way of saying tart. He might have guessed
some people would talk, if only the likes of Mrs. Minton. But
he had never laid a finger on Emma, and he felt a flush rising
to flood his face. It was with a rush of guilt that he recalled
those nights when he lay awake in his chaste bed, hardly able
to breathe, his desire for Emma blazing until he could not
bear it. For desire her he did. On those terrible nights he
envisioned himself running his hands over Emma's beautiful
body, pressing his mouth to hers, stroking her firm breasts,
and ultimately taking her to him passionately. He shivered
and closed his eyes, trying to obliterate those erotic images,
those lustful and sensuous fantasies that haunted him.

After a few moments Joe felt calmer. Wanting a woman and
craving to possess her was one thing, but it was scarcely a
reality, and he resented the ghastly implications of Mrs.
Minton's words. Joe sighed wearily, recognizing that Emma
had ruined the harridan's business, albeit unintentionally.
She made sure her products and the shops themselves were
more appealing and attractive than others in the vicinity. Her
specialties, such as her delicious homemade foodstuffs, were
renowned, as was her dressmaking, and she had captured the
carriage trade for miles around. With her audacity and her
superior merchandising, her two shops had become the busiest
in Town Street in just under three years, and her profits were
high. Joe was aware of that from his weekly inspection of her
ledgers. So enormously high, in fact, she could now afford to
invest two thousand pounds in David's business, as he himself intended to do. That kind of success was guaranteed to
provoke jealousy and vicious talk.

Joe stood up, determined not to dwell on Mrs. Minton's
accusations. He would go and see Emma right away and tell
her that Mrs. Minton was about to vacate the premises.
Emma could now have her third shop. Although she had

never said a word to Joe, he knew that she had been angling for it for some time. It made sense, he had to admit that. With Mrs. Minton gone Emma could indeed expand and the three adjoining shops would be like the department store she envisioned owning one day. He caught sight of the clock. It was well turned nine. He shrugged. To hell with the neighbors. I don't care what they believe. He went upstairs to put on a clean shirt.

Emma stood in the middle of the food shop and surveyed her handiwork with satisfaction. Everything looked beautiful, she decided, and it certainly had been well worth getting up at four-thirty that morning to create her special displays for Christmas. Her keen eyes spotted a particle of dust on one of the glass cabinets and she flew over with a cloth. She flicked it off and stood back, scanning the cabinets that sparkled in the bright light from the gas fixtures on the walls. Now they were absolutely perfect and nothing marred their pristine glitter. The food inside looked delectable. There were Christmas cakes topped with almonds; round fat plum puddings wrapped in fresh muslin, each one tied with a gay red ribbon; a selection of mince pies of various sizes; and yule logs made of sponge cake, thickly coated with rich dark chocolate and decorated with sprigs of marzipan mistletoe. Emma, assisted by the Long girls, had spent endless hours baking all of this seasonal fare but she knew her industriousness would be rewarded. Every item would be sold, along with the additional supplies stored in large tins in the cool collar.

Emma smoothed the fresh white cloth on the table in front of the glass food cabinets and regarded her arrangement of foreign imports, delicacies she had purchased for the holiday season and which no other shop in Armley carried. She moved a blue-and-white china crock of crystalized ginger so that the French glazed fruits and the Turkish delight were easily visible, and deftly straightened the boxes of Egyptian dates and figs from Greece. She then hurried behind the counter and returned with a tray of small straw baskets containing marzipan fruits and jolly little pigs, which had arrived yesterday from Germany. The night before, Emma had lined the baskets with strips of crinkled green cellophane paper, and tied red bows on the handles. She was heavily stocked, but she anticipated a brisk business in the next few days. This was her third Christmas in the shop, and she was now so well established in the district she had no qualms about sales. She was convinced she would be inundated with customers, both her regulars and new ones.

Emma gave the shop a final glance, her eyes critically seeking out the tiniest imperfection. Not one was visible. The innumerable shelves, running around the walls and soaring up to the ceiling, held tins of ham, pork, and game, great black-and-gold canisters of varied teas, all manner of other staples, and her own bottled fruits, vegetables, and jams. Ranged below were jars of candied peel, glazed cherries, mincemeat, and cranberry and apple sauces for the Christmas turkeys and geese. Three huge barrels, to the right of the side counter, were filled to overflowing with nuts, apples, and oranges for the children's traditional Christmas stockings, and the faint aroma of fruit wafted sweetly on the air to blend with the mingled scents of the pungent herbs and spices from the Indies, the fragrance of the newly baked confectionery, and the mouth-watering smells of cheeses and cooked meats. Oh, how she loved her shop! Here she was secure, far away from the Fairleys and protected from them. She thought, too, and with enormous pleasure, of the forthcoming sales and her spiraling profits, and her face immediately broke into a smile.

Now Emma crossed to the door, pulled up the blinds, and drew back the bolts in readiness for her first customers. These would undoubtedly be the cooks and housekeepers from the fine mansions, who usually came trooping in early in the day to place their orders. Emma hoped their shopping lists would be longer than ever this week.

As the clock struck eight Emma took up her usual position behind the counter, seating herself on a stool next to the paraffin stove. She bent down and opened a cupboard, taking out the ledger for the haberdashery. In the year she had been renting Joe Lowther's second shop business had far exceeded her wildest dreams. Laura, whom she had persuaded to manage it for her, had proved to be both capable and efficient, and sales had doubled in the first six months. Emma perused the columns of those beautiful figures and sighed in gratification and relief. Edwina's future and her own were now assured.

The tinkling of the bell brought Emma's head up sharply

and she put the ledger away and locked the cupboard. She stood up, smiling at the woman entering. It was the housekeeper from one of the fine residences in the elegant and exclusive row known as the Towers. "Good morning, Mrs. Jackson," Emma said. "You're out bright and early."

"Morning to you, Mrs. Harte. By gum, it's nippy today. I'm glad to be in your lovely warm shop. I don't know why the other shopkeepers don't follow your example and heat up their premises." Mrs. Jackson shivered as she approached the counter with two large baskets. "I thought I'd best get my order in first thing, though I won't be sending the gardener's lad for it till later in the week." She handed over the baskets and sat down on the stool at the other side of the counter.

Emma stowed the baskets away and said, "Can I offer you a cup of nice hot tea, Mrs. Jackson?"

The woman's face, white and pinched from the freezing weather, lit up. "You can that, luv, if it's no trouble. It was a right frosty walk down Town Street, I can tell you."

Emma always kept a huge pot of tea prepared in the cold weather, which she dispensed generously to her clientele. She had discovered that a little hospitality cost nothing and paid enormous dividends. She lifted the pot from the table next to the stove, adjusted the tea cozy and poured the tea. "Milk and sugar, isn't it, Mrs. Jackson? And how's your little Freddy doing? Has he recovered from the measles?" Emma asked. She made a point of knowing about her customers' children and husbands, and their aches and pains, and she was always ready to offer a sympathetic ear.

Mrs. Jackson accepted the tea, beaming with delight. "Well, isn't that nice of you to remember Freddy. He'll be up and about for Christmas." She opened her handbag and took out a piece of paper. "Here's my list, Mrs. Harte. I think it's complete, but I'll have a look round, if you don't mind and—" Mrs. Jackson paused midsentence. The bell was tinkling and the door opened.

Emma's face broke into a surprised but delighted smile. "Blackie!" she exclaimed, "I didn't expect you until tonight."

"Top of the morning to ye, Emma, and to ye, ma'am," Blackie responded cheerily, inclining his head in Mrs. Jackson's direction. "I hope I'm not disturbing ye, Emma."

"No, not at all. Come around the counter and help yourself to some tea, while I finish with Mrs. Jackson," said Emma, turning her attention to her customer. She looked over the list quickly. "Yes, everything seems clear, Mrs. Jackson. Still, perhaps you should—" Emma paused and gave the housekeeper a thoughtful look. "I wonder if you should take some extra mince pies and yule logs. You know how the children love them, and it *is* a long holiday season this year. To be honest with you, I have a large number of orders to meet. I can't promise there will be much left at the end of the week, if you did decide you wanted more."

"Ooh, I hadn't thought of that. Well, perhaps you'd better increase it. I don't want the missis upset with me. Make it three more of each and pop in another Christmas cake as well," said Mrs. Jackson. Her eyes caught the display of imports and she walked over to the table, carrying her mug of tea. "By gum, these look real fancy." She examined a box of Turkish delight and read out Emma's carefully lettered card. "Exclusive to Harte's. Supply limited."

Emma pretended to check the shopping list, watching Mrs. Jackson from beneath her lashes. She had chosen those words deliberately last night, knowing they would appeal to her customers' snobbishness.

Mrs. Jackson continued to look over the foreign sweetmeats and then said, "I'm not so sure about any of these. They look interesting, but maybe they're just a bit too fancy for my missis."

"Oh, do you think so, Mrs. Jackson? I've always found the gentry to be partial to such delicacies," Emma said pointedly. "Actually, I'm sorry I didn't order more. Those items are going like wildfire. Why, only yesterday, one of the cooks from the Towers asked me to save her two of everything," she improvised swiftly. "Still, I realize they are a little expensive."

Mrs. Jackson gave Emma a sharp look. "My missis isn't concerned about the price of anything, Mrs. Harte," she said defensively. "I'll take *three* of everything!"

Emma smiled. She had learned to take advantage of the competitiveness between the local cooks and housekeepers, who were always trying to better each other. "Very good, Mrs. Jackson. I'll make a note and put them away immediately."

Mrs. Jackson's eyes roved over the shelves behind Emma. "While you're at it, you'd best add a tin of that imported ham and four bottles of your chutney to my list. *My* lady's expecting a lot of *posh* guests over the holidays. It's wise to be prepared."

"Yes, that's true. And you can always send the gardener's boy down later in the week, if there's anything else you've forgotten. You know I'll always do my best for *you*, Mrs. Jackson."

The housekeeper preened. "It's nice to know I'm a favored customer, Mrs. Harte. I know I can rely on you. Now, do you think I've missed anything off the list, being as how you know so much about catering? I do want the missis to be pleased with my menus for the holidays."

Emma made a show of thinking hard. "I would add two tins of pork and three jars of apple sauce, if I were you. For emergencies. And perhaps a selection of cheeses to go with the Christmas cakes. Leave it to me, Mrs. Jackson. I'll pick out the very best of my cheeses, and perhaps a couple of other items."

Mrs. Jackson placed the mug on the counter, looking as if Emma had just done her an enormous favor. "Thank you, Mrs. Harte. It's thoughtful of you to take so much trouble for me. I must say, you've made my life easier since you've been in Town Street. I don't have to do so much cooking these days. Well, I must be on me way. Merry Christmas to you, luv." She paused at the door and waved.

"Merry Christmas, Mrs. Jackson. And remember, don't you worry about a thing. I'll see your order is filled exactly," Emma called after her.

"I bet you will," Blackie said with a grin as he came around the counter and lowered himself onto the stool Mrs. Jackson had vacated. "Ye could sell coal to the natives in darkest Africa. I've never seen anything like it, Emma. Why, ye must have doubled that poor woman's order."

"Tripled it," said Emma with a smug little smile.

Blackie shook his head and adopted a serious expression. "Well, Emma, I just stopped by to pay me condolences to ye."

"Condolences?"

"Aye, I understand ye sailor husband passed away unexpectedly a few weeks ago. Died of typhoid fever in the Indian Ocean, so I be hearing. How very sad." He threw back that great head and roared. Emma laughed with him. "My God, Emma, what an imagination ye have. It's ye who should be an aspiring writer and not Frank. Typhoid fever in the Indian Ocean indeed!"

"Well, I had to kill him off," Emma said. "It was becoming a real nuisance—having a husband. Even one who had deserted me. I thought it was best to have him die far away and be buried at sea."

Blackie chuckled. "True. True." He eyed her red wool dress. "I can see ye are not in mourning."

"My friends wouldn't expect me to wear black for a man who deserted me, now would they? I suppose Laura told you."

"That she did. She said ye had received a letter from the Admiralty the other morning. Ye certainly lay it on thick, don't ye?"

"I had to make it sound authentic, Blackie. They were only white lies. I can tell the truth from now on."

"Oh, ye can, can ye?"

"Yes, of course," Emma said firmly. "But not about Edwina. We have to protect her at all costs. Nobody must know that she's illegitimate, Blackie."

"I won't be betraying ye, mavourneen. Ye know that. By the way, I saw David Kallinski yesterday. I went to look over the factory, so I can make me plans for the alterations. I hope ye don't mind, but I told him about ye husband passing on."

"Oh! What did he say?" she asked cautiously.

"He said he was sorry. But to me he looked like a man who'd just inherited a million pounds." Blackie scrutinized her carefully. "What's going on between the two of ye, Emma?"

"Why, nothing," she said evenly. "I'm his business partner, that's all."

"Oh, aye," said Blackie thoughtfully. "Well, it strikes me he thinks otherwise."

"Stuff and nonsense. It's your Celtic imagination getting the better of you. Yours is a sight more vivid than even Frank's."

Blackie did not reply. He reached into his overcoat, pulled out a sheaf of papers, and handed them to Emma. "Here are the plans for renovating the middle shop and then joining all three together like ye wanted, mavourneen. I aim to go into Mrs. Minton's on either side. That is, from the haberdashery and through that wall over there. I'll make a sort of passage that links all three. How does that sound?"

"Wonderful, Blackie! You know I trust your judgment. I'll look at the plans tonight. When will you start?" she asked eagerly.

"Knowing ye, I suppose ye'd like me to start immediately, but it'll have to be after Christmas, Emma. We'll do a fast job, though, and ye'll be in the shop by the middle of January."

THIRTY-FIVE

D avid Kallinski leaned back against the sofa in the kitchen-parlor behind Emma's food shop and thoughtfully regarded the last of her sketches. He held it away from him, his eyes narrowing perceptively.

As he continued to gaze at it David experienced a flash of excitement and his hands tightened on the drawing. If anything, her designs for their winter collection were even more striking than her summer outfits. They were superb, in fact. The lines were understated and elegant, balanced by fine detailing, and she had cleverly combined the colors for wholly different effects. Her color sense was extraordinary, even if it was a little daring. Only Emma could have conceived of such unusual mixtures—burgundy trimmed with bright pink, navy blue highlighted with apple green, vivid cyclamen flashed with lilac, and, on the other side of the spectrum, a mélange of rich autumnal tones enlivened by pure white, misty grays, and blues combined with violet, plus fir green sparked with rose. And they all worked beautifully together. Not only that, because of the simplicity of their basic construction, their clean lines and general lack of fussiness, her creations were ideal for the mass-manufacturing techniques he was employing at the factory.

David smiled with pleasure and pride in Emma. He did not know where her artistic gifts sprang from, but they were indisputable and her taste was matchless, her flair unrivaled. He had long come to recognize, and with not a little wonder, that Emma possessed natural genius. There was no other term appropriate to describe her incredible talent and, coupled with her prodigious energy, it made her formidable.

Apart from her brilliance as a designer, she had an innate understanding of the public's whims, an uncanny knack of discerning ahead of time what they wanted and, more importantly, what they would buy. It was as if she had a daemon telling her things, and all of her ventures were instantaneous successes. David suspected that Emma Harte would make money at whatever she decided to turn her hand to, for her touch was golden. Both he and his father had been staggered at her total grasp of financial matters and her capacity for structuring complex monetary schemes, all of which stood up to their accountant's scrutiny and won his astonished approval. She read a balance sheet the way other people read a newspaper and she could pinpoint its flaws and its virtues in a matter of minutes. She was only just twenty-one and already she was scaling ambition's ladder with the swiftest and most determined of steps. It seemed to David that nothing could hold her back—it would have been like trying to harness lightning, he had long ago decided. She continually managed to amaze him and he dare not speculate where she would be in ten years' time. At the top of that ladder, he conjectured, and the prospects were dizzying.

David placed the sketch with the others and lit a cigarette. Things were proceeding on schedule and exactly as he had planned. He had been in business for four months, with Emma and Joe Lowther as his partners. Emma also acted as the designer and stylist, and his brother, Victor, was the factory manager. In one month David would be twenty-five, and he had no doubts whatsoever about the future of the Kallinski Clothing Company, or his own destiny. He intended to be a rich and important member of the community; and the whole of Leeds, indeed, if not Yorkshire, would take notice of him one day. That was a promise he had made to himself years ago and he had every intention of keeping that promise.

David had launched into business on his own with flair, assurance, and aggressiveness and it had been a fortuitous start. At the initial showing of the summer collection, the first samples had been received with enthusiasm by the buyers from the big emporiums in Leeds, Bradford, Sheffield, and Manchester, who had fortunately followed up their accolades with surprisingly large orders. The tremendous energy that Emma, Victor, and he had expended, and the long hours they had put in to get the first collection under way, had certainly been justified.

David could not resist shuffling through the sketches once more. He spread them out on the floor and his excitement was barely contained. Yes, by God, she had done it again! This new line could not be bettered by any other manufacturer in Leeds, or even London for that matter. He was absolutely confident that after the winter showing the orders would be huge. He had heady visions of tripling the amount of business he would do in the next few months, for, like Emma, David Kallinski was a born salesman—charming, suave, and utterly dedicated to business.

Emma interrupted his thoughts as she came into the room carrying a steak-and-kidney pie from the storage cellar. David looked up and caught his breath. She had changed into one of their samples and it was enormously becoming to her. Although the style of the dress was not particularly revealing, being tailored and dignified, the fine wool clung to her lovely figure, gently outlining the high curve of her breasts, the rounded smoothness of her thighs, and the length of her graceful legs. The dress was of a dark bottle green and this color served to emphasize the brilliance of her eyes and the translucency of her skin. He noticed she had done something different with that magnificent and abundant hair. It was pulled back as always, so that the widow's peak was highly visible, but she had brushed it loose for once and then captured the thick tresses in a dark green net, a sort of snood topped by a small green velvet bow. The netted russet hair fell to her shoulders and framed her incomparable face and it gave her an innocent look. She's the most alluring creature in the world, David thought wonderingly.

Uncomfortably aware of his prolonged examination of her, Emma halted, frowning. "Don't you like the designs, David?" she asked, misunderstanding the expression on his face.

"Good God, yes!" he cried. "They're excellent, Emma. No, that's an understatement. They're outstanding. You've done a fantastic job. Truly."

Emma smiled. "Don't exaggerate," she demurred, but she sighed with relief. After she had placed the pie in the oven, she glided over and sat on the floor at his feet, her back to the fire. She sorted through the sketches, expounding quickly on each one, her face revealing her zeal. She suggested minor changes to some of the designs, explained her ideas on the cutting and manufacturing processes most suitable, and volunteered her thoughts about costing. When they had first started, Emma had applied strict cost accounting to every phase of manufacturing and because of this they would be able to produce more for less than their competitors. She reiterated those points and David leaned forward, eagerness washing over his fine young face. He listened carefully, making mental notes of everything she said. Her advice had proven to be sound, and he always followed it.

When Emma had finished, David said, "There's only one thing we didn't think about—a name for the line. We must come up with one immediately, because I've already put the summer collection into production and I must order the labels. I don't think Kallinski Clothes is a very exciting name, do you?"

Emma looked up quickly. Not wanting to hurt his feelings, she hesitated before saying, "Not really. It's not—well—it's not very feminine, David. But I don't have any ideas. Why don't you ask Victor? He's very bright about such things."

David broke into a grin. "I guessed you'd suggest that and so I did already. Victor came up with one name this afternoon. I sort of like it, though I'm not sure that you will approve. He suggested we use the name of your famous namesake."

"My famous namesake? Who on earth does he mean? I didn't know I had one."

"I didn't know either, I'm ashamed to admit. Just goes to show how ignorant we are. He meant the first Emma Hart. That's Hart without the *e*."

Undisguised curiosity flickered onto Emma's face. "The first Emma Hart," she echoed. "Who is she?"

"The first Emma Hart was quite a famous lady, or infamous, depending on how you look at it. Let me explain. Your namesake married Sir William Hamilton and became Lady Hamilton. *That's* the name Victor suggested we adopt." David laughed at her bewilderment. "Emma Hart was Nelson's Lady Hamilton. His great love. His mistress. His bequest to the nation in his renowned will, so Victor tells me. Don't you remember your history books, my girl?" he teased.

"Oh, *that* Lady Hamilton! Mmmmm. It's not a bad name actually. Not bad at all," she mused. "Rather distinguished,

when you think about it. Lady Hamilton Dresses. No, since
we are making suits and coats as well, it would have to be
Lady Hamilton Clothes, wouldn't it?"

"Yes, it would. Do you really like it, Emma? To be honest
with you, I took to it at once, but I wanted to discuss it with
you before I had the labels made. What do you say?"

Emma pondered, repeating the name in her head. It did
have a catchy ring to it and it was rather classy. She remembered that Nelson was Winston's great naval hero. Perhaps
this was a good omen. Maybe the name would be lucky.
"Yes, I do like it! Let's use it, David."

"What about Joe? Shouldn't we ask his opinion?"

"Good heavens, David, surely you know Joe will approve
of anything we suggest. You don't have to worry about *him*."
She laughed. "What would we do without Victor? We're such
a couple of illiterates, aren't we?"

"Perhaps we are, but we know how to make money. Anyway, how about a spot of sherry to celebrate selecting the
name?" David stood up, bending over Emma. He offered her
his outstretched hands and helped her up off the floor.

As Emma rose she lifted her head and smiled into David's
face. Their eyes met and held. They stared at each other for a
suspended moment, unable to look away, bright blue gaze
impaled on one of vivid green. Emma felt an internal quivering, as she always did these days whenever David touched
her. A flush rose to her face, and her heart began to pound
unreasonably. She continued to stare into his adoring face,
hypnotized by that sapphire blaze so full of yearning.

Long aware of her hesitancy and reserve, David moved
swiftly. He pulled her into his arms, his mouth seeking hers.
His lips touched her lips and he parted them gently but
firmly. Emma felt the warm sweetness of his tongue and her
senses overwhelmed her. Her fingers flew to the back of his
head involuntarily and ran through his crisp black hair, and it
was as if her touch was a firebrand. David held her closer to
him, his strong hands sliding down over her shoulders to the
small of her back. His palms pressed her slender body into
his own muscular one and, as his embrace tightened, Emma
felt the rise of his own desire against her thigh. It had been
like this for several weeks now—the kissing, the touching,
the ardent glances. Every time they were alone together they

vere both engulfed by a consciousness of their bodies strain-
ng for fulfillment in each other.

David assaulted Emma's emotions in a way that made her
reathless and reeling. Her latent ardor, only tentatively and
leetingly awakened years before and then submerged, was
urfacing with increasing persistency when David kissed her
nd held her in his arms. Emma trembled with a mixture of
pprehension and alarm, old familiars that constantly assailed
er in his presence. She tried to fight her clamoring feelings,
ut her mind floundered and she gave herself up to his
ensual kisses.

They gravitated to the sofa without releasing their hold on
ach other and fell onto it. David bent over Emma, his eyes
ocked on hers and brimming with longing. His image filled
er vision until she was lost in it, and she closed her eyes.
David stroked her face and kissed her eyelids, her forehead,
nd her lips. Very carefully, he untied the green velvet bow
nd removed the net so that her hair was released in a
ascade over her shoulders. He ran his hand through it,
narveling at her beauty and the fervency of the passion she
roused in him. He burned to possess her fully, and he knew
e would never let her go.

David's vivid eyes roved over her body, lying so languor-
us on the sofa, and he was unable to restrain himself further.
Ie began to caress her face, her neck, her shoulders, and her
reasts, and a choking sensation filled his throat when her
ipples hardened under his touch through the fine fabric of
ne dress. His desire spiraled into an exquisite pain that was
lmost unendurable.

Emma opened her eyes and she saw a fleeting flash of
nguish smudge out the blueness of his eyes so that they
ecame dark and intense. David moved closer to her and
ripped her shoulders, and his mouth was demanding and
ard on hers. He covered her body with his own, pressing
own on her, and Emma rejoiced in the weight of him.

His voice was rasping in the hollow of her neck. "Oh,
mma! Emma, darling! I can't stand this!"

"I know, David, I know," she murmured. She smoothed
is darkly curling hair and held his head against her breast,
radling him in her arms. Her hand stroked his broad shoul-
ers and a cry of longing trembled on her lips. She bent her
ead and rested it on his and her hair drifted down around

them like a silken veil. A long sigh rippled through her an
she acknowledged that she loved David Kallinski and wante
him for herself, for the rest of her life, but her natura
rectitude, coupled with her terrible fear of the consequence
of sexual intimacy out of wedlock, would not permit her
succumb to her overwhelming emotions. It was not that sh
did not trust David. She did. She knew he would neve
betray her. He was no Edwin Fairley. And yet she bit dow
on those insistent desires, stifling them, and finally she de
nied him in her mind if not in her heart.

Very quietly Emma whispered into his hair, "We have t
stop this, David. It's getting worse every time and it's not fa
to you. We must not let the situation get out of hand." Sh
pushed him away from her with the utmost gentleness an
sat up, dizzy and shaking.

David leaned back against the sofa and picked up a stran
of her hair. He kissed it and then let it fall. He half smile
"Emma, I love you so much. Don't be afraid of me. I won
hurt you. Ever."

Emma flinched at this deadly echo from the past. "I'm n
afraid of you, David," she answered quietly. "I'm afraid
myself when I'm with you like this and what might happe
when we get so—so—"

"Please don't." He placed a finger on her lips. "I agre
with you. We can't go on like this. It's insanity. But w
must be together, Emma. I can't bear this torment for muc
longer." He grasped her hand, his face earnest. "Marry m
Emma. As soon as possible," he implored. "We must g
married, you know that."

"Married!" she cried.

David smiled. "Yes, married. Don't sound so shocked. I'
wanted to marry you for the last few years. I've only hel
myself in check because of your circumstances." He chuc
led. "Did you think I had dishonorable intentions, Emma?
would never attempt to compromise you. I love you far t
much—" David stopped abruptly, staring at her, his ey
wide with surprise. "Emma, what's wrong? You're as white
a sheet!"

"I cannot marry you, David," Emma said in a low strangle
voice.

"But why not? Don't be ridiculous!" He actually laughe
so disbelieving was he of her words. "I told you I love yo

nd I know you love me. It's the most natural outcome, isn't
? For us to get married. That's what people do when they
ve each other, Emma."

Emma stood up unsteadily and moved across the floor. She
oked out of the window and her eyes filled with tears. She
iscovered she was unable to answer him.

David gaped at her stiff back, her tensely set shoulders,
affled by her behavior. "What is it, Emma? For God's sake
nswer me!" he demanded.

"I cannot marry you, David. Please, let's leave it at that,"
mma said, blinking back her tears.

"Of course you can!" David asserted fiercely. "There is
othing to stop you now. Your husband is dead. You are
ee." David paused, and when he spoke again it was with
uiet intensity. "Emma, I love you more than anyone or
nything on this earth. I want to cherish and protect you with
y life, for the rest of my life. We belong together, Emma. I
now that deep in my heart. And so do you. There is some-
ing very special between us—an unbreakable bond." Still
e did not respond and another thought occurred to David.
s it because of Edwina?" he asked quickly. "You don't have
worry about her. I'm not afraid of responsibility. I will
dopt her, Emma, and the three of us can live together.
e'll be happy and I—"

"It's not because of Edwina."

"Then give me a good reason why you won't marry me!" he
ommanded, his face pale and washed with anxiety.

"David, I cannot marry you because your mother would
ever accept me. She would never approve of you marrying
ut of the faith. Surely I don't have to point that out to you.
he wants you to marry a Jewish girl who will give her Jewish
randchildren—"

"To hell with all that!" David interrupted, his voice rising
ngrily. "I don't care what my *mother* wants, Emma. I want
ou for my wife and that's all that counts."

"I can't hurt your mother," Emma whispered. "She's been
onderful to me, almost like a second mother. I love her and
won't betray her. You're her eldest son, David. It would kill
er if we married. I admit she's very fond of me, but it would
ot be quite the same thing—welcoming me as a daughter-in-
w. Me a Gentile and she so Orthodox. Please listen to what
say, David. It's the truth and you must face it."

David leaned forward on the sofa, his hands tightly clenched "I want you to look me in the eye and tell me you do not lov me, Emma. Turn around and tell me that."

"I can't," Emma said quietly.

"Why not?" he shouted, his voice breaking.

"Because I do love you, David. Just as much as you lov me." Emma swung around slowly and crossed the floor. Sh knelt down at his feet and stared up into his face. Sh touched it fleetingly.

He clasped her tightly in his arms, smoothing her hai kissing her tearstained cheeks. "Then that's all that matter my darling. That's all that matters."

"No, David." Emma pulled away and rose, seating herse next to him. "Other things matter in life. I am not going be responsible for creating heartache and pain for your pa ents. I will not divide your family. They have been too goo to me. Besides, I couldn't live with myself." She searched h obdurate face. "David, don't you understand that it's no possible to build happiness on other people's misery? It mig be all right at first, if we did marry, but eventually the anguish and disappointment would come between us. It wou chip away at what we have, and finally destroy it."

David had been staring at her capable little hand claspin his tightly. It was so small and curiously defenseless. At la he raised his eyes and saw the candor in her green gaze an he knew she had meant every word. But he could not pre vent himself from crying, "Are you trying to tell me that yo are willing to sacrifice our happiness, mine and yours, ju because of some religious beliefs that are not only outdate but utterly ridiculous! I can't believe it. Not *you*. Not *n* Emma. The stalwart Emma who would fight the world f anything she wanted!"

"Yes, I suppose I am. But it's not really like that, Davi please, try and understand—" She broke off. She had hu him profoundly and she could not bear it.

David extracted his hand from hers and moved it across h face. He felt horribly faint to a point of nausea and an intole able pain moved across his chest. It seemed that his life wa draining away. It was as if someone had suddenly snatche his hopes and dreams and the promise of the future from h grasp. But he knew what Emma said was indeed true. H knew, too, that she would not change her mind, just as his mother would not.

David leapt up and paced in front of the fire. Finally, after a few minutes, he stopped and turned to Emma, staring at her. "Is that your last word?" he asked so quietly she could scarcely hear him.

"Yes, David. I'm sorry, but I can't destroy your mother."

"I understand, Emma. You must excuse me. I have to leave. Sorry about the dinner, but I seem to have lost my appetite." He strode out before she could see the tears swimming in his eyes.

Emma stood up swiftly. "David! Wait! Please wait!" The door slammed behind him and she was alone. She gazed at the door for a long moment and then picked up the sketches and placed them in the cupboard. Vaguely she thought of the dinner spoiling in the oven, but such intense feelings of dejection and misery overcame her she did not have the strength to remove the food. Her thoughts centered on David and not on herself, for unconsciously she had always known their relationship was doomed. They could be friends and business partners, but that was all. She had spent enough time with Janessa Kallinski to understand that David's mother would not tolerate anything else. Emma sat for a long time looking into the empty room and David's face swam before her. She would never forget that awful look of hurt on his face as long as she lived.

About an hour later Emma was roused from her stupor by a loud banging on the door. David had come back! She flew out into the small hallway, her heart leaping, his name on her lips. She flung open the door with eagerness and found herself staring into the bulbous face of Gerald Fairley.

Emma was so dumbfounded she momentarily lost all power of speech. But immediately her hand tightened on the knob and she stiffened, alerted for trouble. She tried to close the door but he had anticipated her. He pushed himself inside and closed the door firmly behind him.

Emma found her voice. "What do you want?" she asked coldly. How had he managed to find her?

Gerald grinned. "Aren't you going to invite me in, Emma?" he asked.

"No. I have nothing to say to you. Please leave immediately," she said, summoning all of her courage and adopting her iciest tone.

Gerald, after all the years of gorging himself, was revolting in his incredible obesity, a mountain of flesh and powerfully strong. There was a derisive expression on his blubbery face. "Not on your life! I have a few words to say to *you*, Mrs. Harte," he exclaimed with disdain.

"I repeat, I have nothing to say to you. Please leave."

"Where's the child?" countered Gerald, his sly eyes full of malicious intent.

"What child?" said Emma coolly, but her legs shook and she longed for help, for David to return.

Gerald laughed in her face. "Come on, don't give me that! I know you had Edwin's child. There's no use denying it. He confessed it to me this weekend. You see, I told him I had found you. Quite by accident, of course, since I wasn't looking for you. The silly fool wanted to come and see you, wanted to help you and his child. But I couldn't permit that." Gerald brought his bloated face closer. Emma drew back against the wall, hardly breathing. Gerald smiled. "It's a small world, Emma. We bought Thompson's mill last week. Imagine my surprise when I saw your name on the old books. You used to work there as a weaver, before you came up in the world. Went into trade, I see," he said disparagingly. "Now, where's the baby?"

"I did not have a child," Emma insisted, clenching her hands by her sides.

"Don't lie to me. It would be very easy for me to check it out. Remember one thing, *Mrs.* Harte. I have money and power. I can go to the local hospital—St. Mary's, isn't it? —and after a few pounds have changed hands in the right quarters I can look at the records any time I want."

Emma's heart sank. She knew he spoke the truth. Despite this she was determined not to admit anything, "*I did not have a child*," she repeated, her gaze unflickering.

"Oh, come on, Emma, tie one on the other leg and pull it. Edwin wouldn't confess such a thing if it were not true, especially since he is about to become engaged to Lady Jane Stansby." Gerald grabbed her arm. "I have the feeling you might use this child to blackmail Edwin later. That's common practice with tramps from the working class. But I aim to circumvent that. The Fairleys cannot afford a scandal. So come on, out with it. Where's the little bastard? And was it a girl or a boy?"

Emma glared at him. "I told you, I did not have Edwin's child," she said harshly, and her eyes blazed with intense hatred. She pulled her arm away. "And if you ever lay a finger on me again, Gerald Fairley, I will kill you!"

He laughed and then his eyes shifted to the stairs illuminated by the dim glow from the bedroom lamp. He shoved her out of the way abruptly and bounded up the steps. Emma recovered her balance and flew up after him. "How dare you push your way into my home! I shall go and fetch the police!" she cried.

Gerald had disappeared into the bedroom, and when Emma hurried in she found him pulling out drawers and flinging their contents all over the room. "What do you think you're doing?" she shouted, shaking with rage.

"Looking for some evidence of the child you say you never had. I want to know where it is and who has it. I want to get to the bottom of this before you can cause any trouble."

Emma stood rigidly still in the middle of the room, and her eyes held a dangerous gleam. Gerald Fairley was a bumbling fool. He would find nothing here that would lead him to Edwina.

Gerald turned, glaring, his great body swaying hideously as he lumbered across the floor. He grabbed her shoulders and began to shake her with such violence her head flew backward and forward. "Bitch! You're nothing but a whoring bitch! Out with it! Where's the child?"

Spots of bright color stained her pale cheeks, but nasty insinuations slid over her, leaving no real impression, for Gerald Fairley was beneath her scorn. "There is no child," Emma said through gritted teeth. "And let go of me, you foul monstrosity."

Gerald continued to shake her harder than ever, his huge hands biting into her shoulders until she winced with pain. Suddenly he released her unexpectedly and threw her away from him so forcibly Emma staggered and fell back onto the bed.

Gerald took in the richness of her tumbling hair, her ravishing face, the provocativeness of her shapely figure, and something stirred in him. He began to laugh as he eyed her lasciviously. "How about a little of what you so willingly gave to my baby brother, Emma Harte? Women like you are usually ready for it any time of day or night. How about a bit of loving, Mrs. Harte? Edwin always did have a sharp eye for a looker. I don't mind baby brother's leavings."

Emma gaped at him, so stupefied she found she wàs paralyzed. He advanced towards her and she saw, to her revulsion, that he was unbuttoning his trousers. She shrank back against the pillows, and then she tried to scramble off the bed. But it was too late. He was on her, his great weight crushing her back. He struggled with her skirt, attempting to lift it. Emma began to kick her legs, and Gerald grinned, holding her down with one arm. His face drew closer and he lowered his lips to her face. Emma moved her head from side to side, fighting with him, pushing him off, but although she was physically strong he was too much for her. He began to roll on top of her, grunting and moaning, pressing his horrendous body against hers, trying to pull up her skirts, without success, for he was hampered by his enormous weight. The grunting and the moaning and the rolling became more violent and then, with a final shudder, he went limp next to her and lay back on the bed depleted. Emma pushed herself up and sprang onto the floor, her breath coming in short, rapid pants. As she moved away from him her hand caught the side of her dress. It was horribly wet. A feeling of repugnance rose up in her throat, and she thought she would vomit. She flew to the tangled mass of clothes and linens scattered on the floor and grabbed a towel. She wiped her dress clean and then leapt to the sewing table. Her fingers curled around the scissors and she picked them up, and swung on Gerald, her eyes filled with murderous lights.

"Get up and get out, before I kill you!" she gasped with such venom he looked at her startled and taken unawares. She moved across the floor, the scissors raised in her hand like a dagger. Gerald's face blanched. She hovered over him. "I tell you, I will kill you, Gerald Fairley, if you don't move that obscene body out of here at once!"

Gerald laughed mockingly. "I don't think you would be foolish enough to do that," he said. He sat up and buttoned his trousers, insolently taking his time.

"Don't tempt me!" she hissed.

Gerald heaved himself off the bed. "I must say, I like a tiger, Emma. Makes it more exciting. I'll be back, my girl.

And next time you'll be more cooperative." He nonchalantly flicked the collar of her dress. "This will be off and everything else. You'll be ready and waiting for me. I want to savor that beautiful body of yours, enjoy a bit of working-class rutting. I hear you're all like rabbits." He grinned. "What's good enough for the handsome Edwin is certainly good enough for me!"

Emma had the most overwhelming impulse to spit in his face, but she exercised restraint, not wishing to lower herself to his level. "Leave my house immediately, Gerald Fairley, and don't ever come back—unless you want to encounter real trouble."

He swung around, stumbling down the stairs, laughing raucously. Emma followed him, her rage fulminating. She stood at the top of the stairs and watched him descend, ponderously dragging his immense weight. She flung the scissors after him angrily and they rattled on the stone steps, landing at his feet. He looked up, leering at her. "That's not polite," he said.

"You're not worth swinging for, Gerald Fairley!" she screamed. Emma now sped down the stairs, propelled by her mounting fury. When she reached the bottom step she stared up at him, utterly fearless and totally in command of herself, her hatred blazing on her face.

She took a step nearer and said with deadly coldness, "But I will ruin you! All of you! The Fairleys will rue the day they ever heard the name Emma Harte. Do you hear me? I will ruin you! I swear I will!"

"You ruin us! You? A whoring little tramp? Fat chance you have." Gerald chucked her under the chin lightly and, infuriated, Emma struck out at him. Her nails clawed his face and brought blood.

"Why, you bloody little bitch!" Gerald shouted, and then he threw back his hideous head and laughed. "I like a tiger, *Mrs*. Harte, as I said before. Don't forget, I'll be back. I'm always in the vicinity. I'll pop in one afternoon for a bit of fun."

"Get out! Get out!"

The moment the door banged behind him Emma turned the key and drew the bolts hurriedly. She went into the parlor and closed the curtains and washed the disgusting stain off her dress, scrubbing it with a cloth until it was spotless. Then she sat down in front of the fire, her body convulsed by dry heaving sobs. She felt sick and shaken and apprehensive. For the first time in years she was once again afraid of the Fairleys. Thank God Edwina was in Ripon. Gerald would never find her there. But he was just stupid enough to come back here and the idea petrified her.

The world's a jungle, she said, shivering in a huddle before the dying fire. And I'm still vulnerable to the animals in it. I do not have enough money yet with which to build a wall around Edwina and myself. We are painfully exposed. I need protection. She thought then of David with longing and despair. What she needed was a husband. That was most palpably obvious to her now. But David, her darling David, was forbidden to her. As much as they loved each other the objections of his family would drive a wedge between them. Her mind raced. Where could she find a husband who would protect her and Edwina? Whom could she marry? It came to her in a flash. Joe Lowther! She knew he loved her. The problem was, *she* did not love Joe. She liked him. How could she not? He was decent and kind and dependable. If she married Joe she would be cheating him of that most important of all things in a marriage—love. She also had to face the fact that she would have to share his bed, submit to his sexual advances, and bear his children. She went cold at this prospect. How could she willingly give herself to another man when David filled her heart and her soul? And yet she had no alternative. Emma began to weep, her sobs reverberating in the stillness of the little parlor.

"Forgive me, David," she cried. "Forgive me for what I'm about to do, my darling."

PART FOUR

The Plateau
1914-1917

Life always gets harder toward the summit—
the cold increases, responsibility increases.
—FRIEDRICH NIETZSCHE

THIRTY-SIX

The boardroom of the *Yorkshire Morning Gazette*, oak-paneled walls hung with antique engravings of renowned English authors, mahogany furniture polished to a ferocious glassy sheen, was smoke-filled and vibrating with tension. Adam Fairley and Lord Jocelyn Sydney sat opposite each other on either side of the immense conference table, their faces morose, their eyes grave as they chain-smoked in brooding silence, the crystal ashtrays in front of them littered with stubbed-out butts that bespoke hours of waiting and strain.

Adam, impeccably tailored in a dark blue suit, shifted restlessly in the black leather chair and ran his hand through his silver-streaked fair hair. His mouth, ringed with fatigue, suddenly tightened and his gray-blue eyes fixedly regarded the clock ticking with relentless precision in the leaden stillness.

"Damn it all!" he exclaimed, no longer able to control his temper. He swung to face Jocelyn. "It's almost one o'clock. If Parker doesn't hurry up we'll miss the first edition. He's been fiddling with that lead story for a good twenty minutes. What on earth can the fool be doing, for Christ's sake!"

Jocelyn peered at Adam through the smoke. "Pondering every word, shouldn't doubt! You ought to know that by now, old boy."

"I'll give Parker five more minutes and then I'm going up to see him—" Adam broke off as a copy boy burst in. The heavy oak door swung back on its hinges and the activity and noise of a newspaper in the heat of production rolled into the quiet boardroom.

"Here's the proof of the front page, sir. And the editor says ter tell yer he's starting the presses in five minutes." The boy slapped the damp newsprint dripping with wet ink onto the table in front of Adam and disappeared. The door banged behind him and silence was fully restored. Jocelyn hurried across the room. Placing one hand on Adam's broad shoulder, he bent down and looked at the proof. The banner headline, set in giant-sized type, was black and stark and it leapt across the page.

BRITAIN DECLARES WAR ON GERMANY

Two pairs of eyes quickly scanned the smaller crossheads on the broadsheet: *The Great Conflict Begun. British Mine-layer Sunk. Belgium Invaded. Two New Battleships for Our Navy. Government Takes Control of Railways. Securing Food Supply. State Guarantee War Risk at Sea.*

Jocelyn tapped the lead story with one finger. "How has Parker handled this, Adam? In my haste to get here tonight I forgot my spectacles and I can't read the small print."

Adam read the proof quickly and said, "I think Parker covered everything of importance." He looked up at Jocelyn. "I've dreaded and feared this war for years. But we're in the conflict now and there's no turning back."

Jocelyn fixed Adam with a glassy stare. "Did you really mean what you said earlier this evening—that it will be a prolonged war?"

"Indeed I did," said Adam tersely. "Contrary to what some of the experts in London are saying, I believe it will last several years. Two at least."

Jocelyn's jaw sagged. "As long as that!"

Adam nodded, his face grim. "Yes. And it will be a war of attrition. A bloody holocaust the likes of which the world has never seen. Mark my words, Jocelyn."

"Oh God, Adam, I pray you are wrong! I sincerely do!"

Adam did not answer. He lit a cigarette and gazed reflectively into space, envisioning the terrible consequences of Britain's entry into the war.

"We both need a stiff drink," Jocelyn announced after a few moments. He hurried to the sideboard and his hands trembled as he prepared two brandy-and-sodas and carried them to the table. He handed one to Adam and sat down heavily in the next chair. Neither man bothered to toast the other on this somber occasion, and they sipped their drinks in silence, preoccupied with their own thoughts.

Adam Fairley, newly appointed chairman of the board of the *Yorkshire Morning Gazette*, had kept up a tireless vigil at the newspaper for the past four days, sifting through the stories pouring in from the London office and Reuters, studying the grave news, watching Britain being inexorably drawn into the European crisis. His old friend Jocelyn Sidney had been a constant visitor, prowling up and down the boardroom yet insisting that as long as peace lasted the folly of war could be avoided. Adam had met Jocelyn's inherent optimism with an absolute pessimism that reflected his clarity of vision and an understanding of the facts, pronouncing that it was far too late to avert onrushing disaster.

That pessimism was apparent in Adam's voice as he suddenly roused himself and said, "We're not as well prepared for this war as the Government would have us believe, Jocelyn."

Astonishment mingled with alarm spread across Jocelyn's face. He opened his mouth, but before he could speak Adam said hurriedly, in an effort to assuage Jocelyn's burgeoning fears, "Except for the navy, of course. Thank God Winston Churchill has been First Lord of the Admiralty for the past three years. Only he and a few other enlightened men saw the menace of approaching war and tried to make ready for it." Adam's tone became guarded as he continued, "I know Churchill has never been a favorite of yours, Jocelyn, but you must admit he had the foresight to recognize the increasing threat of German sea power as early as 1911, when he set about reorganizing the Fleet. Good job, too. By withdrawing our ships from China and the Mediterranean and concentrating the Home Fleet and the Battle Fleet in the North Sea, he has increased our strength immeasurably."

"Yes, that's quite true," Jocelyn conceded. "And Churchill has had one aim I've always found most worthy—reinforcing the invincibility of the Royal Navy."

"Yes, the navy is strong, but that's the only service that is, Jocelyn. The army is not at all well organized and our air power is minimal, even though Churchill has endeavored to boost it lately." Adam paused, drew on his cigarette, and concluded. "The War Office has always been grossly inefficient. Actually, what we need now is a new Secretary of State for War!"

"Do you think Asquith will appoint one?" Jocelyn asked.

"I'm positive he will have to," Adam responded firmly. "He cannot function as Prime Minister and run the War Office as well, not in a time of crisis such as this. I'm certain, knowing Asquith the way I do, that he will have the good sense to recognize that. And I hope he will have the wisdom to pick Lord Kitchener for the job. That's the man we need in our hour of peril. Not only for his tremendous ability but, for the uplifting effect on public morale his appointment will have."

"Yes, I see what you mean," Jocelyn agreed. "After all, Kitchener is a national hero."

"He's more than that, Jocelyn. He's a national institution. He symbolizes success to the public. Every military engagement he undertakes comes off beautifully." Adam swirled his drink, pondering. "He will have to raise new armies, of course. The Territorial Army is not very large. In point of fact, whoever is appointed Secretary of State for War will have to embark on a campaign immediately to recruit single men to go to the front."

Jocelyn's pale face had grayed. "A campaign to recruit single men," he repeated shakily. "I hadn't thought of that."

"Since we don't have a compulsory draft system, the country has to rely on volunteers—usually single men between the ages of eighteen and thirty." Adam stopped, aware of the sick expression on Jocelyn's face. "Are you all right, old chap? You look positively ghastly."

"The boys," Jocelyn said in a whisper. "I'm not going to be able to restrain them, Adam. They'll both volunteer immediately. You're lucky, Adam. Gerald would never pass the physical and Edwin is married. Also, *he* has a sense of responsibility to you, and to Jane."

"I'm not so sure about Edwin, to be very honest with you. He's also impulsive at times. Don't think being a married man will stop him if he makes up his mind to go to war. Edwin will consider his responsibility is to his King and country and not the family, or even to Jane. I have a sneaking suspicion they will take precedence over everything else."

Jocelyn bit his lip nervously. "This is a bloody foul mess-up, isn't it? Who would have thought a few years ago that we would be plunged into this disastrous situation, Adam."

"Bruce McGill warned me ten years ago that there would be a great war," Adam said quietly, his eyes brooding, "He was right. That was in 1904—"

"Was it, by Jove!" Jocelyn interjected. "I didn't know old Bruce was a political pundit."

"I'm not sure that he is," Adam remarked. "But he does happen to be a tremendously rich and powerful man, and he has friends in high places. When Bruce was in London last year with his son Paul he was full of foreboding, and I ignored him. I'm beginning to think I'm an ostrich like everyone else." Adam stood up. "I presume you're canceling the shoot, Jocelyn."

"Naturally. I don't expect anyone will be interested in grouse at a time like this," Jocelyn replied with a weak smile. "Thanks for inviting me down to the newspaper. I really appreciate it, old chap."

"I've been glad to have your company, Jocelyn. Now let's be off. This room is beginning to suffocate me."

An hour and a half later Adam's new Daimler motorcar was pulling into the driveway of Fairley Hall. Adam bade the chauffeur a crisp good-night and bounded up the steps.

Murgatroyd was hovering in the dimly lit entrance hall. He hurried forward when he saw Adam, as obsequious as always. "Mrs. Fairley came down ter the kitchen ter tell me and Cook that we was at war. Aye, it's horrible news."

Adam cleared his throat. "Yes, indeed it is, Murgatroyd. The days ahead are going to be difficult for us all. But we must pull together and be strong in the country's hour of need." He noticed the light streaming out from the library. "Has Mrs. Fairley not retired yet, Murgatroyd?"

"No, sir. She's been waiting for yer. I built up the fire and made her some hot chocolate a bit ago, being as how it's a right nippy night."

"I see." Adam strode across the hall.

Olivia had heard Adam's voice and she was halfway across the floor when he entered the library. "Oh, Adam, this is all quite dreadful," she cried as she flew into his arms.

He held her close for a moment, stroking her hair. "Yes, it is, my dear. However, we've been expecting it and we must be courageous." He moved away from her and looked down into her face. "You shouldn't have waited up for me. It's awfully late, darling."

She returned his smile. "I was terribly anxious to see you."

"I'm afraid I am a little done in."

"Perhaps a drink will help," she suggested.

"It might indeed. I'll have a nightcap before we go to bed. A brandy, please."

Olivia gave him a soft loving look. Adam watched her gliding across the floor, his spirits lifting as they always did when he was with her, the war momentarily forgotten. She was wearing a deep blue crepe de chine evening dress which flattered her lissome figure and reflected the color of her eyes. Her face was still unlined and the white streak that shot through her dark luxuriant hair was most arresting. At fifty-four she was a striking woman, and in Adam's opinion she grew more beautiful with age. They had been married for six years. In 1907 the Deceased Wife's Sister Marriage Act, legalizing a man's marriage to his sister-in-law, had been finally passed by Parliament after its defeat in 1901. Adam had convinced Olivia to become his wife in 1908, and they were so completely happy, so perfectly compatible no one else existed for them.

"Incidentally, Edwin telephoned earlier. I told him about the grim developments," Olivia said, returning to the fireplace with the brandy.

Adam stiffened. "How did he react?"

"With surprising mildness, I thought. He and Jane are driving over from Kirkby Malzeard tomorrow, to stay with us for a week as we had planned."

"Well, that is good news," Adam said. "Knowing Edwin, I had visions of him careening back to town to be in the thick of things. I'm glad they are coming. At least you will have some congenial company when I'm absent during the day."

"Do you think they are happy, Adam?"

"I'm damned if I know. Why do you ask?" It struck him then that perhaps Olivia had also noticed the curious lack of warmth between his son and daughter-in-law.

"I can't really put my finger on it," Olivia said thoughtfully. "There's a distance between them. Oh, Edwin is outwardly charming and most considerate. But not very affectionate. They don't seem like a couple to me. And sometimes I have noticed the most awful empty look in Edwin's eyes." Olivia paused and stared at Adam. When he made no response, she pressed, "Haven't you noticed it, darling?"

Wary though he was of embarking on this discussion, Adam admitted, "Well, yes, I have, to be truthful. If there *is* anything wrong there it's definitely to do with Edwin. He's changed radically in the past few years. He devotes twenty-four hours a day to the law, or so it seems to me. He has no other interests and appears to be determined to become the most outstanding young barrister in England before he's reached thirty. And I feel he neglects Jane frightfully."

"Yes, he does," Olivia agreed.

"And yet he has every reason to be happy with her. Jane is charming and pretty and comports herself in the most mature and dignified manner. Pity they haven't had a child. I must say, I was rather looking forward to having a grandchild. Expected one by now. After all, they've been married three years."

Olivia stared into the fire and after a long moment turned to Adam. "Did you believe that nasty story Gerald told you a few years ago? The story about Edwin and Emma Harte?"

"Certainly not!" Adam exclaimed, wishing he meant his words. Intensely protective of Olivia, he did not wish to upset her tonight by dragging out old skeletons. And so for once in his life he lied to her. "Gerald has no regard for the truth. His story was not only preposterous but quite unfounded. It was undoubtedly engendered by his desire to denigrate Edwin in my eyes. You know Gerald has always been inordinately jealous of his brother."

Olivia was not entirely placated. "I remember you made discreet inquiries at the time, about Emma and the child, but are you sure your information was correct, Adam?"

"Of course I am!" He put down the brandy balloon and took Olivia's hand. "Now, why are you suddenly worrying about that old story? It's long forgotten."

"I really don't know, darling. I suppose because we began to talk about Edwin's marriage and his happiness. If you say the story is not true, then Edwin can't have anything on his conscience." Her eyes roved over Adam's face searchingly. "And yet it has often crossed my mind that he does. Perhaps its the peculiar look in his eyes that troubles me, Adam."

Adam frowned. "Now, come, my darling," he said softly. "You are being imaginative. Gerald told a pack of lies. I'm absolutely convinced of that. As for that look in Edwin's eyes, well, maybe it simply springs from his disappointment in his marriage. You should know as well as I do that not all marriages are as happy as ours."

"Yes, that's true," she murmured, and sighed. "Poor Edwin. How terrible for him if he does not love Jane. It must be painful for her, too."

Adam wanted to terminate the discussion and so he said firmly, "It's very late, my darling. Let us go up to bed."

As they left the library Adam acknowledged to himself that the state of Edwin's marriage did not particularly concern him at this precise moment. His consuming worry was that Edwin would volunteer for the army, for Adam knew that the boy no longer put much store in personal safety. Tragically, that most human of all instincts had died in Edwin the day Jack Harte had died. Adam believed that his younger son did not care whether he lived or not, and this attitude, coupled with his strong sense of patriotic duty, would propel Edwin into military service.

THIRTY-SEVEN

Emma clutched the telephone tighter, and her heart began to beat more rapidly then usual. "I don't want you to do this, Frank! You're putting yourself in danger needlessly. It's foolish and—"

"No, it's not," Frank interrupted, his voice echoing hollowly over the long-distance wire. "Look, Emma, I'd even toyed with the idea of joining up, but I know the army would never take me. Not with my poor eyesight and weak chest. But somebody's got to report the war over there. I *must* go, Emma."

"But not *you*, Frank. You're only a boy!" Emma cried heatedly.

"No, I'm not. I'll be twenty-three next month." His tone became intense. "*I want to go.* Please try to understand, Emma. Also, the editor wants me to go. In a way, it's a kind of honor."

"*An honor!*" she gasped incredulously. "Well, in my opinion it's an honor you can easily do without! You'll be in the trenches. In the thick of the fighting. The conditions will be terrible, and you said yourself you're not strong physically. Please, Frank, reconsider this. Think more carefully before you make a final decision!" Emma implored.

"I've already made up my mind," her brother said firmly. "Anyway, it's too late. That's why I'm ringing you now. I'm leaving for the front at five this morning."

"Oh, Frank! I wish you hadn't done this without talking to me first," she remonstrated.

"I'll be fine, Emma. Honestly, I will. Don't make it harder

for me," he pleaded. "Now, take care of yourself and give my love to everyone. I'll be in touch, when and if I can. You'll know where I am from my dispatches in the *Chronicle*. Keep them for me, Emma, and try not to worry about me. Goodbye, love."

"Oh, Frank! Frankie!" Her voice broke and she had to swallow hard to regain her control. "Goodbye, Frank. And take a raincoat and strong boots—" She stopped, unable to continue.

"I will. Bye."

The telephone went dead. Her mind froze at the idea of Frank hurtling across the battlefields of Flanders. This development was the last thing she had anticipated and she was stunned by her brother's news, and afraid for him. It was bad enough that Winston was somewhere with the Battle Fleet without Frank flinging himself into the fray. For the past few weeks she had consistently reassured herself that if England did go to war at least her younger brother was in no danger because of his frail constitution. And that would have been so if he had not made such a name for himself as a journalist. Frank, already a rising star in the newspaper firmament, was the type of young reporter editors sought out. He had an enormous command of the English language, was incisive and perceptive, a master of the descriptive phrase and matchless at capturing mood and atmosphere. Not only that, by nature he was romantic, adventurous, and oblivious to danger. She might have guessed he would want to be a war correspondent and now, as she reflected, she realized he had actually sounded excited about going.

Suddenly and quite irrationally, Emma wished that Frank was not so talented and then he would have been a failure. And safe. Indirectly perhaps it was all her fault, and if Frank was killed she would never forgive herself. *I should have left him where he was—working on that nothing of a weekly newspaper in Shipley, where he would have stagnated,* she said to herself angrily. *But I had to go and interfere, because I was impressed with his ability, and ambitious for him. Too ambitious by far,* she decided. She chided herself, but after a moment her natural pragmatism rose to the surface, as it generally did, for at twenty-five Emma was nothing if not practical, a characteristic that had been magnified in her over the years. *You're being ridiculous,* she told herself firmly, recognizing that Frank would have been just as successful without her help. His kind of incandescent talent could never be held back for long; furthermore, he had always been perfectly sure of his own destiny. She had merely propelled him to the top a little faster and that was all. Her role had been of minor importance. She had simply engineered a job for him as a junior reporter on the Leeds *Mercury*, through her friendship with the assistant editor, Archie Clegg. There had been no holding Frank back after that. He had risen with meteoric swiftness, astonishing her as much as Archie and his colleagues. Of course, there was the matter of the book. If she was honest with herself, she had to admit that she had been instrumental in bringing it to the attention of the right people. But if she had not, Frank would have done so himself eventually. When he was twenty he had shown her a novel he had been working on for two years, shyly requesting that she read it and mumbling that it was "not very good, really."

As busy as she was, Emma had stayed up all night reading it and had swooped down on Frank at the newspaper the following morning, "Why do you say it's not good?" she had cried, barely able to contain her excitement. "It's marvelous! And it's going to be published. *Leave it to me*." She had swept Archie Clegg off to an expensive lunch at the Metropole in Leeds and thereafter had badgered him relentlessly, and on a daily basis, until he had undertaken to send the book to a publisher friend in London. It was accepted by Hollis and Blake immediately and she herself had negotiated a favorable contract for Frank. When they brought it out some months later it was received with critical acclaim. More importantly, to Emma at least, the novel was also a resounding success commercially. Frank had become a celebrity overnight and several months after the book's publication he had been offered a position on the *Daily Chronicle* and had departed for Fleet Street with Emma's blessing. Today he was considered one of the most brilliant young writers in English journalism and his future was assured. Or rather, it had been until tonight.

"Damn this rotten war!" Emma cried aloud, filled with a helpless fury. She viewed it as a terrible inconvenience, for it had disrupted her most carefully made plans. Yet in spite of her single-minded preoccupation with her business, she was wise enough to recognize that it had graver consequences.

The war would throw the world into a turmoil and shatter thousands of lives, a prospect that filled her with dread.

Abruptly she stood up. Reflecting on the past and morbidly anticipating the future was a waste of time, that most deplorable of sins to Emma. There was nothing she could do to change what had happened or control impending events obviously beyond her control. She pulled her blue silk dressing gown around her, shivering slightly, although the night was warm, and walked across the hall, her slippers clicking with a metallic ring against the marble floor, the sounds fading as she mounted the carpeted staircase. The grandfather clock, positioned at the turn of the stairs, struck two, its musical chimes reverberating loudly in the stillness of the sleeping house. Emma tiptoed into the bedroom, shrugged out of her dressing gown, and slipped into the great four-poster bed.

Joe stirred. "Emma?"

"I'm sorry, Joe. Did I wake you?" she whispered, pulling the covers over her.

"No, the telephone did. Who was it?" he asked in a sleep-filled voice.

"Frank. He's going to the front as a war correspondent. He's leaving in a few hours. I couldn't persuade him not to go, Joe. I'm so afraid for him," Emma said in a low voice.

"It's a bit soon, isn't it? We've only been at war a few days. Couldn't he have waited?"

"I begged him to change his mind but he wouldn't listen. Now I have the two of them to worry about—" She shivered and clutched the pillow, pressing back her incipient tears.

Joe became aware of her shivering. He moved closer to her. "Don't worry, Emma," he murmured. "They'll be all right. Anyhow, this mess will be over in a few months."

Emma groaned, suppressing the anger that flared in her. Joe had no conception of the facts. She had been predicting the war for months. Her words had fallen on stony ground and she no longer bothered to argue with him. Joe touched her shoulder tentatively. His pressure increased and he pulled her over on her back. He raised himself on one elbow, peering into her face in the dim light. Emma felt his warm breath against her cheek and she instantly stiffened. He smelled faintly of onions, beer, and stale tobacco and she moved her head away from him, filled with distaste. Joe began to kiss her face and his free hand slid under the bedclothes to grasp her breast.

"Joe, *please*. Not now!"

"Don't be cold to me, Emma," he muttered thickly.

"I'm not being cold. I just don't feel up to—"

"You never do," he snapped.

"That's unfair and you know it," she said, bristling, "It's been a long day and I'm upset about Frank. How can you be so inconsiderate? Anyway, you aren't very careful these days. I don't want to get pregnant again."

"I'll be careful, Emma. I promise," he said in a wheedling tone. "Please, love. It's been weeks."

"Ten days," Emma said flatly, infuriated by his insensitivity and selfishness.

"But I want you," he moaned, and ignoring her protestations, he pulled her into his arms. "Please, Emma, don't turn me away."

Emma did not answer. Mistaking her silence for acquiescence, Joe fumbled with her silk nightgown, his breathing now rapid and belabored. He began to explore her body, his hands roughly insistent as they roamed over her legs and thighs and breasts. Emma averted her head, avoiding his kisses. She closed her eyes, crushing down on the impulse to push him away. In the four years they had been married Emma had made a tremendous effort to accommodate Joe Lowther's physical demands, and she knew she would yield yet again. It was easier than repulsing him and prevented violent quarrels later. Also, she had made a bargain with herself, to be a good wife to Joe, and she never reneged on a bargain. She had not reckoned with Joe's unflagging sexual aggressiveness and his voracious appetite, which seemed to increase rather than lessen with time.

It was too late to pull away without creating an explosive scene and so Emma automatically let her body go limp. And then she detached her mind, thinking of other things, fleeing into her private world. She began to do complicated mathematical calculations pertaining to her latest financial ventures, seeking refuge in her business to block out the reality of the moment.

Joe rolled on top of her, panting, his pounding against her relentlessly sustained. Her body was his anvil. His momentum increased and rudely shattered her self-induced detachment, and just as she had known he would, he lost all restraint, became utterly unconscious of her in his wild abandonment. He grasped her legs and roughly pushed them up against her chest and at that moment Emma thought her control would snap. She swallowed a scream of unexpected pain and rage and revulsion as he lunged at her time and time again, a charging bull mindlessly intent on its purpose.

He was still. Thank God he was finally still. Depleted, Joe fell against her, his breathing harsh but returning to normal slowly. Emma stretched out her cramped legs and moved her head wearily on the pillows, tears of humiliation seeping out of the corners, the taste of blood bitter in her mouth where she had bitten her inner lip. Unwanted sex was nauseating, was becoming unendurable, for Joe did not attract her physically and he aroused neither desire nor passion in her. Furthermore, he had never even tried to do so. Despite his own preoccupation with sex, or perhaps because of it, he was oblivious to her unresponsiveness. Perhaps if he had shown more consideration, had been sensitive and understanding of her female needs, the situation might have improved. As it was, Emma believed it was inexorably disintegrating. She did not truly know how long she could continue to tolerate his unremitting assaults on her body as she had done for so long. Joe seemed to be in a perpetual state of heightened potency and this frightened her.

Joe put his arms around her and buried his head against her bosom. "That was wonderful, love," he said quietly in a voice that was oddly shy. "You're too much for any man. I can't get enough of it with you."

Don't I know, she thought angrily but made no comment. Joe moved away from her, turned his back, and within minutes was fast asleep. Why, he didn't even say good night, Emma thought with a flare of irritation and she was mortified. She slid carefully out of bed and glided across the floor to the bathroom, her bare feet sinking into the thick pile of the fine Wilton carpet. She locked the door firmly behind her, threw off her crumpled nightgown, pinned up her hair, and stepped into the bath. Crouching in front of the faucets she ran the water until it was steaming hot, almost too hot to bear, soaping her body generously, scrubbing energetically at her delicate white skin until it was bright red. And then she lay back in the water, hoping to soothe her aching body and calm her jangled nerves. After a while she began to feel relaxed and she climbed out of the tub and toweled herself dry. Moving across the elegantly appointed bathroom, Emma caught sight of herself in the mirror. She paused and looked at her face. There was not a trace of anguish or despair on that pale oval, but then there never was. Blackie was forever telling her she had the inscrutable face of an Oriental and she was beginning to believe him. But then my inscrutability serves my purpose most admirably, she said to herself. She took a clean nightgown out of a chest of drawers, slipped it over her head, picked up her slippers, and hurried downstairs.

Emma went immediately into the small study next to the drawing room, intending to work for an hour. She was wide awake and restless, and she always retreated into work when she wanted to avoid dwelling on unpleasant matters. But moonlight was pouring in through the french doors and she stood staring at the garden, admiring its beauty.

Impulsively Emma pushed open the doors and stepped out onto the long flagged terrace that ran the entire length of this side of the house. It was a lovely August night, so still and balmy the soft air seemed to enfold her. Emma breathed deeply, feeling a sudden sense of release, an easing of her worries. She looked up. The sky was soaring and hollow, a deep pavonian blue, clear and without cloud, and the new moon was a perfect sphere whose glassy surface was unmarred, and its sharp radiance cast a silvery sheen on the trees and shrubs, the rolling lawn and the glorious flower beds that punctuated the perimeters of the garden in the dusky shadows of old stone walls matted with ivy.

Emma swept along the terrace and stood poised at the top of the flight of stone steps that led down into the garden, her hand resting on one of the great urns positioned at their edge. Her eyes roved over her garden, so typically English, pastoral in its gentle beauty and filled with tranquillity. It was hard to believe there was a war raging on the other side of the Channel or to accept the fact that thousands of young Englishmen were preparing to enter that grim and bloody battle.

Emma proceeded slowly to the bottom of the garden, heading for her own special spot, the sheltered corner she loved the most. Here, near an old sundial, magnificent rhododendron bushes and great clutches of peonies spilled forth their translucent pinks and mauves and whites. Joe had wanted to grow roses in this area, but Emma had objected in the strongest possible terms, not permitting one single bush to be planted anywhere in the garden. She had never told Joe that she could not abide that particular flower or that its perfume sickened her to the point of violent nausea.

A splendid beech tree, huge and spreading with its branches dipping down to touch the ground, was a protective arch of interwoven greens above an old garden seat. "Mummy's seat," the children called it, for it was here that she always came when she wanted to escape the activities of her busy household, to think and to relax, and they had learned never to trespass on her solitude in this private place. Thoughts of Joe intruded into her mind, piercing her recently acquired composure. She stiffened as she recalled with dismay his arduous lovemaking. And then she found herself thinking: Poor Joe. He really can't help himself. Her anger was evaporating so unexpectedly Emma was astonished at this change in her emotions.

Earlier, pinned under Joe and raging with resentment, Emma had contemplated leaving him. Now she reviewed this idea and faltered. A separation was unthinkable, not only because of the children and their loving attachment to Joe and his to them, but because she herself needed Joe for a number of good reasons. Furthermore, Joe would never let her go. He loved her to a point of distraction. Sometimes she wished Joe was a philanderer and that when she spurned him, on those rare occasions, he would seek solace in more responsive arms. She had come to realize this was perfectly ridiculous. Joe wanted only her. No other woman could satisfy his urgent needs because she was the sole object of his desire.

Emma sat back on the seat and considered her marriage with objectivity, finally admitting that she had no intentions of changing the circumstances of her life. The alternatives did not appeal to her, and whatever else Joe was, he *was* a buffer between her and those who might wish to hurt her or Edwina. Also, she had to acknowledge that despite her basic unhappiness in her marriage, she was fond of Joe. He was considerate most of the time and he had never interfered with her business enterprises. Of course, he was phlegmatic and opinionated, and often flew into tantrums if she thwarted him, or sulked for days about inconsequential things. Yet despite these traits, which singularly irritated her, he was not a bad man.

Emma was too big a woman to harbor grudges and she acknowledged anew that Joe Lowther had been a good husband in a variety of other ways. She remembered some of his generous gestures now. He had bought her this house, for one thing, in December of 1910. That had been four months after her marriage, when she was carrying their child. In the preceding June, just before their wedding, Joe had come into another unexpected inheritance, one far more impressive than his mother's legacy. His ancient great-aunt, on the maternal side of the family, had died at the age of ninety-one. Since she was childless and without any other relatives, Joe had been the sole beneficiary in her will. Apart from the one-hundred-and-fifty-thousand pounds in cash and her large house in Old Farnley, he had become the new owner of four commercial properties in the center of Leeds. These were operating factory buildings permanently rented to a tanner, a shoe manufacturer, a printer, and a wholesaler of dry goods. The annual income from these properties so far exceeded Joe's expectations he was astounded. He had weighed his financial situation and decided he could easily afford to buy the vacant house in the Towers, and maintain its upkeep on a comfortable scale.

The house stood in a private and secluded little park in Upper Armley that was surrounded by high walls and fronted by great iron gates. A circular driveway led up to the eight fine mansions situated within the park's precincts, each one self-contained, encircled by low walls and boasting a lavish garden. The moment Emma had walked into the house on that cold December day she had wanted it, marveling at its grandness and delighted with its charming outlook over the garden and the park itself. There were numerous airy and well-proportioned reception rooms on the main floor, including a formal drawing room, an impressive dining room, a parlor, and a small study. At the back of the house there was a huge kitchen, a butler's pantry, servants' quarters, and a washhouse. Upstairs eight bedrooms of various dimensions and three bathrooms provided ample space for Joe's family, soon to be increased with the impending arrival of the baby.

The third floor, under the eaves of the old gray stone house, was composed of two attics and a cedar-lined room for storage.

Because of its size, and Emma's insistence that she continue to run her business after the child's birth, Joe had eventually agreed to engage a small staff. Mrs. Fenton, a local widow, had been installed as the housekeeper-cook, and Mrs. Hewitt, Joe's former charwoman, came daily to clean. Mrs. Hewitt's niece, Clara, originally engaged as nursemaid for Edwina, had remained with them to take care of Christopher, born in June of 1911.

The day Emma, Edwina, and Joe moved into the house Emma had experienced such a profound sense of security she had relaxed for the first time in years. In this fine mansion, so elegant and secluded, Emma was at last convinced she was absolutely protected from the Fairleys, and in particular Gerald Fairley. Emma shivered, recalling his unanticipated and violent intrusion into her life four years ago. That hideous April evening was still vividly etched on her mind and Emma knew she would never forget it. She had lived in a state of burgeoning anxiety for months after that visit.

It had taken Emma several weeks to convince David Kallinski that she would not reverse her decision. Eventually he accepted it with sorrow, and although they remained friends and partners, David wisely limited their association to business. Understanding his motives, whilst yearning for him, Emma had disguised her feelings, displaying no emotions, hoping this would help to ease his pain.

And then with calculation and consummate feminine wiles, she had set out to inveigle Joe Lowther into marriage. Already in love with her, overwhelmed by her beauty and impressed with her industriousness and business acumen, Joe had been an easy and willing target. As their friendship had developed he had grown bolder in his courtship. Receiving no rebuff, he had nervously proposed one month later and had been overjoyed when she accepted him, not recognizing that it was he who had been courted and maneuvered.

The night he had proposed and after she had accepted him, Emma had told Joe that Edwina was illegitimate. She had done so with absolute candor, at the same time sagaciously omitting the identity of the father. She had simply repeated the story she had invented for Blackie O'Neill years before. Joe, impressed with her honesty, had been admiring of her stoicism at carrying such a burden alone. He had told her that her past did not interest him, and it truly did not. He was so besotted with Emma the only thing that mattered was her acceptance of him for a husband.

Emma, who had not wanted to start their marriage with deception about her circumstances or her child, was, nevertheless, aware that she had no choice but to tell Joe the truth. Joe believed she was the widow of a sailor called Winston Harte. How then could she conceivably explain her brother to him—also a sailor with the same name as her deceased nonexistent husband? For this reason, she had confided those same half-truths to Laura, and eventually to David, some weeks after her marriage. Neither one had appeared to be shocked and they accepted her explanation with understanding.

Emma's worst moment had been her confrontation with Winston and Frank, for it was also necessary to explain to her brothers the existence of a three-year-old daughter, who was obviously not Joe's offspring. Frank, still in awe of Emma, had not dared to offer one word of criticism. Winston, on the other hand, had placed Emma on a pedestal, and he had flown into a rage, disappointed in her and full of recriminations. After he had calmed down, he managed to convince himself she had been duped and unwilling, so that he could absolve Emma of all blame and keep her image untarnished. He had cursed the scoundrel who had violated his innocent sister in naval-barracks language so colorful both Emma and Joe had been flabbergasted.

Conscious of her brothers' intelligence and perception, Emma had colored her story for their benefit, inventing a nebulous gentleman of doubtful background as the father of her child, whom she said she had met in Leeds. She had alerted Joe in advance, saying that she dare not tell them a boy from Fairley had taken advantage of her. There would be reprisals in the village if she did so. Joe had agreed there was sense in this and was her ally. For her part, Emma was relieved that she no longer had to fabricate stories about her past, for by nature she was not a liar.

Yes, Joe has been decent, Emma said to herself. He had insisted on adopting Edwina after their marriage and he had given her his name. And he loved Edwina as much as he loved his own child, if not more, Emma sometimes suspected.

As these wandering thoughts sifted through Emma's head she felt an unprecedented stab of guilt about her anger with Joe. He had behaved like a gentleman and had shown a degree of generosity towards her, and Emma reproached herself. The gift of her body and wifely devotion was a small price to pay when she considered everything dispassionately.

It would not be easy, Emma knew, when she thought of his wanton lust in the privacy of their bedroom. But she took hold of herself with cold determination, and resolved to be more understanding and warmly attentive to her husband in the future.

THIRTY-EIGHT

The following morning found Emma at her desk in her department store earlier than usual. Elegantly dressed in a severely tailored black silk dress and pearls—"the Harte uniform," Joe called it—she sat studying two fat ledgers. Her deep absorption in those minute black figures running in punctilious columns down the wide pages was so complete she was only dimly aware of the store coming to life and of the sounds of traffic outside.

Emma's attention was riveted on the books for the department store, which she had bought in the latter part of 1912, renovated and modernized with Blackie O'Neill's assistance, and opened with fanfare in January of 1913.

The store had been an instantaneous success. Brilliant advertising, personally conceived by Emma, attracted the public to its doors. They came in droves to scrutinize and criticize this lavish and exotic emporium that had flowered within the hallowed precincts of Lister's, formerly the most conservative of stores, which had been taken over by some parvenu, an ambitious young woman with newfangled ideas. To their incredulity they were captivated by the glamorous ambiance and the air of exclusivity that pervaded every floor. Lulled into a state of euphoria by the elegant interiors with their glittering mirrors, plush carpeting, harmonious lighting effects, and the specially perfumed air, they remained to browse, to exclaim and admire, and were inevitably induced into buying, unaware that they had been cajoled by the tasteful and tranquil surroundings into spending money through a psychological approach far ahead of its time.

Emma's skillful displays of all her products attracted marveling eyes to its quality, its stylishness, and the reasonable prices. The merchandise was the *dernier cri*, so elegant the ladies of Leeds and other nearby towns found themselves unable to resist temptation, dipping into their purses with enthusiasm, under the gentle encouragement of the charming and pleasant-mannered salesgirls, rigorously trained by Emma in what she termed "the art of the understated sell," and which in later years she was to call "the soft sell."

Another contributory factor to the store's popularity was the café Emma had opened on the second floor. She had decorated it in the style of an English country garden, utilizing pastoral scenic wallpaper, white-painted trellises, artificial topiary, and birdcages housing exquisitely rendered copies of colorful birds. She named it the Elizabethan Gazebo and dressed the waitresses in simple pale green uniforms, frilled white organdy aprons and caps. The enchanting setting, a refreshing change from the overblown pomposity of Victorian decor, the serene atmosphere, superior service, and the simple but tasty dishes made the Elizabethan Gazebo all the rage. It became the chic gathering place for morning coffee, light luncheons, and afternoon tea. Smart women took to rendezvousing there and few left the store without making some kind of purchase, just as Emma had shrewdly anticipated. This innovation, a wholly unique departure for a department store, immediately started a trend in Leeds. It prompted her envious competitors to follow suit, but their rococo imitations were tasteless in comparison, and her stylish café was so well established its business was unaffected.

The gift wrapping of merchandise was another idea dreamed up by Emma, who remembered her own excitement at receiving that brightly wrapped gift from Blackie on her fifteenth birthday. This small service was not performed by other local stores and it gave her yet another sales advantage. With her unerring understanding of the public, Emma was convinced this token gesture, costing relatively little in time, effort, and money, would delight her customers, especially since she made no charge for it, and she was proven right. A gift wrapped in silver paper, tied with silver ribbon, and decorated with a tiny spray of silk violets became the cachet of Harte's. So did the courtesy and helpfulness of the doorman who assisted with packages, opened carriage and motorcar doors, and performed other gallant little duties, and in his splendid gold-braided uniform of deep royal blue he added a touch of distinction to the main entrance. Finally, in an effort to persuade her customers to buy everything they needed from Harte's, and in greater quantity, Emma offered door-to-door delivery of goods three times a week. Her customers came to rely on this service, and it boosted sales to such a staggering extent she had to revise her timetable and send out her royal-blue vans five and sometimes even six days a week to fulfill the orders.

On this Saturday morning, twenty months after the store had opened its doors, Emma Harte was in the black and profits were soaring. She had more than sufficient cash in hand to carry her for several years, she decided, as she reviewed the figures. Nonetheless, she was loath to pull fifty thousand pounds out of the store's bank account at this moment, even though it was hefty with deposits. The country had only been at war for four days, but with her prescience Emma knew they could be in for a long siege, and she might suffer serious setbacks if trade fell off because of the public's depressed mood, and their reluctance to buy in the grim days ahead. She recognized that she must not endanger the stability of the store by making rash moves or by overextending herself.

Emma turned to the ledger for the Gregson Warehouse, a wholesale supply company she owned. Her eyes swept over the figures and she did some swift mental arithmetic. Her cash reserves for this company were considerably higher than the store's bank balance, chiefly because she had owned it for a longer period, was selling products in bulk to the mass market, and had virtually no overhead. Moreover, she was heavily stocked and she would not need to buy new merchandise from the manufacturers for a year, and so she did not anticipate heavy cash expenditures.

She turned the page. Her glance settled on the Accounts Receivable columns. A quick tabulation of the figures reminded Emma that she was owed almost one-hundred-and-eighty-thousand pounds by the various stores in London, Manchester, and Scotland who bought from the wholesale warehouse on a regular basis. She was not worried. The money would start trickling in within the next thirty days. However, she had been aware for some weeks that a number of stores were tardy in their payments. She jotted down the names of those customers whose accounts were overdue and running into the ninety-day period, determining that pressure must be exerted on the delinquent companies immediately. Her terms were thirty to sixty days, although she often extended credit for longer periods to old and valued customers. Now that practice will have to cease, she concluded with detachment. Emma, who could be understanding of problems on a personal level, was hardheaded and without sentiment when it came to business. Joe had once accused her of having ice water in her veins and she had responded, "Yes, that's true. Just like a banker."

Emma sat back in her chair, tapping her teeth with the end of the pencil, lost in thought, and then she leaned forward and picked up the clipping from the *Financial Times*, which had been on her desk for the past week. The story in question detailed the closing of the London Stock Exchange and the raising of the bank rate from 4 percent to 8 percent on Friday, July 31. Both measures had been sensational, and to Emma they were indicative of the grave view of the crisis taken in financial circles. Emma had realized that the first action was simply intended to avoid panic in the City, by giving dealers time to steady themselves before being called upon to settle their disorganized Stock Exchange accounts. But she was aware that the raising of the bank rate was meant to hinder the drain of gold out of the country. To Emma, watchful and weighing all the odds, this had been the most ominous sign of all. Whatever the politicians said, war was imminent.

These developments had prompted her to take action regarding a business venture she had been contemplating. Rather than intimidating her into abandoning this new enterprise, it had actually encouraged her to plunge ahead with it. At the same time, the rise in the bank rate had induced her to reject the idea of borrowing from the bank to finance the project, as she had originally intended, and despite the fact that she had never been reluctant to use the bank's money in the past.

In point of fact, when Emma began to extend her business in 1910, she had entered the arena of high finance with many powerful psychological advantages. By nature she was an optimist and totally unafraid of taking chances, believing she could make her own luck in business. Her risks were calculated risks and in a sense she was a guided gambler, as she was to be all of her life. David Kallinski understood her, being cast from the same mold himself.

Emma also had nerves of steel, and these characteristics set her apart from many of her male contemporaries and competitors who were unimaginative and fearful of losing what they had patiently accumulated. Emma was not at all inhibited by these fears, for she was dauntless, and responsive to all manner of business opportunites, which she seized with tenacious hands. Neither was she fazed by paper transactions or long-term borrowing. She had used all to her advantage in the past four years and would do so again if necessary.

But not at this moment, she said to herself, thinking of that 8 percent bank rate. It was outrageous interest to pay. She had all that cash in the Gregson account and was owed a vast amount from the stores. She could easily take the fifty thousand pounds she needed without endangering the warehouse business. Removing the checkbook for the Gregson Warehouse from the drawer of her desk, she wrote out a check, put it in an envelope, addressed it to Frederick Ainsley, and returned the checkbook to the drawer. She looked at her watch, picked up the telephone, and dialed the warehouse.

Her manager, Vince Hartley, answered, as she had known he would. "Good morning, Vince. I've been going over the ledger and I notice that a number of our customers are behind in payment," she said.

"Morning, Mrs. Harte. Yes, I know. I was going to talk to you about them—"

"I want you to start pulling that money in, Vince. First thing on Monday morning," Emma interrupted. "And don't write the usual dunning letters. Telephone and follow up with telegrams. I want immediate results. If they can't pay in full, insist on part payments. And you might point out to the stores whose accounts are outstanding for sixty days or longer that I intend to start charging interest. At once. Bank rates of eight percent."

Vince Hartley sucked in his breath. "Mrs. Harte, that's a bit stiff, isn't it? I don't think they'll like it. They might not buy from us again—"

"I don't give a damn whether they like it or not. And I certainly couldn't care less if they don't buy from us."

"But we're bursting at the seams with stocks. We'll have it on our hands if we're not careful."

"No, we won't," Emma said firmly. "There's a war on now. Merchandise is going to be in short supply and hard to come by. I can use up those stocks in the store if necessary. In fact, I'll probably need them. Many of the manufacturers we buy from will be turning their factories over to the production of government supplies. Uniforms and such, and so I'm not at all concerned about the stocks in the warehouse. In a sense, they're a godsend."

"Yes, I see your point," Hartley conceded, wishing he had thought of that himself. But Emma Harte was always three jumps ahead of everyone else. Now he said, "There's another problem I wanted to mention. Two of our commercial travelers, the ones covering Scotland, have given notice. They're joining up today. That leaves us short-staffed. Shall I take on some new men to replace them?"

"No, don't bother. The two working Manchester and London will be sufficient. As I said, I may well need that merchandise for the store and I don't want the warehouse to be completely depleted. Get onto those overdue accounts on Monday and let me know the results at the end of the day. I expect you to be tough about this, Vince. I don't have time to deal with it myself, but I will if necessary."

"Please, Mrs. Harte, don't worry. You can rely on me," Hartley said nervously, knowing she meant every word.

"Until Monday, Vince. Goodbye." Emma sat back in the chair, wondering if she should let the two remaining travelers go and cease all selling to other retailers, to reserve the stocks for herself in case of shortages. A knock on the door interrupted her musings. Emma looked up as Gladys Barnes, her young secretary, poked her head around the door.

"Mr. Ainsley has arrived, Mrs. Harte."

"Show him in, Gladys, please."

"Yes, Mrs. Harte."

Emma stood up, smoothed her skirt, and automatically patted her hair, walking across the floor to welcome her solicitor, whom she had been expecting. She was therefore taken aback, and also irritated, when Ainsley's son, Arthur, appeared on the threshold.

Arthur Ainsley, tall, slender, and with the blond good looks of a juvenile lead, was conscious of his physical attributes and the effect they had on most women. Elegantly dressed in a somewhat dandified manner, he played the part of the dashing young buck to the hilt and now he sauntered in with debonair aplomb.

He's forgotten his tennis racquet, Emma thought disparagingly, but she proffered him a charming smile. "Good morning, Mr. Ainsley."

"Good morning, Mrs. Harte. You look as splendid as always." Ainsley flashed his perfect teeth and took her outstretched hand, his clasp lingering too long for Emma's comfort.

"Why, thank you, Mr. Ainsley. Please, do sit down." She glided to her desk and sat behind it, still smiling, sheathing her annoyance. In her opinion, Arthur Ainsley was a fop and she regarded him as his father's errand boy, even though he was a junior partner with the law firm. "Is your father joining us?" she asked in an even tone.

"No, I'm afraid he can't. He came down with a frightful cold last night. Hence my presence instead of his," Arthur replied, suavely apologetic.

"I am sorry," Emma murmured.

"However," Arthur went on quickly, "he did ask me to tell you that you may telephone him at home, if you consider it necessary after our meeting. That is, if you feel I am not able to help you with your—er—er—problem."

"I don't have a problem, Mr. Ainsley," Emma said coolly. "I merely wished to bring to conclusion a certain matter I have been discussing with your father. I think you will be able to handle it quite adequately, since all the major work has been done already."

Arthur Ainsley ignored her patronizing tone, although he winced. He had been trying to ingratiate himself with Emma Harte for the past year without success, and this infuriated him. Nevertheless, he responded with studied charm. "I sincerely hope I can, Mrs. Harte. I always aim to please, you know."

"Indeed," Emma said dismissively. "When I spoke to your father yesterday morning I did not explain why I wished to see him today, so obviously he was unable to brief you. Let me fill you in. Several weeks ago I started negotiations with Mr. William Layton, of Layton's woolen mill in Armley. Mr.

Layton has wanted to sell for some time. He's getting too old to run the mill efficiently and his business has fallen off drastically. Mostly due to the poor quality of the cloth he has been producing and indifferent selling. In fact, it's my opinion he's only a few steps away from bankruptcy. Mr. Layton agreed to sell the mill to me for fifty thousand pounds. I considered this a fairly reasonable figure, although the mill is small, there's virtually no good will to speak of, and his customers are few. He's also stuck with an enormous quantity of shoddy cloth which I will have to practically give away, simply to get rid of it—"

"It doesn't sound like a good proposition to me," Arthur cut in, hoping to impress her.

Emma frowned and held up her hand. "Please, Mr. Ainsley, let me finish!" Her voice was chilly. "The machinery is good and the building is sound, if in need of a few renovations. Also, Layton's is carrying huge stocks of raw wool, of major importance to me. Anyway, to come to the point, Mr. Layton agreed to my terms, which were fifteen thousand on signing of the purchase agreements, ten thousand after three months, and the final payment of twenty-five-thousand pounds at the end of six months. That is approximately the length of time I require to turn the mill around. We were about to go to contract when Mr. Layton backed down. His excuse was that he no longer wanted to sell. I found this hard to swallow, but naturally I had to respect his decision."

"You probably could have held him to that agreement, you know, even though it was verbal," Arthur interjected. "I'm sure my father told you that, didn't he?"

"He did indeed," Emma said. "However, I decided at the time not to do so. Mr. Layton is an old man and I didn't want to back him into a corner. After all, it was his prerogative to change his mind. I told your father I would look around for another suitable mill, since I was anxious to acquire one. Then a few days ago I discovered, through a reliable source of my own, that Mr. Layton had received another offer," Emma explained. "This offer was not higher than mine, but the terms were seemingly more appealing to Mr. Layton. My competitor was prepared to make two payments instead of three, each one of twenty-five thousand pounds. The first on signing, the second after six months. I am not an unreasonable woman, Mr. Ainsley, but Mr. Layton's duplicity appalled me. After all, we had shaken hands on the deal and then he turned around and reneged. Moreover, he did not have the integrity to inform me of that bid, and so give me the opportunity to match it."

"I appreciate your feelings, Mrs. Harte," Arthur said with a fawning smile. "I suppose you want to match this new bid?"

"No, better it, in a sense. I have decided to pay the purchase price in full. On Monday."

Arthur Ainsley sat up smartly, rubbing his chin nervously. "But that's not bettering it, is it? You're simply changing the payment schedule, that's all. What makes you think the other party won't do the same thing? Then you'd be faced with an impasse, and Layton still might not sell to *you*. Also, how do you know they haven't concluded the transaction?"

Emma smiled confidently. "They haven't, and I happen to know that the party in question does not have the ready cash to make payment in full at this moment. He has just modernized the mill he owns and has put in costly machinery. I realize, of course, that he could borrow from the bank to purchase Layton's. That would have been very good business practice a week ago, but today, with the bank rate up to eight percent, I think the rival buyer may well have second thoughts about doing that. I've been informed that he's overextended and well into the bank already. They may not wish to oblige him with further credit. It is my belief that if I move swiftly I can knock him out of the picture completely."

"Yes, perhaps you can," Arthur agreed cautiously.

"It is also my understanding that Mr. Layton does not want protracted negotiations. His creditors are on his back and he wants a fast sale. And so I am dealing from strength, wouldn't you say?"

Arthur nodded, obviously impressed. She was constantly surprising both him and his father. Then another thought struck him. "Look here, let's think about this for a second. Are you sure you want to invest fifty thousand in a new business at a time like this? Since we are at war, I'm not so sure this is a moment for taking risks."

"I'm not taking any risks and, furthermore, this is exactly the right time to buy Layton's, because I intend to obtain government contracts to produce cloth for the armed forces. Cloth for uniforms, Mr. Ainsley. With those contracts I can have that mill on its feet and in profit overnight!"

"Well, I must say, you certainly think of everything!" He had no doubts she would get the contracts, yet he felt compelled to say, "*Are you sure?* Really sure you can get them? It occurs to me the established cloth manufacturers in Yorkshire will be after the same contracts. They could beat you to it."

"I don't think so, Mr. Ainsley," Emma said softly, and with a self-assured smile. "*Naturally* they will go after them, but I have connections in London. And, in any event, the government is going to need plenty of cloth for uniforms, believe me. There will be enough business to go around."

Dazzled, Arthur said, "My father has always considered you to have remarkable vision and certainly you seem confident. What would you like me to do, in regard to the Layton mill?"

"Telephone Mr. Layton and tender my offer as soon as you get into your office on Monday. Arrange an appointment with him for Monday afternoon. I will go with you and we can sign immediately. And make sure he has his solicitor there. I don't want any procrastination."

"Yes, I understand," Arthur said, echoing her businesslike tone.

Emma picked up the papers on her desk and handed them to him. "These are the original contracts. I have made various changes, those I considered necessary. However, I am sure they are in order. In fact, the changes are so minor you should be able to redraw the contracts by noon."

She certainly knows how to give her orders, Arthur thought with a stab of resentment, but nodded. "That's no problem," he asserted.

"And here is my check for the full purchase price." Emma gave him the envelope and went on, "I want you to take it today so that you can tell Mr. Layton, in all truthfulness, that you have it in your hands when you speak with him." Emma's green eyes, now brilliant, rested on Arthur. To her amusement he appeared to be dumbfounded. "I don't think you will have any problems with Mr. Layton. I am making him an offer he will find extremely difficult to refuse under the circumstances," she said. "I know my rival will not be able to move as rapidly as I can."

"Oh, I endorse that wholeheartedly!" Arthur then said,

with a disarming smile, "May I invite you to lunch on Monday, before we go to Layton's? It would be my pleasure."

Emma feigned dismay. "Oh dear, I can't. It's very kind of you to ask me, but I already have an appointment for lunch that day. I will meet you at your office at two o'clock, if that is convenient, and we can go over the contracts before our appointment with Mr. Layton."

Arthur concealed his disappointment, aware that his charm had no effect on her. "Yes, that's fine. Is there anything else you wish to discuss?" he asked, anxious to prolong his visit.

Invariably pressed for time and having no use for idle chatter, Emma said, "No, that's about it." She rose abruptly. Arthur jumped up, reaching for his briefcase. Emma accompanied him to the door. "Thank you for coming in, Mr. Ainsley. And do give my best to your father. I hope he feels better soon." She stretched out her hand, shook Arthur's quickly, and opened the door. He found himself whisked out of her office with such speed he barely had a chance to take his leave of her courteously.

Emma smiled when she was alone. Arthur Ainsley fancies himself, she thought, and then forgot all about him, turning her attention to the store's business. A few minutes after Ainsley had left the office Joe marched in unexpectedly. Having determined, the night before, to be her most affectionate with him in every way, Emma greeted him warmly, only to be rebuffed by a gruff response. Despite her irritation at this intrusion on her busiest morning, and her bafflement at his obnoxious manner, the smile on Emma's face did not falter. She opened her mouth to ask him why he was upset when he saved her the trouble.

"What the hell was Arthur Ainsley doing here?" he growled, flinging himself into the chair recently vacated by the young man.

"Because he's our solicitor. Don't tell me that has *slipped* your mind, Joe."

"His *father* is our solicitor," Joe snapped.

"Frederick Ainsley is ill. I had some urgent business to be dealt with and he sent Arthur in his place."

"I don't like that chap!" Joe announced.

Joe's tone was so harsh Emma was further startled. "For goodness' sake, don't be so snippy, dear. Arthur Ainsley is pleasant and also able, I think."

"He's charming to you, Emma. You wear skirts. That chap's a real womanizer. He's a rake!"

Emma laughed. "Oh, Joe, don't be so silly. Anyway, his private life is his own affair, I think."

"Well, I don't like the way he behaves around you, Emma. I've noticed how young Ainsley dances attendance on you, and he positively leers at you. He's too bloody cocksure of his so-called *fatal* charms, if you ask me."

Emma bit back a smile. Joe was jealous, an emotion he had not hitherto displayed before. But then, she never gave him any reason to be jealous, nor did she have any inclination to do so. Men were the last thing on her mind.

"Look here, Joe, you're getting excited about nothing. I don't encourage Arthur Ainsley's attentions. In fact, I've never noticed them, to tell you the truth. It's hardly my fault that Mr. Ainsley sends him here on business matters. Come along, love, don't be childish," she said cajolingly.

Joe felt suddenly foolish and he grinned, looking shame-faced. "Yes, you're right, but what was so urgent that you had to deal with it on Saturday?"

Emma told him about her decision to buy Layton's mill, explaining some of the ramifications and the necessity for moving with a degree of swiftness. "Surprise is often the best weapon," she pointed out. "Percy Lomax thinks he's got Layton's mill. He thinks he's outsmarted me, but he's wrong. Nobody outsmarts *me*. Ever!"

Joe was staring at her askance. "Don't you think you're biting off more than you can chew?" he cried.

"What do you mean?" she asked in surprise.

"Between the store, the Gregson Warehouse, and Lady Hamilton Clothes it seems to me that you have enough to keep you busy twenty-four hours a day, without that blasted mill."

She laughed. "I'm not going to be running the mill, Joe."

"Knowing you, Emma, you'll want to take an active interest in the administration. You never leave anything to chance, and you'd have to be involved out of necessity. From what I hear, Layton's needs reorganizing, doesn't it?"

"Yes, it does. But I've thought everything out well in advance. I'll get a good manager."

"Who? They're hard to come by, you know."

"Ben Andrews. I've—"

"Ben Andrews! Good God, Emma, he's been at Thompson's mill for donkey's years. You'll never get him to leave."

"That's where you're mistaken, Joe. I've had several meetings with Ben and he wants to leave Thompson's. I only have to say the word. He hasn't been too happy there since the new owners took over four years ago. He's itching to get out, if you want to know the truth."

Joe grinned. "I've got to take my hat off to you, Emma. You certainly know how to pick 'em. Ben is a hell of a good man. The best in the woolen business. He's made Thompson's, that's a certainty."

Emma nodded. "I know. And that's the secret of my success. Finding the right people and being willing to delegate authority to those who are capable of handling it. I'm also very generous. I made Ben an offer Thompson's would *never* match, even if he wanted to stay with them!"

Observing her with grudging approbation, Joe saw her delighted smile turn into one of triumph. He could not help laughing. Shaking his head, he said, "I suppose it tickles you to death to be in a position to employ Ben Andrews, considering he was your boss when you worked at Thompson's. I can't say I blame you."

"No, it doesn't," Emma said softly and in all truthfulness. It was the idea of luring Ben Andrews, three top foremen, and twenty of the best weavers away from Thompson's that intoxicated her. Without Ben's superior management and those experienced workers, Thompson's output would be crippled and the mill would be in disastrous trouble. A thrill of pure elation ran through her. She had just made her first move against the Fairleys, owners of J. P. Thompson and Son.

"Congratulations, Emma. You're a millowner at last."

"Don't congratulate me yet, Joe!" Emma exclaimed. "I'm superstitious about celebrating before a transaction is final."

"Oh, it will be, Emma. I don't doubt that for one minute," he said with an odd smile. "You always get what you want, don't you? There's no stopping you once you've made up your mind. You rush in, sweeping everybody to one side, so intent on your purpose you don't care who gets trampled underfoot."

Emma looked at Joe, surprised at his harsh words and the sarcastic edge to his voice. Normally she disregarded his taunts, but now she could not help saying angrily, "You make me sound ruthless and hard. And I'm not. I'm simply a good businesswoman. Furthermore, nobody has ever handed *me* anything on a plate. I've had to work like a dog for everything I own, Joe."

"I can't deny that. Work *is* your consuming passion, though, isn't it?" His eyes were as hard as pebbles, and condemning.

Emma sighed. She began to shuffle her papers, impatient for him to leave and in no mood to joust. "Why are you in town so early this morning?" she asked gently, changing the subject.

"I'm going to the office. I'm behind with some of the ledgers for the properties," he said offhandedly, and stood up. "Then I'm meeting Blackie for lunch at the Metropole. I want to talk to him about putting new roofing on the tannery and reinforcing the top floor. He's been too overwhelmed with building contracts to attend to the work before now, but both jobs are long overdue."

"Give him my love and tell him I'll come to see Laura on Sunday." Emma's face changed, softening as she spoke of her friend. "I'm worried about Laura, Joe. She hasn't seemed at all strong since the last miscarriage. She needs building up. I wish there was something I could do to—"

"There's nothing you can do," Joe exclaimed. "That's Blackie's problem. He should exercise a little self-control and stop getting her—" He bit off his sentence, flushing.

"In the family way," Emma finished for him with chilly disdain. "Look who's talking!"

Joe dismissed this dig with a wave of his hand, although his flush deepened. "Besides, you do enough for Laura as it is, Emma. Why, the way you dote on that woman anybody would think she's a member of the family."

"She is!" Emma snapped. "She's like my sister, my dearest friend. I would do anything for Laura. Anything in this world."

"That I know!" He strode to the door. "I'll see you at home, Emma. Bye."

"Good-bye, Joe."

After he had left, Emma stared at the door he had so harshly banged behind him, shaking her head. *He's* got a bee in his bonnet this morning, she thought wearily. She did not have time to worry about Joe and his infantile bursts of petulance. She picked up the ledgers and carried them to the safe where she always kept them and locked them away securely. She walked back to her desk, a spring in her step, her head held high. She was about to become a millowner and stick a knife in Gerald Fairley's back at the same time. She laughed aloud. The idea of being able to enhance her business enterprises whilst damaging the Fairleys appealed to her sense of irony. She looked at the photograph of her eight-year-old daughter reposing in a silver frame on her desk. "That's called poetic justice, Edwina," she said to the photograph. "Justice for both of us. And it's just the beginning."

Emma rested her head against the chair. Once again she contemplated the war, endeavoring to gauge the effect it would have on commerce and industry. Her considered reflections prompted her to make a sudden decision. She would definitely discontinue selling certain types of merchandise to other retailers. She was undoubtedly going to need most of the warehouse stock for Harte's in time, and she had no alternative but to curtail the activities of the two remaining commercial travelers to a degree, and enforce limitations on their supplies. She began to selectively tick off the goods she could readily dispose of in her own store. Good old Gregson's, she muttered under her breath. It's the best investment I ever made.

And indeed it was. In 1910, a few months after her marriage to Joe, Emma had learned that the Gregson Warehouse, a wholesale company acting as the middleman between the manufacturers and the retailers, was in trouble and up for sale for a song.

Emma wanted it. More accurately, she craved it passionately. And she determined to have it, recognizing its enormous potential as a moneymaker of no mean proportions. It was also the vehicle she had been seeking, one that would enable her to implement two of her most potent schemes— rapid expansion for a small investment and volume buying from the manufacturers to obtain quality merchandise at low prices. She purchased Gregson's for two thousand pounds and, with her own brand of initiative and expediency, smartly divested herself of its dated and second-rate goods with lightning speed. Her technique was simple but foolproof. She slashed prices drastically and sold everything to local stores that were in constant need of bargains for their semiannual sales.

As she had shrewdly suspected, she actually made money from the stocks. With this money, and by persuading the manufacturers to give her extended credit, she bought in bulk. Some of the smaller clothing manufacturers even began to produce solely for her; consequently much of her merchandise was exclusive as well as reasonably priced. Utilizing the services of four veteran commercial travelers, who worked on a commission basis, she then became a wholesale vendor to retailers in London, Scotland, and Lancashire. Emma was also now in the enviable position of being able to stock her own three shops at no cost to herself, and by cannily supplying stores located in distant areas she kept her wares select and suffered no competition.

Early in 1911, when Gregson's was operating smoothly, Emma had asked Joe to sell her the three shops she rented from him and the other five he owned. He had not wanted to sell to her, even though she had offered him five thousand pounds. Since he received a trifling annual income of fifty pounds from each shop, she had pointedly remarked he was making an immediate profit, and from his own wife.

"I don't want to make a profit at all," Joe had rejoined defensively, going on to grouse that he was disinclined to sell, preferring the income.

"But I'm willing to give you the equivalent of ten years' rent for each shop, plus an extra thousand pounds," Emma had cried, on the verge of losing her temper.

Joe was adamant, being reluctant to diminish his property holdings. But as a compromise, and in order to restore tranquillity to their home life and appease her, he had suggested she could rent the five other shops, leaving ownership in his hands. This was a lackluster alternative to Emma, who had her own motives for wanting the shops, and she flatly refused to consider the proposition.

The deadlock was broken by Frederick Ainsley, who, to Emma's surprise, became her champion and backed her unstintingly. His remarkably persuasive talents and smooth tongue were fortunately not altogether lost on the recalcitrant Joe. "It is only because of Emma's unflagging work that the three shops are such a success. They were failures and vacant half the time before she rented them from you, Joe," Ainsley had adroitly pointed out. "Under the circumstances, don't you think she deserves to own what she has so assiduously built up? It's her investment for the future. And what do you have to lose, Joe, my boy? She's prepared to pay an excellent price, one that more than recompenses you for the income you would receive, whilst relieving you of the burden of maintenance and repairs. Do be a good chap and at least consider selling her the eight shops, Joe. It's to your advantage. That five thousand could easily be invested in something more lucrative."

Privately, Frederick Ainsley had expressed surprise that Joe had not offered to give her the deeds to the shops. "As a wedding present, perhaps," the courtly solicitor had gallantly murmured. He was much taken with Emma, being aware of her superior brain and her business acumen. Skill with finances and nerve to gamble were a redoubtable combination in his eyes. They added up to business genius.

Emma had shaken her head vigorously. "No! I want to *buy* them from him. Then I know they're really mine and no one can ever dispute that fact!" she had cried.

Frederick Ainsley, appreciating the sagaciousness of her comments, and accurately guessing her ultimate goal, had readily concurred. The solicitor had resorted to another tactic to help Emma attain her wish. He had simply presented Joe with several potential investments guaranteed to pay high dividends. "Think about selling to Emma. It's an opportunity that doesn't present itself every day," Ainsley had casually remarked. "And you could have that five thousand working for you most profitably."

Joe thought and eventually sold, if somewhat reluctantly, feeling vaguely uneasy about the whole affair.

Emma had known she would have to mortgage Gregson's to raise the money for the shops, but this did not deter her. And she wanted to pay Joe the total amount immediately. Six months later she had repaid the mortgage on the warehouse and within another twelve months she was ready to put the second and most ambitious part of her well-conceived plan into operation—the acquisition of a department store in Leeds.

To finance this venture Emma sold her eight shops in Armley for a total price of twenty thousand pounds. Joe, dumbstruck, implied she was guilty of sharp business practice, insisting she had willfully inflated the price of the shops above their real market value to suit her own ends. He warned of repercussions.

"Nonsense!" Emma had countered icily, infuriated by his accusatory tone. "I'm not selling the buildings *only*, as you did, Joe. I'm also selling large stocks of quality merchandise and enormous good will. And what about all the renovations I've made? Which I paid for."

Joe had shrugged, disguising his disapproval behind a façade of studied indifference, and had announced he was washing his hands of the whole questionable business.

With the nerve and monumental self-assurance of a seasoned entrepreneur, Emma had taken out a new and far higher mortgage on the warehouse, borrowed from the bank by pledging the new store as collateral, thrown the twenty thousand into the kitty, and purchased Lister's. She had redeemed her promissory notes from the bank in a relatively short space of time, anxious to have title of the department store free and clear, and the mortgage on the warehouse had been paid off within a year.

A sharp knock on the door interrupted Emma's careful examination of the inventory of Gregson's current stock. She looked up.

Gladys came in. "It's only me with a cup of nice hot tea. I thought you'd like one before you go down on the floor, Mrs. Harte."

"That was thoughtful of you, Gladys. Thank you." Emma pushed her chair back, propped her elegantly shod feet on the desk, and sipped her tea, reviewing the Gregson inventory in her head. She could easily keep Harte's well supplied for the duration of the war, she concluded, and with a little of her gambler's luck she would survive without too many losses.

She recommenced her perusal of the last page of the inventory, wanting to complete her assessment before going down into the store. But thoughts of the mill intruded. She could not wait to get her hands on Layton's. It was a potential gold mine. Then she pictured Gerald Fairley's face when his manager, three foremen, and his best weavers walked out.

That bastard's in for a real surprise, she thought, and with not a little vindictiveness.

THIRTY-NINE

Edwin Fairley loitered outside Harte's department store, gazing into one of the windows, trying to summon up enough courage to go inside. It was always like this when he arrived on the doorstep. His nerve inevitably failed him for ten minutes or so, and sometimes altogether.

He pretended to be studying the chic evening gowns in the window, thinking of the first time he had walked past the store on Commercial Street. That had been over a year ago and he had stopped dead in his tracks, instantly struck by the name, staring in astonishment at the silvery metal letters which spelled out E. HARTE against the royal-blue woodwork over the door. Concluding that it was a coincidence, he had proceeded down the street and then suddenly retraced his steps, his curiosity whetted.

Edwin had approached the doorman and inquired about the ownership of this fine new establishment. The doorman had politely informed him that a Mrs. Harte was the proprietor. A few more probing questions had supplied some startling answers, and he had hastened off, considerably shaken. There was no question in his mind, from the glowing description of Mrs. Harte he had wrung out of the doorman, that this was indeed Emma's store. Within a few hours he had received confirmation from Gerald, who had been unable to resist adding a vulgar warning to keep his trousers buttoned. Edwin had turned away in disgust, concealing his anger and repressing the violent urge to punch his brother in the nose.

And the store had attracted him like a magnet ever since. Whenever he visited Yorkshire he made an excuse to Jane to go into Leeds alone, automatically gravitating to Harte's, propelled by a mixture of emotions. Eventually he had found the nerve to enter the store, and had been overwhelmed by the elegance of the interiors and staggered at Emma's singular achievement, which he considered awesome. And he had experienced a curious sense of pride in her. He had returned on several occasions afterwards, nervously walking around, wondering if he would catch sight of Emma. But he never had, and he cursed himself for his juvenile behavior, always vowing never to torture himself in such a ridiculous manner again.

Still, here he was on this warm August Saturday, a day he should have been at Fairley with Jane and the family, longing to go inside, hoping for a brief glimpse of Emma Harte, yet, conversely, afraid he might bump into her. Fool, he muttered, filled with angry frustration at his own indecisiveness.

After several moments of window-gazing Edwin took a deep breath, adjusted his tie, and pushed open the doors. Feeling ill at ease amongst the women shoppers thronging the main floor, he immediately headed for the men's haberdashery.

In his haste and preoccupation he was unconscious of the admiring glances bestowed upon him by some of the ladies who stepped aside to let him pass. At twenty-six Edwin Fairley was a good-looking young man. Tall and firmly built, he had a dashing air and, since he had inherited his father's penchant for elegant clothes, he was always impeccably dressed. But it was his face that caused many women to look twice and speculate. Finely drawn and ascetic, there was, nevertheless, a marked sensuality about his mouth, and his eyes held an indefinable expression that hinted of passion.

Arriving at the haberdashery, Edwin asked to see some silk cravats, examining them whilst surreptitiously glancing over his shoulder, anxiously seeking that one incomparable woman in the crowd. He finally bought a gray silk tie he did not want, because he was embarrassed to walk away after the salesgirl had been so obliging. Declining to have it gift-wrapped, he paid, picked up the package, and moved on.

After making this initial purchase Edwin discovered he was beginning to relax, and he strolled through other departments with a degree of self-assurance, browsing to waste time. He halted at the perfumery counter and bought two bottles of expensive French scent for his wife and his aunt. In order to linger in Harte's he asked to have them individually gift-wrapped. The young woman nodded, smiled, and busied herself with this task. Edwin leaned nonchalantly against the counter, his light gray eyes scanning the main floor. He swung around and looked up at the main staircase.

And it was then that he saw her.

Emma was coming down the stairs. Edwin sucked in his

breath. She was more beautiful than ever, fashionably dressed in black silk that fell in fluid lines around her shapely figure. He recognized at once that she had poise and distinction, and in young womanhood her loveliness was in full bloom. She paused at the turn of the stairs to speak to a customer, her face lighting up, full of vivacity. Edwin gazed at her with intensity, mesmerized by that exquisite oval face, unable to pull his eyes away, and his heart twisted inside him.

He had not set eyes on Emma Harte for nine years, but now, to Edwin, it might have only been yesterday that he had held her in his arms in the cave on the moors. He longed to rush over to her, to beg her forgiveness, to ask about their child. He dare not. He knew, with a sickening sense of despair, that she would repudiate him just as surely as he had repudiated her so long ago on that ghastly morning in the rose garden.

Emma continued to the bottom of the stairs and glided across the floor with infinite grace and aplomb, obviously in command of herself and her store. And then, to his immense horror, Edwin realized she was walking directly towards him. He was rooted to the spot, incapable of moving or even turning his head, and his heart was thundering in his chest. To his supreme relief she paused at another counter and became engaged in conversation with a sales assistant. At one moment she looked over her shoulder and stared right at him, or so it seemed. He stiffened. There was an engrossed expression on her face and her eyes swiveled to the jewelry department. She shook her head, leaned forward, and continued her discussion. Had she seen him or not? Or had she simply not recognized him? He dismissed this idea instantly. That was inconceivable. He had not changed very much and, in any case, his resemblance to his father was now so pronounced it was difficult for anyone to mistake his identity.

The salesgirl spoke to him. Startled, he pulled himself together and gave her his attention. She handed him the packages and the bill, all the while chatting to him pleasantly. He heard her voice faintly through the crashing noises reverberating in his head. It required all of his self-control to keep his hands from shaking as he reached for his wallet. Through the corner of his eye he saw Emma approaching and he dropped his head, his heart in his mouth.

Emma brushed so close to him he could have touched her.

He heard the soft swishing of the silk of her dress and caught the faint whiff of her perfume, something light and fresh like lily of the valley. His anguish was acute, and he had to suppress the urgent desire to reach out and take her arm.

And then she was gone. He watched her disappearing into another department, smiling and nodding graciously to customers.

He completed his business and stumbled out of the store without looking back, feeling sick and undone. He stood in the street experiencing that awful sense of loss again, and the gnawing hollowness in his heart, which never left him, was more chilling than ever.

Edwin walked towards City Square, moving blindly through the crowds, unaware of the traffic or the bustle, seeing nothing but her face. The face he would never forget as long as he lived. It was burned on his brain like a brand stamped on steel. By taking deep breaths Edwin managed at last to steady himself and he struck out determinedly towards the main post office, suddenly intent in his purpose. He had just made a decision and nothing would induce him to reverse it.

Within a short while his business in the post office was completed. He made another stop, attended to the matter at hand with remarkable swiftness, and left. He found the Daimler, parked near the railway station, told the chauffeur to take him home, and fell onto the back seat feeling wretched and depleted.

On the drive back to Fairley, Edwin thought of Emma. The impact of seeing her had been so tremendous he knew at last why he had dreaded it whilst striving towards that goal. She had awakened old longings and also made him painfully conscious of the emptiness of his life. She had rekindled his guilt and shame, never far from the surface anyway.

The memory of her tortured him. Why could he find no satisfaction in the arms of other women? And there had been plenty in the last five years. Why, oh God, why did he persistently seek out women that resembled her if only vaguely? Searching, always searching for another Emma. Irresistibly drawn to green eyes, russet-brown hair, silken white skin, only to be disappointed, dissatisfied, and torn apart in the end. Awake or asleep, Emma haunted him.

He contemplated their child. He had a compelling yearning to see it. It must be eight years old now, if it had lived.

Of course it has lived, he told himself firmly, wanting to believe that part of Emma and himself existed in another human being. Was it a girl or a boy? Did it favor Emma or himself? Or was it a mixture of them both?

A bitter smile slid onto his pale face, gaunt in the dim light of the car. How ironic that Emma had borne him a child out of wedlock, a child forbidden to him, whilst Jane had never conceived and given him the son or daughter he craved. Had she presented him with a child their union might have been more bearable. He pictured Emma, and then Jane. He should never have married her. He should have resisted all that family pressure. His barren, dull, insipid wife. *She* was the cross he had to bear in life. No, that was a dishonorable thought and unfair. He could not condemn poor Jane. She was lovely, and adoring, and it was hardly her fault that he had nothing of himself to give her. He belonged to Emma Harte; that was unalterable and would never change except in death.

Edwin's bleak mood engulfed him all afternoon and well into the evening. He struggled through the family dinner, which seemed more interminable than usual to him, making polite but strained conversation. He was glad when his father suggested they retire to the library. Edwin was also vastly relieved Gerald was absent, for he had been seeking an opportunity to speak to his father alone since his return from Leeds.

Adam poured the drinks and they settled themselves in front of the fire. His father chatted amiably about inconsequential things until finally Edwin could no longer contain himself. "Father, there's something I must speak to you about," he announced abruptly.

Adam looked at him closely, frowning. "You sound serious, Edwin. In fact, you have been very morose all evening. Nothing wrong, I hope."

"No, Father, everything is fine." Edwin hesitated and cleared his throat. "I wanted you to know that I made a decision today. A decision about joining the army. Immediately."

Adam's face changed radically and he placed the brandy and soda on the table with the utmost care. "Edwin, I think you are being hasty. These are early days yet. I don't want you rushing off to war until we have more news, see what the developments are. I beg you to reconsider, my boy."

"I can't, Father. I don't want to upset you, or worry you, but I must go. Please, do try to understand my point of view."

"Edwin, you don't have to volunteer. Only single men have been asked to go to the front."

"Yes, I know that, Father. Nevertheless, I have made the decision." Edwin stood up, reached for the *Yorkshire Morning Gazette* on the library table, and said, "I don't *have* to read this government bulletin to you, Father. You must be familiar with it. The paper has been running it for several days now. But I *am* going to read it to you."

"Look here, Edwin—" Adam began.

Edwin held up his hand and looked at the newspaper, reading from it carefully and slowly.

"Your King and Country Need You! Will you answer your country's call? Each day is fraught with the gravest possibilities and at this very moment the Empire is on the brink of the greatest war in the history of the world. In this crisis your country calls on all of her young men to rally round the Flag and enlist in the ranks of the army. If every patriotic young man answers her call, England and Empire will emerge stronger and more united than ever. If you are unmarried and between eighteen and thirty years old, will you answer your country's call and go to the nearest recruiting office, whose address you can get at any post office. AND JOIN THE ARMY TODAY!"

Edwin dropped the newspaper on the chesterfield and sat down, his eyes resting on his father.

Adam shook his head wearily. "Oh, Edwin, Edwin, don't try to appeal to my own sense of patriotism. I *know* the country is in grave danger, but I am concerned about *you*. That government bulletin asks for *single* men. I beg of you, Edwin—"

"It's too late, Father. I joined up this afternoon when I was in Leeds. I have to report on Monday."

"Oh, my God! Edwin!"

"I'm sorry, Father. Please don't be angry, and please give me your blessing. I don't want to leave here with your disapproval—"

"Good heavens, Edwin, I wouldn't let that happen for the

world." Adam sprang up and joined his son on the sofa. He put his arm around Edwin's shoulder and for a horrible moment he thought he was going to cry. "Now, my boy, enough of that nonsense. I do wish you had waited, of course. But naturally you have my blessing."

"Thank you, Father."

Adam rose and fixed himself another drink. He propped himself against the mantelshelf and gazed down at Edwin, filled with anguish. I've known for days he would do this; nonetheless, it doesn't make it any easier to bear. "I imagine I would do the same, if I were your age, and I'm quite certain my father would have felt the way I feel." Adam shook his head. "But you're so young, Edwin. So young."

"So is every other Englishman who's going, Father."

Adam glanced at Edwin. "Have you told Jane about this, my boy?"

Edwin nodded. "I told her when we were dressing for dinner. She was upset, but she understands. There has been a long line of soldiers in her family, you know. Her brother told us that he intends to volunteer this coming week."

"I see." Adam said, looking thoughtful. "Will Jane come and live with us in South Audley Street? We'd like that, you know, and I don't think she should be on her own in Eaton Square. She will be awfully lonely in that big house by herself, with only the servants."

"Thank you, Father. I appreciate your kindness. However, Jane told me she wants to go to London next week, close up the house, and return to Yorkshire. She would like to be with her father, since her brother will be going. She likes the country and I think that would be the wisest thing, under the circumstances. Don't you?"

"Yes, of course, Edwin. Well, it seems it's all settled," Adam finished, staring gloomily into the fire.

After a small silence, Edwin said, "Father, there's something I want to give you. I've had it for years." He reached into the pocket of his dinner jacket and removed a silk handkerchief. He handed it to Adam, who took it absently.

As his father unwrapped the object in it, Edwin went on, "I found it years ago. Now I'd like you to have it. I know you painted it, and also that it bears a striking likeness to Aunt Olivia."

Adam was staring at the round flat pebble in the silk

handkerchief, his eyes resting on that sweet face. The oils were remarkably well preserved. He smoothed one finger over it. "Did you varnish this again, Edwin?"

"Indeed I did, Father. To protect the paint."

Adam continued to gaze at the pebble, faded memories returning. He had painted this stone when he had been seventeen or thereabouts. The decades dropped away. He saw her standing under the crags at the Top of the World, her dark hair blowing in the breeze, her eyes as blue as speedwells and radiant with light, and he heard her voice echoing faintly across the years. "Adam, I'm going to have a baby."

Edwin was looking up at his father, puzzled by the expression on his face. "It is Aunt Olivia, isn't it?" he said insistently, shattering Adam's memories.

Adam did not respond. He smiled, remembering. But then he had never really forgotten. He wrapped the stone in the handkerchief, almost with tenderness. He returned it to Edwin. "You keep it, my boy. You found it. I want you to have it. One day I will tell you the story behind that stone, but not now. This is not the time." He flashed Edwin a curious look. "I presume you came across it in that old cave up on the moors by Ramsden Crags."

Edwin was watching his father intently. "Yes, I did." He swallowed and said, "There's something else, Father. Something I have wanted to tell you for years. Unfortunately my courage has always failed me. It's been on my conscience for so long. I must unburden myself to you before I go off to war."

Adam sat down in the wing chair, nursing his drink. "Then unburden yourself, Edwin," he said gently. "Perhaps you will feel easier after you have spoken to me. Certainly I shall give you all of my understanding."

"Well, you see, it was like this," Edwin began nervously. "Oh God, I need another drink," he cried, and leapt up, hurrying across the room.

He not only resembles me in appearance but in every other way as well, Adam said to himself, staring after Edwin. He lit a cigarette and leaned back in the chair, waiting. He's going to tell me about Emma Harte and the child, Adam thought, and his heart went out to his son.

FORTY

Lord Kitchener had been appointed Secretary of State for War and had raised an army of one hundred thousand volunteers with his first appeal. Winston Churchill already had the Fleet on standby and between August 6 and August 20 the first four divisions of the British Expeditionary Force had crossed the Channel and the fifth and sixth divisions followed early in September. Not a ship was sunk, not a life was lost, and it was a triumph for Churchill, militant trustee of the British Royal Navy. The rest of Great Britain mobilized for war with ferocious speed and not one of its citizens was unaffected as the grim days rolled by.

The guns of August roared on through September, October, November, and December of 1914, and into 1915. They wreaked slaughter, ruin, and misery. Hundreds of thousands of young men, the hope of a new generation, were felled on the bloody battlefields of France and Belgium.

The stakes were terrifying to the British and their allies: annihilation or survival. They understood this was not a war for the possession of a fortress or a country, but for the inalienable right of any nation to live and develop as it wished.

Like every other intelligent person, Emma Harte Lowther often contemplated the aftermath of the war, the conditions they would be facing, and the future of business, but she did not dwell unduly on the years stretching ahead. Her priorities were all immediate, leaving no room for speculation. She was not blind to the commercial opportunities now presenting themselves, nor was she adverse to accumulating money, and whenever she felt a prick of conscience about making a profit from war she dispelled her discomfiture with logical reasoning: Somebody had to produce the uniforms for the fighting men, and if she did not do it, others would. In fact, were doing it. The majority of the cloth manufacturers of the West Riding were making khaki and navy and air force blue for Great Britain and the Allies, and millions of yards were coming off the looms of Yorkshire to clothe the forces.

Lately it struck Emma that she devoted herself entirely to work these days and shamefully neglected her family. But guilty feelings were swept away by the pressure of her business and the knowledge that she had no choice but to steer the same course. She raced between Harte's, the Gregson Warehouse, Layton's mill, and the clothing factory at breakneck speed, handling everything with her own brand of efficiency, charm, and assertiveness. And yet somehow the days were never long enough for her.

To her relief, Harte's was steady and holding its own. Although business had fallen off to a degree, she did not envision any serious setbacks. The stock housed in Gregson's Warehouse was lasting because she allocated it sparingly and she had also found several new sources of supplies. Layton's, under the skillful management of Ben Andrews, was running smoothly and the mill was meeting the huge government contracts with apparent ease and more promptly than many of her competitors. David and she had temporarily discontinued the line of Lady Hamilton Clothes at the outset of the war, and the factory's entire production had been turned over to the manufacture of uniforms. All in all, everything was under control, her business enterprises were stable, and, in particular, the mill and the factory were operating at a high level of super-efficiency and were flourishing moneymakers.

But now, on this cold afternoon in December of 1915, Emma's mind was not preoccupied with business. Sitting next to the driver in one of Harte's vans, on her way to a meeting with David, her mind dwelled on the Christmas holidays. She was determined to make it as festive an occasion as possible, despite shortages and the depressed mood that engulfed everyone.

Frank was coming to stay for several weeks and she was looking forward to it with the excitement of a child, thrilled at the prospect of seeing her brother again. He had been wounded in November, but his injuries were fortunately not serious. He had been hit by a bullet in the right shoulder and had been shipped back to England to recuperate. If only Winston could get home on leave the family would be complete, but she acknowledged realistically that there was not the remotest possibility of that. The navy was in the thick of the fighting and the news was grim on all fronts. Nevertheless, there would be a Christmas tree, and a turkey dinner with a plum pudding and all the traditional trimmings, mulled wine, and presents for everyone. Most importantly, Frank would receive the love and rest he needed so badly, and all the comforts of home she could provide.

The van arrived at the clothing factory in York Road within minutes. Emma told the driver to wait and hurried inside. As she entered David's office she was surpised to see Abraham Kallinski ensconced with David.

Her old friend stood up and embraced her warmly, his bright dark eyes twinkling behind his spectacles. He scrutinized her appraisingly and said, "Well, Emma, you look wonderful. And it is a pleasure to see you. So long it has been."

Emma smiled. "How are you? And how is Mrs. Kallinski?"

"She is well. I am well. Janessa is always asking for you. She misses you, Emma. I miss you."

"I am sorry I have neglected you both lately," Emma said. A rueful smile touched her lips. "But business does seem to take up all my time these days."

"Ah, yes! My little Emma has become the lady tycoon," Abraham exclaimed, regarding her with affection and pride. She continued to amaze him with her success, which he considered remarkable, and especially since she was a woman.

David was standing behind his desk, obviously in the throes of a mountain of paper work. He laughed. "Don't sound so surprised, Dad. I always predicted she would go far." He came around the desk, took her by the shoulders, and kissed her cheek. Her arms automatically went around him. She felt the strength of his hands gripping her tightly as the pressure of her own fingers increased gently. They pulled away without releasing their hold on each other and exchanged a long gaze.

Abraham Kallinski, observing them paternally, thought with an unexpected flash of dismay: My son. My son. He holds her too long. Ach, and I know that look in a man's eyes! I pray to God that his wife Rebecca and Joe never notice it. Clearing his throat, Abraham said, "Come, Emma. Come, sit here next to me." He indicated the other chair in front of David's desk.

She sat down and said, "There's nothing wrong, is there? Why did you want to see me so urgently, David?"

David leaned back in his chair, his vivid blue eyes focusing on hers. "I have a proposal to make and I hope you will approve. And go along with it."

Emma laughed lightly. "You know I trust your judgment implicitly. What is it?"

"Dad has been harassed of late. He'd like to ease up a little. Not work so hard." David lit a cigarette. "We've been discussing his problems and I think I have a solution that would be beneficial to everyone concerned. It occurred to me that we could merge his company with ours, take over his factory and its management with relatively no problems at all. That would relieve him of running it entirely on his own. He would continue there, of course, but he wouldn't have to work such long hours." David looked at her expectantly. "Well, what do you say?"

Instantly recognizing the enormous potential inherent in this proposition and visualizing a means of simple but swift expansion, Emma did not have to think twice. "It's an excellent suggestion." She turned to Abraham. "Would you be happy if we did that, Mr. Kallinski?"

"I would, Emma. And so would Janessa. She worries about me. Worries so much I worry about her worrying," he responded with a wry laugh.

"Then let's combine the two companies, David," Emma said. "I'm all for it. And now is certainly the right time to do it."

"There are a number of details to be worked out, Emma. But before we get into those I would like you to know my personal feelings about the proposed idea," David said. "If you're agreeable, I think we ought to purchase Dad's business outright, for a fair price that would give him a decent profit. After all, he has devoted years to building it up. We would make him a director of the parent company and pay him director's fees. I also think he ought to share in the profits, as we do. In addition, he would receive a salary for running his factory. How do you feel about these terms, Emma?"

"I'm in accordance with you, David. Your father should have something to show for all the years he's been in business. Why don't the two of you settle on an equitable price? Whatever you decide will be acceptable to me, I'm quite certain." She laughed and shook her head, giving David a fond look. "I can't imagine why you thought I would object. This is basically your business, David. You run it and you're the majority shareholder."

"You pull your weight and you are my partner." He smiled, looking relieved. "Good. Dad and I will thrash it out. You and I can go over the final details later. Then I'll talk to Frederick Ainsley and have him draw up the agreements in a week or so."

"That's perfect," Emma said. She shifted in her chair and gave her attention to Abraham, asking him questions about his government contracts, his cloth supplies, his work force, and his output. Whilst they were engaged in this protracted conversation, David sat back, regarding Emma with intensity.

Winter sun was pouring in through the windows, bathing her in its bright light. She really has that special kind of English beauty that looks its best in the daytime, David thought. That inimitable beauty that Gainsborough and Romney immortalized. And yet curiously Emma was unaware that she was a great beauty. Certainly she was devoid of personal vanity and that was also part of her charm. She was so fresh and radiant and filled with a vitality that was almost sensual in nature. No wonder she is irresistible to all men of all ages, David reflected. Funny, but she was not conscious of this either.

"Don't you agree, David?"

Startled, David sat up abruptly. "Sorry, I was wool gathering."

"I said I thought we ought to take over immediately. By consolidating our work forces we could probably increase production and operate both places even more efficiently. Your father is willing."

"That's an excellent thought! I'll have Victor move in there tomorrow." He looked at his father. "Is that all right with you, Dad?"

"I shall be glad to have him back," Abraham said. "It will put my mind to rest and your mother's."

Emma stood up. The men also rose. "If you'll excuse me, I should be going," she said. "I promised Edwina I would be home early today, to help her dress the Christmas tree. She has been looking forward to it. I don't want to disappoint her."

"No, you must not do that," Abraham said. "It is wrong to break a promise to a child." He gave David a pointed stare. "Which you so often do to my grandsons," he said, sighing heavily.

"But only because of the business, Dad," David rejoined defensively.

"Ah, yes. The business. Always the business. Well, you be off, Emma. Give my best to Joe."

"And mine to Mrs. Kallinski. Tell her I'll stop by soon."

"I'll see you out," David said, helping Emma into her coat and taking her arm possessively.

The Christmas tree was just the right size, Emma decided. She had purposely chosen this particular tree, even though grander specimens were available, in order to avoid ostentatious display, which she felt would be inappropriate in wartime. The housekeeper had potted it the previous evening, and now it reposed on a skirted table in a corner of the drawing room, next to the fireplace. Emma stepped back, her head on one side, viewing it with a critical eye. It was a healthy young fir, a rich dark green, and its branches were thick and luxuriant.

"Hello, Emma. You're home early."

Emma swung around as Joe entered the drawing room and strode to the fire, rubbing his hands together.

"Hello, Joe. Yes, I promised Edwina I would help her to dress the tree."

"Oh, that's right. I'd forgotten."

Continuing to unwrap the decorations, Emma told him about her meeting with the Kallinskis. "I think it's an excellent idea to join forces, don't you?" she finished, glancing at him over her shoulder.

Joe was frowning. "I'm not so sure. Won't it mean a lot of extra work and worry for you?"

"Why me? David bears the brunt of that business."

"It strikes me you both have enough on your plates as it is. Particularly you." Joe sounded grouchy, and as always he was opposed to innovation.

"Don't be so negative, Joe. I don't understand you sometimes," Emma said quietly. "And anyway, there's Mr. Kallinski to think about. He's not been well lately. The merger is the best solution for him."

"The old man could have sold his business to someone else," Joe suggested.

"Yes, he could. But why should he? It was only natural that he would come to David," Emma explained. "Besides, Abraham Kallinski has always been good to me. I'm delighted to help make his life a little easier."

"I'm only thinking of you, Emma. However, if you believe it's such a wonderful idea, who am I to criticize? You and David always do what you want with the factory anyhow."

"We always tell you our plans," she countered swiftly, detecting that disgruntled tone in his voice.

"Yes, I know. After the fact."

"Oh, Joe, please don't be sour. It's almost Christmas. Let's not bicker now."

"Bicker! Who's bickering!" Joe retorted. "Really, Emma, I can't open my mouth without you accusing me of—" He stopped short and his voice changed, became tender, as he said, "Hello, sweetheart. Come in. Don't stand there."

Emma turned around. Edwina was hovering in the doorway. She skipped across the floor. "Daddy! Daddy!" she cried, flinging herself at Joe. He picked her up and swung her around. Her blue velvet dress billowed out and her waist-length hair, of a blond so pale it was almost silver, flew out behind her, gleaming in the lamplight. She laughed delightedly and after a few more whirls Joe put her down on the floor, holding her arms to steady her.

"You're not dizzy, are you, angel?"

"No, Daddy." She smiled up at him, her exquisite little face dimpling prettily.

"Well, there you are, darling," Emma said. "I've been waiting for you. I've unpacked all the ornaments and we can start."

"Hello, Mother," Edwina said without looking at Emma. She grabbed Joe's hand. "Daddy, will *you* help me to dress the tree? Please. Please. Oh, do say yes, Daddy." She fixed her luminous silvery eyes on him appealingly.

Joe laughed and patted her head. "Of course I will, love." Edwina dragged him to the tree. She climbed onto the stool Emma had placed next to the table, still clutching Joe's arm.

Emma was holding a silver bell in her hand. "Where shall I put this, dear?" she asked, smiling at her nine-year-old daughter.

Edwina made no response. She looked up at Joe and flashed him a radiant smile. "Where do you think it should hang, Daddy?"

"Well, I'm not such an expert at these things. Perhaps here." He indicated a branch.

"May I have the bell please, Mother?"

Emma handed it to her silently. Edwina immediately gave the bell to Joe. "You put the bell on the tree, Daddy. Anywhere you want. I think you should be first."

This little ritual continued for several minutes. Whenever Emma picked up an ornament and suggested a spot for it, Edwina took it from her quickly, ignoring her suggestions, deferring always to Joe. Stunned, Emma stepped away from the tree uncertainly, acutely aware of the slight. She was the interloper, and unwanted. She retreated to the fireplace, watching them laughing happily together. She experienced a small stab of dismay and pushed it away quickly. She should not be envious of their relationship. She should be happy they were so adoring of each other.

Joe and Edwina were so engrossed with each other and the tree they did not notice Emma glide quietly out of the room. She closed the door softly behind her and leaned against it. She swallowed hard, conscious of the prick of tears behind her eyes, the ache in her throat. After a moment she was in control of herself and her step was firm as she walked across the marble-floored hall. She took her coat from the closet, picked up the two baskets standing on the floor, and slipped out of the house quickly.

It was a cold night, dark and without a moon, and snow was falling in light flurries. Fortunately the lamps on the iron gates of each house were burning, and their dim glow lighted her way as she turned up the flagged walk that fronted the mansions in the Towers. The snow was beginning to settle. It would be a white Christmas after all, just as Edwina had so fervently wished. Emma bit her lip. Christmas had suddenly lost its appeal for her. She reflected on Edwina's snubs, filled with regret, her mind fogged by the hurt she was still experiencing.

A few seconds later Emma was pushing open the gate of the last mansion in the row, where the O'Neills lived. Blackie had bought it in 1913, two years after his marriage to Laura. If it was not the fine Georgian edifice he had talked about building years before, it was rather imposing, and he had made many grand improvements.

The little Irish maid greeted her cheerfully. She took Emma's

oat and scarf along with the baskets, inquiring politely after
ιer health. Emma was just about to ask her where Mrs.
)'Neill was when Blackie appeared at the top of the red-
·arpeted staircase.

At twenty-nine Blackie O'Neill was a commanding figure
nd the years had treated him generously. He and his Uncle
²at had done well and the building firm had grown into one
ιf the largest in Leeds. Success sat well on him. Not yet the
nillionaire he had bragged of becoming, he was, however, a
·ich man and he had certainly turned himself into the "toff"
ιe had always yearned to be. He dressed elegantly and
·xpensively. After his marriage to Laura she had tactfully
·ersuaded him to curb his predilection for flashy ties, colorful
·rocade waistcoats, and gaudy jewelry. Most of his rough
·dges had been smoothed away and he was even sophisti-
·ated to a degree. His thick Irish brogue had all but disap-
·eared, except for an almost indiscernible lilting burr. Laura
ιad had a refining and gentling influence on him, yet without
·estroying his natural ebullience. And there was still quite a
ot of the actor in him, a trait he had discovered was an asset
n business.

He waved to Emma and ran lightly down the stairs, his
ace merry. "Emma, me love. You're a sight for sore eyes,"
ιe cried, sweeping her into his arms so forcefully her feet left
he floor. He swung her around, planted her firmly in front of
ιim, and, as was his way, tilted her chin and looked down at
ιer. "And what kind of a face is this to be making? You look
ιs if you've lost a pound and found sixpence."

Emma laughed in spite of herself, as always infected by
3lackie's good humor. "I'm all right, Blackie. Just a bit under
he weather, that's all."

"*You* under the weather! That's hard for me to believe."
Ηe looked at her closely. "Are you sure nothing is upsetting
·ou?" he asked, his eyes surveying her perceptively.

"No, truly not. Where's Laura?"

"In the parlor waiting for you." He hurried her across the
ιall. "She thought you might drop in."

Laura was sitting by the fire knitting a khaki scarf and she
hrew it down and flew to Emma, embracing her lovingly.
'Emma, darling. I hoped you would have time to visit us
onight. Do you realize it's been almost a whole week!"

The dismal look on Emma's face lifted at the sight of her

dearest friend. "I know. I've really been up to my neck." She smiled. "I brought you the things you wanted from the store For the Sunday-school Christmas party. The maid took them Incidentally, I put in a few extra things I'm sure you can use for the needy children."

"Oh, Emma, you're so good. Thank you." Laura linked her arm through Emma's and they walked back to the fireplace chatting.

"I can see when a fellow's not wanted," Blackie teased. "I'll be leaving the two of you to your female gossipings. But make it brief, me darlin's. I'll be back shortly to have Christmas drink with you."

Sitting in the charmingly decorated parlor, listening to Laura's light tinkling voice, Emma discovered that her tension was beginning to slip away. Emma knew these feelings of warmth and ease now enveloping her did not come from the heat of the roaring fire, but from Laura's comforting presence. This gentle woman, so dear to her heart, always managed to soothe her. Laura was talking about the party she had arranged for the children who attended her Sunday school classes and as Emma listened she observed her friend with mounting pleasure. Laura looked remarkably lovely this night. Since her last miscarriage, two years ago, she had completely regained her strength and was blooming and full of life. In her dark blue dress, with her honey-blond hair bound in a chignon to reveal that calm and tender face, Emma thought she looked more Madonna-like than ever. Laura was happy with Blackie, and the only thing that marred her joy was her disappointment that she had not given him a child.

"The party seems to have taken up most of my time these past few weeks," Laura explained. "Blackie found me a beautiful tree for the church hall. I'm going to decorate it tomorrow."

Emma stiffened and she knew her face was tightening.

Laura looked up from her knitting. She stopped, staring at Emma. "Goodness, darling, you look awful. Whatever's the matter?"

Emma shook her head. "Nothing. Really," she managed and glanced quickly at her hands.

"Yes, there is. I know you too well. Please, dear, if you are fretting about something, do confide in me. It might help."

Emma cleared her throat. "Well, Edwina was so cutting with me tonight. It really upset me." Taking a deep breath, Emma recounted the incident with the Christmas tree.

Laura frowned and then said, "Girls always gravitate to their fathers, Emma. *You* know that. It's nothing unusual. She'll grow out of it. I'm sure it's just a stage she's going through."

"She's always seemed to prefer Joe to me," Emma countered softly. "Not that I mind. I'm happy they're so devoted. It's these occasional displays of coldness which disturb me. I do try so hard to win her affection."

"I know you do." Laura sighed and reached out, squeezing Emma's arm. "Children can be *so* unkind. They don't mean to be cruel. They're simply thoughtless, that's all."

"Yes, perhaps you're right."

"And she is a very good child, isn't she?"

"Yes, almost too good in a sense. I've often thought that Edwina was born an adult." Emma pondered, and continued, "Sometimes I feel Edwina lives within herself, Laura. She can be very distant. And she always has a faraway look in her eyes."

Laura laughed, trying to dispel Emma's obvious anxiety. "Oh, darling, that's only natural. Girls are always daydreaming."

"I suppose so," Emma said, wanting to believe this.

"As for being distant, I think she's simply rather reserved by nature. Why, Blackie was saying the other day—"

"What was I saying?" Blackie boomed from the doorway, strolling into the room. He hovered over Laura and Emma, puffing on a cigar.

"I was about to tell Emma that you think Edwina is refined and quite the little lady with charming manners," Laura told him.

"She is that. And a beauty!" He turned away, moving to the sideboard. "What can I offer you, ladies?" he asked gaily, pouring himself an Irish whiskey.

"What would you like, Emma? Please do have a little something for once," Laura urged gently.

"I believe I will!" Emma laughed. "I think I need a drink tonight. I'll have a sherry, Blackie. Thank you."

"And the same for you, Laura, me darlin', I presume."

"Yes, please, Blackie. But only a small one."

"A Merry Christmas to my best-loved ladies," Blackie said

with his typical show of exaggerated gallantry, lifting his
glass.

"Merry Christmas," they said in unison, and Emma added
tartly but in a teasing tone, "I should hope *we* are your
best-loved ladies. We'd be very angry if there were any
others."

Blackie grinned. "Laura tells me we are joining you on
Christmas Day. I'm looking forward to it. We must make the
most of this one and have a bit of festivity."

They both stared at him. "What do you mean by that
Blackie?" Laura asked.

"Oh, nothing, love," he responded smoothly, regretting
the remark.

"Blackie, please don't hedge. Answer me, dear. Do you
know something—something about the war that we don't
know?" Laura persisted.

"Not at all, at all," he said, reverting to a thick brogue
"Come along, no talk of the war tonight, darlin'." He joined
Laura on the sofa and took her hand in his. Glancing carefully
at Emma, he said, "I hear Thompson's mill is in a bad way
Producing poor cloth and falling down on their government
orders as well."

"So I believe," Emma said dispassionately. Her face was
inscrutable and she adroitly changed the subject.

The New Year brought more disastrous news for Britain and
her allies. Men were dying in thousands in the trenches, and
the overall losses were so monumental the world was horror
struck. On January 4, 1916, Prime Minister Henry Asquith
stood up on the floor of the House of Commons and intro
duced a bill for the compulsory military service of all single
men deemed fit for enlistment in the army. The bill met
enormous opposition, especially from the diehards and de
fenders of the old voluntary system of military duty. But on
Monday, January 24, the bill passed its third reading by a
majority of 347 votes, the opposition having fallen to a mere
36. And so the first Compulsory Service Act came into force
on March 2.

Although this measure at first applied only to single men
Emma began to experience a feeling of rising alarm as the
days passed. She read the newspapers carefully, analyzing

he developments in the war, aware that more soldiers were
needed, and on a continuing daily basis, because of the toll of
Britain's manhood. And she recognized that it was only a
question of weeks before married men were called. And she
was right.

Reading the *Times* one morning at the beginning of May,
she saw that her fears were indeed becoming realities. She
quickly scanned the story which reported that the Prime
Minister had asked leave to introduce into the House a new
Military Service Bill.

"Joe, I think married men are going to be *forced* to enlist,"
she said quietly.

He looked at her across the breakfast table, his eyes grave.
It was bound to come, Emma. Kitchener's been shouting for
more men for weeks."

Emma nodded. "The new bill lays down the rule that *every*
male British subject between eighteen and forty years of age
is to be deemed duly enlisted in the regular forces for general
service, unless he's exempt for some reason." She proffered
him a weak smile. "I don't suppose you're exempt, are you?"

"No, love, I'm not."

A few days later she read with gloomy resignation that
although the House divided on the bill, the majority of Members were in favor. Finally, on May 27, the new Military
Service Act received royal assent.

That evening Emma sat in the drawing room with Frank,
who was staying with them again, discussing the news. "What
exactly does that mean—royal assent?" she asked.

"It means that in the great crisis of its destiny the British
nation has reverted to the method of Norman and Saxon
times, when the King had the right to take in men, ships, and
every available chattel in his dominion for the purpose of
defending the nation," Frank told her solemnly.

She understood. But understanding did not necessarily
ease her troubled thoughts.

Emma, having previously always complained, and in the
most vociferous voice, of the procrastination and red tape of
bureaucracy, now cursed its deadly efficiency. The three men
most prominent in her life went with the hordes. First David, with the infantry, and then Joe and Blackie, who left
together. At the end of May they had both joined the Seaforth

Highlanders, her father's old regiment, and one that was particularly favored by Yorkshiremen.

"Except that I'm not a Yorkshireman," Blackie had declared. "An Irishman living in England, married to a Sassenach, lapsed from the Church, serving in a Scottish regiment and wearing a skirt to boot. Unique, eh?" Laura and Emma had joined in his laughter but their hearts were heavy.

Joe and Blackie had been immediately dispatched to Ripon for field training. This picturesque and ancient garrison town was a place of old memories for Emma. Two weeks later they came home on leave for twenty-four hours, en route to Tilbury for embarkation to France. On a damp June morning Emma accompanied them to the railway station. Laura, who was now pregnant, begged to go along, but Blackie was adamant.

"Not in your condition, darlin'," he said gently, stroking her hair. "I don't want you getting distraught and upsetting yourself and the baby."

At the last minute Blackie almost had to forcibly restrain Laura, who clung to his arm fiercely, endeavoring to hold back the tears without success. But her strained white face was filled with immense courage as they took their leave of her. She stood at the window, a pale image against the glass, waving to the three of them as they walked down the garden path and disappeared from view.

It was a silent journey into Leeds. Emma was staggered when they arrived at City Station. Crowds of troops, from many other regiments as well as the Seaforth Highlanders, were filing through the gates. The gloomy grime-coated platforms were jammed with hundreds more, and women and girls of all ages and classes, wives and mothers and sweethearts saying farewell to their men. Blackie took their kit bags onto the train and Emma and Joe stood on the platform holding hands.

"You'll be fine, love," Joe said, tightening his grip on her fingers. "Don't worry about me. Just take care of yourself and the children."

Emma bit her lip, striving for composure. Joe had been surprisingly tender and considerate over the past few months, obviously realizing the time for separation was drawing near, and they had become much closer in many ways. "It's you who must take care, Joe," she said softly.

Blackie rejoined them after a few seconds. Emma reached for his hand, pulling him to her. "And you, too, Blackie." She attempted to laugh. "Don't either of you get into any scrapes—" She stopped, her lips shaking.

Joe lifted her face to his gently. "Now, where's that famous smile of yours, love?"

"I'm sorry."

The whistles began to hoot and clouds of steam and smoke enveloped them as the trains revved up to roll on their journey south. Blackie put his arm around her. "Goodbye, mavourneen. Stay well and look after me darlin' Laura for me. See she takes it easy and don't let her fret." He kissed her cheek, his eyes wet.

Emma swallowed, looking up at Blackie. "I will. I promise I won't let anything happen to her or the baby."

Blackie leaped onto the train steps and stood hanging on to the bar, turning away to give them a moment of privacy.

Joe took Emma in his arms. "You've been the best wife, sweetheart." Seeing the look of fear cross her face, he added hastily, "And that's why you can be damned sure I'm coming back to you!"

"I know you will, love. And you've been a good husband, Joe. Be careful over there."

He nodded, choked and unable to reply. He kissed her again and she felt his tears mingling with her own on her cheeks. Joe released her abruptly and sprang onto the steps to join Blackie. The wheels started to grind with a high-pitched screech against the rails and the train began to pull out. It was moving so slowly Emma was able to walk alongside it, holding on to Joe's hand.

Unexpectedly a lone soldier's voice rang out, sweet yet melancholy. "Keep the home fires burning, though your hearts are yearning . . ." Another voice joined in and another and another, until the immense station hall reverberated with the song as troops in other trains and many of the women picked up the refrain, and Blackie's baritone rose above them all, as rich and magnificent as always.

The train gathered speed. Joe dropped Emma's hand and she halted on the spot, waving to them. And her luminous valedictory smile was courageous despite her moist eyes. She watched the train until it was lost from sight and then she turned and left, jostled by the crowds, blinded by tears and wondering despairingly if she would ever see either of them again.

FORTY-ONE

Emma sat on the edge of Christopher's bed, the storybook in her hand, the lamp infusing her face with roseate tints and casting an aureole of light around her head. She closed the book and smiled at her son. "Now, come along, Kit. It's time to go to sleep."

Kit's wide-set hazel eyes regarded her steadfastly and his small round face, covered with a dusting of light freckles, was very intense for a five-year-old. "Please, Mummy, just *one* more story," he begged. "*Please,* Mummy. You promised to read to me a bit longer tonight and you never break a promise, do you? At least that's what you're always saying."

Amused at his unsubtle brand of persuasion but unswayed by it, she laughed and rumpled his hair playfully. "I *have* read longer to you, Kit. You must go to sleep now. It's well past your bedtime." She put the book on the table and, leaning forward, kissed his cheek.

His sturdy little arms went around her neck and he nuzzled closer to her. "You smell so nice, Mummy. Just like a flower. Like a whole bunch of flowers," he murmured in her ear.

Smiling, Emma drew away and smoothed back his hair. "Snuggle down, Kit. Good night and sweet dreams."

"Good night, Mummy."

Emma turned out the light and closed the door quietly behind her. She paused at Edwina's door, hesitating uncertainly before tapping lightly and entering. Edwina was sitting up in bed reading, her pale blond hair tumbling in luxuriant waves around her thin shoulders visible through the light cotton nightgown. She lifted her head and focused her cool silver-gray eyes on Emma, looking as if she resented this intrusion on her privacy.

"I just came to kiss you good night," Emma said carefully,

crossing the floor. "And don't burn the midnight oil for too long, will you, dear?"

"No, Mother," Edwina said. She placed the book on one side and continued to gaze at Emma, a patient expression on her face.

Emma hovered near the bed. "Our little nursery dinner *was* fun tonight, wasn't it?" she gaily remarked, wishing to reinforce the rapport, tentative though it was, which had recently sprung up between them.

Edwina nodded. "Yes." The child studied for a moment and then said, "When is Uncle Winston coming to stay with us, Mother?"

"I'm not quite certain, dear. Very soon, I hope. He said in his last letter he expected to get leave imminently."

"I'm glad he's coming. I like Uncle Winston," Edwina volunteered.

Surprised at this unexpected confidence and encouraged by it, Emma lowered herself onto the bed gingerly, always acutely conscious of Edwina's abhorrence of close physical contact. "I am happy that you do, Edwina. He loves you very much and so does your Uncle Frank."

"Will Uncle Frank be coming, too? I mean, when Uncle Winston gets his leave?"

"Yes, that was the plan, Edwina. We'll have some jolly evenings together. We'll play charades and have singsongs. You'll like that, won't you?"

"Oh, yes, it will be nice." Edwina proffered Emma a rare smile, a deliquescent smile that softened her cold young face and brought a hint of warmth to those enormous argent eyes.

Emma, observing Edwina intently, felt her heart miss a beat. There it was again. *That smile.* That melting smile she remembered only too well. She dropped her eyes, aware that a flick of fear had entered them, and nervously straightened the coverlet. "We'll make plans for your Uncle Winston's visit tomorrow," she said in a low voice, and stood up abruptly. Bending down, she kissed Edwina fleetingly, afraid of being repulsed, and went on, "Good night, darling, Sleep tight."

"Good night, Mother," Edwina responded dutifully in a stiff tone, and returned to her book without giving Emma a second glance or a second thought. Her mother, this woman whom everyone claimed was beautiful and charming and clever, hardly existed for the ten-year-old girl. Edwina lived in a world entirely of her own making and she did not permit anything or anyone to penetrate it, and the only two people she loved were Joe and her Cousin Freda in Ripon.

The child was an enigma to Emma. She ran lightly down the stairs, Edwina's smile lingering in her mind as she entered the study. She grows to look more like *her* every day, Emma thought with a stab of acute discomfort. But it's only a *physical* resemblance, she reassured herself, hurriedly dismissing those characteristics which were becoming more pronounced in her daughter and which disturbed her from time to time. The desk was covered with a pile of papers that needed Emma's immediate attention and she sat down, determined to wade through them that evening, After half an hour she realized her powers of concentration had fled and she put down her pen in irritation and leaned back in the chair, wondering what ailed her. Strain? Tiredness? She had fel distracted and restless that morning, feelings unprecedented for her. But they had persisted throughout the day and she had left the store earlier than usual, conscious of a need to break loose from the fetters of her business and assailed by a desparate longing to be at home with her children.

It was the housekeeper's day off and Emma had shooed Clara, the devoted nursemaid, out of the kitchen and prepared the dinner herself. Emma had enjoyed the simple pleasure of working with the food and using her hands instead of her brain for once, and this brief domestic sojourn had refreshed her. Later she had joined Clara and the children for their evening meal in the nursery, and she had experienced such a profound sense of serenity in their untroubled world her own cares had disappeared.

It was a lovely interlude, Emma said to herself, and vowed she would stop depriving herself of her children's company as she had done so often lately. She was not going to allow business to interfere so relentlessly with her hours with them. This time in their lives was precious and she wanted to share it. Even Edwina was warmer in disposition and more outgoing than usual during supper, Emma reflected with genuine pleasure, and the child's sudden declaration of her liking for Winston was quite remarkable in view of her dismaying lack of feeling for most people. It had been a revelation to Emma, and she was hopeful that it signaled a change for the better.

Emma's drifting thoughts settled on her daughter. She's a Fairley through and through and there's no mistaking that. Emma had long recognized the striking likeness Edwina bore to her grandmother on the paternal side. She was a faithful reproduction—a mirror image—of Adele. Have Winston and Frank ever detected it? she wondered. They had never passed one comment. Blackie, on the other hand, was a wholly different matter. Emma suspected he had arrived at the truth years ago, although he, too, had been discreetly silent on the subject and had never displayed even the slightest hint of his suspicions, either by a knowing look or by a careless reference.

Emma thought then of Edwin Fairley. Her hatred for him remained constant, yet it had changed in nature and now sprang from her intellect and not from her heart. Consequently, it was deadlier than before, for it had objectivity and thus direction.

Even if she had wanted to forget the Fairley family, Emma would have found that virtually impossible, since the *Yorkshire Morning Gazette* consistently reported their activities, social or otherwise. She knew a great deal about Edwin. He was a captain in the army and had been awarded the Victoria Cross "for bravery above and beyond the call of duty." Bravery indeed, she thought, her lip curling with contempt. She had also seen the announcement of his son's birth in the paper only yesterday. His wife, the Lady Jane Fairley, daughter of the Earl of Carlesmoor, had been delivered of a seven-pound boy, to be baptized Roderick Adam in honor of his two grandfathers.

But Edwin Fairley's life was of no concern to her—at the present time. Adam and Gerald Fairley were her primary targets and for a simple reason: *They* controlled the Fairley mills and therefore the Fairley fortune. The family's destiny was in *their* hands. Over the years Emma had come to understand that the most potent way to strike back at them was through business. She had already created immense problems for them at Thompson's mill, because they had found it practically impossible to replace the work force she had stolen. There was nothing she did not know about their holdings and the general state of their commercial affairs. Her information had been acquired with limitless patience, incalculable diligence, and in the utmost secrecy, and she was already formulating her plans for the future.

They were exposed and vulnerable to her and they did not know it! Adam Fairley, always negligent about business, had become excessively so of late. Olivia Wainright Fairley had recently been struck down by some strange illness and he rarely, if ever, came to Yorkshire. The reins were in Gerald Fairley's hands, and *he* was a bumbling fool. *He* was the weak link in the iron chain which she intended to dismantle and cast to one side, just as her father and her daughter and she herself had been cast aside by them. And it was mainly on Gerald Fairley that her vivid green eyes rested with virulent loathing. No woman ever expunged the terrifying memory of the man who had attempted rape on her and Emma was no exception. Yes, Gerald was the key to their downfall. All she had to do was stick out her foot and trip him and the others would come tumbling behind. There were no doubts in her mind about the final outcome. Once she had set herself a goal nothing could deter her from achieving it.

The doorbell rang, echoing through the silent house. It brought Emma up with a start and pulled her away from her contemplation of the Fairleys. She rose and went into the hall, her silk dress swishing as she moved with her usual rapidity. She opened the front door, wondering who could be calling at this hour, to be confronted by a telegraph boy.

"Evening, missis," he said, deferentially touching his cap. He handed her the telegram, touched his cap again, and ran down the steps. Emma closed the door and glanced at the yellow envelope. It was undoubtedly from Winston, announcing his arrival.

Emma glided into the center of the hall and stood under the crystal chandelier where the light was brighter and ripped it open. Her eyes traveled quickly across the top line and they widened and widened, and the smile on her face faded as she read:

"It is with deep regret and the greatest sympathy that the War Office must inform you that your husband Private Joseph Daniel Lowther of the 1st Battalion of the Seaforth Highlanders was killed in action on July 14 in France . . ."

The remaining words blurred and ran together and, recoiling, Emma sat down on the hall chair with a thud, stunned and for a moment disbelieving. She stared blankly at the opposite wall, the light in her eyes dulled, her mouth trembling. Eventually she brought her reluctant gaze back to the telegram crumpled in a ball between her clenched fingers. She straightened it out and read it again. The devastating words slowly sank in and her heart plunged.

It can't be true! There has been a mistake! A ghastly error! Emma cried inwardly, moving her head from side to side, denying the words. Joe could not be dead. Her throat thickened as reality struck at her, and she sat frozen in the chair, as rigid as stone, held in the grips of the most paralyzing shock.

After what seemed like an eternity to Emma she pushed herself up out of the chair, forcing her shaking legs to move forward, blindly making her way to the stairs. She held on to the banister to steady herself, a sensation of fainting weakness trickling through her entire body. She maneuvered herself up the staircase, dragging one leaden foot after the other, moving with laborious care like an old woman crippled by arthritic pain. She stumbled into her bedroom, collapsed onto the bed, and lay motionless, staring at the ceiling in a trance-like state, her eyes dark pools of sorrow.

Poor Joe. Poor Joe. Struck down after only a brief few weeks at the front. He was too young to die. It was unfair. Unfair. Emma began to weep, the tears streaming down her face unchecked. She would never see Joe again. The children would never see him again. Her mind floundered at the thought of Kit and Edwina sleeping so peacefully in their beds. She could not tell them the news. Not now. Tomorrow would be soon enough.

Her anguished mind began to race. How had Joe died? And where was his body? She wanted Joe's body. Irrational as the idea was under the present circumstances, she wanted to give him a proper burial. The thought of Joe's body lying smashed and neglected somewhere in France haunted her. It was a horrendous image that wobbled in the very center of her brain.

Emma lay in the bedroom, unaware of the hour, watching the night descend, abandoned and lonely in her misery. And she grieved inconsolably for Joe. He had been honorable, and kind in an infinite number of ways, and now she dismissed all the traits that had irritated her, forgot the revulsion she had experienced in their marital bed. She carefully obliterated everything that had been distressing, remembered only the good and the best.

And she wept all night for the loss of a decent man, for all that he had been and had represented, and for the life they had shared together.

It was a glorious Sunday afternoon in late October, one of those unexpected Indian-summer days, radiant with crystalline light that flooded the periwinkle-blue sky. The garden was bathed in a golden haze and the trees and the shrubs were already turning color, the autumnal foliage a glowing mixture of yellows and orange running to scarlet and burnt sienna.

Laura O'Neill sat on the garden seat lost in contemplation. Her thoughts as always were with Blackie in France. She had not received a letter for several weeks. On the other hand, that dreaded telegram had not arrived either. Despite the lack of news of any sort, Laura hold the deep conviction that Blackie was safe and would continue to be safe and that he would come home to her when the war was over. Her unwavering faith in Almighty God was the rock upon which her life was built, and she knew with absolute certainty that Blackie was under His divine protection. Laura, always devout, now went every day to mass, disregarding Emma's advice that she stay in bed and rest. She lit innumerable candles for Blackie and Winston and for all of the other fighting men. And her gentle heart overflowed with grief for those who had lost sons and husbands and sweethearts, and most especially for Emma, widowed four months before.

Emma was working at the other end of the garden, filling a basket with magnificent gold and copper winter chrysanthemums. Laura's hazel eyes rested on her dearest friend and her heart tightened with love and sympathy. She's painfully thin, Laura thought. And she's exhausted. She works like a Trojan and her responsibilities would crush anyone else. Even the strongest and most determined of men would stagger under the burden.

It seemed to Laura that Emma had been imbued with an almost inhuman strength since Joe's death. She not only ran her own businesses and managed Joe's properties as well, but played a major administrative role at the Kallinski factories. Yet withal she still found time to devote hours to the children, trying to surround them with love and security. That is Emma's way of coping with her sorrow, Laura decided. The only way she knows how to go on. Her work and the children have become her citadel.

Laura sighed deeply. Death was never final. The person loved was gone but there were always the others, the ones left behind to mourn. The sadness of life is ever present, Laura thought, and yet there is joy in life, too. Joy like the child she was carrying. The child she yearned to give Blackie. She placed her hands across her stomach protectively and with love, and she thanked God she had not miscarried this time. Yes, there was death, but there was also birth. A continual renewal. . . the endless cycle that was eternal, that was man's inexorable fate.

Emma, having completed her tasks, pulled off her gardening gloves and joined Laura on the seat. "You're not feeling chilly, are you?" she asked. "I think we ought to go in shortly. I don't want you to catch a cold. Not now when you've been so well." Emma eyed Laura lovingly. "You only have two more months to wait and then you'll be presenting Blackie with that son and heir."

Laura nodded, her happiness overflowing in her eyes. "This pregnancy has been so easy, Emma. A miracle. I offer thanks for that every day."

"So do I, love."

Laura took Emma's hand in hers and said softly, "I haven't wanted to upset you by bringing it up before, but is Edwina any better?"

"A little." Emma's voice was low. "If only she would cry then perhaps her grief for Joe would be alleviated. As it is, it's all pent up and her self-control frightens me. It's not natural."

A look of sympathy crossed Laura's face. "No, it's not healthy to repress that kind of anguish and pain. Poor Edwina, she did adore Joe so much."

"I've talked to her for hours, tried to give her comfort and understanding, without much success. It's as if she wants to bear it alone. Stoically. I don't know what to do anymore—" Emma stopped. After a moment she added in a dim voice, "Sometimes I think I misjudged Joe."

"What do you mean?" Laura asked in puzzlement.

"Well, now when I look back, I realize how kind he was, and so generous in a variety of ways. His will, for instance. I was thunderstruck when Mr. Ainsley read it to me and I learned Joe had left all the properties to me. I expected him to make Kit the sole beneficiary, willing him the business and everything. I haven't been able to get over that gesture. After all, Kit is the only son."

"Joe left all of his money to Kit, dear," Laura cut in swiftly. "Except for the annuity for Edwina. Look, Emma, Joe always appreciated your business acumen. He wasn't cheating Kit. He was simply being wise, knowing you would handle everything with efficiency and in doing so provide for the children's future. He trusted you, Emma. He knew you would do the right thing."

"I suppose so. But I still feel I did Joe many injustices when he was alive."

Laura squeezed Emma's arm affectionately. "You were a good wife. Don't start chastising yourself now for things that happened in the past. And don't forget, human relationships are never static. They change from day to day, because they are highly complex and also because people are changeable. And life intrudes. Problems intrude and create tensions. You gave Joe a great deal, even if you did have disagreements occasionally. I know you made him happy. Please, Emma, you must believe that."

"I hope I did," Emma murmured.

Noting the sad echo in Emma's voice and wishing to distract her, Laura said briskly, "Shall we go in, dear? I'm getting cold and I would like some tea." As she spoke she stood up, pulling the yellow shawl closer around her shoulders.

Emma took Laura's arm as they walked across the lawn. "What would I do without you, my sweet Laura? You're so wise, and you always make me feel better."

"I can say the same thing about you, Emma. Why, you're the best friend I ever had."

FORTY-TWO

" A h, there you are, Mrs. Lowther," Dr. Stalkley said, hurrying through the swinging doors of the waiting room. "Mrs. O'Neill has been asking for you."

Emma stood up, clutching her handbag tightly. "Please,"

she said anxiously, "is everything all right? I don't understand what happened so suddenly."

The doctor gave her an avuncular pat on the shoulder. "It was a question of operating or going through with the natural childbirth. Because of her religion, Mrs. O'Neill was quite adamant about the operation—"

"What do you mean? I'm not following you, Doctor," Emma interrupted peremptorily.

"Mrs. O'Neill would not permit us to operate because there was the possibility—in fact, the great probability—that she would have lost the child. The operation would have been wiser, safer, of course. However, she would not take any chances with the child's life."

"*But is she all right?*" Emma demanded.

"Weak," the doctor responded quietly, avoiding Emma's eyes.

"And the baby?"

"A fine boy, Mrs. Lowther."

Emma's stare became more penetrating. "Mrs. O'Neill isn't in any danger, is she?"

"She's tired, naturally. It was a difficult birth," the doctor said. "But let's not stand here chattering. She's waiting to see you. Please come this way."

Emma followed him down the corridor, her mind racing as she tried to assess the gravity of the situation. Instinct told her Dr. Stalkley was hedging and this frightened her. When they reached the door of Laura's room the doctor paused and turned to Emma. His face was unreadable as he said, "We've sent for the priest."

"Priest! Why?"

"Mrs. O'Neill asked for him." The doctor shook his head. "She is very weak. Worn out. Please don't excite her."

Emma clutched his arm. "She's not—"

The doctor opened the door for her. "Please, Mrs. Lowther, let's not waste time." He ushered her in and closed the door softly behind him.

Emma hurried to the bed, her eyes sweeping over Laura, who lay propped against the pillows. She was at once aware of Laura's terrible exhaustion. Her lovely face, so wan in the cold light, was etched with lines of extreme fatigue and there were dark smudges under her huge eyes, which lit up at the sight of her friend. Emma's heart sank, for she recognized all the distressing telltale signs, but the smile on her face did not falter for an instant. She bent over Laura and kissed her cheek. Smoothing back the honey-blond hair that tumbled over the pillows, she said softly, "How are you feeling, darling?"

Laura smiled. "So happy. And grateful. It's a boy, Emma."

Emma sat down on the chair next to the bed. Swallowing hard, she adopted her most cheerful tone. "Yes, it's wonderful. Blackie will be thrilled."

Laura nodded, her eyes shining. She reached for Emma's small hand, took it in hers, and squeezed it. "Have you been waiting long, dear?"

"No," Emma lied. "And you mustn't worry about me. You're the one who needs all the care and attention now. I expect you'll be discharged in a week and then you're coming to stay with me and the children. I'm going to look after you like you looked after me when Edwina was born. You will come, won't you, darling?"

A faint smile flickered on Laura's white lips. She said, "I want him to be called Bryan."

"That's a lovely name, Laura."

"And Shane Patrick, after Blackie and Uncle Pat."

"They will be pleased, love."

"Come closer to me, Emma," Laura murmured, "so that I can see you better. The light seems to have dimmed, doesn't it?"

"Yes, it is getting dark outside," Emma said, even though the light was still very bright.

Laura's fine eyes searched her face. "I want Bryan to be brought up as a good Roman Catholic. You know what Blackie is like. So careless about some things. You'll see to it for me, Emma, won't you?"

Emma's fear flared again. "What do you mean?"

"I want you to promise me that you'll make sure Uncle Pat does the right thing while Blackie is away, and that you'll take care of Bryan for me until his father comes back from the war."

"But you'll be doing that, love."

Laura's brilliant eyes remained unwavering, "I'm dying, Emma."

"Don't say that!"

"Emma, listen to me. *Please listen.* I have so little time left," Laura whispered, her faint voice now vibrating with urgency. "Promise me that you'll make certain Uncle Pat has Bryan christened in the Roman Catholic Church and that he attends to his religious training as long as Blackie is gone. And promise you'll look after Blackie for me."

Emma was unable to speak for a moment. "I promise," she finally said, her voice thick with emotion and quavering.

Laura lifted her hand weakly and touched Emma's face. She smiled at her. "I love you, Emma."

"Oh, Laura, I love you, too." Emma could no longer suppress the tears and they spilled down her cheeks and splashed onto Laura's hand.

"Don't cry, dear. There's nothing to cry about."

"Oh, Laura—Laura—"

"Hush, darling. Don't cry."

Emma took a deep breath and endeavored to pull herself together. "Laura, listen to *me* now. You must fight. Try harder, love. Please fight to live," she implored with great intensity. She gathered Laura's frail body into her strong arms and cradled her close, pressing Laura harder against herself, as if trying to infuse her dying friend with some of her own enormous strength, her own stubborn will, as she had done so long ago with her mother.

A small sigh escaped Laura's lips, a soft fluttering sigh that was hardly audible. "It's too late," she said in a fading voice.

Emma placed her back on the pillows, her lips shaking, her face white and strained. "Please try, love. Try for Blackie. For the baby. For me."

There was a rustling noise as the priest came in carrying a black bag. He touched Emma on the shoulder lightly. "She must receive Extreme Unction, Mrs. Lowther," he said.

Emma stood up and moved away with a degree of self-containment, although her knees were buckling. Tears rolled unchecked down her face and then it darkened as she watched the priest bending over Laura. She wanted him to leave. He was a harbinger of death. If he left, then Laura would live. *There is no God! No God, do you hear me!* Emma shouted at him, but the shouts reverberated in her head unuttered.

Emma thought her heart was surely breaking. The room was very quiet; the only sounds were the faint swishing of the priest's cassock as he moved nearer to the bed, the low murmur of his voice and Laura's as she confessed and he absolved her of her sins. *Sins*, Emma thought bitterly. *She*

has never sinned. Laura never did anything to hurt anybody.
She's only given love to everyone she knows. She's never
sinned against God. Never sinned against the world. Never.
Ever.

The priest administered Holy Communion, made the sign
of the cross, and put the wafer in Laura's mouth. He was
anointing her. Emma turned away and looked out of the
window. It was all so wasteful. Yes, even sinful. The operation would probably have killed the baby, but Laura would
have been alive. This dogma of the Catholic Church was
barbaric. Insane. Who cared about the baby? It was Laura
they knew and loved.

When the priest had finished the last rites he came to
Emma. "Mrs. O'Neill wishes to speak with you," he said
dolorously.

Emma brushed past him rudely and flew to the bed. She
brought her face close to Laura's. "I'm here, my darling.
What is it?"

Laura's eyelids lifted slowly. "I'm sorry to keep asking you
to promise me things. Just one more favor. Be brave for
Uncle Pat. He's so old now and he's going to need your
courage, Emma."

"Oh, Laura, Laura, don't slip away from me!"

Laura smiled and her face was glorious, incandescent, and
her eyes, so large they seemed to engulf her face, were
steady and full of peace.

"There is no such thing as death in my lexicon, Emma. As
long as you live, and Blackie lives, I will live, too, for you will
both carry the memory of me in your hearts always. And
there will be Bryan for Blackie."

Emma had no words. She pressed her hands to her mouth,
her shoulders heaving.

Laura said, "Tell Blackie that I love him."

"Yes, darling." Emma bit her lip and blinked back the
blinding tears. "Oh, Laura, what will I do without you?" she
gasped, choked and grief-stricken.

"You'll be fine, Emma. I'm very sure of you. You're so
good; so brave. And remember, God never gives us a burden
that is too heavy to bear."

"Oh, Laura, I can't—"

"And don't forget my Christmas presents for the children,
will you? The dog is at the kennel for Kit and the jasmine

scent for Edwina is all wrapped. In my bedroom. You'll find it. There's something for you, too, my dearest Emma—" Laura closed her eyes and the smile, so radiant a moment before, was a mere fleeting shadow on her face.

"No, I won't forget, darling."

Emma felt Laura's hand go slack in hers. "Laura! Laura!" she cried, pressing the cold hand to her lips.

Dr. Stalkley had to forcibly uncurl Emma's fingers from Laura's hand, so tightly was she grasping it. The priest led her out of the room, murmuring words of condolence. Emma closed her ears, drained and numb in her terrible sorrow.

After a few minutes the doctor joined them. "I think we will be able to discharge the baby in a few days, Mrs. Lowther. We'll let you know when you can come and fetch him. That was Mrs. O'Neill's wish."

Emma hardly heard him. "Yes, I understand," she responded automatically, in a low voice. "You have my address and telephone number." She left them abruptly and without saying goodbye.

Emma pushed open the door of St. Mary's Hospital and walked along the drive and out through the iron gates, moving like a somnambulist. She turned and headed up over Hill Top, climbing steadily, gazing ahead yet seeing nothing. It was a cold December afternoon and the empty sky was bloated with snow and sunless, and the harsh wind blew hard over the hill and dried the tears coursing down her cheeks.

Emma trod the path of her grief in measured steps—steps that sometimes faltered and often slowed but which never failed completely. She buried her pain deep and the world saw only that face of inscrutability, and as the weeks and months passed she learned to live with her heartbreak and the crushing loneliness of her life.

The baby, Bryan, lived with her and the children. Blackie, who had come home briefly on compassionate leave, had agreed this was the most sensible course to take under the circumstances, recognizing that his son would be in a more normal atmosphere with her than if he was put in charge of a nurse at his Uncle Pat's house. Blackie, unconsolable, and burdened down by his grief, had returned almost at once to the front, and Emma was alone again.

At first Emma had resented the baby, seeing it as the

instrument of Laura's death, but one day it struck her, and most powerfully, that she was being unjust and bitter. She came then to understand that she was betraying Laura's love and trust in her and was also negating her own abiding love for Laura with her attitude. This was Laura's son, the child she had yearned for and had died for so that he might live. Emma was seized by remorse and became ashamed of herself and she took the child to her compassionate heart as if he were her own. Bryan had Blackie's dark coloring and jet-black hair, yet his eyes were Laura's, large and limpid and of the same soft hazel. He was a good baby, with Laura's sweet disposition, and when he smiled it was Laura's smile that Emma saw and she would pick Bryan up out of the crib and hold him fiercely to her breast, overcome with love, and she determined to cherish him always.

Sometimes Emma forgot that Laura was dead, and her hand would automatically reach for the telephone whenever she had a special confidence to impart, and then it would fall away and she would sit for a while, lost in memories of the past ten years, her eyes moist, her heart aching. But there were always the children to help dispel her sadness and pain. Emma devoted all of her free time to them, aware that they needed her more than ever now, with Joe gone and in their most formative years, and she gave of herself unstintingly. Winston came home on leave and Frank visited her regularly and she found solace in her family.

PART FIVE

The Pinnacle
1918–1950

He who ascends to mountaintops, shall find
The loftiest peaks most wrapt in clouds and snow;
He who surpasses or subdues mankind
Must look down on the hate of those below.

—LORD BYRON, "Childe Harold's Pilgrimage"

FORTY-THREE

"Why are you angry, Frank?" Emma asked, staring at her brother across the dinner table in the Ritz Hotel.

Consternation swept across Frank's sensitive face and he reached out and squeezed her arm. "I'm not angry, love. Just worried about you, that's all."

"But I'm feeling so much better, Frank. Truly I am, and I've quite recovered from the pneumonia," she reassured him with a vivid smile.

"I know, and you look wonderful, Emma. But I do worry about you. Or rather, your life," he responded quietly.

"My life! What do you mean? What's wrong with my life?" she exclaimed.

Frank shook his head regretfully. "What's wrong with your life? you ask. Oh, Emma, don't you ever stop to think? You're on a treadmill, love. In fact, you're as much a drudge now as you ever were at Fairley Hall—"

"That's ridiculous!" Emma interjected, her face clouding over.

"You're not scrubbing floors, I'll grant you that," Frank countered quickly, "but you're still a drudge, albeit in luxury. You've put yourself in bondage with your business, Emma." He sighed. "You'll never break free."

"I don't want to break free," Emma said, suddenly laughing, "Hasn't it ever occurred to you that I might enjoy my work?"

"*Work!* That's all you do, and that's exactly what I'm getting at. Isn't it about time you had a bit of fun in life? Now, while you're still young." He threw her a wary look and his tone was cautious as he added, "Also, you're going to be twenty-nine in a few months. I think you ought to consider remarrying."

Laughter rippled through Emma. "Remarry! Frank, you're absolutely crazy. Who would I marry? There are no men around. There's still a war on, you know."

"Yes, but it's bound to end later this year. When America got in, the situation started to change and the Allies are making great headway. I'm positive armistice will be declared within nine months or so, and men will be coming back."

"But it's still only January," Emma gasped, still laughing, her eyes wide. "All the young men are noticeably absent. You're a little premature, darling."

"What about Blackie O'Neill, for one thing?" Frank suggested, watching for her reaction. "He's always adored you. And you're both free now. Not only that, you've been looking after Bryan as if he were one of your own for the past year." Noting she was not perturbed, he grinned and finished, "It's not as if you are strangers."

"Oh, Frank, don't be so silly," Emma said dismissively, with an airy wave of her hand. "Blackie is like a brother to me. Besides, I'm not sure I want to remarry. Apart from anything else, I don't think I would like a man interfering with my business."

"That blasted business, Emma! I don't understand you sometimes." His eyes were thoughtful when he glanced up at his sister. "Surely you must feel secure these days. You are a rich woman in your own right and Joe left you well provided for. How much is going to be enough money for you, our Em?"

A small smile flitted across her mouth on hearing this affectionate diminutive from their childhood, and she shrugged casually. "It's not the money, really. I *do* enjoy business, Frank. Honestly, I get a lot of gratification out of it and I do have the children to think about as well. Their futures. And I can handle my life without any help from anyone, or advice, however well-intentioned."

Frank held up his hand. "I simply think you ought to take it a bit easier and relax for once in your life."

Emma leaned forward. "Look, Frank, do stop worrying or I shall get awfully cross and take the next train back to Leeds if—" She broke off and dropped her eyes.

"What's wrong?"

"Nothing. Well, it's the two men at the table directly opposite. They keep staring at us. I wondered if you knew them. But don't look now, they'll see you."

"I noticed them when they came in. The maître d' was bowing and scraping all over the place. However, I don't know them. But I do know that the younger one, the hand-

some major, is an Australian, from the insignia on his uniform. He's with the 4th Brigade of the Australian Corps."

"A damned colonial! No wonder!"

Amused at the anger flaring in her eyes, Frank said, "And
what's that supposed to mean?"

"He's been quite insufferable since he sat down. Every
time I look up I find his eyes on me. And speculatively so,"
she said furiously.

"Come on, Emma. What do you expect? I don't think you
realize how beautiful you really are, love." Frank took in the
bottle-green velvet gown, the creamy pearls at her throat and
ears, the sleek hair pulled back in a chignon. "You look about
eighteen, Emma. And I'm glad you don't wear all that muck
on your face most women have taken to using lately." He
smiled. "Yes, you're undoubtedly the best-looking woman in
this room."

"There's not much to choose from," Emma replied pithily,
but she smiled and asked in a curiously shy voice, "Am I
really, Frank?"

"You are indeed."

The waiter approached the table and said deferentially,
"Excuse me, sir, but you're wanted on the telephone."

Frank nodded and turned to Emma. "I won't be a minute.
Excuse me." He pushed back his chair and stood up. "Why
don't you look at the menu and decide what you want for a
pudding?"

"Yes, all right, dear." Emma watched Frank cross the floor
of the Ritz Hotel dining room. He looked so distinguished
and well bred in his dinner jacket, and she was extremely
proud of his achievements and the shape his life had taken.
He was a dear, and always concerned about her happiness.
Emma smiled, wondering what Frank would say if he knew
about the Emeremm Company. He'd probably give me another lecture and say I was taking on too much, she mused.
But that company's going to be the making of my real fortune. The new business had been a brilliant concept, even if
she did say so herself. It was an acquisition and holding
company, which she had financed by selling Joe's shoe factory
and the tannery for exorbitant prices, and in the eleven
months it had existed it was already in the black. The name
Emeremm was her invention, a contraction of the words
emerald and Emma. One day she intended to call it Harte

Enterprises, but for the moment she did not want the world to know she was associated with it. For her own reasons she sought concealed ownership. Although she was the sole shareholder she did not appear on the board, nor was she an officer of the company. Ostensibly it was run by the managing director and the two other directors she had appointed. Men bought by her and therefore owned by her. Men of straw who would do her bidding.

Emma looked around the elegant dining room absently, her mind dwelling on the Emeremm Company and its endless financial possibilities. As her glance swept past the other tables her eyes inadvertently met those of the Australian major, and Emma found to her amazement she was momentarily unable to look away. He's too handsome, too sure of himself, Emma thought with a stab of annoyance. The sleek hair, the thick brows, the clipped mustache above the sensual mouth were too glossily black against the deep tan of the rugged and arresting face. And those eyes were of a blue so deep they were almost violet. Even the cleft in his chin was more deeply indented than was normal. His wide mouth lifted in a tantalizing smile, brought dimples to his cheeks, and his gaze was now so bold and so provocative she flinched. Blushing, she turned away. Why, he's positively indecent, she thought, her cheeks burning. She had the odd feeling he knew exactly what she looked like stark naked. Embarrassed, Emma reached for the glass of wine and in her nervousness she knocked it over. Further mortified, she began to dab at the cloth with her serviette.

The waiter promptly came to her rescue, murmuring that he could easily repair the damage, and quickly placed a clean serviette over the stain. He cleared off the dirty dishes and Emma thanked him as he moved away. The major was once again in her direct line of vision and she saw to her indignation that his audacious gaze still rested on her. There was an amused smile playing around his mouth and undisguised challenge in his eyes. Emma picked up the menu angrily and buried her flaming face behind it. She cursed the intolerable fool across the dining room who was so blatantly trying to flirt with her, and doubly cursed Frank and his interminable telephone call.

* * *

Bruce McGill's tanned and weather-beaten face was a study in fond amusement and his clear blue eyes twinkled as he said, "If you can drag your gaze away from that fetching creature for a brief moment, perhaps we can have a little decent conversation with dinner, my boy."

"Oh, sorry, Dad," Paul McGill said. He shifted in his chair and gave his father his full attention. "But she is undoubtedly the most fascinating woman I've ever seen. Don't you agree?"

Bruce nodded. "I do, my boy. You inherited my taste for the ladies, I'm afraid. Never could resist a beauty. However, I would like to talk to you, Paul. I don't get to see you that often these days."

"You'll be sick of the sight of me in a few weeks. This blasted wound is taking a hell of along time to heal."

Bruce looked concerned. "Not too painful, I hope."

"No, just aggravating and especially so in this lousy English weather." Paul smiled wryly. "I shouldn't be grumbling, should I? Instead I ought to be thanking my lucky stars. It was a miracle I got through the Gallipoli campaign without a scratch. Then this had to happen in France."

"Yes, you were lucky." A sober expression crossed Bruce's face. "I had hoped you would get out after this, so that you could come back to Coonamble with me. But I suppose there's no chance of that. Will you be going back to France to join Colonel Monash?"

"I expect so. But let's not worry about that tonight. I intend to have a whale of a time while I'm in good old Blighty."

"Glad to hear that, son. You damn deserve it after the hell you've been through. But take it easy, laddie." Bruce laughed, his eyes merry again. "No more little scandals this time. Dolly hasn't let me forget that last romantic encounter you had with her friend."

"Oh, Jesus, don't remind me, Dad. I swear off women every time I think about that particular mess. When are we supposed to be at Dolly's?"

"Any time after dinner, my boy. You know Dolly and her theatrical friends. Those parties of hers usually last until dawn. Incidentally, I hope you don't mind, but I've decided not to go. You can pop along there alone. You'll enjoy it. Give her my regrets. Afraid I'm not up to it tonight. Also, I would like to drop in at South Audley Street and see Adam Fairley."

Paul's dark head came up sharply. "How is he these days?"

"Not well at all, poor chap. Very sad really—that whole business. He was never the same after Olivia's death, and now the stroke. It's hard for me to see him confined to a wheelchair. He was always so active. Olivia's death was a tragedy and he's taken it hard. Leukemia, you know. Such a vivacious, lovely woman. I remember the first night I met her, about fourteen years ago. Rather fancied her myself, to tell you the truth. I can still remember the way she looked. Ravishing. Wearing a kingfisher-blue dress and sapphires."

At this moment Emma and Frank rose and left the dining room. Paul McGill's eyes were riveted on Emma for every step she took. He observed the proud set of her head, her straight back, her total self-assurance, and her regal bearing as she glided out, and he was further intrigued.

Paul caught the headwaiter's eye and motioned to him. To his father he said, "I'm going to find out who she is right now. . . . Charles, who was the gentleman who just left with the lady in the green velvet?"

"That was Frank Harte, sir. *The* Frank Harte of the *Daily Chronicle*. Fine young gentleman. Made quite a name for himself as a war correspondent."

"And the lady?" Paul asked.

"Forgive me, Major, but I'm afraid I don't know."

"So Mr. Harte is well known, is he?" Bruce interjected.

"Oh yes, indeed, sir. He writes on politics now. I understand he was, and is, quite a favorite of Mr. Lloyd George's."

"Thank you, Charles," Bruce said. "You've been most helpful." He leaned forward and fixed his thoughtful gaze on his son. "Look here, Paul, I don't want you doing anything foolish. Just watch your step. I'm heavily involved with a number of politicians in this country. I would hate to have problems because of your romantic philanderings. That might easily be the chap's wife, you know, and since he's well connected it could be a dangerous game you're contemplating."

"Don't worry, Dad. I won't embarrass you. However, I am going to find out who she is if it kills me." Paul sat back in his chair and took out a gold cigarette case. He lit a cigarette, his mind turning rapidly. His father's immense fortune had opened every door for him, all the right doors, and he began to enumerate his friends, wondering who would be the most suitable candidate to arrange an introduction to Frank Harte.

There were a dozen or so people in Dolly Mosten's drawing room when Emma and Frank entered it later that evening. Emma had only taken three small steps into the room when she halted abruptly and grabbed Frank's arm. Startled, he turned to her quickly.

"Frank, we've got to leave!" she hissed.

Surprise flickered onto his face. "Leave! But we've only just arrived."

Her fingers tightened on him and her eyes were pleading. "*Please*, Frank! We've *got* to leave. Immediately!"

"Don't be foolish, Emma. It would seem most odd and I don't want to offend Dolly. That's a fate worse than death. Anyway, apart from the fact that she's London's leading actress and not to be slighted, she's been very helpful to me in the past. She would never forgive me. Why the sudden turnabout? You wanted to come earlier."

"I feel—sick," Emma improvised. "Faint."

"Sorry, but I'm afraid it's too late, old girl," Frank muttered. Dolly Mosten was descending upon them, a cloud of yellow chiffon and canary diamonds, her flaming red hair a fiery nimbus around her superb but vacuous face. And in her wake was the Australian major they had seen at the Ritz. *So that's it!* Frank thought. His eyes were teasing as he looked at Emma and said pointedly, "He won't bite."

Emma did not have a chance to reply. Dolly was greeting them warmly and making the introductions, her famous bubbling voice ringing with laughter, her theatrical vivaciousness enveloping them in an intimacy Emma found curiously distasteful. She averted her head to avoid the major, who loomed up in front of her, all too predatory. Emma felt cornered, and then she found her hand being tightly grasped by a much larger, stronger one. Emma was in a quandary and she stared down at the fine black hairs speckling that hand, almost afraid to raise her head.

"I'm most delighted to meet you, Mrs. Lowther. It is an undeniable pleasure and one I did not anticipate experiencing quite so soon, although, to be frank, I had determined to make your acquaintance. How fortuitous for us both that I stopped by Dolly's tonight," the resonant voice drawled, the faint Australian twang hardly discernible.

Why, the impertinent and conceited devil, Emma thought, the embarrassment and discomfiture she had experienced at the Ritz flaring within her again. She had the overwhelming desire to slap his face, but her innate good manners prevented her. Instead, she lifted her head and finally looked up into that face staring with such intensity at hers. Her mouth parted. No words came out. She blinked, conscious of the roguish expression in those stunning eyes, the sardonic smile as he waited for her response.

Emma felt the insistent pressure of Frank's hand on her back and then to her horror, and before she could stop herself, she said coldly, "I understand you are an Australian, Major McGill. I hope the deplorable manners you so patently displayed earlier this evening are not typical of your nationality, but merely spring from your own lack of upbringing. Otherwise your fellow countrymen will find a frosty reception in this country, where women are treated with respect. This is not the Outback, Major."

Dolly gasped. Frank cried, "Emma, you are being ungracious!"

But Major McGill was apparently amused. He threw back his head and roared with laughter, and he held on to her hand all that more firmly, so that Emma winced.

Emma turned to Dolly. "Forgive me, Dolly. I don't mean to be discourteous to you. Please excuse me. I must leave. I feel perfectly dreadful. *Something definitely disagreed with me at dinner*." She endeavored to extract her hand, but the major had tightened his grip like a vise.

The major said, "*Touché*, Mrs. Lowther. I deserved that, I do believe." Paul bent forward, lowered his head, and offered his right cheek to Emma. "Want to slap it and get it over with?"

Flushing, Emma took a step backward. The major immediately pulled her forward into the group again. He said, "I think I had better take Mrs. Lowther for a glass of champagne. And I hope I will be able to convince her that even colonials are civilized." He tucked Emma's arm through his in a proprietary way. Emma tried to disentangle her arm, but he instantly clamped his free hand over it and shook his head slowly. "Come along, Mrs. Lowther," he said commandingly.

She saw that his eyes were irreverent and taunting, and she loathed him more than ever.

"Do excuse us," Paul said to Dolly and Frank, obviously well pleased with himself as he swept her away.

"A little champagne will cool you off," Paul said, bowing elaborately to a couple he knew but without slowing his pace.

"You can lead a horse to water but you can't make it drink," Emma hissed, her blood boiling.

"Even the most stubborn and temperamental fillies eventually get thirsty, Mrs. Lowther," he said in a low voice, his eyes roving over her boldly. "Depending, of course, on when they last quenched their thirst. You look positively parched to me."

His words, appearing innocent enough on the surface, were full of innuendo and the unconcealed desire flickering in his eyes was revealing of his thoughts and his intentions. Emma's cheeks were scarlet as they walked across the floor, and to her considerable irritation she discovered she was acutely aware of Paul McGill's physical proximity—of his fingers biting into hers, of his arm brushing so intimately against her bare shoulder. He was taller and broader than she had realized at the Ritz, and he seemed to overpower her. He exuded a sheathed strength, an earthy and domineering masculinity that disturbed her. The room swam before her eyes and she was overcome by faintness. A peculiar tingling sensation invaded her entire body and her heart quickened, beating so rapidly underneath the green velvet she thought it was about to burst. She was flustered and unnerved. It's only anger, she told herself, and she truly believed this was the real cause of her sudden distress.

Dolly's drawing room appeared to Emma to have tripled in size and she thought the long stretch of chartreuse carpet would never come to an end. "Please, I would like to sit down," she said breathlessly. "Over there. You can go and find a waiter—"

"Oh no, not on your life! You're not going to escape quite so easily," Paul cried.

"Where are you taking me?"

Paul stopped in his tracks and swung her to face him. He peered down at her, his violet eyes filled with speculation. "Well now, I'm not quite sure. There are hundreds of interesting possibilities and alternatives—" Observing the chilly expression on her face, he laughed that bantering laugh and remarked softly, "Don't look so terrified. I'm not going to abscond with you. I merely wanted to get you away from your brother and Dolly." He scanned the room and inclined his head to the left. "Over there perhaps, near the potted palm. That seems a likely place for us. A quiet and secluded spot."

Emma attempted to break free from him. "Please let me go."

"Never."

He maneuvered her into the corner with great adeptness. Emma realized, and with mounting dismay, that there was now no opportunity for immediate flight, and she also acknowledged that she owed it to Frank to stay at Dolly's for a respectable interval. She sat down on the sofa, relieved to be released from the major's grip, and grudgingly took the glass of champagne which he whisked off the tray as the waiter glided past.

But she had no intention of pandering to this arrogant devil of a man, nor would she spare his feelings, and so she said icily, "I suppose this rough and masterful technique you adopt is successful with most women, Major."

Paul nodded and crossed his legs nonchalantly. "Generally speaking, I would say," he said lazily. He looked her over with an insolence that brought a deep flush to her chest and neck.

"Let me assure you it won't be with me!" Emma exclaimed, her face haughty. "I am different from most women."

"I am aware of that," he admitted, the roguish glint still lingering in his eyes. "In fact, I do believe I detected that characteristic in you at once. I think that's what attracted me to you, apart from your staggering looks." He grinned. "You are seemingly staggeringly blunt as well, Mrs. Lowther. And strong-minded and sassy to boot. Yes, very different, I would say. Fire and ice perhaps?"

"*All ice*, Major," Emma parried.

"Ice can melt, you know."

"It can also be very dangerous. People have been known to have fatal accidents with ice," Emma snapped.

"Danger has always attracted me, Mrs. Lowther. I find it exciting. Challenging. It brings out all my masculine instincts."

Emma threw him a scathing look, turned away contemptuously, and glanced around the room, her eyes seeking Frank. This man elicited an immediate and direct response from her, and one that both infuriated and baffled her. With his monumental egotism, his astonishing appearance, his swaggering self-assurance, and his flippant tongue, he was quite unlike any man she had ever met. And no man had ever had the temerity to be so brash with her or address her in such a suggestive manner. She detested the major and resented his assumption that she was about to fall swooning at his feet. There was also a ruthlessness about him that oddly enough did not trouble her and she was nonplussed, momentarily not understanding that ruthlessness was a trait she was familiar with and could easily handle.

Paul leaned back in the chair, his eyes reflective as he studied Emma's exquisite profile, and he marveled at his incredible luck in meeting her quite by accident this very night. He thought: She *is* very different. An original. She must belong to me. I won't rest until I have her for myself. All of her. Not only her body but her heart and her mind as well. He was shaken to his very core, for no woman had evoked such a violent reaction in him before. Paul McGill, at thirty-six, was lusty, adventurous, worldly, and charismatic, with a down-to-earth sexuality that cut across class lines to awaken a fervent response in all women. Shopgirls and upper-class ladies equally found him irresistible and, consequently, his conquests had been all too easy, and so numerous he had long ago lost count of his romantic entanglements. His approach, until this precise moment in his life, had been based on a "take me or leave me" attitude. Women fell over themselves to take him, and with an eagerness that was almost indecent, before he sauntered out of their lives, the rakish grin intact, his heart untouched.

For all that, and despite the debonair and hedonistic stance he struck, Paul McGill was intelligent and possessed shrewdness and psychological insight. Much smarter than he pretended to be, he now recognized, with a sudden flash of clarity, that Emma was a wholly different proposition. *She* was not going to succumb to his brash charm or his potent virility. This was a woman to be conquered only through understanding, honesty, and subtle strategy. Ruefully admitting he was antagonizing her unnecessarily with his raillery, he decided to change his tactics and cease his baiting of her at once.

He leaned forward and said, "Let's stop this silly bantering. We're spoiling it."

"Spoiling what?" Emma asked snappishly.

"Our first meeting. Our first evening together."

"And our last!"

Paul brought his face closer to hers. "I like a woman with spirit, Mrs. Lowther. I presume Mr. Lowther has the same preference."

Taken by surprise, Emma gaped at him. What a blundering imbecile he is, she thought with irritation. Her stare was glacial. "I am a widow, Major McGill. My husband was killed eighteen months ago. In the Somme offensive."

Oh, my God, Paul thought. He said quickly, "Please forgive me. I am so terribly sorry. I had no idea. I am a thoughtless fool." He swore under his breath and sat very still. Emma was silent and unresponsive.

Paul now said, "It was very tactless of me. One should be more careful in wartime. I am truly sorry. I hope you will also accept my apologies for my appalling behavior at the Ritz. It was quite unforgivable."

Emma heard the sincerity in his voice, detected sympathy in his eyes, saw that the mocking expression had been wiped off his face, and she was amazed at the radical change in his manner.

"Will you accept my apology?"

"Yes," Emma murmured.

Frank joined them and handed a walking stick to Paul. "Dolly asked me to give you this." He turned to Emma. "How are you feeling? Better, I hope."

"Yes, thank you," Emma said. "I am sorry, Frank, I didn't mean to embarrass you."

"Look here, Frank, it was all my fault," Paul cut in. "Let's forget the incident, shall we?"

"Of course, Paul." He grinned at them and strolled off to join a well-known politician holding court at the far end of the room.

Emma was eyeing the walking stick. Paul said, "I'm wounded. But you probably didn't notice the limp." There was a sheepish look in his eyes as he said, "I have to admit I was trying my hardest to conceal it when we walked across the room."

"You succeeded very well." Emma found herself smiling at him and she discovered this small admission of pride on his part induced her to revise her opinion of him. She knew all about self-esteem, and she softened a fraction. She leaned back against the sofa feeling more relaxed. With that grin he looked like the eternal little boy. "I hope your wound is not too painful, or serious," she remarked softly.

"No, not at all. In fact, I'll be going back to France shortly." Paul regarded her thoughtfully, his face serious. He was aware he had gained ground with her, but he hesitated before saying, "I'm on leave for a few more weeks. Would it be possible for us to meet again? I know you think I'm some sort of scoundrel, but I'm not, really. I have no excuse for my ghastly display at the Ritz, other than to confess I was bowled over by your beauty. Still, I should not have caused you discomfort. Can we lunch tomorrow so that I can make amends?" His eyes twinkled. "I promise I'll behave—like an officer and a gentleman and not a scallywag from the Outback."

"I have a luncheon engagement," Emma said.

"Is it terribly important? Couldn't you break it?"

"I don't think so. It's with Frank and I don't see him very often. He would be disappointed."

"Yes, I understand." Paul's face lit up. "I don't want to seem forward, but could I join you? May I invite you both to be my guests?" He smiled engagingly. "After all, you would be chaperoned with your brother present."

Emma smiled. He was quite transparent. "I would have to ask Frank. I'm not sure how he would feel."

To Paul's annoyance Dolly sailed up to them and he stood up, offering her his chair. She declined and said, "I see you two have recovered from your little contretemps." Her eyes swept over Emma and settled on Paul. "How is the wounded warrior? I do hope you're enjoying yourself, darling. We must keep our valiant soldiers happy, mustn't we?" She patted his arm playfully. "I can see you're in good hands. I presume I shall see you at your father's luncheon party tomorrow."

"No, I'm afraid not. I have a long-standing appointment. With destiny."

"Destiny?" Dolly's brow puckered in puzzlement. "I don't think I know her."

Paul kept his face absolutely straight. "I don't believe you do, Dolly."

Dolly shrugged. "One can't be acquainted with everyone in London, I suppose. Do excuse me. I must circulate, my darlings."

Paul leaned closer to Emma, his face sober. "I am, aren't I?"

"You are what?"

"Lunching with destiny."

She looked up at him and smiled, that unique smile that illuminated her face with incandescent radiance. "I thought you were lunching with Frank and me," she said.

Frank said, "Why are you doing this, Emma?"

"Doing what, dear?"

"You know exactly what I mean. Leaving London so unexpectedly."

"I only intended to stay in town for a few days. I've been here two weeks. I have to go back to Yorkshire."

"I never thought I would see my sister running away."

"I'm not running away."

"Yes, you are. It's Paul McGill, isn't it?"

Emma looked at him and bit her lip. She sighed. "Yes, it is."

"I guessed as much. But I still don't understand why you are rushing off."

"Because he's getting to be a nuisance and, anyway, I don't particularly like him."

"Emma! How can you say that! If you don't like him, why have you spent so much time with him? Every night, as far as I can gather. The theater, dinners, parties, and luncheons, too. I've hardly seen you alone, and I must say you have certainly given the impression you are mesmerized by him."

"That's not true, Frank Harte!"

Frank shook his head and looked out of the taxi window. He brought his eyes back to Emma. After a moment's reflection he said, "He's fallen for you like a ton of bricks."

"Oh, phooey!"

"Yes, he has. I can tell. Everyone who sees the two of you

together can tell. He positively devours you with his eyes.
And I know *you* like *him*, Emma."

"Frank, will you please leave me alone."

"Give me a good reason why you don't want to see him
anymore."

"Because he's too charming, too handsome, too fascinating.
And too much—for me to handle. Besides—" She broke off,
her voice faltering.

"Besides what?"

"I'm afraid I'll get more involved if I stay."

"I knew it! But surely you mean fall in love with him, don't
you?"

"Yes." Her voice was a whisper.

Frank took her hand. "Does he know you're leaving?"

"No. There's a note for him at the Ritz. He'll get it tonight
when he comes to collect me."

"That wasn't a very nice thing to do to the poor chap."

"It was the *only* thing to do. Now, darling, please shut up
about Paul McGill. And tell the taxi driver to hurry. I'll miss
my train."

FORTY-FOUR

Calculating of brain though she was, Emma could be
impulsive of heart and especially when her deepest
emotions were involved, and she had acted on impulse the
day she had returned with such abruptness to Yorkshire.
Recognizing that she was falling under the spell of the mag-
netic Paul McGill, she had fled, propelled by panic and fear.

Long ago, Emma had come to the conclusion that she was
unlucky where men were concerned. They either hurt her or
she hurt them. Her relationships had never been balanced.
She doubted that she could ever inflict pain on the self-
assured Paul McGill, but he was a terrible threat to *her*.
Contentment with her life, such as it was at this moment, was
at stake. She could not afford to risk emotional upheaval.
Only in business was she prepared to gamble.

But now, after two days, she was beginning to feel perplexed by his total silence. Aren't you also a little disap-

pointed? a small voice nudged at the back of her mind, and she smiled wryly, her eyes straying to the telephone. Perhaps you are, but you're also relieved, she said inwardly, and looked down at the latest report from the Ememm Company. Almost immediately her attention wandered again, her thoughts returning to Paul.

He had danced attendance on her every day for two weeks. He had been charming, gallant, and amusing, and a gentleman, more or less. He *had* taken her in his arms and his kisses had been sensual and his passions had been fully inflamed. She knew that he was aware that he had aroused the same desire in her, but ultimately he held himself in check. He had made no untoward proposals or attempted to seduce her, and his constraint had baffled her, despite her profound relief at this display of chivalry.

She shivered, recalling his amorous embraces, and instantly crushed down the memory of him. He had apparently forgotten *her* immediately. Or perhaps he was stinging from the blow to his pride. For a proud devil he was and his self-esteem had more than likely been seriously damaged. She was positive no other woman had ever run out on him. So much for Major McGill, she thought. He's dangerous and disturbing. Nevertheless, disappointment flared again and she shook her head, musing on her own inconsistencies, and then brought her eyes back to the papers. Her business needed her undivided attention.

Gladys knocked and came in quietly, looking pink and flustered. "You have a visitor, Mrs. Harte," she said, hovering in front of the desk.

"I don't have any appointments this morning," Emma frowned. "What's the matter, Gladys? You look very fluttery—" Emma paused and her heart missed a beat. She guessed what Gladys would say. Only one person in this world could bring that special look to a woman's eyes.

"It's a Major McGill, Mrs. Harte. He said you weren't expecting him but that you would see him anyway."

Emma nodded, her face inscrutable. "Yes, of course I will see him, Gladys."

He strode in, closed the door firmly behind him, and leaned against it. He was wearing a trench coat over his uniform and his cap was pushed rakishly to one side. He was carrying a picnic basket in one hand but he was no longer using the stick.

Paul gave Emma a hard look. "Coward," he said.

"What are you doing in Yorkshire?" Emma managed unsteadily. Her heart was pounding and her legs had turned to water.

"I've come to have lunch with you." He held up his hand and wagged a finger at her. "I know, don't say it. You always eat lunch in the office." He glanced down at the basket. "I anticipated that and brought a picnic. So you have no excuse. I can't answer for the Metropole's food, but the champagne is Dom Pérignon."

"That's very enterprising of you," she said quietly, recovering some of her composure.

"Yes, isn't it just!" He put the basket on the chair, threw his cap after it, and limped across the floor. He put both of his hands on the desk and leaned forward, his gaze fixed unwaveringly on her pale face. "You ran away. You were frightened," he said.

Unable to deny it, she did not respond.

"Who were you afraid of? Me? Or yourself?" he demanded, his voice unexpectedly harsh.

"I don't know." She looked down at the desk. "Of you, I suppose."

"You silly little fool! Don't you know I'm in love with you!"

He came around the desk and pulled her into his arms, his grip powerful and crushing, his mouth hard and unrelenting on hers. Emma could not resist. Her arms went around him and she returned his kisses, the excitement he aroused in her manifest again, racing through her like fire. Her head swam and she was assailed by a weakness that trickled into her thighs. He pulled away suddenly, as he had done so often in the past, and gazed down at her. He tilted her face to his. His eyes, so darkly violet they looked as black as the brows curving above them, were filled with seriousness.

Paul shook his head. "Did you think a few hundred miles would discourage me?" He laughed. "I'm an Australian. Distance means nothing to me. And you haven't learned much else about me, Emma, have you? Or you would know I'm very tenacious." He put his arm around her, hugging her to him, and laughed again. "What am I going to do with you, my Emma? My stubborn, willful, but adorable Emma. Tame you? But I wonder, would a bridle sit well on you, my sweet?"

Emma clung to his trench coat. She was speechless and her mind was chaotic. What had he said? That he was in love with her. Her heart was tight and her legs shook and she dared not open her mouth. If she did she knew she would tell him that she loved him, too.

Paul seemed unconcerned by her silence. He said, "First of all, we are going to have lunch. Then you are going to show me around your store. After that I want to see Layton's mill." He grinned that engaging lopsided grin, and said, "Later I want to meet your children and I hope you will invite me to stay to dinner. You wouldn't abandon a lonely soldier to an evening by himself in this godforsaken city, would you?"

Emma shook her head.

"We're in agreement, then?"

"Yes, Paul," she whispered, and her voice was surprisingly meek.

Paul McGill stayed in Yorkshire for three days and during that time Emma came to know a very different side of him. In London she had felt there was a deep core of sincerity in him, and although he had often given the impression he lacked the inner conviction to remain serious for very long, she had suspected otherwise. She was not wrong. That thoughtful side was now revealed to her. He was also a gentle man, a characteristic that was displayed most obviously with her children. He listened attentively to Edwina, responding with kindness to her questions about Australia, and he treated Kit like an equal. Kit hung on his every word, and was thrilled when Paul took him sledging down the drive and played with his trains in the nursery.

It seemed to Emma that Paul brought out the very best in her children, and even Edwina, always so distant, emerged from her shell under his vivacious influence. Emma watched Paul closely, reveling in his genuine interest in her family, but she frequently noticed a curiously yearning look flickering in those violet eyes when he believed he was unobserved. She speculated on the reason for it and wondered about this extraordinary man who was so contradictory and compelling.

The day he departed he said, "I don't have very much time

left, Emma. I'll be going back to France shortly. Will you come and visit me in London? Very soon?"

Emma did not think twice. "Yes," she said, smiling up at him.

He touched her cheek lightly. "When?"

"I have a meeting tomorrow morning. But I could come the day after. On Friday."

"Couldn't you make it tomorrow afternoon? Time is running out."

"All right, then."

He tilted her face to his. "Are you sure about this, Emma?"

"Yes, I am." As she spoke she knew that she had made a commitment to him.

It was a bitterly cold February evening and drizzling when Emma stepped off the train at King's Cross. She saw him before he saw her. He was standing at the ticket barrier, the cap pushed back to the same jaunty angle, the collar of his trench coat turned up. Her heart leapt and she began to run. It was undignified but she could not help herself. She did not stop until she was in his arms, breathless and laughing, her face resplendent with happiness.

He held her close, told her she looked beautiful, found the porter with her luggage, and bustled her into his father's car, taking command in his usual way. As they drove through the evening traffic Emma became aware of a difference in Paul, and although he held her hand and chatted to her casually, his voice light, she sensed a disquiet under the surface. It was a controlled tension but, nonetheless, quite evident to her.

The Daimler came to a standstill before they reached the Ritz Hotel, where Emma was staying. Paul said, "I'm going to get out here and walk the rest of the way."

She stared at him. "But why?"

He grinned. "I know how circumspect you are. I would hate to compromise you the moment you arrive. Check in alone and I'll join you for a drink in an hour. Anyway, you need a little privacy. Time to change and bathe."

"Very well. In an hour, then."

He nodded, jumped out, and slammed the door. Emma sat back against the seat, touched by his thoughtfulness. And then she suffered such a sharp sense of loss, and acute loneliness, she was jolted. How silly she was being. She would see him very shortly.

The sitting room of the suite overlooked Green Park. A fire blazed in the grate, the lamps had been turned on, and there were masses of flowers everywhere, all of them from Paul, Emma discovered on reading the amusing messages on the white cards reposing in each arrangement. She smiled with delight but did not pause long to admire. She hurriedly unpacked, hung up her clothes, and took a bath in the huge marble tub.

The bath dispelled the chill in her bones and revitalized her, and Emma slipped into a white silk robe and sat down at the dressing table, humming under her breath, feeling happier than she had in years. She brushed out her long hair until it gleamed in the lamplight and slowly began to coil it on top of her head. She was pushing the last hairpin into the coil when she tensed and remained perfectly still, experiencing the strange sensation that she was not alone. She swung her head slowly and jumped back in the chair. Paul was leaning casually against the door of the bedroom, his legs crossed, a glass in his hand, observing her with great concentration.

"I'm sorry. I didn't mean to frighten you. I should have knocked," he said. "You make a very pretty picture, my sweet."

"How did you get in?" Emma gasped.

"Why, through the door of course." He strolled over to the dressing table and placed a small jewel case in front of her. "These are for you," he said. "Put them on."

Emma threw him a quick, puzzled glance and opened the case. The emerald earrings shimmered like pools of green fire against the black velvet and she drew in her breath. "Oh, Paul! They're beautiful." She frowned. "But I can't possibly accept them. They are far too valuable."

"Put them on," he ordered.

Emma's hands trembled as she screwed the emeralds onto her ears. She gazed at Paul through the mirror. "They're incredible. How did you know emeralds are my favorite stone?"

He smiled. "I didn't. But with eyes your color you should only wear emeralds. See how they echo the light in your eyes." He put down his drink and cupped his hands underneath her chin and, tilting her head back, he bent forward and kissed her forehead. "If you don't accept them I'll be terribly offended. I might never speak to you again."

"In that case I suppose I must. But it was very extravagant of you." She smiled at him tenderly. "Thank you, Paul."

He moved away from her. "Come into the other room and have a drink," he said, pausing at the door.

"I'll just put my dress on."

"No, don't bother. I want to talk to you. You're decent enough."

Emma pulled the white silk robe around her and followed him, feeling self-conscious, but concerned by his tone and unable to protest. He sounded grave and her heart sank. Was he leaving sooner than expected for France? Was that the reason for his tension? When she walked into the sitting room she saw immediately how he had managed to enter the suite so silently. The door at the far end was open and beyond she could see another identical suite. She faltered, unprepared for such an intimate arrangement and unnerved by the implication.

"So that's how you got in," she remarked, and there was a hint of anger in her voice.

He ignored the comment. "I'm drinking scotch, but I know you prefer wine. I'll get you a glass of champagne."

Her eyes followed him as he strode out, and her resentment spilled over into quiet rage. Paul had assumed too much. Assumed she would be an eager and willing partner in this—this—little game of his. She bit her lip. She was being inconsistent again. Had she not known when she stepped onto the train earlier in the day that there would be no going back? This scene now being enacted should not shock her. It was exactly what he had intended from the beginning, and anticipated once she had agreed to come back to London. And she had probably led him to believe it would be so.

Paul returned with the champagne, interrupting her racing thoughts. He handed her the glass and sat down opposite her, and as if he had read those thoughts, he said, "I don't blame you for being angry, Emma. I know you're also upset and uncomfortable as well, aren't you?"

She did not answer him, but stared down at the glass and took a fast sip to hide her nervousness.

"I'm a damn fool. It was presumptuous of me and now I

apologize for that presumption. I feel quite certain you understood what my intentions were when you saw that open door and the other suite. Seduction, of course. I had planned it all very carefully for weeks." His mouth lifted in a small self-deprecatory smile. "I'm not too subtle, am I? However, I realized in the car that I had maneuvered you into a situation which you would have great difficulty extracting yourself from. So, I am going to do that for you." Paul went on, "I am going to finish this drink and then I am going to walk through that door. You will lock it. When you are dressed I will come and fetch you. We will go out to dinner. No obligations. Now, or later. All right?"

Emma stared at him. "Yes, of course. But why have you changed your mind?"

He laughed ironically. "Yes, it is out of character, isn't it? The reformed rake doing the honorable thing." He shrugged. "I'm amazed at myself."

"Why do you want to do the honorable thing?"

"Because I love you, and too much to manipulate a situation to suit my own ends, my own advantage, without giving a thought to you and your feelings."

"I'm not sure I quite understand."

"You have to love *me* and want *me* as much as I love and want you, Emma. Otherwise there is no point to all this." He gulped down the drink and stood up. "Now run along and dress. I'll be waiting for you and we'll go out to dinner."

He stopped at the door. "Lock this after me," he said without glancing back. Emma did as he said and turned the key, her face as grave as his. She sat down on the sofa. She did not know what to do. He loved her. She loved him. She had come to London knowing there was an unspoken commitment between them, and yet now she was acting resentful and outraged. Yes, and being a hypocrite, she reproached herself. Her behavior did not make sense. She closed her eyes and pictured him behind that closed door, waiting to take her to dinner. But also waiting for her decision, one which would determine the outcome of their relationship. Had he passed the decision over to her to avoid responsibility? No, that was unfair. There was no duplicity in him. Why am I frightened of taking this step? she asked herself. And the answer struck her with such force her head spun. She was not afraid of Paul or of her own emotions. She was afraid of the final act of love, of consummation, because of her distasteful sexual experiences with Joe. And she was afraid of hurting Paul by recoiling from him, afraid of failing him as a woman. Perhaps if she explained . . .

Emma flew across the room, unlocked the door, and stood on the threshold. Paul was hunched over the fireplace, his head bent. He appeared to be in the grips of a terrible anguish.

"Paul—"

His dark head swung around and he stared at her. She walked to him slowly. "I—I—would like to talk to you."

He nodded, looking down at her soberly. "I know I put the burden of the decision on you. But only because I wanted to be absolutely sure of you. I also wanted you to be sure of yourself."

Emma put out her hand and touched his lapel, her mouth quivering, her eyes darkly green. She had lost all power of speech and she had certainly lost the courage to discuss her feelings.

Paul took her hand in his and kissed the fingertips. "Such a small, dear hand," he said.

"Oh, Paul!"

Her face, blazing with her love, told him everything he wanted to know. He pulled her to him and kissed her deeply and then he swept her up in his arms and carried her into the bedroom. He kicked the door shut with his foot and walked over to the bed. He laid her down on it and sat on the edge. "Say it, darling," he commanded hoarsely. "Say it!" His eyes burned into hers.

"I love you, Paul."

"And?"

"I want you."

"Oh, Emma, Emma, you always have, my darling. Don't you understand? This was fated to happen from the first moment we set eyes on each other." He traced a line down her cheek. "*I knew*. But you had to recognize it, and that is why I would not force the issue tonight. I wanted and needed you to come to me of your own free will."

He stood up and unbuckled his Sam Browne belt, throwing it to one side. His jacket followed and his tie and his shirt. As he undressed her eyes did not leave his face, and the fear was dissipating, and she thought: I have never seen a man completely naked before. Why, he has a beautiful body. It was tanned and firm with muscle. His shoulders were broad, his waist narrow, his legs long, his stomach flat.

"Take your robe off, my love," he said softly, as he came towards her.

He covered her body with his own and cradled her in his arms, smiling down into her expectant face. "It's such a pity to ruin this exotic hairdo," he murmured as he began to pull the pins from her hair. The russet tresses spilled around her shoulders, porcelain fragile and pink in the warm glow of the lamp, and he gasped at her loveliness now so perfectly revealed to him. He ran his hand through the heavy lengths and held her by the nape of her neck, bringing her face up to his own. His lips met hers, savoring their warmth and their sweetness, and they were both engulfed by their longing and the emotions which had been denied release for weeks. He moved his mouth into the hollow of her neck, kissing her shoulders, her breasts, and the deep valley between, and his strong hands smoothed over her firm skin and he caressed every part of her until he knew her fervor matched his own.

Emma was suffused with an unfamiliar warmth, a burning heat that flooded her being. Her whole body arched up, cleaved to him. She ached to be joined to him, to become one with him, and she marveled at her pleasure in his body and in her own, was astonished at the ease with which her reluctance had fallen away as if it had never existed. And she willingly gave herself to him, receiving his kisses and responding wildly to his demands.

With a stab of surprise he was aware of her lack of sexual sophistication and this touched him, thrilled him further. It was as though he was the first man to possess her. But he also recognized the latent sensuality in her and he drew out that hidden voluptuousness, brought her along the fine edge of desire until she quivered under his touch and called his name, and pledged her love for him.

Paul finally took her to him with flaring passion, his ardor gentled but in no way muted by his tenderness. Silken arms and legs entwined him, fluid and weightless, yet they pulled him down . . . down . . . down. He was plunging headlong into a warm blue sea filled with slanting sunlight, carrying her with him. Down faster, into darker, greener depths, green the color of her eyes. Down into a bottomless ocean.

Waves crashed around him. His heart thundered in unison. He thought he was losing consciousness as he spiraled into infinity with her. He felt the warm enveloping softness of her flesh, the rise of her thighs and breasts thrusting against him, the velvet strands of her hair entwined in his fingers. His body locked to hers, spasmed, was submerged in hers. Oh, God! Oh, God! This was the only way it should ever be! A man and a woman joined together, the perfect communion of twin bodies, twin souls. His endless quest was over. That ultimate joy which had so long eluded him was surging through him and he was reborn in her. *This* was the secret of life, the ecstasy of life, so fleeting in that final moment of truth, but overpowering in its brief intensity. He was floating up, taking her with him to the surface. Up into that radiant light. She *was* that light. Pure golden light.

He opened his eyes and looked down at her and he saw the flush of unprecedented pleasure on her face, the pulse beating in her neck, the eyes so wide and green and spilling her adoration. And there was a vulnerability in that face, and perfect innocence, and his eyes unexpectedly filled with tears. He kissed her with tenderness and pulled her to him, vowing never to let her go.

Emma lay with her head on his shoulder, dazed, languorous with euphoria, basking in her love. She was filled with peace and the first real fulfillment she had ever experienced, and there was wonderment in her eyes as she contemplated the mysterious transformation he had wrought in her, the joy he had given her, and her heart crested high with love for him. Her hand rested on his chest, fingers buried deep in the black hair covering it and she thought: He is a man just like any other man, but with him *I* am different.

Paul passed his hand over the crown of her head and kissed her hair. There had been so many other women before her, but just as he had believed he was the first man to take her, now he felt she was the only one who had ever truly possessed him. She was in his blood and he would never be free again. The light in his eyes changed, darkened, became anguished as he stared into space.

"Emma, darling."

"Yes, Paul?"

"I'm married."

The hand on his chest did not move and she remained

utterly motionless in his arms, but she felt as if she had been struck in the face and her stomach lurched. Finally she said in a small voice, "You certainly picked an inappropriate time to make your startling announcement."

He tightened his embrace, resting his head against hers. "It's not inappropriate. I purposely picked this time."

"Why?"

"Because I wanted you in my arms when I told you. Intimately, like this. So that I could hold you closer and make you understand how unimportant my marriage is. So that I could love you again and tell you that *you* are the reality." Emma did not reply and he went on anxiously, "I wasn't trying to hide the facts, Emma. It's not a secret and it might easily have been mentioned in your presence by any one of my friends. I prayed it wouldn't, of course, because I wanted you to hear it from me. I simply delayed telling you because I was afraid of losing you. I knew you would have disappeared if I'd told you sooner. That you would never have permitted our relationship to go this—"

"You clever devious bastard!"

She struggled to get off the bed. He pulled her back and pinned her under him with roughness, gazing into her cold white face. Emma thought she was being swamped by the startling blueness of those eyes swimming above hers.

"It's not like that, Emma!" Paul cried furiously, his face blazing. "Please believe me. I know what you're thinking— that I wanted to accomplish my own ends before telling you. But all I wanted to do was make you love me, so that you would be bound to me irrevocably. Once loving me, I knew you would not let the circumstances get in the way. Stand between us. I love you, Emma. You're the one thing of value in my life."

"And your wife?" she whispered.

"We have not lived together for six years. And we ceased being man and wife a year before that."

"How long have you been married?" Her voice was almost inaudible.

"Nine years. Emma, it is a meaningless marriage. It's not even a marriage. But right now I am tied to her because of— Tied to her legally. After the war is over I'll sort it all out. I want to spend the rest of my life with you, if you'll have me.

You are my life now. Please, darling, you must believe me."
His voice shook.

Emma stared at him, her turbulent thoughts clouding her judgment momentarily, and then her head cleared. She could feel the tension rippling through him. His haunted face was naked in its agony and his sincerity leapt from his eyes, stunning her. "I believe you," she said slowly, in a stronger tone, and ran one finger across his lips. "Yes, Paul, oddly enough, I do believe you."

FORTY-FIVE

The weeks that followed were enchanted, endless hours filled with rapture so dreamlike in quality time might have been suspended. Days merged into nights, nights drifted into dawns, and every single moment was spun out, intertwined with desire and joy that bound Emma and Paul inexorably together.

They existed only for each other, wanted only each other, rejoiced in each other. They remained in the two adjoining suites at the Ritz Hotel, rarely venturing out except for walks in Green Park and an occasional quiet dinner in a secluded restaurant off the beaten tracks of fashionable society. They were so wildly, so passionately in love they could barely contain their feelings for each other, were reluctant to share even a minute with friends and jealously guarded their privacy. Plans were canceled, invitations declined, Bruce McGill and Frank held at bay, and the world was well lost for them both.

They were so overwhelmed by their sexual attraction and their growing love they were unnerved, and they would stare at each other in wonderment that this miracle had occurred. A mere glance was as devouring as a kiss, a simple gesture as meaningful as an embrace, and every word they uttered to each other was cloaked with its own significance.

Emma was filled with incredulity and overpowered by the intensity of her compelling emotions. But for once she did not pause to analyze. She was ecstatic with happiness. Fulfillment and soaring joy now dislodged the grief and hurt and humiliation of years. Love ripped the mask of inscrutability from her face; love exposed her heart in all its vulnerability; she was brought to life by the touch of love. Paul's adoration, and his deep understanding of her, made dust out of the suspicion and self-protectiveness which were inherent in her nature and which hitherto had ruled her life. She was her true self with him in a way she had never been with another soul. All the guards were finally lowered for the only man she had ever really loved and to whom she had given herself with no reservation.

Paul was a revelation to her. His rakish pose and sardonic manner had long been dropped, but now she was also permitted to know him as no other woman had been allowed before. The reflective and introspective side of him was disclosed and she discovered there was a fine mind behind that handsome and polished façade. She was impressed by his brain and his vast knowledge of the world. She was captivated by his sophistication, and admiring of his savoir-faire that unmistakably sprang from security engendered by old money, the privilege that accompanied great wealth, and an education at Wellington and Oxford. And she was constantly entertained by his swift wit. In short, she was spellbound.

Paul, in turn, was equally besotted, held in the grips of the only genuine love he had experienced in his years of romantic dallying. He believed her to be the most beautiful woman he had ever seen in his wanderings around the world; he also thought she was the most intelligent he had known, and her vividness of mind startled him. But the one thing he marveled at continually was her incredible presence, that quality of personality that set her apart and made her so unique. It was as though an incandescent glow emanated from her innermost core. He could only compare it to that vitality and indefinable charisma that made an alluring actress a great star. For them both it had been a *coup de foudre*—as though struck by lightning, they had fallen blindingly in love instantaneously.

The days passed in a dreamy haze of passion flaring and assuaged and flaring again with a stronger brighter flame, of animated talk that continued far into the nights, of thoughts and emotions unveiled and shared. They discovered in each other all they had yearned for in a lover and a companion and their communication was a fusion of minds and souls as well as bodies.

One afternoon when they were lying in each other's arms, exhausted by their passion, Paul said, "You won't mind if I go out for a little while, will you, darling? I have a few things I must attend to."

"Not if you promise to hurry back," Emma replied, brushing her lips against his chest.

"Nothing could keep me away from you for longer than an hour. I'll be back by four," he said, kissing the strands of her hair. He released his hold on her and disappeared into the bathroom. He emerged a few minutes later freshly shaven, his black hair slicked back, a towel wrapped around his waist. From her position on the bed Emma observed him stealthily like a cat, her intent green gaze riveted on him, and she discovered she derived enormous pleasure from watching him occupied in so simple a task as dressing. He picked up his shirt from the chair and the muscles on his wide back rippled and she had to suppress the impulse to run to him and enfold him in her arms. She thought: He has become my whole world.

He buckled the Sam Browne belt on over his army jacket and strode over to the bed. He bent down and kissed her and her arms went around his neck. He removed her arms gently after a moment. "I have to go, sweetheart."

"And I wonder just *where* you are going," Emma said, fluttering her eyelashes coyly. "Shaved and groomed and scented to high heaven. Why, Major McGill, if you have a rendezvous with another woman I'll scratch your eyes out. I swear I will! And hers, too!"

He grinned and touched the tip of her nose playfully. "O tiger's heart wrapp'd in a woman's hide!"

"Waxing poetic, Major?" she teased.

"Stolen from Shakespeare, I must confess. *Henry VI.*" Paul kissed her fingertips, his hand tightening, his eyes penetrating. "And if *you* ever so much as *look* at another man I will kill you." He stood up. "Be a good girl. I won't be long."

After he had left, Emma busied herself with telephone calls to her secretary at the store and to her housekeeper, anxious to reassure herself that all was well in Yorkshire during her absence. Relieved that everything was still under control since yesterday's calls, she then spoke to Frank at the *Chronicle*.

"Good Lord! No wonder it's snowing!" Frank exclaimed on hearing her voice. "So he's let you out of his clutches long enough for you to ring me." He laughed. "I'm only joking. I'm happy for you, Emma."

"Oh, Frank, I'm happy, too. So very happy I can't believe it. And you're wrong for once. I'm the one who's let Paul out of *my* clutches for an hour."

"Mmmmm! I see! Well, I must say, he's apparently very good for you. I've never heard you sound better. But why didn't you tell me who he actually is?"

"What do you mean?"

"That he is the only son, the only child, of *the* Bruce McGill. A millionaire and one of the most powerful men in Australia. I suppose you know Paul stands to inherit a fortune. A vast sheep ranch. Mineral rights and mining. Coal fields, and God knows what else."

"He's mentioned the family's various business interests, of course. But how do *you* know so much all of a sudden?"

"I was with Dolly Mosten the other day and she was telling me a few things about Paul—"

"What else did she tell you?" Emma asked suspiciously, her heart sinking.

"Nothing. That was all. She simply remarked that the McGill family was extremely rich and powerful. What's wrong? You sound edgy."

"No, I don't." She laughed. "How are you, Frank? Are you all right, dear?" she inquired, quickly changing the subject.

"Yes, everything is fine. But I'm afraid you've caught me at a bad time, Emma. I can't really talk right now. I have to go into an editorial conference. Can you call me tomorrow so we can chat longer, love?"

"Yes, of course."

"Take care now. Give my best to Paul. Bye."

"Goodbye, Frank."

Emma put the telephone down and stared at it, her face brooding, her thoughts weaving a tortuous web in her head as she contemplated the McGill family, or, more precisely, the mysterious Mrs. Paul McGill. The wife he had never referred to again and about whom she had not dared to question him; had not wanted to know about. But now Emma was unexpectedly eaten up with curiosity. What did she look like? Was she beautiful? How old was she? Why had the marriage gone awry? Did they have children? Was that the reason Paul had never divorced, in spite of his long separation? Emma closed her eyes, crushing the questions flaring in her mind. She would not open Pandora's box. He would tell her everything eventually, she was certain of that, and she did not want anything to mar the time they had left together. This very precious time.

She looked at the clock on the mantelshelf and to her surprise she realized Paul had been absent for over two hours. It was already five-thirty. For no logical reason she was seized by panic. This feeling was irrational, but nonetheless, her nervousness increased, and she had the sudden premonition that Paul would be leaving her imminently. He had carefully refrained from mentioning the date of his departure, but she was aware that two weeks had flown by. In Yorkshire he had told her time was running out. Has it now done so? she asked herself, dismay trickling through her.

To still her disquieting thoughts, Emma hurried into the bathroom and preoccupied herself with her toilet. She took a hot bath, toweled herself dry, sprayed her body with perfume, and went into the bedroom. She put on a long powder-blue panne velvet housecoat she had designed herself and which Paul admired on her. It was in the French Empire style with a high waist, tight bodice, long sleeves, and frogging from the low square neckline to the hem, and it gave her the air of an ingenue. She brushed her long hair and left it hanging loose the way he preferred it, and after she had added a little lip rouge and the emerald earrings she drifted through into the sitting room to wait. By seven o'clock agitation swamped her, and the panic began to disintegrate into real fear. Where was he? Had he had an accident? She clenched her hands in her lap, every muscle tense. And then instinctively she knew. Paul was at the War Office receiving his orders. He was leaving. She was positive this was so. The war! Forgotten for days whilst they had lived blindly in their ecstasy. He might be killed . . . he might never come back . . . She pressed her hands to her aching eyes.

"Here I am, my sweet," he said, coming through the door that linked his suite to hers.

Emma dropped her hands, jumped up, and ran to him, her

face taut. "I thought something had happened to you!" she gasped, grabbing the lapels of his trench coat.

"Nothing is going to happen to me," he reassured her. "I have a guardian angel. And anyway, my time's not up yet. There are all those years earmarked for me. Years to be spent with you. You haven't forgotten that you are my destiny, have you? It hasn't been fulfilled yet, my love."

Her heart began to beat more normally. She looked up at him, smiled, and pulled away. "Your coat is wet through," she said. "You'd better take your clothes off before you catch your death."

His eyes crinkled at the corners with laughter. "That's the best proposition I've had in the last four hours, madame." He winked suggestively.

"Oh, you know what I mean, you wretch!"

"I hope I do," he said. "Give me ten minutes. I've already ordered dinner for nine o'clock, and there's a bottle of champagne cooling in my suite. Excuse me, angel, I'll be right back," he called over his shoulder.

When Paul returned he had changed into civilian clothes. He wore a white silk shirt, a pair of black worsted trousers, and a silk smoking jacket striped in burgundy and black. He looked casually elegant as he carried the champagne bucket to the console. "I think it's cold enough," he said, opening the bottle of Dom Pérignon.

Once more Emma watched him alertly. Just as his eyes normally followed her every moment, now hers were concentrated on him, and she saw him afresh. When he had been gone for a period of time, however brief, she was always startled by the impact his looks had on her when he reappeared. It was no one thing in particular but the sum total of the man. And she was inevitably struck by his commanding manner, the panache with which he did everything.

He caught her staring at him and pursed his lips, grinning with fond amusement. He strode over and handed her the glass of champagne. "I 'aint bin wiv anover leidy, I swear I 'aint," he said, adopting a Cockney accent.

"I 'opes yer 'aint," she said, responding in kind. But her eyes were serious, searching his face, and she was afraid to ask where he had been. "You were gone so long, darling," she murmured softly.

"I had to see my father about a few things. Business

matters to discuss," Paul said, clinking her glass. "Here's to you, my lovely Emma."

"To us."

Paul leaned back in the chair. "I'm afraid I've neglected the old man these last few weeks—"

"It's all my fault!"

"No, it's not. It's nobody's fault," he countered swiftly, and flashed her his boyish grin. "He has an understanding heart—when it comes to matters of the heart."

"Nevertheless, I've deprived him of your company at a crucial time, and kept you away from all of your other friends."

"Ah, but you must think only of the happiness you have given *me* and not be concerned with them. I'm not. It was my choice. I do believe I made the rules, didn't I? Anyway, we could have seen people if I had considered it important. I didn't. There wasn't a soul in the world I wanted to be with but you. Others would have profaned our private world. This special world we have created for ourselves, here in our little cocoon. I didn't want anything to intrude, to shatter the illusion."

"You make it sound as if what we have exists only here!"

He stared at her and an eyebrow went up in a quirk. "No, I don't! Good God, Emma, surely you know this is real wherever we are, and wherever we might be in the future. This is no illusion. This is reality. I've told you that before."

Her heart lifted. "I'm glad it's not an illusory world we have been living in. I would hate to wake up and discover it has all been a dream—"

Paul saw the smile slip, the cloud cross her face. Acutely in tune with her moods, he leaned forward and touched her knee and asked, "What is it, Em? Is something troubling you, darling?"

"You were at the War Office. And then you went to see your father, to say good-bye, didn't you? You're going, aren't you, Paul? And very soon."

"Yes," he admitted quietly.

"When?"

"Tomorrow."

"Oh, my God!"

He crossed to the sofa and took the glass of champagne from her shaking hand and placed it on the table. He drew her close to him, looking into her anxious face. "I read something at Oxford years ago, about lovers who were about to be separated. It has always stayed in my mind. It went something like this: 'This parting cannot be for long; for those who love as we do cannot be parted. We shall always be united in thought, and thought is a great magnet. I have often spoken to thee of reason, now I speak to thee of faith.' "

He saw that her eyes, so steadfastly fixed on his, were filled with tears. He tenderly brushed them away from her long lashes with his fingertips. "Don't, my darling. Please don't."

"I'm sorry, Paul. It was those words. They moved me so. Who said them?" she asked tremulously.

"Abélard to Héloïse. They were uttered centuries ago, but they are as true now as they ever were then. Don't forget them, my Emma, and please have faith. And believe that we will always be united in thought and therefore as one. And know, too, that I will carry you in my heart for the rest of my life."

"Oh, Paul! I love you so much! I cannot bear to be without you!"

His clenched fist came up under her chin, moving against it lightly. "Come along, sweetheart. You must be brave. And we're not going to talk about my leaving anymore. We are going to think only of *now*. There is only *now*. At least until this mess is over." The roguish smile crossed his wide mouth and his eyes swept over her in the old appraising way. "And we do have hours of pleasure ahead of us yet. The whole *night*, in fact," he said. He leered at her theatrically, endeavoring to distract her, wanting to make her laugh. "And, my dear, I must honestly confess that one night with you is worth—"

"Why, you wicked letch! You—you—reprobate," she exclaimed, smiling lovingly through her tears.

"A fairly accurate description of me, I would say, especially when it comes to you." He took her in his arms and moved his lips along the soft curve of her cheek and down the line of her neck. He began to speak in a low voice, using expressions of such love and intimacy the blush rose to her cheeks. She clutched at him, her fingers biting into his arm. Her heart raced as he pushed her back on the sofa, pressed his body against hers, and began to unfasten the buttons on her robe. His eyes were so brilliant she was blinded. She closed her eyes as he brought his lips to hers.

FORTY-SIX

"Amputate!" Emma cried, her face turning deathly white. "But he has been so well for the last few days."

"No, he hasn't. Your brother has been hiding the facts from you, Mrs. Lowther. He has also been refusing to have the operation. Despite our warnings he has been fighting us. But you can't fight gangrene. It's virulent, and ultimately deadly."

Emma sat down abruptly, her eyes pinned on the doctor. "Isn't there an alternative?"

The doctor shook his head. "No, there isn't. Unless you want to call death an alternative." Seeing the fear registering on her face, the doctor seated himself next to her and took her hand. "I'm so sorry. I don't mean to be brutal. But circumstances necessitate honesty, even bluntness, I'm afraid. Time is of the essence."

"What happened, Doctor? I thought you had been able to remove all the shrapnel from his foot and calf."

"We did, but the gangrene set in several days ago and it travels rapidly. It's already above his knee. You *must* sign the papers giving us permission to operate. Otherwise—" He lifted his hands helplessly, his face grave.

Emma swallowed, "But—but—Winston has to make that decision—"

"Mrs. Lowther, don't you understand? Your brother is incapable of making the decision in his present state of mind. *You* must take the responsibility. Now. *Today.* Tomorrow will be too late."

Emma bit her lip and nodded. Her heart was heavy as she said, "Give me the papers, please."

The doctor stepped to his desk, returned with the documents, and handed them to her with the pen. "You are doing the right thing, Mrs. Lowther. The only thing you can do. Your brother will be grateful to you for the rest of his life. Please believe that."

Emma looked at him somberly but made no comment. She signed, and although she was quivering inside, her hand was steady. "May I see my brother now?" she asked dully.

"Yes, of course. I'll take you to him right away," the doctor said. His face was sympathetic as he led her out of the office.

Winston was in a ward with other sailors who had been wounded. Screens had been placed around him, and as Emma walked past them and approached the bed she saw that his eyes were glazed over with pain and beads of perspiration stood out on his forehead. She leaned down to kiss him and he let out a stifled scream, his eyes febrile. Emma pulled back hurriedly in alarm. "Whatever is it, Winston, dear?"

"You touched the bed," he moaned. "I can't stand the slightest movement. The pain is excruciating." He drew in his breath sharply and closed his eyes.

Emma watched him with consternation. After a moment she said with the utmost quiet, "Why didn't you tell me you had gangrene, Winston?"

He opened his eyes and glared at her, the old bravado of childhood momentarily invading his face. "I'm not having it off, Emma!" he cried vehemently. "I'm not going to be a cripple for the rest of my life!"

Emma sat down on the chair near the bed and nodded, her heart aching for him. "I know how you must feel, dear. It's a terrible thing to have to face. But if they don't amputate you'll—you'll die."

"Then I'll die!" he shouted, defiance now supplanting the feverishness in his blue eyes. "I might just as well be dead with only one leg! I'm a young man, Emma, and my life will be over. Finished."

"No, it won't, darling. You will be incapacitated to a certain extent, I realize that. And the prospects must seem terrifying to you right now. But isn't amputation preferable to not being here at all?"

"I'm not having my leg off," he mumbled in a tired voice.

Emma's tone was pleading as she continued, "Winston, listen to me. You must have the operation. *You must*, dear. And immediately. If you delay any longer your whole system will be poisoned." Her voice broke at this thought. "If you won't do it for yourself, then do it for me. *Please! Please, Winston!*" she begged. "I love you very much. Apart from the children, you and Frank are the only family I have—" She groped in her bag for a handkerchief, pulled it out, and blew her nose, attempting to control herself. "I've had too many losses in the last few years, Winston. Mam, Dad, Joe, and Laura. And then Aunt Lily only last week. I don't think I could endure the loss of another loved one. I just couldn't. It would kill me." Tears filled her eyes, and she finished tremulously, "I just couldn't stand it if you died, too, love."

"Don't cry, Emma. Please don't cry, pet." A spasm of pain streaked through him like a ripping knife and he flinched, his face ashen and sweating more profusely now. He sighed. "All right, then, let them cut it off. To tell you the truth, I don't think I can take the pain much longer." A faint smile touched his white lips. "Half a loaf is better than no bread at all, I suppose. You'd better sign the papers and get it over with, Emma."

"I already did."

He mustered a grin. "I might have known. Old Miss Bossy Knickers."

Emma smiled weakly. "It's going to be fine, Winston. I know it is. The doctor is preparing the operating theater now. In a few minutes the nurses will be coming in to get you ready." She stood up. "I have to go. The doctor said I must make it brief. Every minute counts now."

"Emma—"

"Yes, love?"

"Will you—can you wait?"

"Of course I'll wait, dear. I wouldn't dream of leaving until it's all over." She blew him a kiss, not daring to approach the bed again.

Emma gazed out of the window of the waiting room of Chapel Allerton Naval Hospital, her thoughts with Winston, now undergoing surgery. How frightening for him to lose a leg. He who had taken such pride in his good looks, and his virility, who had loved sports and dancing and was so physical by nature. She acknowledged that he would indeed have a number of major readjustments to make, and in many ways he would have to start a new life. But, despite the restrictions the amputation of his right leg would impose, she was thankful he was alive. He had been wounded during a naval battle in the North Sea. His battleship had staggered into Hull half crippled, and it was nothing short of a miracle that the ship had made it to that great Humber port, so fortuitously close to Leeds and the naval hospital. Otherwise he might be dead by now.

Emma leaned her head against the window, closing her

eyes. In a few weeks she would be twenty-nine. Only twenty-nine and yet she felt like an old woman, weary and worn out from her responsibilities these days. A nurse thoughtfully brought her a cup of tea and Emma sat down to drink it—and to wait. That seemed to have become one of her chief occupations of late: *waiting*. Mostly she waited for letters from Paul, feeling crushed and apprehensive when she did not receive one, filled with soaring relief when there was a note, however brief and hastily written.

She took Paul's last letter out of her handbag and read it again. It was worn from too much handling and some of the words had blurred from her tears. He had returned to France to rejoin Colonel Monash and the Australian Corps in the middle of February. Now it was the beginning of April. But he was still safe and well. When Paul had left he had taken an essential part of her with him and she felt incomplete, only half alive without him.

The minutes ticked by slowly. Almost two hours had passed since Winston had been wheeled down to the operating room. Had something gone wrong? Had they been too late? Quite unexpectedly, just when she thought she was going to scream from frustration, the doctor strode in. He was nodding and smiling. "He's fine, Mrs. Lowther."

Emma closed her eyes and exhaled with relief. "Are you sure?"

"Absolutely! He's a little woozy from the anesthetic, but he's young, healthy, and strong. He'll mend well." The doctor's eyes clouded. "There is just one thing—"

"*What?*"

"We had to amputate very high. The gangrene was well above the knee and we had to cut a good four inches above that, to be certain we got it all."

"What does that mean exactly?"

"It means there's the possibility he might not be able to wear an artificial limb."

"My brother's not going to spend the rest of his life on crutches," Emma cried. "Or in a wheelchair. He's going to wear an artificial leg if—if I have to damn well design a special one myself! My brother is going to walk, Doctor!"

And walk he did. But it was a grueling period for Emma. Winston's mood swings were erratic and, not unnaturally, highly emotional. He plunged from relief in being alive to depression, from depression to rage, frustration, and self-pity, and then unexpectedly the euphoria returned, but soon to be replaced by foul black moods. Emma cajoled, threatened, screamed, implored, and challenged, using every ruse she knew to shatter the melancholia that engulfed him and lift him out of it, her only tools her stubborn belief in the indomitability of the human spirit and her conviction that anything was possible in life, *if* the will was strong enough. Slowly she made progress with Winston, badgering him relentlessly, and after several weeks she managed to instill in him the determination to lead a normal life. She gave him strength, and her optimism bolstered his own natural courage.

The Limb Fitting Center at Chapel Allerton Hospital in Leeds was already renowned throughout England for the remarkable feats of rehabilitation accomplished there since the outset of the Great War. The doctors worked painstakingly with the men, especially those who had lost legs, endeavoring to get them ambulatory in the shortest possible time. Winston was no exception. His flesh healed quickly and within two months the doctors had him moving about on crutches. He was fitted for a leg, released from the hospital, and went to live with Emma during his recuperation period. To Emma's relief, when the leg arrived he was able to wear it, in spite of the shortness of the stump. All that was required were two extra stump socks to cushion the stump against the metal. Three times a week he was driven to Chapel Allerton Hospital in one of the Harte vans, where he underwent physical therapy and wore the leg for half an hour at a stretch. And so he commenced the long and difficult task of adjustment to the artificial leg and learning to walk with it correctly.

One day in October, eight months after the amputation, Winston literally strolled into Emma's office, self-confident, smiling, steady on his feet, and in absolute control of the leg, and it was one of the most gratifying moments of her life. His limp was negligible and he had taken her advice, proffered months before, to make the leg an integral part of him.

"I can't dance, but there's not much else I can't do," he informed her proudly. He placed his walking stick on a chair, moved across the room without it, and sat down. "I can certainly move with great speed if I have to and I can climb and descend stairs easily. Believe it or not, I can also swim.

And now that I have the final release from the hospital I am going to look for a job."

"But, Winston, I told you months ago you could come and work for me. Why don't you?"

Winston frowned. "Here at the store? But what would I do?"

"You've always liked figures. I could put you in bookkeeping until you get used to things, and then I would like you to become my assistant. I need somebody I can trust implicitly. Don't forget, I have other businesses, Winston, as well as the store." Emma paused, eyeing him carefully, and finished, "For instance, there's the Emeremm Company."

"What's that? You've never mentioned it before." Winston looked at her with alertness.

"It's a holding and acquisition company, which I formed in 1917." Emma leaned forward. "I financed it myself and I own one hundred per cent of the shares, but it's run for me by a man called Ted Jones. Apart from Ted, and the other directors, no one else knows I'm behind it. Except for you now. I want to keep it that way, Winston. Not even Frank knows, so don't ever discuss it with him."

"I would never talk about your business to anyone," he said quickly. "But why all the secrecy?"

"Mostly because men don't like doing business with a woman, especially in areas of high finance. There are other reasons, personal reasons, but they are not important for the moment."

Winston grinned. "You are a dark horse!" he exclaimed. "And even more successful than I realized. You know, I think I'd like to work for you, Emma. It sounds challenging."

"I'm delighted. You can start on Monday if you like. It's up to you. However, there are a few things you should know about me, Winston, if you are going to work here. First of all, I don't like surprises, especially nasty ones. So you must always tell me everything. And if you make any mistakes, don't hide them. As long as I'm informed they can be corrected. Secondly, I want you to understand something else and this is *imperative*. I never deal from a position of fear. Only from strength, and if I don't have that strength I make damned sure the world thinks I do. You will have to learn to do the same if you're going to act on my behalf. Do you think you can?"

"Yes, Emma."

"Good." Her eyes focused on him intently. "I believe the key to success in business is discipline, dedication, concentration, and patience. And I won't tolerate temperament in business. It is immature. I am not suggesting you are temperamental, but I want you to comprehend that you must always keep a cool head and you must never let emotions get in the way." She smiled. "Any questions, Winston?"

"Yes, quite a lot." He grinned engagingly. "But they can wait until later. Until I start working for you on Monday. Right now I have an appointment."

"Who with?" she asked in surprise.

"With one of the nurses from the hospital. That pretty brunette—Charlotte. I'm taking her out to tea."

Emma laughed gaily. "You don't waste much time, do you? But I'm glad to hear it. Now I know you're really your old self."

Emma had told Winston only half the truth about her attitude towards business. Over the years she had embraced a merciless philosophy—never show weakness, never lose face, never confide. She had also mastered the art of compromise and this instinct towards accommodation had served her well, permitting her to negotiate and maneuver with more flexibility than many of her competitors, who were rigid. Since she had a particular aversion to conflict and confrontation, she preferred always to move in roundabout ways and if necessary with stealth, and she was to acquire much of her power by stealth.

Later that afternoon, when Winston had left, she moved covertly in the direction of the Fairleys and struck a deadly blow at their business enterprises. Her strategy was simple: she manipulated a weak and foolish man, who blithely, if unwittingly, put Gerald Fairley exactly where Emma wanted him—in her clutches.

This development had not occurred by accident. One of the first purchases the Emeremm Company had made in 1917 was Procter and Procter, a wholesale cloth warehouse in Bradford. Emma bought it for several reasons. It was a sound investment, even though it had been mismanaged over the years. Also, the sprawling warehouse sat on a prime piece of land in the center of Bradford, and Emma knew this land

could only increase in value over the years. But aside from
the company's potential, Alan Procter, the owner, was a
crony of Gerald Fairley's and Emma had recognized that here
was a conduit to her sworn enemy, a source of vital informa
tion about the latter's activities.

At first Alan Procter had been reluctant to sell, despite the
fact that he had run the company into the ground, had
innumerable creditors and personal debts, many of them due
to his inveterate gambling. However, the Emeremm Compa
ny's terms were so appealing they inevitably won Procter
Emma had made the terms irresistible. The purchase price
was fair without being so excessive as to create suspicion
More importantly to Procter, he was offered a contract to
remain as chairman of the board at a salary he could no
afford to dismiss. There was one clause—Procter must no
reveal the change of ownership of his company. If he did his
contract would be instantly terminated.

Seeing his problems miraculously disappearing before his
eyes, the venal and exigent Procter had not bothered to
question the necessity for this secrecy. In fact, he had rather
welcomed it, envisioning a means of continuing to run his
company, at the same time solving his personal and business
debts and saving face in Bradford. He sold, signed the em
ployment contract with its secrecy-of-ownership clause, and
in so doing became the property of Emma Harte. Emma had
instructed Ted Jones to put an Emeremm man inside Procter
and Procter. "Procter is merely a front. I want his hands tied
so that he cannot do any further damage to the business. And
whoever you put in must ingratiate himself with Procter
Become his confidant."

Her scheme worked. Procter had a loose tongue, especially
after it had been well oiled over splendid luncheons with the
new managing director—the Emeremm man. All manner of
useful information came filtering in to Emma about Procter's
associates in Leeds and Bradford, many of them her com
petitors, and prominent amongst it was a great deal about the
Fairleys.

Through Procter Emma learned early in 1918 that Gerald
Fairley was in dire straits with Thompson's mill and wanted
to sell. "Buy it for as little as possible," she coldly told Ted
Jones. Using Procter and Procter as the purchaser, the
Emeremm Company acquired Thompson's. Believing he was

selling to Alan Procter, an old and trusted friend, and because of his strained financial situation, Gerald Fairley had accepted a quarter of the mill's true value, to Emma's immense satisfaction.

Now a piece of new information had landed on Emma's desk that very morning, and it had brought her head up with a jolt. Gerald Fairley had lost heavily at cards and had gone running to Alan Procter. He wanted to borrow two hundred thousand pounds. Procter had blabbed to the Emeremm man and had inquired about the possibility of making a corporate loan to Gerald Fairley.

Emma's vivid eyes rested on the memorandum again and a curious glint entered them. She recognized that here was the opportunity she had been waiting for and she seized it, moving with her usual swiftness. She picked up the telephone and spoke to Ted Jones at the Emeremm Company in London. "You can inform Alan Procter he can make that corporate loan to Fairley."

"What are the terms, Mrs. Harte?"

"I want a noncontestable one-hundred-eighty-day note. But I want the note collateralized."

"What kind of collateral, Mrs. Harte?"

"The deeds to the Fairley mills in Armley and Stanningley Bottom."

Ted Jones sucked in his breath. "Rather steep terms, wouldn't you say?"

"Those are my terms," Emma said icily. "Gerald Fairley can take them or leave them. It's no skin off my nose either way. He won't be able to raise the money anywhere else. He's in too deep with the banks. I also happen to know he has borrowed heavily from some of his father's old business associates. He owes Procter money personally as well." She laughed dryly. "Where is Mr. Gerald Fairley going to go, Ted?"

"You have a point there. I'll pass on the terms to our man at Procter and Procter and he can relay them to Alan. I'll get back to you later this afternoon."

"I'm in no hurry, Ted. I'm not in trouble. It's Fairley who is sinking."

"Yes, he is. The damned fool. It takes some sort of genius or ineptness to suffer losses in wartime when every other

cloth manufacturer has made a fortune from governmen
contracts."

"That's very true. Goodbye, Ted." She hung up.

Emma leaned back in her chair and a gloating smile settlee
on that beautiful face. It's all happening sooner than I ex
pected, she thought. It struck her then that she did not have
to make a serious effort to destroy the Fairleys. Gerald wa
doing it for her. Ever since Adam Fairley had been felled b
a stroke Gerald had been in total control of the mills an
without his father's guidance he was floundering. All I have
to do now is sit back and watch him dig a pit so deep he wil
never climb out, Emma said to herself.

Later she acknowledged that Gerald would undoubtedl
fight the Procter and Procter terms, but he would have t
accept them eventually out of the necessity to save his skin
And he would never be able to raise the money to pay off th
note on its due date. But she could afford to be generous
She would extend the note for a few months and thus lul
Gerald Fairley into a greater sense of false security. Whe
she was ready she would foreclose on the note and take ove
the Fairley mills. Emma laughed. She had Gerald Fairle
cornered and he was in complete ignorance of the fact.

As she had suspected, Gerald Fairley at first balked at th
terms and backed off from the proposition for longer than sh
had anticipated. To her considerable amusement she hear
he was running around endeavoring to raise the money h
required. He was miserably unsuccessful. After four days
panic-stricken and dealing from a position of increasing des
peration, he finally slunk back to Alan Procter and signed th
noncontestable corporate note to which he had been forced t
attach the deeds of the two Fairley mills. He did so because
once again, he thought he was dealing with a friend whom h
believed would never make a move to endanger the owner
ship of his mills.

One week later, when Emma placed the note and th
deeds in her safe, her triumph was unalloyed.

FORTY-SEVEN

David Kallinski pulled the car to a standstill outside Emma's house, and turned to her. "Thanks for working this morning, Emma. It was good of you to give up part of your Sunday with the children."

Emma smiled. "I didn't mind. Really, I didn't, David. Actually I was glad to get the summer sketches for the Lady Hamilton line out of my hair, and I knew you were anxious to put them into work immediately." She opened the car door. "Are you sure you won't come in for a drink?"

"No. Thanks anyway, but I've got to be going. I promised my father I'd stop in to see him." He caught her arm abruptly. "Emma, there's something I want to tell you."

So intense was his voice Emma was alarmed. "Is there something wrong, David?"

"I'm thinking of getting a divorce."

Thunderstruck, Emma gaped at him in disbelief. "A divorce! My God, David!" She hesitated, and then said, "Aren't things quite right between you and Rebecca?"

"No better than before the war." He cleared his throat. "I'm finding life intolerable since I came home. I might as well be honest with you—" He broke off, staring at her closely. "I'm still in love with you, Emma. I thought if I was free— Well, I had hoped you would marry me."

Emma stiffened, taken unawares, and shaken by his proposal. "Oh, David, David." She touched his hand clenched on the car wheel and said, "My dear, you know that's not possible. I didn't make that sacrifice nine years ago, when you were single, in order to create a catastrophe now that you are married. It would kill your mother. Besides, you have two young sons and I have two children. There are other people to think about, as well as Rebecca and yourself. I told you years ago that it's not possible to build happiness on other people's misery, and I know I'm right."

"But what about you and me, Emma?" he asked, his eyes filling with pain.

"There is no you and me, David." Sharply conscious of his

disappointment, she said softly, "I hope I haven't done anything to encourage you, David. Surely I haven't built up your hopes, have I?"

He grinned ruefully. "No, of course you haven't. And I haven't spoken out before now because I've been doing a lot of soul searching. Finally, last week, I knew I had to tell you how I felt. Being silent was accomplishing nothing. You see, I always thought you loved me, even after you married Joe. All through the war I believed that. It kept me going, kept me alive, in a sense. My feelings are exactly the same as they were and so I assumed yours were, too. But you don't love me anymore, do you?"

"Oh, David, darling, of course I do. As a dear friend. To be truthful, I *was* still in love with you when I married Joe. Now I have a different kind of love for you, and I am different. The vicissitudes of life do intrude and ultimately feelings change as well. I've come to understand that the only thing that is permanent is change."

"You're in love with someone else, aren't you?" he exclaimed with a flash of intuition.

Emma did not answer. She dropped her eyes and clutched her handbag tightly and her mouth slipped into a thin line.

David said, "I know the answer to that, although you are silent. You don't have to spare my feelings," he announced crisply but without rancor. "I ought to have guessed. Nine years is a long time. Are you going to marry him?"

"No. He's gone away. He doesn't live in this country. I don't think he will ever come back." Her voice was muffled.

David detected the sorrow and defeat in her and, despite his own hurt, sympathy surged up in him, for he truly loved her and had her welfare at heart. He put his hand on hers and squeezed it. "I'm awfully sorry, Emma."

Emma looked at him through dulled eyes. "It's all right. My wound is almost healed—I hope."

"There's no chance for me, is there, Emma? Even with him out of the picture."

"That's true, David. And I will always tell you the truth, although it is often distressing to hear. I would not intentionally hurt you for the world, and there's very little I can say to comfort you, I suppose. Please forgive me, David."

"There's nothing to forgive, Emma. I can't condemn you

for not being in love with me anymore." His eyes were soft. "I hope you find peace yourself, Emma darling."

"I hope so, too." She opened the door. "No, please don't get out." She kissed him on the cheek. "Think carefully before you do anything rash about Rebecca and your marriage. She is a good person and she does love you. And remember that you are very special to me, David. I'm your friend and I'm always here if you need me."

"Thank you for that. And I'm your devoted friend, too, Emma, and if there's anything I can do to make things easier for you, now or later, you know I will." He smiled. "It seems we're both crossed in love. If you need a strong shoulder— well, it's here."

"Thank you for being so kind and understanding." She attempted to smile. "I'll see you at the factory as usual next week. 'Bye."

"Good-bye, Emma darling."

Emma walked up the garden path without looking back, her feet crunching on the hard snow, her head bent. She was filled with compassion for David, conscious of his dejection, and his suffering was her own. Her face was stark in the bleak winter light as her thoughts swung abruptly to Paul. She stopped at the front door, and took a deep breath before going inside. She took off her coat and hat in the hall, looked in on Mrs Fenton, who was preparing Sunday lunch in the kitchen, and then wearily climbed the staircase to the nursery.

It was the week before Christmas in the year 1919. Exactly twelve months ago Paul McGill had been in this house with her and the children and her brothers. The Great War had finally ended in November, and Paul had come to stay with them before returning to Australia to be demobilized. It had been a joyous Christmas, full of gaiety and love. Emma had been giddy with happiness, and more deeply in love with Paul than she had believed possible. She had felt as if everything she had always yearned for and desired was hers at last. Hers forever. But now she had nothing . . . a broken heart and loneliness and despair. How foolish she had been to have believed it could be otherwise. Personal happiness always eluded her. And how different this Christmas would be. Her hand rested on the doorknob of the nursery. She thought: I *must* make an effort and be cheerful for the children's sake.

Kit was seated at the table painting. His eyes lit up and he jumped down and skittered across the floor. He flung himself at Emma. "Mummy! Mummy! I'm so glad you're home," he shouted, hugging Emma's legs.

She kissed the top of his head. "Good gracious, Kit, whatever have you been doing? You seem to have more paint on yourself than there is on the paper. And what are you painting, sweetheart?"

"You can't see it! Not yet. It's a picture. For you, Mummy. A Christmas present." Kit, who was now eight years old, looked up at Emma, wrinkling his nose and grinning. "You can have a peek if you want."

"Not if it's meant to be a surprise."

"You might not like it, Mumsie. If you don't, I can paint another one. It's bestest you have a look, just in case. Come on." Kit grabbed Emma's hand and dragged her across the room.

"Best, not bestest, darling," Emma corrected, and looked down at the painting. It was childlike, awkwardly composed, out of perspective and splashed haphazardly with gaudy colors. It depicted a man in a uniform. Emma held her breath. There was no doubt in her mind who it was meant to be. Not with that thick black smudge across the upper lip and the bright blue eyes. "It's very good, darling," Emma said, her face pensive.

"It's Uncle Paul. Can you tell? Does it look like him? Do you really like it, Mummy?"

"I do indeed. Where's your sister?" Emma asked, changing the subject.

"Oh, stuffy old Edwina's in her room, reading or something. She wouldn't play with me this morning. Oh well, who cares! I want to finish this painting, Mummy." Kit climbed back onto the chair, picked up the brush, and attacked the painting with renewed vigor and enthusiasm. A look of concentration settled on his freckled face. "I must get it just right for you, Mums. I think I'll put a kangaroo in it. And a polar bear."

"Don't you mean koala bear, Kit?"

"Well, a *bear*, Mummy. Uncle Paul told me there were bears in Australia."

"Yes, dear," Emma said absently. "Lunch in half an hour, Kit. And don't forget to tidy up before coming down." She rumpled his hair and hurried out to her own room, feeling the need to be alone to collect her scattered thoughts.

Winter sun was pouring in through the tall windows and the room was awash with rafts of pristine light. The deep peach walls and the matching carpet had taken on a golden hue and the pale green watered silk covering the bed, the sofa, and several small chairs held a faint shimmer as though shot through with silvery gray. Georgian antiques, their patinas mellow, punctuated the room with dark color and the crystal lamps with their cream silk shades cast a warm glow against the rosy walls. A fire blazed in the white marble fireplace and the ambiance was cheerful. Emma hardly noticed her surroundings. She stood in front of the fire warming her hands, the old iciness of childhood trickling through her limbs. Her head throbbed and she felt more depressed than usual.

David's declaration of his love for her and her subsequent rejection of him had served to underscore the searing torment Paul McGill had caused her. Always prominent in her mind, this feeling was now more rampant than ever, and she felt utterly defeated. After a moment she crossed to the chest of drawers and opened the bottom drawer. She pushed her hands under the silk nightgowns and lifted out the photograph of Paul. She had placed it there weeks ago, no longer able to bear the sight of it on her dressing table. Her eyes rested on that well-loved face, took in the direct gaze of the eyes underneath the thick brows, the smile on the wide mouth, and her lacerated heart ached. Unexpectedly, a furious anger invaded her and she hurled the photograph across the room with great force, her eyes blazing.

The moment it left her hand she regretted her immature action and ran to pick it up. The silver frame had been dented and the glass had shattered, but to her relief the photograph was undamaged. She knelt on the floor, gathering up the broken glass and placing it in the wastepaper basket. She sat down in the chair by the fire, hugging the photograph to her, thinking about Paul. The photograph had been taken the preceding January, just prior to his leaving England, when they were staying at the Ritz together. He was wearing his major's uniform and looked incredibly handsome. She saw him then, in her mind's eye, standing on the platform at Euston, before he boarded the boat train. He had tilted her

face to his and looked deeply into her eyes, his own spilling
with love. "I'll come back, my dearest darling. I promise I
will be back before you know I'm even gone," he had said.
And she, imbecile that she was, had believed him.

She looked down at the picture. "Why didn't you come
back. Paul? You promised! You vowed nothing could keep
you from me!" Her question echoed hollowly around the
room, and she had no answer for herself, once more baffled
and wracked with despair. Paul had written to her twice and
she had replied immediately. To her surprise he had never
responded to her second letter. At the time, wondering if it
had gone astray, she had written again. This letter had also
remained unanswered. Finally, swallowing her immense pride,
she had penned a circumspect note, and then had waited for
word from him. The weeks had turned into months, and the
silence had been absolute. In a state of bewilderment and
shock, she had done nothing. She had lost her nerve. By
October, Emma had miserably resigned herself to the fact
that Paul was not man enough to write and tell her that he no
longer loved her. That it was over. It was the only conceivable conclusion she could draw in her heartsick state. He
simply has no further use for me, she thought. I served a
purpose when he was alone in England. He has resumed his
old life in Australia. *He is a married man*.

Emma leaned back, staring into space abstractedly, her
face cold and set, her eyes wide and tearless. She had cried
all the tears she would ever cry for Paul McGill, night after
night for months past. Paul McGill did not want her and that
was that. There was nothing she could do about it. . . . .

"Mother, may I come in?" Edwina asked, poking her head
around the door.

"Yes, darling," Emma said, slipping the photograph under
the chair and forcing a smile. "Did you have a nice morning?
I'm sorry I had to go to the factory on your day. It was an
emergency."

"You work too hard, Mother," Edwina said reprovingly.
She sat down in the opposite chair and smoothed her tartan
kilt.

Emma disregarded the remark and the offensive tone and
said cheerfully, "You haven't told me yet what you would like
for Christmas. Perhaps you would like to come to the store
with me next week and look around, darling."

"I don't know what I want for Christmas," Edwina said, her silvery eyes observing Emma. "But I would like to have my birth certificate, please, Mother."

Emma froze in the chair. She kept her face bland. "Why do you want your birth certificate, Edwina?" she asked, adopting a mild voice.

"Because I need it to get a passport."

"Good heavens, why do you need a passport?"

"Miss Matthews is taking the class to Switzerland next spring and I am going, too."

Emma's sweeping brows puckered together. "I notice you have simply assumed you are going. You haven't asked my permission. I find that quite dismaying, Edwina."

"May I go, Mother?"

"No, Edwina, you may not," Emma said firmly. "You are only thirteen. In my opinion that's far too young for you to be traveling to the Continent without me."

"But we will be chaperoned. Most of the girls are going. Why can't I?"

"I have *told* you why, dear. You are too young. Furthermore, I find it hard to believe that most of the girls are going. How many exactly will there be in the group?"

"Eight."

"That's more like it! Eight girls out of a class of twenty-four is merely a third. You are prone to exaggerate sometimes, Edwina."

"So I can't go?"

"Not this coming year. Perhaps in a couple of years. I will have to give it some careful thought. I'm sorry to disappoint you, but you should have discussed it with me first. And my decision is quite final, Edwina."

Knowing that it was useless to argue with her iron-willed mother, Edwina sighed theatrically and stood up. *She hated her*. If her father were alive he would have let her go abroad. She smiled at Emma, craftily concealing her dislike. "It's not that important," she said, and glided across the room to Emma's dressing table. Picking up the brush, she began to brush her waist-length silver-blond hair, staring with total absorption in the mirror. Emma watched her with mounting annoyance, her eyes narrowing as she saw the self-gratified smile on her daughter's face revealed in the glass.

"You know, Edwina, for a little girl, you are terribly vain. I don't think I've ever seen anyone gaze into a mirror as often as you do."

"Now *you're* exaggerating, Mother," Edwina countered haughtily.

"Don't be impertinent," Emma said crossly. Her patience was worn thin this morning and her nerves were on edge. But regretting her flash of temper, she said in a lighter tone, "Your Uncle Winston is coming to tea today. You'll enjoy that, won't you, darling?"

"Not particularly. He's not the same since that woman got him."

Emma suppressed a smile. "Your Aunt Charlotte hasn't *got* him, Edwina, as you so curiously put it. She's married to him. And she's awfully nice. You know, too, that she is very fond of you."

"He's still not the same," Edwina said stubbornly. She stood up. "I have to finish my homework, Mother. Please excuse me."

"Yes, dear."

When Emma was alone she returned Paul's photograph to the drawer, her mind preoccupied with Edwina's request for her birth certificate, a disastrous development she had not anticipated. She ran downstairs to the study, closed the door firmly behind her, and telephoned Blackie in Harrogate.

"Hello, me darlin'," Blackie said.

"Blackie, something perfectly dreadful has happened!"

He heard the fear in her voice. "What's wrong, Emma?"

"Edwina just asked me for her birth certificate."

"Jaysus!" He recovered himself swiftly. "Why does she suddenly want her birth certificate?"

"To get a passport for a school trip to the Continent next year."

"You refused, I presume."

"Of course. But the day will come when I can't stall her, Blackie. What am I going to do?"

"You'll have to give it to her. But not until she's old enough to handle the situation, Emma." He sighed. "This was bound to happen one day."

"But how will I explain your name on the certificate? She thinks Joe was her father."

"You could let her think that I really *am* her father."

"But that's such a responsibility for you, Blackie."

He laughed. "I have a broad back, me darlin'. You should know that by now." His voice changed perceptibly, and he went on, "Of course, you could tell her who her real father is. But I don't suppose you want to do that, do you, Emma?"

"No, I definitely do not!" Emma made a decision, drew in her breath, and plunged. "You know who he is, don't you?"

Blackie sighed softly into the phone. "I can hazard a guess. She looks too much like Adele Fairley for me to be in doubt any longer. It was Edwin, wasn't it?"

"Yes, Blackie," Emma responded quietly, and felt a sudden rush of relief that she had finally told him the truth. "But Edwina will never know. Must never know. I have to protect her from the Fairleys all of her life."

"Then you will just have to let her believe that I am her true father. I don't object, Emma." He chuckled quietly. "Come on, me darlin', relax. I can feel your tension coming over the wire. Forget this little problem for the moment. Delay as long as you can. You're a clever woman. You can skirt the issue for several years. At least until she's seventeen or eighteen."

"I suppose I can," Emma said slowly. "We're never free of the past, are we, darling?"

"No, mavourneen, that's the sad truth, I'm afraid. But let's not dwell on the past. It's fruitless. Now you haven't forgotten me party on Boxing Day, have you?" Blackie went on in an effort to distract her. "The party for me new house. It's a beauty, Emma, even though I do say so meself."

"Of course I haven't forgotten. I wouldn't miss it for anything. Frank is coming to Yorkshire for Christmas and he's promised to bring me. And I'm longing to see the house. You've been so secretive about it."

"Ah, but you'll be recognizing it the minute you see it, Emma. It's exactly the way I described it to you all those years ago on the moors. Me fine Georgian mansion right down to the last detail."

"I'm so thrilled for you, Blackie. It was always one of your dearest dreams."

"Aye, that's so. Emma, I must hang up. I can see me beautiful Bryan coming up the drive with Nanny. Now don't you worry about that birth certificate. Forget it for the next year or so. We'll deal with it only when it's absolutely necessary."

"I'll try. And thank you, Blackie. You're always such a comfort to me."

"Sure and its nothing, mavourneen."

Emma hung up the telephone and sat lost in introspection, her mind dwelling on her daughter. There was something so unapproachable about her, an innate coldness in her nature, and Emma was aware at all times of a curious disapproval in Edwina's manner, and she was often at a loss to deal with it effectively.

How will I ever find the courage to face that child with the truth? she asked herself. How can I tell her without losing the little affection she has for me? She flinched at the thought of a confrontation, however far off it was, and for the first time in months Emma momentarily forgot about Paul McGill and her own misery.

Blackie O'Neill strolled across the magnificent entrance hall of his Georgian mansion in Harrogate, his arm around Winston's shoulders. He ushered him into the library and locked the great double doors behind them.

"Why are you doing that?" Winston asked, looking puzzled. "I thought we came in here for a quiet brandy."

"True. True. But I want to talk to you privately and I don't want any interruptions."

"Who would interrupt us? Everyone's too busy enjoying the party."

"Emma, for one."

"Ah! You want to talk about my sister. Is that it?"

"It is indeed." Blackie busied himself at the console, pouring generous amounts of the Courvoisier into two brandy balloons.

From his stance by the Adam fireplace, Winston watched Blackie, wondering what he had on his mind. He shook his head in bafflement and glanced around with admiration, appreciating the elegance of the furnishings and the beauty of the setting. The bleached pine walls, interspersed with bookshelves, were balanced by forest-green velvet draperies, and a carpet of the same color covered the center of the mahogany parquet floor. A number of deep sofas and armchairs were upholstered in lighter green velvet and rose damask, and this warm color highlighted the cool greenness. Tables, consoles, and a fine desk in the mingled designs of Sheraton and Hepplewhite graced the room, and a spectacular Waterford crystal chandelier dropped down from the soaring ceiling. The library, like the rest of the new house, was a splendid tribute to Blackie's sense of perspective and color and his knowledge of the decorative style of the Georgian period.

Looking exceptionally handsome and prosperous in his dinner jacket, Blackie handed Winston a balloon of the cognac. "Cheers, Winston," he said.

"Cheers, Blackie."

Blackie selected a cigar, clipped off the end, lit it slowly. He puffed on it for a few seconds and finally fixed his bright black eyes on Winston. "When is she going to stop all this foolishness?"

"What foolishness?" Winston demanded with a frown.

"Throwing money around. She's gone crazy in the past six months. At least so it seems to me."

"Emma's not throwing money around. In fact, she's not very extravagant with herself at all."

Blackie raised a black eyebrow quizzically and a faint smile flitted across his mouth. "Now, Winston, don't play the innocent with me. You know damn well what I mean. I'm talking about the way she's been plunging into the commodities market. Recklessly so, I might add."

Winston grinned. "Not recklessly at all. She's made a fortune, Blackie."

"Aye, and she can easily lose it! *Overnight!* Speculating in commodities is the most dangerous game there is, and you know it."

"Yes, I do. And for that matter, so does Emma. She *is* something of a gambler in business, Blackie. We're both aware of that. However, she's also astute and she knows what she's doing—"

"It's all much too chancy for my liking! She could easily be ruined!"

Winston laughed. "Not my sister. You've got to admit it takes real genius to start out with nothing and build what she has so brilliantly built. Only an idiot would be stupid enough to risk throwing it all away. Emma's nobody's fool and, anyway, she stopped buying and selling commodities several weeks ago."

"Thank God for that!" Blackie looked relieved, but his tone

was worried as he continued, "Still, I am concerned about all this rapid expansion she's undertaken. The new stores in Bradford and Harrogate were admittedly good buys, but the renovations she insists I make are going to be very costly. And I couldn't believe my ears tonight when she told me she's thinking of building a store in London. As usual, her ideas are pretty grandiose. To be honest, Winston, I was dumbfounded. How the hell is she going to pay for it all? That's what I want to know. It's my opinion she's overextending herself."

Winston shook his head adamantly. "No, she's not! She's as smart as a whip and never does anything rashly. How is she going to pay for it? I just told you she made a hell of a lot of money in commodities. And she has been selling off Joe's remaining properties for very high prices. In fact, she's gradually divested herself of all the real estate he left her, except for that plot of land in the center of Leeds. She's hanging on to that, because she thinks it will increase in worth, and you know she's right. The store in Leeds is in profit and, also, this boom in the cloth trade since the end of the war has turned Layton's into a bigger moneymaker than it ever was. Orders are pouring in from all over the world and Ben Andrews has had to put most of the workers on overtime to meet them. The Gregson Warehouse is fully operating again, and don't forget, Emma is David Kallinski's partner—"

Pausing, Winston eyed Blackie with amusement. "Does that answer your questions about how she intends to pay for everything?"

Blackie had the good grace to laugh. "Aye, me boyo, it does." He shook his head wonderingly. "She's obviously become a very rich woman—richer than I had imagined, from what you tell me."

Winston nodded, a proud look on his face. "How much do you think she's worth?" he said with a spontaneity he instantly regretted, since he could not tell the truth.

"I couldn't even hazard a guess."

Winston took a sip of brandy to hide his hesitation. He could not admit Emma's true worth, because he dare not reveal the existence of the Emeremm Company and her ownership of it. Therefore he selected a conservatively low figure and said, "A million pounds. That's on paper, of course."

"Jaysus!" Blackie exclaimed. He knew Winston was not

lying or exaggerating and he was immensely impressed. Blackie lifted his glass. "That deserves a toast. Here's to Emma. She has surpassed us all, I do believe!"

"To Emma." Winston eyed Blackie thoughtfully. "Yes, she has. Do you know why? Do you know the secret of my sister's great success?"

"Sure and I do. I attribute it to a number of qualities. Shrewdness, courage, ambition, and drive, to name only a few."

"*Abnormal* ambition. *Abnormal* drive, Blackie. That's the difference between Emma and most people. She won't allow anything to stop her and she will go for the jugular with a business adversary, especially if her back is against the wall. But those are not the only reasons for her success. Emma has the killer instinct to get to the top."

"Killer instinct! That's a hell of a thing to say about her. You make her sound ruthless."

"She is in some ways." Winston could not help laughing at Blackie's startled expression, and said, "Don't tell me *you've* never recognized that trait in her!"

Blackie pondered, recalling incidents from the past. "At times I have thought her capable of ruthlessness," he murmured slowly.

"Look, Blackie, enough of all this. I hope I've alleviated your worries about her."

"Yes, you have. I'm glad we had this talk, Winston. I've been concerned about that commodity lark ever since she mentioned it. Scared the hell out of me, if you really want to know. Well, now we've got that out of the way, shall we go back to the party?"

"Whenever you wish. Incidentally, talking of killers, I notice the lady-killer is on the prowl tonight. He can't take his eyes off Emma and he's certainly fawning all over her."

Blackie was alert and interested. "Who are you talking about?"

"Why, Arthur Ainsley, of course. The great hero of the war—according to him. Conceited bastard."

"I always thought Emma didn't like him."

"I wouldn't know about that. I wasn't around, remember? But she did tell me that he'd changed and she seems unperturbed by his attentions tonight."

"I hadn't really noticed," Blackie said curtly, and stood up with abruptness. He was preoccupied as they returned to the drawing room. Immediately upon entering, Winston drifted off to join Charlotte and Frank, and Blackie ambled over to the piano. He leaned against it nonchalantly, but his full attention was focused with intensity on Emma, who was engaged in conversation with Frederick Ainsley and his son Arthur.

Blackie thought Emma looked particularly lovely tonight, if a little paler and wistful. Her hair was worked into a coronet of plaits atop her head and the upswept style made her face seem more delicate than ever. She wore a white velvet gown, cut low and off the shoulder, and pinned onto one of the small sleeves was the emerald pin he had given her for her thirtieth birthday. It was the exact replica of the cheap little green-glass bow he had bought for her when she was fifteen, but larger and more exquisitely worked. He had been gratified at her obvious surprise that he had remembered a promise made so long ago, and thrilled at her delight in the costly gift. Now, to him, it looked like a trumpery bauble in comparison to the magnificent emerald earrings that sparkled with such brilliance at her ears.

Automatically his hand went into his pocket, his fingers curling around the jewelry box that reposed there. It contained the diamond ring he had purchased last week. He had intended to ask Emma to marry him tonight. After their recent conversation about Edwina's birth certificate and the dilemma it posed, he had finally made the decision he had been toying with for months. Lately he had come to understand that if he did not love Emma in quite the same worshipful and spiritual way he had loved his Laura, love Emma he did. He had always loved her, ever since she had been an innocent child, his starveling creature of those bleak and misty moors. Her happiness was important to him. He found her physically alluring, she amused him, and he valued her friendship. Apart from his own deep attachment to her, Bryan adored her and his darling Bryan needed a mother. Also, Blackie had concluded, if he married Emma perhaps the sting would be taken out of the blow Edwina would receive when she discovered her illegitimacy. He would be like a father to the child, would try to replace Joe in her affections. If she learned to love him in return, then she might not be so resentful when she saw his name on the birth certificate, and he would willingly give her his name legally.

All in all, he had thought his idea foolproof—until Winston's revelations a few minutes before. Suddenly Blackie saw Emma in a wholly different light, saw her now as a woman of undeniable power and enormous wealth. He had never underestimated her, for he was too intelligent by far for that. He had simply not realized or, in fact, recognized exactly what she had become, being too subjective to focus on her as a woman of the world and a successful tycoon. He himself had done well, but she had more than outstripped him, and David Kallinski, and in the most staggering manner. Furthermore, he now admitted that she would never be like a normal woman, dedicated to a husband, a family, and a home. She could never be wrested from her business. In many ways it *was* her.

Blackie was no longer sure she would accept him as a husband and, perhaps more cogently, he was uncertain of his ability to handle her. And so Blackie O'Neill, thirty-three years old, charming, rich, and hitherto a man of self-assurance and élan, lost a fraction of his confidence because of Emma's incredible achievements. And he faltered in his determination to propose.

He caught Emma's attention and she excused herself from the Ainsleys and glided over to him. "It's a lovely party, Blackie, and I can't get over the house. It's superb." She looked up at him, her eyes glittering vividly in that pale oval. "And it *is* exactly as you said it would be, with your light greens and blues and fine Georgian furnishings." She laughed. "Do you remember when I asked you who Hepplewhite, Chippendale, and Sheraton were?"

"I do. I also remember I told you then that you would be a grand lady one day. My prediction came true."

She smiled.

Blackie became aware of Arthur Ainsley's eyes on them and he said with a frown, "I always thought you couldn't stand young Ainsley, but tonight you appear to to quite kindly disposed towards the fellow."

"Oh, he's not so bad. He's much more intelligent than I thought and amusing. Actually, I find him rather charming as well."

Blackie's eyes flared. "Aye, he is. If he weren't a Sassenach I'd swear he'd kissed the Blarney stone," he pronounced.

Emma laughed at Blackie's sarcastic retort and admitted, "Yes, I suppose he is a bit too smooth sometimes. But at least he's entertaining and easy to be with."

"Have you been spending a lot of time with him?" Blackie asked evenly enough, although he experienced a twinge of jealousy.

"No, not at all. I only see Arthur on business matters. Why?" She gave him a puzzled look.

"No particular reason. I just wondered. Incidentally, talking of business, where do you intend to build your store in London?"

"I've found a large piece of land in Knightsbridge, and I can get it for a good price. I would like you to see it." She touched his arm. "Could you come to London with me next week, darling?"

"Sure and I'd be delighted. If you go ahead with the purchase I can start the plans immediately. I'll build you a magnificent store, Emma. The best in London."

They talked for a while about the intended department store. Emma expounded her ideas, which were grandiose, but her enthusiasm was so infectious Blackie found himself growing unexpectedly excited about the challenge she was presenting to him and his talents. After a little further discourse, Blackie seated himself at the piano and began to play. He sang a number of amusing Irish jigs and Emma sat back, as always enjoying his marvelous voice. Many of the guests thronged around the piano, just as they had done in the Mucky Duck, and Emma remembered the old days, and smiled to herself. And then she froze as Blackie's rich baritone rang out again, pure and clear, in the opening strains of "Danny Boy." Familiar words invoked in her a terrible yearning and a sadness that was overwhelming.

His voice swelled and filled the room as he commenced the second verse: "But when ye come, and all the flow'rs are dying—"

Emma could not bear to listen any more. She slipped out of the room, her heart tearing inside her, and her throat was choked as she thought of Paul, and only of him: gone from her forever.

Frank and Winston exchanged alarmed glances and Frank

shook his head as Winston rose. "I'll go. You stay here with Charlotte." Frank followed quickly on Emma's heels and caught up with her in the entrance hall. He took her arm and propelled her into the library without saying a word. He closed the door, put his arm around her shoulders, and then said, "He's not coming back, Emma. You might as well face the facts."

"I have, Frank," she responded in a low resigned voice.

"You know I would never interfere in your life, but I can't stand to see your heartbreak any longer, Emma. There are certain things I must tell you. That you must know. I can't hold them back."

Emma looked at him warily. "What do you mean?"

"Paul McGill is married."

"I know, Frank dear. I've always known."

"I see." His sensitive mouth settled into a grim line.

"I suppose Dolly Mosten told you," Emma ventured.

"Yes, she did."

"Dolly's a gossip! She had no right to—"

"I asked her, Emma. Forced her to tell me, in point of fact. Only out of concern for you, though."

"Oh," Emma said, and stared down at her hands miserably.

"So Paul told you he was married. I suppose he also promised to get a divorce."

"He said he'd sort it all out after the war," Emma whispered, conscious of the venom in Frank's voice.

She fell silent and Frank went on furiously, "Did he tell you he's married to the daughter of one of the most prominent men in Australian politics and that her mother is from one of Sydney's first families?"

"No, he never discussed his wife."

"*I bet he didn't!* I bet he didn't tell you he had a child either."

Emma gaped at Frank, her lip trembling. "A child!"

"Yes. A boy. I gather he refrained from passing on that piece of vital information."

"He did," Emma confessed, her heart sinking. A wife he was estranged from she might have been able to compete with, but she could not fight a child. A son. Men as wealthy as Paul McGill pinned all of their hopes on the new generation, on the heir to the dynasty. He would never give up his son for her.

"I need a drink," Frank said, standing up. "And so do you, by the looks of you." He poured a glass of champagne for Emma and a brandy for himself, observing his sister closely. By God, she *is* a strong woman, he thought admiringly. He knew she was shocked and distressed, but she was in full control of herself. He said, "I'm so sorry I had to hurt you, love, but you had to know."

"I'm glad you told me, Frank." She laughed bitterly. "You certainly gave Dolly a grilling, didn't you?"

"You'd be surprised what a woman will confide to her lover, especially in the intimacy of the bedroom."

"You and Dolly! Frank, I don't believe it!" she cried incredulously.

"Yes, for the moment anyhow."

"But she's years older than you."

"Ten to be exact. However, I don't think my relationship with Dolly is the issue right now, is it?"

"No, it's not." Emma leaned forward intently. "How does she know so much about the McGills?"

"She used to be Bruce McGill's mistress several years ago."

"Philandering seems to be a family characteristic!" Emma exclaimed contemptuously. "What else did she tell you? I might as well know all the details."

"Not much, really. Mostly Dolly talked about their wealth and their power. Actually, she didn't seem to have much information about Paul's wife or his son. In fact, I rather got the impression there was a bit of a mystery about the wife. Dolly said something about Paul always appearing alone in public, even in Sydney before the war, and she indicated that he is a—" Frank stopped short, and looked down at his drink.

"A *what?*"

Frank cleared his throat. "Well, if you must know, Dolly implied he is a womanizer."

"I'm not surprised, Frank. Don't be upset you told me."

Frank tossed down the brandy. "I'm not upset. I'm just angry that you have been hurt." He rose and crossed to the console, returning with the bottles of cognac and champagne. He filled Emma's empty glass and said, "I always liked Paul. I didn't think he was such a bastard. Just goes to show you how wrong one can be in life. Why don't you tell me about it, Emma? It sometimes helps to unburden yourself."

Emma smiled grimly. "I doubt it. But I'll tell you anything you want to know, Frank. Perhaps *you* can explain his behavior to me."

As Emma confided in Frank she slowly drank the whole bottle of champagne and for the first time in her life she deliberately got drunk. When Winston appeared in the doorway an hour later he stared at her in surprise. "You're three sheets to the wind, Emma!" he cried, moving with unusual swiftness across the floor.

Emma lifted the glass and waved it in the air, spilling half of the champagne. "Splishe the brashemain. I mean splishe the mainbrashe," she slurred, and hiccuped.

"How could you let her get so pie-eyed, Frank!" Winston exploded in an accusatory tone. He regarded Emma reclining languorously on the sofa, her eyes half closed, her mouth twitching with silent laughter. "She'll have some head tomorrow," he muttered crossly.

"So what? Don't be so harsh, Winston," Frank said quietly. "For once in her life I think she really needed to let her hair down."

FORTY-EIGHT

Edwin Fairley's face was grim and there was a cold anger in his eyes as he said, "You put the noose around your neck all by yourself, Gerald. There is absolutely nothing I can do to help you."

Gerald gaped at his brother in stupefaction. His sly black eyes, narrowing in the bloated face, appeared smaller and more evil than ever. "Are you telling me that Procter and Procter are really within their legal rights? That they can take over the mills just like that?" he asked fearfully.

"Yes, I'm afraid I am, Gerald. A noncontestable note is just that—noncontestable. And since you attached the deeds as collateral you don't have a leg to stand on if you can't pay off the note. That was most foolhardy. Why did you do it?"

"I needed the money," Gerald muttered, unable to meet Edwin's direct stare.

"To pay off your blasted gambling debts! I *know* that. I

mean, why did you hand over the deeds to the mills without seeking legal advice first? If not from me, at least from the family solicitor."

"There would have been no point to that. I needed the money desperately. I had nowhere else to go and those were the only terms acceptable to Procter and Procter. My talking to the family solicitor wouldn't have changed *their* minds. I had no option, and anyway I thought Alan would be reasonable. Give me time to repay the loan." A bitter look slid onto Gerald's face. "As it is, Alan Procter has turned on me. He's a bloody thief! He's stolen my mills!"

"Don't be ridiculous, Gerald," Edwin countered impatiently, staggered at his brother's lack of business acumen. "Alan hasn't stolen the mills. You handed them to him on a plate. I'm appalled by your lack of foresight. Furthermore, from what you have just told me, Alan has been very understanding. The note was for six months. It's been extended three times, for an additional period of eight months all together. I would say he has been exceptionally considerate under the circumstances. After all, it was a company loan. Alan has a board of directors to answer to."

Gerald dropped his head in his hands, overcome as always by self-pity. After a few minutes he looked up and said in a demanding voice, "You have to lend me the money, Edwin."

Edwin sat bolt upright on the chesterfield and stared at Gerald in amazement. "Are you joking! I don't have two hundred thousand pounds, plus the interest due. You must be mad to think I do."

"Father left you a trust, Edwin. You *must* have it. You don't want to help me out of a jam," Gerald whined.

"The income from my trust is meager and you know it!" Edwin cried, infuriated. "Father lived lavishly all of his life and spent lavishly, particularly after he married Aunt Olivia. What he left me was negligible compared to what you received, and you've thrown most of it down the drain." Edwin glared at Gerald with disdain. He then said, "Besides, as little as it is, I need the income from the trust. *I* have a wife and son to provide for and a household to maintain."

"But you're doing well in your law practice—"

"Yes, but not well enough to support your bad habits!" Edwin snapped peremptorily.

"Father left you the majority of his shares in the *Yorkshire*

Morning Gazette. You could borrow against them," Gerald said, scowling at his brother.

"I could, but I have no intentions of doing so. I promised Father I would hold on to them and take an active interest in the newspaper and I will not renege on my promise," Edwin responded with firmness. "I can't understand how you could get yourself into such a predicament—"

"Don't start giving me another bloody lecture!" Gerald shouted, lumbering out of the chair. He began to pace up and down the library, his cringing fear palpable.

He is a coward and a fool, Edwin thought, scrutinizing his brother. Gerald's gluttony had only increased over the years and he was now elephantine and gross in his ugliness, and the dissipation of his life was revealed on his ravished face. To Edwin, Gerald appeared obscene and he looked away in revulsion.

Gerald plodded over to the black-walnut chest and poured himself a large neat whiskey. "I don't suppose you want a drink, do you?" he mumbled without looking around.

"No, thank you," Edwin snapped. "I have to be going."

Seating himself opposite Edwin, Gerald pinned his crafty eyes on him. "You believe yourself to be the brain in the family, so you tell me what to do, brother," he said scornfully.

"Listen to me, Gerald. Things could be worse for you. After all, you still own the mill here in Fairley and the brickyard. I suggest you tighten your belt, cut down on personal expenditures, stop gambling, and retrench in every way. Devote your attention to the one mill you still have. I don't know much about the woolen business, but only a fool could fail to realize the cloth trade is booming. Actually, I don't understand why the Fairley mill isn't going better. Surely you can turn it around."

Always full of self-justification, Gerald countered in a defensive tone, "Things are different than they were in Father's day. You don't know the burdens I have to carry. There's a hell of a lot more competition now, Edwin. Thompson's makes the same cloth as us and they've swiped many of my customers of late. So has your bloody Emma Harte. She owns Layton's mill, in case you didn't know, and she's giving me a run for my money as well. If the truth be known, she helped to ruin me. My problems started when she stole Ben Andrews and some of the best workers away from Thompson's in

1914." Gerald's voice echoed with invective as he declared, "Yes, your bloody whore has been a thorn in my side for a long time. The bloody little whoring bitch. She's—"

"Don't let me hear you call Emma a whore ever again! Do you hear me, you filthy bastard!" Edwin cried, clenching his hands and leaning forward threateningly. His face had whitened and his eyes blazed.

Gerald grinned derisively. "Still carrying the torch for the servant girl, eh, Edwin? Whatever would the Lady Jane say if she knew you had an itch in your crotch for that bit of working-class—"

"That's enough, you rotten swine!" Edwin shouted, springing up. It took all of his self-control to restrain himself from hitting Gerald in the face. "I drove over to Fairley with the best of intentions, hoping to help you with legal advice. I did not come to listen to your obscenities about Emma," he said furiously. He glowered at Gerald and his contempt was so clearly written on his face Gerald shrank back in the chair. Edwin went on, "I happen to be very proud of Emma. She's made something of herself and she's a damned sight better than you. You—you—piece of scum!" Edwin stepped away from his brother abruptly, conscious that he was prepared to inflict bodily damage on him if further provoked. "Good-bye. You won't be seeing me for a long time."

Gerald taunted, "You're too transparent, Edwin. So Emma Harte's in your blood, is she? My, my, my! She must have something sweet between *her* legs to hold your interest all these years. Tried to make it with her myself once when I found her living in Armley—"

"You did what!" Edwin, who was halfway to the door, spun around and shot across the library. He leapt at Gerald, clutched his lapels, and shook him fiercely, his rage exploding. "If you so much as rest your eyes on Emma I will kill you! Kill you! I swear to God I will!" Edwin's face, so close to his brother's, was twisted with a mixture of loathing and deadly intent, and this registered forcibly with Gerald, who flinched, suddenly afraid.

Edwin let go of Gerald's lapels and wiped his hands on his trouser legs with the utmost distaste, his lip curling. "I don't want to soil myself by touching you," he hissed. *"You are a foul specimen of humanity! You are contemptible!"* He turned on his heel and walked out, his limbs shaking, his head spinning with unbridled hatred and disgust.

FORTY-NINE

Emma stepped out of her shoes, took off the tailored black dress she always wore at the store, removed her jewelry, and placed it all on the dressing table. Discarding her underwear, she slipped into the silk robe the maid had put out for her and hurried into her bathroom.

As she stood in front of the oval gilt-framed mirror tying a chiffon scarf around her recently bobbed hair, she smiled as she always did when she entered this particular room in her new mansion. It was too opulent by far, and when Blackie had shown her the original plans for its remodeling she had told him it looked like a cross between the Hall of Mirrors at Versailles and a courtesan's boudoir. Not that she had ever seen anything like the latter—only the former, when she and Arthur Ainsley had gone to Paris on their honeymoon three years before. Over her mild protestations that it was excessively grand, Blackie had insisted on executing the design intact, exhorting her to trust his judgment. To her amazement, she had actually liked the bathroom when he had finally completed the overall decor, deriving a certain sensuous satisfaction from its luxurious appointments.

The walls were lined with shell-pink marble, intersected with wide panels of mirror running from the floor to the ceiling for an infinity of endless reflections. The domed ceiling was a pale turquoise blue across which cavorted pink dolphins and sea urchins intertwined with delicate green tendrils of seaweed and vivid pink and mauve sea anemones. The turquoise oval tub was sunken into the pink marble floor and two leaping silver dolphins, each one foot in height, stood sentinel at the top and bottom, and the taps were miniature silver dolphins. On a narrow mirrored console table reposed innumerable bottles of French perfumes and Floris bath oils and silver-topped crystal pots for her creams and lotions. Blackie had also included a chaise longue upholstered in rose silk at one end, along with a mirror-and-glass Art Deco coffee table. At the other side of the chaise a huge garden basket painted pink overflowed with all the latest

fashion and illustrated magazines and financial journals. The
ambiance was feminine, and this one room in the house had
become Emma's haven, a place of repose where she could
retreat to unwind after her busy days at the store.

Emma poured Floris gardenia bath oil into the water the
maid had already drawn and, removing her robe, she stepped
into the tub. She stretched out her long legs, luxuriating in
the heavily scented water, her thoughts turning to the supper
dance she was giving that evening. Since her marriage to
Arthur they had entertained on an increasingly lavish scale,
yet this was undoubtedly the most elaborate social event she
had planned to date and she was looking forward to it. The
dance was to celebrate Frank's engagement to Natalie Stewart, the daughter of a prominent London politician, a match
Emma had approved of from the beginning and which she
had enthusiastically helped to foster. Apart from the fact that
Natalie was a lovely young woman, Emma had been relieved
to see her brother released from Dolly Mosten's clutches.
Natalie was a lady to the manner born, and if her exquisite
blond beauty seemed somewhat delicate, Emma knew it
belied a stalwart heart and a backbone of steel. Increasingly
she reminded Emma of her beloved Laura.

Emma had spared no expense on the dance, determined to
do justice to Frank's engagement. The house looked magnificent, each one of the spacious reception rooms resplendent
with fine antiques and paintings, filled with color and banked
with masses of spring flowers. Since the elegant mansion was
three times as large as the house she had formerly owned in
Armley, it lent itself to entertaining in the grand manner and
Emma had become a charming hostess whose spontaneous
grace put her guests at ease.

The catering department of Harte's had provided a superb
supper and the dishes had been arranged on a long buffet
table in the formal dining room. Emma considered the menu
she had chosen. There were two soups, jellied consommé and
cream of watercress served in cups, salmon mousse, smoked
salmon with capers and lemon wedges, lobster patties, may-
onnaise of turbot, beef Wellington, turban of chicken and
tongue, quenelles of pheasant, roasted spring lamb with mint
sauce, tomatoes à la tartare, French beans, and pomme soufflé.
The desserts were baba au rhum, compote of fruit, trifle,
parfait, apricot snow, and almond cake, and there was an

assortment of drinks, including champagne, claret cup, white and red wines, cider, fruit juices, coffee, and tea. The selection was wide enough to appeal to the most discerning or pernickety of palates, Emma decided, and made a mental note to congratulate the chefs at Harte's, who had surpassed themselves for the occasion.

The one hundred guests would dine at small tables covered with pink cloths and partnered with gold chairs, which had been arranged in the dining room, the library, and the morning room. After supper there would be dancing in the long marble gallery overlooking the gardens, and those who did not wish to dance could enjoy conversation in the two lovely drawing rooms. The band engaged for the evening had already arrived and when she left the gallery the musicians were setting out their instruments. Faintly, wafting up on the night air, came the strains of a popular song as the band warmed up. Everything was in hand. Nothing had escaped her, and there was a small army of waiters and maids, plus her own staff, to look after the guests. Arthur had told her earlier that she had organized everything with the efficiency of a general planning war maneuvers. Emma closed her eyes, feeling languorous as the tensions of the day slipped away.

Meanwhile, in the adjoining suite of rooms, Arthur Ainsley dressed for the evening, as preoccupied with the details of his appearance as Emma was with the plans for the dance. He stepped back from the cheval mirror and regarded his reflection with immense concentration, well pleased with what he saw.

At thirty-two Arthur still carried the air of a juvenile lead, this impression further emphasized by his dandified dress and elegant mannerisms that often bordered on the effeminate. He shot his cuffs below his jacket sleeves, adjusted the black-onyx-and-diamond dress studs on his shirt, and reached for the comb on the nearby commode. For the fourth time he ran it through his soft blond hair, patted the waves precisely into place, and smoothed one manicured finger over the neat blond mustache he favored. He then put down the comb and drew himself up to his full height, raptly absorbed with his image.

Regrettably, Arthur Ainsley did not have much to recommend him in his character. All of his life he had been so concerned about his exterior beauty he had made no effort to acquire any inner resources. Consequently, he was a shell of a man, and his very shallowness caused him to put store only on what was readily visible. Not unintelligent, educated at the best schools, Arthur was, however, so indolent and self-involved he was utterly unable to retain any serious thoughts for very long. He was cursed with a single-minded concern for pleasure, and his perpetual need for instant gratification was infantile in nature. Thus, although he loved the outward manifestations of wealth and success, he did not have the ability to acquire them for himself, being averse to hard work, lacking in diligence, and without the power of concentration.

Arthur moved away from the mirror, glancing at his platinum-and-diamond pocket watch. He had dressed too early and now he had an hour to waste before the guests were due to arrive at ten o'clock. He reached into one of the drawers of the commode and took out a bottle of brandy. He started to pour himself a drink and then hesitated, grimacing at the thought of Emma's disapproval.

Arthur Ainsley had been seeking refuge in the bottle for the past eighteen months, ever since he had discovered he was impotent with Emma. He believed he drank because of his impotency but, in point of fact, he drank to excuse it. It was so much easier to blame the liquor than face the real reasons for his inadequacy, which were highly complicated. Critical self-examination was alien to Arthur's vainglorious nature and so he was uncomprehending of the causes. In truth, he had become impotent with Emma because he was a latent homosexual and also because his wife was everything he was not.

Emma had done nothing at all to emasculate him. Simply by being herself she had caused him to suffer damage to his self-esteem. Thus, he now sought out women who bolstered his male pride. Chiefly his targets were shopgirls, waitresses, and barmaids, who, flattered by his attentions, fawned over him.

Arthur's feelings about Emma were continually vacillating. He frequently desired her, yet his constant fear of sexual failure isolated him from her; he needed her strength and her wisdom, whilst resenting these attributes; he boasted of her achievements but was envious and insecure because he did not measure up in his own career. In his way, Arthur loved

Emma. Unhappily, he also harbored many grudges against her, at the root of which was his terrible sense of powerlessness. This manifested itself in repressed rage, and sometimes he actually experienced a real hatred for her.

Always drawn to Emma during her marriage to Joe Lowther, he had pursued her unavailingly for months after his return from the war. Then unexpectedly, at Blackie O'Neill's on Boxing Day night of 1919, she had seemed to thaw toward him and, being exceedingly opportunistic, Arthur had pressed his suit with a rare show of determination in the new year, egged on by his ambitious parents. After a whirlwind courtship of three months they had been married in the spring of 1920.

Arthur had believed that Emma was as smitten with him as he was with her, his vanity not permitting him to think otherwise. In all truth, Emma had married him for wholly different reasons. The terrible implications of Paul McGill's silence and continuing absence from England had devastated her and her anguish had become too painful to bear. Her increasing loneliness had prompted her to reassess her life. Plain common sense had led her to conclude that there was no future for her with Paul, and she acknowledged that to yearn for him was not only foolish but inevitably self-destructive. She tried to put Paul out of her mind completely, deciding that she must lead a more normal life for her children's sake as well as her own. Convinced that she would never again experience the same kind of sublime love she had had with Paul, she sought instead a companion, a man who was easy to be with. She also wanted a father for her children and a suitable male head for her household. In short, she was prepared to compromise, to settle for less out of necessity and in the belief that great love was not always a prerequisite for a happy marriage.

At first amused by Arthur's most transparent and eager overtures, Emma had come to view him as the perfect solution to her problems. He was a gentleman and came from a good family. He also had charm and handled himself with a degree of elegance in all situations. He was amusing, attentive to her needs, and enamored with her. Furthermore, Emma liked beauty and had strong aesthetic instincts, and she found Arthur attractive. If he aroused no great passion in her, he likewise did not repulse her, and she had decided she could easily tolerate the physical aspects married love entailed, concluding that other factors in their relationship were of more vital consideration to her. Emma knew Arthur was weak, yet curiously she turned a blind eye to faults in his character for several fundamental reasons: Arthur did not threaten her; she recognized that he would never interfere with her business or the manner in which she led her life; she instinctively knew that she would always retain the upper hand. These reasons aside, he had a winning way with her children and treated them with a naturalness she appreciated.

Emma wanted to obliterate Paul McGill by involving herself in a new relationship. She was determined to marry quickly, and Arthur appeared to be the most suitable candidate on the horizon. Expedient by nature, she plunged ahead, seeking action and commitment in preference to waiting. Her unprecedented imprudence stunned her brothers and Blackie, who met such icy imperiousness when they tried to interfere they immediately retreated, recognizing it was fruitless to offer advice once she had made up her stubborn mind.

Ruefully Emma acknowledged her error after only a few weeks of marriage, but by then it was too late. She had conceived on their honeymoon. It had not taken her long to discover that Arthur's charm was meretricious, and his wit often as cruel as it was entertaining. He was captious, and his shallowness and indolence appalled her. Also, his sexual appetite was as voracious as Joe Lowther's had been, although Arthur displayed more finesse and he did not induce physical revulsion in her. Nonetheless, Emma soon found their lovemaking burdensome because it was only Paul she loved and desired.

But she was honest enough to admit that she had made the mistake, and because she took her obligations seriously, Emma endeavored to maintain a civilized front and simulated passion whenever necessary. In the beginning the union was relatively tranquil, mostly due to Emma's expert dissembling. Arthur, unaware of her feelings, was euphoric at his good fortune in winning this beautiful, accomplished young woman, and he basked in Emma's prestige and enjoyed the privileges that came with her money. He was, for the most part, considerate and acquiescent. Unhappily, after the twins, Robin and Elizabeth, were born in 1921 he grew careless and offhand with Emma, confident that his marriage was secure now that he had fathered two children by her, and convinced of her devotion to him.

During Emma's confinement, Arthur had taken to amorous adventuring, and having acquired a taste for the excitement inherent in illicit relationships, he found them increasingly impossible to forgo. Then when he and Emma resumed their marital intimacy, he was unable to fire up his ardor sufficiently for effective consummation. After several disastrous experiences Arthur had retreated into his own room. To his relief Emma never questioned his absence from her bed. In his vanity he ascribed this to her preoccupation with her business, the children, the demands of a large household, and her nervousness about becoming pregnant again so soon after the birth of the twins. It never occurred to him that she loved another man, and as the months passed his complacency increased, as did his arrogance.

As Arthur contemplated his appearance, Emma climbed out of the tub and dried herself briskly. She stood for a moment in front of one of the mirrored panels, gazing at her body with detached interest. Her full breasts were high and firm, her thighs gently rounded, her stomach flat. She had kept her figure; considering she would be thirty-four next month, and had borne four children, she looked amazingly youthful. There was nothing matronly about her shape, thanks to her busy schedule and her singular distaste for rich foods that sprang from the deprivations of her spartan childhood. Turning away, she put on the silk robe and padded into the bedroom.

Seating herself at the dressing table, Emma picked up a silver monogrammed hairbrush, her head held on one side. She was delighted she had decided to cut off all her hair last week. She liked this new bob that was all the rage. The style suited her and was absolutely perfect with her new haute couture clothes from Vionnet and Chanel. There was a sudden loud knock and Emma swung around as Arthur strode in. Emma stared at her husband, surprised by his unexpected appearance. She pulled the robe around her swiftly and suppressed a stab of impatience, resenting the intrusion. She was finding it increasingly difficult to maintain a cordial front with him these days.

"Really, Arthur, you quite startled me."

"Did I just!"

Emma's eyes lighted on the drink in his hand. "You're starting a bit early, aren't you?" she said, striving to hide her annoyance.

"For God's sake, don't start that again!" he cried, walking over to the yellow velvet sofa. He draped himself on it and threw her a scathing look. "You can be such a crashing bore, my dear. A real killjoy, as a matter of fact."

Emma sighed, recognizing his mood. "We are facing a long evening, Arthur. I don't want you to—"

"Get drunk and disgrace you, my pet," Arthur interjected. "Emma must never be upset. God forbid that should happen," he snapped with a flash of arrogance. "What am I supposed to do all evening? Tread in the Queen's shadow?"

Ignoring the jibe, Emma turned to the dressing table and picked up a bottle of Guerlain's L'Heure Bleu. She dabbed the crystal stopper behind her ears and, not wanting to provoke a quarrel, she changed the subject. "I had a sweet letter from Kit today. He sends his love. He's enjoying school. I'm so glad I sent him to Rugby. He's in his element."

"Yes, that was a good idea of *mine*, wasn't it?" Arthur smirked. "I do have quite a lot of them, you know, if only you would give me half a chance. Instead you treat me like an idiot."

After a moment's silence, Emma said, "I have to finish dressing. Did you come in for something in particular, Arthur?"

"Oh yes, I did, by Jove!" Arthur answered, looking up. "I thought I had better glance at the guest list. Refresh my memory."

"It's on my desk." Emma shifted in the chair and took a pair of superb teardrop diamond earrings out of a jewel case and screwed them on absently.

"Rather a distinguished crowd we're having," Arthur remarked, scanning the list and noting the names of a number of beautiful and possibly acquiescent ladies amongst the guests. Wanting suddenly to make his escape, he threw the list on the desk and edged to the door. "I think I'll go downstairs and take a look around." He pulled out his watch. "It's nine-thirty. I'll leave you now so that you can dress."

"Thank you. I would appreciate that." Emma watched him saunter out. She shook her head, pondering on Arthur. If he was a fool, then she was surely a monumental fool. This mess was all her fault. How curious it was that she never made the same mistake twice in business, yet continually repeated them in her personal life. Loving David Kallinski, she had deliberately married Joe . . . loving Paul McGill, she had plunged into matrimony with Arthur. But the circumstances were different, she told herself. David had been forbidden to her because of the Orthodoxy of his mother. Paul had abandoned her because he did not want her. Still, it seemed that she had a penchant for picking the wrong men as husbands. Joe was decent, though, she mused, whereas Arthur is worthless. "Marry in haste, repent at leisure," she said, remembering her brother's words of warning. Damn my stubbornness, she muttered.

Emma stood up purposefully. She could not dwell on this disastrous marriage tonight. She would think about it later. Tomorrow. She hurried to finish dressing and stood staring at herself in the mirror of the armoire. Her gown was a long slender sheath of turquoise silk encrusted with thousands of tiny bugle beads in shades of pale blue and emerald green. When she moved, however slightly, it undulated and changed color in the way a summer sea ripples from blue to green to aquamarine. The gown emphasized her svelte figure and brought out the color of her incomparable eyes. With her diamonds and pearls she was the epitome of elegance. If outward appearances counted for ought, then apparently she had everything. A handsome husband, lovely children, good looks, wealth and power. The world envied her.

The carriage clock on the mantelshelf chimed ten and roused Emma from her reflections. She left her bedroom and stood poised at the top of the curving staircase for a brief moment. And then she picked up one side of her skirt and swept down to greet the first of her guests, who were just arriving. Her famous smile was intact, but her heart was covered with a layer of frost.

FIFTY

The butler who opened the door of Fairley Hall was a middle-aged man they did not know.

Blackie said, "Good afternoon. My name is O'Neill. I have an appointment with Mr. Gerald Fairley."

"The Squire's expecting you, sir," the butler replied, opening the door wider. "Please come this way." He led them across the huge gloomy entrance hall and showed them into the library. "He will be with you in a moment. Please make yourselves comfortable." He bowed and retreated.

When the door had closed Blackie said, "Murgatroyd must have retired."

"He's dead," Emma said. "He died two years ago."

"And Cook?" Blackie asked, remembering Elsie Turner with fondness.

"She's still alive. But she doesn't work here anymore. She's too old. She lives in the village."

Blackie strolled over to the fireplace and stood with his back to the flames, warming himself. "Well, how does it feel—being back in this house after all these years?"

Emma threw him a swift glance. "Rather strange, I must admit." Her cool green gaze swept around the room and she laughed mirthlessly. "Do you know how many times I dusted this paneling, beat these carpets, and polished this furniture?" She shook her head wonderingly, and her mouth unconsciously tightened into a grim line.

"So many times I expect you've forgotten by now," Blackie said.

"I never forget anything," Emma replied crisply.

She walked slowly around the library, regarding the furnishings with interest. She had once thought this room so impressive, but in comparison to the library in her house in Roundhay it looked dreary and there was an unmistakable air of dejection about it. April sunshine was flooding in through the tall windows and the bright light focused attention on the overall shabbiness. The Persian carpets were threadbare, their once vibrant red-and-blue jewel tones dimmed by time, and

the velvet draperies at the windows were faded, the uphol-
stery on the wing chairs badly worn. Even the ruby-colored
chesterfield was dark and muddy, and the leather was cracked.
Emma recognized that the antiques were fine and obviously
of value, as were the many leather-bound books and hunting
prints, but withal the room's dreadful neglect was patently
obvious.

Emma shrugged and glided over to a window to look out.
In the distance the wild implacable moors soared up before
her eyes, a grim black line undulating beneath a clear spring
sky, a sky the color of her mother's eyes. She had a sudden
longing to go up to the moors, to climb that familiar path
through the Baptist Field that led to Ramsden Crags and the
Top of the World. The place her mother had loved the most,
up there where the air was cool and bracing and filled with
pale lavender tints and misty pinks and grays. That was not
possible today. Innumerable memories assailed her, dragging
her back into the past. She closed her eyes, and heard the
sweet trilling of the larks, could almost smell the scent of the
heather after rain, could feel the bracken brushing against
her bare legs and the cool wind caressing her face . . .

From his position at the fireplace Blackie scrutinized Emma,
held in the grips of his own memories. He thought of the day
he had first met her, so long ago now. This imperious and
distinguished woman standing before him bore no resemblance to his poverty-stricken colleen of the moors. He shook
his head, marveling at her and all she had become. At thirty-
four, Emma Harte Ainsley was undoubtedly at the height of
her beauty, a beauty so staggering it startled and bewitched
everyone. Today she wore an expensive and fashionable silver-
gray wool-crepe suit trimmed with sable and a smart sable
hat. His emerald brooch gleamed on the collar of her gray
silk blouse, matchless pearls cascaded from her slender neck,
and the magnificent emerald earrings were just visible below
her stylishly bobbed hair. She was not only elegant but
cultivated and self-assured and she exuded an aura that bespoke undeniable power.

Emma swung around unexpectedly and was immediately
aware of Blackie's eyes resting on her with such intensity.
She laughed lightly. "Why are you staring at me? Is my slip
showing?"

Blackie grinned. "No, I'm just admiring you, me darlin'. Just admiring you. And also remembering—so many things."

"Yes," Emma said slowly, a thoughtful look drifting onto her face. "This place does evoke all kinds of memories, doesn't it?" She smiled faintly, stepped to the desk in the corner, and placed her suede bag on it.

"Aye, it does." Blackie lit a cigarette, drew on it, and shifted his stance. "Fairley's taking his sweet time. I wonder what he's trying to prove."

"Oh, who cares." Emma shrugged. "Anyway, we're not in a hurry." She sat down at the desk, the desk which had once been Adam Fairley's, and leaned back in the chair. She pulled off her gray suede gloves slowly, smiling to herself. She examined her hands. Small strong hands and certainly not the most beautiful in the world. But they were white and soft and the nails were polished to a soft pink sheen. They were no longer red and chapped from scrubbing and scouring and polishing . . . no longer the hands of the skivvy who had been in bondage in this grim house.

The door flew open and Gerald Fairley entered, dragging his great weight, his steps lumbering. He did not see Emma, who was in the shadows, and he hurried over to Blackie, his hand outstretched.

"Good afternoon, Mr. O'Neill." He looked Blackie over with unconcealed interest. "I thought your name was familiar when you made the appointment. Now I remember you. Surely you used to do repairs here when I was a boy."

"That's correct," Blackie said, stepping forward and shaking Gerald's hand. "Pleased to meet you again, Mr. Fairley." Not having set eyes on Gerald for many years, Blackie was astounded at the man's hippopotamic body, his ruined face, and his apparent dissipation. Gerald was so physically repugnant Blackie shuddered with distaste.

"Never forget a face," Gerald went on. "Now, may I offer you a drink before we get down to business?"

"No, thank you," Blackie declined politely.

"I need a brandy myself. Always do after lunch." Gerald plodded over to the black-walnut chest and poured himself a generous measure of cognac. As he turned around, glass in hand, he spotted Emma seated at the desk. His porcine eyes opened wide and a look of disbelief spread itself across his blubbery face. "What the hell are *you* doing here?" he bellowed.

"I am with Mr. O'Neill," Emma responded softly. Her face was without expression.

"*You* bloody well know how to make yourself at home, don't you!" Gerald exploded, still incredulous. "How dare you take such a liberty! Sitting at my desk!"

"I believe it is my desk now," Emma said in the softest voice, her eyes fixed unwaveringly on Gerald.

"Your desk! What the hell are you talking about?" Gerald stomped into the middle of the room and swung to face Blackie, his manner bellicose. "What does she mean, O'Neill? What is the explanation for all this! I sold Fairley Hall to Deerfield Estates. You yourself told me on the telephone that you represented them, and had been engaged to do the renovations. So why in God's name is *that* woman in my house? You had no right to bring *her* here." He did not wait for Blackie's answer, but heaved his monstrous body to face Emma. "Get out! Get out!" he yelled. "Get out, do you hear me! I will not tolerate your presence at this private meeting."

Emma remained perfectly still. Not even an eyelash flickered. She smiled darkly. "I have no intentions of leaving. And I do have every right to be here, *Mr*. Fairley," she pronounced with cold disdain. "You see, *I am Deerfield Estates*."

For a moment Emma's words did not sink into Gerald's befuddled mind. He continued to glare at her uncomprehendingly, and then, as if a veil had been miraculously lifted, he stuttered, "Y-y-y-you are Deerfield Estates—"

"I am indeed." Emma opened her purse and took out a piece of paper. She gave it a cursory glance and looked across at Gerald. "Yes, this desk *is* listed on the inventory, just as I thought. I purchased it along with some of the other contents. And, since you have already cashed the check from Deerfield Estates, this is *my* desk, as this is undoubtedly *my* house. I have paid for them."

Reeling, Gerald fell into one of the wing chairs. What had she said? That she was the owner of Fairley Hall? Emma Harte, the servant girl they had once employed! Never, not in a thousand years! The idea was unthinkable, outrageous. Gerald's eyes swiveled to Blackie, standing calmly at the fireplace, his hands in his pockets, a faint amused smile playing on his mouth.

"Is it true?" Gerald asked, his voice unsure. "Is she telling the truth?"

"Yes, she is," Blackie replied, endeavoring to keep his face straight. By God, he would not have missed this scene for the world.

"Why didn't you tell me she was coming with you when you made the appointment?" Gerald now demanded in an accusatory tone.

"It was not my prerogative to do so," Blackie said, taking out his cigarette case.

Gerald stared at the drink in his hand, all manner of vindictive thoughts flashing through his addled brain. Good Christ, if he had known this little tramp was connected with Deerfield Estates he would not have sold the house to them. He must cancel the sale at once Yes, that was undoubtedly the right thing to do. And then sickeningly he recalled her words of a moment ago. He *had* cashed the check and spent all the money. He had used it to pay off some of his gambling debts. He was trapped. He lifted his shaking hand and tossed down the drink in one gulp.

Emma flashed a glance at Blackie and her green eyes below the curving golden brows sparkled. She rose and walked sedately over to the chesterfield. She sat down, gracefully crossed her legs, and studied Gerald. "Under the terms of the sales contract you should have vacated this house by now," she said in a light, clear voice. "I will give you one more week to do so."

Gerald blinked and shook his head so vigorously his chins wobbled. "That's not long enough," he whined. "You've got to give me more time."

"One week," Emma repeated. She paused and her gleaming eyes narrowed. "Furthermore, I must insist you remove all of your personal belongings from your office at the Fairley mill immediately. Today. By five o'clock, in fact. Otherwise they will be packed in cardboard boxes and deposited in the mill yard to be retrieved by you at your convenience. By five o'clock today."

Gerald was jolted upright in the wing chair, and he stared at Emma thunderstruck. He opened his mouth to speak but no words came out, so undone was he. He sat gaping stupidly, paralyzed by his spiraling fear.

Emma continued icily, "I am not wrong in thinking you sold the Fairley mill two weeks ago, am I? To the General Retail Trading Company."

"What's that got to do with you?" Gerald spluttered, rousing himself. He was obviously perplexed as he added, "General Retail Trading is a division of Procter and Procter, which is owned by my friend Alan Procter."

"I am well aware of General Retail Trading's connection with Procter and Procter," Emma said. "However, you are slightly misinformed. Procter and Procter is, in turn, a subsidiary of the Emeremm Company. It does not belong to Alan Procter. It has not belonged to him for some years. He is merely an employee of the parent company." She sat back, watching him.

"Alan Procter never mentioned that to me," Gerald muttered. A most terrible and unacceptable thought now entered his swimming head. He asked haltingly, "Who owns the Emeremm Company?"

"I do," Emma said, smiling thinly and enjoying the expression on Gerald's face. "Consequently, I control Procter and Procter and the General Retail Trading Company, as well as Deerfield Estates." She leaned forward, clasping her hands together. "Therefore, I now own all of your mills, as well as Fairley Hall."

"You!" Gerald screamed, half rising. "It was you!" He fell back into the chair, seized by an uncontrollable shaking, and then he experienced a stab of pain in his chest, one so acute it knocked the breath out of him. He clutched his chest and the shaking increased. He thought he might be having a seizure. Suddenly the reality of her revelations overwhelmed him and with dawning horror he recognized the ghastly truth. Emma Harte now possessed all that had been his. Most of the Fairley enterprises were in her hands. And so was his family home. His ancestral home. She had smashed his life. All he had left were a few shares in the *Yorkshire Morning Gazette* and the brickyard, neither of which he gave a damn about. He shuddered and dropped his head into his hands.

Blackie gazed dispassionately at Gerald. He saw a devastated and broken man and yet Blackie felt no sympathy for him. He turned and glanced at Emma, who sat poised and calm on the sofa, in command of herself and the situation, and then he sucked in his breath. Her beautiful face was a bronze mask, her eyes as deadly as steel, and his hackles rose. There was power and stealth in this room, and a ruthlessness so tangible the air seemed to vibrate with it. And it emanated solely from Emma. Blackie swallowed and looked away, finally truly understanding what a force she was to be reckoned with.

Gerald lifted his head slowly and glared at Emma venomously. "You conniving bloody bitch!" he hissed from between clenched teeth. "You have been behind all the dreadful things that have happened to me. Why, you deliberately set out to steal my mills. You ruined me!"

Emma laughed sardonically and for the first time that day her virulent loathing for Gerald was fully revealed. "Did you think I made an idle threat that day, thirteen years ago, when you tried to rape me? I will never forget that day. And now, neither will you. It will haunt you as long as you live, Gerald Fairley." She gave him a curious icy smile. "Yes, I set out to ruin you, as I vowed I would when you forced your way into my house and attacked me. But you were my willing ally. You made it very easy for me. If the truth be known, you really ruined yourself. I simply helped you along the way."

Gerald's monumental fury and humiliation pushed aside all reason. He stood up unsteadily. He wanted to put his hands around her neck and squeeze and squeeze until she had no life left in her. He *must* destroy her. He stepped towards Emma, his hatred blazing, his eyes bulging in his twisted face. He raised his hand as if to strike her.

Blackie, astonished and enraged by what he had just heard, moved with swiftness, catching Gerald's arm as it came down, neatly deflecting the blow. Although Gerald was huge, he was weak and his weight was cumbersome, and so he was no match for Blackie's strength and speed. Blackie spun Gerald around roughly and grabbed him with both hands, pinning his arms to his sides. He increased his vice-like grip and forced Gerald down into the chair.

"Don't try that again, Fairley!" Blackie cried, anger suffusing his face with dark color. "If you so much as breathe on her I will give you the worst thrashing of your life!"

Foolishly disregarding Blackie's warning, Gerald struggled upright, mumbling foul imprecations. He heaved himself to his feet, sweating profusely, and glowered at Emma. He seemed about to attack her and then suddenly he changed his mind and lurched at Blackie. Blackie was prepared and stepped aside adroitly, swung his right fist, and caught Gerald a glancing blow on the jaw. A look of stunned surprise crossed Gerald's purple face before he crumpled and collapsed in a heap at their feet, overturning a small mahogany table as he fell.

"Oh my God!" Emma exclaimed, rising,

"That bastard asked for it!" Blackie muttered, and gave her a sharp, puzzled glance. "Why didn't you tell me he tried to rape you when it happened? I would have knocked the living daylight out of him! He would have been crippled for life, after I'd finished with him!"

"I know. That's why I never mentioned it, Blackie," Emma said quietly. "I thought it advisable to keep it to myself. I didn't need any more trouble in those days. My life was difficult enough as it was." Emma righted the table and smiled wanly. "But thank you for interceding now. I really think he meant to hit me."

Blackie looked at her askance, as always surprised at her fearlessness. "What do you mean, *think* he did? I know he intended you bodily harm. The nasty piece of work."

Emma gestured at Gerald. "What are we going to do with him? We can't just leave him lying there."

A malicious gleam entered Blackie's black eyes. "I can think of a lot of things I'd like to do with him. But he's not worth going to jail for, I can tell you that." Blackie spotted a jug of water on the walnut chest. He brought it over to Gerald and threw the contents on him unceremoniously. "There, that should do it!" he exclaimed, and stood regarding Gerald coldly.

After a moment Gerald struggled into a sitting position, spluttering and wiping the water from his face. Blackie pulled him to his feet. "No more violence, Fairley. Do you understand me? Otherwise I won't be responsible for my actions," Blackie said harshly, his manner threatening. He maneuvered Gerald into the chair with a degree of roughness and hovered over him. "Now, let's get down to the business at hand. You know why I came. Presumably you are going to permit us to make a tour of inspection. I don't think you have any alternative under the circumstances, do you?"

Gerald ignored Blackie and snarled viciously at Emma, his enmity for her more palpable than ever. "I'll get you for this!" he shouted, shaking his fist at her. "You're not going to get off scot-free," he blustered. "Or as easily as you think, Emma."

"Mrs. Ainsley to you," Blackie said as Emma walked over to the desk.

Emma picked up her gloves and handbag and said, "Please leave us now. I believe you have something to attend to—removing your personal belongings from your office at the mill."

Gerald stood up uncertainly. He held on to the back of the chair and his tone was venomous as he said, "I give you fair warning—" His voice broke and tears welled in his eyes. "I am going to—"

"You can do nothing," Emma said, and she turned away in disgust.

Blackie said firmly, "You heard the lady, Fairley. You had better do as she says and be quick about it. I think it would be rather embarrassing to find your stuff dumped in the mill yard."

Gerald stumbled out of the library, his shoulders hunched in defeat. He slammed the door behind him and the wall sconces rattled in their sockets.

Emma, who abhorred violence, had been alarmed by the altercation, as brief as it was, but she had not lost her composure. She glanced across at Blackie and said dismissively, "So much for fools. Shall we look around the house?"

"Why not? That's why we're here, isn't it?"

"One of the reasons," Emma said.

Blackie's eyes rested reflectively on Emma. Revenge generally came at a high price and, whilst he understood her motivations, he wondered, abstractly, if the price had been worth it to her. Superstitious Celt that he was, Blackie shivered unexpectedly. The desire for revenge was not unnatural, but it could curdle and embitter the soul, and it often destroyed the avenger. Was it not perhaps infinitely wiser to abjure the wicked and abandon them to the fates, and trust in God to make retribution in His own good time? He found himself saying, almost inaudibly, "Vengeance is mine; I will repay, sayeth the Lord."

Emma gave him a peculiar look, and then she laughed. There was a hint of irony in her voice as she retorted, "Don't start getting mystical with me. You know I don't believe in God. Besides, even if I did, I would still have taken matters into my own hands. You see, Blackie, I didn't have time to wait for the Lord."

"And you also wanted the satisfaction of seeing Gerald Fairley's face when he discovered you had been his adversary all these years," Blackie asserted.

"Do you blame me?" Emma asked, one eyebrow raised.

"I don't suppose I do," Blackie admitted, and regarded her for a long moment. "And tell me, Emma, how do you feel, now that you have accomplished what you set out to do?"

"Why, I feel wonderful. Why shouldn't I? I have waited twenty years to see the tables turned on the Fairleys. Twenty years, Blackie! And let me tell you something. Revenge is sweet. Very sweet indeed."

Blackie did not reply. He put his arm around her shoulders and gazed down at her. To his relief that cold and implacable mask had been discarded, had been replaced by the sweetest of expressions, and the hard glint in her emerald eyes had disappeared. A thought struck him. "And what of Edwin Fairley?" Blackie asked curiously. "Do you have something special in store for him?"

"You will have to wait and see," Emma said cryptically, and smiled. "Anyway, don't think Edwin won't be upset by all this, because he will. For one thing, he will be mortified by the scandal, the terrible disgrace. Gerald is practically bankrupt and the whole of Yorkshire's business community knows it. Furthermore, Edwin's income is going to be most seriously affected. He had an interest in the Fairley mills, under his father's will. Now that's gone up in a puff of smoke," she finished triumphantly and with an eloquent wave of her hand.

Blackie said softly, "Is there anything you don't know about their affairs?"

"Nothing."

Blackie shook his head. "You're an amazing woman, Emma."

"Aren't I, just. I amaze myself sometimes." Emma laughed. "Well, let's do what we came here to do and make our grand tour of Fairley Hall."

They went out into the entrance hall and slowly mounted the great staircase washed in the eerie light sifting in through the huge stained-glass window that soared high above the central landing. They walked down the endless dusky corridors that reeked faintly of wax and gas and dust and that peculiar mustiness that seeped out of the walls, and the wood creaked and the wind moaned in the eaves and the light dimmed, and it seemed to Emma that the ancient house was expiring all around them. They looked in on various rooms where grimy dust sheets draped the furniture and then moved on into the main corridor of bedrooms.

Emma paused at the door of the Blue Suite and glanced back at Blackie standing behind her. "These were Adele Fairley's rooms," she remarked, and hesitated, her hand resting on the knob. And then she braced herself, flung open the door, and went in purposefully. Motes of dust rose up from the carpet in eddying whirls and danced in the sunlit air as they disturbed the room, which had obviously been unused for years and held an aura of neglect more pronounced than the library. Although Emma had never liked this room as a child, she had been awed by the quality of the antiques and some of the other furnishings. Now she saw it through the eyes of the connoisseur she had become, and she grimaced. Here poor Adele Fairley had lived out her life in her introverted world, isolated from her family and escaping reality by fleeing down the neck of a bottle. Emma had long ago acknowledged that Adele had been an alcoholic. But was she also mad? She pushed aside the troubling thought of inherited insanity and drifted through into the adjoining bedroom, pausing by the huge four-poster bed swathed in faded green silk. The silence was overwhelming and, in the way the imagination can play queer tricks, Emma heard Adele's tinkling laughter and the rustling of her peignoir, caught a faint whiff of her Jasmine perfume. She blinked rapidly and gooseflesh speckled her arms. She laughed at herself and then swung around and hurriedly returned to the sitting room.

Blackie followed her, assessing everything as he did. "These are fine rooms, Emma," he said, peering about. "Beautifully proportioned. They have a lot of potential. Of course, you'll have to get rid of most of this junk Adele Fairley collected."

"Yes, I will," Emma said, and thought: What a pathetic memorial to Adele Fairley. She who was so beautiful.

Emma inspected the other bedrooms perfunctorily yet with a degree of curiosity. She hovered in front of the dressing table in the Gray Room, once occupied by Olivia Wainright

Fairley, musing on her. Unexpectedly, a wave of reluctant affection surfaced in her. Olivia *had* been kind; *had* eased her burdens in this terrible house. She wondered if her empathy for Olivia had been unconsciously engendered by that woman's marked resemblance to her mother. Perhaps. Emma's face softened and she turned and left the Gray Room. But her expression changed radically when she pushed open the door of the Master's Room. Her eyes were stony as she surveyed the austere furnishings, thinking of Adam Fairley. And Emma remembered anew all that had happened to her at Fairley Hall and she felt no compunction about what she had done. Her revenge had had a long gestation period, but it had been surely worth it.

Fifteen minutes later Emma and Blackie descended the main staircase and quickly traversed the reception rooms on the ground floor. All the while Blackie chatted enthusiastically about the renovations he would make, and outlined his plans for transforming Fairley Hall into an elegant home for her. Emma listened and nodded but said little. At one moment, when they were viewing the drawing room, she touched Blackie's arm and asked, "Why was I so frightened of this house when I was a child?"

Blackie squeezed her hand lovingly. "You weren't afraid of the house, Emma. You were afraid of the people in it."

"I suppose you're right," she replied softly. "And now those people are just ghosts."

"Yes, me darlin', just ghosts. And this is only a house, after all. I once told you it could never harm you."

"I know you did." Emma took Blackie's arm. "Let's go outside and look at the grounds. It's chilly in here, and rather depressing."

Emma blinked when they stepped out into the bright sunlight. "Do you know, it's warmer out here than it is in there," she remarked, and stared up at the grim edifice soaring in front of her. Emma's face became introspective as she walked along the flagged terrace, regarding Fairley Hall from time to time. This daunting house was enduring—and inescapable; a bastion of wealth and privilege, a monument to a society long outmoded, to a cruel class system she detested, and it sorely offended her.

Inclining her head towards the house, she murmured, "My father used to call this Fairley's Folly."

"And so it is."

"Tear it down," Emma said with cool deliberation.

"Tear it down!" Blackie echoed, gazing at her incredulously. "What do you mean?"

"Exactly what I say. I want you to tear it down. Brick by brick by brick, until there is nothing left standing."

"But I thought you were going to live in it," Blackie exclaimed, still flabbergasted.

"To tell you the truth, I don't think I ever really intended to do that. You once said it was a monstrosity and that's a decided understatement. There is no place in this world for monstrosities. I want it wiped off the face of the earth as if it never existed."

"And the furniture?"

"Sell it. Give it away. Do as you wish. I know I don't want one piece of it. You can take anything you like, Blackie." She smiled. "You might consider keeping Adam Fairley's desk. It is quite valuable, you know."

"Thank you, Emma. I'll think about it." Blackie rubbed his chin. "Are you sure about this decision? You did pay a lot for the house."

"I am very sure." Emma swiveled and tripped lightly down the terrace steps until she stood at the entrance to the rose garden. In her mind's eye she saw herself as a young and desperate girl, and she recalled the day she had told Edwin she was pregnant, and remembered his repudiation of her as clearly as if it had happened yesterday.

"And destroy this garden," she said icily. "Demolish it completely. I don't want one rosebud, one single leaf left growing."

The villagers were agog at the news that Emma Harte, Big Jack's daughter, was now the owner of Fairley Hall and the mill. It was a reversal of circumstances so unlikely it staggered the imagination, and, in turn, they were stunned, astonished, and finally wryly amused at the ironic justice so inherent in the turn of events, which was quite unexpected. Hidebound as they were by tradition and prejudice, and trapped in a rigid caste system that kept the workers in their place, they nevertheless marveled at her audacity in daring to defy that system and break all the rules set down by the Establishment for centuries.

The following morning women stood on doorsteps and leaned over garden gates, arms akimbo, shaking their heads and exclaiming about the remarkable success story of one of their own. That night in the White Horse, the men at the bar, most of whom worked at the mill, crowded together, speculating about the future of the mill and chuckling at the demise of the Fairleys' power. Although Adam Fairley had not been particularly liked, because he was not of the same ilk as his bluff and hearty father, being too "fancy" for their north-country tastes, he *had* been respected since the men recognized his basic integrity and fairness. However, Gerald, who was a tyrant and a fool, was loathed, and no one was unhappy to see his downfall, nor did they have a shred of pity for him. "Good riddance to bad rubbish" was the phrase most often heard in the ensuing days as the villagers waited eagerly for the arrival of their new employer and the future mistress of Fairley Hall.

But Emma did not come to the village—at least not until Gerald Fairley had vacated Fairley Hall. Two days after his departure her silver-gray Rolls-Royce pulled up into the mill yard and she went into the mill to hold a meeting with the workers. The manager, Josh Wilson, son of Ernest, who had served Adam so well, assembled the men and women in the weaving shed. Emma, wearing a navy-blue tailored dress, a navy cloche, and pearls, cordially greeted some of the men she remembered from her childhood and then addressed the gathering.

She was direct: "As you are only too well aware, there has been a slump in the cloth business for almost eighteen months, ever since the price of wool hit rock bottom, to be followed by the price of cloth. Due to the inferior management of the previous owner, Fairley mill has been limping along and I know that many men were laid off over the past few months." Emma paused and cleared her throat. "I am afraid I cannot reinstate those men." She held up her hand as loud groans and mutterings rippled through the audience. "However, I am going to give a small pension to the men who have been laid off and who have not found work in the nearby towns. I would also like to say now, and most definitely, that I have no intention of closing the mill, as I believe many of you thought I would. But under the present circumstances, I must re-trench, economize, reorganize, and decrease the staff. Therefore, all men of retiring age and close to it will be retired immediately. Each man will receive a pension. Younger men, especially those who are single, will be offered jobs in my other companies, if they are willing to leave Fairley and carve out a niche for themselves in the cities of Leeds and Bradford. Those who do not wish to take advantage of this offer may remain. Of course, I hope some of you will consider it, so that I can reduce the work force here in older to operate more economically. As I told Josh, I am going to sell the quality cloth we produce to the three Kallinski tailoring factories in Leeds, but even their orders will not be sufficient to keep the mill in full production. I have a solution to that problem. I am going to start making a lower-quality cloth immediately, to be sold at cheaper prices abroad, and I hope there will be a demand for it here, too."

Emma smiled confidently. "I am fortunate in that I can afford to ride out this slump, and with a little luck, and your cooperation, I know we can turn this mill around and put it on a paying basis quickly. Let me say again, I am not going to close the mill, so I don't want any of you to worry about your jobs. I don't intend to let this village starve."

They cheered her rousingly, and one by one, clutching their cloth caps, the men came to shake her hand, to thank her, and to welcome her back to Fairley. "I knew yer dad, luv," one man told her, and another added, "By gum, Big Jack'd be right proud of yer, lass."

After a meeting with Josh Wilson, Emma stepped into her Rolls and told the chauffeur to drive her to Fairley Hall. Blackie O'Neill's workmen were already swarming all over the house, scrambling up ladders and across the roof. Windows were being removed, chimneys dismantled, and slates ripped off. Emma smiled to herself, and returned to Leeds.

At first the villagers believed the Hall was being renovated and they were excited about this development and looked forward to welcoming Emma Harte as the lady of the manor. But within the space of a week, they realized, to their shock, that the house was being slowly demolished, and they were baffled.

In the middle of May, Emma made a second trip to Fairley Hall. She walked along the terrace, which still remained intact, and regarded the great tract of rough bare ground where the house and stables had formerly stood. Not one brick was left and the rose garden, too, had disappeared. Emma felt an enormous surge of relief and an unexpected sense of liberation. Fairley Hall, that house where she had suffered such humiliation and heartache, might never have existed. It could no longer hurt her with the painful memories it evoked. She had exorcised all the ghosts of her childhood. She was free at last of the Fairleys.

Blackie, who arrived a few moments later, put his arm around her shoulders. "I followed your instructions down to the letter and removed the monstrosity, mavourneen. But like the whole of the village, I am eaten up with curiosity, Emma. Tell me, darlin', what are you going to do with this land?"

Emma looked up at him and smiled. "I am going to turn it into a park. A beautiful park for the villagers of Fairley, and I am going to name it after my mother."

FIFTY-ONE

A week later, on a lovely evening at the end of May, Emma stepped out of a taxi at the Savoy Hotel in London and hurried through the lobby to the American Bar. She saw Frank before he saw her. He was seated at a table facing the lobby, and as she mounted the short flight of steps into the bar she noticed that he looked reflective and brooding as he nursed his drink.

"Penny for your thoughts," she said, coming to a standstill in front of him.

Momentarily startled, Frank raised his head quickly and his eyes lit up. "There you are!" He rose and pulled out a chair for her. "And don't you look lovely, our Em."

"Why, thank you, darling." She smoothed the skirt of her lime-green silk dress and took off her white kid gloves. "It is a scorcher, isn't it? I think I'll have a gin fizz, Frank, please. It will refresh me. I had quite a hectic day at the store."

Frank ordered the drink and lit a cigarette. "I'm sorry to drag you all the way down to the Strand, but it is closer to Fleet Street and I've got to be back at the paper in a short while."

"I didn't mind coming here. I rather like this bar. Anyway, why did you want to see me? You sounded urgent when you phoned me at the store. I was a little worried, to tell you the truth."

"I'm sorry, Emma. I didn't mean to do that. Actually, it's not all that urgent, but I did want to talk to you."

"What about?"

"Arthur Ainsley."

Emma's shapely brows shot up. "Arthur. Good heavens, why do you want to talk about *him?*"

"Winston and I have been worried about you lately. You're sitting in a hopeless marriage and it disturbs us both. In fact, we think you should divorce Arthur. I promised Winston I would broach the idea to you."

"A divorce!" Emma laughed gaily. "Whatever for? Arthur doesn't bother me."

"He's not right for you, Emma, and you know it. There's his terrible drinking, for one thing, and the way he carries on with—" Frank swallowed and drew on his cigarette.

"Other women," Emma finished for him. She looked amused. "I realize the wife is always supposed to be the last to know. However, I've been aware of Arthur's activities for a long time. You don't have to spare my feelings."

"And it doesn't upset you?" Frank asked.

"My monumental lack of interest in Arthur Ainsley and the way he conducts his life must surely negate the idea that I *care* for him. Actually, I have no feelings for Arthur whatsoever."

"Then why not get a divorce, Emma?"

"Because of the children, mainly."

"Fiddlesticks! You're using them as an excuse. Edwina and Kit are away at boarding school. They wouldn't be affected—"

"I was thinking of the twins, Frank. They are Arthur's children and they need a father."

"What kind of father is Arthur?" Frank snorted.

Emma picked up the drink the waiter had placed before her. "Cheers."

"Cheers. Now, come on, give me an answer."

"Well, he is a presence in their lives. He's very fond of them, and quite good with them, really."

"When he's sober," Frank pointed out with a degree of acerbity.

Emma sighed. "There's a grain of truth in what you say, of course. But look here, Frank, I honestly don't want to divorce Arthur, even though I have grounds. At least, not right now. You know I hate upheaval and I really *do* think it's the wrong time. Perhaps when the children are older I'll consider it." Her voice trailed off and she looked pensive. She cheered. "I'm reasonably content. Arthur doesn't interfere with me, or the business, and you know how much I love that."

"You can't take ledgers to bed with you, our Em. They don't keep you warm on a cold night, and they certainly can't cherish and love you as you should be cherished and loved."

Emma laughed. "Why is it you men are always thinking of sex?"

"I did say 'cherished' and 'loved.' You're a young woman. You should have some companionship, a relationship with a decent man. My God, you must be bloody lonely!"

A cloud passed over Emma's face and her eyes were briefly sad. She shook her head slowly. "I don't have time to be lonely. I'm very busy these days, as you well know, constantly traveling between here and Leeds. And I am adamant about the divorce, Frank. Now, let's not waste any more time talking about Arthur. Tell me about the house you found in Hampstead. Does Natalie like it?"

Frank groaned, acknowledging it was useless to pursue the conversation, and said, "Yes, she does. So do I. It's ideal for us. But I would like you to take a look at it, and give me your opinion. It's quite expensive, you know."

"I'd be delighted. And don't worry about the price, Frank. If it's more than you can afford, I'll give you the difference."

"Oh, Emma, I couldn't take it," Frank protested.

"Don't be ridiculous. Years ago Blackie told me that money was meant to be spent and he was correct. I want you to have a nice house, to start this marriage off on the right foot. I want you to be happy, Frank." She laughed. "Whoever said money doesn't buy happiness was misinformed, in my opinion. It buys a lot of happiness, for a lot of people. And frankly, I'd rather be miserable with money than without it." She squeezed Frank's arm. "You know anything I have is yours and Winston's. It will be part of my wedding present to you and Natalie."

"You're so generous, Emma. I really appreciate it. And what can I say but thank you very much." Frank sipped his drink and continued, "Can you spare an hour to view it tomorrow?"

"Indeed I can. How is dear Natalie?"

Frank beamed. "She's marvelous. A treasure. I love that girl, Emma. I really do."

"I know. You're lucky, Frank. You're going to have a wonderful marriage. She's—" Emma stopped and caught her breath. From her position at the table, a vantage point in the bar, Emma could see a major portion of the lobby and her eyes were now riveted on two men talking together near the reception desk.

Frank, watching Emma carefully, said, "What's wrong?"

Emma glanced at Frank, white with shock. "It's Paul McGill!" She looked down the steps again. "Oh my God! He's coming this way. I think he's heading for the bar. I must leave immediately, before he sees me."

Frank put a restraining hand on her arm. "It's perfectly all right, Emma. Don't get excited. And please don't leave," he implored softly.

Emma's eyes blazed. "Frank! You knew he was in London, didn't you?"

"Yes."

"You didn't—you couldn't possibly have asked him to join us?"

Frank did not answer. He looked down at his drink.

Emma hissed, "My God! You did!"

"Guilty, I'm afraid," Frank murmured.

"Oh, Frank, how could you?" Emma half rose, and Frank pressed her gently back into the chair.

"Please, Emma. You have to stay."

She looked at him furiously. "This sudden desire to talk about Arthur and the house was just a ruse, wasn't it?" she cried accusingly.

"No!" Frank exclaimed. "It wasn't! I did want to discuss your marriage. I have for a long time. I told you, Winston and I are very perturbed. And I do need your advice about the house. However, I did agree to arrange this meeting."

"My God! What am I going to do?" Emma whispered hoarsely.

"You are going to be your civilized self and have a drink with Paul."

"I can't," she wailed. "You don't understand. I must go!"

As she spoke, Emma knew it was already too late to make a graceful exit. Paul was bounding up the steps and then he was standing at the table, his bulk casting a shadow on them. Emma lifted her eyes slowly and looked at him looking down at her. She was relieved she was seated. Her legs had turned to jelly and her heart was palpitating.

"Hello, Emma," Paul said, and stretched out his hand.

Automatically she gave him hers. "Hello, Paul," she responded in a strangled voice, shaking internally. She felt his strong fingers tighten on hers, felt the bright color flooding her face. She extracted her hand quickly and gazed blindly at the table.

Paul greeted Frank like an old friend and sat down. He ordered a scotch and soda, leaned back, crossed his legs nonchalantly, and lit a cigarette. He turned his attention to Emma. "It's good to see you, Emma. You look lovely. You haven't changed a bit. And I must congratulate you. Your store in Knightsbridge bowled me over. It's magnificent. A monumental accomplishment. You should be proud of yourself."

"Thank you," she murmured, not daring to look at him.

"I must congratulate you, too, Frank. Your new book is splendid. Thanks for the copy. I was up half the night reading it. Couldn't put it down, in fact."

Frank grinned with pleasure. "I'm glad you like it. I'm also happy to say it's doing very well."

"And so it should. It's one of the best novels I've read in years." Paul's drink arrived and as he lifted it he said, "Here's to old and dear friends, and your impending marriage, Frank."

Emma was silent. She had never thought her brother capable of duplicity, but he had certainly been devious in this instance, and was obviously on cordial terms with Paul.

Frank said, "I'm delighted you will be here in July. Natalie and I hope you can come to the wedding."

Emma could not believe her ears. She glared at Frank, who ignored her penetrating look and continued, "And thanks for the invitation to dine with you later this week. Natalie suggested Friday, if you are free."

"I am. And I wouldn't miss the wedding for anything." Paul's eyes rested on Emma. "Could you join us for dinner on Friday, Emma?"

"I'm quite sure I can't," she responded, avoiding his eyes.

"Why don't you check your appointment book later?" Frank suggested.

"I don't have to. I am positive I have a dinner engagement," she enunciated clearly and in a firmer tone, her eyes signaling her displeasure to Frank.

Recognizing the stubborn expression settling on her face, Paul refrained from pressing the point and, turning to Frank, he said, "Where are you planning to go on your honeymoon?"

"We've been considering the South of France, although we haven't definitely decided yet."

Emma sat back in the chair, no longer listening to them. Their conversation washed over her as she retreated into herself. She had been utterly thrown off balance by Paul's unexpected arrival and she could, at this moment, have cheerfully killed Frank for his participation in the scheme. She felt dazed, and many mixed emotions, so well controlled over the years, broke free in her. The impact of seeing him was devastating. Paul McGill was sitting *here*, unconcernedly chatting to Frank, smiling, nodding, and behaving as if nothing had happened between them. She felt the enormous power of him, his sheathed strength and virility, and she remembered every detail of the days they had spent together at the Ritz. And then she recalled, with a stab of sadness, how she had yearned for him. Pined for him. Needed him in the past. Now he was only inches away, and she stifled the impulse to reach out and touch him, to reassure herself he was real. Instead she looked at him surreptitiously. He was as immaculate as always, dressed in a dark gray chalk-striped suit and a gleaming white silk shirt. Sapphire-and-gold links glittered in the French cuffs and he wore a deep blue silk tie, and a white handkerchief flared in his breast pocket. She knew he had been forty-two at the beginning of February, but he looked exactly the same as he had in 1919, except that his face was more deeply tanned and there were additional character lines around his eyes. His coloring was as vivid as it had ever been, and his chuckle was deep and throaty. How well she knew that amused, sardonic chuckle. Sudden anger swamped her. How dare he come back here so casually and expect her to treat him with civility after all the pain he had caused her! What audacity. What arrogance. Resentment edged out all other feelings, and she steeled herself against his potent charm.

Dimly, she heard Frank saying good-bye. He was leaving her alone with Paul. The idea terrified her.

"I must go," she said, picking up her gloves and her purse. "Please excuse me, Paul. I have to leave with Frank."

"Don't go, Emma. Please. I would like to talk to you," Paul said in the softest of voices. It was imperative that he detain her at all costs, yet he dare not exert obvious pressure on her.

Frank threw Paul a conspiratorial glance and addressed Emma. "I have to get back to Fleet Street. I'm running late." He kissed her on the cheek perfunctorily and departed before she could protest further, and she knew she was trapped.

Paul summoned the waiter and ordered more drinks, and then he leaned forward intently. His eyes were serious, his face grave. "Please don't be angry with Frank. I persuaded him to arrange this drink."

"Why?" Emma asked, and for the first time she looked at Paul fully and with coldness.

Paul winced. He knew he had a difficult time ahead of him, but he was determined to convince her of his sincerity. "As I said, I wanted to see you and to talk to you. Very desperately."

"Desperately!" she echoed, and laughed cynically. "That's a strange word to use. You can't have been all that desperate, otherwise you would not have let so many years elapse."

"I understand your feelings only too well, Emma. But it does happen to be the truth. I have been *really* desperate. And for the past four and a half years," he insisted.

"Then why didn't you write to me?" she demanded, and her voice shook unexpectedly. She took furious control of herself, determined not to show any emotion whatsoever.

"I did write to you a number of times and I also sent you three cablegrams."

Emma stared at Paul, a look of disbelief crossing her face. "Don't tell me they all got lost in the post! And that the cablegrams disappeared into thin air! I would find that very hard to swallow."

"No, they didn't. They were stolen. As your letters to me were stolen," Paul said, his eyes not leaving her face.

"Stolen by whom?" Emma asked, returning his intense stare.

"By my private secretary."

"But why would she do a thing like that?"

"It's rather a long story," Paul said quietly. "I would like to tell it to you. That was the reason I wanted to see you. Will you at least give me the courtesy of listening, Emma? Please."

"All right," she murmured. It would do no harm to hear what he had to say and her curiosity also got the better of her.

"When I returned to Australia in 1919, the only thing on my mind was seeing my father and then returning to you as quickly as possible."

Paul paused as the waiter appeared with the drinks. When he was out of earshot he went on, "I walked into quite a mess when I arrived in Sydney, but I won't go into that now. Let me first tell you about the letters. Years ago my father befriended a young girl who worked in our Sydney office. He groomed her to be his private secretary during my absence. After I was demobbed I had to take over the reins of the business at once, because Dad was not at all well, and so I inherited her. Marion Reese was a godsend in those first few weeks. Anyway, for a couple of months I was working very long hours with Marion at my side, guiding me, helping me, and filling me in on most things. My father was gradually getting worse and he was confined to bed. Frankly, Emma, I relied heavily on Marion. I had enormous responsibilities thrust upon me and I was out of touch." Paul lit a cigarette, inhaled, and continued, "Marion had been like a member of the family before the war. My father was very fond of her and I looked on her as a friend, as well as a valued employee. She was like an older sister in a sense, since she is about four years my senior. One night, after we had been working rather late, I took her to supper, and I confided in her. I told her about you and my plans for the future, my intention of marrying you, once I had sorted out my marital problems."

A regretful smile played around Paul's mouth and he shook his head. "Confiding in Marion was a terrible mistake, as it turned out. A mistake I made when I had had a few drinks too many. Of course, I didn't realize it was a mistake at the time. Marion was most understanding. She promised to help me pull everything back into shape as quickly as possible, so that I could come to London for a few months and—".

"Why was it a mistake?" Emma interrupted, frowning.

"I didn't know it at the time, but Marion Reese was in love with me and had been for many years. There had been nothing between us ever, and I had never done anything to encourage her. Naturally, the last thing she wanted was for me to leave Australia, and especially to go to another woman, although I was not aware of that then. In any event, I went on furiously reorganizing the business and writing to you, not realizing that my devoted secretary was confiscating my letters to you instead of posting them. I was puzzled and unnerved when you didn't reply to my letters, other than the first one. I sent two cablegrams, begging you to at least let me know you were well. Of course, they were never transmitted. Marion destroyed them. Still, in spite of your silence, which I couldn't understand, I was determined to see you and, as soon as I could, sailed for England."

Emma, who had been listening attentively and digesting his words, knew with absolute certainty that he was speaking the truth. She looked at him alertly. "When was that?"

"About a year later. In the spring of 1920. I wrote out a cable and gave it to Marion before I departed, announcing my arrival, and I prayed you would meet the boat. You didn't because you never received the cable. The first person I telephoned was Frank. He told me you were on your honeymoon. That you had married Arthur Ainsley just one week before."

"Oh my God!" Emma cried, her eyes flaring open. Dismay swamped her.

Paul's smile was pained and he nodded his head. "Yes, I was a week too late to stop that. *Unfortunately*."

"But why didn't you come before? Why did you wait a whole year?" Emma demanded, her voice rising.

"I simply couldn't get away, Emma. You see, my father was dying of cancer. He passed away about eight months after I had returned to Australia."

"I'm so sorry, Paul," Emma murmured, and genuine sympathy was reflected in her eyes.

"Yes, it was sad. And Dad was very dependent on me in those last few months. Well, to continue. I had hoped to leave immediately after Dad's funeral, but then my wife—" Paul hesitated and grimaced slightly. "My wife, Constance, became very ill, and I was further delayed. Just when I thought I could get away at last, my son fell sick." Paul eyed Emma carefully. "I have a son, you know."

"Yes, so I heard. You could have told me, Paul. I wish you had," she reproached.

"Yes, I should have, Emma. But Howard, well, he has problems, and I have always found it difficult to talk about him." Paul sighed heavily and his eyes dulled momentarily. He straightened up in the chair. "Once Howard recovered I was able to leave for England."

"And you met with Frank?"

"Not at first. Frank was a little reluctant to see me. I don't believe he thought very highly of me. However, he did know how devastated I was when I learned of your marriage and I suppose he took pity on me, especially since I had told him on the phone that I had been writing to you diligently over the whole of the previous year. When he told me that you had never received my letters, and that you had also been writing to me, I was flabbergasted and baffled."

"How did you discover the letters had been stolen?" Emma asked, her face as grim as Paul's.

"It struck me immediately, and most forcibly, that someone had been tampering with my mail. Several letters going astray was one thing, but not a dozen or so. It didn't take much to deduce it was Marion. She was the obvious culprit, since she handled my correspondence in both Sydney and at the sheep station in Coonamble. And she also mailed all of my personal letters as well."

"It's a pity you didn't post them yourself, isn't it?" Emma said quietly, cursing Marion Reese under her breath. Her penetrating eyes focused on Paul.

"Yes, that's true. I must admit I was careless. On the other hand, I had no reason not to trust her. Also, I was facing monumental problems. I was overworked and preoccupied."

"I presume you confronted her when you returned to Sydney," Emma ventured.

"I did indeed. She denied it at first. But eventually she broke down and confessed. When I asked her why she had done it, she said she had hoped to sabotage our romance, so I would not leave."

"She succeeded," Emma said dryly, and thought of the wasted years.

"Yes." Paul searched Emma's face, which was unreadable. He reached into his inside breast pocket and pulled out an envelope. "This is a letter from her solicitors. In it they acknowledge her guilt, on the understanding that I would not prosecute her, which I had threatened to do. Theft of mail is a felony, you know. I demanded this," he explained, tapping the envelope, "because I hoped one day to have the opportunity to show it to you, to prove that I am not the blackguard you undoubtedly think I am." He handed her the envelope and finished. "They also returned my letters to you, and yours to me, by the way."

Emma looked at him askance. "You mean she kept them! How peculiar!" she exclaimed.

"I thought that, too. Please, Emma, read the letter from her solicitors. The story is so incredible it has occurred to me that you might think I have invented the whole thing."

Emma was reflective for a moment, and then she took the letter out of the envelope and perused it rapidly. She returned it to Paul, smiling faintly. "I would have believed you without this letter. Nobody could invent such a yarn. Thank you for showing it to me, though. And what happened to Marion Reese?"

"Naturally I fired her at once. I've no idea where she is today."

Emma nodded. She pondered, looking down at her hands, and then she lifted her head and met Paul's gaze directly. "Why didn't you wait for me to return from my honeymoon four years ago, so that you could tell me you had written, Paul?"

Paul gave her a swift glance. "What would have been the point of that? It was too late, Emma. I didn't want to interfere with your marriage. Besides, you might not have believed me. Remember, I was only speculating on what had happened to the letters. I had no proof until I returned to Sydney."

"Yes, I understand. However, I am surprised Frank never told me."

"In all fairness to him, he did want me to stay and meet with you. And he even wanted to tell you himself. I asked him not to do so. I thought it pointless. I felt you were lost to me." Paul shrugged. "At the time, it seemed wiser for me to simply disappear, quickly and quietly."

"And why are you telling me now, after all this time?"

"I have always wanted to explain, Emma. To exonerate myself with you. The knowledge that I caused you suffering has haunted me. I've seen Frank on previous trips to London and he's kept me informed about your life. But I thought it was inappropriate to come to you, under the circumstances, although I longed to. Last week, when I first arrived, I lunched with Frank. Almost at once he said your marriage wasn't working. When I heard you were unhappy with Arthur and spending a lot of time alone in London, I decided I would no longer be upsetting anything if I saw you. I insisted Frank arrange this meeting. I did want the chance to vindicate myself," he finished, praying fervently that he had.

Paul leaned across the table, his face tensely set. "I know you were shocked to see me, and perhaps it *was* a little unfair of me to spring myself on you without warning, but quite honestly, I didn't know what else to do. I hope you're not angry with me, or with Frank."

"No, I'm not. And I'm glad we met." Emma looked down at the table contemplatively, and when she raised her head to meet Paul's unwavering gaze her face was grave, her eyes moist. "I was as unnerved and as perplexed as you were, when I didn't hear from you, Paul. And very hurt. Heartbroken, in fact," she found herself admitting. "It helps knowing the facts, even now so long afterwards." Emma smiled wryly. "I suppose, really, we are both victims of circumstances—and of Marion Reese's possessiveness. How different our lives might have been if she had not interfered." She shook her head. "Why is it some people want to play God?" she asked, her face wreathed in sadness.

Paul sighed. "I don't know, Emma. In her case, I imagine it was a truly sick mind at work. You know the old saying, 'Hell hath no fury like a woman scorned.' But I will never understand what she hoped to gain. I did not display the slightest interest in her as a woman."

"People can always hope," Emma murmured. "And fantasize."

"That's so," Paul acknowledged. He scrutinized Emma closely for a few seconds and then said quietly. "Do you still hate me, Emma?"

A look of surprise flashed across her face. "I never hated you, Paul!" She half smiled. "Well, at least only fleetingly, when my emotions overcame me. You can't blame me for that."

"I don't blame you at all." Paul shifted in the chair and lit a cigarette to hide his nervousness. "I wondered—would it be possible—could we be friends, Emma? Now that the air is cleared between us. Or is that too much to ask?" He held his breath.

Emma dropped her eyes, feeling suddenly wary. Dare she expose herself to him again, if only in friendship? She had been acutely conscious of him as a man from the moment he had arrived. He was just as dangerous to her as he had been in the past. Despite her inherent caution, she finally said slowly, "Yes, Paul, if you want that."

"I do," Paul responded firmly. He looked at her in his old appraising way, his eyes admiring. She was composed and as beautiful as always. Time had not marked her exquisite face, although he detected a certain sadness in her eyes when her face was in repose. He had to curb the compelling desire to take her in his arms and kiss her. He did not even dare to touch her hand. He must be careful if he was to win her back and possess her completely again. He saw her glance at her watch and his heart sank. He said quickly, impulsively, "Have dinner with me, Emma."

"Oh, Paul, I can't," she said, flustered.

"Why not? Do you have another engagement?"

"No, but I—"

"Please, Emma. For old times' sake." He smiled engagingly and his brilliantly blue eyes danced. "I'm not afraid. Are you?"

"Why should I be afraid?" Emma countered defensively, staring at him. Her heart missed a beat. He was hard to resist.

"You have no reason at all, I can assure you," Paul chuckled, relaxing for the first time. As the tension slipped away he took command with his usual panache. "Then it's settled. Where would you like to go?"

"I don't know," Emma said, feeling curiously weak and so overpowered she was incapable of declining the invitation again.

"Let's go to Rules across the street in Covent Garden. Do you know it?"

She shook her head. "I've heard of it, but I've never dined there."

"It's a charming old place. I know you'll like it," he said, and motioned to the waiter for the bill.

*   *   *

They were halfway through dinner when Paul said, somewhat abruptly, "Why did your marriage go wrong, Emma?"

Emma was so startled by the unanticipated question she did not answer for a long moment. Because I still loved you, she wanted to say. Instead she murmured, "Because Arthur and I are incompatible."

"I see. What's he like?" Paul questioned, riddled with curiosity and not a little jealousy.

Emma said carefully, "He's handsome, charming, and from a good family. But he's also a little weak. And rather vain." She glanced back at Paul and said quietly, "He's not the type of man you would have much in common with."

Nor you apparently, my love, Paul thought, but said, "Are you going to get a divorce?"

"Not at the moment. Are you?" she retorted, and caught her breath, regretting the question.

Paul's face changed, settled into harsh lines. "Well, I asked for that one, I suppose," he responded quietly. "I want a divorce, Emma. I have for many years. However, I have some serious difficulties with Constance." He paused, ruminated briefly, and went on. "My wife is an alcoholic. She was a heavy drinker before the war. That is one of the reasons the marriage broke up. By the time I returned to Sydney she was a lost cause. I put her in a nursing home at once. She ran away, just after I had buried Dad. It took me five weeks to find her and she was in a pretty ghastly state. Physically debilitated and mentally deranged as well. That was why I couldn't come to England when I wanted to—I had to see her settled first. Believe me, I was infuriated. I don't want to sound callous, but I have tried to help Constance over the years, to no avail. She won't help herself. I lost my patience a long time ago."

"Yes, I know what you mean," Emma said grimly. "I'm sorry, Paul. Truly sorry. It's a terrible situation for anyone to cope with. Is she still in the nursing home?"

"Yes, she is. They have dried her out, but she is very weak in every way and not capable of looking after herself, or functioning normally. She will have to be institutionalized permanently, I imagine. Constance is a Roman Catholic, Emma, so that is another impediment to the divorce. Nonetheless, I haven't given up hope of gaining my freedom one day." Paul took a sip of Montrachet. After a moment he continued, "There is something else I must tell you, Emma. It's about my son." He hesitated. "Howard is—well, he's retarded, I'm afraid. That's what I meant earlier when I said he had problems."

Emma was stunned. The pain on his face was raw. "Oh, Paul! Paul! How awfully tragic. And what a heavy burden for you to carry alone." Compassion flooded her face and her eyes softened. "Whyever didn't you tell me years ago? Surely you knew I would have been sympathetic, and talking about your son might have helped you."

Paul shook his head. "Perhaps I should have told you, Emma. I think I was a little ashamed, to tell you the truth. Especially after I had met your children. Also, I have always found it hard to discuss Howard. I love him, of course. However, my emotions are mixed. My heart aches for him. I also carry enormous guilt. And sometimes I—" Paul frowned. "I am reluctant to admit this, and I never have to another soul, but at times I almost hate him. I know I shouldn't. Yet I can't help it. I hope you don't despise me for that."

Emma's heart went out to him. "I don't despise you, Paul. I know that parents of retarded children often do experience hatred. It apparently springs from frustration and despair. Truly, your feelings are not abnormal." Impulsively she reached out and touched his arm. "You must feel very helpless. How old is Howard?"

"He's twelve, Emma. And, yes, I do feel absolutely despairing most of the time." He shook his head. "Nature plays strange tricks. You know, he is a lovely looking boy. He has a sweet, almost ethereal face and the most gentle eyes. And the mind of a five-year-old." Paul ran his hand across his face wearily. "And he'll never be any different!"

Emma was silent, filled with sorrow, and she did not know how to comfort him. Eventually, she asked, "Where does he live?"

"Out at the sheep station in Coonamble. He has a male companion-nurse who is devoted to him. My housekeeper is there and quite a large domestic staff. When I'm at Dunoon I spend a great deal of time with him, although I'm quite sure he doesn't really know I'm around. He lives in his own very special world." Paul lit a cigarette. "I'm sorry, Emma. I didn't mean to pile all my problems on you tonight. I never discuss them with anyone." He grimaced. "I must admit though, I have felt rather defeated by my personal life in the past few years. It is so arid and unrewarding. Thank you for listening, for being so understanding."

"I have been far enough down to know what the realities of life are, Paul," Emma said. "My life has never been easy. Whatever you might think."

He looked at her attentively, his eyes narrowed. "I'm sure it hasn't, Emma."

"But then life *is* hard, Paul. The important thing is how one copes with the hardships and overcomes them." She smiled her dauntless smile. "Let's face it, Paul, neither of us are too badly off. Not when you look around and see other people's problems. We are both successful. Wealthy. In good health. We are also fortunate in that we have our work."

Paul gazed at her. He thought: She truly is a rare woman. He said, "Yes, I have buried myself in work these last few years, as I'm sure you have. And you are right, Emma. Our lives are not too bad. We must be grateful for all the good things we do have." He smiled at her lovingly. "Thank you again. I'm glad I told you about Constance and Howard. I feel a great sense of relief."

"I'm glad, too."

Paul lifted his glass. "Here's to you, Emma. You are a wise and understanding lady. I'm so happy we are going to be friends again, aren't you?"

Emma touched his glass with hers. "Yes, I think I am, Paul."

"Well, enough of all this misery. Let's talk about something more cheerful."

Emma smiled at him. "Tell me about your oil fields in Texas, and the Sydney-Texas Oil Company. I was very intrigued when you mentioned your new venture earlier."

After dinner Paul escorted Emma home to her small house in Wilton Mews, just off Belgrave Square. He helped her out of the cab, told the driver to wait, and saw her inside. He kissed her tentatively on the cheek. "Thank you for a lovely evening, Emma. May I call you soon?"

"Yes, Paul. And thank you. Good night."

"Good night, Emma."

Later, when she was in bed, Emma lay awake for a long

time, musing on the evening. Paul McGill's dramatic reappearance in her life was the last thing she had ever anticipated. Life was full of staggering surprises. She dwelt momentarily on Marion Reese. *If* Paul had not been the man he undoubtedly was, then perhaps that frustrated woman might never have loved him . . . might never have stolen the letters. *If* Paul had only written to Frank . . . *If* she had not rushed into marriage with Arthur. If . . . if . . . if. She sighed inwardly. It was such a waste of time dwelling on what might have been. And surely their characters had made their destinies. Her heart filled with sadness as her wandering thoughts settled on the tragic circumstances of Paul's life. He who was so virile, and extraordinarily brilliant, must surely chafe under the burdens he had to carry. His life was as difficult and sterile as her own. She realized then, with a flash of surprise, that she had enjoyed the evening, once she had recovered from her initial shock and anger. She wondered if he had merely wanted to see her to set the record straight, or if he had been motivated by other reasons. Did he still love her? She did not know the answer to that. She shivered. One thing she did know: She was mortally afraid of his persuasive charm and of being engulfed by it again. She endeavored to push him out of her mind, but when she finally fell asleep she was still thinking about Paul McGill.

FIFTY-TWO

"**Y**ou look as if you're about to commit murder," Winston said quietly, drawing to a standstill next to Paul McGill. He followed Paul's gaze, which was resting with loathing on Arthur Ainsley. "He's asinine," Winston went on. "Don't pay any attention to him. Frank and I don't."

Paul swung to Winston, his expression one of mingled anger and disgust. "He makes my blood boil! The preposterous fool has embarrassed Emma all through lunch and now he's compounding his execrable behavior. The bloody imbecile. Apart from the fact that he can't hold his liquor, he can't keep his hands off the other women present. Emma must be mortified."

Winston smiled thinly, his animosity for Arthur barely concealed. "I know. You don't have to tell me. He's a dyed-in-the-wool bastard. And furthermore, I'm quite sure he does it on purpose. As for Emma, she appears not to notice. That's sheer defensiveness, of course. You know my sister. She doesn't miss a trick." Winston shook his head. "I'll be glad when Frank and Natalie are married next week, and these interminable luncheons and dinners end. Then we won't have to suffer Ainsley's continuing presence."

"He's a bit of an unsavory character, isn't he?" Paul probed. Winston was silent, and Paul continued, "I know a lot of Englishmen of his particular upbringing and education do have somewhat effeminate mannerisms, and that these don't necessarily indicate a lack of masculinity, but, if I didn't know differently, I'd swear to God he was a raving homosexual. Don't you agree, Winston?"

"It's crossed my mind, and more than once lately. I've noticed a change in Arthur over the past few months. Certain tendencies seem to be coming out. Being married to Emma and fathering the twins doesn't necessarily preclude sexual deviation, although I've no evidence to prove that about him. And he does go after women all the time."

Paul frowned. "Perhaps he likes both sexes. That's not unheard of, you know—bisexuality."

"I wish to God my sister had never married him. We all tried to stop her, but she's very stubborn. She was on the rebound, of course."

"I realize that only too well," Paul muttered, and looked down at the drink in his hand. "You don't have to rub it in."

Winston drew Paul into a secluded corner of Lionel Stewart's drawing room, where the guests had gathered after a prenuptial luncheon. Winston, who had always liked Paul, had discovered that his admiration and empathy for the Australian had only increased over the past ten days when, at various social functions, they had been thrown together and had gravitated to each other. Now he said, in a confidential tone, "Frank tells me you have been seeing quite a lot of Emma during the last month. I'm happy about that." Observing the look of astonishment flit across Paul's handsome face, Winston grinned. "I know you regard me as the protective older brother, so I just wanted you to know that I approve, in spite of the complications in your very complicated lives.

Emma needs a man like you, Paul. To be accurate, she needs *you*. You're about the only man I know who is strong enough to handle her on a permanent basis. She can be quite intimidating. Most men can't cope with an independent and brilliant woman—albeit a very alluring one!"

Paul smiled engagingly, a trifle startled, but delighted at this endorsement. "Thanks, Winston. I'm glad to hear it. And I agree with you." His eyes crinkled with laughter. "Do me a favor and tell that to the lady in question. I need all the help I can get."

"I have told her. So has Frank. But you know Emma. She has to make up her own mind." Winston regarded Paul keenly. "Perhaps she thinks you'll take off for Australia at any moment. After all, you do have vast business interests there."

"True enough. However, I've told her that I intend to be around for a long time. It doesn't seem to make a dent. Actually I've reorganized my business enterprises so well in the last few years I will only need to make an occasional trip to Australia from now on—maybe once a year, twice at the most. Emma is also aware that I expanded my London offices last year and that I'm going to operate from here in the future." He shook his head. "I don't say much anymore because she always looks skeptical. I can't say I blame her."

"Maybe you've been *too* subtle," Winston volunteered. "You know what women are like. Sometimes you've got to spell everything out for them."

"Emma's hardly like most women."

"That's the understatement of the year." Winston laughed. "Give her a chance to get used to the idea that you're here on a permanent basis. She'll come around to accepting it eventually."

Paul nodded and glanced about the spacious, elegantly appointed drawing room, seeking out Emma. He spotted her talking to Frank and Natalie and the latter's parents. It was a scorching July day and everyone was suffering from the heat. The guests looked uncomfortable and a little wilted—except for the incomparable Emma. She was wearing a yellow silk summer frock that was simply styled, crisp and fresh. It gave her a carefree girlish air, as did the gay confection on top of her russet bobbed hair. She looked exceedingly feminine, and the other women paled in comparison. It was not only her beauty that set her apart, but that incandescent glow which emanated from her. It took one hell of a woman to conduct herself so elegantly and with such composure in the light of Ainsley's antics, he conceded. Then he saw, to his surprise, that Emma was leaving. He handed his drink to Winston hastily. "Look after this, old chap. I'll be back in a minute. Excuse me."

Paul caught up with Emma in the entrance hall. "Where are you off to in such a hurry?" he asked, taking her arm possessively and turning her to face him fully. "Running out? I thought I was the only one who did that." He chuckled.

Emma could not help laughing. "I am also fleet of foot when I want to be, Mr. McGill," she said. "I felt it would be simpler if I made a quiet exit. I didn't want to break up the party, and unfortunately, I have to get back to the store."

Like hell you do, Paul commented dryly to himself, guessing she wanted to escape her ludicrous husband. "I'll drive you," Paul asserted swiftly, taking charge and propelling her to the door.

At first Emma made a little desultory conversation as Paul edged his Rolls-Royce through the Saturday-afternoon traffic congesting Mayfair. But after a few moments she fell silent, ruminating on the luncheon. She was seething. Arthur's tasteless display had appalled her. He had not only demeaned himself but her as well. Usually indifferent to him, she had experienced real discomfiture during lunch and afterwards. She had handled it well, concealing her fury behind a dignified façade, yet, nonetheless, Arthur's disregard for the social amenities rankled. She could no longer afford to turn a blind eye. After Frank's wedding she would not expose herself in social situations. In part, her embarrassment sprang from the fact that Paul had witnessed it all. And yet, curiously, his presence had also been comforting.

Emma stole a glance at Paul, wondering what he was thinking. His face revealed nothing, On her recent trips to London she had dined with Paul on a regular basis. He had taken her to the theater and the opera, and to parties. He had been charming, gallant—and oddly detached. She had half expected him to make overtures after their first few evenings together, but he had not, somewhat to her relief. In all honesty, she had wanted to see him, to spend time with him, and she could not deny he held a fascination for her. On the other hand, her inbred sense of self-preservation still made her wary of him. Her marriage was no marriage at all, yet the rest of her life was orderly. She could not permit anything to jeopardize her tranquil state of mind, acquired at such cost, and Paul could easily do that because he had the ability to hurt her. She was determined never to suffer for love again. An unprecedented feeling of depression swamped her. She looked at her watch.

"Perhaps you had better take me home, Paul," she said. "It's a bit late to go to the store. It's almost five o'clock."

"Of course," Paul said. "Anything you want, Emma." He noticed that her expression was pensive and a wave of tenderness swept through him. As he stopped at the traffic lights he pondered on her, trying to gauge her feelings for him. She was pleasant and gay whenever they met, yet she held herself apart, and he had admitted days ago that she was impervious to his charms. He knew she was riddled with insecurity about him and he had acted accordingly, endeavoring to dispel this, but apparently without success. He wondered if his strategy had been all wrong. As he herded towards Belgrave Square he made a snap decision, drove around the square, bypassed Wilton Mews, and headed back to Mayfair.

"Where are you going?" Emma asked in a puzzled voice. "I thought you were taking me home."

"That's exactly where I am taking you. *Home*. With me."

Emma gasped. "But—"

"No buts, Emma," he said forcefully and with a finality that forbade argument.

Emma held herself stiffly in the seat, clutching her bag. A protest rose on her lips, remained unspoken as her mouth went dry. Taken aback at this sudden bold move on his part, she found herself in a quandary. She had never been to his flat and was petrified of being alone with him. A self-deprecatory smile slid onto her face. She, who was afraid of nothing and no one, was actually frightened of Paul McGill! Yet he was only a man. After all, she was a grown woman and perfectly capable of looking after herself. Anyway, was not life full of risks?

His face was rigidly set and determined and he appeared to be perturbed. The tension in his broad shoulders conveyed itself to her, and she shivered involuntarily. Her eyes focused on his strong hands, which gripped the steering wheel so

fiercely his knuckles protruded sharply, and, to her consternation, her heart began to beat with unusual rapidity.

Paul brought the car to a stop in Berkeley Square. Silently
he helped her out and took hold of her arm firmly, maneuvering her across the lobby and into the lift. His fingers bit
into her flesh, yet she welcomed his support. She thought her
legs would buckle at any moment.

He did not release her even after they had entered his flat.
He slammed the door shut with ferocity and swung her to
face him. He lifted her veil with the other hand, searching
her face, and then he pulled her to him roughly. His lips
crushed down on hers, hard and insistent. She tried to push
him away, but he was too strong for her. He tightened his
hold on her, tremors rippling along his arms, and she heard
his heart banging like a sledgehammer in his expansive chest.
His mouth suddenly softened on hers. He parted her lips
gently and found her tongue with his. Emma ceased struggling as a swooning faintness enveloped her. She found herself yielding to him, clinging to him, returning his kisses. Her
handbag fell to the floor unheeded. His hands slid down her
back and onto her buttocks, and he pressed her slender body
into his so that they were welded together. He shifted his
stance slightly and she felt the hardness of his rising passion
through the thin silk of her frock and her legs almost gave
way, and she was suffused with that old familiar warmth
which spread like fire through her body. He pushed her head
back against his wide shoulder and covered her breast with
one hand, his fingers rubbing against it and playing with the
nipple with increasing urgency. She was overwhelmed by
him, and filled with exquisite sensations long forgotten but
now so well remembered. She was helpless in his arms.

Paul's fervent kisses ceased abruptly, and he looked down
into her face. She gazed back at him dizzily, saw the wild
desire leaping from his clear blue eyes, took in the burgeoning impatience congesting his face, recognized the physical
and emotional pressures driving him beyond endurance, and
new tremors swept through her. Her lips opened and a cry
strangled in her throat. His face closed in on her, his eyes
darkening to brooding violet, and he was kissing her again,
ravaging her mouth almost savagely, and she did not want
him to stop. Prayed he would not stop. Desire engulfed her,
and all of her true feelings surfaced, obliterating her fears,

both rational and irrational. Her defenses crumbled like a sand castle before an onrushing tide, and she willingly surrendered to him, her sensuality, so long submerged, taking hold of her completely, dazing her.

He placed her away from him, but he did not remove his hands from her shoulders. His mouth curved up in a small challenging smile. He leaned forward, pressing her against the door. "Now tell me you don't love me!" he whispered hoarsely in her ear. "Now tell me you don't want me!" His breath was warm and tantalizing against her throat. Before she could respond, he said in a low voice thickened by desire, "You can't deny either, Emma, because I know you do!" He peered deeply into her burning face and perceived the yearning in her eyes that surely reflected his own, and he finally released her. He took her hand gently in his and led her into the bedroom.

Late-afternoon sunlight was streaming in through the windows and Paul left her to draw the curtains. The room was suddenly cool and dim. Mesmerized, she stood in the middle of the floor watching him. He swung around and strode back to her, moving lithely, like a great panther, and he appeared taller and broader and more domineering in his masculinity than ever. He removed her hat and tossed it onto a chair. He pulled off her gloves slowly. He unbuttoned her dress and slipped it over her shoulders. It fell to the floor, a rippling pool of yellow at her feet. He guided her away from the dress and sat her down on the bottom of the bed, all the while smiling at her faintly, and his eyes did not once leave her face. He discarded his jacket, his tie, and his shirt, and she caught her breath, stunned at the sight of his handsome torso and the sheer physical size and beauty of him.

He knelt before her. He took off her shoes and kissed her feet, and then he buried his head in her lap. Automatically she ran her hands through his crisp black hair and bent to kiss the crown. She smoothed her fingers over his enormous shoulders and down his sunburned back, and she felt his muscles rippling under her touch.

"There hasn't been a day I haven't thought about you, Emma. A day I haven't wanted you. Longed for you. Needed you, my love. Never in all these years," he cried in a muffled voice. He gripped her thighs, burying his face deeper into

her. He finally raised his head and looked up, his eyes
brillant. "I've never stopped loving you, Emma."

"And I've never stopped loving you, Paul," she said softly,
and her eyes grew huge, turned dark, and swam with tears.

He stood up and pressed her back onto the bed. He
stretched himself on top of her, encircling her with his arms,
kissing her face, her throat, and her shoulders. It seemed to
Paul that the rest of their clothes just fell away. They were
naked and in each other's arms again, and he was blinded by
his searing passion, the feverishness of his unendurable desire. He could hardly wait to possess her, to become one with
her, but he controlled himself rigorously, leading her along as
he always had in the past, arousing her as only he could. He
covered her entire body with kisses, and caressed every
intimate and erotic part of her until she gasped with delight,
and her unbridled excitement only served to inflame him
more than ever.

She thought: *There is only him. He is the only thing that
matters in my life. He is the only man I have ever truly loved
and desired. If he goes away, and I never see him again as
long as I live, this moment will have been worth it. It will last
me forever.*

He felt her fingers gripping his shoulders. She stiffened
and spasmed and then her body was wracked by shudders,
and she called his name in a low moaning voice and he knew,
with the utmost certainty, that only with him had she experienced this special kind of ecstasy and fulfillment. He lifted
his head and trailed his lips up over her smooth flat stomach
until they reached her breasts. His mouth lingered there a
moment and moved on into the hollow of her neck. She
sighed and quivered under him, her arms entwining him, her
hands sliding voluptuously down his back. He thought he was
going to explode. He arched his body over hers, his arms
braced on either side of her, and gazed down into her pleasure-
filled eyes. Her deepest emotions were explicit on her face,
that best-loved face that haunted him always, and he was
moved by the wonder of it all, by the wonder of her, and his
heart twisted.

And he took her then, his manhood at full flood, thrusting
deeply into the very core of her, to touch her heart, and she
responded with a rush of enveloping sweet warmth, sponta-

neously, wildly giving herself with no reserve. And her need for him was as clamoring as his need for her.

Memory became reality. Pain was transmuted into joy. Anger was diffused by passion. They were fused together in desire and exquisite bliss. Having suffered for each other and their love, there was a new awareness between them, an intensity of feelings heightened, a rare poignancy in their breathless consummation. And as perfect as their lovemaking had been in the past, this time it was more stunning than ever before, and they were devastated by the impact of their reunion.

Much later, when they lay clasped in each other's arms, unable to tear themselves apart, shattered and exhausted, Paul said, "I will never leave you again, Emma. Never, as long as I live. I know you're afraid I will hurt you. But I won't. You must believe me, my darling."

"I'm not afraid, Paul," she said against his chest. "And I do believe you. I know now you will be with me always."

He felt her smile. "What is it?"

"Years ago someone called me Doubting Emma. Perhaps I was. Do you remember when you quoted Abélard to me and told me to have faith, before you went back to the front?"

"Yes, I do, my love."

"Well, if I had had that faith, when you were absent in Australia in 1919, perhaps all this anguish and torment we have experienced could have been avoided. I'll never doubt you again."

He smiled and pulled her closer to him and kissed a strand of her hair. "We'll make up for the lost years," he said.

FIFTY-THREE

Emma let herself into her house in Roundhay, shivering slightly from the cold December wind. She slipped out of the sable coat, which Paul had bought for her the previous winter when they had been in New York together, and threw it onto a chair. She walked briskly across the hall, thinking of Paul with a rush of tenderness. She must telephone him immediately to let him know she was arriving in London tomorrow.

She went into the library and stopped dead in her tracks on the threshold, astonishment flashing onto her face. "Good heavens, Edwina! What are you doing at home? I thought the winter term didn't end until next week."

"It doesn't," Edwina snapped, staring coldly at her mother.

Her daughter's face was unusually pale, and the girl's distress instantly communicated itself to her. Upon reaching the sofa Emma made a motion to kiss her, but Edwina swiftly averted her head. Faltering, Emma sat down opposite Edwina. On closer inspection the girl seemed positively ill. Or was it that gray school uniform which drained the color from her face? Edwina looked almost gaunt in the winter afternoon light.

"Whatever is it, darling?" Emma asked with real concern. "What are you doing at home? Did something happen to upset you?"

"No, it didn't. I came home because I wanted to see you," Edwina retorted. "To talk to you about this." She pulled an envelope out of her pocket and tossed it to Emma.

"Whatever it is they are teaching you at that expensive boarding school, it certainly isn't manners," Emma remarked softly, and bent to pick up the paper at her feet.

Edwina cried shrilly, "You don't have to bother looking inside. It's my birth certificate. You wouldn't give me the original, so I wrote to Somerset House for a copy. You *know* what's on it. And now I know why you have hidden it from me all these years."

The envelope fluttered in Emma's shaking hand and she stared at it blankly, the blood draining out of her. She looked at Edwina, a feeling of nausea overwhelming her, and her mouth was stiff and white-lipped. She could not speak.

In turn, Edwina regarded Emma fixedly, a scornful expression on her face. "Why are *you* looking so shocked, *Mother*?" she spat. "I'm the one who should be shocked. After all, I'm the one who is illegitimate." She pronounced the word with such harshness, and her contempt was so evident, Emma flinched.

Edwina now leaned forward and her silver-gray eyes were febrile with hatred. "How could you let me go on believing Joe Lowther was my father all these years, when it was

Blackie O'Neill?" She laughed with derision. "Blackie O'Neill! Your dearest friend. I'll bet he is. Hanging around you like a lovesick dog for as long as I can remember, and through two marriages!" Her eyes narrowed. "You disgust me, Mother. I grieved for Joe for years after he was killed, and you let me. How cruel of you!"

Emma managed to pull herself together, but her voice shook as she said, "Would my telling you have helped, Edwina? Would it have assuaged your grief, or lessened it? Joe *was* your father, in the best sense of that word. He loved you as much, if not more than his own child. You loved him, too, and you would still have grieved for him if you had known the truth. Any man can father a child, Edwina. It's what a man does after the child is born that makes him a *real* father, a *good* father. And although you were not of Joe's flesh and blood he certainly treated you as if you were. And that's all that counts."

"You were just protecting yourself! You—you—lying tramp!"

Emma gaped at the eighteen-year-old girl sitting before her and she did not know what to do, or to say, to calm her, to deflect her obvious pain.

"And what am I supposed to call myself, might I ask, Mother *dear?* I don't have a name, do I? Is it O'Neill? Or Harte, perhaps?" Edwina sucked in her breath harshly and her eyes were metallic. "You are a lying, immoral bitch!"

Emma recoiled as if she had been slapped but she ignored the abusive remarks and took control of herself. "Your name is Lowther, Edwina. Joe adopted you and gave you his name."

"Thank you. That's all I wanted to know." Edwina rose and held out her hand. "I'll have my birth certificate, since I went to so much trouble to get it." She grabbed it from Emma rudely. "I am leaving."

Emma also rose. She took hold of Edwina's arm, but the girl snatched it away angrily. "Don't touch me!" she screamed, and darted across the library.

"Edwina, please sit down," Emma said quietly. "You are old enough to discuss this with me calmly and intelligently. In a sensible manner." Her voice took on a pleading note. "Please, darling. I know you are terribly upset and hurt, but let me explain. Please give me a chance to tell you—"

"Nothing you have to say interests me. I'm leaving," Edwina rejoined.

"Where are you going?" Emma asked agitatedly, and stepped forward, stretching out her hand imploringly to her daughter. "Please, Edwina, don't go. Let us talk this out. I want to make you understand, and then perhaps you will forgive me for hiding the truth. I had good reasons. I wanted to protect you. I only had your welfare at heart, my darling. I love you."

Edwina gave Emma a scathing look and her voice was tinged with bitterness. "I told you I am not interested in your explanations." She drew herself up haughtily. "I am leaving this house and I will never set foot in it again."

"But, darling, you can't leave! Where will you go?" Emma's throat ached with suppressed tears.

"I am going to stay with Cousin Freda in Ripon for Christmas. After the holidays, I intend to go to finishing school in Switzerland. The one I asked you to send me to, but which you refused to consider. Please make the necessary arrangements now." Edwina smiled contemptuously. "You're rich enough to pull all the right strings to get me in at this late date. I presume you will continue to pay my school tuition, Mother. And that you will not stop my allowance."

"How could you even think that?" Emma cried. "I have never deprived you of anything and I never will. Please stay." Emma's eyes brimmed and her voice was unsteady. "Don't leave like this. Let us discuss—"

"I have said all I want to say to you." Edwina stepped purposefully to the door. Her hand rested briefly on the knob. She turned and looked at Emma and her delicate face twisted. "I hate you, Mother! I never want to see you again as long as I live!"

The door slammed behind Edwina. Emma stared at it, her face crumpling, and she staggered into the nearest chair. She dropped her head into her hands and the tears rolled silently down her cheeks. She had dreaded this day for years, had tried to avert this ugly confrontation. And now that it had finally happened she felt incapable of dealing with Edwina, who was so unbending. She had always known her daughter would react violently, just as she had always known she would lose Edwina's affection, scant as it was, when the truth was revealed. Edwina had never had any deep feelings for her. Edwina had loved only Joe and Freda. All the devotion and tenderness she had showered on her firstborn had fallen on stony ground. Edwina had rejected her, even as a small child. She wondered suddenly if she should go and tell Edwina who her real father was. But that would not assuage Edwina's pain and terrible humiliation. She would still be illegitimate. It was better to let matters rest for the moment. A jumble of painful memories and stark images danced around in her head. She thought of her struggles, the sacrifices she had made, the fears and humiliations she had experienced. And she thought, too, of all she had done to shield Edwina. Had it all been for nothing? Surely not. Besides, she had not known what else to do, and she *had* done her best.

Emma wiped the tears from her face, and her inherent optimism surfaced. Perhaps in a few weeks, when Edwina was calmer, there would be a chance for a reconciliation. This new thought cheered her and she hurried upstairs. She would persuade Edwina to meet with her after Christmas, beg her to do so if necessary, and surely somehow they could reach an understanding. But to Emma's dismay the girl was nowhere to be found. Emma stood in the center of Edwina's room, staring at the open armoire where empty coat hangers told their own story. She crossed to the window, looking down into the driveway. The Rolls had disappeared. Edwina had obviously asked the chauffeur to take her to the railway station. Emma pressed her throbbing head against the windowpane and she knew, with a terrible sinking feeling, that there never would be a reconciliation. Her daughter was lost to her.

She turned away, her face ashen and troubled, and walked with leaden steps into her own bedroom. She must speak to Blackie. She reached for the phone and then her hand fell away. He was in Ireland until next week, which would be soon enough to break the news. Emma sat down wearily, overcome by a sense of loss. And her heart ached for Edwina, who was suffering such agonies, and she longed to comfort her.

Eventually Emma stood up, pulling herself together with effort, and went into the bathroom. She splashed cold water onto her aching face and her swollen eyes, and redid her makeup. When she was sufficiently composed, Emma telephoned Arthur at the office. "Are you coming home for dinner tonight?" she asked quietly when he came to the phone.

Arthur was taken aback. "No. Why?" he asked in his usual peremptory tone.

"I must see you, Arthur. It's rather urgent, actually, since I am leaving for London tomorrow. I won't take up much of your time. Just half an hour at the most."

"Well—all right," he acquiesced grudgingly, although more from curiosity than a desire to please her. "I'll be there in about twenty minutes."

"Thank you, Arthur." Emma hung up and went downstairs to wait for her husband.

When Arthur entered the library a little later he gave her a guarded look and said, "What's ruffled your feathers? You look bloody awful." He poured himself a drink and carried it to the fireplace. He sat down opposite Emma and scrutinized her with great interest. "What's wrong?"

Emma said, "Arthur, I have something important to tell you."

"Go ahead, my dear. I'm all ears."

"I'm going to have a baby," Emma said evenly.

Arthur had the drink in his hand halfway to his mouth and for once in his life it did not reach its destination. He banged it down unsteadily and gawped at her, for a moment nonplussed. And then he threw back his head and laughed. "Oh my God! That's rich! Little Miss Goody Two-shoes has finally taken a lover. He must be a brave man indeed to want to tango with you!" he cried. "And who's the lucky fellow?"

"I have no intention of telling you that, Arthur. I merely wanted you to know that I am almost four months pregnant. I am going to have the child, and you will recognize it as yours."

"You don't think I'm going to give some bastard my name, do you? That's preposterous. I shall divorce you immediately, Emma."

"I don't think you will, Arthur." Emma fixed her cool gaze on him and smiled faintly. "I don't want a divorce. At least, not at this moment. And neither do you."

"I bloody well do. You're not going to rear your illegitimate brat as mine."

Emma rose and walked across to the bookshelves. She pressed a button and a panel swung open to reveal a concealed safe. She opened it, removed a pile of documents, and returned to the fireplace. She looked at Arthur thoughtfully and said, "Your father is a conservative old gentleman, Arthur. And as fond of him as I am, I have to admit he is also narrow-minded and decidedly old-fashioned. If I give him these documents he will cut you out of his will at once, and without the proverbial shilling. And I fully intend to hand them over to him if you make trouble for me, or attempt to divorce me. And these do make fascinating reading." She smiled her icy smile. "Your father may not be surprised to learn of your gross infidelities to me over the years, or of your excessive drinking and gambling. However, Arthur, I am quite certain he will be shocked to discover his son, his heir, has questionable relationships with young men of dubious character who are known sexual deviants."

Arthur looked like a man who had been handed a death sentence. "That's a damnable lie!" he shouted. "You're bluffing!"

"No, I'm not, Arthur. You see, I have had a detective on you for several years. There is absolutely nothing I don't know about your private life. Unfortunately you have not been very discreet."

"I say you are bluffing!" Arthur yelled.

Emma offered him the documents. "See for yourself."

He snatched them from her anxiously and shuffled through them, his eyes widening. He paled, and then an embarrassed flush suffused his neck and face. He looked at her, and very deliberately began to tear the papers into shreds, throwing the pieces into the fire.

Emma let him continue without a word and, when he had disposed of them entirely, she laughed. "Oh, Arthur, you do underestimate me. Those were copies. I have the originals safely locked away. And, furthermore, I won't hestitate to use them if you force my hand. I promise you I *will* go to your father."

"You bloody cow! That's blackmail!"

"Call it what you will, Arthur." Emma sat back and folded her hands in her lap.

He stood up unsteadily. "What a nerve you have! Expecting me to live in this house with you, when you're carrying another man's bastard." He laughed hollowly. "I'm not going to tolerate your adultery."

Emma looked at him coldly. "Don't be a hypocrite. That's exactly what I've been tolerating for years."

He stepped away with abruptness, glaring at her with

unconcealed animosity. He was shaking now and his face was strained and gray. He looked down at her. "You bitch!" he hissed. "You may have won this round, but we'll see about the next."

Emma remained utterly still, and she was silent. Arthur continued to glower at her for a prolonged moment and then he walked across the room in swift deliberate steps. When he reached the door he swung to face her. He was livid and fuming with rage. He drew in his breath. "God, how I hate you!" he cried, then he left the library, banging the door behind him with a thunderous crash.

FIFTY-FOUR

Paul McGill paced the floor of Emma's living room in Wilton Mews with restless impatience, his hands plunged deep into his pockets, his shoulders hunched. He stopped at the window and gazed out, and when he eventually turned his head his eyes focused on Emma with intensity. He observed her reflectively, his face troubled.

Finally, he said, "I don't understand why you didn't ask Arthur for a divorce, Emma. I really don't. I thought we had agreed we would seek your freedom immediately. Why are you procrastinating? Is it because Constance won't divorce me? Don't you trust me? Don't you know that I intend to be with you always? I would like an explanation, Emma."

"Come and sit down next to me, darling," Emma said gently.

Paul joined her on the sofa and she took his hand in hers. "Of course I trust you, Paul. My decision had nothing to do with your situation. I know you are doing everything you can to rectify it. And I *will* divorce Arthur. But not until after the baby has been born, registered, and christened. I want the baby to have a name, Paul. I don't want the birth certificate to show that it is illegitimate."

"What you are actually saying is that you want *my* child to be brought up as Ainsley's! I don't like that, Emma. I'm not sure I will stand for it!"

Emma stared at him in surprise. This was the first time he

had ever spoken harshly to her. She must make him understand her motives. "I know how you feel," she placated. "But
we must think about the child, Paul. You see—"

"I *am* thinking about the child. I want it to have the benefit
of my love and protection and all the other things I can give
it, and I don't want it growing up not knowing *me*. Furthermore, I want my child reared under my influence and not
another man's. I won't have it living under Ainsley's roof
under any circumstances. You know my opinion of him. I
thought I had made myself clear about all this, Emma."

"Yes, you did, darling. I told you the baby would remain in
London. But I must protect the child. It must not carry the
stigma of illegitimacy all of its life."

Paul sighed impatiently. "My money will protect the child,
Emma. Give it immunity from scandal. Besides, I told you I
would adopt it immediately. Please, Emma, you must consider naming me as the father on the birth certificate. I wish
to acknowledge paternity."

"No! We can't do that!" Emma cried fiercely, her eyes
flaring. Instantly recognizing the hurt flickering on his face,
she brought his hand up to her lips and kissed it. She looked
at Paul long and hard. She drew a deep breath and very
slowly, in a sure voice, she told him.

She told him first of her confrontation with Edwina the
preceding day, and of the way she had handled Arthur. She
told him about her early life as a servant at Fairley Hall. She
told him about Edwin Fairley, her pregnancy, his repudiation of her, and her anguished flight to Leeds as a terrified
young girl. She told him about her struggles and her poverty,
her deprivations and the punishing days of toil she had endured. She told him of Gerald Fairley's attempted rape of
her. She told him everything there was to know, and she
spoke with candor and with eloquence, and she neither
embellished nor dramatized. Very simply, she gave him the
facts without any show of emotion.

Paul listened attentively, his eyes riveted on her face, and
he was moved as he had never been before by anyone. When
she had finished he took her in his arms and stroked her hair,
and pulled her closer to him, overwhelmed by feelings of
protectiveness and abiding love.

"Whoever passed around the ridiculous story that this is a
civilized world we live in?" he murmured into her hair, and

kissed her forehead. He fell silent and then he said softly, "Oh, Emma, Emma. I have to make up for so much—all the pain you have suffered over the years. And I will. I promise you that."

Paul held her away from him and looked deeply into her eyes. "Whyever didn't you tell me all this before?" When she dropped her eyes and did not answer, he continued gently, "Did you think it would have made any difference to the way I feel about you?" He bent forward and kissed her on the lips. "You don't know me very well if you think your past matters to me. I love you all the more for what you have made of yourself, what you have become. And for your indomitability and enormous strength. You are a very special woman, Emma."

"I didn't deliberataly avoid telling you," Emma said quietly. "There just never seemed to be the right opportunity."

Paul gazed at her, his heart bursting with his love. He thought: Oh, my darling, what cruelties and humiliations you must have endured and how bravely you have dealt with life.

Emma said, "You do understand now, don't you, Paul? I mean, about my not divorcing Arthur just yet. I don't want our child to turn on me one day. I couldn't bear a repetition of yesterday's scene with Edwina."

"That would never happen. Not with our child. But yes, I do understand," he said. "I will do whatever you want, Emma."

Their child, a girl, was born early in May of 1925, at a private nursing home in London. It was Paul who paced the waiting-room floor. It was Paul who took Emma in his arms after the delivery. It was Paul who chose the baby's name. She was to be called Daisy after his mother.

The following day Paul visited Emma, his face wreathed in smiles, his arms filled with flowers and gifts. "Where's my daughter?" he asked.

"The nurse will bring her in momentarily," Emma said, smiling radiantly.

He settled himself on the edge of the bed and embraced Emma. "And how's my love?"

"I'm wonderful, Paul. But you must stop spoiling me."

"You might as well get used to it. That's the way it is going to be from now on." He took her hand in his and to her amazement he pulled off her wedding ring before she could protest, opened the window, and threw it out.

"Good heavens, Paul, whatever are you doing?"

He did not respond. He reached into his pocket and took out a platinum wedding band. He slipped it onto her finger and then he added the great square-cut McGill emerald which had belonged to his mother and his grandmother before her.

"We may not have had the benefit of clergy, but as far as I'm concerned you are my wife," he said. "From this day forward until death do us part."

Since his return to England in 1923, Paul McGill had made his feelings for Emma obvious in every way. He was passionately in love with her and his emotional involvement transcended all else in his life. He admired her as well, and was filled with a sense of pride in her achievements. After the birth of their daughter these feelings were only intensified. She and their child became the core of his life, his reason for living. They gave shape and meaning to everything he did, to the way he ran his life and his enormous business enterprises. Old disappointments and defeats, and the hurts which had accumulated over the years, were swept away and he was filled with burgeoning hopes for the future. Daisy might not bear his name, but she was his child, of his blood, and in her he saw the continuation of the McGill line and the dynasty founded by his grandfather, the Scottish sea captain who had settled in Coonamble in 1852.

In all truth, he worshipped Emma and Daisy and he had no intention of letting either of them out of his sight, or his presence, for very long, despite the complications of their lives and the obstacles presented by their marital entanglements. He took matters firmly into his own hands in the late summer of 1925, when he purchased an unusually beautiful mansion in Belgrave Square, immediately giving the deeds of ownership to Emma. He then set about remodeling it into two flats, sparing no expense. The smaller bachelor quarters on the ground floor he retained for himself. The three floors above became an exquisitely appointed maisonette for Emma, Daisy, a nanny, a housekeeper, and a maid, whom he engaged. To the casual observer the two flats were entirely separate and self-contained, each having its own entrance. But they were linked by a private interior elevator.

They lived together, but discreetly so, with an eye to all the proprieties, for Emma was reluctant to flaunt their relationship in view of her other children and her responsibilities as a mother. Paul was constantly astonished at the duality in her nature. He would tease her, calling her a bundle of contradictions, and point out that she, who was so fearless in business and scorned what the world thought of her, was curiously sensitive about public opinion regarding her personal morals. "Once I'm divorced I won't give a damn," she would temporize, and Paul would simply smile, realizing that her self-consciousness about their life sprang from the experiences of her early life.

As it happened, the divorce came sooner than anyone anticipated. In June, acutely aware of Emma's overwhelming desire to protect their child, Paul permitted Emma to take Daisy to Yorkshire, agreeing she could be christened at a local church in Leeds. However, he insisted on being invited and traveled to Yorkshire with Frank and Natalie for the occasion. As a long-standing friend of the family, his presence was not unseemly, and, because of an unexpected turn of events, it actually went almost unnoticed. Several days prior to the christening, Arthur Ainsley's mother collapsed and died of a heart attack. The baptism, following so quickly on the heels of the funeral, was a glum affair and Frederick Ainsley and Arthur were so grief-stricken they were hardly aware of the proceedings or of the other guests, and, also, Arthur had no interest in the event. Daisy was duly christened without incident and the next day Emma took her back to London. Three months later Frederick Ainsley, old, frail, and long in ill health, followed his wife to the grave. Arthur came into his inheritance and, in an unprecedented show of gallantry that stunned Emma's brothers, he allowed her to divorce him on the grounds of adultery. Emma was not stunned. She had cannily bought Arthur's gallantry for ten thousand pounds.

Once the decree nisi was granted, Emma's life changed radically. She brought the twins, Robin and Elizabeth, to live with her in Belgrave Square, and, just as she had guessed, Arthur made no objections. Apart from being happy to be free of him at last, she also welcomed the idea of bringing up the twins without his influence.

Kit, who was at boarding school, spent half terms and vacations with Emma and made no secret of the fact that he approved of Paul and was devoted to him. Nor did he shed any tears about the abrupt disappearance of Arthur Ainsley from his young life. Emma also reorganized her business drastically, so that she could spend most of her time in London. Winston was appointed managing director of the Yorkshire shops and the mills, and Emma supervised her northern industries from her headquarters at the Knightsbridge store, making a monthly trip to Leeds, where she spent five hectic days, working long hours with Winston.

She and Paul were as circumspect as possible, especially in front of the children, but as time passed no one seemed to care about their unusual living arrangements and their rather extraordinary household filled with her diverse children by different fathers. Very early Paul had established himself as the titular head of the household and with his strength, plus his inherent gentleness, he was both respected and adored by the children, and he quickly became the father figure to them all. Slowly Emma began to relax. Paul had patiently explained to her that their combined wealth set them above the usual conventions, making them invulnerable to social censorship, and she admitted the truth in what he said. Her natural self-confidence and courage soon overcame her earlier misgivings.

Paul and Emma were inseparable. He bedecked her in magnificent jewels and furs and lovely gowns. He entertained on a lavish scale with her at his side as his hostess. They went to the theater, the opera, concerts, dinners, and parties. They mixed with the wealthiest and the most influential people in London and in other cities across the world—politicians, tycoons, socialites, and men and women from the arts and letters on three continents. He took her to the capitals of Europe when he traveled, whether for business or for pleasure. She went with him to New York and to Texas, where his oil fields were located, and twice she accompanied him on his annual trips to Australia. Just as she had fallen in love with New York and Texas, so, too, was she captivated by the Antipodes. Paul was still endeavoring to gain his freedom, but continually met implacable opposition from Constance, who would not agree to a divorce. This was the one thing that marred his happiness. Although he had legally adopted Daisy, and had provided for both her and her mother, he desperately wanted to marry Emma and put their lives in order. However, so secure was Emma in their relationship by this time she was unperturbed by the situation and constantly tried to alleviate Paul's anxiety. Now it was she who told *him* to relax and not to fret so much, optimistically remarking that things would work out in the end, reiterating her love for him and reassuring him of her happiness.

The only disturbing factor in Emma's life was Edwina's continued estrangement, for she had not been able to mend the rift between them. Her only tenuous communication with her eldest daughter was through Winston, who took care of Edwina's financial affairs on Emma's behalf. After two years at the finishing school in Switzerland, Edwina had taken a flat in Mayfair and was leading a dizzy social life with her upper-class friends, enjoying her status as the well-heeled daughter of a very rich woman. Emma had not curtailed Edwina's spending, and had set up a trust fund for her which gave the girl an annual income of no mean proportions. Emma longed to see Edwina, to draw her back into the bosom of the family, yet she was wise enough to refrain from making overtures, understanding that the first move must necessarily come from the girl.

And so for the most part Emma was content, more so than ever before. Paul's abiding love, and hers for him, sustained her at all times. Emma also took great consolation in Daisy, who was her particular pride, and even though she was reluctant to admit it even to herself, she loved Daisy more than any of her other children. This was the child of love, the one child she had truly carried with joy. There was a closeness between them she had not experienced with those born before, and it only became stronger with time. Sometimes, when she looked at the growing child, Emma's heart would clench with the most overwhelming feelings of tenderness, seeing her beloved Paul so perfectly reflected in her. For Daisy was undoubtedly her father's daughter, favoring him in every way. Being his constant companion, she unconsciously copied many of his mannerisms and when she smiled her face became as mischievous and as endearing to Emma as his. By nature Daisy was sweet and loving, and because of the affection and attention showered on her by her parents she was a self-confident, outgoing little girl, yet she was utterly un-spoiled and natural with everyone. There was much of Emma in her character. She had inherited her mother's sunny dispo-sition, her optimism, and her stubborn will.

When Daisy was five years old, Paul had insisted she accompany him and Emma to Australia. After a week in Sydney he took them up to Coonamble and they spent four weeks at Dunoon. An unusual rapport sprang up between the vivacious little girl and her half brother, Howard, and Emma and Paul were touched by the relationship. Daisy seemed to reach the boy in a way no one else ever had before, and her devotion to him and his dependency on her warmed their hearts. They returned every year thereafter with Paul, who did not want to deprive Howard of the joy his little step-sister so apparently brought to his restricted life.

The years slipped by so quickly Emma often wondered what happened to time. The children were all growing up and leaving the house in Belgrave Square. Kit, a fine-looking young man who much resembled Joe Lowther, went to Leeds University, and the twins departed for their respective board-ing schools, bitterly complaining about being seperated for the first time. If Daisy was Emma's best-loved child, then Robin was undoubtedly her favorite son, and she missed him more than she had realized she would during school terms. Robin had none of Arthur Ainsley's annoying characteristics or habits, and bore a strong likeness to Winston. He was a thin vital boy, with a vivid intelligence, a quick wit, and inbred charm. Scholarly by inclination, he was a brilliant student and Emma had high expectations for him.

His twin, Elizabeth, being identical, naturally also favored the Harte side of the family. Emma would sometimes look at her and catch her breath, seeing striking echoes of her own mother in the girl, and occasionally she even caught a fleeting glimpse of Olivia Wainwright in Elizabeth's lovely face. She would ponder briefly then on the past, recalling the uncanny resemblance between those two women from such different worlds which had so startled her as a girl. Of all Emma's children, Elizabeth was the real beauty, willowy, graceful, her exquisite face delicately translucent, surrounded by a thick cloud of dark hair. She, too, was blessed with an abun-dance of charm. Unfortunately, Emma had long detected

other traits in her, which she found dismaying. Elizabeth was
violent of temper, flighty, and often difficult to control. Paul
agreed with Emma that she needed a firm hand, and they
hoped that the discipline of boarding school would tone her
down without breaking her spirit.

Emma's businesses continued to grow. The Knightsbridge
store became world-famous, the Yorkshire stores a household
name in the North; the mills flourished, as did the Kallinski
clothing factories; the Emeremm Company, now known as
Harte Enterprises, blossomed into an enormously rich organization with diverse holdings throughout the world. By following her own shrewd instincts and listening to Paul's advice,
Emma invested her money wisely and multiplied her worth
threefold, as well as that of Winston and Frank, whose personal financial affairs she supervised. By the time she was
forty-six years old she was a millionairess many times over
and a power to be reckoned with, not only in London and the
North of England, but in international business circles as
well.

Despite her happiness with Paul and her family, and as
preoccupied as she was with her gargantuan business enterprises, Emma's interest in the Fairley family had not waned
one iota. Their affairs continued to obsess her as they always
had. Gerald Fairley, after she had ruined him in 1923, spent
the last few miserable years of his life depending on the
largesse of Edwin, since the brickyard was not a profitable
concern. He died in 1926, "obviously from the gross excesses
of his nature," Emma had remarked to Blackie on hearing the
news, and in the ensuing years her icy gaze had rested solely
on Edwin. She followed his career with undivided interest.
How she had longed for him to be a failure! But he had made
a name for himself as a criminal lawyer of great brilliance,
and there were constant rumors in the Temple that he would
be made a K.C., although this had not yet happened. He
resided and practiced in London, but he had not entirely
severed his ties to Yorkshire. He was often in Leeds, where
he devoted an unflagging amount of energy to the *Yorkshire
Morning Gazette*, just as Adam Fairley had done before him.
He was chairman of the board and the majority shareholder,
and thus wielded the power on the newspaper.

Emma wanted that paper and she would stop at nothing to
get it. Both Winston and Blackie pointed out that she had

done enough to cripple the Fairley influence in Yorkshire, and remonstrated with her to drop her vendetta and forget about the newspaper. But Emma, as self-willed as always and still vindictive about the Fairleys, would not listen. She was determined to acquire their only remaining holding. Gradually she began to buy up the common shares as they came onto the market, moving with her usual stealth, and waiting patiently until she could find the right opportunity to move against Edwin. Although the paper was losing money, Edwin somehow managed to keep it operating and he clung to his shares, much to Emma's frustration. Until she could wrest those shares from him she was powerless to move in and take over. She dreamed about the day she would oust Edwin. Only then would her revenge be complete.

"And I do have the patience of Job," she told Winston one day in the summer of 1935. "I won't rest until I own the *Yorkshire Morning Gazette*, and I will own it one day."

"I know you will," Winston said, and shifted in his chair. He lit a cigarette and went on, "I had a call from Joe Fulton yesterday. He's prepared to sell you the remainder of his shares in the *Sheffield Star*. If you buy, you will have control. Do you want them?"

"I do indeed," Emma declared, and her face brightened. "I also think you should talk to Harry Metcalfe again. He's been hankering to sell the *Yorkshire Morning Observer* for a long time. I think I'd like to own it, after all. I can certainly use it as a vehicle against Edwin Fairley. Give him a run for his money and a lot of stiff competition. If we do buy the shares in both newspapers, I will really have a foothold in publishing in the North." Her eyes lit up. "Let's start a new company, Winston. What shall we call it? How about the Yorkshire Consolidated Newspaper Company?" she suggested, and rushed on, before Winston could reply, "Yes, that's a strong-sounding name. Let's do it!"

"I can't think of any good reasons why you shouldn't take over both papers, Emma," Winston said, suddenly infected by her enthusiasm. "They can easily be turned around. All they need is good management, an infusion of money, and some top-notch journalists to inject new life. Maybe Frank can recommend the right men. I'll get onto it first thing tomorrow."

"I do wish we'd thought of this before," Emma exclaimed, hardly able to contain her excitement at the prospect of becoming a publisher, and going into competition with Edwin Fairley.

"Obvious ideas are generally the last ones we think of, you know," Winston remarked casually, and stood up.

He walked slowly across the lovely upstairs parlor at Pennistone Royal, the great house near Ripon, which Emma had purchased three years before, and stood in front of the oriel window gazing down into the grounds. It was a glorious August Sunday, the sky a blaze of crystal blue above the clipped lawns, fanciful topiary hedges, and luxuriant abundance of trees, so verdant and lush and shimmering in the summer air. The gardens were spectacular, Elizabethan in design and so very English with their overwhelming greenness and profusion of vivid flower beds.

In the distance, he heard the plopping of tennis balls and he wondered how Paul found the energy to play three sets on such a grueling day. His thoughts now turned to the news he had to impart to Emma, edging out all else as he sought the simplest way of doing it. His common sense told him to be direct. He looked at Emma sitting on the sofa, coolly beautiful in a white shantung dress and with her russet hair falling to her shoulders. Well, he might as well tell her. He said, "I spoke to Edwina yesterday. She's getting married."

"Married!" Emma repeated, sitting bolt upright on the sofa. She put down the balance sheet she was reading and gave him her full attention. "To whom, might I ask?"

Winston cleared his throat. "To Jeremy Standish."

Emma stared at him open-mouthed. "Jeremy Standish? The Earl of Dunvale?"

"That's right. The wedding is in two weeks. In Ireland, of course, at his estate, Clonloughlin."

"But he's so much older than she is, Winston," Emma said. "I'm not so sure about this marriage." She frowned. "It's not a very likely match, in my opinion."

"There's absolutely nothing you can do about it, Emma," Winston pointed out, relieved her reaction had been so mild. "After all, she is twenty-nine. Besides, it might just be the stabilizing influence she needs. And he does have pots and pots of money, you know."

"Perhaps you're right," Emma mused. She looked at Winston. "I don't suppose she is inviting any members of the family."

Winston shook his head. "No, I'm afraid she's not. But she did ask me to give her away. How do you feel about that? Do you mind, dear?"

Emma leaned forward and clasped her hand over his. "Oh, darling, of course not. I think it's wonderful of her to ask you. It would please me enormously. She won't seem quite so alone if you're there." Emma paused and then asked hesitantly, "Did she mention me?"

"No, Emma, she didn't. I'm sorry."

"I must send a nice wedding present, of course." Emma changed the subject, realizing there was nothing further to add, but her eyes were reflective as she continued her business discussion with her brother.

When Winston returned from Ireland, Emma was full of questions about Edwina, the Earl of Dunvale, and the wedding. Winston satisfied her curiosity, and assuaged her anxieties about Edwina's marriage to the man, who was twenty years her senior. It had been apparent to him that Edwina was deliriously happy, although he was not absolutely certain whether this was because she had become the Countess of Dunvale and a member of an ancient and celebrated Anglo-Irish family, or because she truly loved her husband. Dunvale, for his part, was besotted with Edwina, and Winston had no doubts about the bridegroom's feelings in the least.

A year later Emma became a grandmother, when Edwina gave birth to a son, baptized Anthony George Michael. As the first-born he had the courtesy title of Lord Standish and was heir to the earldom. Emma wrote to her daughter congratulating her, and sent a gift, as she had done at the time of the wedding. Emma received a courteous but cool thank-you note from Edwina and she was hopeful that it would lead to a complete reconciliation one day. And she determined to enlist Winston's help to effect this. Kit was not so positive. Feeling slighted at not having been invited to his sister's fancy society wedding, he took to making derogatory remarks about her disregard for family, and her snobbishness, whenever the opportunity presented itself. Paul constantly admonished him and finally, in exasperation, forbade him to discuss Edwina with his mother. He himself encouraged Emma's belief that she would be on friendly terms with her eldest daughter again, knowing that this was the only possibility acceptable to her, and he dare not demolish her hope.

One of Emma's greatest assets was her ability to shelve unsolvable problems, and eventually she managed to put Edwina out of her mind. The present was her first priority, her true imperative. Her own life was as demanding as always. There was her work, her relationship with Paul, and the other children. She had no complaints about them and in general things were harmonious. Kit was working in the mills and learning the woolen business. Robin, in his last year of boarding school, was preparing to go up to Cambridge to study law. Elizabeth had expressed a wish to follow in Edwina's footsteps and was at a fashionable Swiss finishing school. Finally the day came when Daisy left for boarding school, and Emma and Paul were alone in the house in Belgrave Square for the first time.

"I'm afraid you're stuck with me, and only me now," he teased her one evening when they were having a glass of champagne in the library.

"I miss them all, particularly Daisy, but I'm glad we have our time together at last, Paul. Just the two of us."

"And we do have lots of time, Emma. Years and years stretching ahead." He grinned. "I don't know how you feel, my love, but I rather like the prospect of growing old with you."

It was the first week of September in 1938. And sitting there in the handsome mellow library, talking quietly as the twilight descended to fill the room with soft drifting shadows, it did not occur to Emma and Paul that anything could happen to destroy their security. They were at peace with themselves and with each other, and still deeply in love. And so they spoke for a long time about their future together, and made plans for the Christmas holidays at Pennistone Royal, and discussed their impending trip to America in the new year. Later they went out to dinner at Quaglino's, laughing and holding hands like young lovers, and it was one of the most carefree evenings they had spent in months.

But the Nazi shadow was spreading itself across Central Europe. Hitler, who gained power in Germany after the burning of the Reichstag in 1933, was on the march. War was inevitable. It was only a question of time.

FIFTY-FIVE

"There will be a war in the Pacific, just as surely as there will be a war in Europe," Paul McGill said quietly. "The facts are incontrovertible. Japan industrialized late, as Germany did, and their success has shaped them both into arrogant, warlike nations with plans for world domination." He paused and drew on his cigarette. "I know I'm not wrong, Dan. America had better be prepared. Europe isn't, unfortunately."

Daniel P. Nelson, one of the most powerful men in the world, and grandson of the most famous of all the great robber barons, nodded thoughtfully. He smiled but his eyes were worried as he said, "I don't doubt you, Paul. I've been saying the same thing for months. Told the President, only last week when I was at Hyde Park, that Japan has real aims in the Pacific. Has had since the twenties, to be accurate. Roosevelt's not blind. He's aware of the situation. On the other hand, this country's still recovering from the Depression. Not unnaturally, his thoughts are focused on the domestic scene. There are still ten million unemployed here, Paul."

"Yes, I know. What worries me is that since Congress passed three neutrality acts a few years ago the prevailing attitude has been isolationist. It still is, I'm afraid. However, America can't possibly remain neutral if Britain goes to war with Germany."

Dan said, "But as far as Roosevelt's concerned, I know he's not an isolationist himself. I feel he will come to Britain's aid if the necessity arises. We've been natural allies for more than a century, and he's also aware he can't let the West sink. But—enough of all this depressing talk of war. Emma is looking far too grave."

"I am concerned," Emma said, "as any informed person is today. My brother is a political writer in London, and he believes Hitler seeks global power and will stop at nothing to get it. Unfortunately, like his good friend Winston Churchill, Frank is patently ignored. When will the world open its eyes and see what is going on?"

Dan smiled faintly. "The prospect of another world war is

frightening, my dear. There is a tendency to dismiss those with the vision to foresee onrushing disaster. The public has a bad habit of sticking its collective head in the sand, as do a great number of politicians."

"I suppose that's human nature—the desire not to face such a terrible reality as war. But some of us must be prepared—" She stopped short, as Paul caught her eye. Aware that he wished to discuss business with Dan Nelson, she murmured, "Well, I'll leave you. If you will excuse me, I must attend to my other guests."

The two men watched her glide across the drawing room, the white chiffon evening gown floating out behind her, the magnificent emeralds blazing at her throat and ears, on her arms and hands. Dan said, "I do believe Emma's the most remarkable woman I've ever met. You're a lucky man."

"I know," Paul replied. He turned his attention to Dan Nelson and went on, "I wanted to talk to you about my oil tankers and a couple of other rather pressing matters. I think we have time before we leave for the opera. Let's step into the library." They slipped out discreetly.

As Emma circulated amongst the other guests assembled in their luxurious Fifth Avenue apartment, the thought of impending war nagged at the back of her mind. She had, only that morning, received a disturbing letter from Frank, who had just returned from a trip to Berlin. He had been full of dire predictions, and, trusting his judgment as she did, she knew he was not exaggerating. He had said Britain would be at war before the end of the year, and she believed him. She glanced at the three other men in the room. They also wielded immense international influence and their combined wealth added up to hundreds of billions of dollars. She saw that their eyes betrayed their fears, even though they, too, were making a show of conviviality that befitted the occasion. Yes, they knew that the world was on the brink of another holocaust. She thought of her two sons with a stab of apprehension. Both of them were eligible to be called up. Another generation of young men in their prime would be sacrificed to the war machine. Despite the warmth of the room she shivered and she thought then of Joe Lowther, and remembered the Great War and the havoc it had wreaked. Had the past twenty-one years been only an armed truce?

Later, when they were seated in their box at the Metropol-

itan Opera, Emma was temporarily distracted by the anticipation that pervaded the air. Her eyes swept over the opulent
red-and-gold decor, took in the glittering beauty of the be-
jeweled women and the elegance of the men in their tails.
And she thought how normal they all seemed, even carefree,
as though they were oblivious to the gathering storm.

Emma glanced down at her program, determined to enjoy
the opera. It was from Blackie O'Neill that she had learned
about music, and as the breathtaking theatrical spectacle
unfolded on the stage she suddenly wished Blackie was here
with them to share the experience. She began to relax, captivated by "Mignon." Risë Stevens, the young mezzo-soprano
who had made her debut two months before, was magnificent
in the title role and at one moment her glorious voice so
moved Emma she felt the rush of tears. What a gift that
superb voice was. Emma was soon transported into a magical
world of make-believe and she let herself be engulfed by the
melodic arias, the performances of Risë Stevens and Ezio
Pinza, the exquisite sets and costumes, and for several hours
her worries were entirely forgotten.

Paul had invited their eight guests to Delmonico's for
dinner, and as they settled themselves at the table Emma
looked across at Paul, endeavoring to assess his mood. Despite the grave conversation with Dan Nelson earlier, he now
appeared to be unconcerned, and as always he was the expansive host, ordering Dom Pérignon and caviar, and beguiling
everyone. He is the most brilliant and handsome man here,
Emma thought with a flash of possessiveness. It was February
3, 1939. His birthday. He was fifty-nine years old, but he
carried his years splendidly, and the wings of white in his
black hair only served to emphasize his dashing appearance.
His eyes had not lost their vivid blueness and the brows
above were still the color of jet, as was his mustache. There
were deep lines around those eyes, but his tanned face was
surprisingly free of wrinkles and his body was as firm and as
muscular as it had been twenty years ago. Emma was always
slightly stunned by the sheer physical size of him, the bulk of
those wide shoulders and the barrel chest. Tonight, in his
white tie and tails, he had an aura of true glamour that was
more electrifying than ever.

His eyes met hers and he winked, and then gave her that
old appraising look she knew so well. Why, the devil's flirting

with me. And after all these years, she thought. She herself would be fifty in April. It hardly seemed possible. She had known Paul for twenty-one years, and they had been together on a permanent basis for sixteen of them. Sixteen incredible years. They had not always been easy years. Paul could be as authoritative and as self-willed as she was herself, and he often felt the need to assert himself forcefully. He was domineering, frequently bossy, and he had made it clear who wore the trousers in their household. She had learned to let him have his way in most things pertaining to their private lives, and he, in turn, was wise enough never to interfere in her business. Paul was also a flirt and he made no secret of the fact that he liked the ladies. Emma suspected he might have had other women when he traveled abroad alone, but he never gave her cause for heartache, or embarrassment, and she never doubted his devotion. Also, since she considered sexual jealousy a useless emotion, she rarely contemplated his infidelities, if indeed there were any. His passion for her had not lessened with time, and she knew she was a lucky woman.

Emma sat back in the chair, and between the champagne, the delicious food, the stimulating conversation, and the gaiety that prevailed amongst their friends, she managed to push aside those troubling thoughts of war that had assailed her at the outset of the evening.

In the following week Paul did not mention the war again and she carefully avoided the subject herself. They went to East Texas to visit the Sydney-Texas Oil Company, recently renamed Sitex at her suggestion, and then proceeded to West Texas, where Paul purchased oil leases in Odessa and Midland, much to Harry Marriott's annoyance. Emma did not particularly like Paul's partner and had not hesitated to say so when she had first met him some years before. It was on their return journey to New York that she reiterated her opinion, and asked Paul why Marriott was so unhappy about the new purchases.

Paul grinned and said, "Because he always wants to play it safe. He never wants to gamble. He's afraid of losing or diminishing what we've already accumulated over the years. The fool. We're one of the richest oil companies in America today, but expansion is necessary. No, vital. Harry means well, but he lacks imagination. Remember how he fought me when I bought the oil tankers? I proved him wrong about that. They've been an enormous asset to the company and more than earned their money back. I'll prove him wrong again, Emma. I have a nose for oil, and I guarantee you it will be discovered in Odessa and Midland within a few years. I plan to start drilling there before the end of the year."

"It's a good thing you own the majority of stock in that company, otherwise you might have really insurmountable problems with Marriott," Emma said.

"You're damned right." Paul chuckled. "You don't think I'd be fool enough to spend the millions I invested initially without having control, do you?"

"No," she conceded, laughing, "You're far too tough and smart for that." She hesitated. "Are you sorry Daisy wasn't a boy?"

"Good Lord, no! Whatever makes you ask that, darling?"

"Well, Howard can't very well follow in your footsteps. And it's often occurred to me you might be disappointed you don't have a son to carry on the business, the McGill dynasty."

"What makes you think I've dismissed the idea of Daisy doing that? After all, if she takes after her beautiful mother she'll make a hell of a good businesswoman. And she'll marry one day and have children. My grandchildren. Ponder on that one, Emma."

She did, never once forgetting his words.

One day, at the end of February, Paul came home early from the Sitex offices in New York, and Emma knew at once that something was terribly amiss. He appeared to be unusually preoccupied, kissed her somewhat absently, and fixed himself a drink, which was also rare in that it was only four o'clock.

Never one to hedge, she said immediately, "You're upset, Paul. What is it?"

"I can never hide anything from you, my love, can I?" He sipped the drink, lit a cigarette, and then he told her, "I have booked a passage for you to England on the *Queen Elizabeth*. I was lucky enough to get a stateroom for you, even at this late date, so you will be comfortable, darling. You sail on Thursday."

"Aren't you coming with me?" she asked as evenly as possible, but her throat tightened.

"No, darling, I can't."

"Why not, Paul? You had planned to return with me."

"I want to go back to Texas for a few days, to take care of certain matters and to reassure myself that Harry fully understands I want to start drilling in Odessa as soon as possible. And then I'm going to Australia."

"But you weren't supposd to go there until later in the year!"

"Later in the year might be too *late*, Emma. I must leave as quickly as possible now, to attend to my interests over there and confer with the men who run my companies. You know how I feel about Japan's threat to the Pacific. I can't possibly leave anything to chance."

Emma's face had paled. "I don't want you to go!" she cried. "I'm frightened—frightened you'll get stuck in Australia if war breaks out before you can return to England. We could be separated for years." She rose and went to kneel at his feet. She looked up at him. "Please don't go, darling. I beg you not to go!" She touched his face lightly, the dearest face in the world to her, and her eyes brimmed.

"You know I must, Emma darling," he said with the utmost gentleness. He smoothed one hand over her head and his eyes regarded her tenderly. "But I won't stay for long. Only two months at the most. Things are in relatively good order out there. They have been for years. However, I must be sure everything will run smoothly, should I have to be absent for longer than the usual year. And I might have to be. We don't know how long this war will last when it does come, do we?" He smiled at her confidently. "I'll get back quickly. I want to be with you in England when the conflict starts. I certainly don't want you to be alone. Now come along, cheer up, sweetheart. I'll only be gone eight weeks. That's not so bad."

Emma did not argue with Paul or further attempt to dissuade him, knowing it would be fruitless to do so. His holdings were so vast they staggered the imagination, and he could not shrug off the responsibilities they entailed, which were of equal magnitude. Power had its undeniable privileges but it brought crushing burdens as well. It was quite apparent that Paul, in all good conscience, could not ignore the world political situation, and the effect it would have on his business. Because of who and what she was, Emma understood his motives and acknowledged the necessity of his plan, even though she was not enamored of it.

And so she put up a gay front for the next few days before she sailed. But the idea of being separated from Paul depressed her more than it ever had before, and that awful sense of foreboding stayed with her during the entire voyage to England. Even when she was settled in their house in Belgrave Square it persisted, gnawing at her peace of mind.

FIFTY-SIX

Torrential rain was falling when Paul left the nursing home on the outskirts of Sydney. He turned up the collar of his trench coat and made a dash for the Daimler.

He was drenched when he got inside and he shrugged out of his wet coat, tossing it carelessly onto the back seat. He took out a handkerchief and wiped his streaming face before lighting a cigarette. He noticed that his hand shook as he did so. He was in a blinding rage with Constance, so that was not very surprising. He had been on the verge of striking her a few moments before, and it had taken all of his will power to control himself, to take his leave of her with a degree of civility. The violence of his emotions appalled him. He had never struck a woman in his life, had not experienced such overwhelming anger in years.

Paul inserted the key in the ignition, pulled out of the parking area, and turned into the main road leading back into the city. His patience with Constance had entirely evaporated years ago, along with his pity, and now he loathed her. *Loathed her.* Damn it, he wasn't going to be tied to her any longer. He would find a way to get the divorce himself. He would talk to his solicitor. There must be a legal loophole, a means of disentangling himself from this ridiculous marriage, which had not been a marriage for twenty-seven years. It was absurd that a man of his undeniable power should find himself in such an untenable situation, shackled to that demented creature, who surely held on to him only out of sheer perversity. He wondered what he had ever done to Constance to make her want to punish him. He had been a good husband in the early years. It had been her drinking and her promiscuousness which had come between them, and inevitably killed his love for her. *He must have his freedom*. For Emma and Daisy. And he was bloody well going to get it, come hell or high water. He gripped the steering wheel and hit the open road with ferocity.

The etiolated sky, bleached out by lightning, rocked with the deafening booms of thunder and, as if there had been a sudden cloudburst, the rain fell more profusely, sluicing down the windows in streaming sheets, dimming his vision momentarily. He took the turn in the road too fast, saw the approaching lorry too late. Instinctively he swerved and braked, but the car was traveling at such high speed it seemed to move with its own velocity. It went into a slithering skid and spun out of control, careening across the wet road. He fought to regain control but despite his enormous strength he was unable to do so. The car slewed up over the embankment, leapt into the air, somersaulted down into the gully, and impacted against a formation of boulders. He felt himself being crushed against the steering wheel, and then he blacked out.

It was the lorry driver who pulled him out of the wreckage a fraction of a second before the car burst into flames. Paul was still unconscious when the ambulance arrived at the hospital in Sydney two hours later. And he remained unconscious for several days. That he had lived at all was a miracle, the doctors said.

Paul maneuvered himself across his study in the wheelchair until he was directly in front of his desk. He lit a cigarette and then settled down to peruse the pile of legal documents Mel Harrison, his solicitor, had left with him a week ago, just before he had been discharged from the hospital. He had gone over them endlessly, searching for any kind of small omission, or a clause that might lack clarity, and so far he had found none. But to be absolutely certain before he signed them, he went through them for the last time, reading each page slowly, weighing each word scrupulously. At the end of three hours he was satisfied nothing could be misinterpreted. As usual, Mel had drawn the documents with his special brand of brilliance. Every one of them was watertight and would stand up in any court of law, in any country in the world, should they be challenged. He did not expect that to happen. He was mostly concerned that his exact intentions were crystal clear, and indeed they were. Paul smiled for the first time in days. Something had gone right for once.

It was almost six o'clock. Mel was due any moment. What a staunch, supportive, and devoted friend he had been in the last three months since the accident, always there when he was needed, and often when he was not. Preparing legal papers; attending to matters too confidential to hand over to anyone else; visiting the hospital on a daily basis; even neglecting his wife and family on weekends, to sit with him and bolster his courage, to pull him out of the black moods which sometimes engulfed him. Since the bandages had been removed, Paul had not wanted any visitors except Mel and the men who worked for the various McGill corporations. He had certainly not wanted his other friends to see his shattered face. He could not have stomached their sympathy, or their pity.

Despair trickled through him and he closed his eyes, wondering how much longer he could go on. Sometimes he thought he could not tolerate another day of living in this wretched state. What a rotten twist of fate. The accident could never have happened if he had listened to Emma in New York and not returned to Sydney. Now here he was, chained to a wheelchair and dependent on others for almost everything he needed. It was a condition that did not sit easily with him. He had always been in the enviable position of being able to bend life to his will, to reverse circumstances to suit himself. But ever since the crash he had experienced a sense of powerlessness so acute it was devastating. It engendered a monumental frustration that spiraled into blazing anger. Even his money and his influence, always potent weapons in the past, had become quite useless to him.

Smithers, the butler-valet who had been in his employ for years, knocked and entered the study, interrupting Paul's thoughts. "Mr. Harrison has arrived, sir. Shall I show him in here, or do you want to go into the sitting room?"

"In here, Smithers, please."

A moment later Mel was grasping his hand. "How are you, Paul?"

"Feeling much better, believe it or not," Paul said, and motioned to the butler. "Fix us the usual, Smithers, please."

"Right away, sir."

Paul swung the chair away from the desk. "Let's sit ove
there by the fire. I always feel chilled to the bone thes
days."

When the butler had left, Paul said, "I should have bee
more forceful with the doctors weeks ago, and made ther
discharge me then. I think being in familiar surroundings ha
helped me a great deal."

"I'm sure it has," Mel said brightly. "Cheers, old chap."

"Cheers," Paul responded. They clinked glasses and Pau
went on, "I've spent a lot of time on the papers, Mel. They'r
in good order now. We can sign them later."

"Fine, Paul. Incidentally, I told Audrey I wouldn't b
home for dinner. If you can stand my company for a secon
night running I thought I'd foist myself on you. Is that a
right?"

"Of course. I'd be delighted to have you dine with me.
He wheeled himself to the bar and poured another scotch
"How's your drink, Mel? Can I freshen it up?"

"Not right now, thanks. Listen, Paul, I've been thinking
lot about Emma these past few days, since you've bee
home. I think we ought to send for her. I've discussed it wit
Audrey, and she agrees with me."

"No!" Paul spun the wheelchair around. He peered int
Mel's face and his eyes blazed. "I absolutely forbid it!" h
exclaimed harshly. "I don't want her to see me like thi
Besides, the news is getting graver every day. We could be a
war with Germany tomorrow. I don't want her travelin
halfway across the world at such a dangerous time."

Mel regarded Paul carefully. "I understand your feeling
But I also dread to think what she'll do to me when she find
out I've lied to her in my letters, just as you have in your
You also used your considerable influence to keep the detail
of the accident out of the newspapers, and so she is in th
dark about the seriousness of your condition. But isn't it tim
you wrote and told her the truth? She should know."

Paul shook his head. "*She's not to know*. Not under an
circumstances whatsoever." He softened his tone. "Not ye
anyway. I'll decide when it's the right time to tell her." Hi
face became morose. "How *does* a man tell a passionate an
active woman like Emma that she's tied to a hopeless cripp
who is paralyzed from the waist down, who has lost half hi

face and—" He paused and looked at Mel intently. "And who is impotent. Who will always be impotent. Not easy, my friend. Not easy at all."

Mel did not know how to respond and such strong feelings of sympathy swept through him he stood up quickly before Paul detected the pity filling his eyes. He stepped to the bar and picked up the bottle of scotch. He said, "I think you might be underestimating Emma. In fact, I'm damned sure you are. She would want to be with you. To give you all of her support and love. Let's cable her, Paul. Now."

"No," Paul said, his voice suddenly tinged with weariness. "I don't want her to be burdened down with me. I'm no use to her. I'm not much use to myself, if the truth be known."

Mel walked back to the fireplace, racking his brains for a way to convince Paul to send for Emma. He needed her more than he had ever needed her in his life, but he was an obstinate devil, and proud. "Emma wouldn't see it that way. She loves you. Why, she worships the ground . . . you," Mel quickly corrected himself, and cleared his throat. Then his face brightened perceptibly as another thought struck him. He said rapidly, "Look here, if you don't want Emma traveling, why don't you book a passage to England yourself? You could be there in a month."

"That's not feasible. I have to go to the hospital almost every day for treatment. There are no medical facilities of the kind I need on board a ship." Paul gulped down the scotch and placed his glass on the table. He brought his gaze back to Mel and his eyes were deadly serious, his tone bleak. "There is something I haven't told you, Mel. The prognosis is bad. Very bad, actually. The doctors don't know how long they can keep the infection out of my kidneys. That's what usually kills paraplegics—kidney failure."

Mel stared at Paul and his ruddy face lost most of its color. "H-h-how l-l-long?" he stammered, unable to complete the question.

"Nine months—at the most," Paul replied in a matter-of-fact voice. He had already adjusted to his death sentence. He had no alternative.

Mel said with a desperate urgency, "I think we ought to call in more specialists, Paul. Surely there must be a way to—"

"No, there isn't." Paul said. "If I had broken my spine the

doctors could have fused it. But the nerve ends of the spinal cord were crushed. There is no known way to repair those."

Mel looked away into the fire. He had no words that would comfort Paul. The accident had been a catastrophe, but he had been led to believe Paul had years of life ahead of him, albeit confined to the wheelchair. But now . . . Oh, God, what a waste of a rare and brilliant man. Eventually, after a long silence, he said, "Is there anything I can do, Paul? Anything at all? You only have to ask me."

Paul smiled gently. "No, old chap. Thanks, though. Don't take this so hard. And for Christ's sake, don't start getting maudlin on me now. I need that cheery spirit of yours, and your optimism. Also, you've become my right arm and you're going to be around me a great deal. I don't want a glum face staring at me. Now come on, let's have another drink and then we'll dine. I've got some great Chambertin, which my father put down years ago. We'll have a couple of bottles with dinner. Might as well drink it now, while there's still—" Paul bit off his sentence abruptly. He picked up the empty glasses, dropped them into his lap, and rolled over to the bar.

Mel was again unable to respond coherently. He reached for his handkerchief and blew his nose loudly. He looked at Paul's wide shoulders and broad back outlined above the chair, and his eyes dimmed with infinite sorrow. It was heartbreaking to see that splendid body so horribly broken, that extraordinarily handsome face so hideously ruined. And yet how stoically this incredible man bore his afflictions. The admiration Mel had always held for his oldest and dearest friend increased inordinately. Paul's unimpaired courage and his strength of character in the face of defeat were immense. He wondered if he could have been so brave and indomitable in similar circumstances. He was not sure. One thing he did know, Paul needed all the support he could get and he was going to do his damnedest to give it to him without reserve.

Much later that same evening, long after Mel had left, Paul sat in his dimly lit study, nursing a balloon of brandy and chain-smoking. His face was calm, his eyes thoughtful as he mused on the conversation of earlier. Perhaps Mel was right. Perhaps he should write to Emma and tell her the truth. In his previous letters he had underplayed the accident and used business as an excuse for his tardiness in not returning to England. Yes, he owed her that. The truth. For all they had been to each other and still meant to each other. And it must be the absolute truth. Nothing less would do for his Emma. He moved the wheelchair up to the desk, pulled a piece of notepaper towards him, and began the letter.

Sydney, July 24, 1939

My dearest darling Emma:
 You are my life . . .

His eyes lifted and rested on the gold-framed photograph of her on the corner of his desk. He picked it up, gazing at it intently. It had been taken a few years after Daisy's birth and Emma looked radiant and she was smiling that incandescent smile that was so uniquely hers. He thought his heart would burst with his love for her, and unexpected tears welled in his eyes and trickled down his cheeks unchecked. Paul held the photograph to his chest for a long time, hugging it to him as if it were Emma herself he held in his arms, remembering the past, pondering on the future. And he did not write the letter.

FIFTY-SEVEN

Frank Harte left El Vino's bar and walked down Fleet Street towards the *Daily Express*, reflecting on the piece he had written earlier that evening. It still sat on his desk, for he had wanted an hour away from the office to think about the tone of it.

The hour in El Vino's had not been restful. The bar had been jammed with reporters from all the newspapers, their faces grim, their voices somber as they had talked about the political situation, which was worsening, and reviewed the depressing news flooding in from all parts of Europe. Now he asked himself if he had been excessive as he considered the piece, written for the Editorial Opinion page. But that fool Neville Chamberlain *should* be kicked out of office. Winston Churchill was, without doubt, the man they needed as Prime

Minister, with war an inevitability. He knew the Old Man agreed with him on that issue. Beaverbrook and Churchill were long-time friends.

Frank crossed Fleet Street and looked up at the *Daily Express*, a shimmering sliver of black glass and steel and blazing lights, the modern architecture incongruous, juxtaposed against the time-worn buildings that flanked it on all sides. It was as if the Old Man had deliberately cocked a snook at tradition when he had built the *Express*, and yet nobody was more traditional than Lord Beaverbrook, tireless defender of the British Empire and all that it entailed. Jealous competitors considered the building to be an eyesore, an offense to the historic Street of Ink, but Frank loved it. He saw it as a tribute to modern journalism and the changing times. The Old Man had been right to build it, for it was certainly the most striking landmark on Fleet Street.

Pushing through the swinging doors of the *Express*, Frank traversed the lobby and took the lift up to his office. He threw his hat on a chair, sat down, picked up the column, and propped his feet on the desk. He read his words with as critical an eye as possible. It was good, damned good, even though he said so himself. He would let it stand. He jumped up and took it in to Arthur Christiansen.

Chris, young editor of the *Daily Express*, was the boy wonder of Fleet Street. Beaverbrook's star protégé, he was the man responsible for changing the look and tenor of English popular journalism. In his shirt sleeves, his face flushed, his hair rumpled, he looked harassed but was obviously in total control behind the paper-strewn desk. He gave Frank a cheery grin. "I wondered what had happened to you. I was just about to send a copy boy over to El Vino's to get you."

Frank handed him the column. "I wanted time to think this over. I thought I might have been too strong."

Chris's bright, probing eyes focused on the pages of copy. He read them quickly. "Good man. It's damned clever, Frank. We'll run it as it stands. No changes necessary. If you tone it down it will lose its impact. The Old Man will like this. You've struck just the right note, as usual."

"You're sure it's not excessive?"

Chris grinned again. "I am. It's very balanced, in fact. But then everything you've been writing about the world situation lately has been thoughtful. And damn it all, let's face it, you *are* dealing with facts. Nobody can deny that." Chris wrote on the first page: *Set as is. No changes.* "Boy!" he called, motioning to a copy boy loitering near the door of his office. "Run this down to the chief sub."

Frank said. "If you don't need me, I'll get off. My sister's expecting me. You have her number if anything comes up."

Chris nodded. "Fine, Frank." He picked up one of the telephones, which was ringing loudly. "Christiansen here. Good evening, sir." He covered the mouthpiece and said to Frank, "It's Lord Beaverbrook calling from Cherkley. Excuse me, Frank."

Frank collected his hat from his office and strolled through the newsroom, as always lingering there for a moment. The bustle and activity had reached fever pitch as the deadline for the first edition of Monday's paper approached and the noise was deafening. There was a sense of immediacy in the atmosphere, and the air was pungent with the smell of damp newsprint and wet ink from the page proofs, which always sent a thrill of excitement coursing through Frank's veins. Popular and successful novelist though he had become over the years, he could no more abandon journalism than he could stop breathing. It was in his blood. And there was no other place quite like the offices of a daily newspaper at this hour, just before the giant presses rolled. It was the pulse, the very heartbeat of the world.

Frank paused at the Reuters wire machine and glanced with quickening interest at the stories coming in. The news was ominous, presaging war. A copy boy dodged past him, tore off the latest Reuters dispatches, and raced away. As he did, Frank's eye caught a new story coming over the wire. His attention was riveted on it. He was motionless for a long time, reeling from shock, and disbelieving, and then he roused himself and moved up to the Associated Press machine. After a moment he went to look at the United Press ticker. All the wire services were carrying the identical story and he groaned. There was undoubtedly no mistake. No mistake at all. He tore off the UP story and had a word with the chief sub about it, who acquiesced when Frank asked to take it with him. Pushing the piece of paper in his pocket, Frank walked out of the newsroom, benumbed and sick at heart.

Within seconds he was in the street and hailing a cab. Despite the muggy August weather, he shivered and his hands were unsteady as he lit a cigarette. He wondered how in God's name he was going to find the strength to do what he must do.

Winston was in London on business and he was staying with Emma, as he always did. They were seated in the drawing room, drinking their after-dinner coffee, when the housekeeper showed Frank in a few minutes later.

Emma's face lit up when she saw him, and she rose to embrace him. "We'd just about given you up!" she exclaimed, hugging him.

"I'm sorry I'm so late," Frank murmured.

Emma said, "Let me get you a drink. What would you like, Frank?"

"A brandy, please, Emma." He turned to Winston. "How long are you staying?"

"A few days. Do you want to have lunch tomorrow?"

"Yes, I do."

Emma handed Frank the drink and sat down in the chair opposite. She looked at him intently and then frowned. "You look awfully pale, Frank dear. You're not sickening with something, are you?"

"No, I'm just tired." He tossed down the brandy and stood up. "Mind if I have another? I need it tonight."

"Of course not." Emma's eyes swiveled to Winston and one brow shot up quizzically.

Winston noticed his brother's weary stance. "Are you sure you're not ill, Frank? Emma's quite right, you don't seem to be your usual self."

Frank swung around and managed a smile. "I suppose the situation is getting on top of me," he muttered, and returned to the chair. "The Nazis are about to move into Poland. We're all convinced of that."

Winston and Emma plied him with questions, and Frank responded automatically, attempting to sound coherent. Emma had been listening thoughtfully and she turned to face Winston, who was fixing himself a scotch and soda, and she said, "I expect we ought to start thinking about our various staffs. They will be badly depleted when the men get called up." She caught her breath and her hand flew to her throat nervously to finger her pearls. "And my God! What about the boys! Kit and Robin are bound to go. And Randolph, Winston. He's also of age."

"Yes, he is. In fact, he wants to join the navy. *Immediately*." Winston's mouth tightened. "He's determined to do it. I won't be able to stop him."

Emma gave her older brother an anxious glance. His only son was the apple of his eye. "Randolph's headstrong, I realize that, and so are my boys. They're not going to listen to us. I don't suppose there is anything we can do. They will ultimately get their papers." She now addressed Frank. "Well, at least your Simon is not old enough to be called up."

"For the moment," Frank said, and rose. He poured a large brandy and brought it to Emma. "You had better drink this. I think you are going to need it."

Emma regarded him with puzzlement. "Why do you say that?" She frowned. "And you know I don't like brandy. It gives me heart palpitations."

"Please drink it," Frank said quietly.

Emma brought the brandy balloon up to her mouth and took a drop of it, wrinkling her nose with distaste. She put the glass down on the butler's tray table in front of her, and focused her attention on Frank. Once more she noted his extraordinary pallor. And when she saw the apprehension, now so clearly etched on his sensitive face, it alarmed her. A dreadful feeling of impending disaster struck Emma and she clasped her hands tightly together in her lap. "Something's terribly wrong, isn't it, Frank?"

Frank felt a dryness in his mouth and his voice was hoarse as he finally said, "I've had some very bad news. Just now, before I left the office." Despite the iron control he was exercising, his voice shook badly.

"Frank dear, whatever is it?" asked Emma, every one of her instincts alerted for trouble.

Winston said rapidly, "There's nothing wrong at the paper, is there?"

"No," Frank responded in a low voice. "It's . . . it's about Paul, actually."

"Paul! You've had bad news about Paul! What's wrong with him?" Emma demanded.

"I don't know how to tell you this, Emma—" Frank stopped. After an awful moment of silence he finished in a faltering voice, "He's—he's—he's passed away."

Emma stared at her brother with stunned disbelief, and she shook her head in bewilderment. "What do you mean?"

she asked, unable to digest his words. "I don't understand what you are saying. I just had a letter from him. Yesterday. *What are you saying to me?*" She had turned so deathly pale she looked as if she was going to faint and she was shaking.

Frank went to kneel at her feet. He looked up at her gravely and took her hand in his. He said with great gentleness, "Paul's dead, Emma. The story came over the wires when I was on my way here."

"Paul," Emma whispered incredulously, and her expression was one of blank stupefaction mingled with fear. She cried in a tremulous voice, "Are you sure there is no mistake? There *must* be a mistake!"

Frank shook his head dismally. "All the wire services are carrying the same story. I checked them out."

"Oh my God," Emma groaned, her blood turning cold.

Winston, as gray as a ghost, managed, "How did Paul die, Frank?"

Frank gazed at Emma, bleakness washing over his face as he sought the appropriate words. But nothing would soften the blow. Frank found himself incapable of speech.

Now Emma tightened her grip, her fingers biting into his hand. "Did Paul—? Was it his injuries? Were they more serious than he told me?" She sounded weak.

'Well, yes, I believe they were much worse than he led you to understand—"

The trilling of the doorbell startled them all, and Emma's eyes widened with apprehension and appealed to Winston. He nodded and pulled himself up out of the chair. As he left the drawing room he prayed it wasn't the press wanting a statement. To Winston's relief the housekeeper was admitting Henry Rossiter, a partner in the private merchant bank which handled all of Paul's business in England, and much of Emma's as well. Henry's face was as dolorous as Winston's. He shook Winston's hand and asked, "Does she know?" Winston inclined his head. "How is she taking it?" Henry murmured.

Winston said, "She's stunned. It hasn't really sunk in yet. There will be a horrible delayed reaction, of course, Henry. I dread to contemplate it."

Henry nodded his understanding. "Yes. They were so close. What a tragic, tragic thing to happen. How did Emma hear about it?"

Winston quickly explained and motioned to the drawing room. "We'd better go in, Henry. She needs us."

Henry entered the living room and sat down next to Emma. "I'm sorry. So very sorry, my dear. I got here as quickly as I could. As soon as I knew."

Emma's throat worked and she passed her hand over her throbbing head. She said, "Did someone in Sydney contact you, Henry?"

"Yes, Mel Harrison. He has been trying to get me all day. I was in the country, unfortunately."

"Why didn't he attempt to reach me?" she asked in a voice echoing with sorrow.

"He wanted me to break the news to you in person, Emma. He didn't want you to be alone when you heard—"

"When did Paul die?" she interrupted, her heart squeezing.

"His body was found on Sunday night. It's early Monday morning there now. Mel put in a call to me as soon as he arrived at the house. He realized he couldn't hold off the press indefinitely, since the police have to—"

"Police!" Emma exclaimed. "What do you mean? Why were the police there?"

Henry looked at Frank with dismay. They exchanged worried glances and both men were silent. Frank now contemplated lying to Emma, but there was no point in dissembling. Better to get it over with. He said gently, "Paul took his own life, Emma."

"Oh my God! No! No! It's not true! I don't believe you! Paul wouldn't do that. *Never*," Emma cried.

"I'm afraid it's true, darling," Frank said, and put his arm around her.

Emma moved her head wildly from side to side, denying Frank. She seemed to shrink in the chair. "How did he—" She could not continue.

Frank bit his lip. "He—he—shot himself." He did not add that Paul had shot himself through the heart. He could not bring himself to tell her that.

"No!" she shrieked, losing control. "*It's not true!*" she gasped. A tearing sob strangled in her throat and she twisted her hands agitatedly. Her eyes, brimming with shock, focused on Henry.

He nodded sadly. "It is true, Emma."

"It's not! It's not!" she cried, her voice rising. "Oh my God! Paul! Paul! Oh, my darling. Why?" Her voice broke and tears welled in her eyes. She pushed Frank aside and stood up, moving to the center of the room. She stretched out her arms, clutching blindly at the empty air, as if seeking Paul, to hold him to her.

Frank sprang up and took her arm, leading her back to the sofa. "Sit down, Emma. Please, darling."

Winston rose unsteadily and walked across the room, anxiety dulling his eyes, and he wondered desperately where she was going to find the strength to bear this tragedy. He picked up the glass of brandy. "Drink this, our Emma. Drink it, love. We're here. We'll stay with you."

She took the glass from him with both hands, which were trembling, and she gulped it down quickly. "I must know everything. Please, Frank, you must tell me everything, I must know it all. For my own sanity."

Frank was alarmed. "I have the UP story with me, Emma, but I don't think I should—"

"Yes, you should. You must. *I beg of you.*"

"I think you had better give Emma the facts, Frank," Winston interceded, adopting a calmness he did not feel. "She won't rest until she knows all the details. However painful they are to hear, you must tell her."

Frank nodded and pulled the piece of paper out. In a slow, saddened voice he read:

"Paul McGill, Australia's most renowned industrialist, was found shot to death on Sunday night at his home in Sydney. Mr. McGill, who was fifty-nine years old, was in a serious automobile accident four months ago, which paralyzed him from the waist downward. One side of his face was also badly shattered. Mr. McGill had been confined to a wheelchair since his release from the hospital and his doctors believe he took his own life in a moment of acute depression, undoubtedly caused by his condition. No note was found. Mr. McGill, who had resided mostly in London for the past sixteen years, was the only son of Bruce McGill and the grandson of Andrew McGill, founding father of the famous Australian family, one of the wealthiest and most influential in the country. It was Andrew McGill, a Scottish sea captain, who began the family sheep station, Dunoon, in Coonamble, in 1852. One of the biggest and most prosperous in New South Wales, the

*sheep station was inherited by Paul McGill upon his father's
death in 1919. Mr. McGill, believed to be one of the richest
men in the world, was chairman of the board of numerous
Australian companies, including the McGill Corporation, which
operated the sheep station, McGill and Smythson Real Estate, the McGill Mining Corporation, and the McGill Coal
Company. He was also chairman of the board of the Sitex Oil
Corporation of America, headquartered in Texas, and president and chief executive officer of McGill-Marriott Maritime,
which owns and operates one of the world's largest oil-tanker
fleets."*

Frank stopped. "There's a lot more about the business, the
family, Paul's war record, and his education. Do you want to
go on, Emma?"

"No," she whispered. She turned to Henry miserably.
'Why didn't he tell me about the paralysis? His face? I would
have gone to him immediately. He should have told me,
Henry." Tears seeped out of the corners of her eyes and
trickled silently down her cheeks. "Did he think his condition
would have made any difference to *me?* And I should have
been with him." She began to sob brokenly. "I loved him."

Henry's voice was sympathetic. "Mel wanted him to send
for you. But you know how stubborn and proud Paul was. He
was adamant, it seems. According to Mel, he didn't want you
to see him that way, or know the seriousness of his injuries,
or to be burdened with him."

Emma was speechless. Not to be burdened with him, she
thought. But I loved him more than life itself. Oh, Paul, why
did you keep me away from you when you needed me the
most? She envisioned Paul's pain and the terrible despair
which had prompted his action, and an overwhelming sorrow
engulfed her.

It seemed to Emma that the whole world had abruptly
stopped. There was no sound in the room, except for the faint
ticking of the carriage clock on the mantelshelf. She looked
down at the great McGill emerald glittering on her finger,
and at the wedding ring Paul had given her when Daisy was
born, and her unchecked tears fell on her hands and splashed
against the rings. And she remembered the words he had
spoken that day: "Until death do us part," he had said. Her
heart twisted inside her. She lifted her head and glanced
about, and a terrible aching numbness entered her body. She

felt as though she, too, was paralyzed and would be quite unable to move ever again. The pain was beginning, and she understood with a flash of clarity that she would never be free of it. She thought: I cannot live without him. He was my life. There is nothing left now. Only the empty years ahead to endure until I, too, die.

Winston and Frank were helpless in their despair. Winston could not stand to see her suffering, and telephoned the family doctor, who arrived fifteen minutes later. Emma was given a sedative and the housekeeper helped her to bed. But wracking sobs continued to convulse her and they did not cease for over two hours, when the sedative finally lulled her into a more tranquil state.

Her two brothers, Henry Rossiter, and the doctor stayed with Emma until she finally fell into a drugged sleep. As they left the bedroom, Winston said, "Her sorrow is only just beginning."

Tragedy had struck at Emma many times in her life. It had caused her to falter, but it had never brought her to her knees. Paul's death felled her with one swift blow.

All of her children, except Edwina, came home to be with her. They had loved and admired Paul, and they were aghast and grief-stricken, most especially Daisy, who had been the closest to him. Each one in their own way tried to comfort their mother, but their efforts were in vain.

Frank's wife, Natalie, came immediately; Charlotte, Winston's wife, and their son, Randolph, traveled up to London from Leeds with Blackie and his son Bryan, the four of them accompanied by David Kallinski and his sons, Ronnie and Mark. None of them could reach Emma and, after a brief visit with her in her bedroom, they assembled in the library, their faces clouded with anxiety.

Blackie attempted to alleviate their worry. He said, "Even the strongest heart can be broken, you know. But a strong heart always mends. I put my money on Emma any day. She's a born survivor and she'll survive this. Also, I think it's much better she gets her grief out. I know she'll be all right." And he meant every word, for he knew the stern stuff she was made of.

But for days Emma lay prostrate, half crazed and incoher-ent with grief. She became so debilitated at one point Winston seriously contemplated hospitalizing her. The dawn hours were the worst for Emma. She would lie motionless in her bed, bereft and without hope, watching the cold gray light creeping in, waiting for the beginning of a new endless empty day, staring vacantly into space like a blind woman. But her vivid and active mind was forever in a turmoil, filled with conflicting and troublesome thoughts. She wondered if she had failed Paul in some way. Failed to properly convey over the years the depth and sincerity of her love for him. She castigated herself for not having gone to Australia when he had first had the accident, believing she could have prevented him from lifting that fateful gun. If she had not listened to him she could have saved his life, of that she was absolutely convinced. The weight of her guilt was heavy to bear, and her despondency and wretchedness only increased.

Henry Rossiter had told her of the doctors' dismal prognosis, and slowly, as the shock receded, she began to dimly understand that a man like Paul, so virile, so powerful, would regard suicide as the only viable solution to his awful predicament, and yet sometimes she felt utterly abandoned and betrayed by him. However, mostly she was able to dismiss these feelings as manifestations of self-pity, a curious anger, which was baffling, and her own sense of powerlessness. It was also incomprehensible to her that Paul had not written, for she was unable to accept the fact that he would kill himself without one last word to her, and every day she looked for a letter, which did not come.

Winston, who had taken charge of the household and the Knightsbridge store, decided to keep Daisy at home from boarding school after the rest of the family departed. It was she who eventually reached Emma and brought her a measure of relief. Emma's youngest child was surprisingly mature for a fourteen-year-old, and understanding beyond her years. Her own sorrow was acute, but she carefully strove to conceal this most of the time, and she finally achieved a real breakthrough with her mother. She persuaded Emma to eat a little every day, and gradually helped to stem the flow of tears with her loving presence. Occasionally Emma would look intently at Daisy and she would see Paul so clearly reflected in the child's face her tears would start afresh, and she would cling to their daughter, calling for Paul. Daisy would wipe away the tears and calm her with soothing words, rocking her in her arms as if she were the mother and Emma the daughter.

One night, after Emma had collapsed again, Daisy tenderly cajoled her into a more peaceful state of mind, and for the first time Emma fell into a natural sleep that was heavy and deep. When she awakened several hours later she felt rested and had even acquired a degree of composure. She at once noticed Daisy curled up on the chaise, dozing. And she suddenly saw her daughter objectively. With a flash of insight Emma recognized she had been burdening Daisy with her own grief when the child herself needed love and support. With a supreme effort she roused herself from her lethargy, and some of that strength, always formidable, began to trickle back into her weary body.

Emma got out of bed unaided and moved slowly to the chaise, her legs shaking and unsteady. Daisy woke up instantly and when she saw her mother bending over her she took hold of her hand swiftly, her eyes apprehensive. "Mummy, what is it? Do you feel ill again?"

"No, darling. In fact, I think I'm a bit better." Emma took Daisy in her arms and held her close, stroking her glossy black hair. "I've been very wrong, Daisy, putting the burden of my grief on you. So wrong. Please forgive me, darling. Now, I want you to get ready for bed and have a really good night's sleep. And I don't want you to worry about me anymore. I will be fine. And tomorrow I am going to send you back to boarding school."

Daisy pulled away and stared at Emma in surprise, and her vivid blue eyes were brilliant with tears. "But I want to stay with you, Mummy. To look after you. Paul would want that. He really would. He wouldn't want you to be alone, Mummy."

Emma smiled gently. "You've been looking after me very well, and now it's my turn to look after you. I am going to be all right, darling. Truly I am."

Daisy began to cry and she buried her head on Emma's breast, sobbing as if her heart would break. "Hush, darling. Hush," Emma murmured. "We must be strong and brave, and help each other in the coming months."

"I've been so afraid, Mummy," Daisy sobbed, her tears drenching Emma's crumpled nightgown. "I thought you were going to die, too."

Emma said, in a voice that was surprisingly steady, "I am not going to die, Daisy, I have you to live for now."

It was a glorious afternoon in late September, sunny and warm and with a cloudless sky that was radiant with light. But Emma shivered as she walked wearily across the drawing room. She huddled in a chair in front of the fire, warming herself, her thoughts on her sons. War had been declared on September 3, and although she had been too bereaved to pay attention then, the situation could no longer be ignored. Britain was mobilizing with the same speed and efficiency it had displayed in her youth, and she knew that they would be in for a long siege.

Feeling warmer, she shifted in the chair. As she did a raft of bright sunlight illuminated the ravages her grief had wrought. She had shed pounds and looked painfully thin in the simple black wool dress, its severity unrelieved by jewelry. The only pieces she wore were Paul's rings, and a watch. But her hair was bright and crackling with life.

"Here I am, me darlin'," Blackie called from the doorway, startling her. She rose to greet him, managing a smile. "It's lovely to see you, Blackie dear," Emma said, embracing him.

He enveloped her in his arms and held her tightly to his broad chest, and he choked up as he felt the fragility of her body. She was a bag of bones. He held her away, looked down into her face, and put his hand under her chin. "You're a sight for sore eyes, mavourneen. It's grand to see you up and about."

They sat in front of the fire and talked for a while about the war and the probability that the boys would enlist imminently. "Bryan is in London with me," Blackie told her. "He wanted to come with me today, but I wasn't sure you'd be up to it."

"Oh, Blackie, I am disappointed. I'd love to see him," she exclaimed, her face brightening. "Could he come tomorrow? You know how dear Bryan is to me."

"Sure and he can. I'll bring him meself." Blackie now gave her a guarded look. "When do you think you'll be fit enough to go back to the store?"

"Next week. The doctor was against it, actually. He thinks I should go to Yorkshire for a rest. But I simply can't neglect the business any longer, and it's just not fair to Winston. He's carrying all the responsibility. Besides, he ought to go back to Leeds. We've a lot of reorganizing to do."

"I know what you mean. I'm facing the same problems. Anyway, Emma, I think it's a good idea for you to get back into the harness again. You must keep your mind occupied, so that you don't dwell on things."

Her face clouded momentarily. "Yes, that's true." The maid knocked and came in with the tea tray. Emma eyed the heavy Georgian teapot warily, wondering if she had the strength to lift it. For days she had been like a woman with the palsy, dropping and spilling things. She lifted it carefully and poured two cups, and to her relief her hands did not tremble for once.

She said, "I spoke to David yesterday. He sounded very down in the dumps. Ronnie and Mark have already joined up. He's going to miss them terribly. They've been his whole life since Rebecca died."

He observed the sudden mistiness in her eyes and said swiftly, "He'll be all right, Emma. Tell you what, I'll take him under my wing when I get back to Leeds. Get him out of that great mausoleum where he lives in such solitary splendor. It'll do him good to start socializing again."

"I wish you would, darling, I do worry about him." Emma looked into the fire reflectively, and when she turned back to Blackie her expression was sorrowful. "How does one go on, Blackie? It's so hard, isn't it?"

"Yes, but not impossible, Emma. Not for someone with your courage."

"I haven't been very strong these past few weeks," she said drearily.

"You can't rush it, Emma. You'll have a lot of readjusting to do. You must give yourself time, darlin'."

"However did you manage after Laura died?" she asked.

"I sometimes wondered that myself at the time." He smiled faintly. "After I went back to the front I tried my damnedest to catch a bullet, to get myself killed. But the good Lord protected me from me own foolishness. After the war it took me a long time to forgive myself for being alive, but once I did I started to live again. I looked around and became aware of my responsibilities, my duty to Bryan. He was a great help, Emma. A great source of sustenance. As Daisy will be for you. That child, of all your children, is the most like you in character. She understands you and she worships you, mavourneen."

"Yes, I know," Emma responded quietly, and looked away again. "I just—just—just don't know how I can go on without Paul."

Blackie took her hand and held it tightly. "You can, darlin'. *You will*. The human soul has great fortitude." He paused and his black eyes swept over her piteous face. He said gently, "Do you remember what Laura said to you when she was dying? I've never forgotten the words since you repeated them to me, and they have helped me many times. Do you remember what she said about death, Emma?"

Emma nodded. "Yes, I remember her words as if she had spoken them only yesterday. Laura said there was no such thing as death in her lexicon, and that as long as I lived and you lived she would live, too, for we would carry the memory of her in our hearts forever."

Blackie said, "Aye, mavourneen, and she was a wise lady, my Laura. She truly believed that, as I have come to believe it, and as you must. It will help you, I know. And just as I have Bryan, you have Paul's daughter. She is part of his flesh, part of him, and you must cleave to that and take strength from it."

His words seemed to give her comfort and so he continued. "You also told me Laura said God doesn't give us a burden that is too heavy to bear. She *was* right, Emma. Think on that." He sighed under his breath. "I know you are heartbroken and that you feel lost and alone. But none of us are alone, Emma. We all have God, and God has helped me over the years. Why don't you try Him on for size?"

Emma's eyes widened. "You know I don't believe in God."

Observing the look on her face, Blackie refrained from making any further comments and wisely talked of other things.

But later, when he left Emma's house, Blackie walked to the Brompton Oratory. He crossed himself on entering that fine old church, sat down in a pew, and lifted his face to the altar. And he prayed to God to give Emma comfort and courage in her crushing loss, and he prayed for her soul.

Before she went to bed that night, Emma sat at the window in her bedroom for several hours, dwelling on those words of Laura's. The sky was a peculiar cobalt blue, clear yet

intense, and shining with hundreds of stars, and a pale silver
moon rode high in the heavens. Its beauty was so perfectly
revealed to her it made her catch her breath and she suddenly had the most overwhelming sense of the Infinite. It
was a feeling she had never experienced before and she was
strangely moved as she sat gazing at that incredible night sky.
And then it seemed to her that Paul was with her in the
room. And she thought: But of course he is, for he is in my
heart always. And she drew strength from this knowledge,
and that night she slept a deep and untroubled sleep.

Two days later Emma received a letter from Paul. It had
been posted the day before his death and it had taken three
weeks to arrive. She looked at it for a long time before she
finally found the courage to slit open the envelope and take
out the letter.

My dearest darling Emma:

*You are my life. I cannot live without my life. But I
cannot live with you. And so I must end my miserable
existence, for there is no future for us together now.
Lest you think my suicide an act of weakness, let me
reassure you that it is not. It is an act of strength and
of will, for by committing it I gratefully take back that
control over myself which I have lost in the past few
months. It is a final act of power over my own fate.*

*It is the only way out for me, my love and I will die
with your name on my lips, the image of you before my
eyes, my love for you secure in my heart always. We
have been lucky, Emma. We have had so many good
years together and shared so much, and the happy
memories are alive in me, as I know they are in you,
and will be as long as you live. I thank you for giving
me the best years of my life.*

*I did not send for you because I did not want you to
be tied to a helpless cripple, if only for a few months at
the most. Perhaps I was wrong. On the other hand, I
want you to remember me as I was, and not what I
have become since the accident. Pride? Maybe. But try
to understand my reasons, and try, my darling, to find
it in your heart to forgive me.*

I have great faith in you, my dearest Emma. You are

*not faint of heart. You are strong and dauntless, and
you will go on courageously. You must. For there is our
child to consider. She is the embodiment of our love
and I know you will cherish and care for her, and bring
her up to be as brave and as stalwart and as loving as
you are yourself. I give her into your trust, my darling.*

*By the time you receive this I will be dead. But I will
live on in Daisy. She is your future now, my Emma.
And mine.*

*I love you with all my heart and soul and mind, and I
pray to God that one day we will be reunited in Eternity.*

I kiss you, my darling.

Paul

Emma was motionless in the chair, clutching the letter, the
tears seeping out of her eyes and rolling silently down her
pale cheeks. She saw him in her mind's eye, tall and handsome, his deep violet eyes laughing, and she remembered
him as he wanted her to remember him. She thought of the
years and the joy and love he had given her. And she forgave
him, now understanding, and with great compassion, both his
dilemma and his motives.

At the beginning of October, Mel Harrison took a four-
engined "C Class," Qantas flying boat from Sydney to Karachi,
and there boarded an English airplane that provided the link to
Great Britain. Several days later he arrived in London. His purpose: to see Emma and present Paul McGill's will to the solicitors
who handled the McGill legal work in England and Europe.

Emma, austerely dressed in black, appeared wan and fragile,
yet she was composed when she arrived at Price, Ellis, and
Watson for the reading of Paul McGill's last will and testament.
Winston, Frank, and Henry Rossiter accompanied her.

"Paul made you the executrix of his estate," Mel informed
her as she sat down. She was taken by surprise, but she
simply nodded, at a loss for words.

There were bequests to servants, to old and loyal employees, and a two-million-pound trust fund had been created to
provide for his wife and son during their lifetimes. Upon
their deaths it was to go to charity. His entire estate he had
willed to Emma in perpetuity, passing to Daisy upon her
death, and from Daisy to her progeny. To Emma's astonish-

ment Paul had left her everything he owned, holdings worth
well over two hundred million pounds. He had made her one
of the richest women in the world and their daughter the
heiress to a great fortune. But the thing that moved Emma
the most was the fact that Paul had accorded her the respect
and consideration generally reserved for a man's legal widow
and not his common-law wife. In death, as in life, Paul had
declared his devotion and love for her, had acknowledged her
to the whole world. And into her hands had passed the
McGill dynasty for safekeeping.

FIFTY-EIGHT

Emma's grief was a mantle of iron, but slowly she came to
grips with her heartache. In all truth, her sorrow did not
really lessen and she missed Paul and yearned for him constantly, but she took control of her emotions, and as the
weeks passed she began to function like her old self. Also,
her anguish was muted by the circumstances of her life and
the world crisis which had developed.

She was beset by the most pressing problems as England
plunged into the European conflict, and consequently her
energies were taxed to the fullest, leaving little time or
strength for self-indulgences. Her sons joined the forces, Kit
enlisting in the army, Robin in the Royal Air Force.

Elizabeth, who had enrolled at the Royal Academy of Dramatic Art in the summer of 1939, was quietly married to
Tony Barkstone during the Christmas holidays. Although Elizabeth was only eighteen and still too flighty to marry, in
Emma's opinion, she did not have the heart to object. Everyone had to grasp happiness when they could, especially in
these terrible times, and, in spite of her misgivings, she gave
her blessing. The young couple were obviously head over
heels in love, and Emma approved of Tony, who was a friend
of Robin's from Cambridge and also a pilot in the RAF.

Despite the austerity, a spirit of gaiety prevailed at the
wedding and all of the family were briefly reunited, with the
exception of Edwina, who was still estranged from Emma,
and Kit, who was unable to get leave. June, his wife of one

year, came up to London for the occasion and stayed with Emma through the New Year. In January of 1940, Elizabeth dropped out of the Royal Academy to become a Red Cross nurse, much to Emma's amazement. "But I thought you always dreamed of being a famous actress and seeing your name in lights," she exclaimed when she heard the news. "Oh, phooey to all that nonsense," Elizabeth quickly responded. "I feel I must be part of the war effort, too, Mummy." Emma was soon impressed by Elizabeth's seriousness and her dedication to nursing, and she began to think the marriage would be the stabilizing influence her most wayward child needed.

The news grew more distressing by the day, and in March Emma contemplated sending Daisy to America to live with the Nelsons at their Hudson River estate. But the more she thought about it, the more she balked, acknowledging that the transatlantic crossing could be hazardous, and she decided that the child's present location at boarding school in Ascot was probably the safest place.

As the year progressed, Emma threw herself into work with a vengeance, but she welcomed the distraction it offered. Henry Rossiter, who had handled some of her business in the past, became her financial adviser on a full-time basis, since she now had all the McGill holdings to supervise as well as her own. She was in constant touch with Mel Harrison in Sydney and Harry Marriott in Texas, and her days were longer and more arduous than ever before as her responsibilities increased. But she took everything in her stride. She was the dynamo she had been in her youth, and most especially during the First World War when she had also been left to cope single-handedly. If Emma's face grew graver by the day, then so did every other face in England, for the country was held in the grip of fulminating desperation as Hitler's blitzkrieg continued unabated.

Towards the end of May, just after his fifty-fourth birthday, David Kallinski came to London to discuss their mutual business interests with Emma. He was still a good-looking man and those penetrating blue eyes had not dimmed, although his hair was iron gray and he had thickened around the waist. His devotion to Emma had remained constant over the years and he was always concerned about her. To his relief, when she greeted him at the house in Belgrave Square, he immediately saw that her face had lost its gaunt look and her beauty was returning, and she had also put on a little weight. Later they were joined by Blackie, and after a light supper they adjourned to the library for coffee and liqueurs, their conversation revolving around the war.

"Do you think we'll be able to get the boys off the beaches in time?" Emma asked, thinking not only of Kit, and Ronnie and Mark Kallinski, but of the thousands of other British troops stranded in Dunkirk.

"If anybody can do it, by God, Winston Churchill can!" Blackie asserted. He shifted in his chair and went on, "He's assembled an armada the likes of which the world has never seen, albeit a motley one. But it's united in one goal—getting our boys safely home to Deal and Ramsgate before they are annihilated by the Germans advancing across the Low Countries into France."

"I read they came from all over England to assist the Royal Navy's destroyers," David interjected, puffing on his cigar. "Volunteers from all walks of life, with their rowboats, sailboats, fishing trawlers, yachts, pleasure steamers, and even barges. It's the most wonderful display of patriotism and heroism I've ever heard of in my lifetime."

Blackie nodded. "Aye, it is, David. Seven hundred vessels of all shapes and sizes, including the destroyers, of course. It seems the volunteers are picking up the men and carrying them out to the bigger ships that can't get close enough to the beaches, while some are even ferrying the boys across the Channel on a round-the-clock basis. Enormously brave men, sure and they are, and indefatigible."

"How long do you think the evacuation will take?" Emma inquired quietly, looking from Blackie to David with consternation.

David said, "A few days longer at least. There are hundreds of thousands of British and French troops to lift off, you know."

"I read today that the Luftwaffe is keeping up a steady bombardment of the beaches," Emma said. "I dread to think of the casualties."

"There are bound to be some, Emma," Blackie said. "But the RAF boys are up there in their fighter planes doing their damnedest to—"

"Bryan, Robin, and Tony amongst them, Blackie," Emma interjected, and she looked away.

"We all feel frustrated and helpless, sitting here in London. But all we can do is pray that our sons will be safe. And we must be cheerful," Blackie said. "Now come along, let's have another drink. It will do us good." As he fixed their drinks Blackie's eyes strayed to the clock on the mantelshelf. "Do you mind if we turn the radio on, Emma? Winston Churchill's about to speak."

"No, of course not. I'd like to hear him myself." She rose and fiddled with the knob, tuning in to the BBC, and a moment later the familiar rhetorical voice rang out: "Good evening. This is the Prime Minister." The three old friends, who had shared so much in the past thirty years, sat back to listen, even more strongly joined together by fear for their sons and all the sons of England. When the Prime Minister had finished, Emma's eyes stung and her voice quavered when she said, "What an inspiration that man is to us all. God help us if we didn't have Churchill."

The epic of Dunkirk gripped the imagination of England and her allies. Out of hell came back all the little steamers and rowboats and pleasure steamers, bringing back the living and the wounded. The evacuation had taken eleven days, and 340,000 Allied troops had been rescued by the time the Germans captured the French sea town. Only 40,000, mostly French, were left behind. Emma and David were lucky. Amongst those to land at Ramsgate on June 1 and 2 were Ronnie and Mark, and on June 3 Kit stepped off the barge that had transported him to Deal across a choppy Channel jammed with vessels and wreckage. Kit told Emma later, when he came home on leave, "I just made it by the skin of my teeth, Mother. I must have a guardian angel watching over me." He embraced her tightly, and, clinging to him, she choked up, thinking of his father, who had died in France in 1916, apparently in vain.

On June 4 Winston Churchill rose in the House of Commons and made a speech on Dunkirk. At one moment he said, "We shall fight on the beaches, we shall fight on the landing-grounds, we shall fight in the fields and in the streets, we shall fight in the hills; we shall never surrender." Six days later the French Government and the Army High Command fled Paris as the Nazi army drew closer. Four days after that the French capital was captured by the Germans, who took it without firing one shot. France had fallen.

Britain stood alone.

That summer was the worst Emma could remember. In July the Battle of Britain began in earnest. Hitler had ordered an all-out offensive against the RAF, specifically Britain's aircraft factories and the fighter bases that ringed London. Day after day, night after night, huge fleets of Dornier and Heinkel bombers swept across the Channel to pulverize Britain, while Messerschmitt fighter planes fought off the RAF Hurricanes and Spitfires that rose up into the sky in swift retaliation.

Awakened at night by the screaming air-raid sirens, Emma would get up and stand by the window in her darkened bedroom, looking out at the night sky starkly illuminated by the searchlights and echoing with the incessant drone of the bombers and fighter planes, her heart in her mouth as she thought of Robin, Tony, and Bryan and the other young pilots up there risking their lives. Some nights she was joined by Elizabeth, who had given up the small flat she had taken during her Royal Academy days, and was again living at home. "Are you awake, Mummy?" she would invariably whisper, gliding into the room in her nightgown. "Yes, darling," Emma would answer, and the two of them would stand together, their arms around each other, watching the planes zooming past.

One night Elizabeth grasped her mother's arm fiercely, and her voice was unusually harsh when she cried out, "Why, Mummy? Why? Why did this ghastly war have to start? What's the purpose of it? They're all going to be killed! Tony and Robin and Bryan, and all of our other boys!"

Emma had no answers for her daughter, or for herself. Elizabeth became distraught, sobbing uncontrollably. Emma put her arms around Elizabeth's shoulders and led her to the bed. "They're not going to be killed, darling," she comforted. "They're going to be all right. I promise you. We must be brave. Get into my bed and sleep with me tonight. We'll keep each other company."

"Yes, Mummy, I think I will," Elizabeth said, crawling under the covers. Emma held her close, as she had done when she was small and frightened of the dark. "Don't cry and try not to worry, Elizabeth."

"If Tony gets killed I won't be able to bear it," Elizabeth said through her tears. "I love him so much. And if Robin—"

"Hush, darling. Try to sleep now. You must have your rest."

"Yes, I'll try. Thank you, Mummy. Good night."

"Good night, dear."

Emma lay in the darkness, waiting for Elizabeth's tense body to relax and go limp in sleep. But it did not, and Emma knew that her daughter would spend yet another sleepless night worrying about her husband and her twin, as she would herself.

Emma had made a habit of walking to the store in Knightsbridge every day, and as the summer drifted on she did so to the accompanying sounds of antiaircraft guns, whining sirens, falling rubble, and shattering glass. She would flinch when she saw a favorite landmark demolished, an ancient church in ruins, old haunts she and Paul had frequented flattened to the ground. Yet in spite of London's devastation, its bleak mood, and the weary expressions on the faces she passed in the streets, Emma would nevertheless marvel at the stoicism and indomitability of her fellow countrymen and countrywomen. Often a cheery Cockney voice would break into a song, perhaps a fireman hosing a pile of smoking bricks or a workman clearing away the debris, and a cab driver would have a breezy comment to make, and they lifted her heart with their courage. It was at times like these that she would remember Churchill's words, "We shall never surrender," and her strength was renewed, a spring returned to her step, her back straightened, and her head flew up proudly. And somehow her burdens seemed all that much lighter to bear.

The summer drew to a close. In September a large portion of the East End docks were destroyed in a massive air attack. The daily raids continued and the RAF pilots were tested to their limits, flying nonstop missions. The usual two- and three-day leaves were canceled and Emma did not see Robin for weeks. The Royal Air Force was Britain's last defense, and even though they were outnumbered three to one, the boys in blue in their Spitfires and Hurricanes outperformed the Luftwaffe. By October the Führer's plan to destroy the RAF and break English morale in readiness for a full-scale invasion had proved a failure. In fact, Hitler had suffered his first major defeat. But the German bombers still continued night raids on the large cities, leveling many to the ground, and the grim years dragged on endlessly. Years of the Blitz; coupons, ration cards, and queues; shortages and deprivations; sorrow and grief as old friends and the sons and daughters of old friends were killed or named missing in action.

But in the midst of the devastation there was the miraculous renewal of life. In 1942, June, Kit's wife, gave birth to a daughter. Emma was fond of June and delighted at the arrival of a second grandchild, and she went up to Leeds for the baptism of the baby, who was called Sarah. The same year, at the end of the summer term, Daisy left boarding school and came home to live with her mother and Elizabeth in Belgrave Square. Now the house did not seem so lonely and there were even moments of gaiety and laughter, especially when Robin came up from Biggin Hill, where he was stationed. He invariably brought one or two of his RAF friends from the 111th Squadron with him, explaining to Emma, "The chaps are going to bunk in with us, Ma. You don't mind, do you? All the hotels are jam-packed." Emma did not mind. In fact, she willingly opened her doors and her heart to those dauntless young pilots.

At Christmas, Robin was fortunate to get a three-day pass at the last minute and he arrived unannounced on Christmas Eve, as usual dragging three friends in his wake. The moment David Amory walked into her living room Emma's heart missed a beat. He was tall and dark, with bright blue eyes and a flashing smile, and there was something about his looks and his engaging manner that reminded her of Paul McGill. David was not as outrageously handsome as Paul had been as a young man, nor did he have his massive size or his audacious personality, yet he struck a chord in her memory of Paul as he had been during the First World War. David was twenty-four, a new arrival at Biggin Hill and already something of a war hero. With an ingenuousness that was quite endearing, he charmed Emma at once.

That Christmas was a particularly merry one and the house rang with peals of laughter, the friendly but unmerciful bantering that went on between the RAF boys and her daughters, the endless sound of the gramophone and the clink of glasses. Emma entertained gaily, taking them all under her wing, enjoying the fun as much as the young people. But whether she was being the gracious hostess or quietly sitting in a corner, looking on and knitting a balaclava helmet, she was aware of David Amory. Her smile was benign but her eyes were watchful as she observed the seventeen-year-old Daisy, her most beloved child, being bewitched and falling under the fatal spell of the dashing young RAF officer. And David appeared to be as enamored with Daisy as she was with him, and he was never far from her side. Emma held her breath, knowing they were falling in love and that there was nothing she could do to prevent it. Nor was she certain she wanted to interfere. After the holidays, David Amory became a constant visitor at Belgrave Square, whether he arrived with Robin or came alone, and over the months Emma took him to her heart. He was from an old Gloucestershire family, well bred and well educated, and had been studying law when the war had erupted. Emma quickly discovered he had integrity and a bright mind, as well as a gentleness that she found appealing, and she could not help but approve of him for Daisy. It did not come as a surprise when David asked her permission to marry her youngest child. He did so in May of 1943, just after Daisy's eighteenth birthday. "But she's so young, David darling," Emma exclaimed, intending to persuade them to wait. But she found herself saying instead, "When do you plan to get married?"

Daisy, who had been hovering nervously by the fireplace, hugged her so furiously Emma winced. Daisy's face was radiant and her eyes sparkled. "Next weekend, Mummy, if that's all right with you."

The wedding was quiet, just as Elizabeth's had been, because of the wartime conditions and Emma's natural reluctance to display her wealth in such troubled times. Daisy wore a blue silk dress, a matching picture hat, and carried a nosegay of summer flowers. Winston gave her away, Robin was the best man, and Elizabeth the matron of honor. David's parents and younger sister came up from Gloucestershire for the wedding and there was a small reception at the house afterwards. The young couple had a one-night honeymoon at the Ritz Hotel before David returned to Biggin Hill and Daisy to her mother's house.

And then, almost before Emma could catch her breath, Robin married Valerie Ludden, a nursing friend of Elizabeth's, in January of 1944, and a few weeks later Elizabeth gave birth to a son, whom she named Alexander. Elizabeth, who wanted to be close to Tony, found a small cottage near the airfield and moved there when the baby was a month old.

"It hardly seems possible they are all married now," Emma said to Winston one day in the spring, when they were lunching together. "Or that I have three grandchildren. I feel as old as the hills."

"Nonsense," Winston declared. "You're the damnedest-looking grandmother I've ever seen. And you'll never get old, Emma. You have the kind of beauty that is indestructible." He grinned at her affectionately. "Furthermore, Frank tells me that the American major you met at his house has taken quite a fancy to you. *You* might find yourself with a suitor before you know it."

"Don't be foolish, Winston," Emma snapped, but she smiled as she spoke.

"I'm not being foolish," Winston responded. "After all, you'll only be fifty-five next month. Besides, you look years younger." He paused and eyed her carefully. "And Paul has bean dead for almost five years."

Emma was silent and Winston changed the subject. He and Frank constantly talked about the possibility of Emma forming a relationship with another man, and they went out of their way to introduce her to their eligible friends. But although she was gracious, she was patently not interested. She would never replace Paul in her life; she did not want to.

The year 1945 began auspiciously for Emma. Daisy gave birth to her first child in January. It was a girl.

"How do you feel, darling?" Emma asked as she walked into Daisy's private room at London Clinic.

"Thin," Daisy said, laughing. She hugged Emma. "I was awfully lucky. It was an easy birth."

"Yes, I know. The doctor told me." Emma moved a strand of hair away from Daisy's face and kissed her. "I just spoke to David at Biggin Hill. He's thrilled to bits. Celebrating with the boys from the squadron, and playing the proud father. He's going to phone you a little later. And good news, darling. He's got a twenty-four-hour pass. He'll be up in town tomorrow."

"Oh, that's wonderful, Mummy. I can't wait to see him." Daisy wrinkled her nose. "I'm not sure who the baby looks like. She's awfully crumpled and red, poor little thing. But she has black hair, and I think she's going to have a widow's peak like yours from the way her hairline is formed. And her eyes are violet. Do you think they'll change color?"

"They might," Emma said, sitting down. "They often do. Still, yours remained blue."

"I've chosen the baby's first two names, Mummy," Daisy announced. "I'm going to call her Paula McGill. After my father."

Emma's face, normally inscrutable, was only too readable for once in her life, and Daisy burst out laughing. "Don't look so shocked. Honestly, Mummy, for a woman as sophisticated as you are, you can be awfully naïve sometimes. Did you think I didn't know Paul was my father?"

Emma said, "I—I—" and stopped.

Daisy laughed again, but it was a gentle laugh and full of love. "Even when I was quite small I thought he was my father. After all, he was always with us and we traveled everywhere with him. Then, as I grew older, I realized how much I resembled him physically. And let's face it, I never knew Arthur Ainsley, whose name I bear." Daisy paused and her bright blue eyes were fixed intently on Emma. "Anyway, when I was twelve Paul told me himself."

Emma's jaw dropped. "Paul told you he was your father! I can't believe it!"

Daisy nodded. "Well, he did. He said he wanted me to know, and that I was old enough to understand. But he said it must be our secret for a few years. He was worried you would be upset. He explained everything to me very directly and carefully, and with so much gentleness. He told me why you and he couldn't be married, but that he hoped to solve the problem one day. He also told me that he had legally adopted me, and he said he loved us both more than anything in the world." Daisy's eyes were moist. She cleared her throat and finished, "Actually, it didn't come as much of a surprise to me, Mummy, because by that time I had guessed. I told him so, and he really chuckled. He said he knew his princess was the smartest girl in the world."

"Didn't—doesn't it bother you, knowing you are illegitimate?" Emma managed to ask.

"Oh, Mummy, don't be so old-fashioned. Of course it doesn't. I'd rather be Paul McGill's illegitimate daughter than Arthur Ainsley's legitimate daughter any day of the week."

Tears welled in Emma's eyes and she fumbled for her handkerchief. "I—I—don't know what to say," she began falteringly.

Daisy leaned forward and held out her arms to Emma. "I love you, Mummy. And I loved Paul. I couldn't have had better parents if I'd chosen them myself. And you have been the most wonderful mother in the whole world."

"But why didn't you tell me you knew before?" Emma asked in a muffled voice, her face pushed against Daisy's shoulder. "Why didn't you tell me when Paul died?"

"I didn't think it was really the right time. My main concern was trying to alleviate your grief."

Emma sat back in the chair, blowing her nose. She smiled weakly at Daisy, her face reflecting her love. "I'm glad you know, darling, I should have told you myself. But I thought you would react like—that you would be upset and that you would hate me and Paul."

"You are a silly goose, Mummy. I could never hate or criticize you or my father for what you did. You loved each other." Daisy took hold of Emma's hand and squeezed it. "I'm proud to be your daughter." Daisy gave Emma a questioning look. "Are you sure you don't mind my calling the baby after my father?"

"I'm thrilled," Emma said.

The nurse came in, interrupting them. Emma held the baby in her arms and her face glowed as she looked down at the small bundle nestling against her shoulder. This is Paul's first grandchild, she thought, and her heart quickened. If only he had been alive to see her. Paula McGill Amory, the first of a new generation in the McGill dynasty.

One week later Daisy came home to Belgrave Square, where her old nursery had been beautifully prepared to receive its new young occupant. Almost immediately the child became the center of Emma's world, and if she sometimes usurped Daisy's role as mother, Daisy did not seem to mind in the least. She was gratified to see Emma so joyous and smiling. And she enthusiastically encouraged her mother when she talked of her plans for Paula and her future.

And the future in general was beginning to look brighter. "It's as if Paula's birth was a good omen," Emma said one morning over breakfast, gesturing to the newspaper she was reading. "The Allies are really making a breakthrough. I think the war will end soon."

She was right in this assumption. As the new year eased into spring, the whole of England took heart. In March, the American First Army crossed the Rhine over the bridge at Remagen and established an invasion bridgehead in Germany. Between April 20 and 25, the Russians entered Berlin, and five days later Hitler and Eva Braun committed suicide. The Third Reich, which the Führer had said would last a thousand years, had disintegrated in humiliating defeat. On May 7, the Germans surrendered unconditionally at Reims in France.

Emma was in Leeds on May 8, which was V-E Day in Britain. She dined that night with Winston and Charlotte and they drank two bottles of champagne in celebration. But in spite of the flags hanging out of windows and fluttering on flagpoles all over Leeds, and the festivities going on around them, Emma felt more relieved than jubilant. And she drew her first easy breath in six years. Her sons were safe, and her sons-in-law, and the sons of her brother and her dearest friends, Blackie O'Neill and David Kallinski. There had been no casualties in their families, and for that Emma was deeply grateful.

And slowly they all came home.

"I just stopped by to congratulate you, Emma," Blackie O'Neill said, striding into the drawing room at Pennistone Royal. "Winston tells me the Yorkshire Consolidated Newspaper Company has taken control of the *Yorkshire Morning Gazette*. So you've finally won!"

Emma smiled at him faintly. "Yes, I have. But then you always knew I would, didn't you?"

"Yes, I did." He threw her a sharp glance and asked, "How did you do it, Emma? I'm very curious."

"Patience, really, and a weak adversary." She folded her hands in her lap, looked down at the McGill emerald and then went on crisply. "My newspapers are the most successful in Yorkshire and they have slowly eaten up all of the *Gazette*'s circulation. That paper's been losing money since the end of the war. To be honest, I deliberately ran the *Gazette* into the ground, and I did so without compunction. Edwin Fairley is not a good businessman. He should have stuck to law." She laughed dryly. "And he's made a few fatal errors, not the least of which was selling a big block of his shares two years ago. He weakened his position. He has not been dealing from strength for a long time."

"But he stayed on as chairman of the board," Blackie interjected.

"Yes, he did. But he failed to recognize the tenuousness of his position, and he also underestimated the other shareholders, both the old and the new. He just didn't seem to realize that loyalty flies out of the window when there's a great deal of money at stake. The board has been worried about the failing paper for years, and when Harte Enterprises approached them to buy up their shares they were willing to sell, almost to the last man. I've been acquiring shares in the company for years, and those, coupled with my last purchases, gave me a lot of power. Those shareholders who didn't at first sell to me finally threw their weight behind me when I offered to step in and put new management into the company. Very simply, Edwin Fairley was outvoted at the last board meeting and had to step down as chairman. Harte Enterprises made an offer for the remainder of his shares and, surprisingly, he sold."

"Quite a coup for you, Emma, eh?" Blackie remarked. "But I'm surprised you weren't present at that board meeting to witness his demise. Winston said *he* represented you."

Emma's face changed radically and a cold glint entered her eyes. She said, "Forty-five years ago I told Edwin Fairley I would never see him again as long as I lived, and I haven't. You don't think I want to set eyes on him now, do you?"

Blackie shrugged. "I suppose not," he responded quietly. "Did Winston say how Edwin reacted when he learned you were behind his fall from power at the *Gazette*?"

Emma nodded. "Apparently he was poker-faced. All barristers are good actors, you know. Then he said, 'I see.' But Winston told me Edwin had a peculiar look on his face, which he found hard to fathom." She paused and stared fully at Blackie. "Winston said he thought Edwin looked gratified. Odd, wouldn't you say?"

"Yes, I would. I can't imagine why Edwin Fairley would be gratified you had taken over his newspaper." He shook his head, baffled. "The paper that's been in his family for three generations."

"God knows," Emma said, "it's a mystery to me. I told Winston it was more than likely sheer relief he witnessed." She laughed ironically. "In one way, you might say I've lifted a burden from Edwin's shoulders."

"Aye, mavourneen," Blackie said, and his face was unreadable as he lit a cigar. Maybe she's right, he thought. Maybe Edwin Fairley *is* relieved, but not for the reason she thinks.

Emma rose. "I must go out and look for Paula. It's time for her lunch. I won't be a minute, Blackie. Please excuse me."

Blackie nodded and followed her out onto the terrace. He stood watching her hurry down into the garden, his eyes trained on her and narrowed against the bright August sunlight. Emma drew to a standstill at the lily pond at the bottom of the garden and bent down to talk to Paula, who was playing with her doll's pram on the lawn. Emma was as lithe as she had ever been, and in the distance, in her light summer frock and with her still luxuriant hair now tinted to the russet-gold shade of her youth, she appeared to be the young girl he had first met on the moors so long ago, and for an instant the decades fell away. He clearly recalled his little servant girl of Fairley Hall, and a slow smile spread itself across his face. Almost half a century had passed and so much had happened, things he had never dreamed possible. How extraordinary life was. And Emma went on forever, as indomitable now as she had been then. He blinked and shaded his eyes. He saw her smooth her hand over the child's head and then she straightened up and returned to the terrace, walking briskly.

Blackie smiled at her fondly. "You're undoubtedly the most doting grandmother I've ever seen," he remarked with a chuckle. "And as for the wee one, why, she's become your shadow."

"I suppose we do seem like an odd couple, the old woman and the five-year-old, but we understand each other." She turned back to look at the child and her face softened. "All my dreams and hopes and expectations are centered in her, Blackie. She is my future."

PART SIX

The Valley
1968

And yet, the order of the acts has been schemed and plotted, And nothing can avert the final curtain's fall. I stand alone. All else is swamped by Pharisaism. To live life to the end is not a childish task.

—Boris Pasternak, *Doctor Zhivago*

PART SIX

The Valley

FIFTY-NINE

Emma sat at her desk in the lovely upstairs parlor at Pennistone Royal, going over the legal documents spread out before her, her sharp eyes flicking swiftly across the pages. She eventually nodded with satisfaction, returned the papers to her briefcase, snapped it shut, and placed it on the floor next to the desk. Half smiling, she stood up and glided over to a small Georgian table, where she paused briefly to pour herself a sherry. She carried it to the fireplace and stood as usual with her back to the flames, endeavoring to warm her icy limbs.

Emma Harte Lowther Ainsley was seventy-eight years old. At the end of April, just a month away, she would celebrate her seventy-ninth birthday. And yet in old age, as in youth, her looks were still so arresting they startled with their vividness and clarity. Years before, she had stopped tinting her hair and it was a blaze of pure silver around her oval face, immaculately coiffed and waved, the prominent widow's peak protruding onto her wide brow as dramatically as always. Those once incomparable green eyes seemed smaller, hooded now by the ancient wrinkled lids, and they were more penetratingly observing than ever, and they missed nothing. Her face was lined and scored by the years and there were folds and creases in her neck, but her excellent bone structure had not blurred with time and her pink-and-white complexion was as translucent as it had been when she was a young woman. Her adherence to a simple diet had enabled her to keep her slender figure, and she easily passed for a woman in her early sixties, without consciously wishing to do so, for vanity had never been one of her frailties.

This evening she wore a stunning black chiffon gown by Balmain, cut on loose flowing lines like a kaftan and with long wide sleeves. Emeralds threw off prisms of intense color at her neck and ears and on her narrow wrists, and the huge square-cut McGill emerald blazed like green fire on her small left hand. In the past ten years she had acquired a different kind of beauty, a beauty that was austere and autocratic, and she looked exactly what she had become—a woman of immense power and substance. She was the true matriarch in every sense, and if she was demanding and imperious, she was also understanding of heart, and even her enemies grudgingly acknowledged she was one of the most extraordinary women of her time. Eleven years older than the century, there was almost nothing she had not seen or experienced, and she was a living legend.

She took a sip of the sherry, turned and placed the glass on the mantelshelf, and looked down into the fire reflectively, musing on the evening that stretched ahead. Her children and her grandchildren had all arrived, either last night or earlier that day, summoned by her to Pennistone Royal, ostensibly for a family weekend after her bout with pneumonia, but in actuality for the confrontation she had been planning for several weeks. Her face changed, and the light in her eyes dulled as she thought wearily of her children or, more accurately, of the first four she had borne—Edwina, Kit, Robin, and Elizabeth. The plotters caught red-handed in their scheming, but as yet unaware that she had been apprised of their duplicity and disloyalty, or that she had already circumvented them.

When her secretary, Gaye, had revealed her children's plotting to her in New York in January, Emma had been shocked. But she had not permitted emotions to obscure intelligence, for it was her vivid intelligence which had saved Emma from disaster many times in her life. She had immediately seen everything with objectivity and without sentiment, and she had moved with speed and with consummate resourcefulness, as was her way when she was facing opponents. Whilst they were still fumbling around, inept in their intriguing, she had taken steps to render them powerless against her.

Emma shook her head sadly. She had lost the taste for battle after she had taken over the *Yorkshire Morning Gazette*, and had buried the sword years ago. She found it regrettable that her children had forced her to take it up again to protect all that which she had so doggedly built up over sixty long years of purpose and sacrifice. The scene which would be enacted that evening was one she did not relish, but her business and the dynasty she had founded must be preserved.

The door opened and Paula came in, interrupting Emma's

ruminations. Paula halted in the doorway, staring at Emma. Her young heart quickened. She's up to something, Paula thought. Despite Grandy's reassurances to the contrary, this weekend was not planned for the reasons she gave me. She's about to do battle. I know that look in her eyes only too well.

"Why, Grandy, you look absolutely fabulous," Paula exclaimed. She kissed Emma and stood away, her expression admiring. "You're really going to knock their eyes out in that gown and with your jewels."

"I wonder," Emma said. Her eyes settled on her favorite grandchild, became softer, and the obdurate look disappeared from her face. She nodded approvingly. Paula wore a deep violet-blue silk evening dress that perfectly matched the color of her eyes and enhanced the translucency of her skin. Her coal-black hair tumbled loosely around her face, giving her a vulnerable quality that touched Emma. She said, "You look perfectly lovely, Paula. Like a bit of spring sky."

"Thank you, Grandy." Paula walked over to the Georgian table and filled a glass with white wine. "But just wait until you see Emily. She looks gorgeous in your red chiffon dress and diamond earrings. I noticed her mother eyeing those, and quite covetously."

"Elizabeth always was acquisitive," Emma said dryly, and picked up her glass of sherry. She took a sip and went on, "I suppose they have all assembled by now and are waiting for me to come down. Riddled with curiosity to see how the old woman is holding up." She laughed cynically. "I really think they thought I was going to kick the bucket this time. But I'm not pushing up daisies yet and it will be a long time before I do."

Paula said, "Yes, they're slowly straggling into the drawing room, where Uncle Blackie is holding court. It doesn't seem possible he's eighty-two and still going strong, He's a miracle, isn't he?"

"He is indeed," Emma said. She was filled with a rush of warmth as she thought of Blackie. They had been friends for sixty-four years and he had always been there when she had needed him. "My dearest friend," Emma added almost to herself, and went on, "Has Jim arrived yet?"

"Yes, he has. The aunts and uncles looked positively flabbergasted to see a *Fairley* in this house, and for a family gathering, no less. Especially Uncle Robin."

"I'm not surprised. He's not particulary enamored of Jim, you know. He thinks I've given him too much power in the newspaper company, that I let him have his head. I do, to a certain extent. But I'm not going to engage a man to run my papers and then manacle his hands." Emma's eyes turned flinty. "Ever since your Uncle Robin has been Member of Parliament for South-East Leeds he has held the misconception that my papers should be vehicles for his socialistic viewpoints. But I've never espoused his politics and I have no intentions of doing so now. He misguidedly blames Jim for the Tory policy of the papers, not appreciating that I dictate policy. I always have and I always will. Anyway, Robin's opinions don't really interest me," she finished dismissively. "He's too damned left-wing for my taste."

"Robin's political philosophy and his way of life don't quite dovetail, though," Paula remarked. "Share and share alike is his motto to his constituents. But that only holds good as long as he doesn't have to share what *he* has. He's a hypocrite and an opportunist, if you want my opinion."

Emma threw back her head and laughed uproariously. "You're quite the stringent one tonight, darling, But enough of Robin. Has Jim spoken to your father?"

"He's doing that right now. They're in the library together. Jim said he'd like to see you privately before dinner, Grandy. Is that all right?"

"Of course. He can come up shortly. I want to see your Aunt Edwina first, but what I have to say to her won't take long. Now come, darling, sit here with me for a few minutes. There's plenty of time, and anyway, I'm in no hurry to go down." She smiled a trifle maliciously. "Let them wait."

Paula joined Emma on the sofa, her violet eyes, so like Paul McGill's, clouding over. "Is there something wrong, Grandmother? You sound serious."

"No," Emma said. "Don't look so worried." She took Paula's long tapering hand in her small strong one and her eyes swept over her granddaughter's face searchingly. "You are happy now, aren't you?"

"Oh yes, Grandy! Very happy." Paula's face was filled with radiance. "Delirious. I do love Jim so much. Thank you for reversing your decision, for giving us permission to marry. You've changed my whole life, given me the one thing I truly want."

"I'm so glad, so very glad, darling," Emma murmured. "Your happiness is more important to me than anything else in this whole world. It was a small gift really, in view of what you mean to me. As I told you last night, I decided it was ridiculous, and yes, even wicked, to let the pride and bitterness of an old woman get in the way of your heart's desire, your future." She looked deeply into Paula's eyes. "The Fairley family have touched my life with pain since I was a girl of fourteen. Perhaps now the last of the Fairleys will touch it with joy." Emma shook her head bemusedly. "It's odd, when I think about it. I went out of my way to protect my children from the Fairley family, to keep them well out of their orbit, and yet it never occurred to me to protect my grandchildren from them, particularly you. I suppose because there weren't any Fairleys left, except Jim."

"And yet you gave him a job with the newspaper company, Grandy."

Emma laughed wryly. "Yes, that I did. I must admit when he applied for the position I was thrown off balance, and then my curiosity got the better of me. I wanted to see for myself what he was like. When he came up from Fleet Street for the interview I was impressed with his ability, despite my terrible prejudice. I knew he was the right man, the best of all the candidates. It would have been self-defeating to pass him over." Emma's mouth twitched with amusement. "I also suspect I derived a great deal of satisfaction at the idea of a Fairley working for me. But in my wildest imaginings I never thought you two would meet, particularly since you have nothing to do with the publishing side of Harte Enterprises." Now Emma leaned forward. "How *did* you meet him? I've often wondered."

"I didn't meet him in Leeds, Grandy, if that makes you feel any better. I met him on a plane coming back from Paris. I'd been covering the fashion shows for the stores, and he'd been on vacation." Paula grinned. "Actually, he'd been eyeing me at the airport, and he went out of his way to get the seat next to me. I was aware of him and attracted to him at once. But when he told me his name, and who he worked for, I almost had a heart attack. It's no great secret you've always hated the Fairleys, and I knew you wouldn't approve if I went out with him. A Fairley in your employ is one thing, courting your grandchild quite another."

Emma gave Paula a penetrating look. "You did go out with him, though, despite your misgivings. She smiled affectionately. "But then you're as stubborn and as self-willed as I am, I suppose."

Paula returned Emma's look steadily. Just as you intended me to be, she thought. Aware of Emma's continuing interest, she said, "Looking back, I think I fell in love with Jim the second time we met. He asked me to have dinner with him the following evening. I knew I shouldn't, that it was asking for trouble, but I couldn't help myself. I wanted to see him again. And in all fairness to Jim, he didn't know who I was. I had been rather evasive about myself. We dined at the Mirabelle and your favorite waiter, Louis, spotted me. Naturally he made quite a fuss of me and sang your praises to high heaven. He wanted to know when you would be in town and dining at the restaurant again. Jim became inquisitive about you. He wanted to know who my famous grandmother was."

As she envisioned the scene, Emma's eyes twinkled. "And what did you say?"

Laughter bubbled in Paula. "I was a bit naughty, really. I couldn't resist saying, 'My grandmother is the chairman of the board of the Yorkshire Consolidated Newspaper Company and your boss.' Jim almost fell out of the chair. He stared at me dumbfounded and then he remarked about us both having a widow's peak, and said that you must have looked like me when you were young. I know you don't think we resemble each other physically, but I do. I've seen all those old photographs of you, and the likeness *is* there, Grandy."

"Your Uncle Blackie would agree with you, but I'm not so sure. Perhaps because I have always thought you take after your grandfather in appearance. Anyway, what happened after you had dinner together?" Emma probed.

"I went on seeing Jim, against my better judgment. We couldn't resist each other. When I realized how involved we were becoming, how serious Jim's intentions were, I pulled away. You know the rest."

Emma looked down at her hands, a thoughtful expression on her face. "So it was a chance meeting. A meeting that would have happened whether Jim worked for me or not. I suppose not even I can control events. It was meant to be, perhaps."

"I think it was, Grandy. Jim is my destiny and I am his."

Emma started and gave Paula a curious look. "It's strange you should say that. Your grandfather told me I was *his* destiny fifty years ago."

There was a knock on the door before Paula could respond, and Edwina walked in peremptorily, carrying a glass of scotch. "You wanted to see me, Mother," she said coldly, and gave Paula a curt, unsmiling nod.

"I did indeed, Edwina. I see you already have a drink, so come and sit down. Please excuse us, Paula dear. Tell Jim I'll see him shortly."

"Yes, Grandy," Paula murmured, and left.

Edwina, Dowager Countess of Dunvale, swept majestically into the parlor and seated herself opposite Emma, her antipathy thinly veiled. She stared at her mother, waiting expectantly, and there was a belligerent look on her face.

Emma regarded Edwina with quickening interest. She thought: If Adele Fairley had lived to be Edwina's age this is exactly how she would have looked. Edwina was sixty-two and she had not worn as well as her mother. Her exquisite blond beauty had been too delicate to weather the years, and her looks had faded long ago. Her hair was still a shimmering silver-gold, but its color now came from a bottle, and the once-lovely argent eyes were dimmed and heavily lidded.

"That's a lovely gown, Edwina," Emma said, and took a sip of her sherry, peering at her oldest daughter above the glass.

"Why did you want to see me, Mother?" Edwina responded with icy disdain. "I'm quite certain you didn't ask me to come up here to compliment me on my frock."

"That's perfectly true," Emma said. She smiled faintly, ruminating to herself. Edwina had not softened with age. "Let me ask you a question before I answer yours. Why did you accept my invitation to come here for the weekend?"

"Invitation!" Edwina exclaimed, her eyes filling with hostility. "It was a command, as usual, Mother. And none of us ever ignores your commands, do we? I was ambivalent about coming. But you said you wanted to see Anthony, too, and when I told him, he insisted we make the trip." Edwina threw Emma a baleful glance. "My son adores you. Neither his mother's wishes nor wild horses could have kept him away from this little gathering. He was also worried about your health. And so, since I love my son and wish to please him, I acquiesced. If it had not been for Anthony I would not have come, let me assure you of that."

Emma sighed audibly. "When your Uncle Winston effected a reconciliation between us in 1951, I hoped we could become friends. But it's always been an armed truce, hasn't it?"

"Yes, Mother. And if you want to know the truth, it was Jeremy who persuaded me to see you again. My husband always did have great family feelings. He felt we should make peace."

"Such as it is," Emma retorted. "But let us not bicker. I wanted to see you alone because I have something important to tell you. I wish to speak to you about your father."

Edwina's face stiffened. "I can't imagine what you could possibly have to say to me about *him*," she snapped, deep color flooding her face. "He's sitting downstairs at this very moment, behaving like the grand seigneur. Frankly, I don't know how you could be so thoughtless as to have him here in my presence, or in the presence of my son, who is, after all, a peer of the realm. That intolerable man makes me feel uncomfortable. But then I suspect you enjoy making us all squirm, don't you, Mother? You are addicted to manipulating people."

"You never did know me very well, Edwina," Emma sighed. "And there is no reason why Blackie O'Neill should make you feel awkward or cause you discomfiture, because he is not your father."

Edwina's jaw dropped. She gaped at Emma, but said nothing. Recovering her speech, she cried quickly, "But his name is on my birth certificate!"

"That's true, but for quite different reasons than you believe. Blackie was my only friend when I was sixteen, alone, almost penniless, and carrying you. He asked me to marry him, out of friendship, I think. I refused. He insisted I name him as your father because he thought the phrase 'father unknown' would be yet another stigma for you to bear. He also thought it would protect us to a certain extent, and in a way it did," Emma finished, thinking of how it had given her the courage to deny Edwina's paternity, indeed her existence, to Gerald Fairley.

"Then who was, or is, my father?" Edwina demanded.

"Your father was Edwin Fairley."

Edwina leaned forward alertly. "Do you mean Sir Edwin Fairley, K.C. The famous criminal lawyer who died last year? One of the Fairleys from Fairley Village?"

"Yes, I do," Emma said quietly, relieved at last that it was out in the open.

"Good God!" Edwina sat back in stupefaction and took a long swallow of her drink. After a moment she said, "Why didn't you tell me this that day I showed you the copy of my birth certificate?"

"You didn't give me an opportunity to explain anything. You fled to Cousin Freda's, if you remember. Besides, I'm not sure I would have revealed his identity then. I might have, but it's doubtful. The Fairley family have caused me a great deal of heartache. I did not want you to suffer or to be exposed. I also—"

"Why *now*? Why are you suddenly telling me *now*? What has prompted this unprecedented display of honesty on your part, and at this late date?"

"Because tonight I am going to announce Paula's engagement to Jim Fairley, your father's only grandson. He will be a member of this family, and also you are his only living blood relative. His parents were killed in a plane crash in 1948. I thought he ought to know you are his aunt. I would also like to wipe the slate clean once and for all." A reflective look entered Emma's eyes. "I want Paula and Jim to start their marriage in the right way. No skeletons in the closet. No ancient secrets to haunt them. But apart from that, I felt I owed it to you to tell you the truth, Edwina. It's long overdue."

The understatement of the year, Edwina commented bitterly to herself. Finally, she said slowly, "Edwin Fairley was a brilliant barrister and renowned throughout the country, and, perhaps more importantly, he was a gentleman. He had breeding and lineage. I'm not ashamed to acknowledge him as my father. You may tell Jim if you want. In fact, I think I would like you to do so."

"Thank you, Edwina."

Edwina stood up. "I wish you had been honest with me years ago, Mother. Things might have been different between us."

I sincerely doubt that, Emma thought, but said, "Perhaps they would."

Edwina walked to the door without another word and

Emma was aware of the gratified look in her daughter's eyes. She's such a ridiculous snob, she said to herself. Her illegitimacy doesn't matter to her anymore, now that she knows her father was gentry. Emma called after her, "Please ask Jim to come upstairs."

Edwina swung around. "Yes, Mother." She hovered and said hesitantly, "You remarked that the Fairleys had caused you grief, and yet you—you named me after my father . . ."

"A mere slip of the tongue, I'm afraid," Emma said pithily, "but then that's another story."

A few minutes later Jim Fairley walked in and Emma straightened up, smiling pleasantly. Jim, who was thirty, was about six feet one in height, with broad shoulders, a narrow waist, and long legs. He had an attractive, rather sensitive face, although his mouth had a sensuality about it that contrasted markedly with his ascetic features and his soulful bluish-gray eyes. His light brown hair, streaked with blond, was brushed loosely across his shapely head and worn slightly longer than the vogue. His appearance was faultless, for he was always impeccably dressed, and he was the epitome of the perfect English gentleman right down to his handmade shoes. He wore a flawlessly tailored evening suit, Edwardian in cut, which was the current fashion, and his fine lawn evening shirt was ruffled down the front and punctuated with sapphire studs.

Jim might have stepped right out of another era into the present, and as he strode towards her, smiling engagingly, Emma was carried back in time to the elegant dinner at Fairley Hall which Olivia Wainright had given in 1904. I always believed Jim looked like Edwin, Emma thought. He drew to a standstill and she recognized that it was Adam Fairley who stood before her tonight. James Arthur Fairley, the last of the line, was the reincarnation of his great-grandfather.

Emma felt unnerved for a second, but she brushed aside the peculiar feeling of déjà vu and said in a gracious voice, "Good evening, Jim." She rose and stretched out her hand. "Welcome to my house. Welcome to my family."

Jim smiled warmly. He revered and almost worshipped this regal old woman grasping his hand, and his admiration was fully revealed on his face. "Good evening, Mrs. Harte. And thank you. I am honored to become a member of your family, and to be in your home." He held on to her fingers and looked down into her eyes. "I love Paula with all of my heart. I will be a good husband to her."

"Yes, I believe you will, Jim," Emma said, extracting her hand. "Can I offer you a drink?" As she spoke she moved towards the Georgian table.

Restraining her, Jim said, "Thank you. I'll have a glass of wine. But I'll get it. Don't trouble yourself."

Emma watched him stride across the room with that easy grace that sprang from self-confidence engendered by breeding and background, and she saw him yet again through newly objective eyes, wondering why she had never detected his uncanny resemblance to Adam. Perhaps it's more apparent because of the Edwardian evening clothes, she decided, and looked into the fire, filled with remembrances of things past.

Jim returned with his drink. "Cheers," he said, moving to the fireplace and leaning against the mantel.

Emma lifted her glass. "Cheers, Jim," she said, and went on, "I understand from Paula you want to speak to me."

"Yes, I do, Mrs. Harte. But first I have something for you." He put down the drink and reached into his pocket. He took out a small silver cardboard box and handed it to her.

Emma looked up at Jim. "What is it?"

"Open it," Jim said.

Emma did so quickly, her curiosity aroused. The box contained a silk handkerchief, its whiteness yellowed by time, and it had been carefully folded so that the initials E.F. were clearly visible, and her hands trembled as she lifted the corners. She caught her breath, staring down at the stone lying on the ancient silk. It was the flat pebble she and Edwin had found in the cave at the Top of the World, and upon which had been painted the miniature portrait of a woman. It was extraordinarily well preserved, the oils almost as vivid as they had been over half a century ago. She picked it up and gazed at it, and then lifted her eyes to Jim's questioningly.

"My grandfather gave it to me the day he died," Jim told her, watching her face. "He told me to bring it to you. He wanted you to have it."

"Why?" Emma asked in a low voice. So Edwin Fairley had

not forgotten her, after all. He had remembered her on his deathbed.

"I'll get to that in a moment, Mrs. Harte. I'd like to explain something else first. My grandfather knew about my relationship with Paula. You see, I took her to meet him at his house in Harrogate, when we first started seeing each other. At the time I couldn't understand why he looked as if he'd seen a ghost when she walked in. Anyway, over the months he grew to love her and he was enthusiastic about the match. It seemed to give him renewed energy. His dearest wish was that we should marry."

Jim paused, lit a cigarette, drew on it, and went on, "Then Paula suddenly broke off with me, explaining that you would never accept a Fairley in the family, that you bore us a hatred she could not understand. She told me she would never do anything to cause you pain, because you had had too much pain and grief in your life. I argued with her, begged her to discuss it with you, or let me talk to you. But she became so hysterical at the mere suggestion of this, I decided to let her calm down, hoping she would have a change of heart. She didn't, as you know."

Emma nodded. "And you explained all this to your grandfather?"

"I did. I implored him to enlighten me. Many times, in fact. He refused point-blank. I knew you had wrested control of the *Gazette* from him in 1950, and I asked him if your hatred towards our family sprang from business conflicts. Again he refused to answer me or discuss you. He seemed to go downhill when Paula left me. He brought me up, you know, and we were very close, but not even I could reach him. He grew awfully frail in the last few weeks of his life, and one day last December he sent for me. I think he knew he was dying—"

"And he gave you this stone to give to me," Emma interrupted. "And he told you the whole story, didn't he? He told you about me and what had happened between us when we were young," she finished in a faint voice.

"Yes. He told me everything. He said he hoped you would relent and give us your blessing, but if you did not, I was to come to you with this stone. He said it was imperative that you knew it was a painting of your mother and not Olivia Wainright, as he had believed when he found it." Jim stopped and gazed at her, trying to gauge her emotions, but Emma's face was a mask of inscrutability.

In point of fact, Emma was not surprised at his revelation. "I thought it was my mother," she murmured softly. "I think I always knew that. Adam Fairley painted it, did he not?"

"That's correct. Grandfather took the stone to his father after Olivia died, thinking he would want to have it for sentimental reasons. Apparently Grandfather had offered it to Adam before, and once again he wouldn't accept it. My great-grandfather then explained why. He said it was a painting of your mother, and he told Grandfather they had been childhood sweethearts."

Emma nodded her head slowly. "That was another thing I suspected years ago—that there had been a friendship between them."

Jim took a deep breath. "Your mother and my great-grandfather were more than friends, Mrs. Harte. They were lovers."

Emma was jolted upright on the sofa and her fingers tightened on the stone. "Are you certain of that, Jim?"

"Oh, yes. Great-grandfather explained it all to Grandfather very carefully and in detail. It seems Adam fell in love with your mother, Elizabeth, and she with him. She became pregnant by Adam and ran away from Fairley. He found her some weeks later in Ripon. He had decided to abandon his military career, defy his father, and emigrate to America with your mother. It was too late. She had miscarried. Adam did not know if it was a natural miscarriage or one induced by some quack midwife. Elizabeth was very ill. She almost died. And she would not countenance Adam's idea of elopement. Eventually she recovered, returned to Fairley, and soon after she married your father, Jack Harte. And she never spoke to Adam Fairley again."

Emma was silent, filled with a terrible aching sadness. I knew it always, she thought. That was probably one of the reasons I hated Adam Fairley with such virulence. But *how* did I know? Did I overhear something as a child? A family quarrel? Recriminations between my parents? Local gossip? She searched her mind and found no answers.

Jim came and sat next to her on the sofa. "I hope I'm not upsetting you, Mrs. Harte, opening old wounds that must be painful for you. However, I felt you ought to know Grandfather had confided in me, and I wanted you to have the stone, even though you had relented about Paula and me of your own accord."

A wistful look flitted across Emma's face. "No, you're not upsetting me, Jim. I'm glad you followed your instincts. I loved my mother very much and I don't have a photograph of her. I shall treasure the stone. Now, please continue. I'm sure there is more."

"Yes, there is. When Grandfather gave me the stone for you, he said that the Harte women had always held a fatal fascination for the Fairley men, but that they had been forever crossed in love. 'Doomed by circumstances of birth' was the phrase he used. He said, 'Tell Emma to let it end now. Tell her to let this generation have the happiness she and I were denied, and which her mother and my father were denied. Tell her that in all good conscience she must end it, once and for all. Tell her it is she, and she alone, who can finally join our two families together in holy matrimony.' He was very emotional, Mrs. Harte. I said I would do as he asked."

Emma took Jim's hand in hers, and her eyes, so old and wise, were moist. "Why didn't you come to me before, Jim? Your grandfather has been dead three months."

"I was going to come to you in January, but then you and Paula left unexpectedly for America. When you returned, you fell ill. I intended to speak to you a few weeks ago, but you were so preoccupied I didn't want to disturb you, particularly so soon after your illness." He smiled. "And then out of the blue you approached me and said you would approve of the marriage if we both still felt the same way."

"I'm glad I made the first move," Emma said. "Somehow it makes me feel better." She shook her head wonderingly. "It is strange, isn't it, that three generations of Fairley men have fallen in love with Harte women and have always been thwarted until now. Three generations, Jim, spanning almost a hundred years." She sighed deeply. "Too long. And there has been too much heartbreak. Your grandfather was right. It must end now." She smiled. "Why, it *has* ended, hasn't it, Jim?"

"Yes. Thank God." To Emma's surprise and astonishment Jim now knelt down on the floor at her feet and took her hands firmly between his. He looked up into her face, his eyes almost beseeching. "Grandfather asked me to do something else, Mrs. Harte. Just before he died, he said, 'When you have told Emma all this, I want you to get down on your bended knees and beg that woman's forgiveness for everything the Fairleys have done to her. In particular, ask her to forgive *me*. Tell her I've never stopped loving her all the days of my life, and that without her my life has had no real meaning. A part of me died the day I repudiated Emma in the rose garden, and I have paid dearly for what I did.' I promised faithfully to do as he wished, Mrs. Harte, but Grandfather suddenly became agitated, and made me promise over and over again. He also said, in the most sorrowing voice, 'Jim, it will be an unquiet grave I lie in if Emma does not forgive me. Implore her to do so, Jim, so that my tortured soul can rest in peace.' I told him I knew you would forgive him, and eventually I managed to calm him. He fell asleep for a short while. When he opened his eyes he didn't seem to see me, and there was a faraway look on his face. He stared out of the window for a long time. When he lay back on the pillows I knew he was slipping away. Quite unexpectedly he smiled, and it was a triumphant, happy smile. He cried in the strongest voice, 'Emma! Emma! I'm going back to the Top of the World,' and then he died peacefully in my arms."

Emma blinked back her tears. "Poor Edwin. Poor Edwin," she said in a voice that quavered. "I think perhaps your grandfather suffered more than I did, after all."

"Yes, I believe he did," Jim said. His face became intense. "You do forgive the Fairleys, don't you, Mrs. Harte? And Grandfather in particular."

"I forgive them, Jim. All of them, and most especially Edwin." She touched Jim's face lightly, and with affection. But it was Edwin she now saw kneeling before her. I've spent a lifetime seeking revenge for what you did to me, she thought. But it wasn't really necessary. Your own conscience did my work for me. If only I had known. What a lot of pain and effort it would have saved. You wanted me to win. It was a salve for your overwhelming guilt. That's why you looked so relieved when I stole the *Gazette* from you. You knew the vendetta was finally over.

"Mrs. Harte, are you all right?" Jim asked anxiously.

Emma blinked and stared at him. "Yes, I'm fine. Now be

good enough to lend me your handkerchief. I can't go
downstairs to announce your engagement with tears streaming down my face, now can I?"

"As far as I'm concerned you can do anything you want,"
Jim said as he handed her his handkerchief.

Emma blew her nose and said, "I was going to tell you
tonight that I had borne your grandfather's child, Jim. I
wanted you to know. My eldest daughter, the Countess of
Dunvale, is your Aunt Edwina. Or rather, your half aunt."

"I guessed as much when I met her this evening." Jim
grinned. "She looks like a Fairley, if you don't mind my
saying so."

Emma chuckled. "She does indeed. She used to be the
spitting image of your great-grandmother, Adele, when she
was younger. Now, give an old woman your arm and escort
me downstairs to greet my family."

"I will be honored," Jim said.

SIXTY

The dinner had been in progress for some time. Emma
sat at the head of the long mahogany table in her splendidly appointed Adam dining room, surrounded by her children, their wives and husbands, and her grandchildren. The
food was superb, the wines were excellent, and now a certain
conviviality prevailed. Everyone appeared to be relaxed, their
jealousies, hatreds, and differences buried or well concealed
behind their smiling façades.

All the clowns wear masks, Emma thought, borrowing a
line from a poem she had once read, for she detected an
undercurrent of tension in the atmosphere, although to a
degree it was less pronounced than when she had arrived in
the drawing room earlier, on the arm of Jim Fairley. Her
grandchildren, who loved her dearly and were fiercely loyal
to her, had greeted her with enthusiasm and great affection,
the camaraderie they shared most apparent. Her children
had been amiable enough, if somewhat reserved, but Emma
had been conscious of a cautiousness in some, veiled hostility
in others, a wariness in them all, with the exception of Daisy.

For her part, Emma had been her gracious self, her face unreadable, all the while recognizing they were unable to look her in the eye, burdened down as they were by their collective guilt.

She had been sardonically amused to see that the four conspirators had assiduously avoided each other. However, she had not missed the apprehensive glances Kit and Robin had occasionally exchanged when they thought they were unobserved, yet they, too, had remained aloof from one another. Even Elizabeth, who was as close to Robin as ever, had adroitly sidestepped her twin, hovering attentively over Blackie, fawning and flattering him. Edwina had remained by the side of her son all through the cocktail hour. The engagement had been announced, champagne toasts given, congratulations effusively offered, and despite their obvious surprise when they learned she had accepted a Fairley into the bosom of her family, her children's expressions had hardly slipped.

Now, in the flickering candlelight, as she toyed with the dessert on her plate, Emma looked up from time to time, surreptitiously regarding the four culprits, her green eyes watchful beneath the hooded lids. She had the advantage. A lifetime's experience in dealing with people had augmented her natural ability to assess her children's individual capacities and handicaps. She had discovered their flaws long ago and they no longer baffled or surprised her. She could read each one like an open book. After tonight she would not have to bother. The book would be closed.

Her eyes rested briefly on Kit. How like Joe Lowther he had become over the years. Plodding, phlegmatic, and lacking in imagination or initiative. And what a monumental fool he had been to throw his lot in with Robin, who would double-cross him at the drop of a hat. She shifted her glance to the latter. How handsome Robin looks tonight, she thought, and experienced a twinge of pain. Robin had always been her favorite son and the knowledge that he had been the instigator of the plot hurt more than she had realized. He was urbane and suave, and she had to admit he was the true dyed-in-the-wool politician, facile of tongue, the deal maker. Unfortunately, like his father, Arthur Ainsley, his overweening vanity was his fatal flaw, and it constantly obscured his judgments.

In many ways his twin sister was much shrewder than he,

except that she rarely bothered to exercise that capacity. Emma glanced at Elizabeth, swathed in silver lamé and turquoise chiffon and dripping diamonds. *Her* problem was a desire to pursue pleasure to the exclusion of all else. Just like her father, too.

At forty-seven Elizabeth was still stunning, the real beauty of the family, but she was more highly strung than in her youth, brittle, and immature in innumerable ways. Emma thought: She's a dreadfully unhappy woman. But then, when was Elizabeth ever happy? And how many husbands has she had since she divorced Tony Barkstone, father of Alexander and Emily? Emma had almost lost count. There had been Michael Villiers and then Derek Linde, by whom she had had the twins, Amanda and Francesca. After their birth Elizabeth had lost the taste for Englishmen, and had sought out more exotic fare. A Polish prince with an unpronounceable name, to be followed in quick succession by the Italian count, who was a good fifteen years younger. Some count, Emma thought dryly. More likely a gigolo.

Emma now observed that the count was being excessively attentive to Edwina, who in turn was playing the role of the Dowager Countess of Dunvale to the hilt, acting condescendingly and with a display of superiority that was nauseating. How transparent Edwina was. After tonight, with the information she now had about her paternity, she would really feel obliged to turn up her snooty nose at the world.

Well, so much for those four, Emma remarked to herself with cold detachment. Little joy or comfort they've offered me in my old age. But they did give me my grandchildren and for that I will be eternally grateful. Emma put down her fork and sat back in her chair, smiling benignly. But her eyes were forever watchful and if any of them had looked more closely they would have detected a cynical light glittering in their ancient depths. She moved her head and peered down the table at Blackie, who sat in the host's chair, stately and distinguished. His hair was snow white but still abundant and wavy, his skin glowed with ruddy health, and his black eyes were as merry as they had been sixty years ago. He had become a majestic figure of a man, his bulk undiminished, his mind unimpaired, and he carried his old age blithely. He had outlived Winston and Frank, who had both died in the early 1960's within a year of each other, and David Kallinski, who had passed on in the summer of 1967. There are only the two of us left now, Emma thought. And Blackie will go on forever. He's an old war-horse. But then, so am I.

Emily, who was sitting further down the table, caught Emma's attention, rolling her eyes upward, silently mouthing words Emma could not understand. She frowned and motioned for Emily to come to the head of the table.

"What on earth's the matter with you, Emily? You look as if you're having a fit!"

Emily bent forward and whispered, "It's Aunt Edwina, Grandy. She's three sheets to the wind, and tilting. As usual. It's all that wine she's guzzled, plus the four scotches and the champagne before dinner. If you ask me, she's got a drinking problem. She's getting awfully snotty with Gianni. I know you don't like him, but he's harmless and he's good to the twins and Mummy. I think she's been abominably rude and he's so uncomfortable. Mummy's bombed, too. Not that that's so unusual these days. Shouldn't Hilda serve coffee?"

Emma patted Emily's arm affectionately. "Good girl. I'm glad you told me. Now, do me a small favor and run upstairs. You'll find my briefcase in the parlor. Put it behind the desk in the library."

"I will, Grandy. In just one minute." Emily returned to her place at the table, reached over, and picked up her glass. She stood behind her chair and cleared her throat loudly. "Please, be quiet, everyone!" she pronounced in a strong voice. The buzz of conversation stopped abruptly and they all looked at her in surprise.

The self-confident Emily, who was never fazed by anything, exclaimed, "Far be it from me, as a member of the younger generation of this family, to suggest that someone here has been remiss tonight. But I would like to point out that no one has proposed a toast to Grandmother, who has just recovered from a serious illness. I think we should drink to her continuing good health. For we all love her very dearly—"

Emily, as dramatic as she could be pithy, paused and glared at Robin and Kit, whom she detested. Her green eyes, so like Emma's, were condemning. "And so *I* am going to propose a toast to her. To Emma Harte. A great lady. To whom we *all* owe so much. May she be with us for a long time to come. To Emma Harte!"

"To Emma Harte!" they said in unison, raising their glasses.

Emma was moved by Emily's gesture. But, perhaps more importantly, she was proud of her twenty-one-year-old granddaughter. She's got guts, that one, Emma thought, and she's not afraid of anyone, least of all her uncles. Emma took in the furious expressions on the faces of her sons, and she concealed a small smile as she rose to her feet.

"Thank you," she said, inclining her head. "And now let us adjourn to the library for coffee and liqueurs." And the last round, she added silently, thinking of the winning cards she had up her sleeve. She swept out grandly, in a swirl of black chiffon, her eyes as brilliant as the emeralds at her throat, her silver head held high, her step as sure and as purposeful as it had been fifty years ago.

SIXTY-ONE

The library was a large room with a high-flung ceiling and mullioned windows looking out onto the grounds. With its western aspect and early eighteenth-century pine paneling, it made a gracious setting for the fine antique tables and cabinets, the grand Chippendale desk, the many books, the comfortable sofas covered in light green floral chintz, the dark green velvet chairs and matching draperies.

Emma walked briskly across the Aubusson carpet that covered the dark wood floor and stood in front of the massive carved stone fireplace, the original that dated back to 1611, when Pennistone Royal had been built. She spread her hands and warmed them in front of the log fire and then looked up at the overmantel that soared to the ceiling. Her eyes settled on the relief in its center. How appropriate, she thought, with a faint ironic smile. It depicted the Judgment of Solomon.

Emma swung around as Emily hurried in breathlessly. She held up the briefcase, grinned, and deposited it behind the desk, and then flitted over to the fireplace, the red chiffon flaring out behind her. She hugged Emma. "I do adore this dress, Grandy. Thank you again for giving it to me."

Smiling affectionately, Emma touched Emily's cheek, the gesture tender. "You may also keep the earrings, dear."

Emily gasped. "Oh, I couldn't! Are you sure?" Emily stared at her grandmother, her eyes sparkling. "You *do* mean it. I can tell by the look on your face. Oh, you are a darling. Thank you. Oh, gosh!" She broke off and her young face fell. "Mummy's going to be as mad as hell. She was furious when she saw me wearing them."

Emma swallowed a smile. "I think I can dispose of my jewelry any way I like, Emily. It's none of your mother's business, or anybody else's for that matter. Don't give it another thought."

Sarah, Kit's only child, appeared in the doorway. She made a striking picture in her bottle-green velvet gown, her russet-gold hair tumbling around her freckled face to soften her angular features. Thank God she doesn't take after her father or her grandfather, Joe, Emma thought, as Sarah joined them at the fireplace.

The twenty-six-year-old tucked her arm through Emma's possessively and said with a frown. "I don't know what's wrong with my father. He's been edgy all evening. I just ran into him in the Stone Hall talking to Uncle Robin. They both looked like thunder and seemed to be having a terrible row. I hope they won't spoil this lovely party with their bickering. They're impossible, as usual."

"I'm sure it's nothing of any consequence, Sarah. Don't worry," Emma said. She thought: So, the conspirators are at each other's throats. Not surprising.

Emily volunteered in her breathless voice, "I think all the oldies have been behaving a bit strange since they got here. Sort of jittery, Grandy. Especially Mummy. But then she's always a bag of nerves. Oh, well, who cares. We're having fun."

"Indeed we are," Emma said, and plunged into an animated discussion about business with her granddaughters.

The others began to stroll in gradually. They seated themselves around the room or clustered in groups. Hilda, the housekeeper, served coffee and the butler dispensed after-dinner drinks and cigars. Blackie strolled over to Emma, nursing a brandy and puffing on a cigar.

"A lovely evening, Emma, sure and it is." He peered down into her face. "And you look wonderful, mavourneen. If I were two years younger I'd be asking ye to marry me. On the blessed heads of the Saints I swear I would," he laughed, lapsing into his brogue as he was wont to do of late.

"There's no fool like an old fool," Emma quipped. Her face sobered. "And talking of fools, don't you think you ought to take it easy with these?" she asked, indicating the drink and cigar.

"I hardly have to worry about my health at my age. I'm living on borrowed time as it is," he exclaimed, and continued, "Me darlin' Bryan sends you his love. And I'm happy to announce that Geraldine's expecting me third grandchild."

"Congratulations, Blackie. That *is* wonderful."

Elizabeth, who was feeling no pain and looked feverishly excited, pounced on Blackie and dragged him away, chattering incessantly as she led him over to her husband. Emily and Sarah drifted off and Emma stood alone in front of the fireplace quietly observing the scene. She felt completely at ease with herself and she was enjoying the company of her nine grandchildren, who in their different ways gave her such happiness. One by one, the younger generation gravitated to her, and they kept her entertained and warmed her tired heart and she basked in the love that flowed out from them. And her conviction that she had been right in all she had done to preserve her dynasty was more strongly reinforced in her than ever.

Philip, whom she had recalled from Australia earlier that week, recounted anecdotes about happenings at the sheep station, and as she listened she was filled with fond memories of Dunoon and of the happy times she had spent with Paul and Daisy in that lovely old house. Paul would be proud of his grandchildren, she thought. They turned out well. Philip was as straight as a die, intelligent, and a hard worker, and he was proving himself a good businessman. Along with Paula he would ensure the continued success of the McGill enterprises.

Emma glanced over at her granddaughter, who was totally absorbed in Jim Fairley and radiating happiness, and her mind turned automatically to the Fairleys. She had brought ruin to that family and she wondered if it had all been worth it. But regrets were a waste of time. She remembered words uttered years before by Paul. "Success is the best revenge, Emma," he had said. Perhaps her own success *would* have been enough in the long run, and yet without her hatred for the Fairleys to goad her on she might not have reached the pinnacle. Revenge had been the spur. Now she was in the valley of her life, and after tonight she could relax, secure in the knowledge that all she had built was intact for this generation, and the ones that followed.

I must get it over with. Be done with it, she said to herself. An hour had already passed and it was time to show her hand. She quietly disengaged herself from the group in front of the fireplace and edged her way around her guests until she was standing in front of her desk at the far end of the room.

"Can I have your attention, please," Emma said, walking behind the desk. The buzz of conversation continued unabated. She picked up a glass paperweight and banged it hard on the leather blotting pad. There was a lull as they stopped talking and all faces turned to look at her. "Please make yourselves comfortable. I have a little family business to go over with you."

Glances were anxiously exchanged by some, and they all did as she asked. When they were settled, Emma sat down at the desk and opened her briefcase. She removed the pile of documents and spread them out before her, taking her time. Her glance caught Jonathan's, who winked and gave her a broad smile. He looks more like Arthur Ainsley than Robin, she mused, shuffling the papers. It's fortuitous his character is more like mine. She smiled at Jonathan. "Please be good enough to get me a glass of water, dear." Jonathan sprang up and did as she asked. Emma took a sip, savoring the moment, purposely keeping the plotters on tenterhooks.

Emma picked up a document at last and her voice rang out:

> "*I, Emma Harte Lowther Ainsley, of Pennistone Royal, Yorkshire, being of sound mind and body do hereby declare this to be my Last Will and Testament, hereby revoking all wills and codicils heretofore made by me.*"

A collective gasp rose on the air. Emma paused and lifted her silver head. All eyes were riveted on her and the silence in the room was suddenly so acute a pin dropping would have sounded like a clap of thunder. Emma smiled, deriving malicious enjoyment from the astonished expressions on the faces of her children. Only Daisy and the grandchildren seemed unperturbed.

Emma smiled, but her eyes were steel blades. "I know it is not the usual practice for a will to be read by the testator, but there is apparently no legal reason why this cannot be done. Unorthodox perhaps, but then, I've never been one to conform to the rules."

"Isn't this a bit morbid, Mother?" Elizabeth exclaimed unsteadily, her face strained.

"Please don't interrupt me! And no, I don't think it is morbid." Emma tapped the will and went on, "This is rather an unwieldy document to read word by word, since it is over a hundred pages long. It is also full of legal terminology. Therefore, I think it will be easier to cut through it all and tell you, in simple language, how I have disposed of my business holdings, properties, and not inconsiderable wealth."

Emma leaned back in the chair. Her eyes swept around the room, keenly observing. No one uttered one word and the four who had conspired against her looked as if they had been turned to stone images in their chairs.

Placing the will to one side, Emma continued, "Before I proceed with the disposition of my estate, I would like to clarify something. I think there is probably a misunderstanding about the McGill empire which I inherited. It struck me recently that there might be those amongst you who believe Paul left me everything unconditionally, and that I can therefore dispose of the McGill fortune in any way I see fit. However, this is not the case."

She took a sip of the water and shifted in her seat. She looked at the gathering at large and said in a solemn tone, "Under the terms and conditions of Paul McGill's last will and testament, his natural daughter, Daisy Ainsley Amory, automatically inherits the entire estate when I die. From her, the estate passes to her two children, Paula McGill Amory and Philip McGill Amory, to be divided in equal shares between them after their mother's death."

Low murmurings broke out. Emma held up a silencing hand. "During her lifetime, Daisy will receive the income from the McGill estate, with the Rossiter Merchant Bank acting as trustees. I have appointed Daisy executrix of the McGill estate and Henry Rossiter as co-executor. Upon my death, Daisy's daughter, Paula, will take my place on the board of the Sitex Oil Corporation and will act in behalf of her mother, as she has been trained by me to do. Also upon my death, Daisy's son, Philip, will take full control of the McGill holdings in Australia and will run them for his mother, which he has been learning to do under my supervision for the past three years. I assume you all clearly understand that in no way can any of my other children, or grandchildren, inherit one single penny from the McGill estate."

No one spoke. Emma's narrowed eyes traveled swiftly across the faces staring at her with rapt intensity. Whatever her other children were thinking, they were keeping their feelings to themselves and their faces were unmoving.

She said, "With the McGill inheritance clarified, I will now commence with the disposition of my own estate." Emma felt the tension and expectancy increase so palpably it seemed to reach out and touch her in waves. Her gaze settled on Edwina's only child, the thirty-two-year-old Earl of Dunvale, grandson of Edwin Fairley and half cousin to Jim. "Anthony, please come here and stand by me."

The young earl, who was rather shy, looked momentarily startled to be singled out, but, nonetheless, he did as she asked and took up a position to the right of Emma. She flashed him a smile and turned back to face the others. "My eldest grandson, Anthony, will receive the income from a two-million-pound trust which I have created for him. I also gave to Anthony my house in Jamaica, British West Indies, and all furnishings therein, with the exception of the paintings currently hanging in that house." Emma looked up at Anthony, who was astonished and speechless. She said, "I have not left you any interest in my business because you have never worked for me, and also because you are fully occupied running your estates in Ireland and the various business ventures you inherited from your father." She paused and gave him a penetrating stare. "I hope you understand and do not feel cheated in any way."

"Good Lord, Grandmother, absolutely not!" he cried, blushing. "I don't know what to say. I'm overwhelmed. You've been generous beyond belief. Thank you." He made to return to his seat.

Emma restrained him. "Stay here with me," she said. Anthony nodded and stepped back, standing behind Emma's chair at the right. "Now to come to my two youngest grandchildren, Amanda and Francesca." She beckoned to the fourteen-year-old twins, daughters of Elizabeth, grandchildren of Arthur Ainsley, who sat on the floor at Blackie's feet. They stood up, looking slightly bewildered, and approached the desk holding hands.

"Stand over there by your cousin, girls," Emma instructed. "I have also established a trust of two million pounds for Amanda and the same for Francesca, who will receive the income from said trusts upon reaching the age of eighteen." She swiveled to regard the twins. "I know you are a little young to understand these proceedings. I will explain everything to you later."

"Yes, Grandy," they said together. Amanda cried tearfully, "You're not going to die, are you, Grandmother?"

Emma shook her head and smiled reassuringly. "No, not yet, dear. But I must make proper provision for your futures. That's what this is all about."

"We can come and live with you, can't we?" Francesca asked plaintively, her face puckering up.

"We'll talk about that tomorrow, dear."

Emma leaned forward, clasping her hands together, and her voice, always strong, sounded more vibrant than ever. "I will now discuss the disposition of Harte Enterprises, the company that controls my clothing factories, woolen mills, Deerfield Estates, the Roe Land Development Corporation, as well as the General Retail Trading Company and the Yorkshire Consolidated Newspaper Company. As you know, it is a holding company worth many millions of pounds and I own one hundred percent of the shares—"

She broke off, took a sip of the water, and leaned back in the chair, her face inscrutable. A faint smile touched her lips fleetingly. As raptly attentive as the four conspirators had been before, they were now mesmerized. She looked pointedly at Robin and then at Kit.

"I bequeath to my grandson Alexander Barkstone, fifty-two percent of my shares in Harte Enterprises."

She heard Kit suck in his breath, incredulity spreading across his face. Robin gasped, "My God!", turned ashen, and half rose. Emma glared. "To continue. I bequeath to my grandchildren Sarah Lowther, Jonathan Ainsley, and Emily Barkstone the rest of my shares in Harte Enterprises. Said shares to be divided equally between these three, each one receiving sixteen percent of the remaining shares."

She motioned to the four beneficiaries to come to the desk.

They stood before her, their faces suitably serious. Emma looked at each one of them in turn and said evenly, "I hope you understand my reasoning behind the disposition of Harte Enterprises. After careful deliberation, I decided the only way to preserve the company, and prevent any dissension or quarreling later, was to put control of the company into one person's hands. In my considered opinion, Alexander is the best equipped, in knowledge and experience, to run the company. But this is no reflection on your capabilities, which are superior. You will continue to work in the subsidiaries and take control of your own divisions upon my death. And of course, you will derive considerable income from the shares I have given you. I have also established a one-million-pound trust for each one of you, Alexander included. I hope you don't think I've played favorites, or been unfair."

They reassured her that they fully understood, individually thanked her profusely, and stepped to the left of the desk. Sarah looked fixedly at the stone fireplace, unable to meet Kit's angry gaze. She knew her father had expected to inherit a large chunk of the Harte Enterprises shares. Jonathan looked down at his feet, avoiding Robin's glaring countenance for the same reason. But the saturnine Alexander and his ebullient sister, Emily, seemed unconcerned about Elizabeth. Their mother's reaction was one of bewilderment bordering on stunned disbelief.

Emma continued, "To digress for a moment from my business holdings. I would like to tell you how I am disposing of my various homes, collections of art, sculpture, and jewelry. To my grandson Philip McGill Amory, I leave the remainder of my art collection and sculpture, with the exception of the paintings here at Pennistone Royal, which currently repose in my various other homes, executive offices in London, Paris, and New York. Philip, please come and join your cousins."

Philip paused at the desk and thanked her. She said, "I am not leaving you anything else Philip, because you are going to be a multimillionaire under your grandfather's will. I hope you appreciate my motives."

"I do indeed, Grandy. You have been eminently fair."

"Now to my other homes. I bequeath the following residences to the following of my grandchildren. To Alexander, the villa at Cap Martin in the South of France. To Sarah, the house in Belgrave Square. To Emily, the Avenue Foch apartment in Paris. To Jonathan, the Fifth Avenue apartment in New York. The same grandchildren will also inherit all the furnishings in said residences. My jewelry, with the exception of my emeralds, is to be divided equally amongst my granddaughters Sarah, Emily, Francesca, and Amanda."

Emma stopped and signaled to Daisy with her eyes. Her youngest daughter, acutely aware of the antipathy in the room, rose and glided swiftly across the floor, positioning herself next to her son, Philip. Emma said, "To my daughter Daisy, I give the McGill emerald ring, earrings, and necklace, given to me by her father. I also bequeath to her this house, Pennistone Royal, and all of its contents, to be used by her during her lifetime. Upon Daisy's demise it will pass to her daughter, Paula."

Mutterings and whisperings rippled in the air. Dresses rustled. Chairs creaked as bodies were shifted angrily. Her four eldest children, seated at the opposite side of the room, were staring at her with such open antagonism Emma flinched, but her gaze did not waver, and her face was implacable. Her eyes focused on Jim Fairley. She lifted a document from the pile. "This is for you, Jim," she said, putting it in an envelope quickly and holding it out to him.

Jim was taken aback, his eyes widening, and then he hurried to her side, a questioning look in his eyes. She handed him the envelope. "This is your new contract, ensuring your employment with the Yorkshire Consolidated Newspaper Company for the next ten years. Peruse it, show it to your solicitors, and return it to me next week. Signed. I am also appointing you managing director of the company, to take effect next month, with an increase in salary."

"Thank you very much, Mrs. Harte. I don't know how to express my gratitude. I will—"

Emma said crisply, "Later, Jim. And please, stay here with the others." Emma lifted the glass of water and drank deeply, emptying the glass. She straightened up in the chair, her demeanor imperious, her face glacial. "I now come to the disposal of the Harte department-store chain. Something I'm quite certain you've all been anxiously waiting to hear about." She stopped, her eyes becoming reflective. "I built that chain from nothing, with the toil of these hands." She lifted them in the air for them all to see. "A lifetime's work has gone into building that chain into what it is today. One of the biggest in the world. I decided several weeks ago that it must pass into the right hands, that it must go to the one person who would ensure its continuation, who would run it efficiently, in the manner in which I have always run it—" She bit off the end of her sentence dramatically. The silence was overwhelming now, the tension almost unbearable.

"I give and bequeath *all* of my shares in Harte Stores to my granddaughter Paula McGill Amory. I also give to Paula the remainder of my emerald collection."

Automatically Paula rose, discovering to her dismay that her legs were unsteady as she traversed the long stretch of carpet. But she kept her face expressionless, her eyes pinned solely on Emma. Alerted for trouble though she had been all week, she had not expected anything quite as dramatic, and she dared not think of the repercussions. She stood in front of the desk. "Thank you for the trust you are showing in me, Grandmother. I promise Harte Stores will be safe always."

"Do you think I don't know that, darling?" Emma said lightly, with a fond smile.

Paula returned her smile and stepped towards the others who ringed Emma like a phalanx. Grandmother's divided the room into two camps, Paula said to herself, and wondered with sharpening interest what was going to happen next. There's bound to be another bombshell, she decided, and groaned inwardly.

"Finally, I have appointed my daughter Daisy Amory as executrix of my estate, and Henry Rossiter, of the Rossiter Merchant Bank, as co-executor."

Edwina, Kit, Robin, and Elizabeth were paralyzed with shock, and Emma saw hatred mingled with bitterness and disappointment gleaming on their cold faces. She sat perfectly still, waiting for the furor to begin. But oddly, and to her astonishment, they were curiously contained. They know I have outwitted them and they are too cowardly to protest.

It was Robin who recovered first. He sprang up, his face apoplectic. "Now look here, Mother. You've been grossly unfair. You have cold-bloodedly cut us out of your will, deprived us of what is rightfully ours. I fully appreciate the ramifications of the McGill estate, but your own fortune and business holdings should have automatically come to your children. *We are your legal heirs.* I don't intend to accept this. I am going to contest the will, and the others will back me. Undue influence has obviously been brought to bear on you. I will prove that you were incompetent when you drew it. You are obviously no longer responsible for your actions. Any court of law will recognize that. Furthemore—"

"Shut up and sit down," Emma said, her voice cutting through the air like a steel blade. She stood up and gripped the edge of the desk. "I did indeed cut you out of my will. And for good reason. You see, I know you four plotted to wrest my empire from me, to get everything for yourselves, even at the expense of your own children." She laughed sardonically. "I think I might have had a grudging respect for you if you had been subtle in your scheming. I've always admired clever adversaries. But you were inept and obvious." She sucked in her breath. "And there was a fatal flaw in your plot. *You underestimated me*."

She gazed at them, her eyes thin green slits beneath the old lids. "Henry Rossiter once described you as a nest of vipers. How right he was. You really don't deserve any consideration in view of your unconscionable behavior. But I am not as vindictive as you might suppose, and as many others would be in my place. And so I have decided not to revoke the trust funds I established for each of you some years ago." Emma's lip curled with disdain. "As for contesting my will, well, I expected that. I second-guessed you on that one, Robin. And I am prepared for that contingency."

Emma picked up an envelope, from which she took four pieces of paper. She held them up in the air and fluttered them between her fingers. "These are checks made out to each one of you. The value of each check? *One million pounds*. A drop in the bucket to what you would have received if you had not betrayed me, but, nevertheless, a lot of money by anybody's standards." She smiled cynically. "Don't think these are outright gifts. They are not. I am simply buying you. And I know you *all* have a price."

Placing the checks on the desk, she picked up a sheaf of documents. "If you each accept your check for one million pounds, cashable on Monday, incidentally, you will sign an individual contract with me." She waved the documents she was holding at them. "They are already drawn, as you can see. Each contract is a legal agreement between us, stipulating that you will not challenge my will. As a lawyer, Robin, you know that by signing such an agreement and accepting monetary consideration, you cannot ever contest."

Her eyes flickered from Robin to Kit, Edwina, and Elizabeth. "Let me warn you now I have made certain my will is irrevocable. Since this is the case, you might wonder why I am prepared to give you each one million pounds. Very simply, to prevent your disturbing my business empire with so much as a single ripple, and to ensure none of you causes trouble for my grandchildren." She took hold of the checks again, waving them in the air. "Let's just say I believe in insurance policies."

She sat down, gazing at them unemotionally. Kit had slumped in the chair. He was flustered, and he could not meet her eyes. Elizabeth was nervously twisting her hands together, held in the grip of obvious indecision, while Robin, the ringleader, had adopted an expression of false bravado. Of them all, it was Edwina who seemed the calmest, the least concerned.

Emma, who had paid no attention to her daughters-in-law or her son-in-law, the count, during the proceedings, now addressed them. "Would you like to confer with your better halves?" she asked, and laughed. "A million pounds is a hell of a lot of money to turn down." June and Valerie, who had always been fond of Emma and were obviously horror-stricken at the duplicity of their husbands, shook their heads mutely. And the count, aware of his rocky position in the family, also politely declined.

"Come on, make up your minds," Emma snapped. "I haven't got all night." She stood up and briskly began to return the documents to the briefcase. "Suit yourselves. But I'm warning you for the last time, you won't win if you attempt to contest the will after my death. Never. I will outsmart you from the grave."

Elizabeth roused herself first. "Where's the pen?" she cried shrilly, standing up, avoiding Robin's furious gaze. Edwina followed her. Robin joined them, sullen and bristling with rage. They all signed the contracts and accepted their checks. Kit was the last. Emma noticed that his hand shook and he was quite unable to look her in the face.

Emma locked the contracts in her briefcase. "Well, now that this little bit of family business has been completed satisfactorily, I suggest we continue the party."

There was a moment of absolute silence and everyone gaped at her, and then the pandemonium she had anticipated earlier suddenly broke loose. They all started to speak at once, thronging around her. Emma picked up her briefcase and said, "Please excuse me for a few moments. I shall return momentarily." She took hold of Paula's arm. "Go up to the parlor with Jim. I would like to see you both alone for a moment. And take my briefcase with you, please."

"Of course, Grandy."

Emma glided across the room. She tucked her arm through Blackie's. "Will you come and have a quiet drink with me?"

"Sure and I'd be delighted," Blackie said. He tilted her face to his, as was his way, and looked deeply into her eyes, his own twinkling. "Quite a performance, Emma. Quite a performance!"

Emma smiled back at him, but she remained silent, and together they left the library, crossed the Stone Hall, and followed Paula and Jim up the great curving staircase. Something prompted Emma to pause at the bend in the stairs. She turned and glanced back. Kit, Edwina, Robin, and Elizabeth were standing in the doorway of the library, watching her ascent, their faces unreadable. But she knew what they were thinking. She straightened up and with one foot she kicked out the back of her chiffon gown in a flippant gesture of disdainful dismissal. And she continued up the stairs, as proud and as regal as ever.

Upon entering the parlor, Emma excused herself and went through into her bedroom. She returned a few minutes later to find Jim and Paula seated on one sofa, Blackie on the other. She stood in front of the fireplace and looked from Jim to Paula. "Have you told Paula the extraordinary story of the Harte women and the Fairley men?"

Jim said quickly, "No, I haven't, Mrs. Harte. I felt it was up to you to do so."

"What extraordinary story?" Paula asked curiously.

"I'll let Jim recount it to you. He'll tell you later. This is not the time." Now Emma uncurled her right hand. "I found this locket amongst my mother's things after she died. It is engraved 'A to E 1885.' I know that it was given to my mother, your great-grandmother, by Adam Fairley, Jim's great-grandfather. I want you to have it, Paula."

Intrigued, Paula took the locket and examined it. "Thank

you," she said. "I will keep it always." She looked at Jim.
"You must tell me the story when we go downstairs. It
sounds fascinating."

"It is," Jim responded.

Emma now turned to Jim. "I also found this gentleman's
gold stickpin with the locket. Could it have belonged to your
great-grandfather?"

"Why, I believe it did!" Jim exclaimed, turning it over in
his hand. "There was a photograph of Great-grandfather in
Grandfather Edwin's desk which I found when I was going
through his possessions. Adam was a very young man when it
was taken and he was dressed in riding clothes. I'm quite
positive he was wearing this in his stock."

"Please keep it, Jim," Emma said softly.

"Why, thank you, Mrs. Harte. I'm very touched. And
thank you for the contract, and the promotion. For everything. I didn't expect—"

"It was the least I could do," Emma interrupted. "Now run
along, you two, and enjoy yourselves. I want to visit with
Blackie for a while. We've hardly exchanged a word all night.
We've a lot of gossip to catch up on."

Jim stood up. He bent down and kissed her on the cheek.
"You are indeed a great lady, Mrs. Harte."

Emma smiled. Paula hugged her grandmother and whispered in her ear, "I knew you were a foxy old thing, and that
you were up to something. But even I was flabbergasted.
You're still full of surprises, Grandy. And I do love you."

Emma watched them leave the parlor together, holding
hands and smiling into each other's eyes. They'll be all right,
she said to herself.

Blackie regarded her carefully, puffing away on his cigar,
his black eyes filled with tenderness. He had loved her for
sixty-four years, his wild young colleen of the moors. They
had come a long way together, shared so much sorrow and
joy, and she never failed to amaze him. Eventually he said,
"So the vendetta has finally ended. You have united the two
families at last. Paula will become a Fairley." He smiled at
her gently. "I'm beginning to think you're a sentimental old
woman, after all, Emma Harte."

"Yes, perhaps I am." Emma settled back against the sofa
and smoothed her gown. "You know, Blackie, if I live long
enough I will have Fairley great-grandchildren to bounce on

my lap. Who would ever have believed that!" Her eyes sparkled. "I'm so glad I relented about Jim and Paula. It's their happiness that counts now. They are the future."

Blackie said, "Aye, indeed they are." He rose and strode across to the Georgian table. "Would you like a drink, Emma?" he asked, pouring himself a cognac.

"I'll have a Bonnie Prince Charlie, please."

Blackie returned and sat next to her on the sofa. They clinked glasses. "Here's to those we've loved and lost, to those we've loved and kept, and to those of ours who are yet to be born, Emma."

"Yes, to the next generation, Blackie."

They sat in silence for a while, ruminating, and as at ease with each other as they had always been since the first day they had met on the moors above Fairley Village. Suddenly Blackie took her hand in his. He said, "It's an extraordinary road you've traveled, Emma, in your quest for power and wealth, and I'm curious. Tell me, did you discover anything special along the way that you would like to impart to your old friend?"

"Yes, Blackie, I did. I believe I learned the secret of life."

Blackie looked at her intently. "And what is that, mavourneen?"

Emma gazed back at him for a prolonged moment. And then she smiled that incomparable smile which illuminated her face with radiance.

"It is to endure," she said.

ABOUT THE AUTHOR

Barbara Taylor Bradford has had a notable career in journalism, both in England and the United States. Since writing the beloved *A Woman of Substance*, she has devoted herself to writing only fiction, and each of these books, *Voice of the Heart* and *Hold The Dream*, have been bestsellers as well. Her most recent novel, *Act of Will*, was on the New York Times bestseller list for sixteen weeks. She lives in New York City with her husband, Robert.